PELICAN COVE

Pelican Cove

GOING HOME

JB Arthur

Bad Cat Studio

A special thanks to Barbara Nash
for her support and love
and for literally putting the
words in my mouth with her
editing and narrative suggestions.
Thanks, Sis!

Prologue

Historic Spanish Point is one of the largest intact, actively preserved archaeological sites of the prehistoric period and is located on the gulf coast bay of Osprey, Florida. The site contains an archaeological record that documents well over five thousand years of Florida prehistory. Human habitation of the site, known to archeologist as the Palmer Ranch site 8s02, spans the Late Archaic period (5,900–3,200 years ago) to the Manasota and Late Woodland periods (3,200–1,000 years ago).

The bay and its surrounding area appear on one of the earliest known maps of what is now the state of Florida as Zara Zote, believed to be an indigenous name. It's theorized that following the retreat of the glaciers; ocean levels rose creating the current coastline and the natural bounty of today's Sarasota Bay.

The location of the Florida peninsula attracted some of the earliest human settlements in the hemisphere. The prehistoric peoples living on the bay's shore saw the introduction of ceramics and implements that precipitated the transition from nomadic hunters and gatherers to settled subsistence societies. They capitalized on the abundant resources provided by the Gulf of Mexico, marsh, woodland and bay ecosystems and developed specialized tool technology to further establish permanent settlements.

Archaic Period sites are not as prevalent on the gulf coast and are often not as well-preserved as Historic Spanish Point's Hill Cottage Midden (a dump for domestic waste). Archaeological excavations and examinations of data place this midden clearly in the Archaic Period of North America. Given its age and the potential for further study, Hill Cottage Midden is among the most important sites in all of Florida, and it is believed to be one of the oldest and largest ceremonial shell ring middens in all the Southeastern United States.

One totem uncovered at the dig site has had archeologist and historians alike stumped since it was first discovered. During the first lab investigations, it appeared to be a Kokopelli-type of fertility deity usually associated with Native American cultures in the Southwestern United States. Similar to other known deities, they would preside over fertility, childbirth, and agriculture. The unusual observation regarding this piece is that the symbol is in the form of what appears to be a man who looks like a tree, or vice versa. He is not the typical humpbacked flute player we are familiar with in today's native cultures, and as one archeologist put it, "He appears to be an extremely well-rooted male tree at that!"

1701 BC

The orange glow cast by the fire's flames danced off the oak tree limbs that embraced an array of roughly hewed thatch huts. No two were exactly alike in shape or size, and none contained doors. Inhabitants could be seen spreading the palm fronds with their hands and stepping outside their meager dwellings and into the circle of longleaf pine needles that carpeted the entire encampment floor.

Conch shells resonated loudly, trumpeted by a group of young males and signifying the end to yet another span of illumination. The great ball of fire could be seen through the gaps in the black mangroves, descending slowly before going below the rippling waves of high tide to sleep on the ocean's floor once again.

Mothers placed their babies in large baskets woven from the sacred coconut palm trees and set them beside their hut, well within eyesight, as they joined the other females already dancing within the fire ring. The roughly shaped circle was created out of local shells such as whelk, cockle, and scallops of various shapes and sizes. At four equidistant points around the pit, not dissimilar to today's compass points, were four different animal skulls. Though each were in various stages of decomposition, some even showing signs of rotting fur and flesh, they appeared to be those of a saber-toothed type of cat, a large crocodilian, a giant sloth, and a cave bear.

The tribal elders were already seated on the far side of the fire but facing the now glistening, moonlit waters of the bay. They chanted and prayed to the abundant long beak and pink spoon mouth fishing birds settled in the distant red mangrove rookery islands to nest for the night. All further tribe activities would wait until the birds were finished providing safe passage to the underworld for any tribal member that had recently ceased being.

When satisfied, the senior tribesmen dipped their feculent fingers in a glutinous mixture of fermented saw palmetto fruit and berries and, unabashed, slurped it off between rotten and missing teeth. All the young males of the tribe were now noticeably missing from the village. Each one had quietly faded inconspicuously into the darkening shadows of the surrounding jungle woods.

The elders, now with glazed eyes and impaired progression, entered the circle offering their fermented mash to the dancers from off their fingers. The women had begun a chant in a manner that started out gentle and barely audible, but now was increasing in intensity as the dancing took on a fevered pitch. What sparse skins and furs they actually wore were randomly shed and stomped upon by the other participants. Some touched themselves in an intimate manner inducing screams and yelps, while others simply shuddered in place and then continued the dance. The scene now included only the fertile women of the village bending over and displaying their womanhood that was swollen and moist.

The elders signaled to their mates who dutifully followed them as they retreated quietly into their own huts. The lone older women rounded up the half-grown children while accompanying the nursing mothers to gather up their babies and baskets and make their way between the fronds and disappear quietly into their shelters for the night. Those remaining young women stopped the feverish dance and encircled the slowly dying fire with their backs to it. They waited, facing out, bleary-eyed towards the darkness of the forest primeval.

Suddenly the rustling sound of whispering leaves could be heard. The jungle began to come alive and move ever so slowly towards them. The actual trees slowly stepped forward while swaying their limbs and branches in the warm and gentle ocean breeze. Each move seemed to be choreographed to the undulating rhythms of the seas pounding waves as they kissed then embraced the shimmering shore. As each figure got closer to its selected female, it would shudder and groan. Only as they approached what remained of the last remnants of fire light could one discern that the trees had eyes.

In fact, it soon became apparent as the effects of the ardent spirits waned that these were not trees at all, but the young virile men of the tribe in elaborate ceremonial make-up and garb. Assisted by the mated men; mud, sand, and dyes from berries had been painted on their naked bodies to approximate tree bark where once was skin. Branches, twigs and leaves had been attached so as to resemble sprouting foliage. Even such details as egret nests instead of hands or cypress knees from their feet had not been overlooked. Only one feature stood unsheathed and in plain view, his manhood, leaving no doubt that each male participant was quite aroused and anticipating the next phase in this ceremonial rite of passage.

1866 AD

Since their arrival in America from Wales, they wanted nothing more than their own land to farm and the chance of a better life for their children. Much like their Welsh neighbors they had left their beloved homeland after years of poor harvests and hungry bellies. Now, the decision for John and Eliza Webb to pack up and leave Utica, New York, in the mid-eighteen hundreds was actually an easy one.

Their sons Jack (John Jr.) and Will were robust young boys with their father's inquiring mind and his ache for the good Lord to provide them all with something more out of life. The daughters Anna, Lizzie, and Ginnie had their mother's fair looks and strong appreciation for the arts, music, and literature. The middle daughter, named Eliza after her mother but referred to fondly as Lizzie by the family, had fallen in love and married a year earlier. His name was Frank Guptill, the son of a farmer, and they had met at the First Presbyterian Church of Utica where they were married. The Webb's, especially John the elder, were so thrilled with his pioneer spirit and determination that they too would join in the venture thus keeping the clan together.

Till now the family, utilizing John's knowledge of dairying, had survived by producing Welsh butter, an extremely desired commodity in the Mohawk Valley area. This allowed them to bankroll enough capital for the family to finally light out on their own. But the big question was whether to seek land ownership out west by way of the Pride of Utica on the Erie Canal or purchase horses and a wagon and trek south.

To the south was yet another new frontier that few pioneers had interest in. The region had just gained statehood and had assumed the exotic name of Florida. Rumors ran rampant about this land where the weather was always temperate, flowers and fruits grew wild for the picking, and water, a commodity those choosing to go out west had to take with them, ran plentiful. Of course, tales of huge man-eating cats, fifteen-foot reptiles with razor sharp teeth, sea creatures that could swallow whole boats, and primal natives balanced these stories out!

Yet, the decision was made one winter's night over a pint of ale when John senior made the acquaintance of a Spanish trader called Gorez Goz at the Nail Creek Pub. The bearded Spaniard told him of an elevated point of land that was rich for the taking and located directly on a flourishing bay. He told of exotic fruits like mango, carambola, and papaya growing in abundance amidst shrubs of huckleberry, dewberry, and blueberry, all just ripe for the picking. His tales of how abundant the fish and game were left little doubt that night in John's mind as to the direction the family would be taking. The next morning, he gathered the family and enlightened them of the promised land he had heard about. He related the Spaniard's tale embellishing it even more by adding elaborate details of the bountiful life they would soon be living in the alluring land called Florida.

February 17, 1867

Prior to their departure Lizzie had kept mum to both her husband and the entire Webb family that she suspected she might be blessed with child. It had been nearly three months since she last bled, her breasts were tender, and most mornings were met with nausea after smelling the aroma of the morning coffee. These were all sure signs she had read about in one of her mother's many collected books. She knew that mentioning it would either put an end to her and Frank joining in on the trip or, worse yet, detain the entire family from going. She couldn't bear to be the one to offset her father's lifelong dream.

So once the journey was well underway and late one night, somewhere in perhaps West Virginia and after the rest of the family had bedded down in the wagons, Lizzie turned to her husband and whispered her news in his ear. It felt good to share the burden finally with someone, and to her joy, Frank reached over and laid his hand on her stomach and gently kissed her. Longing to feel close, she opened herself up to him and guided him deep into the sultriness between her legs. Quietly they made love and then they lay by the fading campfires light, embraced in each other's arms till the first light of dawn.

June 26, 1867

No one was quite sure if they were in southern South Carolina or northern Georgia when the labor pains came on markedly strong and steady. Her mother, Eliza, and the girls had been of great support since learning the news of the baby that was on the way. However, Eliza would discreetly share her concerns with her husband, John, regarding the dangers of giving birth out in this God forsaken wilderness. Stories she read in the Utica Dispatch of Indian attacks resulting in scalped settlers and kidnapped babies had left an impression on her. John did his best to point out that to his recollection those reports originated mostly from the Wild West.

As if a blessing, the trail exited the dense forest and opened up to a beautiful valley filled with the aroma of confederate jessamine and surrounded by gentle green foothills.

"It's a sign!" declared Eliza, and they made camp early this day under a lone shagbark hickory tree.

The labor was a long and painful one and, being her first child, left the young woman exhausted and filled with fear. Only her mother's reassurance and tales that she herself had indeed survived this ordeal five times would calm her. Eliza couldn't help but recall the birth of her second youngest, Will, born in steerage on their long crossing of the Atlantic. She remembered how much she longed for the comfort of her own mother left behind in Wales. That night Lizzie delivered a baby girl who was perhaps on the small side, perhaps on the early side, but healthy nonetheless. The slap on her bottom by her teary-eyed grandmother and subsequent cries could be heard by all of God's creatures echoing throughout the valley.

That morning the family held an informal service in the field and praised God for his miracles and prayed for his protection over this new young life. Although not ordained, John ceremoniously baptized the child using a dipper of drinking water from the wagon's barrel.

"*Beth ydych chi wedi enwi'r plentyn hwn o Dduw* [What have you named this child of God]?" he asked while lifting the baby skyward.

Lizzie who was being supported at the back of the wagon by her husband Frank.

"Floy," she weakly replied.

"We have named her Floy Webb Guptill," said her husband. "It means flowers since that's where she was born. In a field of beautiful wildflowers!"

After only two days and with little rest for the new mother, they moved on with haste. While out hunting for fresh meat to feed the family in the nearby woods, John and Frank both were seized with the disarming feeling that they were not alone. This part of the country was known to have Cherokee Indians in it, yet they saw no braves to instill such fear.

"It's almost like the trees are watching us," said Frank, his voice low.

The family continued on and made their way through the Florida wilderness following a map John had acquired from a federal land grant agent in New York representing the Armed Occupation Act. The grant, opened up the territory to private ownership by those of European descent, consisted of land not totaling more than 160 acres. The Webbs' had surmised that it would easily be more than enough land for the family to build their dream on.

Their first time they saw the sea was when they arrived at Fort Brooke located at the mouth of the Hillsborough River on Tampa Bay. Many of the town's residents were pioneers who, following similar maps themselves, had decided they either would not or could not go any further. This is where the marked map ended, showing only a dense wilderness with a few unmarked trails ahead for those who ventured even further south. Many of the others residing here were simply seeking shelter and protection from the nearby Seminole population that lived and hunted there, claiming the area as their own.

After spending not quite a week at the outpost, a decision was made to move on and continue their search for the utopia described by the Spaniard. They restocked their provisions with staples like coffee, flour, salt, and sugar and then continued following the shoreline of the large bay. Fishing was bountiful and a welcome addition to the hard tack, jerky, and occasional fresh deer or rabbit they had depended on for so many months.

September 5, 1867

Along the way, the family came across the remains of a deserted fort. The structure, situated on the bay, was not outlined on the map. It stood near a point that would much later be designated as Indian Beach, Sarasota. The framework and charred remains stood in various stages of decomposition from nature. A broken and rotting sign reading Fort Armistead lay on the ground at what must have once been the fort's entrance. To the left of the settlement were apparent graves. They were unkempt and those not covered with stones were eroding. The disturbing part, as the family and wagons passed slowly through them, was there were so damn many.

Later that week, on September 11, they arrived in what would become known as the Osprey area and exited the steaming, humid canopy of the Florida wilderness at what they believed to be the exact location described by the Spaniard some nine months earlier. The Webbs found themselves standing on a knoll above a beach providing a long-desired ocean breeze. They stood looking out at a cove filled with emerald blue glistening water. Further out was an island covered in low growing mangroves and flocks of white birds. The gentle waves breaking at the shore made an agreeable cadence as the pelicans and gulls chortled a hearty welcoming call. Three dolphins broke the surface of the water as they swam parallel to the land. John turned to face his family.

"We've arrived... we've reached Spanish Point. I so call this land by that name in honor of the Spanish trader that guided us here!"

1868–75

The Webbs' began to build a small homestead with timber from the land as well as materials from their wagons. The family commenced to plant citrus trees, sugar cane, and various vegetables for their own sustenance as well as for retail to the nearby fishing village to the north of Sarasota and Fort Myers to the south. Eventually they built a packinghouse to prepare their produce for market. To transport the produce there, John's sons Jack and Will, along with son-in-law Frank, built a ten-ton schooner they called *The Vision*. Eliza and her sister Emily, who had joined them a year later in the fall of 1869, and daughters Anna, Lizzie, and Ginnie did the cooking and household chores. Everyone shared in caring for little Floy and farming the homestead daily. The entire family worked extremely hard during these early years.

Eliza Writes a Letter to Her Sister Nell Still in Utica, New York

Spanish Point, June 19th, 1875

Dearest Sister Nell,

I thank you for your good long letter, which I received a long time ago. I will make no excuses for not having written before, except want of time. Lizzie has told you how we live and that we are almost a self-supporting household. We make all the clothes for the men even to their hats, which we braid from the palmetto a kind of palm that grows all around us. The only thing we don't make for them is their shoes. We women want little in the way of dress because we have no church to go to show off our finery.

We make our own sugar and syrup and have some six or seven barrels to sell. We raise vegetables for a Key West market and send them in our little schooner, The Vision, that brings us back our supplies. For three months in the summer we can get turtle and their eggs on the gulf beach. There are four kinds which are all good to eat, but the green turtle is the best, it makes an excellent soup, and salted is quite as good as the beef we get here, which is not first quality, for the cattle are all so feral and scraggy. One turtle will lay from a hundred to a hundred and seventy-five eggs, which they bury in the sand. Each laying twice in three months. The eggs are almost as good as hens' eggs and almost as large for cooking. Then our bay is filled with the most excellent fish and oysters. Game is quite plentiful, but it is not often that I can look out of the kitchen window and see three deer feeding within gunshot as I did a few days ago. Jack shot one of them and they have not been quite as bold to return since.

We shall have quite a little show of fruit on our orange trees this year and lemons, limes, citrons and guavas in abundance, also bananas. How I wish you could come down this winter and see for yourselves, as all these things would be so new to you. And then our winters, why you know they seem to me to be a foretaste of that better place to which we all hope to go some time, God willing. Never too hot and seldom too cold. No insects to annoy you as there are in our summers, very little rain. As Professor Webster (who spent a part of the winter with us this year) says, "You need not tell me this is winter for it seems like June." Also, Professor Meek, our visitor from the Smithsonian, says he wishes the institute was on our farm and this was his home. As soon as we get a good line of steamers on this coast, we shall have northern people spending their winter here as we hear tell they do on the eastern coast of Florida now.

Willie and Lizzie's husband Frank have gone to Cedar Key to get lumber to finally finish our big house, which we hope to do this summer. We shall expect to have a house full of boarders in it this next winter. John's father has written to let us know he is quite out of health and that he and his new wife will spend the winter here and if they like the country they will move down here. Lizzie and Ginnie have gone up to Manatee, which is forty miles from here, they have been gone about two weeks now. They will return when The Vision goes after them. One of our hands has just returned from Manatee and he says the girls are creating quite a sensation. There is but one organ in all of Manatee, and no one knows how to play on it there. We have had one now for two years, and Ginnie you may know has not lacked for time to practice and she has wonderful musical ability, so everyone says that has heard her play. Lizzie plays well too, but she has not had as good a chance as Ginnie to practice since she's rearing Floy and expecting yet another. The boys can play a little, all these things help to make our home pleasant.

Will is a grown man, and Jack is a big boy now. I say to you, Nell, they are all good, dear children, all in all a family to be proud of. Anna's health is quite poor, that is she can't endure much. A little work tires her out. I think it is well for her that we came south as she could not have endured the cold winters of the north, what with her chest tightness and breathing problems. Our one doctor, Thom Wallace from Sarasota, has prescribed a chest rub of chloroform liniment that has brought her great relief during her spells. Floy is now seven years old, a big girl as well for her age, and we think she is quite smart.

Now don't laugh at my tales, and me, as you know this is a private letter to you and I would not say as much to anyone but my own kinfolks. And I thought you would like to know these things. I hope you will see for your-self some time by making the journey. The train line coming south all the way to Tampa is due for completion as soon as the next year or two.

Remember me to Uncle and Aunt Eaton and Uncle Isaac. Kiss the little ones for their Aunt Eliza. With lots of love for yourself, I remain your ever-dear sister.

Eliza

1876

The Webbs started to encouraged winter boarders and family from New York to come stay with them. Eliza would set time aside two nights a week to write letters, an early attempt at marketing, touting what she called, "The Many Wonders of Spanish Point." Once arriving these board-ers enjoyed the extremely mild climate of winter, walks along the nearby beaches, fishing in the bay, hunting in the forest, sailing the Gulf of Mex-ico and other leisure activities of the day. Thus, around 1876 the very first tourist resort in the area was established. They named it Webb's Winter Resort at Spanish Point and built the first of several dormitories for guests and named it Hill Cottage.

1881

John Webb became the postmaster in 1881. He'd requested from the government that a post office be placed at Spanish Point so the family wouldn't have to sail the fifteen to twenty miles to get their mail in Sara-sota each week. He began to set the postal unit up in the offices of the re-sort under the heading of Spanish Point. The United States Postal Service informed him that the location needed to have a one-word postal name, so John chose "Osprey," no doubt inspired by the birds so commonly seen in this area every day.

Daughters Anna and Ginnie liked to sketch their surroundings and used to encourage guests at the Webbs' Winter Resort to do the same so as to have memories of their stay to take back home with them. For the postal card rate of one-cent, guests could mail small sketches embellished with watercolors back home showing the beautiful surroundings of where they were staying. With any luck, they might be delivered via coach and railcar before the sender returned back north, that's if they ever got there at all.

One family, the Sherrills, were regular winter visitors to the resort for years. Their young daughter, Mary Sherrill, adored taking drawing lessons from the two talented Webb sisters. She would produce incredible detailed drawings of the flora and fauna of the area but had an innate obsession with the native trees. She repeatedly told her tutors of how she loved the trees, and they in turn loved her back. She was known to go unescorted into the woods for hours on end with sketchbook and charcoals in hand.

Late in the day, just about sunset, she would return with what to most untrained eyes appeared to be some strange and abstract representations of Florida live oaks. Albeit containing the expected limbs and boughs, their forms were unmistakably human-like and extremely virile in nature. Her mother would repeatedly tear the sketches from the book, destroying them as her father read aloud about the sin of impure thoughts from the bible. Both parents feared what other visitors to the resort would make of their daughter's blatant bawdiness.

One day young Mary went out for one of her usual sketch sessions and never returned. As night fell, the family was frantic and they and the Webbs organized a torchlight search. Hours passed and finally her sketchbook was found at the base of an enormous oak tree. Her parents frantically opened it and searched the pages for some clue, anything that might help in their search for their missing daughter.

Most of the pages had been aggressively ripped out, but one remained that caused them to catch their breath. It appeared to be Mary from the back completely naked and almost erotically embracing what looked to be the very tree that stood before them. The details and artistry of the piece were undoubtedly one of her best and well beyond the young artist's skills. As the Sherrills leaned in closer and illuminated the sketch page with their torchlight yet another detail made them gasp. The majestic oak tree in the drawing had eyes that were glaring straight back at them!

1986

The original Mary's Chapel was built in Webbs' Winter Resort, Osprey, at the request of Mrs. Sherrill. It's said that it was constructed as a memorial to her daughter Mary, who had sadly disappeared and was presumed dead at a very young age, after her mother had traveled to the small, central Florida town of Cassadaga. There, she was advised by a spiritualist that they were channeling her daughter and that her soul was wandering lost in limbo. She was advised to build a religious offering to God and that it wouldn't hurt if she gave a generous gift to the medium as well.

The Sherrill family members stayed seasonally at Webb's Winter Resort for many, many more years after the tragedy and found great comfort in having a place on the property in which to worship. Eliza, too, appreciated finally having a place for prayer.

In the early 1900s the Webb family placed parcels of the old homestead for sale hoping to settle some unfortunate debts by selling to new settlers. Since the completion of the Plant Train Line and Plant Steamship Line, the territory was growing by leaps and bounds. One widowed philanthropist named Bertha Palmer arrived from Chicago and bought up almost every square inch they had to offer.

All members of the original pioneer Webb family are buried in the Pioneer Cemetery located next to Mary's Chapel except for son Jack Webb who had moved to California to propagate his line of Moro oranges. Like anything built out of wood and sitting in a subtropical rain forest for well over a hundred years, the structure deteriorated. The first thoughts of the Gulf Coast Heritage Association and its Board of Directors were to have the building raised. Fortunately, it was determined it played a significant part in the legend of Historic Spanish Point, and the chapel was reconstructed in 1986, using the original stained-glass windows and bronze church bell. Little did this small committee know... this story was far from over!

When I hear music, I fear no danger. I am invulnerable. I see no foe. I am related to the earliest times, and to the latest.

—Henry David Thoreau

Throughout the creation of this novel there was a playlist of songs running through my head, much as is customary in a movie soundtrack. Copyright regulations and their related costs do not allow this debut author to include the complete lyrics to these works. However, it is permissible for me to include the title, performer, lyricist and year written. It is my hopes that perhaps you'll find yourself humming along as you read, or perhaps take a moment to look up the tune and have a listen.

https://open.spotify.com/playlist/7boeACWkgO0jA9ERUgLlML

—J.B. Arthur

All Alone Am I
—Brenda Lee (1963)

Lyricist: Arthur Altman

1

June 2011

So here I sit—all alone with my heart pounding from anxiety—at the airport in Tampa, Florida, waiting for my ride. Actually, a realtor if you can believe it. A realtor I've never met in person is coming to pick me up. Inside the air-conditioned luggage claim area, the non-stop opening and closing of the automated doors has allowed the temperature inside to soar. The electronic sign scrolling Welcome to the Suncoast has the time and temperature flashing on it, and at only ten-thirty a.m. in the morning, it's already 87 degrees.

Why the hell did I wear long sleeves?

I ponder this as I frantically search my purse and carry-on bag for a tissue. All I can find is a slightly used napkin with Applebee's printed on it stuck in an outside luggage pocket.

This'll do. I dab at the perspiration on my face and then automatically check to see how much make-up I have wiped off.

Why did I even wear make-up?

"What the hell does it matter?" I mutter aloud. My hair is starting to frizz in this humidity and I'm so emotionally drained I could lie down on one of the lousy plastic benches

I chastise myself for sitting here worrying about how I look for some guy I haven't even met. Heck, we've only talked on the phone and via emails so far.

"*Well ma'am,*" he'd said on the phone. "*If I'm fixin' to find y'all your dream house in paradise, I need to get a better feel for what it actually looks like!*"

Speaking of looks, I'm imagining he's probably a fat, old, balding southerner, wearing some shabby suit like most male realtors do.

Why do they all wear suits anyway? It's not like they're bankers or something. My mind wanders.

Several months ago, I started looking for a new address to call my own by searching online. I would be retiring at the end of the year from Procter & Gamble and had made the major decision every mature adult makes: I'd wanted to run away from home!

You're still young, I told myself. Well youngish, and sixty is the new fifty they say. *There's plenty of time to start over...*

Anyway, it's what I have kept telling myself.

Heck, you're even relatively attractive... well, when you work on it you can be.

But the real decisionmaker had come when my inner voice answered back loud and clear one day.

Besides my dear, you're currently extremely unhappy with your lot in life!

Even though I'm rather well-traveled, without any research or further contemplation, I chose Sarasota, Florida, as my future refuge. Actually, I was quite familiar with the place as a vacation destination. For countless years, my husband and I would come to Florida when our children were young. That was long ago, and in my heart of hearts I know viewing it as a permanent residence—and without my family—is going to be a very different experience indeed.

Why choose a place with so many memories?

I pondered this time and time again. Perhaps it is because I know, deep down inside, they were some of my happiest ones?

And now the well-worn napkin comes in handy to dab the tears streaming down from the corners of my eyes.

My phone begins playing "By the Seaside" (I have recently changed my ringtone to help support this life decision with each and every ring) signaling an incoming call that instantly snaps me back to reality. I answer the thing.

"Hello, Elizabeth Blum speaking, how may I help you?"

I immediately scold myself mentally for answering like I'm some sort of work geek. Old habits die hard!

"Hello, Miss Blum?" The male voice on the other end rises like a question.

"This is she."

"Great, this is Frank Landers with Sunshine Real Estate. I believe we have an eleven a.m. appointment today. Are you at the airport?" He sounds different somehow down here, neither old nor bald.

"Yes, yes, I am Mr. Landers. I am waiting for you."

"Great!" he says quite pleasant and enthusiastic. "Grab your bags and find the sign that reads 'cabs and buses this way' and exit there. Wait to the left of the cab queue. I just entered the airport grounds, so I'll be by in about five minutes to pick you up. I'm driving a black Infinity G37."

"Okay," I say, though I am not sure what a G37 is and still a bit overwhelmed by this entire adventure.

"Oh," he says, "and what color are you wearing?"

"Red." I blurt it out then look down at myself. Even though the predominant color I am now and usually always do wear is black. "Actually, it's only a red scarf."

"Well ma'am," he says, amused, "if I might be so bold, a woman in nothing but a red scarf shouldn't be hard to spot!"

2

I collect up my belongings and make my way down the concourse following the directional signs. About halfway through I come to one stating, Salir de Autobuses y Taxis. Below that in small print but English: For Buses and Taxis Exit Here.

Note to self: purchase Rosetta Stone for Spanish when you get back home. Florida isn't in America!

I exit the set of automated doors and am greeted by the hustle and bustle of luggage dragging travelers, searching frantically for their particular long-term parking shuttle or hotel bus. A beefy man in a Tampa Bay Rays T-shirt and matching ballcap whacks me in the shin with his golf bag. As I limp onward, a small child wheels her red and white polka dot Minnie Mouse backpack over my left foot and chirps, "Watch it lady."

I bite my lip and hobble on noticing that straight ahead there's a long line of individuals waiting for cabs.

I navigate my way to the right of the queue and stake my place on the curb, placing my carry-on between my good foot and my aching left while making sure my shoulder bag strap is secure across my chest. I stand as directed, facing the oncoming traffic and glance inside every passing black car as if I'll recognize the driver the moment I see him. I scan my phone and see its been over fifteen minutes since I first spoke to Mr. Landers. I watch the line of people before me waiting for taxis slowly inch forward as each yellow cab moves ahead, after the driver has loaded the luggage into the trunk and hopped back in before speeding off with their fares.

I suspect perhaps Mr. Landers is stuck in traffic and am amazed at the number of dark colored cars that seem to be flying by in the outer two lanes. It's difficult to tell black from blue or navy in this glaring sunlight. I search my purse for my sunglasses. Checking the time again, I see it's now going on twenty-five minutes.

I consider calling him back when I hear the seaside song and see it's the same number on the screen as before.

"Hello, is that you Mr. Landers? Where in the world are you? I'm about to melt out in this heat!"

I dab at my cleavage with what's left of the napkin before tossing it in a nearby trash receptacle while doing a sort of wiggle, wishing I could discretely adjust my undergarments.

"The better question, Miss Blum, is where are you?"

"Why I'm standing on the curb to the right of the taxi stand just like you told me to!"

"Well, that there explains it, ma'am." He laughs. "Because I asked you to wait to the left of it!"

There is a pause while I take this in.

"Oh… I'm so sorry! Where are you now and can I come to you?" I ask trying to sound sincerely as bad as I actually feel.

"Well, ma'am, I believe I see your red scarf off in the distance. Since you weren't where I was expecting you, the traffic and the cement lane dividers forced me to join the cab line. I believe if you look up, I'm now about five cars back from the front of the line!"

Apologizing profusely, I cut my way across the queue of travelers avoiding all eye contact and indignant remarks.

'Mira a dónde vas señora!' – I really must learn Spanish.

'Für wen zur Hölle hält diese Schlampe sie?' – and was that German?

I approach the black Infinity, and the guy inside is wearing a Panama hat, red sunglasses and some wild multi-colored Hawaiian shirt with various beer bottles screen-printed on it. He reaches over and opens the passenger-side door while apologizing.

"I'm so sorry, ma'am. I would normally get out and help get you and your things into the car. However, this traffic keeps moving and per the signs posted on every pole, cab drivers are not permitted to exit their vehicles unless assisting their fares with their luggage at the point of pick-up. Again, I do apologize."

"I assume you're Mr. Landers?"

The vehicle continues to inch slowly forward.

"At your service ma'am!" he says cordially.

I struggle to jump in while swinging my carry-on into the back seat and my purse and computer bag onto my lap, all while slamming the door shut on the slowly rolling car. I immediately check to see that there's a door handle and accessible lock on my side and, when convinced I can escape if he turns out to be a rapist, allow myself to finally take a much-needed deep breath followed by a long cleansing sigh.

3

Before leaving the airport, he pauses to put the top down on the Infinity and then jockeys his way onto I-275 south, weaving in and out of traffic like a psychopath.

"Can we slow down a little?"

I yell in an attempt to be heard over the blowing headwind. By now my hair is in my mouth and my neck scarf is flapping around somewhere behind my head.

"Sorry, ma'am," he yells back, "but I'm just trying to make up for a little lost time so we're not late for our showing in Venice!"

"Venice? I'm not looking in Venice. I'm interested in Sarasota!"

"Oh, I know, ma'am. But I would be remiss not to show you all of the opportunities available to you along the Suncoast region. There's a spot just south of Venice called Englewood that has some great deals on homes. They appear to be exactly what you wanted and just a little on the high side of your budget!"

"How the heck can they be what I wanted," I say trying to get more hair out of my mouth, "if they're not even where I wanted to live?"

I try to straighten myself up a bit as we're slowing down to a manageable speed now. "What's that ahead where all the traffic's stopped?"

"Oh, that's just the toll booth, ma'am, before the Sunshine Skyway."

"The *what?* Oh my, GOD! You don't mean that long, tall, frickin' bridge that fell down, do you?" I scream and grab my chest and start panting for air. "We can't go this way I... I have a fear of heights and, well, bodies of water, and so bridges..." My voice is rising ever higher in pitch. "Well, my husband always took I-75 all the way around Tampa for me!"

"Besides taking about twice as long to travel while going in the same direction, ma'am, it's now too late to go back." He attempts to explain in a comforting way. "There's nowhere to turn around out here."

My mind starts racing trying to recall what I know about the damn bridge that lay ahead. I remember it being some several miles long and my experiencing one of my more memorable anxiety attacks while crossing it.

Was that the summer of ninety or ninety-one?

"My husband Scott," I say as much to myself as Mr. Landers, "he talked me over it by counting down every tenth of a mile until we reached the other side."

My psychiatrist would later give this episode a name, *gephyrophobia*: a fear of bridges. I remember thinking at the time it was one of about thirty fears I have, and wondering how long it would it take for him to discover the others.

I believe it was shortly after one of our trips down here back in the eighties that the old bridge actually fell down. Hell, the thing was hit by some kind of boat and collapsed. People died as their vehicles went into the water.

"TURN THIS DAMN CAR AROUND NOW!" I yell as I start gathering up my things, grabbing at the door handle, and preparing to jump out.

At which point, Mr. Landers flies past the toll booth. "Too late now, ma'am. Fortunately for us, I have a SunPass and we're able to shoot right on past the cashier without so much as a Howdy do."

I frantically search my purse, spilling the bulk of its contents onto the car floor, in a desperate search for my tiny cloisonné pill case I always carry with me. I find it and slide the lid open revealing four Librium, three aspirin, two Pepcid, and a gummy multi-vitamin. I grab two of the Libriums and pop them in my mouth struggling to create enough saliva to dry swallow them down my throat.

"Wahh… wuh…" The capsules seem to stick in my esophagus and induce further panic, as now I'm sure I can't swallow or breathe. *Water!*

"What's that ma'am?" he asks with a concerned glance in my direction while trying to keep an eye on the busy road. "Did you ask, how much farther? Would you like me to count the miles off like what you were just telling me about? One tenth, two tenths, three…"

"Water," I blurt grabbing his right arm with my sweating palms and yanking on it like I'm ringing a church bell. "Coke, beer, anything wet!" My heart is pounding and I am growing ever more wide-eyed.

"I keep a little cooler in the back-seat, ma'am, for my clients. There's not a big selection, and if your heart's really set on a beer, I don't think I have one. But there are always a few waters and possibly half of a Mountain Dew. The Dew is one of my favorites in the morning instead of coffee!"

I release my death grip on his arm, unbuckle my seatbelt and kneel in my seat bending over to the back in search of the cooler as he continues.

"It gets pretty hot down here and lots of northern folks don't think to bring something to drink with them when they're out house hunting, so I like being able to offer them somethin' to wet their whistle."

I am frantically digging beneath a damp beach towel, a pair of bright yellow Speedo swim trunks, jeans, a white dress shirt wadded into a ball and a bra top with dolphins on it until finding a small red and white Igloo cooler.

"Did you find it, ma'am?"

I open it, pull out a water bottle labeled Zephyrhills and chug it, water dripping off my chin. The pills move on and for a moment I feel slight relief while looking backward at the fading shoreline of St. Petersburg.

I turn around, retaking my seat and adjusting my seatbelt so that the strap is under my armpit and doesn't press against my tightening chest.

"Better, ma'am?" Mr. Landers sounds confused yet concerned as he continues to try to drive at seventy miles an hour in bumper-to-bumper traffic while keeping one eye on me.

"First stop calling me ma'am!" I snap. "And second, punch it, Margaret... show me what this fancy little sports car of yours can really do!"

As he starts weaving in and out of traffic, I place my head between my knees, and using index fingers from each hand I keep checking my temples for my racing pulse.

"I'll be singing Hello Dolly at the top of my lungs now," I say. "I'll be trying for Barbara Streisand but sounding more like Carol Channing!"

After a few moments of silence from him, I can hear above my singing.

"Okay ma— I mean miss, I mean missus... or would you rather I call you Elizabeth, ma'am?"

4

The next time I come up for air we're barreling down the ramp at the end of I-275 and pass under a sign that reads I-75 south to naples. I take another deep breath while attempting, yet again, to pull myself together. I sit up straight, coercing a bit of a smile, and muster my composure.

"Liz… Calling me Liz will be just fine."

To which he beams. "Well that's just dandy, ma'am. And you can call me Frank!"

We continue on in silence. Me too embarrassed to speak after the scene I just caused. And he, I'm guessing, wondering what he's gotten himself into. We cross the Manatee River, which is quite scenic with several kayakers and a sailboat navigating it. Along the way we pass wetlands where the grasses look like ocean waves as the breezes cause them to sway. A little further and the reeds turn to a brownish-mauve that reminds me of mink fur. Although we're driving in bright sunshine, further down the road the sky seems to darken. Even as I watch it fills up with the most mountainous, rolling clouds I've ever seen. My mind's eye instantly flashes to the clouds in *Close Encounters of the Third Kind.*

I decide to break the now uncomfortable silence.

"How much further to Sarasota, Frank?" I ask, keeping an eye on the sky.

"Well once we pass State Road 64 for Bradenton and 70 at Lakewood Ranch the next four expressway exits are for Sarasota. There's

University, Fruitville, Bee Ridge, and Clark. But we're going to the exit after that at Laurel and cutting over to 41 in Nokomis then heading on down toward Venice. We'll then make our way back up north on the trail as we stop for our other showings."

"Funny, I don't remember Sarasota being a large enough city to merit four exits."

"It's really not ma'am, um, Liz." He smiles. "It's just extremely skinny and very long with a lot of expensive oceanfront property on the number one beach in America. You need to consider that the city's actually three-sided since the entire west side is the Gulf of Mexico."

Frank reaches into his car door pocket and hands me a folder that contains printouts of all the listings he hopes to get in today and suggests I give them a look-see before we get there. We continue our drive, making friendly banter, with Frank mostly explaining what insider realtor information he can recall about each of the listings.

"Seems one's an estate settlement," he says. "This can work to your advantage if the kids are up north and have no desire to live down here. Heck, I've seen these come completely turnkey, furnished and with a car! There's a divorce. Those can go either way... in your favor if both parties are fed up and just want to get out of Dodge, ridding themselves of any and all memories of ever having lived together." Glancing in my direction he smirks before going on. "Not so great if one of them still maintains hope and wants to hang on to the past."

Suddenly the air is filled with the deep rumblings of thunder.

"Summer rains!" he says. "A few movin' on ups, you know... bigger is better, and two short sales." The latter he explains are a sign of the times and economy that can work to my advantage if I'm not in a rush to move in soon. "The banks don't want them, but they sure as heck take their time with the paperwork."

"The last property my husband and I bought," I say, "was well over twenty years ago. I'm sure the game has changed somewhat since then."

"I reckon some, but probably not so much ma'am, uh Liz... Find a place you love, make an offer, settle on how you're paying for it, and move on in." He chuckles. "It's pretty simple really."

"Most of the property virgins find signing the mountains of paperwork at closing the hardest part. But heck, at your age you've probably financed quite a few big purchases and are used to that sort of thing!"

I now know my Librium is in full effect as I let his final comment regarding my maturity roll right off my back with only a bristling, roll of my eyes in his direction.

As we're passing the Bee Ridge Road exit of Sarasota, it begins to drizzle. Then abruptly, the sky opens up with a thunderous deluge containing the largest raindrops I've ever seen.

"Put the top up!" I cry out.

"I can't until we stop!"

He yells back, both of us struggling to be heard over the tumult of the storm. We take the next exit at Clark Road and he pulls into the parking lot of a joint called Wings'n'Weenies. Frank works on putting the top up while I excuse myself.

"I'll be inside using the ladies room!"

Of course, once located down a hall towards the kitchen, the bathroom door is locked, so there I wait dripping wet, creating a puddle on the black and white linoleum. I look down at my brand-new Michael Kors sandals and, yet again, wonder what the hell I was thinking when I got dressed this morning to go house hunting.

After watching two men come and go out of the men's room, the women's room door finally swings open and a young girl with a jet-black sculpted Mohawk, various face piercings, and tattoos galore steps out.

"There ain't no TP in there, lady," she says, "so y'all may wanna grab yerself some napkins before ya squat." She makes her way to a table, where a leather clad biker is dunking a weenie in a beer.

"Thanks," I mumble and then enter the bathroom, locking the door behind me.

I take one look in the mirror at my wet hair, runny mascara, and dazed eyes and start to cry.

Dammit, Elizabeth! The girl told you there's no toilet paper, there's no hand towels either, only a damn hand blower. And you threw away your Applebee's napkin back at the airport!

5

We finally reach our first destination inside the Royale Boca Golf &
Country Club. It's a beautifully landscaped gated community whose entrance signs boast Spend Your Days Living in Endless Summer. After
advising the gate attendant that we're here for a showing. we make our
way down a palm-lined street of identical looking homes.

"These all seem to be houses in here," I say. *And they appear to be
pricey, I think.* "Are there condominiums mixed in?"

"I don't think so." Frank's ambiguous reply.

"Well, I distinctly told you I want a condominium lifestyle when we
first spoke. I'm single and have no intentions of caring for a home and
lawn anymore!"

"Oh, that's not a problem, ma'am, the fees here cover various portions of the common areas maintenance, and everyone hires their own
landscapers, gardeners, pool man, etc. Why you wouldn't have to lift a
finger!"

We pull into the drive of one of the carbon-copy houses. Each unit
appears to be made up mostly of a huge garage door from the front. The
first thing I notice upon exiting the car is it's so quiet. No kids playing,
nor cars passing by, no music from a distant radio.

"Well, what do you think so far?" asks Frank, beaming.

"It seems extremely... peaceful!" I say. It was all I could come up
with.

Considering the rain we drove through getting here, the ground is
already dry, and the sun is back out in the sky brighter than ever. I

search for my sunglasses, even feeling the top of my head, and come to the realization that the last time I saw them was in the bathroom at that chicken and hotdog place. It feels like about a hundred percent humidity now, and instead of feeling like my clothes are finally drying out, I feel like they're sticking to me down to my undies.

I attempt to discreetly adjust a wedgie issue as Frank fumbles with the lockbox. He's looking at his phone and somehow getting the combination from it. We step through the double, glass paneled front doors.

"Wait here, ma'am, while I turn off the alarm."

We went through a gate with two guards, I think. There are walls around the entire community and the neighborhood looks very safe and actually quite lovely. So why, I wonder, do these people need an alarm system? Again, he somehow gets the code off the phone and the system gives three short, happy beeps announcing it's safe to come in.

The entryway opens directly into what Frank calls the great room. From this vantage point the dining room is directly before me, the living room is behind that, divided on the right by a countertop bar in the kitchen. Continuing to look further, there's another dining area that I assume to be a breakfast nook. Even from here I can see the dinette and kitchen sets are identical patterns, only the dining set has seating for eight and the kitchen seats four.

The entire back wall consists of several sets of sliders and outside is a caged-in pool area. All the wood furnishings are bamboo looking with large carvings of palms and tropical leaves on them. The color scheme is also tropical with furnishings covered in various shades of green leaves with lots of orange, red, and pink flowers.

The walls are adorned with huge bird paintings giving me the overall feeling that I'm in the Tiki Room at Disney. I smile, realizing that from this reference I'm now thinking about Scott for the second time today and now the children. I pause experiencing the all too familiar pang of loss that pops up unexpectedly at the strangest times.

The emotion quickly fades leaving behind a grimace and watery eyes as Frank brings me back to the present.

"It's what they call a split-plan down here, ma'am. The master on one side and the kids, uh mother-in-law, or perhaps a male guest on the other. Each side has their own full bath and lots of privacy."

I take a look-see and grab a couple tissues from behind the commode in the master bath and stuff them in my slacks pocket.

We finish off with a tour of the yard, which is actually non-existent. The giant birdcage, attached to the rear and filling the entire backyard area is referred to as a 'lanai.' This I find out when I refer to it as a lovely, screened-in patio.

The strips of spongy grass on the sides of the building are all of two feet wide. I realize the only windows on the sides of the houses are the bathrooms and they are non-opening glass block squares. Otherwise, if they did open, you could easily reach out and borrow some body wash from your next-door neighbor. The front yard is so heavily landscaped that there's only a small patch of the strange grass that might measure twenty by twenty feet. I immediately wonder where in the heck would my dog do his job.

We hop back in the car.

"One down, six to go!" says Frank, as he whips it in reverse and out of the driveway.

"Would you like the top down again, ma'am?" he asks, somehow oblivious of our earlier ordeal.

"Oh, I'm just fine like this," I say. "But it would help if you could turn that air up a little!"

We make our way back to Route 41 north as I confuse him even more by rolling down my window, trying to regulate my internal body heat from the post-menopausal hot flash I'm having, while also feeling a bit claustrophobic in his tiny car with the top up.

The remainder of the day goes pretty much the same; we look at more places that aren't at all what I'm looking for. Granted, to Frank's credit, I haven't been the clearest in describing what I actually want. Basically, that's because I don't know what I want. But I'm pretty sure that what he's showing me somehow fulfills his dreams, not mine. When we finally see a condo unit, it is on the thirteenth hole of a well-groomed golf course. I don't play. The next is on a very scenic lake complete with a fishing pier and a resident gator. I don't fish.

He takes me to where I tell him I'm staying—the Best Western Midtown on 41 near downtown.

"Not quite where I pictured you staying," he says. "And if you're going to be a local, you better start referring to it as the Tamiami Trail or better yet just the trail!"

"Yes, well," I say, "by the time I finally decided to take you up on the offer to show me around, there wasn't a room to be had. Seems there's something called the Sarasota Music Festival going on, and everywhere else was booked. Well, anywhere near downtown which is where I wanted to stay that is."

He pulls under the motel portico to let me out. "It's actually a great event and brings a lot of talented musicians to town. You like Jazz?" he asks, giving me a quizzical look including a sheepish grin.

"I like my soft jazz served with a glass of red wine," I laugh.

"Great!" he says. "I'll pick you up around eight thirty."

Frank then speeds off in his little black car before I have any chance to respond. I'm so dumfounded by what just transpired—not to mention exhausted from my travels and viewings—it's all I can do to trudge into the lobby dragging my body and my bags.

Well, you wanted a major lifestyle change, old gal.

I just pray to God it includes taking a nap first!

Take Five

—Dave Brubeck (1959)

Composed by Paul Desmond

6

Startled, I sit straight up in bed as my phone alarm goes off playing "Slow Rise" and wonder where the hell I am.

The room comes into focus and it all starts to come back to me. To help shake off my disorientation I get up and jump in the shower rinsing off, but not doing my hair. I dry off, then wrap the towel around me before brushing my teeth and hair. A little lipstick, a clean white cap sleeve tee, black capris, and this time my red Vans. One more look in the mirror and I'm good to go. In fact, I wonder why I didn't wear it to fly the day before.

I walk to the lobby and ask the girl at the desk about getting some coffee.

"We have a continental breakfast till ten… well, toast and hard-boiled eggs in the breakfast room. There's one of those machines that whips up coffee, but it's not that good. Actually, I only like the hot chocolate with marshmallows!"

"I see. Is there someplace nearby that's good?"

"Well, there's a Panera right across the street!" She smiles and points out the window at the shopping center across the way. "But I think they're kind of pricey and they don't have donut holes!"

A short walk later I'm sitting at an outside table and downing a spinach and artichoke egg soufflé with a large, skinny caffè mocha, skim no whip, while pondering whether the little gal at the motel ever tasted a decent hot chocolate.

I also take the time to think about what a nice time I actually had last night with Frank. Sipping away at my hot coffee, I realize that once you get past his southern drawl, loud fashion, and polite ma'am-ings, he is actually a very nice guy. My bad for thinking his slower mannerisms and manner of speech possibly translated into dimwitted. He actually proved himself quite knowledgeable about many things last night when we finally got talking about something other than real estate. I gather up what's left of my drink and carry it with me back to my room.

He picks me up outside the lobby precisely at nine o'clock as scheduled and we start the day viewing a luxury condo built in 2005 at 100 Central Sarasota. It's on the fifth floor above the Whole Foods garage in downtown. It's only 991 square feet with one bedroom and two baths at the bargain price of $435,000.

I have to ask: "Why in the world are you showing me something that is well over twice the budget I shared with you?"

He dons his now becoming familiar grin. "Because I've had clients like you before, ma'am. You won't know what you want until you see it. And how are you going to know it's the right one when you see it if you don't have a mental picture of what's out there to compare it to?"

I give him what I'm guessing has now become my way too customary quizzical look through a squinting left eye.

The unit is actually quite lovely with its cathedral ceilings, large windows, granite counter tops, and a very workable kitchen. It also shows well—whoever decorated it spared no expense. It looks like a showroom that no one has actually lived in… ever! I walk over to a slider that glides open and step out onto a large balcony terrace. It, too, is beautifully appointed with Brown Jordan furnishings and live plants.

I consider that somebody has to water them, and guess that it's hired help.

I look over the side and down towards the street at the bustling scene below. The Sarasota Farmers Market is in full swing and a wonderful beehive of activity.

"I can't remember," I say, turning to Frank. "Did you say this happens every weekend?"

"Every Saturday!"

"My husband and I lived near a market the year we took an apartment in Rome. What was that area called? Cipro, I think… yes, Cipro. I loved buying fresh foods from the market every day and then taking them home, trying my hardest to channel and cook like Lidia Bastianich, that thin-haired chef on television."

As always, he brings me back around by announcing that in order to stay on schedule for our viewings we need to be going. He continues speaking as we take the elevator down and exit the garage.

"We're going to shoot over to Long Boat Key, then see one in Anna Maria, cross over to Bradenton where we'll catch I-75 to Lakewood Ranch and end our day with one on Fruitville and two on Siesta Key. Since you said you wanted to keep Sunday open, we have quite a lot of running around to do today. That sound alright, ma'am?"

"Yes sir!" I snap a salute, trying to make light of his insistence on calling me ma'am.

But he just smiles. "Well, alright then let's get going!"

7

Since a long weekend was all I was able to negotiate with work, I had wanted to keep Sunday free to explore the area by myself. Funny, but as my final time with P&G is getting ever closer, the more work my boss has been piling on me. The irony is I am teaching two different individuals how to do my single job. Kind of ludicrous that it took my announcement of retirement for my boss to finally perceive all I did for him. These days I'm carrying around a lot of emotional baggage, and I know it. But, somehow, I've always been able to separate my personal life from my work, and I'm a damn good performer, and now they realize it!

I had arranged for the motel to get me a one-day car rental through Enterprise so I could do a little driving around Sarasota on my own, and then drive myself to the Tampa airport on Monday morning. It was a welcome change to be out on my own and with no itinerary other than walking a beach.

I decided to face the demons straight on by returning to Siesta Key via Siesta Drive off of 41—*the trail*, I think, remembering what Frank had said about talking like a local.

I slow down on the bridge as I cross over onto the Key and glance at the homes, the water, the boats, heck the entire view.

Honestly, Liz, what's not to like?

I round the corner, heading south where the road changes to Higel. I pass the juncture of Midnight Pass on the left and then take a quick right onto Ocean Boulevard. The homes I've passed are mostly behind gates and walls, but once in a while I get a glimpse of the beach and the good life on the key. If nothing else, the plantings and lush foliage are spectacular and help reinforce that this place is nothing like landlocked Ohio.

I enter Siesta Key Village, and to my amazement find an open parking spot on the street in front of the Daiquiri Deck. I remain in the car with the air on while digging through my purse for loose change. I come up with a quarter, three dimes, five nickels and eleven pennies...

Ninety-one cents; let's see how long that gets us!

I jump out without looking and nearly lose the driver's door and my left arm to a SCAT bus.

"Whoa!" I make my way around the front of the vehicle and onto the curb.

"There are no parking meters?" I mutter looking at both sides of the street. *This place just keeps getting better and better.*

I walk in and out of the shops with the intentions of mingling with the locals and getting a feel for island life. However, I'm soon very much aware that most, if not all, of the individuals I encounter are not only tourists, but they're not even Americans. I hear foreigners speaking the familiar languages of French, German, and of course Italian. The latter of which I even understand bits of what they are saying.

But there are numerous other dialects being spoken around me of which I haven't a clue. In fact, other than the scantily clad teens in their bikinis and surf shorts that are talking teen-speak, it becomes apparent that the only locals are the shop owners and their employees.

I cross the street and enter the Beach Bazaar, an eclectic mix of everything for the beach from swimsuits to surfboards. So that the kids will spend even more of mom and dad's money while on vacation there is a section of beach toys, kites, and rubber sharks.

For those seeking the tacky Gatlinburg shopping experience, there are items like bikini-clad salt and pepper shaker girls whose left boob is salt while the right one's pepper. And, who couldn't add to their home décor with a plastic Jesus figure enshrined in a grotto created from seashells and illuminated from behind by a night light bulb. I reminisce on how this place use to be a 'must stop' shopping experience for my vacationing family.

In the far back room, there's actually some very nice ladies' items, and I find what I'm looking for. Hats. There's a mirror handy and I try several of them on until I find one that immediately suits me. It's simple, unpretentious, plain white, and the tag states it's "Wad'n'Wear" plus it's great for backpacking, travel, and provides beach goers a UPF of 50!

I make my purchase from a pleasant woman at the back counter, who looks about my age, and exit the building crossing to the other side of the street. Making my way back towards the car, my stomach grumbles loudly. Realizing I didn't even take advantage of the motel breakfast, I unexpectedly walk up to the deck of SKOB, the Siesta Key Oyster Bar.

The girl at the hostess station gives an unrestrained sigh when I say there'll only be me. Table for one. It's early so there are lots of empty four-tops on the front deck, but she looks about pondering where she can stick me.

"Inside or out?"

"Out," I say and wonder if she's trying to hide the loner someplace inside.

"I'll be right back!" she says and disappears around the corner.

In the meantime, a line has now started to form behind me. I half consider asking if anyone could use a fourth to round out their three-some.

The hostess returns. "Follow me."

She leads me around the corner and through the outside restaurant to a back-bar area.

"I hope you don't mind eating at the bar, they'll take good care of you!" She gives a coy wink at the bartender. "Won't you, Sunny?" And then she prances away before I'm given any chance to object.

I belly up to the bar thinking how it's a bit early on a Sunday morning to be seen here. The bartender, an extremely young, but really cute, guy with tat sleeves over bulging biceps and a braided ponytail suggests starting off with a bloody mary and to even my surprise I oblige.

He hands me a menu. "I'll build you a Mary you won't soon forget while you check out the menu, babe!" And he takes off towards the kitchen.

Glancing at the lunch listings my eye catches the Blackened Bleu Cheese Burger. I smile remembering how my husband, Scott, would always order them. I wonder just when the awareness of each and every little detail that sparks a reminder of him daily start to wane. Ever?

After all these years, it's hard to believe so many little things are coming to mind down here. It's odd because, back home, I may think about him perhaps once a day, and then usually only when I'm very tired and let my guard down. Or when I need a hug. It's funny, I struggle with the loss of intimacy and sex, but I miss snuggling on the couch while watching a movie even more.

Sunny returns, setting down two drinks in front of me. "Ready to order?"

To cover up that I've been off in a dream and not looking at the menu, I say, "Everything looks so good, what do you suggest?"

"Depends." He grins showing incredibly straight and brilliantly white teeth surrounded by a day-old beard and bronze tan. "Breakfast or lunch?"

It's not quite eleven o'clock. "Let's do breakfast!"

"Well my favorite is the SKOB Benedict," he says, explaining that it consists of a crab cake, with a poached egg, asparagus, and hollandaise sauce.

"That sounds perfect if you can finagle getting the sauce on the side," I say. "Oh, and I only ordered one drink."

"For you, babe, no problemo—sauce on the side," he says. "Oh and our Sunday brunch always includes twofers!" Then with a playful wink of his big brown eyes he spins around displaying a firm buttock under jogger shorts before heading off back towards the kitchen.

I feel the warmth of a blush on my cheeks. *Yes, this move may be just what I need after all!*

8

The breakfast is glorious, and once finished, I tuck a purple Karma orchid—I'm pretty sure he's placed on my plate as a flirtatious token—behind my ear, bid him Goodbye, and leave a generous tip. I turn around, sliding off the stool to see that the restaurant behind me is now quite full. I instantly comprehend why using an entire table for me was a possible dilemma for the poor girl working the door. As I make my way towards the exit, I start to notice that just about every plate I pass has an orchid garnish on it.

Well, they would have labeled me a cougar anyway! I chuckle to myself.

A short walk and I'm back in the rental car. I drive down to the Siesta Key Public Beach parking lot. It's not as crowded as I had remembered it being in some of my past visits. Perhaps they're all still in church?

I find a parking spot and make my way towards one of the beach access boardwalks. After crossing over the sea oats and grasses, I pause for a moment to just stare straight ahead at the immense crystal quartz beach and the magnificent water before me.

The sand is as white as Ohio's first snow—the water a beautiful emerald blue. I slide my shoes off and carry them as I step onto the sand. The walk to water's edge is surprisingly long, four hundred feet I'm guessing. The sun is out, and it's getting hot, but the sea breeze makes it actually quite bearable. I walk towards the colorful scene of lifeguard stations, one blue, one yellow, one red, and an array of multi-colored chairs and beach umbrellas.

I smile. *I'm smack dab in a Tommy Bahama commercial!*

As far as the eye can see, along the shore in both directions, are walkers… lots and lots of walkers. Some individuals appear determined or on a mission of sorts and move along briskly and with little to no conversation. In contrast many other couples appear animated and in constant prattle while walking with their Dunkin' Donuts coffee or water bottles in hand. Others, many wearing heart-rate-target monitors, appear alone and are carrying hand weights or pumping their arms in exercise motions. Then there are the meandering few who zigzag in and out of the surf, bending over every few steps to pick up treasures from the sea. With the abundance of condominiums built on this beach, it's no surprise how many individuals there actually are.

I continue trudging through the sand towards water's edge and momentarily consider what effort it must take to cross the Sahara Desert as perspiration is now staining my T-shirt. At about thirty feet from shore I enter the zone of butts, boobs, and bulges consisting of beautiful bronzed bodies on blankets, beer bellied men in skimpy Speedos, and parents, flopped into their beach chairs, half eyeing children digging holes in the sand… lots and lots of holes!

I weave through them all and then negotiate an opening—similar to a game of Frogger—before crossing the path of the multitude of walkers. Standing at the shoreline, I allow the warm surf to kiss my toes and feel the gentle tug as the sand is pulled out from beneath my heels. Looking down I am delighted to see the small and colorful coquinas, or butterfly shells, reburying themselves after each and every pass of the undulating water.

I bend down and pick up a beautiful shell the shape of the Shell Oil logo only with purple speckles and place it in my pocket.

Which way to go? I ask myself. *Left, or right?*

Right appears to go around a bend off in the distance, but I can't currently recollect to where it leads. Left I know ends at an outcropping quite a good distance away.

"Point of Rocks!" I say, surprising myself that I remembered the name, and start walking in that direction.

I walk along, keeping my feet in the water, listening to the rhythm of the crashing waves and the laughter of the gulls. Three pelicans skim the water, gliding along motionless before one makes a dead drop into the ocean and then comes back up with a fish. The others follow in unison repeating the process.

I tip my head back looking up at the amazingly clear blue sky overhead and take in an incredibly deep breath. I hold it for a moment and then slowly let it out through my nose...

Yes, this place is just what the doctor ordered!

Then I see it, the Casa Mar. It's unpretentious amongst the other huge condos along this stretch of the beach. In fact, it's mostly one story like an old motel with only two small buildings facing my way having a second floor. This is where Scott and I brought the kids so many years ago on our first vacation to Florida. Although employed, we were a young family, house poor and living on credit. We not only still owed on our own school loans; we'd started paying tuition for both children. We found out after becoming urban pioneers and purchasing a hundred-year-old row house in the Clifton area of Cincinnati, that if you have kids of school age, and live in the city, you're pretty much left with no other choice but a private education. Yet, somehow, we had come up with the ways and means for our first real family road trip.

Suddenly, across the long expanse of white sand, I visualize Scott coming from the condo towards me on the beach with two ice-cold beers dripping with condensation in one hand, and our son, Tommy in tow in the other—Tommy grinning ear-to-ear as he kicks at the sand.

Ahead of them is our daughter Maggie, shovel and pail in hand, running straight towards me.

"Mommy, mommy... can we make another sand mermaid today? I found two great shells for her boobies!" She breaks into little girl laughter. "Please, can we! Huh, can we?"

Suddenly I smell the familiar scent of Coppertone suntan lotion and then the smell of Tommy's hair when freshly washed. It's Johnson &

Johnson. I smile. *Were we all really ever this young and happy?* Then I become sullen. *Were we all really ever that alive?*

Two teens tossing a Frisbee that whizzes past my right ear startle me back to the moment.

"Sorry lady!" apologizes a boy in striped Rip Curl board shorts as he snatches up the disc and flings it back to his friend before even straightening upright.

"No problem," I say and glance back at the beach front and the backside of the Casa Mar knowing perfectly well, even before looking, that my family would be gone.

9

The next morning, after prepping with a Librium, I'm off to the airport. This time using the Magellan that came with the rental, I negotiate taking I-75 to the Lee Roy Selmon Crosstown Expressway to prevent any possibility of crossing that damn bridge again. Once I return the car, I experience check-in, security, finding one's gate, inevitable delays, zone boarding, sitting on the runway, rude passengers, halfhearted service from air personnel... yes, flying is just as fun as ever.

When I finally arrive home later that afternoon, there's a note taped on my front door.

Liz,

DON'T EAT!

Come pick up Mac, I'll make dinner.

Love,

Jack

I smile, drop my keys on the porch floor, check the mailbox, pick up my keys, and let myself into the house. I'm always aware of how quiet the house feels when Mac doesn't come noisily running to greet me, nails clicking on the hardwood floor, accompanied by what I call his under-his-breath grumbling.

Scotties are talkers, constantly grousing or barking... they are terriers after all! These actions are why my friend, Jack, has dubbed him my Scottish Terrorist. I've had my guy for five years now, and wouldn't give him up for the world, but there's no denying that, behaviorally, he's possibly the worse pet I've ever owned. Truth-be-told, he was kicked out of puppy preschool—the teacher's final remark:

"That dog's going to cause you nothing but trouble. I'm not going to say untrainable Mrs. Blum, but he's a stubborn one!"

I set my carry-on, purse, and the mail on the kitchen table and take another look at the note. Jacqueline Hernandez has been my best friend since I started at P&G back in the eighties. We no longer worked together, but she had started in the same department a whole six months before me and subsequently felt compelled to take this fledgling under her wing.

She demonstrated all the little ins-and-outs of working for a large corporation while also showing me how to fit in a bite to eat and a little shopping during lunch hour. Albeit almost ten years younger than me, we had immediately hit it off, becoming fast friends and dubbing each other with the monikers Jack and Liz. Thus, making her the only person at work to call me anything other than my God given name of Elizabeth Katherine.

I grab my bag and head upstairs, then strip down and jump in the shower. How can traveling make one feel so dirty? The shower feels so damn good! I howl while tilting my head backwards allowing the water to rinse the shampoo out of my hair. I luffa, check my legs, decide to skip the shave and then quickly dry off. A brush through my hair, my favorite Paige jeans, a red boyfriend tee and I'm good to go. Another thing I love about my bestie Jack; a dinner invitation doesn't require any make-up.

I arrive at her place, a bottle of Cabernet Sauvignon in hand, and I can already hear my Mac barking on the other side of the door. He knows it's me. The door opens and Mac jumps up on my leg while Jack simultaneously gives me one of her great big bear hugs. Jack's always big on hugging, and since I can sometimes appear a bit cold or standoffish, she's been really good for me. I now hug back.

"Hope red's okay," I say, handing her the bottle.

She laughs. "Perfect! It pairs well with fish."

"Whatever!" I say, getting her dig and grabbing it back from her. "Let's just pry it open and find a glass."

"Only one?"

"Not if you want to hear about my crazy time in Florida. Grab two and have a seat!"

10

The next day at work is mostly spent playing catch-up for having taken an extra day off.

Recently the demands from my boss started—then continued—to increase. I had to wonder whether the guy remembers that I am going to retire or not. Perhaps he's just trying to get everything he can out of me before I leave.

Today I am leaning toward the latter. If he had his way, I'd be here working late into the night with him, side-by-side, as he seems to never, ever, go home on time.

Thank heaven for my dog as he's my fallback excuse.

"Well Greg, I really have to call it a day as I have no one to let Mac out. I'll see you first thing in the morning! What? Oh, yeah sure, I can try to come in a little early tomorrow. Have a good night!"

Once home, I hop on my laptop as Frank emails me new listings every few days. I look at each by first reading the details and then viewing the pictures. I then reply regarding each with what I feel have become repetitive comments: Too big, too small, remember I want to be in Sarasota, too expensive, too cheap, remember I don't golf. I sigh aloud and close the computer.

Has that man even heard a single word I've said?

So now, each and every night, I find that I'm compulsively searching the web for Sarasota condominium listings for myself. I seem to run into the exact same type of listings that Frank continues sending to me. Just how many designer-planned, fifty-five plus, gated, guarded, golf course, active living, near or on the water condo communities can there be in Sarasota?

Then I happen upon a listing I haven't seen before. Pelican Cove Condominiums for Sale – Updated Daily! The post reads:

Harbor House... Very rare listing a FIRST-FLOOR END UNIT!!! Secluded and private botanical setting overlooking immense oaks, gardens and canal. Large deck off the lanai, perfect setting for entertaining or to enjoy Florida living at its finest. This 2-bedroom 2-bath boasts granite countertops in the newly updated kitchen, and a large dining/living room combo. This condo is a must see! The grounds, for sure, make this community one of a kind. Yet, only minutes to Siesta Key and a short drive to downtown Sarasota or Venice. Pelican Cove is your answer to a beautiful resort lifestyle in a 75-acres/gated community on Little Sarasota Bay. And best of all, it's west of "the trail." It offers access to sailboat, canoe, kayaking & fishing from your own private docks. 6 pools, 4 tennis courts, a private harbor, 3 clubhouses with a bevy of social activities, plus its own university-accredited classes. Pelican Cove continues to be recognized as a wildlife and bird sanctuary and a national awards winner for its landscaping and its superior management. Excellent opportunity for your personal get away, full-time home or next investment property. Call us for details today!

I make my way through the numerous pictures and am overwhelmed by what I see. The place is absolutely gorgeous! Oh, the actual interior condo pictures are just okay, and not as up-to-date as most of the places Frank has been showing me. I research a little further checking out several other listings and see that the community was developed in 1979. That explains the look of some of the bathrooms and kitchens I'm seeing. But the grounds are absolutely beautiful! They show flower gardens, trails, pools, tennis courts, boardwalks, docks, water views and my word... even a peacock!

Where the hell is this place?

Early the next morning I anxiously call Frank from my office and inquire about the where and whats of this Pelican place. I explain that I found several listings and that I'm quite interested in them.

"What do you know about the place, Frank?"

"Oh goodness me… you don't want to look at Pelican Cove, ma'am," he says right away. "It's outdated and extremely overpriced for the square footage and the condo fees are shockingly outrageous!"

"But I like the way it looks. I like all the pictures of the property. It reminds me of that Marie Selby place, you know, the botanical gardens by downtown!"

"Well ma'am, I don't really know much more about the place except the tales other agents tell here in the office."

"Like what?"

"Well… it seems they're quite a different group of people they got livin' there. You know… artists, musicians, writers, liberals… umm free spirits… and, well… the majority of owners, so they say, appear to be well… Jewish!"

I'm a bit taken aback by his remarks but not put off whatsoever.

"I want you to start following all the listings in this place and send the availability and property information to me as soon as it becomes available. I'll review the listings you send me, and we'll go from there."

"Well, I'll be glad to do just that for you, ma'am, but once again I'm not sure that place is right for you!" He sounds genuine. "There's a brand-new community of villas they're building on Palmer Ranch that we haven't even seen yet. And over off of University is where it's really happening. Why they're even buildin' a new upscale mall over there!"

"Either way," I say, "this Pelican Cove place has definitely piqued my interest!"

Stranger On the Shore

Written for Clarinet, Acker Bilk (1962)

Performed by the Drifters (1962)

11

So, Frank does as I have requested, and within a few days, the listings for Pelican Cove begin flowing to my inbox. I remain over-whelmed by the beauty of the place. Can it really look like that in person? I wonder. Seems there are one-, two-, and three-bedroom options with one or two bathrooms available. The square footage is on the small side, but heck, I think, *It's going to be just for me.*

I say it out loud. "Just for me!"

Only me... will I be lonely? Will Jack come to visit? Hell, of course, she would... wouldn't she? Will I make new friends? How will Mac adjust to condo life? Will my Maggie ever visit? Do I really know what the heck I'm doing?

About three weeks in I decide I'll never know if I'm wasting time fantasizing about this place unless I go see it in person. By now I've convinced myself that the property pictures—that continue to repeat themselves on almost every listing—have got to be bogus... or at least drastically photoshopped. Hell, the darn Jungle Cruise at Disney doesn't look that tropical!

I pick up the phone to call Frank.

We setup another weekend visit to take place in a little over two weeks. I advise Frank to set up as many showings inside Pelican Cove as he can for the time I'm there. He and I are both a bit confused over just how many properties are actually on the market as numerous real estate sites and rental management companies have the same proper-ties listed over and over again.

Frank finally admits to me that he's never actually toured the property before. Everything he knows is based on hearsay. He admits that he's actually looking forward to my visit and seeing it first-hand. I hang up the phone and for some reason I'm more excited inside then at any point since I started to look.

"This thing is really going to happen, Mac!" I say, and his ears prick up at the sound of his name.

I call up Jack. "What are you doing the last weekend of this month? You're open for suggestions… well then, how about a road trip?"

I put the back seat of my Escape down and place Mac, tail wagging, in his crate behind the passenger seat so I can see him, and vice versa. He does his usual grumblings, turns around three times and settles in for what lies ahead. We pick up Jack and pull out of Cincy early Thursday morning. The trip down does us both good as I share my apprehensions about the move, and she shares hers about my going. Two days, sixteen long hours confined in a moving, metal box together and you start admitting what's really on your mind.

"You're my best friend, Liz!" she says. "There's nobody else in that entire damn city that I could call up and say, I need you NOW, and know they'd be there within minutes!"

"Trust me," I say, my voice quivering with emotion. "For you I'll fly back standby should you really need me!"

Our travels go without incident except for a slowdown in Tennessee due to fog in the Smokey Mountains and the HOV lane in Atlanta coming to a dead stand still because of an accident. We spend the night at a dog-friendly La Quinta in Macon, Georgia, and pull into Sarasota around three pm, Friday. We get off I-75 at Clark Road and have a good laugh as we pass the Wings 'n' Weenies place and I'm obliged to retell my tale.

"I've learned that Clark turns into Stickney Point and that takes you straight over the bridge to the key!" I boast proudly.

"Well," Jack says, "with your sense of directions I'm not counting on it!"

This time I was able to secure a reservation at the Tropical Sun Beach Resort on Siesta Key. Before checking in we pull into Davidson Drugs on Midnight Pass and purchase two bottles of wine and some Banana Boat SPF 30 sunscreen. We quickly unpack the car, give Mac a short walk to do his job, throw on our suits, and with wine and lotion in hand, run for the beach.

"Now this makes that long ride worth it!" Jack says while spreading a towel on the sand.

"I know. And imagine being able to get here within minutes on any given day you desire!"

Jack rolls her eyes. "What I'm imagining is that, amidst all this exposed flesh, we both better go to a tanning booth and start on the Nutrisystem diet with Marie Osmond!"

We both laugh and plop onto the towels and quickly open the wine.

"And a boob job for me." I grin pulling at my ill-flitted swim top. "The girls are heading south!"

And that comment brings on yet another round of laughter. "Damn right we are!" she says and pours into a plastic motel room glass.

12

The next morning I'm up early, and since I'm not a quiet dresser, that means Jack is up too. I feed Mac and take him for a walk on the beach way before the crowds show up. In fact, at this hour we only pass a handful of people coming towards us.

Suddenly from behind: "Slow pokes!"

Jack goes jogging by dressed in only hot pink bikini bottoms and a black racer-back sports bra.

"We'd join you but Mac's not a runner," I yell after her. "His legs are too short!"

While Jack showers off, I make coffee in the room. We then both nosh on a couple honey oat granola bars the motel left in a basket in the kitchenette while waiting for Frank to pick us up. He shows up exactly at nine in a huge van with Sunshine Florida Real Estate plastered down the side including a larger-than-life colorful picture of a happy family of four waving in front of a beach house. He's also donning yet another loud Hawaiian shirt and khaki messenger cargo shorts.

"What happened to your fancy wheels?" I say, as he slides the rear side-door open, causing the house to reduce to half size while the mom and dad completely cover the two children and reducing the company name to read unshine Flo.

"It's in the shop, ma'am," He says. "I also thought you'd be a bit com-fier in here since you brought along company. Oh, and I got you some cold waters this time, they're right there in the cup holders." He grins and gives a wink. "You know, ma'am… just in case!"

After the introductions, as we buckle-up and are pulling away, I lean into Jack.

"He really is terribly sweet," I say under my breath.

She answers in a whisper. "You never mentioned he was cute!"

I am taken aback that in just ten minutes from Siesta Key we're at the entrance to the property. The first thing I notice are the two identical wooden signs bordering the gate publicizing Pelican Cove with a cartoonish looking pelican on them in bright orange, green and white. I jest that it looks like the entrance to an amusement park.

"It reminds me of Scooby-Dooby-Doo!" Jack says.

We wait our turn in line at the guardhouse. Once the guy working the gate has permitted the two vehicles before us to proceed, Frank pulls up.

"Howdy doo! It's yet another beautiful day in paradise, isn't it?"

"Hello sir," comes an unemotional reply from an older, grey-haired—yet ponytailed—gentleman. "How can I help you?"

Frank then explains to him that he has several showings set up for today, some are lockboxes, a couple the residents will let us in, and one we need to go to the office in order to get the key. The guard seems extremely business like as he searches his clipboard, withdraws back into the building, and appears to be doing a search on the computer. He's interrupted a couple times by incoming phone calls and then appears to make a phone call himself where we can only hear a few key words. Realtor... showings... three of them.

He hangs up and asks Frank for a picture ID plus his real estate license. He takes them and jots down the information on the clipboard and then hands them back.

"Remember the speed limit in here is only fifteen so keep it slow, and don't park under any carports, they're for residents only!"

Frank then shows him the list of all the properties we're planning to tour.

"I wonder, sir, if you could tell me where we might find these?"

He's met with a scowl but handed a map of the entire property and advised to move along, as there is now a line of cars five deep behind us.

As the gate rises, I can't help but point out: "That took longer than the trip from the motel to here!"

"I'll plan accordingly when I come to visit you," Jack says. "Oh… and I'll be sure to carry a picture ID!"

We enter Pelican Cove on an extremely narrow blacktop road. Once inside, it immediately becomes apparent that you've entered the forest primeval and that Highway 41, the traffic, the mall, hell… the real world was left somewhere behind you at the entrance. Considering how busy the gate appeared, it's amazing how few other cars are actually moving about in here.

The road is lined with huge melaleuca trees, their enormous trunks sloughing their skin and towering so tall one cannot easily define their exact height from within the vehicle. I'm feeling dwarfed by their immense presence. The canopy forms a tree bridge blocking out any direct sunlight, and even the van's headlights automatically come on due to the intense shade. Upon closer inspection, the bark almost appears cork-like in texture and seems to be shedding as if in long sheets of tan paper.

The undergrowth is filled with a variety of tropical plantings. The grounds by no means appear manicured, but sort of wild and natural. Yet, you can tell they are well tended to and kept in check, or they would quickly swallow the narrow drive. The shrubs include *Fatsia japonica*, beautyberry, bird of paradise, bougainvillea, gardenia, hibiscus and so much more. Huge golden pothos vines scale the trees, their ends hanging down creating scenes reminiscent of old Tarzan movies. And here and there, mixed in at ground level, are flowerbeds of summer impatiens of various colors in full bloom.

I almost gasp at what I am seeing. "It's even more beautiful than the pictures."

"I've never seen anyplace like it, Liz!" says Jack as we both twist and turn in our seats trying to take in every aspect of the views.

"I just knew you'd like it, ma'am." States Frank rather matter-of-fact.

And I give him a quizzical look. *Weren't you the one that told me not to look in here? Once a realtor, always a realtor!*

We continue down the road until we come to a four-way stop. The enormous street sign before us couldn't be more confusing. It lists at least eight different roads with directional arrows pointing out in every conceivable direction. All eyes turn to the large yellow colonial house trimmed in white on the corner.

"Who lives there," I say, "the president of the condo association?"

A small sign out front reads The Wilbanks, and there's a male peacock strutting his stuff on the front lawn.

"My God, there really is a peacock!" I stammer.

On the opposite corner is a less pretentious beige building with a sign over the door, stating condominium of the year winner and on the door, it says office. Frank decides to pull in there first and see about getting a key and maybe, if he's lucky, a little more help with directions.

13

Jack and I stay in the air-conditioned van while Frank goes in.

"So…"

"I just love it!" I say.

"It looks like Jurassic Park," says Jack.

"I'm anxious to see inside the condos."

"No offense, Liz, but the ones we were able to see through the trees while driving in kind of look like a Girl Scout camp!"

About twenty minutes later, Frank comes out, that grin on his face again, but this time he's shaking his head. Before his bottom is even back in the driver's seat he's already talking about what he went through in the office.

"Goodness gracious ma'am!" he says. "Even after the frisking I took at the gate, I had to again show my ID, sign my life away, and promise my first born as collateral in order to obtain this here front door key."

He holds it up for us to see. "And the lady behind the counter just laughed herself silly when I handed her the addresses of the listings and asked her if she would be kind enough to aim us in the right direction."

He starts the engine and backs out of the spot. "She just handed me this here map and brochure about the place, along with a couple Tootsie Rolls, then wished me good luck all the while chuckling to herself!"

He hands it all, along with the map, back to me. "If I give you an address, you mind seeing if you can make heads or tails of this place, ma'am? I'll try the Garmin again, but it doesn't seem to be able to get a signal since we came in here."

Jack grabs the map out of my hands. "Not only doesn't she know east from west, but she pretty much has problems with left and right as well. I've got you covered, buddy boy!"

I shoot her a look and then we both laugh, mostly because it's so true. I have a great knack for always going the wrong direction.

Frank glances at his list. "Let's start with 1717 Pelican Cove Road."

"Okay," Jack says. "We came in on Pelican Cove, right? So, we should just keep going straight ahead."

Straight ahead is short-lived as the road comes to a fork. However, left appears to be a continuation of the roadway and right looks more like parking behind the office we just departed.

We veer left and meander through numerous twists and turns, trying to figure out the numbering system on the mailboxes. The mailboxes on one side are in the 1600s, but on the other they are in the 1500s. Then to add more confusion, we round yet another corner and the road splits again.

"The sign reads Pelican Point Drive," says Frank, "but it points in both directions."

"The numbers are getting smaller," I point out.

"Found it!" says Jack. "We're on Pelican Point and we need to be on Pelican Cove. Turn around and aim back the way we came."

Frank dutifully does as he's told from his two back seat drivers, as now both of us are mulling over the map. We end up passing the office again and are back at the four-way stop.

"Turn right," says Jack, "and continue going straight past the Wilbanks. Apparently, the main road coming in makes a turn."

We continue on, having to pause briefly to let an oncoming car pass as there is literally a huge tree covered with enormous orange blooms growing into the pavement on our side of the road.

Glancing closer at the map for myself, I now add to the confusion.

"I'm seeing no less than three different units at different locations on this map that are labeled 1717. What's up with that? How do you know which 1717 you're looking for?"

"The addresses may be the same, but they're on different streets," says jack.

"Well that's even more confusing!"

We come to a section where the road forks around a kumquat tree and splits into two one-way streets. However, our side takes us through a parking lot full of carports and blind spots as Frank screeches to a stop to allow a car to finish backing out of its spot and proceed before us. The individual who is manning the vehicle is so small that, due to the headrest, we can't see a head. We follow the creeping car through the parking lot where it signals and takes such a long pause before making a slow, exaggerated U-turn that we almost think it's parking. The invisible driver then continues driving back the way we came on the other side of the one-lane road.

We pause as well, at a stop sign, as one has to apparently make a sharp right turn to continue on Pelican Cove Road. The view is drastically obstructed by a row of mailboxes and additional dense landscaping.

"Well this little maneuver isn't clearly marked on the map!" says Jack.

We continue straight all the way to the end, and again the road leaves us with the choice of taking a sharp right, onto what appears to be yet another road, or curving to the left and continuing on.

"This place is like a maze…" says Frank. "Which way now, ladies?"

Jack feels that if we take the left, we should still be on a continuation of Pelican Cove Road, adding, "Who designed this place?"

I point out to her that the map shows something called the Pelican Pavilion and a pool on the left side of the road. So, we round a corner whose view is mostly obscured by a huge fuchsia-colored bougainvillea in full bloom hanging over the road.

We now find ourselves on a long straight road with two-story buildings on the left and an extremely tall chain-link fence on the right. The fence is covered with star jasmine, but through some of the gaps in the vegetation, we can see what appears to be the street of another community. It is lined with huge Italian-style villas and appears to be a much more manicured community than Pelican Cove.

"What's that place?" I ask.

"I believe it's called Portofino On the Bay, ma'am. And that should be Assisi Drive you're glimpsing. All those homes are around the million-dollar mark over there," Frank says. "The property abuts Pelican Cove to the south along with Bay Village Retirement Community as the other neighbor to the east. It's that big pink towering building you may have seen out on Vamo Road when we first arrived."

We continue driving slowly down the road noting that this time the numbers on the mailboxes are in the 1700s.

"That's a good sign!" quips Frank.

"But I don't see any sign of a pool," I say.

"The numbers are getting bigger!" adds Jack. "Look, this one is 1708!"

We come to the final unit before the road makes yet another sharp left turn and its address is 1716.

"I think we may have found it, ladies!" says Frank, as we make the turn and stop in front of the next unit, which is 1720. "wait now, what the heck happened to 1717?"

Confused and frustrated he pulls into a parking place and states he's going to look around on foot.

"Hopefully I'll bump into someone that can explain where 1717 is hiding!"

He disappears down a mulch path and into the foliage between the buildings as Jack and I take the opportunity to jump out and stretch our legs. Jack carries on about how huge and confusing this place is.

"What smells so good?" I ask.

I walk over to the fence that's in full bloom with small white flowers and take a deep breath. Unexpectedly, I'm suddenly in my grandmother's backyard and surrounded by the scent of honeysuckle bushes in the summertime. I snap off a small sprig and bring it back for Jack to sniff.

"Get a load of the other side of this crazy map," she says, handing it to me. "It's an unbelievably long list of rules and regulations."

I quickly scan it. "Well considering the front-page states big as day, Welcome to Pelican Cove, it doesn't come off as being all that friendly so far does it?"

Frank shows up at the other end of the building, separating the plants with his hands as he makes his way out.

I smirk. "Remember Artie Johnson from *Laugh-In?*"

Jack giggles. "I kind of do… but your real-estate buddy is way too young to ever make the connection."

"I found it!" he shouts. "Let's get back in the van!"

We do as we're told as, Frank poses the rhetorical question as to how 1717 can be around the corner after 1720 when we passed 1716 first.

"I'd hang onto that map ma'am," he says. "Just in case you purchase here and want to find your house again."

"A lot of good that would probably do me," I say, "with my poor sense of direction. Plus, we haven't even found the doggone pool yet!"

14

We stand in front of the unit but now have to decipher yet another confusing numbering system as all the doors we see have two letters followed by three numbers on them.

"This must be where the GL-431 comes in on the listing address," Frank says. "Seems the bottom condo is GL-331 and the top one is 431, the one we're looking for."

"Wonder what the GL stands for?" I ask.

"Good luck!" says Jack.

Frank shakes his head. "Why not 131 on the first floor and 231 on the second?"

He uses the key from the office and finally lets us in for our first viewing of a Pelican Cove condominium in person. I share with Jack that my heart is actually beating rapidly in my chest with excitement. She's quick to point out that we have just climbed an amazingly steep set of open stairs. Always the gentleman, Frank gestures towards the open door.

"Ladies first."

And we all go in.

We stand just inside the entry, which actually seems to be the dining room, and as usual Jack's the first to speak.

"Well, now we know where Don Johnson's been hiding!"

As the condo's décor is straight out of *Miami Vice*. The color scheme is teal and peach plus plenty of oversized all white furnishings. A huge Naugahyde sectional sofa almost fills the entire living area and is accompanied by two matching chairs that appear to have come from the deck of the Starship *Enterprise*. A gigantic square coffee table of clear Lucite sits in the middle of it all. Atop it there's a mirrored tray with what appears to be various alcohols in cut-crystal decanters. There's a huge glass ashtray and a clear acrylic box filled with cigarettes. The finishing touch is the tall cylindrical glass lighter.

Huge paintings of ocean scenes, beaches, and palms fill most of the wall space and there are nautical accents and shells everywhere.

"These look like the paintings they show on those 'starving artist' commercials back home," I say.

"I don't know," says Jack, "It looks like the gift shop at Sea World in here to me."

There's a pass-through opening to the kitchen in the dining area with a countertop. Above it hangs an actual taxidermy sailfish. The kitchen appliances seem to be newer, but the walls are covered in a wallpaper of brown, wooden ship's wheels on an ocean blue background and the soffit over the cabinets has a border of maritime sailing flags.

"It's kind of kitschy," says Jack.

"Do you sail, ma'am?" Frank asks of her.

"Only through life," she says, eyeing him up and down. "Only through life."

The bedrooms are surprisingly non-descript. One has a queen bed, and the other two twins each covered by heavily washed and faded, floral spreads.

But the bathroom doesn't disappoint. "Liz, quick…" yells Jack, "get a load of this!"

What with the blue foil wall covering and the mermaid themed décor, I'm a little taken aback.

"It's not every day you see a mermaid and merman, possibly coupling on a shower curtain"

I note that the bedroom and living area both have huge sliders that lead to a back porch.

Frank again points out: "It's a lanai down here, ma'am, and besides offering a fantastic view, you'll be able to open everything up come wintertime and let the air flow right on through."

Jack and I both make eye contact as I point out that the view is pretty much lacking since all you can see is the side of the next-door building.

"I may be wrong, but I believe we're looking at the backside of 1720!" I say, and Jack and I laugh while Frank scratches his head.

We leave the condo and my initial excitement is a bit faded.

"Well what did you think of it, ma'am?" asks Frank.

"You honestly don't know?" says Jack.

I try to be a bit more tactful. "Well, it was a bit dated. I don't care for the stairs. It felt kind of small, and I obviously didn't care for the furnishings… they don't come with it do they?"

"I don't believe so, ma'am. But if you saw something that caught your eye, we can always write it into the offer!"

"Well thank goodness," says Jack. "You'll never find another shower curtain to replace that one!"

15

We weave our way around "the Cove," referencing the map and reading the street signs trying to find Brookhouse Drive. At one point we find ourselves back at the front gate. With cars behind us, we're forced to exit and make a U-turn, all as the guard is watching us out the windows of the building. We then pull back up to the guardhouse as Frank slowly rolls down the van's window while also expelling a faint sigh.

He tries to explain the error of our ways and how we exited by mistake. But, unbelievably, we're left to deal with the guard entirely anew. In fact, he requests that Frank show his ID and licenses once again.

"Does he honestly not remember us?" I whisper as he again fills out his clipboard.

"He's like the gate Nazi," Jack whispers back.

Frank hears us and laughs out loud, and the guard fixes him with a stare.

"Is there something humorous going on that I need to know about, sir?"

This time, however, when Frank composes himself and builds up the nerve to ask the whereabouts of Brookhouse Drive, the guard does recommend that we might consider the first right off Pelican Cove Road once he has granted us entrance.

The gate arm goes up, we re-enter, and I can't help it. "Oh my God," I say, "it's just so damn beautiful in here!"

Jack says, "It's starting to feel more like the haunted forest in *The Wizard of Oz*. Remember the sign? 'I'd go back if I were you!'"

We turn right onto Brookhouse Drive and each of us questions how we missed it the first time. We pass over Clower Creek Drive and cross a small one lane bridge spanning a scenic little creek. What shouldn't be surprising to us by now is that the road then forks. The sign pointing right reads Brookhouse Circle and to the left Brookhouse Court.

"What's with this place?" Frank says again.

As Jack is again twirling the map around trying to read it, I suggest going right since it says circle.

"Common sense says it will circle around and we'll end up right back here! With a little luck we'll hopefully find the next listing somewhere along the way. What's the house number?"

Frank looks at his list. "This time we're looking for 1617 Brookhouse Drive unit # BR160."

So, on we twist and turn until the road makes a sharp left turn. We continue until we make another left turn.

"This is looking good!" says Frank as, yet again, we make another left.

"See, we're making a circle!" I exclaim building on Frank's excitement. We proceed down a small hill and the road slightly curves right until we come to a complete dead end.

There's a small sign reading Brookhouse Pool and a mulch path leading to a fence with a gate.

"Now what?" I say, as Frank throws it in reverse and, on the tight road, maneuvers back and forth several times until he's forced to pull into the only open carport in an attempt to turn the van around.

"We go back the way we came ma'am!" he says, and for the first time ever I detect an all-out frustration in the tone of his voice.

Back at the fork this time, we turn left onto Brookhouse Court and make our way through a parking lot until we come to a sharp right with a sign for Brookhouse Drive. The address of the corner unit is 1637, across from that is 1606. Remaining confused over the numbers, we turn the corner and the next building is 1627. Unbelievably, the road turns right yet again. We proceed down another small hill to another dead end, but this time Jack looks up from the map and yells.

"I found it!"

"Great," I say, "but so did we!" As the mailboxes of the unit in front of us are numbered 1617!

We again go on a hunt for the actual condo unit and Frank finally finds the door with BR160 on it. "This one's a ground floor and has easy access!" he says. "Well, easy once you've actually found it in this place."

"I think I've figured the house numbers out!" I suddenly squeal. "We're on Brookhouse Drive and the BR tells you what street the condo is on."

"Well that would make perfect sense," says Jack. "But do you care to explain why the one on Pelican Cove Road was a GL? It should have been PE or even PC."

"Well, perhaps PC wouldn't have been Politically Correct!" I blurt out, chuckling while following Frank up the walk.

Jack just smiles. "Not bad Liz, you're learning!"

There's a small walled-in patio area out front, and it seems to be accessible from the sliders in the kitchen. There's a set of steps up to the second-floor unit beside the front door. Under the steps, there are two air-conditioning units both running loudly. The noise level is such that when Frank opens the door he has to yell when gesturing for us to make our way in.

"This way ladies. Watch your step!"

The unit is empty. Frank advises that it sometimes makes it hard to visualize how furniture would look or work within an empty room space. But, overall, it shows better than the last condo as it's completely updated and extremely clean. The blonde hardwood flooring looks brand new and runs the length of the room. The unit has a bit of a trailer feel to it, as it is long and narrow. There's an attractive chandelier hanging down in the area where we entered again signaling that we're in the dining room. Having no separation, we assume the area beyond that to be the living room and after that is a large lanai. There are no sets of sliders separating the lanai from the other rooms, so the entire area has a much longer and more open feel to it.

Out back is a substantial size pond containing a rather large fountain spraying quite high into the air. Even with the doors and windows shut tight and the air running we can hear the spattering sounds of the water.

"I need to pee!" Jack grimaces.

"Imagine hearing that all the time?" I say.

Frank advises that many communities turn off the fountains at night for sleeping. To which Jack says, "That's great, but I really gotta go now! Think the waters turned on?" Without waiting for a reply, she scurries off to find the bathroom.

The kitchen is lovely, with granite countertops and cherry wood cabinets. Some have glass fronts, and all have decorative handles in brushed nickel, and inside each has sliding shelves and other upgrades. All the appliances match and are high-end La Cornue brand including the wine fridge, and they all look brand new and unused. There are decorative ceiling fixtures and under-the-counter lighting that, when turned on, give the room a warm and inviting glow.

The unit has three bedrooms and two bathrooms. Again, each bedroom is empty, but the master bath looks like high-end hotel luxury. A louvered closet at the end of the lanai area also contains a fully equipped laundry area with washer, dryer, and lots of shelving and cabinets.

"Well this sure is a big difference from our visit back to the eighties at the last place." I look out at the pond. There are a couple steps down to ground level and little-to-no grass in the backyard to speak of. "I like it being a bottom unit far better," I say. "I've got Mac, he's my dog, and taking him out for walks to think about. But I was hoping for a little more yard for him to do his business in."

I turn around looking back towards the front door. "And, I'm not at all sure how one goes about decorating this long, skinny room!"

Jack returns to join us as we move toward the front door. As we're exiting the air-conditioning unit kicks back on and some sort of lid flips up with a loud *BANG*.

"Who in the world thought placing those things at the front door was a good idea?" says Jack, swinging her damp hands back and forth Girl Scout style. "No towel," she adds noting my questioning look.

One Particular Harbour

—Jimmy Buffet (1983)

16

The scenario of first finding and then viewing the condos plays itself out several more times until collectively we decide we've all had enough and need a break. The map shows numerous boardwalks along the bay and a yacht basin with harbor.

"Even with all the viewings so far," I say, "we haven't seen hide-nor-hair of any of it."

"Heck," says Jack, "we haven't even seen a body of water other than that dang pond with the tinkle fountain."

She then suggests we pull into the parking lot of the Harbor Club and pool and that from the map there appears to be access to the yacht basin across from it.

"Since it's a club maybe we can get something to drink," I say. "Plus, now I also could use the little girls' room."

We park, get out, and stand in front of the van watching a game of doubles being played on the tennis court before us. They are all women and are actually wearing tennis whites. There are several umbrella tables outside the fenced-in court area and lying beneath one is a golden retriever. He lifts his head, looks our way, blinks and then lays it back down, closing his eyes and returning to his nap in the shade.

We make our way up a ramp, stopping to admire a metal sculpture of a pelican on the wall before entering the clubhouse.

"Let's keep moving," says Jack. "I have my sights on an ice-cold Bud-weiser!"

We're in a small lobby that apparently was decorated by the same person that did the first condo we saw. It's very nautical and in a red, white, and blue motif. Why, even the lamp on the end table next to a rattan couch boasts the carved image of the Gorton's Fisherman.

I see a door that reads Ladies Room. "I'll be right back, order me a white wine spritzer with a lime wedge!"

When I come back out, I find Jack and Frank in the next room and it quickly becomes evident that we won't be having cocktails in here anytime soon.

It's a large, undecorated area with a kitchen down one side and opposite it a small stage containing an upright piano and a podium. Several rows of seats are set-up facing the stage. There's a dry-erase board on an easel with "Grounds Committee Meeting" written across the top and then an agenda outlined underneath. Point one written in bold is: Eradicating the Brazilian pepper tree – the most aggressive non-native invaders! HOW DO WE DEFEND OUR FENCE LINE?

"Sounds like Orson Welles might be the guest speaker," wisecracks Jack.

The back wall contains windows and out of them we can see an extremely nice pool and spa area off a deck. In the pool someone appears to be swimming laps, while a short older gentleman in long pants and dress shirt, arms behind his back, attempts to keep pace by walking the pools edge, and incessantly talking to the swimmer.

We exit the rear door, and to the right is a pottery studio. The door is locked, but out amongst the trees there's an array of pedestals. Several contain what appears to be clay creations set out to dry, while others are wrapped in damp towels.

"I wonder if there are wheels and a kiln in the room?" I say, excited by the prospect. "I used to throw pots many moons ago and loved it."

"You could channel your inner Demi Moore," says Frank, to which Jack and I exchange surprised glances and crack up.

"Good one Frankie boy!" she says.

To the left we re-enter the building through another door and find ourselves in a fully equipped nautilus workout room. The ceiling mounted TV has CNN's Anderson Cooper on. He has a panel on discussing the Mitt Romney/Obama head-to-head debates.

There is a shirtless, trim, and extremely fit middle-aged man working his obliques and possibly his significant other is jogging on the treadmill. Her well-endowed breasts are stuffed into a thin, white, racer tee revealing her nipples, yet nothing seems to bounce. She has on skintight, zebra print, Lululemon yoga pants, and the entire ensemble is accessorized with an abundance of clanking gold jewelry. She gives us a slight smile showing her perfect white teeth between Julia Roberts' lips.

He grabs a white towel and wipes the sweat from his face and chest with well-defined, vascular arms.

"Well, hello there, ladies!" He cheekily grins with his own set of pearly whites, while adjusting his junk and giving a nod our way and completely ignoring Frank. Both the specimens before us are bronze, buff, and flawlessly beautiful.

We spot an exit on the other side of the room, and as we make our way across, Frank notices there's even a Swedish sauna. The exit places us back in the lobby where we entered.

"Nothing like a little eye candy huh, Jack!" I say.

Frank again takes us by surprise. "Yes ma'am, she sure was!"

"Frank," says Jack, "that candy store you were shopping was all bought and paid for big time!"

17

We exit the Harbor Club and take the boardwalk path that is directly across the street. The walkway takes us under the shade of more large oaks and beautiful plantings. At the end we find ourselves with a grand view of the yacht basin harboring a variety of moored boats. At the far side sits a covered shelter with a large American flag, hanging limp from the mast of a nautical flagpole.

We make our way down several steps and pass through another structure, where kayaks are stacked four high on racks, before setting foot directly on the harbor boardwalk. Now unblocked by the tropical trees and foliage the sun shines down unrelentingly. Not a breath of air seems to be moving.

"It's hot out here," I say. The reflection of the sun glistening off the water seems to be intensifying the effect. I dig through my purse for my sunglasses and curse myself under my breath for apparently leaving them back in the car. Jack overhears me and pats the top of her head.

"You might want to check up top!"

At this point on the boardwalk one can either go left or right and both appear to take you to the other side of the yacht basin. There's also a small portion of dock that juts straight ahead into the middle of the harbor, but one can see that it soon dead ends. Frank suggests left towards the covered shelter, and we all follow on the narrow walkway in single file like ducklings.

We pass an array of boats from simple Jon boats and Sun Tracker pontoons to large sailing vessels like Catalina yachts. Along the walk are neatly coiled rope lines and hoses, some attached to boats, others awaiting their watercraft's return to the dock.

Halfway around, Jack and I are sweating profusely. My bangs are plastered to my forehead and Jack has twisted her long dark hair into a makeshift ponytail in an attempt to get it off her neck. Perspiration is starting to show up on the white cotton blouse I'm wearing. Only Frank seems to charge along unscathed by the afternoon sun pulsating straight down overhead. I guess that proves he's a true Floridian, I think, wiping my sweaty upper lip with the back of my hand.

We come to the shelter, and Jack and I both plop down at a picnic table in the shade, while Frank seems to be reading some sort of notice posted on a pole.

"What I'd give for a water right now!" I mutter through dry, sticky lips.

"They're back in the damn van," says Jack, putting her forehead down on the table. "I think I'm going to be sick!"

"That's right," I say wryly, "he gave us water just in case."

Frank has overheard us. "Just maybe ma'am singing that 'Hello Dolly' song again might help you?" He then casts a concerned look at both of us.

Jack raises her head up just long enough to catch his glance and then lays it back down. "My God… he's bone-dry and smiling!"

He offers to go back and get them for us.

"No thanks, Frank," I say. "Let's just make our way back to the van as a group in case one of us dies along the way. First one there turn the air-conditioning on high."

"You two go ahead," says Jack slapping a mosquito off her arm. "I'll try crawling out of here come nightfall!"

18

Stumbling back into the van we all vote to call it a day. Frank says, "I'll see what I can do about rescheduling the remainder of the showings for tomorrow, ma'am. I'll also check to see if anything new has come on the market that I may have overlooked."

We weave our way around some more until we finally arrive at the four-way stop that by now we all have come to recognize.

"Hallelujah!" I say. "Now if we can just make it past the guard, we're home free."

Jack holds a cool water bottle to her forehead. "Oh… something tells me we'll get to start all over again with him tomorrow morning!"

Back at the motel, I quickly run Mac out, as it appears he's been anxiously waiting at the door. He only makes it as far as a nearby flowerpot full of geraniums before lifting his leg.

"Sorry, boy," I say. "We were gone a lot longer than I expected!"

Jack and I then both pass out on our beds and take long needed naps.

We're startled awake by a loud banging on the door that causes Mac to growl and bark vehemently.

"Quiet down, boy!" I say. "You want to get us kicked out of here?"

After checking out my puffy face in the mirror and running a brush through my hair I answer it. Jack has hastily retreated to the bathroom closing the door swiftly behind her.

To my surprise it's Frank with two brown paper Publix grocery bags in his arms. He's wearing one of his outlandish shirts, shorts, and flip-flops. I consider yet again how this guy looks like anything but a real-tor.

"Evening ma'am!" he says with the grin. "Sorry to show up unan-nounced like this, but I thought after the day y'all had, well… just maybe you two fine ladies might enjoy a little picnic on the beach. Oh… and maybe the company of a fine southern boy?"

He stands there grinning and for the first time I look deep into his eyes and notice what an unbelievably dark, steel blue they are. Jack, who's been obviously eavesdropping from behind the bathroom door, suddenly pops out, crowing. "Hell yes, we never really had lunch and I'm starving!"

I tell Frank to give us fifteen minutes to pull ourselves together and we'd be pleased to join him. I mention that in the courtyard out front there are tables, chairs and even some chaise lounges.

"You go have a seat and we'll be right out!"

I shut the door, and Jack jumps right in. "What in the heck do you think he's up to?"

"He's just a nice guy, and he knows we were tired and alone."

"Well, aren't you oblivious!" she says. "I say this has ménage a trois written all over it!"

We freshen up—I twist my hair into a low bun then wrap it with a scarf, apply a little lipstick.

"Finished!" I look one more time in the mirror over the dresser. "This is as good as it gets in fifteen minutes for me." I glance at the clock on the nightstand and see it's been more like thirty.

"Me too," says Jack as she digs through her cosmetic bag, finds a small bottle of Marc Jacobs Daisy, and dabs it behind her ears and dé-colletage.

"Well isn't that going just a bit too far for a beach picnic?" I ask.

She laughs. "Not if I happen to be right!"

We enter the courtyard and to our surprise Frank has quite a spread set up on one of the umbrella tables.

"I hope you don't mind, ladies, but I took the liberty of setting up our picnic out here. This way we have a table and chairs and we don't have to deal with sand in the food."

"It looks fabulous!" I exclaim.

"Hand me a paper plate," says Jack, "and make it snappy surfer boy!"

He has supplied us with an assortment of cheese and crackers, crab spread, and cold prawns with cocktail sauce. There are Kalamata and blue cheese stuffed olives. There's a whole roasted mesquite chicken, and he's included holiday grapes, a couple apples, and a pear. Best of all my eyes spy a container of chocolate brownies iced with additional chocolate.

"You sure know how to throw one heck of an impromptu picnic." I smile as he takes out a package of plastic wine glasses from the bag, followed by two bottles of wine.

"Red or white?" he asks while holding one up in each hand.

To which we simultaneously answer, "Both!"

Frank sits next to Jack on a bench, and I situate myself in a chair on the other side of the table. We eat lots, drink much, and talk even more. The conversation is pleasant and gentle with not a mention of real estate or condos. I can't help but notice that most of Frank's attention is directed at Jack. He cleverly interjects questions into the conversation like a trained investigator.

"Where do you live? Here, have some Brie, ma'am. What do you do? Let me pour you ladies some more wine. Do you live alone?"

This is the one question he seems to hang on, waiting for her answer. It comes to my attention that this evening the man has spoken more than at any time since I met him, and yet for some reason, I feel like I've known him for years.

The sky above the motel begins to glow pink as the pre-show for the sunset has begun.

"Oh, I'd love to see another sunset before going back to land-locked Ohio!" exclaims Jack.

"Well, how about we all refill our glasses and head for the beach?" Frank is already filling Jack's glass to the top.

I put my hand over mine. "No more for me, please, I've had quite enough. Why don't I stay here and clean this stuff up while you two take a walk? Plus, I need to feed Mac and take him out again."

Jack gives me a quizzical look, her eyes saying, *What's up?*

Frank grabs both their glasses while gesturing, *Right this way ma'am!*

I finish putting the leftover picnic items away in the mini-fridge in the kitchenette. I feed the dog, pour myself a half glass more of Cab Sav, grab the James Patterson book I've been reading out of my bag, put Mac on his lead, and aim back out to the courtyard. After a quick search for a grassy spot with Mac, I curl up on a chaise precisely as the sky shifts to a brilliant orange and the lampposts flicker to life for the evening.

Well, so much for reading in this light. I chuckle just as a couple of guys, possibly a few years younger than I, exit their room with wine bottle in hand and come join me.

"Hi," I say, and we immediately strike up a friendly conversation as Mac begs each of them for attention.

Seems the one is a professor from New York visiting the other one who's on faculty at the Ringling College of Art and Design. The one from New York further explains that it's time for the Annual Ringling College Faculty and Staff Exhibitions, and he wouldn't miss his friend's current showing for the world. He further clarifies that he also teaches art at the Cooper Union and that is how they met.

"It was more like on the beach during a spring break vacation sweetie!" says his companion. The more wine they drink the more obvious it becomes these two are partners.

We continue chatting, with them repeatedly offering me some of their wine, to which I unsuccessfully try to decline. It's only after one of them runs back to their room to grab another bottle that I finally take my phone out of my pocket and check the time. It's just after nine thirty and the sun's been down for a while now. I have to wonder if Jack is okay, and whether I go look for her—or whether she's A-okay, in which case I should leave her alone!

19

Curled up in bed, with Mac at my feet, I finally get the chance to continue reading my book, *Sail*. I'm completely lost in the story as the sailboat the family is sailing on explodes. I gasp at the same instant that I hear a key turn in the lock. Jack enters, shuts the door, then leans back against it with a smile on her face that I haven't seen in a long while.

"Well?" I say.

"You were right," she replies. "He's a very nice guy!"

She flops across the bottom of the bed alongside Mac and begins the play-by-play account of what transpired.

"Basically, after the sun went down and the beach cleared of people, we continued walking. Have you ever heard about the green flash?"

"The what?"

"Never mind, anyway before we knew it, we were all the way to the Village. He offered to buy me a drink and we ended up at the Old Salty Dog. We talked and talked until I suddenly realized it was eleven o'clock, and knowing how you worry, I suggested I should be going. Seems our Frank is a bit of a regular, and he knew the bartender who called us a cab that brought us back, and the rest, as they say, is history."

"What on earth did you have to talk about in all that time with a total stranger?"

"That's the odd thing," says Jack. "Everything and nothing at all. It just felt right being together!"

"So…" I push harder. "How did the date end?"

"What date?" Jack defends. "It was a walk on the beach with your re-altor!"

"Well…?"

"Well… honestly, I think he would have kissed me if I'd have leaned in further!" Jack giggles with a blush.

The next morning, I feed Mac and take him out before we go. After seeing numerous dogs around Pelican Cove, I plan on taking him with us. Heck! I think, he's got to live there too so we might as well get his opinion.

When Frank arrives, I get the usual "Mornin' ma'am," but Jack gets a "Well, hello Miss Jackie."

As he slides open the door letting us both into the van I whisper, "Miss Jackie. When have you ever let anyone call you Miss or Jackie?"

She smirks and whispers back. "Somehow when he said it, well it was okay. You know, sort of a 'when in the south' thing?"

We pull up to the guardhouse, and Mac has made his way onto Frank's lap so he can see out the open window. I can literally hear Frank take a deep breath, bracing himself for what's about to come. To our surprise we're greeted by a hefty, round-faced fellow. He sets down what appears to be a bologna on white bread sandwich and smiles.

"Good morning folks, how can I help you today?" He requests the same documentation and proceeds with the same lines of questioning. However, he is so less pretentious than the guard yesterday and some-how warm and welcoming.

Frank jests with him about yesterday's experience and of our trouble finding some of the listings, to which this guard generously offers up yet another map of the place.

"You folks keep that Scotch hound on a lead. Okay?"

Frank thanks him, the gate goes up, and we're back inside in a frac-tion of the time it took to enter yesterday. He hands back the extra map to us.

"I still have yesterday's maps up here. You may want to keep that one with you in case we get split up!" And I catch a glimpse of that devious smirk of his in the rearview mirror.

The day's viewings pretty much progress exactly as yesterday. We hunt, we search, we finally find, and then we view one-by-one the condos on his list. We actually look at something called a tree house this time, which is basically a two-story unit. It feels more like a house, and I like the additional space. However, the master bedroom and bath are both on the second floor, and I'm pretty set on not having steps in my life this time.

We also view a condo out on a point with views of the Little Sarasota Bay. Unlike yesterday, there's a breeze, and one could tell it would be quite pleasant to sit on the lanai of this unit and watch the boats go by.

"I'm seeing rattan furnishings, a good book, and me sipping wine out here," I say.

"I'm seeing me overstaying my visits, and you with a pitcher of margaritas pouring for me!" laughs Jack.

Frank is quick to point out that this particular unit has an asking price of almost twice that of all the others we've seen in here.

The more we tour, the further convinced I become that this place is it. Sensing my thoughts perhaps, Frank asks me what I think.

"It's beautiful and I love being so near the water," I say. "Unfortunately, we haven't found the right floor plan and the right setting for Mac and me yet."

"We still have a few more to see, ma'am, and now that y'all narrowed the condo community down to this place, well, that's half the battle. We'll just keep on a lookin'."

And continuing to look is what we do. He announces that this next one just came on the market and that he came across the listing in a search back at his office yesterday afternoon. He voices his concern that the description boasts: "Handy Man's Special and a Real Fixer Upper!" And that the price is quite a bit below what all the other units are listing for.

"Well that's a good thing!" I say. "I'm not adverse to some paint and papering."

"Well to be honest, ma'am, they usually need a lot more than just a little TLC."

20

Ironically this condo is back on Pelican Cove Road, exactly where we started first thing yesterday. It's across from the Pelican Pavilion and pool, both of which we have yet to see. Frank parks and we perform our now synchronized maneuver of all jumping out together. We easily spot the pavilion and hear the sound of water splashing from behind plantings and a gazebo.

Directly across from it are a visitor parking lot, a small four-space carport, and a tall dense hedge. Above it all we can just make out the roofline of a building peeking out between a tall swamp chestnut oak and several queen palm trunks. We're looking around for a way to get to the other side of the blockade of plantings when Frank shouts, "Over here!"

Mid-center and under the awnings of the carport is a narrow break in the hedge. After passing through it we find ourselves crossing a small wooden bridge over what appears to be a dry creek bed lined with decorative lava rocks. The plantings are lush in front of what appears to be four condo units. The small cement block path we're following splits in three directions. One path goes immediately right to a bottom unit while a much longer one goes left to another. A center path leads straight ahead to the base of two sets of stairs, each leading to individual upper units.

"Which one's GL-359?" asks Frank, as the unit's numbers are not easily visible from our vantage point, nor are they on the front doors like previous units we visited.

Of course, it ends up being the last one we check, and furthest from the bridge, when we find it. It's the bottom left unit and it has a cute green café table with two matching chairs sitting on the small patio area in front of the kitchen sliders. There's a decorative watering can on the table, and it is home to a silk, red geranium plant. As well, there's a wreath hanging on the wall by the front door and it, too, has red geraniums adorning it.

From our current point of view on the covered porch, we can see that a mulch path passes by the property and crosses yet another wood bridge with a view of what appears to be a dry retention pond, and it too is lined with large rocks. Overall the look is quite charming and welcoming.

"I like this!" I say. "The place reminds me of a fairy tale."

"Which one," says Jack, "Three Billy Goats Gruff and the troll bridge?"

"No!" I say, "Hansel and Gretel!"

"You do know that's about a cannibalistic witch, don't you?"

As always, Frank allows us to lead the way and I stop dead in the doorway after its opening.

"What the heck is that smell?" I ask as Mac gives one of his low guttural growls while sniffing raucously at the fetid air exiting the building.

"Smells like something or someone died in there," says Jack. "But then like they sprayed it with what... bug spray?"

"Or possibly, somebody left Limburger cheese sitting out?" I suggest.

Frank insists he go first and asks us to step aside and let him have a look around. The place is extremely dark inside, and when he flips the light switches, just inside the front door, nothing comes on.

"Seems the electricity is turned off," he says back to us. "That explains how hot and stuffy it is and partly the smell problem. Please leave the front door open, if you would ma'am, to let some more air and light in here."

He pulls a small keychain flashlight from his pocket and quickly disappears off around the corner, while Jack and I are left standing there in the entry with Mac.

"Should have known he's a boy scout and always prepared," states Jack.

After my eyes adjust, the first thing I notice, by sticking my head inside, is that large sections of the popcorn ceiling in the living area appear to be peeling and falling off onto the floor. There are sections of it all over the rug. I peek around the corner, and because of the glass sliders providing ambient lighting, I can easily see around the kitchen. It looks like something straight out of the seventies.

Frank returns. "Just another minute, ladies, and I'll have all the blinds open so we can try to see something!"

Jack and I, led by Macs sniffing nose, continue in. All the appliances are old and original.

"Good grief, Liz," she says, "you think they even work?"

"Hard to tell with no power," I say.

I open the fridge door and suddenly we both know what the source of the bad smell might be. Mac comes scurrying over and sniffs at the air with tail wagging. Unrecognizable food items have been left inside and even in this low light they resemble some kind of science project more than anything that was once edible.

Jack quickly slams the fridge back shut and pinches her nose. "Pee-yew!"

Mac licks at the outside of the refrigerator door and I have to pull him away by his lead.

"Gross!"

There's some sort of yellowed, plastic, domed ceiling overhead, and the walls are overlaid in a daisy pattern vinyl wall covering. I'm compelled to try the light switches, which again don't work, and I'm even further grossed out by how sticky they are. In fact, as I look around and make the mistake of opening a cabinet, I come to the realization that everything in the kitchen is covered with a thick layer of cooking grease. However, I'm surprised to see a colorful set of Fiesta dinnerware and a couple of juice glasses inside.

It's just about this time that I let out a scream, and Mac responds with a bark, as a huge roach runs out of the cupboard and up the wall.

Frank rejoins us. "Everything all right ma'am? Did you find the body?"

We quickly bring him up to speed on what we've found in the kitchen.

He advises us that the master bathroom vanity is for some reason torn out and sitting in the middle of the bedroom. There's a large hole in the master bathroom wall and the guest shower has a bit of a mold problem.

"It's hard to tell how bad the place really is without lights, but I don't believe anyone's lived here for quite a long time."

We make our way to the rear of the condo and the lanai area. Here Mac sniffs and snorts profusely along the sliding glass door edges and grumbles at the chameleons running on the screens. Most of the other units have had gorgeous views to the outside. This one is blocked by huge, overgrown, foliage and right outside the door within arm's reach are the trunks of two huge trees.

We open a double set of doors to the right and find an extremely dated Maytag stackable washer and dryer that look one step away from induction into the Smithsonian. The entire laundry area is filled with rusty paint cans, old buckets, a toilet plunger, two dirty brooms, and a squeeze mop.

Frank pries at the rear slider door that seems to have not been opened for many years and then struggles with a broken screen door latch. He finally gets them open, and we step out into a small jungle with a few round pavers scattered here and there, making a haphazard kind of wobbly path out to the backyard.

Once we make our way out to the clearing Frank takes a deep breath. "Goodness gracious, ma'am, I'm sorry to waste your time on this one. What a mess."

Jack laughs. "Wow Liz, he's right... this one's the pits!"

I look around at the large, grassy backyard with its beautiful garden directly behind the place, the regal and tall trees embracing the building, the colorful Picasso's paintbrush and gold dust crotons, and the last remains of azalea blossoms surrounding it all.

"I'll take it!"

And with that, Mac lifts his leg and pees on Frank's shoe.

This Is Home

—Switchfoot (2008)

(Songwriters: Adam Watts, Andrew Creighton Dodd and Jonathan Foreman)

21

Returning back home I quickly jump into wrapping up my old life. My house has been on the market for several months and my extremely staunch, suit-and-tie Cincinnati realtor and I agree to lower the asking price since I now own two places. He concludes that this new price point will most assuredly get some additional traffic through the place and hopefully sell it fast.

Through the years I have accumulated way too much "stuff" I reflect, as I walk around my first floor taking it all in. Recently, while at work, I viewed an Oprah segment with a focus panel of housewives waiting to be questioned about their retention of content from commercials they saw during an hour of typical afternoon TV viewing. The topic of the show dealt with a "less is more" theme, and somehow intuitively I knew they meant me. The theory was that all the things we collect and surround ourselves with are actually burdening and weighing us down.

Oprah's guest, Peter Walsh, advised that as we release our emotional attachment to inanimate objects, and by giving things away, we literally and spiritually become lighter, and in turn we feel less stress. The stress that is induced by our constant caring for and worrying about everything we own. Seems we also internalize a fear that we actually need to keep them in our possession in order to be happy. I distinctly recall Oprah's words: "I'm not just cleaning my closet out. I'm cleaning out my life. And I'm keeping only that which delights me or enhances my well-being." Whatever the case, less stress and lightening my load is exactly what this move is all about for me.

I continue walking around the house opening cupboards and cabinets and looking at all the QVC on-line purchases, garage sale finds, and passed-along antique family heirlooms I have amassed. Where previously I saw treasure, I am now seeing clutter, and lots and lots of dust. Where I once staged collectibles in curios for bragging rights, I now see unused and gratuitous items. I suddenly come to the realization that we don't really own anything… we just borrow it for a while and then someone else gets to love and hopefully use it.

"Yes, yes, yes!" I proclaim aloud. "The time has come for me to let go!"

Jack has offered to help me whenever she has free time if I can use her assistance. I know part of the offer is because that's the kind of person she is, always ready and willing to help others. A big part of what I love about her. But the actual motivation, and more important one, is because I'm leaving soon and she wants to get as much face-time in as possible. Heck, we both do! Either way, I'm just super glad to have her as my best friend.

The entire process, however, is bittersweet and starts out with only the least attractive or chipped items making the first cut. I'm flabbergasted to find I have eight full sets of dishes to choose from; each includes cups, saucers, and dessert plates. Several even have sugars, creamers and matching salt and peppers. Also, I have enough glasses of various types and sizes to host a party for one hundred individuals before we'd have to start washing them.

Jack gets a twinkle in her eye and selects one representation of each dinner plate and lays it on the dining room table.

"Okay, Elizabeth Blum, which one's your absolute favorite?"

I scan the line of plates and easily pick-up my grandmother's Bavarian china. "I love this one not only because the flower pattern is so beautiful," I say. "But because I think of my Gram each and every time I use them." And then always emotional me begins to tear up.

"No time for that crap! You old softy," says Jack. "Okay, you just picked the good china, now what's your second fav?"

I walk up and down the table looking at each several times, as I believe I now know exactly where this is headed.

"I think I would have to pick the set of dishes Scott and I bought and used when we lived in Italy. We ended up shipping them back home as our souvenirs to ourselves."

"Great job sweetie, say hello to your everyday setting!"

Jack brings in two moving boxes and wrapping paper from the garage while I'm directed to grab the packing tape, scissors, and permanent marker from a kitchen drawer. We put the boxes together and start wrapping. She takes Gram's Bavarian and I take the Italian, packing each set carefully in its own boxes. I spend the majority of the time re-telling tales of our Italian travels, and some of the great meals from the local market that were served on these plates to our newfound Italian friends and neighbors.

Once packed and the boxes marked with; dining room, dishes, fragile, this side up! I ask, "What the heck am I going to do with all the others?"

"Grab your Canon camera and MacBook Pro!" orders Jack. "Now stack one set at a time on the table and take a picture of each. First, you're going to post it on Facebook where your neighbors, friends, and co-workers can all see it. For the status write: This stuff will be available to whoever wants it for the next three days… Come-And-Get-it! What's still left over after that goes to Goodwill, and you'll have a great tax write-off."

I do as I'm told and then we move on to the glassware, handling it in much the same way. Except Jack jokes, "Keep any and all wine glasses, as we know you'll definitely be using them, plus you always tend to break them."

"Only when we kill two bottles at once!" I say, and we both break into laughter followed by a well-needed break for a hug.

The laughter fades, and then Jack turns somber. "Have you told your daughter anything?"

"I tried calling Maggie," I say. "And got her voice mail, per usual. I left a short message for her yet again, but only included that I was definitely moving and wanted to talk to her about it. I totally left out the fact that it's to Florida. She'll probably conclude that I'm moving to an assisted living community here in Cincinnati!"

And again, we laugh. "She's so wrapped up in her acting career and social life in New York City that now I probably won't hear from her until the holidays, and only then because she feels guilty for... what? Successfully cutting all ties with her past life? At least I might see her on TV performing in the Macy's parade!"

"And your sister-in-law, Margaret?" she pries further while giving me an inquisitive glance.

"You know darn well, Jacqueline, that I have no idea what country she even calls home these days, and I haven't heard directly from her since last year's Christmas card!"

"Sorry I asked, it's just that you two were so close once," she says. "And I know darn well I've pushed too far when you refer to me as Jacqueline. Let's move on to the library, shall we...? Now, you're not taking all those damn books of yours, are you?"

22

Finally, it appears that my manager realizes the countdown is on. So now instead of piling on the work he just looks forlorn and keeps saying, "What in the world am I going to do without you?"

And, although possibly construed as inappropriate behavior by co-workers, he hugs me at least once a day now advising, "I'm sure going to miss you, kiddo!"

I sincerely believe he means it as we have worked together for quite a long time now. I also start to realize how many other people I'm going to miss throughout the rest of the company.

Since the condo was vacant at the time of purchase, and it's an estate settlement between two estranged sisters with neither one wanting anything to do with the place—or each other—the closing moves along quickly. Almost too quickly! To my surprise I don't even have to return to Florida for it. Several days prior, the mortgage company sends an overnight FedEx to all parties involved that include copies of all the paperwork to be signed.

Next they send a representative—a notary—to my house in Ohio, and she witnesses my signature. There is some exchanging back-and-forth of checks to cover various expenses or balances due and then she shakes my hand.

"Congratulations, Mrs. Blum on your new home purchase. I'm sure you'll enjoy it!" Afterwards she exits swiftly out the front door.

Suddenly I feel a bit apprehensive, then anxious, and finally sick to my stomach.

Oh my God... I own two places, a situation I can't possibly afford, and I'm voluntarily leaving my source of income soon!

I try to reflect on how I wasn't given any choice regarding being handed a mandatory retirement package from P&G at my age. And now, standing alone amongst the boxes and packing materials, I scream out loud. "What in the hell am I doing?"

After a Librium, washed down with a wine chaser, I begin to relax. Thinking back now, the hardest part of the entire closing process was finding somewhere to sit, as my dining room table was full of that day's giveaway items. This time my Facebook page was filled with small kitchen appliances and various cooking utensils. Jack had returned yesterday to help tackle the kitchen cupboards and pantry, which explains why we couldn't use my kitchen table either. Besides, she had sold it to my neighbor, Pam, when the woman merely stopped by to see how I was doing and to bid me well on the move.

I have confirmed a mover—Two Men and A Truck—to arrive December 31 to load the U-Haul I reserved. In turn they will have a couple of their movers from their company in Bradenton meet us on the other end to unpack it. The plan is that Jack will drive the truck down while Mac and I follow in my Escape. Jack will stay a few days in Florida, eat some seafood, and then fly out of Sarasota—my treat for helping me move. Per her I'm getting off cheap!

The days fly by faster and faster as the house becomes emptier and emptier. I have taken to stacking the packed moving and copy paper boxes I bring home from work in the two-car garage and am amazed at how quickly it has filled up. Of course, this means I must keep my car outside on the driveway. So now I have to add on additional time in the mornings to defrost and scrape ice from the windows or brush off snow before leaving for work. Both are chores I won't miss one iota after the move.

The showings have all but stopped, as we are now smack dab in the middle of the holiday season. My staunch old realtor advises me that only buyers that sincerely must move for employment reasons actually look at homes this time of year. He ensures me it will pick up come springtime. I contemplate the idea of waiting till spring to sell and think how far away that date seems.

"Don't worry," he says. "I will keep an eye on the place and hire someone to shovel the snow if necessary. You should keep the heat on 65 degrees and leave a water faucet dripping on an outside wall like the kitchen sink. If you can leave a couple lamps behind for nighttime showings that would be helpful too."

"What about the keys?" I ask.

"I'll put a lockbox on the front door. These McMansions don't always show well when they're empty. But if you can arrange to have the carpets cleaned, it helps to get rid of the furniture marks."

We shake hands, extremely businesslike, and he scampers out the door. "Safe travels, and I'll be in touch."

December 31 comes, and a mere four hours later, the movers have finished packing up the truck and left as well. Now I sit all alone, in an almost empty house, on a folding lawn chair, next to the ugliest lamp I have ever owned that's sitting upon an old TV tray with a crowing rooster picture on it.

I'm treating myself to my favorite pizza from LaRosa's prior to the big move tomorrow. It contains mushrooms, red onions, and black olives on traditional crust, and I savor every bite. I suspect it'll be the last LaRosa's pizza I ever eat. I pick up my half-full glass of wine, while standing up and grabbing the bottle of Happy Camper Cabernet and proceed to walk around the house realizing it feels so empty, so lonely... so sad.

I pause in the living room and picture my family being in it together during happier times. There's a fire in the fireplace and the smell of cinnamon and spice Yankee candles fill the air. I'm directing my children, Maggie and Tommy, on the fine art of properly trimming the Christmas tree, while Scott is stirring his infamous hot chocolate on the stove in the kitchen. Maggie delights that he always sticks a candy cane through several marshmallows before placing them in the steaming mugs as stir-sticks.

A holiday special is on the TV, and we snuggle in under one of Mema's afghans on the couch to all watch it together. Sipping at our mugs of hot chocolate, the kids' laughter fills the room at the appearance of the Snow Miser. Even the thought of the afghan, now safely packed away on the moving truck, conjures up more emotions regarding my leaving Cincinnati. It was hand crocheted by my mother who was born, raised, and buried here.

My God, am I really leaving?

I sigh, take a sip of wine, and open the front door to the night's frosty air.

I step outside on the front porch and take a deep breath, hugging myself for warmth, and glance up and down the street. The twinkling of all the neighbors' Christmas lights, in contrast to the darkness of my house, and the complete silence of the scene blanketed in new fallen snow brings on more melancholy.

"You're on the verge of a great adventure my dear," I say to myself. "It's a New Year and a new you. CHEERS!" I yell out while lifting my glass towards the sky. And as snowflakes kiss my cheeks goodbye, I finish off the last of the wine.

23

January 1, 2012

I wake up in my sleeping bag, stiff from lying on the random-peg hardwood floor of the family room, with Mac curled up next to me. Jack had offered for me to stay at her place since mine was empty, but I somehow felt the need to spend the last night right here. I get up reflecting on last night's emotion-fest and scratch Mac's ear.

"You know what, good boy? I think we're ready to go now!"

I let Mac out to do his business in the fenced-in backyard while I go into the first floor half-bath to wash my face and brush my hair and teeth. Searching my purse, I apply a little lipstick in an attempt to look presentable. I blot my lips on a tissue and then rub the residue on the apples of my cheeks.

A lot of good that did. I smirk checking the mirror one last time. There's a "shave and a haircut knock" on the front door and in pops Jack, Dunkin' Donuts bag and two cups of coffee in hand.

"Time to rise and shine sleepy head!" she bellows. "We should have been on the road a half hour ago."

"Hand me one of those!" I beg.

She hands me a cup. "Skinny, French Vanilla, Latte for you. Straight up, strong and black for me!"

Jack then hands me the bag. "There's a flat bread egg white veggie sandwich in there for you. I ate my pink frosted donut with sprinkles on the way here so you wouldn't have to see it."

Then, seeing Mac scratching at the patio door, she walks over and lets him back in. He stops in the middle of the hardwood floor and shakes vigorously to get the snow off his fur leaving a puddle of wetness.

"Well, that's one mess I won't have to deal with in Florida," I say and grab a roll of paper towels off the kitchen counter.

I place my personal items in my travel bag, roll up the sleeping bag, pack up Mac's food and a few last-minute things, and then pause in the entry hall before going out the door.

"Aren't you going to take a last tear-filled look around?" says Jack. "You're leaving a lot of history behind here. I even brought Puffs-To-Go!"

To even my surprise I smile. "Been there, done that last night… I'm good to go!"

The trip down takes FOREVER. It's actually only two and a half days, but my bottom says I've been sitting much longer. It seems the truck's fastest speed is around sixty-five miles per hour—less when it encounters uphill grades. Throw in crossing the Smokey Mountains after Jellico, Tennessee, and we're mostly in the slow lane crawling.

At a rest stop I question Jack's knowledge of shifting and if she's using the correct gears while driving. She in turn reminds me of how fully loaded the moving van actually is, and while pointing a finger to the warning label on the back door suggests, "Perhaps you exceeded the recommended weight capacity limit of 7,500 pounds."

"You know darn well I got rid of tons of stuff," I say. "Why I'm practically down to the bare bones. Per Oprah, I'm so damn light and stress-free right now I should float!"

"Oh, I see," she says with a chuckle. "Is that why you snuck that third set of dishes onto the truck?"

We finally pull up to the gate at Pelican Cove around five-thirty p.m. on Sunday, and the strict guard with the gray ponytail sticks his head out. I put on my brightest smile and muster up my friendliest "Hello there! I'm Elizabeth Blum." Then I explain my new ownership of unit GL359 and that I'm moving in today, all while dangling the new door keys that were mailed to me in his face as proof of my honestly belonging here. I further expound about my friend Jack and the truck behind me and throw in how we've been on the road for days now and that a hot shower would feel really great about now. Finishing with "And your name would be?"

I swear the man's expression doesn't change one bit during my entire award-winning performance. When it appears that I'm finished he stares me in the eyes.

"It's after five-thirty p.m., Miss Blum, and no delivery trucks are permitted in Pelican Cove after five, and never, ever on Sunday. Here's a parking pass for your vehicle for tonight, but be sure to report to the office first thing in the morning to get your visitor's permit."

But I'm a resident?

He continues, "Since it's Sunday night, and the employee lot is empty, you can park your truck there for the evening. However, you must have it out of there prior to seven a.m. when the employees start to arrive."

"That's fine," I say. "I'll just call the movers and tell them they can arrive earlier than we planned tomorrow."

To which I'm met with a frown and a stern warning. "No contractors or service personnel are permitted entry prior to nine am."

"Okay…"

"And that truck's too large to be permitted into the cove. It may damage our delicate tree canopy. You need to tell your movers they'll need to off-load it into a pick-up truck or van and then move the items individually by hand. I recommend that, in the morning, you move your truck to the empty Kmart parking lot on the corner of 41 and Beneva and have them move everything from there."

The gate goes up slowly, and as I pull forward, I faintly hear him say, "I hope you enjoy your visit with us."

24

Prior to my arrival I had spoken to the office where they advised me they were replacing something called 'the stacks' and that Pelican Cove was responsible for repairing my bathroom walls and resetting the vanity in place. As well, they had helped me secure a company to come in and deep clean the condo. However, during Jack's stay, after thoroughly cleaning the kitchen again, we put away things like dishes, glasses, and pots and pans in the obvious places we think they should go. We're now left with moving furniture around and approximately fifty or so additional unpacked boxes. We've made some of the boxes into temporary end tables complete with lamps.

Going from almost three thousand square feet of living space down to fourteen hundred, I keep wondering what I would have done if I hadn't gotten rid of three quarters of the stuff in my other home. And even now, after the move, Jack and I have to take several loads of items to the Goodwill drop-off out on the Tamiami. Somehow numerous pieces of framed art and various pieces of furniture just didn't look right once I see them in this setting. They're too dark, too heavy, and too northern. And what about all that kitchen stuff and glassware? Well, only so much can fit in the minimal number of drawers and cabinets these places have.

I didn't bring my bedroom set, or my living room couch, so I have nowhere to sleep except my trusty sleeping bag. Jack has made a makeshift bed out of a stack of blankets and topped it off with one of my mom's granny square afghans. Again, what I love about her, she goes with the flow even referring to our few days together as a camp-out in the Pelican Woods.

And with that thought in mind, we both agree upon Jack's original description of the architecture and look of Pelican Cove. It's a glorified Girl Scout camp. Unbeknownst to both of us, before this trip, each had attended sleep-away camps with the scouts when we were kids—me in Ohio and Jack in Chicago, Illinois. We both recall staying in non-descript, beige and brown cabins or lodges nestled into their wilderness surroundings, almost as if they'd popped up and grew naturally in the woods, much like a mushroom or how an alder bracket nestles in at the base of a tree. We quickly start referring to walks in the cove as hikes, the pool as the swimming hole, and assisting some of the elderly neighbors as earning our merit badges.

On this, our last hike prior to Jack leaving, we stroll the boardwalk along the Little Sarasota Bay with Mac. The breeze is gentle through the palms, the air smelling fresh, and the sun setting over the Turtle Beach end of Siesta Key.

"You know, Liz, Girl Scout camp never had anything quite like this," says Jack, taking in the magnificent view.

"I know… trust me I know! The closest thing at mine was the campfire we had by the lake."

Jack chuckles. "I thought you were going to say the jungle breakfasts where they hung our food from the trees!"

25

The three days have flown past, and it seems like we have both been avoiding the inevitable goodbyes to come. Oh, we have hugged as we pass on the way to the bathroom. We give a peck on the cheek before bed. We hold hands while walking the dog. Each quiet sign of affection loudly expressing, *I'm going to miss you so damn much!*

Mac and I drop Jack off at the SRQ Airport, and I'm suddenly hit with the realization that I'm now all alone and living in Sarasota, Florida.

"Hell, I don't even have a doctor or a shrink to run to during an anxiety attack! Was that a hospital we passed on the way here?"

I'm talking to Mac but know darn well that the statements are directed at my inner, worrisome self. My palms are getting sweaty on the steering wheel, and I feel my mind racing as I overthink how I'm going to die alone in my dilapidated jungle hut of a condo. I contemplate how no one will find the body until the mailman can't cram another piece of forwarded mail into the mailbox, and finally stops by the Pelican Cove office to bring it to their attention.

I crank up the air and turn on the car radio in an attempt to distract myself by singing along to Taylor Swift's "Everything Has Changed." Then I quickly turn it off as the beat of the music has made me even more anxious.

"Damn, damn, damn!" I yell at myself, and Mac curls up in the passenger seat while giving me his famous Scotty eye roll, and sighs as if to say, *"Here she goes again!"*

I feel the need to jump out of the car, possibly while it's still moving, so I quickly take a right turn attempting to get off busy 41. Finding myself now on the John Ringling Causeway I am forced to proceed across the Ringling Bridge.

"BAD CHOICE!" I scream. "Now I'm on a damn bridge."

On the far side, I quickly pull into Bayfront Park, driving straight ahead into a spot and throw the car in park.

Surprisingly, instead of bailing, I sit facing the water and its rippling waves. I open the car windows, take a deep breath, and stare at the blue-green beauty of the lagoon before me. Mac makes his way over the center console and places himself smack-dab in my lap with his chin on my chest.

I gently stroke his head and back while continuing to look straight ahead. I'm oblivious to the other cars coming and going in the lot or the park walkers crossing the bridge on foot to the right of me. I feel my chest loosen and realize my breathing is slowing down. The tunnel vision is retreating, and my peripheral vision slowly returns. I finally move my head and take in the city view, the boats, and the group of board paddlers going by on the water. The sun, sparkling like crystals across the tops of the curling waves in Sarasota Bay, makes the scene almost surreal. It's an unbelievably beautiful time of the day.

"How lucky we are to have the chance to live here," I whisper to Mac, who climbs up and licks my face. "Thanks for the kiss." He's really just after the remnants of a salty tear. "Actually, big guy… how lucky we are to have the chance to start over here in paradise!"

And that's when I suddenly realize it's the first time EVER that I have made it through a full-fledged panic attack without the aid of a Librium.

I place the car into reverse and slowly back out of the parking spot. I pull back onto the road, leaving the windows open this time. In fact, I even open the sunroof on the Escape and my hair blows every which way. Mac puts his paws up on the passenger-side armrest and happily sticks his head out the window, sniffing the air. Usually these episodes leave me completely exhausted and in need of a nap to recoup. However, this time I feel better than I have in a long, long time. I'm actually exhilarated, left with a new feeling of having conquered something... "My demons," I mutter and then turning to Mac, "We're going to be just fine fella!

He looks back into the car from the window and gives me a Scottie wink.

I'll Be There for You

—The Rembrandts (1994)

26

Settling into a routine has been challenging for Mac and me. Back home I had a fenced-in yard, so our regular regimen basically consisted of my opening the rear door, letting Mac out, and then getting a cup of coffee. Down here, per Pelican Cove rules, all dogs must be kept on lead and the only fences are the ones around the perimeter of the entire compound. This is actually a bit of a relief to me as I figure, if Mac were to accidently get out, the only true exit is the front gate with the guard. That is unless he aims towards the bay and the water where there is no fencing. But that thought comes with additional worries as I think about the gators and the bobcats that are purported to be in here.

So, now we start our day at six in the morning with Mac nuzzling me in the face, grumbling in Scotty fashion until I get up. This part of the routine is completely new, as usually I'm not lying on the floor at eye level to him. I grab my robe and we quickly run out the front door, across the bridge and over to the large southern live oak across the street, where he relieves himself. We both then quickly retreat back to bed. As I snuggle back in place, I contemplate how I wanted a place with a yard for him, but since I'm not strong enough to pry the broken backdoor open, we've had to resort to going out the front one.

Around eight am we get back up and Mac eats breakfast while I prep my Mr. Coffee. We then go for our morning walk. I was apprehensive and a bit self-conscious at first about walking the grounds, as I wasn't yet familiar with my surroundings. I had kept the map Frank had given me, but that only showed the main roadways and did little to ebb my anxiety regarding the unknown. I quickly find that this place is a maze of shell and mulch paths, walking trails and boardwalks. Actually, there are no real sidewalks to speak of anywhere. Even the walkways to the condo units consist of only landscape pavers.

So today I take off with Mac, tethered into the new red harness I got him at PetSmart at the Landings Plaza grasped in my left hand and bottled water in the right. We head, yet again, across the street to the large grassy spot under the big oak that Mac believes he has not yet significantly marked as his own... and he does so yet again by doing both his jobs. We continue on behind a row of treehouse condos, passing the Pelican Pool, and onto a dirt trail that soon connects with a shell path.

That path continues connecting us to Treehouse Circle and we turn left onto the roadway, where I'm glad to find a semi-hidden dumpster. It's discretely surrounded by a privacy fence and landscaped with plantings around its perimeter. I open the gate and deposit the waste bag of Mac's poo I've been toting. Picking up daily after Mac is yet another new experience for me, as basically up north it's mostly a summertime ordeal, since in winter the snow covers it over and it disintegrates by spring.

We continue on making our way between the end of a condo unit and a dense jungle bordered with tall switch cane bamboo. The path ends up coupling with yet another one that runs directly along the entrance road of Pelican Cove, thus allowing me to finally know where I am. We choose to go right, and Mac has a great time sniffing at the base of each and every tree that lines the route, then stopping at about every third one to leave his calling card as well.

"You know that you're merely just going through the motions," I say. "By now there can't be a single drop left in you!"

To our right is a half basketball court with some benches, and behind that is an area in the woods with the signage, dog park. We take the path to the dog area and it appears to be a completely fenced enclosure with additional benches for owner seating.

"Well, now we know there's somewhere to let you run off lead," I tell Mac while bending over to scratch behind his ears.

As the path continues through a forest of loblolly pines it curves around a huge pineapple palm where we come face-to-face with a husky man and his schnauzer.

"Well, howdy do!" he says.

"Hello."

"Correct me if I'm wrong, but I don't believe we've ever met?"

He sticks out a large hand for me to shake while I proceed to introduce myself. Mac and his dog do their own form of introductions by exchanging sniffs.

"This little gal's name is Patty," he says, "short for Patty Cake. And yours is?"

"Mac," I say, "short for MacArthur."

After exchanging pleasantries, he takes off in the opposite direction calling back over his shoulder. "Hope to see ya 'round!"

Just before coming to the guardhouse, we cross Pelican Cove Road and continue on Brookhouse. We then walk left onto Clower Creek Drive, making our way under the tree canopy and passing what appear to be additional two-story condos set back from the road.

Surprisingly, partway down the road the sky opens up as the tree limbs thin and eventually the pavement is drenched in bright sunshine. The plantings and landscaping appear a bit more kept and formal around the houses here. The temperature in the sun feels at least twenty degrees hotter than it did while under the shade of the forest canopy, and I'm glad I thought to bring a bottled water. I smile as I take a big swig and a bit dribbles off my chin. I cup my left hand, filling it with water, then lower it to Mac's level.

"Here you go, boy!"

He eagerly laps at the cool drink and then yaps as if to say, "*Thanks!*"

We pass one of the tennis courts on the left and that sort of gives me my bearings yet again. We then find ourselves in front of the Harbor Club.

"Okay, home should be about half a mile straight ahead," I mutter, and then start laughing as I recall Jack, Frank, and I believing we might get a refreshing piña colada here, complete with umbrella, during our first visit.

"Well, Mac, I believe I'll go mark my territory since I know where a lady's room is before we move on!"

<h1 style="text-align:center">27</h1>

Jack and I can't seem to go more than three days without calling each other. This time she calls me while I'm watching the sunset down on the covered dock that juts out into the actual cove which is surrounded by black and red mangroves. Mac likes to tag along and sun himself here. I've come to calling it the birdwatching station as I have seen so many different species fly by while sitting here pondering their names and contemplating how I need to get a Florida bird book the next time I'm at Books-A-Million in Gulf Gate.

"Guess who called me today?" she says with nary a hello.

"Ed McMahon," I say, "and you won the Publishers Clearing House."

"No silly," she says. "Anyway, I think he died a few years ago. It was Frank!"

"*My* Frank?" I say. "Why in the world would my Frank call you, and how would he even get your number?"

"Well... I didn't know he was exclusively yours, and I do get gentleman callers from time to time." She sounds defensive.

"Good grief, you know I didn't mean it that way. I meant, why in the world would my realtor in Florida be calling you in Ohio?"

"He called to see how I was doing, that's all."

"We talked about everything, yet nothing at all... just like the night we walked the beach. That's actually when he got my phone number by the way. I had shared with him my concerns about your living alone in Florida and me being so far away in Cincinnati, and heaven forbid if something should happen and I'd be unable to reach you quickly."

There is a momentary pause to sip what I'm guessing to be wine. "Get this, he said just call me, and I can get to her in a matter of minutes for you! He gave me two of his business cards advising me to keep the one near, and if I ever needed anything just give him a call."

"Well that's a new pick-up line, but actually that was really sweet of him," I say, touched by his sincere behavior (I note Mac giving a low growl). "So what was the other card for?"

Jack chuckles and says, "Well, that's how he got my number. That night he also said to me, 'If you're comfortable giving me your phone number as well, ma'am, just write it down on the back of this here other card. I promise I won't misuse it!' He then hands me his pen, and to my surprise, I did it!"

"Oh my God, that sounds so much like Frank," I say, "but nothing like you!"

Mac is growling now as he gets to his feet and begins sniffing and snorting between the floorboards of the dock.

"Well don't laugh at him too much, Liz, because I think I kind of like him... actually I kind of like him a lot!"

We continue chatting, her filling me in about recent goings on at work and me filling her in on living in the Cove, when suddenly there's a loud growling sound from under the dock that causes me to jump out of my seat with a scream.

"Liz, LIZ... What's the matter? Answer me dammit! Do I need to call Frank already?"

Mac lunges on his lead for the dock's edge closest to the water. I hear the sound again only this time it reminds me more of a giant bullfrog on steroids.

"I'm here..." I whisper, while slowly creeping my way to the edge to look over, as Mac looks between the railings and barks incessantly. I grab the rail top and cautiously peer down.

There in the water of Pelican Cove are two large eyes and a snout looking right back at me. It opens its mouth and out comes the indescribable sound yet again, now accompanied by the dog's constant yapping.

"What the hell's going on Liz?" Jack begs.

"I'm fine! I'm fine," I say. "But I think Mac and I just met one of our grumpier neighbors. Let's get out of here Mac before that gator makes you its dinner!"

28

As for our evening routine, it's not dissimilar to the morning one. Mac eats and we go out for our walk. However, the big difference is we usually bump into at least six different dogs—and their owners, of course—somewhere along the way each and every night. In fact, sometimes we come upon an entire group of dogs and owners forming an impromptu circle in the middle of the road. The humans are all talking a mile-a-minute amongst themselves while the dogs sniff each other *Howdya do,* and eventually settling at their owner's feet.

It is during these times that I have begun to meet many of my new neighbors. They say dog people are friendly people, and this seems to be the fact here. Individuals actually go out of their way to cross the road and introduce themselves and their pet, while inquiring about Mac and me. Generally, we get asked (1) if we're a new owner or a renter, (2) our names and (3) where we're originally from. Many of these inquiries lead to warm introductions and handshakes. This really helps, and I no longer feel quite so all alone.

Then there are the walkers without dogs. You can pass by them at just about any hour. Some are groups of all male, others all female. Some appear to be married couples while others walk alone. Some stroll, while others power walk. There are even those with trekking poles that I recall seeing people use during several of my business trips to Germany.

Most are quick to bid me a Hello or Good evening; however, there's some who simply wave, or just nod in recognition, and a peculiar few that make no eye contact at all. The latter group I notice is increasing recently, and when I mention them to the dog people, they all laugh.

"That's the last of the snowbird's honey, they'll all be flying north soon. You'll get used to them!"

There's a woman that I keep crossing paths with, and she doesn't seem to fit any of the categories. She appears to be around my age, quite attractive in a plain Jane kind of way, and gives off artistic vibes in her choices of clothes and jewelry. Her most distinguishing feature is a head of beautiful gray hair that curls wildly, yet attractively around her beautiful smile and twinkling brown eyes. It makes me slightly jealous when I think of the hours I spend both blow-drying and flat ironing to straighten my own hair. She's quick to say Hi when she sees me, but then always seems to be running off somewhere, like she's constantly on a mission. I'm in hopes someday she'll stand still long enough for me to really meet her as I'm desperate to develop some close friendships in here!

I've also befriended an elderly neighbor named Marilyn. She's short, a bit plump, and uses a walker to get around. She slowly makes her way out in the mornings with her teacup poodle, Tookie, at about the same time as Mac and me. I often find her bent over the walker with the dog's lead twisted all around her ankles and the walker's legs, as she searches the ground, facial tissue in hand, for Tookie's #2 waste. I can hardly believe she even bothers—she often asks me to help look for it, and once located it's usually about the size of an almond.

The leaves are falling this time of year from the abundance of live oaks, making it even a greater challenge in locating it. On one particular morning, both she and I are scanning the ground for Tookie's doodies as she calls them.

I say, "This is kind of like going on an Easter egg hunt together every morning. Isn't it?"

Marilyn straightens up and looks me directly in the eyes. "You're not Jewish, are you, honey?"

From that day on, our bond grows stronger. I have taken to searching the web and reading what I can about Judaism in an attempt to learn more about her, and many of my other neighbors, unfamiliar habits. Thankfully, there are free Wi-Fi hotspots at all the clubhouses and pool locations.

My first search was to learn more about the ornamentation on the upper right portion of Marilyn's doorframe. I had seen them in *Fiddler on the Roof*, noticing that Tevye would touch it when entering the cottage, but I had no idea of its true purpose. I learn it's a mezuzah and inscribed with Hebrew verses from the Torah. They comprise the Jewish prayer Shema Yisrael and begin with the phrase:

"Hear, O Israel, the LORD our God, the LORD is One."

The mezuzah contains a piece of parchment. A qualified scribe, or Sofer Stam, who has undergone many years of meticulous training, has prepared it. The verses are written in black indelible ink with a special quill pen. The parchment is then rolled up and placed inside the case. Many individuals recite the prayer every time they pass through the door. Others kiss their finger and touch the mezuzah thus feeling closer to God in that way.

How lovely, I think, *to thank God prior to entering and receiving all that he has given you.*

I then find myself searching the web for Presbyterian churches in the area and considering my own spiritual needs for the first time in quite a long time.

I have started taking leftovers from dinner, excluding pork, to Marilyn. Always quick to reassure that my kitchen may not be kosher, but I definitely keep it clean! She just laughs.

"You're ruining my girlish figure, honey!"

She has yet to say no to anything I've offered.

One morning on our walk—actually more of a shuffle with Marilyn and her walker—she stops and looks me in the eyes as best a woman who is four foot six can to another one who's five eleven. "Have you ever wanted to go to temple, my dear?"

I think about the question. "I think I would be interested in seeing inside and attending a service. I've attended pretty much all other religions at some point for weddings and funerals and the like and have enjoyed the experience."

"Good!" she says, "I'm in need of a ride to synagogue tomorrow!"

29

Growing tired of sleeping in a sleeping bag, sitting in garden chairs, and moving boxes around for end tables, I begin my search for furnishings amongst the numerous furniture stores in Sarasota. I drive north on the trail to a place called Kane's, just before the Landings, a shopping plaza off South Tamiami. It's huge!

"And how can I help you?" asks a short, chubby man. He is stuffed into his suit and scurries up to me.

"I'm just looking today," I say.

"For anything in particular?"

I attempt to veer off to the right and begin circling the big showroom floor.

"Not really," I say, and as I glance in a mirror over a dresser on the wall in front of me, I catch a glimpse of him tailing me from afar, like a wolf stalking weak sheep.

I attempt to forget about him, but I'm constantly aware of his presence lurking just off in the distance. There are various room settings, and some are actually quite nice. The colors, styles, and patterns are all so... well, so *Florida,* and nothing like the dark furnishings of up north.

I start fantasizing about how I want the new place to look and sit down on a plump blue and yellow floral couch that's lined with a mixture of coordinating plaid pillows across the back.

"Oh my God!" oozes out of me as I sink in deep and close my eyes. "This is more comfortable than a bed."

I smile, and then it hits me… I do have something I'm looking for, and my first purchase needs to be a bed. The mere thought of spending another night on the floor sends me off looking for my chubby stalker who, of course by now, is nowhere to be found.

I pop into the Rooms-To-Go next door and this time announce aloud to the approaching salesperson: "Where are your beds?"

This place is a mix of modern and Tommy Bahama knock-offs. The prices are extremely reasonable, but I soon notice you actually get your best deals by buying the entire room of furniture. Most sets consist of headboard, footboard, dresser, chest, two nightstands and even include a set of matching bedside lamps.

"You know we have fifty months same as cash going on right now don't you?" offers the young man. "And, you're not locked into the two lamps shown in the display. You can have your choice of any pair you see in the entire store. That beauty you're looking at there is called Berkshire Lake and it also comes in white as well. That will only run you about forty dollars per month unless you need to add on the mattress and box springs. We'll even take your old set away for a small fee. So, what size bed are you replacing?"

I quickly circle the store and come to yet another realization. I don't want to have to be back out shopping to replace everything again in a few years because I bought things too inexpensively. I'd rather purchase quality and something classic that I really like even if it takes me a while to find it. I thank the guy, and he hands me his card.

"You can just call me, and we can get this ordered over the phone if you like. Did I mention we also offer delivery for a small fee?"

Back in the car, I start heading south towards the condo and stop at Drexel Heritage. The lobby is appointed with such beautiful furnishings that I wonder what I'll see once I actually enter the store. An impeccably dressed, accessorized, and well-coiffed woman approaches me.

"How do you do?"

Suddenly I'm made quite aware that I'm due for a haircut, desperately need my nails done, and that denim jeggings and a boyfriend tee weren't the best choices I've made today.

"I'm looking for a bed," I state.

"Right this way," she smiles, and we weave our way through some of the most beautifully appointed showrooms I've ever seen. Everything including the accents and artwork are all lovely.

"Do you have a particular style or taste in mind?" she asks.

"I've honestly just started looking, and I'm not sure."

"Well, are we trying to match any other heirloom or existing bedroom pieces?"

I chuckle, "Only a sleeping bag with a Scotty probably lying on it."

She pauses and, to her credit, doesn't so much as bat an eye. "There are pieces that merely furnish a home, and then there are those that define it!"

She leaves me in an area of bedroom settings. "Why don't I just allow you to peruse these rooms at your leisure, dear. Should you have any questions, my name is Grace. I'll be right up front." And off she saunters.

Well, she's a soft sell. I smile. *And she definitely lives up to her name.*

I reach over to look at the tag on a beautiful headboard.

"Oh my God!" literally blurts out of me when I see the price.

After doing a double take, I look around to see in front of whom I may have embarrassed myself.

Simultaneously my phone starts playing "By the Seaside," and I set my purse on the bed to dig through it while thinking how juvenile my ringtone sounds in here. I finally find it.

"Hello, Elizabeth Blum here."

"Are you working again?" asks Jack. "Should I call back later?"

"No Miss Smarty Pants, old habits die hard, and once in a while I forget I can just say hello now!"

"What are you up to?" she asks.

"I'm looking at beds."

"Anyone cute in them?" She chortles at her own joke.

"If there were, I couldn't afford them in this place!"

I use her call as an excuse to exit the store, waving at the salesclerk as I pass her desk and pointing to my phone. She gives an understanding nod and reaches out with her business card.

"Give me a call if I can assist you in any way."

I fill Jack in on the furniture adventure thus far.

"You know this would be a lot easier if you were here to help me!"

"Funny you should say that because I was calling to see if you could handle a house guest in a couple weeks. How's June 22nd look?"

30

The next day I wake up, grab my white spa robe and take Mac out to do his morning business. The sky is a beautiful blue, and it's still cool out as the sun has yet to make it above the tree line.

Suddenly cars start pulling into the parking lot beside the grassy area where I'm encouraging Mac to speed things up. Elderly ladies, also in white robes, jump out of their vehicles, toting gallon milk jugs half-filled with water in both hands. They are talking a mile a minute and aiming for the Pelican Pavilion pool.

Two of them pass me and one says, "If you're joining us for swim-mercize class, honey, you can't bring that dog, and if you don't have your own jugs I have another set in the trunk!"

Then they scurry off letting the pool gate slam behind them. One comes hurrying back out aiming straight towards me in a panic.

"We can't find our boom box anywhere. Have you seen it?"

Once back inside, I start the coffee brewing and start thinking about what Jack shared with me yesterday on the phone.

"You know Frank and I have been calling each other, and things have been going great. We actually have a surprising number of things in common. He just really caught me off guard by inviting me to come down to Florida for the weekend and the offer for me to stay at his place."

She had picked up on my questioning tone at that point. "In his guest room of course!"

"I advised him that I would love to come and yes, going out together in person would be a preferable method of getting to know each other better. However, I think it's a bit premature to be staying under the same roof and that I would check to see if you would have me. I was so afraid of coming off a prude, especially at my age, but you know what he said, Liz? Imagine this… 'Well ma'am, I can surely respect that decision. Let me know so I can make your plane reservation!'"

"Of course!" I had responded. "Come on down!" And already I was beginning to get excited over the prospect.

Oh, I knew in my heart that this would be different from our usual one-on-one girl time together, but I couldn't have been happier for her and the new spark I heard in her voice whenever she talked about Frank.

I decide I better continue looking for furniture, especially in light of my upcoming visitor. So, after a quick shower, I make a towel-dried messy bun and look in the mirror to apply a little lipgloss. Suddenly a flash memory of yesterday's faux pas of being extremely underdressed comes to mind, and I quickly pull out the scrunchy and begin to blow dry my hair. I laugh to myself recalling being told by my sister-in-law, Margaret, prior to my spending time in France, to always remember that the Parisians even dress to take out the garbage. Somehow, Pelican Cove and Sarasota seem the same.

After choosing a crisp taupe DKNY blouse, navy slacks, strappy sandals, and even earrings I'm ready to go.

It's a wonder my holes haven't closed up, I think while taking a final glance in the mirror at the amethyst earrings Scott bought me for my birthday the first year of our marriage. I actually smile thinking about him and the happy memory instead of being overwhelmed by a wave of sadness.

My Wellbutrin must finally be working, I think, *and after only ten years!*

I actually laugh out loud then bend and pet Mac on the head. "You guard our little hobbit hole!"

And, yet again, I head out the door to shop.

You're My Best Friend

—Queen (1975)

31

This time I decide to heed the advice given me by several of the dog walkers and aim south towards Venice and check out the consignment shops along the way. My first stop is at the Pelican Cottage. To my surprise, they have a mixture of new and used furniture and decorative items. It's very much a Florida and Caribbean vibe in the front room. Teals, pinks, and yellows dazzle the eyes and palm prints and hibiscus patterns are everywhere. There's even a thatch roofed tiki bar, complete with a swimsuit-clad mannequin sporting a kinky, blonde wig "tending" it.

"Might want to rethink that hair-do," I suggest to her as I make my way into the next area.

It's actually a large warehouse with several sets of garage doors opened wide to the outside world. It allows for a slight breeze and some air to ventilate the space, accompanied by Florida's high heat and humidity. I immediately come across a sectional sofa I love. Everything I've seen so far is way too large for my place. This one is diminutive without appearing out of scale. I like the fabric as it seems durable, and it's actually comfortable to sit on. I look at the tag and am amazed at how reasonably it's priced. I flip it over and it has *Sold* written in bright red sharpie.

Well bummer! I think and stand up to look at it again.

"Can I help you?" asks a tall slender saleswoman.

"Well somebody got a deal on this one," I say. "Guess that great price was because it's gently used? It appears to be in excellent condition!"

She smiles. "That's because it is brand new. Not everything here is consignment. We actually have made to order furnishings available." And she points to a large book of fabric samples splayed on the coffee table.

"Nicki, the owner, likes to keep some samples mixed in on the floor to show people, and more often than not we sell them pretty fast."

"You mean that's the price for a brand-new piece?"

"It is!" She beams.

"Well then, how do I order?"

She takes me back to the front room where my northern blood is thankful to be back in the air-conditioning. She motions for me to have a seat on yet another sofa and plops several books full of fabric swatches on the coffee table in front of me.

"That style sectional can be covered in any one of these fabrics. The books also show some recommended companion prints for the two throw pillows that come with it and also ideas for matching chairs. As well, I'm an interior designer and am at your beck and call should you need me!"

Later I'm back on the Tamiami Trail, head spinning, thinking aloud.

"Well my dear, I guess you finally have a direction for your condo that you can hopefully build on."

The sofa fabric I've picked out is called sea-foam mist. I'm also having an overstuffed chair done in a floral print that contains various shades of orange, green, red and the same blue of the sectional on a linen cream background. The two couch pillows are being made up to match the chair and the saleswoman has even convinced me to order two matching bar stools for the kitchen pass-through.

Next, I stop at House of Lords, a large warehouse-style building with some funky geometric eighties shapes and colors on the front of the building. Near the street is an LED sign showing pictures of furniture and an occasional photo of a smiling guy that looks like Mr. Clean. Two sandhill cranes stand sentinel at the front door to check me out as I enter. Inside, behind a sales counter of estate jewelry, stands a petite elderly woman who greets me with perhaps an Austrian accent.

"Velcome, lets me know if I can be of any help to you!"

The place is enormous and filled with huge pieces of furniture and statuary. There are large mirrored mahogany chifforobes, gold gilded sideboards with marble tops, French tapestry settees, and silk embroidered fainting couches. Why there's even a full-size Egyptian pharaoh statue that appears to be made out of onyx.

My first thought: *Where in the world did all these museum pieces come from?* Followed quickly by: *Who in the world buys these things, and if their condo is anywhere near the small size of mine... well, how in the world do they get them in the front door?* There's an entire area of complete sets of fine china stacked on display shelves. Amidst it all is a passageway, with a sign and pointing arrow reading more this way.

The long hallway I proceed down is lined with artwork for sale, some of it is actually quite lovely; there are windows to side rooms filled with fine crystal—Waterford, Swarovski and Tiffany. There are other rooms that have shelves of collectibles like Hummel's and Lalique. The hallway ends into what looks like a fine art gallery. I had thought the meager art in the hall was impressive, but this room soon dazzles with not only well-known names in the art world, but with many being signed and numbered prints and originals to boot. Each commissioned piece boasting an equally impressive price tag to match.

There's a doorway to yet another room, and this one appears to contain all the mismatched leftovers and odd pieces. Some of the pieces are Early American, such as a maple dinette set whose captain's chairs have seat cushions boasting eagles with flags in their talons. Or a sleek, mid-century piece in cleat Lucite with Champagne chairs and extremely modern lines.

To the side there's an array of single chairs, and one in particular catches my eye. The frame is of painted wood in a cream color. The finish is a bit crackled as if aged by time. The arms are carved into swans' heads whose beaks are pointing down. The legs are further detailed with elaborate carvings. The chair wraps around in a curved, almost half circle fashion. The upholstery of the back and seat is a little darker blue than the couch I just selected, but the small check pattern and piping are exactly sea-foam mist. I can't help but find humor in my remembering the exact name of the color of the couch. I then break out into unrestrained laughter as I conclude that this chair looks exactly like the non-moving seat on a merry-go-round.

I really want this thing!

I check out the tag and find it a bit confusing. There are four calendar dates accompanied by four different prices. Each date is in ascending order and accompanied by a dollar amount in descending. A gentleman pushing a dolly, with yet another chair on it, comes wheeling by.

"Excuse me, but do you work here?"

"Yes, I do and how can I help?"

I ask about the price tag, and he explains that the item's cost starts at the highest price on the first date it's available and then subsequently goes down each date after that if it hasn't sold.

He takes a look at the tag I'm referencing.

"This piece started at $250.00 on May 20th. In two days on June 20th it will be at its lowest price $125.00 and remain there until sold or picked back up by the consignee."

I thank him and contemplate whether it's worth paying $175.00 now and securing the chair or taking a risk that it will still be here in two days and saving $50.00.

After mulling it over I decide, *This whole adventure has been a gamble thus far so why change now?*

I leave without buying, while mentally planning my return visit first thing Wednesday when they open.

"If it's still here, then it was meant to be!" I say to the two cranes still present outside the front door.

32

I decide since I'm this far down 41 to continue south to Venice and go to Save-a-Lot to buy Mac some green beans. It's sort of a grocery store but nothing like Kroger back in Ohio or my Publix in Palmer Ranch. It has a lot of the staples, but they are all some off-beat brand. The produce usually looks a little questionable, but the avocados are always ripe and delicious. There are also some unexpected things, like two entire aisles of Mexican cuisine and Hispanic household products.

As well, there's an entire aisle, and several other remote locations throughout the store, of bottled wines. The vineyards are actually not bad—usually middle-of-the-road $10 to $15 bottles anywhere else, but here they range around $6.99 with a store coupon. However, there really isn't an actual store coupon available and the cashier automatically takes off the price at the checkout. Go figure.

As for the green beans, Mac's new vet at the Sarasota Animal Hospital has deemed him chubby and placed him on a diet. It consists of half-a-cup of dry kibble with a full can of drained and rinsed beans in the morning, and the same for dinner in the evening. Also, we're to cut back on the cookies, treats, and people food. The off-brand beans at Save-a-Lot are only forty-nine cents per can. That's a huge savings over Libby's for a buck twenty-nine at Publix, and well worth the drive since I buy four flats of forty-eight cans at a time. The dog walkers have commented on Mac's weight loss since our arrival and inquired as to how we're doing it. I advise them of the beans.

"Plus all this walking around the cove isn't hurting us either."

Traveling through Osprey on the way back home I decide I'm up to one more stop before I need to get home to let the dog out. There's a hidden little shop near Historic Spanish Point whose difficult-to-read sign promises fine antiques and rare collectibles within. My tires grumble as I pull into the gravel parking lot.

I question the wisdom of entering such a place alone when a young woman exits the front porch.

"Thanks again for everything," she calls back over her shoulder. "It literally changed my life!"

She walks down the path towards me, gets into her car and starts it. I get out of mine and decide I'm overthinking this—a tendency of mine—and lock up by way of a button on my key fob. The woman gives a smile my direction as she passes by and pulls out onto 41.

The cottage sits well off the trail and is surrounded by a dilapidated picket fence the color of driftwood. There is an arched trellis supporting a vine of trumpet creeper blanketed in yellow blooms and a shell path that leads to a sort of faded orange sherbet building with peeling teal trim.

One must negotiate a set of steep steps, with no banister, to reach the huge covered porch housing a floor to ceiling jumble of items for sale. There are pots and pans, ceramic planters, glassware and furnishings. Shelves running the lengths of the porch are filled with everything from children's games to antique dolls and block the large square paned windows of the building. However, when able to catch an occasional glimpse inside there is such an assemblage of "stuff" actually in the windows that you can't begin to see in, even if you wanted to.

The front door sign reads enter here and where the hours of operation should be filled in is hand-written: if the open sign is up then we must be open! I step through the door, causing electronic chimes to bellow throughout the store. It takes my eyes a moment to adjust, as the room is rather dark partly because of the aforementioned blocked windows, but also because there is no overhead lighting. The only lights are an array of vintage table lamps that all appear for sale given the tags hanging off their shades.

I'm apparently standing in the entry hall from when it was a home, and the area is filled with dark wooden cases with locked glass door fronts lining the walls. Their shelves are jammed with various collectibles that appear to be somewhat categorized by, *what...* themes? One shelf has a collection of skulls, from those of an actual human to ones created out of crystal or carved stone. Another has a collection of Asian items including intricately carved ivory figurines, charms and buttons. An entire case is devoted to graven African fetishes, intricate ceremonial masks—some even including human teeth and hair—tribal pipes, and amazingly detailed basketry.

The overall feel of the cottage is that of a museum, but the smell of the place is a mixture of your grandmother's house, tobacco, and... candy canes perhaps? Something rubs my right leg, then my left, and I about jump out of my skin until realizing it's a tabby cat. I pat my chest and take a calming breath thinking aloud,

"Well kitty, you're just about the only thing I didn't smell!"

"Wit y'all in da shake of da tail feather!" echoes a voice from another room. "Y'all just have a gander till I git there. I be needin' to throw a beescuit in da attic for da iguana!"

This is followed by a trailing laugh mixed with a smoker's cough.

I feel like this may be my best chance to cut bait and run, and I'm squandering the opportunity, but I'm finding some of the items exhibited before me to be quite intriguing.

Making my way further and into what may have been the dining room there's a shelf full of kaleidoscopes (which have always fascinated me). I pick one up, hold it towards a light, close one eye and peer in. Without even rotating it or turning the end piece I'm seeing what appears to be the Milky Way passing by—but no, I quickly realize, it's more like I'm actually flying through space at the helm of a speeding rocket ship. This expanding universe is complete with shooting stars, planets, black holes and more. I take it away from my eye and quickly glance at the other end where you usually spin random objects that in turn make pretty patterns... it's solid black.

The next one I peer into produces some sort of jungle scene. However, it appears I'm running through the dense undergrowth, pushing large leaves and palm fronds out of my way. I realize it's actually a rainforest and a light rain and mist fills the air and I can actually feel it on my skin. There's a low guttural growl from somewhere right behind me and I have the distinct sensation I'm being stalked and in grave danger. The feeling that I'm fleeing for my very life is so strong that I immediately take the kaleidoscope away from my eye and set it back on the shelf with trembling hands.

Wow, those things aren't merely toys! How does it appear so real?

Continuing further on, in the living room there are shelves full of rocks and crystals. Many sparkle as I move towards them. I'm familiar with the fact that some people believe they hold healing powers and involve chakras. I believe some religions, like Buddhism, even worship with them.

There's an extremely large cluster of amethyst crystals with a sign on a small easel that reads peace + prosperity. There's a large grouping of amber and their signage reads good luck + happiness. Next to that is a beautiful display of clear quartz that reminds me in miniature of the Chris Reeve Superman movie and the place he takes Margot Kidder to meet his parents on Krypton. It apparently provides meditation + alignment. There are additional shelves containing chrysocolla, carnelian, citrine and so many more. The clamp lights affixed to these displays show them off wonderfully.

Of course, amethyst being not only my favorite gem but also my birthstone, I'm compelled to pick the large cluster up. Suddenly I am filled with an inner peace that I haven't known since childhood. I reflect to the end of a long summer's day at play, and I'm a child again and my mother is kissing my forehead as she tucks me in bed for the night.

"You can't sleep with that jar of lightning bugs honey. Give it to me and I'll place it on your dresser where you can gaze at your treasure all night long."

She closes the window blinds and, smiling, sings, *"Night, night, sleep tight, don't let the bedbugs bite."*

As she slowly closes my bedroom door, I am about to call out to her...

I suddenly realize a single tear is running down my cheek, and I reach up and wipe it off while setting down the crystal.

Curious, I pick up a piece of gypsum that states it provides awareness + insight. Just as unexpectedly I suddenly think of my daughter Maggie in New York City. I see her clear as day talking with a heavyset man in a suit regarding an upcoming Broadway show. I can feel that she's concerned. Then the image shifts to a tall attractive young man holding both her hands in his. She's crying as he leans in, tenderly kisses her cheek, glances down taking in her figure and then let's go and walks away. I'm suddenly filled with the knowledge that she needs me in some way. And yet again, I'm left with a feeling of downheartedness.

What in the world? I quickly replace this stone to its spot on the shelf. *What's with this place?*

Suddenly I'm brought back to the moment as a small wisp of an elderly woman comes around the corner. Her long, dishwater grey/blonde, braided hair, leathery tanned skin and vaguely cowboy attire immediately brings to mind the saying "Ridden hard and put away wet."

"Well, well," she states while giving me the once over from head to toe.

"What in tarnation be bringin' y'all dis ways and dis far south missy?" she asks, staring me dead in the eye.

I shift my feet in place as I'm now left feeling a bit uncomfortable.

"Oh, I only live a couple miles up the road," I say perhaps too quickly. "It really isn't that far!"

She grins from ear to ear showing coffee or tobacco stained teeth. "Oh, I reckons y'all been travelin' a bit more than dat on dis current journey y'all are on."

She reaches in her pocket and pulls out several wrapped red and white striped peppermint balls and then holds her weathered hand out offering me one.

"Y'all helps yourself ta one," she offers with a wink of the eye.

I can't help but notice all the turquoise and silver rings on almost every finger. They match the ornate, heavy necklace she's wearing around her crepey skinned neck.

"Da mint has da power to clears up da brain," she says and then gives that same laugh and cough that I heard earlier.

I'm obliged to accept her offer and unwrap the candy and pop it in my mouth. The intensity of the peppermint flavor is so strong it's almost overwhelming. It goes right up the back of my nose and sort of zings my cerebrum, not dissimilar to an ice cream brain freeze.

"Y'all be betters now, honey?"

"Sure, uh maybe… I think so." But suddenly realize I don't remember much after entering the front door.

"Now what's dat you be a lookin' fir?" she asks with a half pleasant smile.

"Oh, I'm just looking. It's my first time in here!"

"Well, y'all have a goody, long, looky-see arounds, ya hear, and holler ifin y'all needs me!"

33

The shop owner makes her way behind a glass display counter and saddles up on a high stool where she starts counting money from a vintage, Cubano cigar box. To even my own surprise, I make my way into the next room as my curiosity continues to get the best of me.

I should probably flee this place. Again, questioning my wisdom of entering this establishment. *They're going to find my dead body under the hollow sounding floorboards someday.*

This area is filled with similar shelves in a similar layout. There are what appear to be cowboy artifacts mixed with American Indian ones almost everywhere. There's an enormous mounted buffalo head on the wall, and its huge ebony eyes seem to follow me no matter where I move.

Jack would tell me it's a security camera. I smile.

And then think about how I'll have to bring her here just for kicks. As I venture further, I observe sections of Chinese and Asian swords, Buddha figures and onyx or jade carved symbols. The next shelves I pause in front of contain Egyptian pieces including Anubis, obelisks, and ankhs. There's signage that reads: the ankh represents the life-giving elements of air and water. it was offered to the king or pharaoh's lips daily as a symbolic ritual symbolizing the 'breath of life'.

I pause a moment to dig for my phone and snap a selfie of me in the room focusing on the life-size cigar store Indian in the corner behind me. I send it to Jack's phone texting:

Should I be reported missing look for me here. LOL! I'll call and explain later. (((HUG)))

There's an arched hallway leading to the last room. On one side of the hall is a closet filled with nautical themed antiques. Directly across from it is an actual bathroom whose doorway has been covered with a plate of plexiglass. Inside, sitting on the lid to the commode is a sign that reads:

Cottage lore is that a female slave originally lived in this small area until her death in the late 1920s and that later, once plumbed, it became the home's bathroom. When the current owners bought the property and were putting in bushes along the fence line, they dug up a cache of her personal belongings (Displayed for you to view within this room). They found her teacup and saucer, several skeleton keys secured on a bulls-ring, a piece of wood with her name, Ruby, scratched into it and a disintegrating silk purse with make-up rouge inside. Current shop employees claim they have felt some sort of ghostly presence of Ruby when working late at night in the Cottage.

Still trying to absorb what I just read I enter possibly the master bedroom where it becomes apparent that its theme is "everything Florida". There is old road signage on the walls. There's a fifties bikini-clad blonde leaning against a palm tree with the tagline vivacious florida, the year 'round vacation-land. Another shows an illustration of an overflowing crate of oranges spilling onto the sand of the beach. There's a border of orange blossoms and a script title, greetings from florida. There are baskets of shells; there are shelves of shells, and everywhere shell lamps provide the light for this room. There's also orange jelly, orange syrup, candied orange slices and even orange gumballs. I spy Gummi gators, chocolate gators, rubber gators, and Florida Gator's sports paraphernalia in the form of caps, pennants and jerseys.

There's a lone set of shelves standing in front of one of the few unobstructed windows in the whole place. It displays fossils, artifacts such as pots, utensils and statuary. Included are several huge sharks' teeth with the inscription: Caspersen Beach, Venice, written in china marker on them. Atop sits an extremely small and poorly handwritten sign reading: Historic Spanish Point, Osprey. There are some other items such as large bone segments and skull fragments along the floor that appear prehistoric.

From behind me: "Oh my oh me, I sees dat y'all found Digger Doug's sellin' spot."

And the shop owner gives that slightly unnerving laugh yet again as she places the stump of a burning carved meerschaum pipe in the cracked corners of her mouth and takes a long drawn out puff. She tips her head back letting the smoke rise towards the low ceiling adding to years of discoloration and then proceeds into a hacking cough.

"Dem dare items be loco finds, honey. Digger's bin diggin' in dis heres area… well, since he been a wee toad!"

"They look like archeological finds and museum pieces to me," I say. "I'm surprised the Smithsonian doesn't want them!"

She takes another tug on the pipe and speaks as the smoke coils out from between her cracked lips.

"He's not da brightest penny, sweetie, and ain't been able to work at nothin' payin' since da axident. He mostly juss be makin' a livin' offs what I can sells um fer. Anythin' catchin' dat pretty leetle eye of yours, missy?"

I'm taken aback that these marvelous pieces are not only in the backroom of a shabby shop in Osprey, Florida. But that the excavator of these rarities appears to be a bit of a local vagrant. I continue eying the artifacts and my eyes keep coming back to one piece in particular. It's a smaller piece carved out of some kind of brownish gray wood. It's obviously a mature, well-endowed and fully aroused male figure. His fingertips are sprouting limbs, and his feet are rooting themselves into the surrounding earth. A pile of leaves reminiscent of fall raking tops his head. His skin appears in transition between being human and becoming bark. Oddly enough, the expression on his face appears one of complete bliss.

I find myself somehow comparing it to *Saint Theresa in Ecstasy*, a white marble piece sculpted by Bernini and located in the Santa Maria della Vittoria in Rome. My husband Scott and I had taken the tube from our apartment and then searched the streets for the location of this church, since I was determined to see this statue in person while we were there. I then immediately realize it's more reminiscent of Apollo and Daphne where she prays to her father Peneus, a river god, to turn her into a tree to escape Apollo's advances after he's been struck by Cupid's arrow. Coincidently sculpted by the same artist and located at the Galleria Borghese, my favorite museum.

"Well I'm quite fond of this one!" I say while gently picking it up to inspect it closer. It's surprisingly heavier than I anticipated.

"The statue is extremely detailed especially items like the leaves and tree bark. Considering the age of the piece and the primitive tools that must have been used to create it, well it's just a spectacular period piece."

"Well, I don't be knowin' nothin' bout those artsy and fartsy kinda tings sweetie. But I do knows dat Digger could be a usin' twenny-fi dollahs in cash right 'bouts now and if y'all have dat on ya, well dat dare totem be yours! Just be handin' it to ole Granny Daisy and I'll be wrappin' it up fer ya."

34

Getting into my car, I place the wrapped *totem*—as Granny Daisy had called it—between my legs and secure it with my left hand for safe keeping on the ten-minute drive home. I pull off 41 onto Vamo Road and then enter the cove, where traffic is backed up five deep at the gate. Aside from needing to empty my bladder, for some reason I'm feeling extremely anxious to call and check on my daughter Maggie. I can see the authoritarian guard running the lead pickup truck driver through the ringer as he hands forth his identification.

I glance up out of my sunroof, no doubt a beseeching look on my face. *Dear God, why can't I just drive into this place and the gate go up?*

Suddenly he allows the truck to proceed, then steps out of the gatehouse and motions for all the other vehicles to stay to the left. He signals me to pull up the drive on the right-hand side, and with some kind of remote in his hand opens the resident gate and gestures for me to drive through.

I'm absolutely dumbfounded as I pull through while mouthing a whispered *"Thank you!"* and start the winding drive towards my home. Never, ever have I experienced anything like that at the gatehouse! Even on the rare occasion that I'm the only individual at the gate, he still takes a great deal of time to scrutinize my Pelican Cove window decal, making a prolonged determination on whether I actually do belong here. Other times he may gesture for me to roll my window down asking some inane question regarding the names on my visitors list or

144

reminding me to call the gatehouse regarding authorizing special deliveries such as Pizza Hut.

I pull into my carport, jump out of the car, and hurry through the hole in the hedge, over the little bridge and down the walk to my front door. All the while noting how I'm not fumbling with my keys as per usual. Once inside I set down the totem on the kitchen counter and dash for the bathroom, begging the pressure on my post-menopausal bladder to give me just a few more seconds to make it. When I walk back into the living room, Mac is sitting at the front door asking to go out.

"So, you have to go too!" I say, and he gives me his quizzical Scottie head cock. I grab his lead, and he drags me full tilt back out the front door.

Once back inside I search for where I have thrown my purse. I spot it in the kitchen sink. *A-ha! Who knows why I just toss things?* I dig through it, per usual, to find my phone and then bring up Maggie's number. To my great surprise the call doesn't go into voicemail and she answers by mid second ring.

"Mom. Hi… is that you?"

At first, I'm stunned because she usually references me as Liz or mother these days. Secondly, the tone in her voice sounds just like when she was eight years old and her best friend and neighbor Amy told her she no longer wanted to be her bosom buddy.

"Yes Mag, it's mom. You've been on my mind recently, what's going on?"

And, for the first time, in since I can't remember when, she starts pouring her heart out to me. Her words flow like a torrent.

"This town is just, just… well, so damn hard. It just chews people up and spits their picked clean bones out into Hell's Kitchen!"

She blows her nose.

"Have you been crying sweetheart?" I ask—gently since we're treading on ground that hasn't been walked on in years.

"Five years of tryouts and auditions while taking theatre classes by day and working as a shitty barmaid by night. Three leads in off Broadway plays, while waitressing during the day, and nary a damn one of them makes it to the Great White Way. And then my fucking manager, Richard Cox... who's such an asshole he goes by Dick, asks me to stop by his office for a chat last week.

"Well some chat, the bastard drops me as a client, saying he has a couple of new kids that are really going to be going places that require his full attention. Currently they're taking up a lot of his time. Then he had the balls to say to me, 'Maggie baby, it just wouldn't be fair of me to not focus entirely on you and getting your career started off on the right foot!' What the Hell is he talking about? MANAGING MY CA-REER has been in his hands since I frickin' moved here... Damn him anyway!"

I continue listening and contemplate how New York City has definitely added color to her vocabulary. She finally takes a breath allowing me to interject,

"Oh Mags, my heart aches for you. I know acting has always been your dream, and I have always hoped someday that your wish would be fulfilled. After everything we... uh, I mean you have been through, there is nothing more that I wish for than for you to be happy. That's all I've ever wanted for you."

"Fat chance now!" Is all she says and then dead silence with a hint of tears, and I refrain from speaking and just let the moment happen wishing I could wrap my arms tightly around her.

When I can't take the silence anymore, I ask, "Did you get the literature I mailed you a few weeks ago about where I'm living? It's called Pelican Cove. They have such a nice brochure, and I also sent the most recent newsletter. Have you ever seen so many activities?"

"It looks really nice, Mom, –sniff– the pictures are beautiful. But I guess I'm still trying to rationalize why you sold the old house. I thought, no actually I always had the preconception that you would live there till... well, you know forever!"

"Sweetheart," I start to say and then pause to think how I want to word this.

"One day, I found myself turning sixty years old, forced to take an early retirement and rambling about all alone in a huge four-bedroom home. The house held a lot of wonderful memories, all of which I have packed up and brought with me. But it also continuously, day in and day out, reminded me of the pain of losing your father and brother. Every day it was right there in my face, your dad shaving in the bathroom, your brother running down the stairs and slamming the front door. Hell, some days even the smell of frying bacon could cause me to weep. It was like living in a haunted house full of friendly ghosts and—"

"Oh mother, I hadn't considered how difficult it must be for you to live by yourself!" She blows her nose again. "I took for granted that you were comfortable there."

I make my way to the lanai and sit in one of the two lawn chairs I have situated there. Mac follows and curls up at my feet laying his head on my left foot.

"Oh Maggie, I haven't been comfortable with things in a long time. I wasn't comfortable in that house, I wasn't comfortable with Cincinnati anymore, and I'm still not comfortable with what's become of us. I love you so much… you do realize that, don't you?"

Suddenly, I fear I've overstepped my boundaries as I'm met with complete silence again save for the sound of yet another sniffle. Until today our phone conversations are more like business calls taken in the office… emotionless and right to the point. In fact, our occasional reunions are planned down to every detail while referring to our calendars for when we can squeeze a couple days in together.

Then, rather humbly, she says, "I'm so sorry mom for how I've treated you. I know the accident wasn't your fault, but I had to blame someone for what happened. Hell, I was a teenager when it happened. Overnight I lost my father whom I adored, and the little brother I loved dearly, my only sibling. It's taken time, counseling, and a lot of soul searching to get where I am. To be honest, I don't know how you carried on at all after losing your husband, son… and for far too many years your daughter!"

And for the next several minutes, all that can be heard from either end of the phone is crying by both of us.

35

Unexpectedly, I laugh. It's so inappropriate for the moment, like when you find yourself giggling at a wedding or funeral, then Maggie joins in. She struggles between bouts of snickering to spit out, "There's nothing funny mother –gasp– about either of our situations."

"I know sweetie –snort– that's what makes this so damn funny." Finally, after wiping my eyes and a few deep breaths I manage: "I think we just dumped many, many years of pent up angst!"

We talk well over an hour and a half, which is something we never do. Once I can tell we're finally wrapping up the call, I say, "I don't think we have had this serious a conversation since we discussed sex and your period."

"Gross! But you know what? I've still got a few questions!"

Thus, we end our call on the notes of continued laughter.

While my ear's still warm, I can't help but call Jack.

"Guess what happened?" I say

"You switched to valium?"

"No, but speaking of that, have I told you how much better I'm doing down here?"

That causes me to remember my bizarre store experience that I then share with her, and finish with what happened afterwards at the gate.

"So, after pulling in and seeing the line of cars, Jorge goes and waves me pleasantly through the open gates!"

"Who the Hell is Jorge?" She asks. "Is that some sort of code for Saint Peter?"

149

"No silly, remember the ponytailed guard at the gatehouse? That would be Jorge," I say. "Anyway, I called Maggie and we talked for almost two hours!"

"Really," she says, shocked. "About what?"

I then give her the blow-by-blow playback version complete with uncontrollable laughter.

"Oh Liz, you have to be so happy right now. When are you going to see each other?" She asks.

"Oh, good grief… I never thought to ask!"

We end the call noting that she'll be here in a few days, and even though she has a date of sorts with Frank, I can't wait to see her.

"Let's eat chocolate and drink too much wine while you're here," I say.

We end the call in our usual way.

"Love you."

"Love you more!"

By now it's time to feed Mac and take him out. I open and drain the green beans, then top them with kibble and he dives in while I again run to the potty to pee. Upon returning he's standing at the front door with one end of the lead in his mouth waiting for me. As I clip it to his harness I think, *Someday I have to get that back door fixed so I can take him out that way!*

We start our walk, and he does his job under his favorite tree by the pavilion. As I'm bagging up his gift and heading for the dumpster, the carillon at the Methodist church just outside Pelican Cove on Vamo road begins to play. Every day at noon and six p.m. it plays various hymns. I actually recognize today's selection as "Be Thou My Vision" and I attempt to sing along.

"Be Thou my Vision, O Lord of my heart
Naught be all else to me, save that Thou art
Thou my best Thought, by day or by night
Waking or sleeping, Thy presence my light.

"Be Thou my Wisdom, and Thou—"

As I turn the corner onto Treehouse Circle I'm face to face with a tiny blue-haired woman. Mac sniffs at her red Grasshopper shoes.

"Oh, don't stop singing, honey, you have such a lovely voice."

I blush as she continues.

"Who do we have here?" she asks while trying to bend down to pet Mac on the head, but she can't quite make it.

"Here, let me help." I pick up the dog to her level allowing her to easily pet him. Her rouge colored cheeks bulge from her smile and her little gray eyes glisten.

"Oh my, my, my," she says while continuing to pet. "You know I had a little black dachshund when I was a girl? I named him Pepper but my father called him shtupper!" She gives a coy glance up at me over her glasses, as if she's been naughty, followed by an old lady's sweet chuckle.

"What's your name, honey?"

"Liz," I say "Yours?"

She doesn't answer. "What's the last name, hon?"

"Blum," I say. "Liz Blum."

"B-l-o-o-m?" She spells it out while squinting at me through her left eye and removing her glasses and placing the temple in the corner of her mouth.

"No, B-l-u-m."

She switches eyes "Well then your name's *Blum*," she says rhyming it with plum. "Most of those are from the New York area. Unless there's an E on the end, then it's pronounced like bloom. Could there be an E on the end of your name, honey?"

"No ma'am, there's no E, and in Cincinnati where my family is from, it's pronounced *bloom*."

"Well dear," she finishes before heading off in the opposite direction, "that's all fine and dandy, but all that really matters is that your name is in the book, you know, the Shemot!"

And off she toddles.

"I know I'm in the Pelican Cove directory!" I shout back.

Blue Skies

—Irving Berlin (1926)

36

I'm ecstatic as June 22nd finally comes, and I drive south on I-75 towards Charlotte Harbor. I pull into the Punta Gorda Airport to pick up Jack and am amazed at how small and easy to navigate it is—although I do have to question why Frank didn't simply fly her into Sarasota. He sold one of his listings and needs to be present at the closing, so I willingly volunteered to pick her up, knowing it would allow me to savor some extra moments with her during this abbreviated visit.

I park the car in short-term and walk through the openings of a split-rail fence to enter the building. It's a single room with one baggage carousel situated in the middle. The area is full of people waiting to pick up their loved ones. Most are in shorts and flip flops, some standing and some sitting on the floor, as seats are few and far between. Many have dogs with them, and I suddenly feel guilty that I left Mac at home. I haven't yet fallen into the Florida lifestyle of routinely taking your dog with you everywhere you go.

There's a single board with DEPARTURE information on the left and ARRIVAL on the right. I quickly scan down the arrivals until I see Cincinnati and next to it are the words DELAYED 2 HOURS. I berate myself for not having checked online prior to leaving to see if her plane was on time. I was just so damn excited about seeing her, that I jumped in the car and raced down I-75.

What now?

It's an hour down here and an hour back, so leaving is silly. I walk around looking for a restaurant or bar that I might kill some time in, and when I ask one of the airport personnel I'm politely directed towards a wall of vending machines. Then I notice in the center of the baggage carousel there is a display of colorful ceramic pots and bamboo plantings. A small sign reads:

This display courtesy of Pottery Express and Bamboo Farm
Punta Gorda, Florida, just 10 miles west from the airport off 765

So, I jump in my car and drive east on Piper Road before realizing I've gone the wrong direction, pull a U-turn, and aim back towards Pottery Express. Luckily there are signs along the way giving encouraging directions.

You're almost there.

Just 5 more miles, keep going.

Prepare to take the next left onto Zemel Road.

I pull into a parking lot surrounded by thousands of pots in a variety of shapes and colors. On the right is a garden with walkways and bridges glimpsed through huge stalks of bamboo. I find an open spot, park the car, and get out to take a look. As soon as the door clicks shut, I become aware that, since I'm inland and away from the water, the humidity and the temperature must both be hovering around 95. I unlock the car and reach in to get the bottled water I've brought.

If nothing else so far, I've learned you always take water with you wherever you go. My condo neighbors, long-time Floridians, have warned me about leaving the house without it. I'm often reminded of the signs out west prior to crossing the desert: last chance for gas and water.

I started trying to remember to leave a bottle in the car at all times until the blonde gal on Good Morning Suncoast News did a story on bottled water. The segment's scare title: Bottled Water Bad for the Boobies, and it claimed that allowing bottled water to sit in your car and heat up all day may contribute to breast cancer, due to the carcinogens being released by the plastic bottle.

Good grief... I had thought as the news anchor just grinned back at me. *Don't go telling a neurotic, hypochondriac like me that type of information. Hell, I just recently started holding my cell phone to my ear again!*

A guy working at Pottery Express and Bamboo Farm swings by in a golf cart.

"Want a lift to the store?"

"Sure thing!"

I jump in and he speeds through the lot, where we pass rows upon rows of skids full of pottery. He lets me out while providing a brief overview of the layout, including information regarding the silk batik demonstration going on at the Art Studio, and also pointing out the restroom facilities before speeding off to round up more customers.

I'm flabbergasted at the size of this place. There are several warehouses full of ceramics and a central courtyard filled with pots, fountains and figurines. I make my way inside and just stop in my tracks and take it all in. The array of colors in front of me is so dazzling I'm compelled to take out my phone and snap a picture. I text it to Jack along with:

Look what I found while waiting on you!

I hit send and swoosh... it's gone.

I'm drawn to an entire display where each planter is created out of broken irregular pieces of ceramic that seem to have white caulking holding them in place. Each one contains various solid colors that coordinate with other patterned pieces like florals or polka dots. Mixed in are things like glazed insects and frogs, and the one large pot I stop in front of has a small oval plaque attached to the front that reads: Jardin. I remember that *jardin* means garden in French and think about my visits to Paris and the Luxembourg Gardens.

Heck, I live in a garden now! And I decide on the spot to buy the giant pot.

'By the Seaside' begins to play and I start digging through my purse thinking, *Maybe it would help if I carried a smaller bag or got one of those purse organizers I saw on QVC?*

The screen name reads Jack Hernandez.

"Hello! Where are you?" I ask.

"Yes I'm –garble–port waiting –garble– Where the –garble– you?"

"Jack… Jack are you there? You're breaking up. Let me pay for my pot and I'll be right there!"

After pulling my Escape around and putting the backseats down, an incredibly dark and handsome piece of Hispanic eye candy comes wheeling the monstrosity towards me. His partially unbuttoned cotton shirt is so drenched with perspiration I can see his nipples, and his bronze muscular body is the color of burnt caramel mixed with sweet cream.

Focusing back on the project at hand, I now ponder whether the darn thing's going to even fit in the car; then: *Where in the hell am I going to place it once I get it home?*

He easily hefts it into the back of the vehicle and offers to get some packing material to place on either side to keep it from rolling around. I can do nothing but smile as I watch his tight butt walk away in well-worn jeans all the while wondering when in the hell my libido came back to life!

I start back for the airport and, for whatever reason, the traffic is a lot heavier and slow moving. I check the car clock and it appears I should still have a half hour before her plane's arrival.

She wouldn't be calling me from the plane would she. Doesn't that cost money? And then speculate that her caller ID wouldn't have come up unless she was using her own phone.

I remember hearing something on Good Morning America about being able to use your phone on planes now. Is that what she did?

I again pull into the airport and park and as I'm aiming for the only door into the terminal, there sits Jack on a bench amidst several dog owners and a couple smokers.

"Well my dear, did you score enough pot for all of us?" Several of her newfound friends break into laughter.

"What?" I answer startled.

"When I called you, you mentioned something about paying for the pot and then you'd be right here. I was just telling these guys that apparently we're going to be partying a lot harder than I thought this weekend!"

37

As we head for the car, I attempt to explain the garden planter purchase while trying to occupy myself during her flight delay. She laughs.

"We actually made good time according to the flight crew even though we had a delayed takeoff. They credited something about a tailwind because of the big storm in the gulf."

"Hmm, seems sunny and beautiful right now!" I say "Maybe we can take in the sunset at the beach tonight unless you're seeing Frank straight off?"

"We're not getting together until noon tomorrow. He says he has an entirely wonderful day planned for us." She is absolutely beaming.

We reach the Escape where I press the button on my key fob and up pops the rear hatch.

"Oh my God! Is that the flowerpot you bought?"

"Yes, siree!" I say, grinning ear to ear. "Isn't it a beauty?"

"It's HUGE!" she squeals. "What in the hell are you going to do with that thing? It's bigger than your living room!"

I take her carry-on and squeeze it in the back then close the hatch. "I didn't buy it for the living room!"

Once back on I-75, aiming north toward Sarasota, I turn off the Blend on SiriusXM and commence with nothing but uninterrupted girlfriend banter. I fill her in on what we've come to call "Tales from the Cove" while she shares her stories dubbed "P&G and Me."

As we enter into North Port, I finally ask what's been on my mind.

"Okay, coming all this way for a man, well, it's not like you. What's up?"

"I've already explained that I really like Frank. We have lots in common, and I enjoy his company. Why does there have to be more to it?"

"Because I couldn't get you to go out with possibly the world's best catch Neil Morris, just down the hall from you at work," I say. "Or that cute bartender at Carlo & Johnny's that always flirted with you during happy hour and who constantly refilled your wine while I sat there with an empty glass of melting ice."

"I don't know, Liz. I guess it's partially the biological clock thing. I'm fifty and unlike you I've never been married. I know it's a bit late for children, but suddenly the aspect of spending the rest of my life without someone scares me. You do know that your leaving me alone in Cincy fueled this fire, don't you?"

And suddenly huge, Florida size, raindrops start hitting the windshield.

I switch on the wipers. "Wow, I hadn't given that much thought. I've been so concerned with making a new start for myself that I just took for granted you'd continue to… well, continue to just be you."

I look over and tears are falling down her cheeks. I reach for her hand.

She says, "I think since your move I know for the first time what true loneliness is and what you must be going through."

And then we're both crying. Between the car windows streaked with rain, and my teary eyes, I'm certain we're going to be involved in a horrendous car accident.

As usual, in an attempt to lighten the moment Jack quips, "Guess the beach is out for tonight?"

I laugh. "It's Florida in summer, sweetie, don't let the rain stop ya! In a half hour's time you won't even know it rained."

And we continue on with lighter conversation until reaching the Laurel Road exit off I-75 to Nokomis.

The light is green and, forgetting my cargo in the rear, I make the sharp left turn onto Laurel a little too fast and the huge pot starts rolling around and hitting the sides of the Escape.

"Good grief!" I yell as it clinks against the car's windowpanes. "I totally forgot it was back there."

Jack undoes her seat belt and climbs over the seat to the back. She positions herself facing backwards, legs spread far apart on either side of the pot and embraces it from the top with her arms.

"Take it nice and easy from here on and we just might all make it home in one piece!" She laughs.

Driving in the tumultuous rain through Osprey, and only moments from home, we come upon the cottage belonging to Granny Daisy. I glance over at the building and swear I see the faint image of the old cowgirl, umbrella over her head, smoking her pipe on the side of the road in the pouring rain. Her head turns and follows our passing as if she had been waiting and expecting us to come by. Startled, I check the road ahead and then wipe at the thin film of fog that has built up on the side windows from running the air conditioning. When I look back in the side view mirror, surprisingly, there's no one there.

38

It's absolutely pouring as we pull under my carport. The rain hitting the tin roof is so loud that we have to scream to be heard.

"Grab your bag and climb back up here!" I yell. "We'll get the pot out later when the rain stops."

We jump out and run for the condo, where first we see Mac nervously pacing at the kitchen slider, before unlocking and entering through the front door. The dog gives a disgruntled grumble in my direction and jumps up on Jack's leg begging to be petted.

"I have no control over the weather," I say while bending down to scratch his head. Suddenly there's a loud clap of thunder, and Mac takes off nervously running for the back lanai.

"How's about some hot tea and an egg salad sandwich?" I suggest.

Jack smiles "White wine might pair better."

That reminds me to show off the retirement present from P&G that was recently delivered. It's a beautiful bar and wine storage unit, and it's currently the nicest thing in my entire living room. It's made of polished maple with black accents and the top is solid marble. The front cabinet door contains one large pane of curved glass, through which can be seen my proudly displayed two bottles of wine and three unmatched wine glasses dangling from the stem holders.

"I'll take the Ecco Domani," says Jack as she saunters towards the guest bath.

"I can't believe you haven't unpacked and done more with this place. The bar looks great, but where are all the nice wine glasses I packed up for you back in Cincinnati? And I love the merry-go-round chair. I'm glad you went back and got it! It will look great when the couch arrives. And the black bookcases you brought with you work well on that wall, but they definitely need more than a couple books and that little, naked and aroused man thingy you have on them."

She glances into the guest bedroom as she passes by and before shutting the bathroom door calls out: "Well I see you at least got me an air mattress! Did you think to buy sheets and a pillow?"

"No, but I did finally buy myself a new bedroom set!" I say.

When she comes back out, she's only wearing her T-shirt, which covers her panties.

"Hope you don't mind, but the bottom of my pants were wet from our romp in the rain, so I hung them in the shower to dry. Then I decided if I'm getting that comfortable, I might as well ditch the bra and give the girls some breathing room."

I hand her two wine glasses and the bottle. "Great idea! I'll be right back. Oh, and I set the egg salad and wheat bread out on the kitchen counter along with the corkscrew."

I go into my bedroom and find my white, spa robe in the walk-in. I strip down to my underwear and place my damp clothes in the hamper then slip the robe on. I glance in the vanity mirror, run a brush through my hair before returning to Jack.

What you see is what you get. Then take a second look at what? A sparkle? *You know you don't look half bad for a drowned rat!*

We take our wine and sandwiches out to the lanai and each take a seat in the two lawn chairs. We both reach out to clink our glasses.

"Salute!" I say as Jack pulls her legs up under her tee.

"Cheers!"

The rain has not let up, and now the gutters can no longer take the deluge and are overflowing causing a waterfall effect in front of the windows. The splattering sound as the water hits the ground is so loud we can barely talk. Suddenly the room lights up from a bolt of lightning. The accompanying thunder causes Mac to run off again, but this time to the bedroom, and both of us in unison commence to pick up our chairs and move deeper into the living room.

"I know your motto is don't let the rain stop ya," says Jack, "but, at this rate it's not going to stop us; it's going to kill us!"

"Maybe we should switch on the TV," I say, "and see if we can get a weather report when the early news comes on?"

I turn on the small twelve-inch monitor that I moved with me from my old bedroom in Cincinnati.

"I haven't gotten a new one yet." I say. "Mostly because I haven't found an entertainment console I like."

"Why buy one?" says Jack. "Those boxes it's sitting on seem to work perfectly well… and they're so très chic."

She shoots me a stern look "Seriously, Liz, if nothing else we're going to take some time this weekend to shop, and I'm going to force you to buy some more furniture! Honestly… college kids live better than this!"

"Have you forgotten I also bought a couch that's being custom made?"

A Special Report suddenly interrupts the Ellen DeGeneres Show. The message: Tropical Storm Debby Flirting with Florida scrolls across the chyron at the bottom of the screen over a background of swirling white and gray clouds. A nice-looking guy appears, and the title on-screen identifies him as Steve Jerve of WFLA. He's standing on Bayshore Boulevard in Tampa, and as his umbrella is blown inside out, his demeanor remains professional and he calmly advises residents to take care as this system moves through the area and be prepared for local flooding.

The camera pans to scenes of large waves cresting over the sea wall. "We expect this storm to move on in a couple hours and proceed across the gulf towards Texas. Model forecasters see no possibility of Debby becoming a hurricane, but she's definitely going to help alleviate the drought situation we've been experiencing and may even bring our water tables back up to normal. Stay tuned to Channel 8 and your NBC News for further details at five o'clock."

And, we're back to the Ellen show where PSY has her, and soon the entire audience, dancing Gangnam Style.

"Well that doesn't sound so bad," I say.

"Sure," says Jack, "except we're not in Tampa!"

I go on to explain that until I get hooked up to cable, the only stations I seem to get are this Tampa one and another PBS one out of Venice.

"Once I set-up a time to have Comcast install cable service, I'll also have Wi-Fi and the ability to Facebook again from home."

Jack stares at me and shakes her head, smirking. "Just what have you been doing with your time since moving here?"

And I sincerely reply, "I don't really know."

Jack's phone rings, and its Frank. She motions to me that she's going in the guest room, and I hear the door shut. As the rains and rumblings continue, I'm left to myself. I stand up and take a good look around my place.

What *have* I been doing? I make my way to the kitchen to grab the Pledge and a dust cloth. Approaching the bookcase, I remove the few books and pick up the totem. I turn him to face me and address him directly.

"We're going to make this a showplace; you just wait and see!"

I give him a good rubdown with the cloth—apologizing for the groin region—before dusting off the entire set of bookcases.

39

By the time Jack finally comes out of the bedroom, I've actually emptied two boxes of books and another full of knickknacks.

"Now that's the ticket." She smiles encouragingly. "Aim me towards the next box and let me help."

As she rips off the packing tape and opens the lid to the box, I stare at her, my hands on my hips.

"Are you really not going to give me a hint of what you and Frank talked about for over an hour?"

She pauses what she's doing and smirks. "You, the weather, you again and when he's picking me up tomorrow, you… happy now?"

"Well, that was vague, but I'm glad I was such a big part of it."

We continue unpacking boxes, and Jack takes charge of arranging the shelves as I continue to dust things off before handing them to her. She organizes my books in groups such as current fiction, travel, and cooking. When I hand her the totem she gives it the first serious look.

"What in the hell is this thing?" Then turns it around so as to inspect it from all angles. "I saw it earlier and meant to ask."

"Remember my text from the strange antique shop saying if I go missing search for the body here? Well this is what I bought."

"Interesting." She takes the totem and positions it in front of some travel books. But then can't resist asking me, "Proportionally speaking… have you ever met a penis that size in real life?"

She digs up a few bookends I saved, but also uses mugs, decorative bowls, and various knickknacks to arrange every shelf far more artistically than I ever could—then she breaks the work momentum. "I need more wine! What about you?"

But before I can respond, she opens up about Frank.

"Liz, I'm as nervous as a high school girl on a first date when I start thinking about spending all of tomorrow alone with him. What if I goof up?"

"Goof up, what do you mean? You keep saying you two get along famously," I say. "What's to goof up?"

"You know me better than anyone," she says, looking straight at me. "I can be slightly nutty, totally opinionated and a complete smart ass at times."

"So… what's not to love?" I say, hugging her.

"You're the best thing to ever come into my life and I love you dearly. I just hope Frank appreciates what the hell he's getting. Remember what I told you on the phone when the subject of a possible relationship first came up? If nothing else comes of you two meeting each other, you've at least both made a new friend in your lives. And who couldn't use a few more friends in this big, crazy world?"

We break for the suggested wine refill and, after Jack flips on the recessed ceiling lights that highlight the bookcases, stand back to admire our work.

"Wow, it really looks great!" I say.

"Yeah! Almost like someone lives here! What do you say we order a pizza?"

"Veggie thin crust?" I ask.

"Deep dish meat lovers!" she says.

"Well, that sounds like we're ordering two."

I find the number for Pizza Hut and each time I dial I get a busy signal. "That's strange," I say. "In this day and age of technology you don't often hear a busy signal."

On the fifth try I get through and then have to listen to a complete audio commercial followed by today's specials. Then: "All our lines are busy right now, but if you'll please hold a member of our team will be right with you!"

I'm now listening to additional Pizza Hut menu banter. A minute later: "All our lines are busy right now, but if you'll please hold a member of our team will be right with you!"

And this scene plays out over and over for the next ten minutes.

In the meantime, Jack has turned the TV back on and is watching the end of the six o'clock news. The same weatherman is now back in the studio and doing a live report on what he's calling troublesome TS Debby.

"...she seems to have virtually stalled out right over the Sun Coast and Tampa Bay region and at this hour just simply isn't moving. It seems Tropical Storm Debby is being fed by the warm waters of the gulf and continues to dump tremendous amounts of rain in areas from Brooksville to Fort Meyers. In other news..."

"Hey Liz, where the hell is Sarasota located in all of this?"

"Smack dab in the middle!"

When someone finally comes on the phone their first response is not to inquire as to what I want to order, but to preemptively advise: "Our delivery is taking well over and hour due to heavy volume and the storm." There follows a deep sigh, then: "Do you still want to place an order?"

I look at Jack. "It'll be well over an hour."

"So where are we going?" she says. "I gave up on the sunset and beach idea hours ago!"

40

I've put off feeding Mac as long as possible due to the inevitable situation that he needs to go out and do his job immediately afterwards. I've put shorts and an old tee back on and decide rubber flip-flops are the best choice for footwear. I put him on his lead, grab an umbrella, and hand Jack a bath towel before exiting.

"What's this for?"

"Just stand ready for when we return."

And Mac and I sprint out into the pouring rain.

Of course, Mac first goes across the street and under the tree to the left of the Pavilion before stopping to pee. The umbrella is only keeping the top of my head dry and my arms and shoulders are becoming soaking wet. He finishes and shakes the rainwater off which splatters all over my legs and then drags me across the parking lot through ankle deep puddles to his other favorite spot to squat and do his other job.

A bolt of lightning strikes nearby as I bend over to pick it up with a doggy bag, and now my entire backside is drenched. I question the sensibility of being under all these large oak trees during an electrical storm.

Being a creature of habit, instead of just aiming back towards my front door and leaving the bag to wait for morning, I lead Mac down the road and around the corner to the garbage dumpster where we usually deposit his waste. Along the way, in the middle of the road, we pass a large storm drain with wide, open grates. The drain is barely able to handle the torrential downpour and has created a kind of whirlpool effect as the water attempts to enter it. Mac continues to pull me straight through it.

I look back at my right flip-flop, that's been sucked off my foot, as it disappears down the drain.

We get to the dumpster which is enclosed like all the others in a box of decorative wooden fencing. I struggle to open the gate with one hand while holding Mac and the umbrella in the other just as another bolt of lightning cracks loudly in a nearby oak, causing a limb to snap and me to cringe.

I then attempt to lift the lid to the dumpster with my only free hand and suddenly I let out an ear shattering scream. Looking back at me from amidst the garbage is a raccoon with the edge of a KFC box in his mouth. He jumps onto the edge of the dumpster, drops to the ground while screeching loudly at me and runs off. I'm forced to let go of the umbrella, which rolls away in the wind, and it takes both hands for me to hang on to Mac's leash as he's determined to take off after the varmint.

I get the dog under control and locate the umbrella that has only been stopped on its journey by becoming wedged between a car tire and its bumper. Now, completely drenched, I only put it over my wet head in an attempt to keep the rain out of my eyes with the hopes of being able to see my way back home. I return to the dumpster tossing in the poop bag, slam the lid, close the gate and limp home.

Jack's waiting at the door, agitated. "I was starting to get worried about you two. I could have sworn I heard somebody scream after that last flash! Did you see anything?"

I pick up Mac and step dripping wet into the foyer onto the entry rug.

"Only a furry dumpster diver," I say.

"Oh, okay…" She ponders the sight we must make. "So who's the towel for?"

I towel off the dog, walk to the kitchen, throw my left flip-flop in the trash bin, and excuse myself to my bathroom. "Keep an ear open for the pizza guy. I'm guessing he's coming by boat!"

I strip down yet again, wringing everything out in the sink, and this time hanging it all on the towel bar to dry. I turn the shower on hot and step inside. I wash my hair with Asian pear shampoo and loofah off with coconut milk body wash—and smell like fruit salad while toweling off.

I put on a pair of Nick and Nora Party Monkey PJs and go out to join Jack in the living room. To my surprise she has located and set up my card table and chairs under the dining room chandelier, found one of my tablecloths, and set the table with plates and utensils.

"I'm bound and determined you're going to start living here," she says. "Not just use this place as a storage locker!"

We pull up the two lawn chairs closer to the TV and having become tired of the now continuous coverage of Tropical Storm Debby, opt for watching the Venice station. We are both thrilled that an episode of *Downton Abbey* is beginning even if it is a summer rerun.

"Oh, remember this one?" asks Jack. "Branson the chauffeur tells Lady Sybil he loves her, and he will only leave if she goes with him."

"I love Sybil's character," I say. "Is this the one where Lady Mary decides she'll marry Sir Richard?" I ask.

"I don't remember," she says. "So, don't ruin it for me!"

We continue watching while talking more about the costuming and the sets than we do the characters.

"How I wish I would have been born in a different time," I say. "Everything was so much more elegant then, more refined."

Jack slyly grins my way. "They didn't have Tampax tampons or Charmin toilet paper… think about it!"

The episode continues with Mrs. Hughes, the housekeeper, finding Ethel naked in a storage closet with Major Charles Bryant.

"Oh my gosh," I say leaning forward as she fires the housemaid on the spot and sends her packing without a reference. "What's she going to do now?"

Again, Jack chuckles at me. "You know this isn't real, right?"

The show ends with the cliffhanger of everyone at Downton worried because Matthew and William are both reported as missing in action during WWI.

"I just love that show," I proclaim as the credit's role. A promo announcing *Antiques Roadshow* from Boston is coming on next appears. "I enjoy this one too! Were you aware they are supposed to film in Cincinnati this year?" I ask.

"You don't remember our entering a lottery to get tickets through work?" asks Jack. "The whole thing was your idea and you made me do it."

"That's right," I say. "I was going to take my grandmothers antique milk pitcher that my mother had from the farm. What were you going to take?" I ask.

"Probably you!" chuckles Jack.

We watch the show, and during a special segment off-site by Mark Walberg focusing on Boston baked beans "By the Sea" plays loud and clear from the other room.

"That's probably about the pizza" Jack says.

I automatically glance at the grandfather clock; another family piece I brought with me before remembering it hasn't worked regularly since the move. I grab the phone and see from the time on it that it's been almost an hour and forty-five minutes since I placed our order.

"Hello, Liz speaking."

"Miss Blum, this is Kenneth the night guard at the front gate. I have Pizza Hut here and they're claiming you placed an order for delivery. I'm denying entrance because we didn't hear from you."

"Oh my gosh, I totally forgot to call," I say. "It so rare I order out, but since I have a friend from Cincinnati visiting, we decided to try it and to be honest what with this weather and all, well going out just wasn't an option. Plus, I had already changed out of my clothes for the first time when we decided to order. Well, I guess I could have gone out and grabbed something once I got dressed the second time, but then my dog had to go out in the rain, and I had to take everything off yet again. Hello… hello Kenneth, are you still there?"

"Yes ma'am, so I'm taking that as a *yes*, you did order a pizza? I'll let them right through."

Dream
—Everly Brothers (1958)
Songwriter: Boudleaux Bryant

41

I gaze out the window at the continuing rain. It's much gentler than it was earlier. Its rhythmic, almost mesmerizing in its cadence. I go back to the vanity and fiddle some more with my hair. I try brushing it out again and then search for some bobby pins as I contemplate wearing it up. I end up pulling it back and putting it in a black eyelet ponytail holder before twisting it into a bun. I hold up the hand mirror to see the back of my head in the vanity mirror and am pleased with the look.

"It's simple and sophisticated," I think aloud, "and, it will work well with the black, strappy Marc Jacobs dress I blew the budget on just for tonight."

I start searching the various little bowls and containers around the bedroom looking for my good diamond studs. I have the bad habit of taking out earrings and leaving them scattered about the house. Scott had given me this particular pair on the birth of our daughter, and somehow, they seem just right in light of tonight's big event.

I've never been to an opening night gala and am excited about the bright lights of Broadway, meeting the cast and of course the after party at Two Times Square, where my Maggie will surely be a nervous wreck waiting for the morning reviews.

I ponder shoes while rummaging thru my closet. The black lace Manolo Blahnik heel on my left foot looks great with the dress but will kill my feet after a few hours. However, the plain black leather Coach one on my right I can wear till morning. I shift side-to-side viewing both in the full-length mirror.

I choose comfort and go back to the vanity mirror to reapply Dolce & Gabbana Devil to my lips. "Damn girl, those red lips make you look hot!" I giggle.

Ever since P&G acquired the D&G brand, I have done everything in my power to get my hands on any and all product samples left behind after marketing events and photo shoots.

Lost in the mirror, Scott sneaks up from behind and wraps his strong arms around my waist.

"Easy big guy, you'll muss me. I worked all afternoon to look this good."

He gently kisses the sides of my neck and then turns me around, looks me in the eyes.

"I love you no matter how you look!"

He bends in to kiss me and I pull back. "My lipstick!"

But he pulls me back in and brings me even closer as his lips meet mine and we gently kiss. He releases me slightly repeating, "I love you so much Kitty." And he then caresses me tight again and proceeds with another kiss. Our lips slightly separate and he gently licks my lips and then brushes my tongue.

"What's got you so worked up?" I ask. "We have to be at the theater to see Maggie's debut in less than two hours."

His hazel eyes twinkle in his occasional bad-boy way and he slowly pulls down the straps to my dress.

"*Scott*, I'm serious we don't have time for this."

He proceeds kissing the front of my neck, and as I tilt my head back, he deliberately moves on to my cleavage. He slides the dress down over my breast and it falls to a pile around my ankles. Picking me up he carries me to the bed and along the way I kick off my heels.

"Whatever you do just don't touch my hair," I say panting for breath while nibbling at his earlobe.

"I can pretty much put the rest of this costume back together, but the hair could take a while!"

As nimble as any magician, he removes my black strapless bra and then stands at the end of the bed pulling on my half-slip. I'm left on the bed only wearing black lace panties.

He then starts undressing in a manner that rivals any scene of Channing Tatum stripping down in *Magic Mike.* He tosses his suit coat and tie in the chair, slowly unbuttons his white dress shirt and then undoes the cuffs and chucks it to the floor. He undoes his belt, pulls it slowly out of the pants loops and drops it as well. He kneels on the bed and makes his way up my body kissing my ankles, behind my knees, my belly button and then caresses my breasts before licking my nipples. I wiggle and groan as he glances up at me and with a wink of his eye then slides himself back down the bed while taking my panties with him.

He stands back up, unzips his pants and allows them to fall to the floor. His underwear shows off an eager bulge. He steps out of the pants and slides his briefs off, again allowing his mouth to find its way up my body. He stops midway and begins licking and stimulating me with his tongue, and then stops and arching his back continues rubbing my clitoris with the tip of his penis.

"Oh Scott, don't stop, I love you… I love you… I love you…"

Suddenly there's a tremendous, ear splitting CRACK of thunder and the sound of pouring rain. Startled awake, I open my eyes and for the moment have absolutely no idea where in the hell I am or what happened to Scott. Flashes of lightning brighten the room, and suddenly I'm all too aware that I'm alone in my bedroom in Pelican Cove, and not in the one I left behind in Ohio.

I lay sweating amongst rumpled sheets in a confused state somewhere between bliss and depression. My heart's beating a mile a minute, and I can barely breathe. I'm startled at the realization that I believe I've just experienced my first nocturnal orgasm.

"Hells bells," I say. "It's been so long since I had any kind of an orgasm that wasn't of my own doing!"

But I'm deeply struck by the realization that my love, my husband, my Scott wasn't really ever here with me and that I miss him so much.

I get up and pull on my robe. Mac stirs from his bed. "Go back to sleep, it's too early to go out. Six o'clock won't be for three more hours."

As usual, he seems to understand me, and I can hear him circle around several times and scratch at his bed before lying back down.

I try to make my way across the living room to the guest room in total darkness for fear of waking Jack. I quietly pull her door closed and tiptoe back through to the dining room, where I have completely forgotten that Jack had earlier set up the card table and chairs. I walk smack dab into them stubbing my pinky toe and causing a metal folding chair to fall against the table, then onto the floor, with enough clanking that it rivals the unabating thunder.

Mac comes running from the bedroom as I let out a yelp from the pain and with the aid of additional lighting I can see, and reach for, the chandelier light switch. I hobble over, upright the chair and take a seat in it while cradling my foot in my lap and inspecting my broken toe. Mac puts his paws up on my leg to get a closer look for himself.

"Guess that helps me make my decision about what heels to wear to the Gala," I jest in Mac's direction. "Looks like I'll be wearing gym shoes to Broadway!"

Jack comes stumbling out of her room, looks the situation over.

"What in the world is going on? Between the clanging, banging and yelling in here, and the sounds of battle going on outside, I thought I was working triage back in Desert Storm. And my God, wait till I tell you about the weird dream I was having!"

42

Jack suggests that perhaps it is the right time for that cup of tea. She fills the teakettle and sets it on the stove then turns the burner on high. From my vantage point at the table, I direct her to where I keep the tea, sugar, honey and cups.

She smirks. "I'm quite aware of where the cups are, since I unpacked them the last time I was here. Let's see… I think I'm having chai. What do you want?"

"Plain old Lipton will do for me," I say. "With a teaspoon of honey please."

I get up and, walking on the heel of my foot with the broken toe, make my way to one of the lawn chairs. Mac follows. I reach over and flip the TV back on and, lo and behold, the same weather guy is still on the air talking about the tropical storm. He's a bit unkempt and has removed his suit coat and tie. His sleeves are rolled up, and a woman rushes in, handing him a piece of paper before scurrying back off camera. He pauses from speaking; holding his finger up for a moment as he quickly scans the page before continuing.

"Debby has veered from her projected track of landfall somewhere between Louisiana or Texas, the storm is now headed in the complete opposite direction, moving slowly north-northeast, and possibly later due east. Currently sustained winds are between thirty-five and forty miles per hour. The storm is dropping immense amounts of precipitation along its path! Recent—"

A high-pitched keening drowns out the TV.

"That's the teakettle!" I yell out to Jack who has wandered into the guest bath. Running across the chyron at the bottom of the screen are flood warnings, and Sarasota County is included. She runs through the room, toothbrush in mouth, and turns the burner off.

"I'll be wiff you im a mimit," she mutters through foaming lips while still brushing.

In a message bar at the top they are showing live twitter feeds, with individuals providing personal up to the minute tweets on conditions from their own neighborhoods in and around Tampa Bay. The weatherman now moves behind the anchor desk joining another meteorologist whom I've occasional seen on the weekends. They both have laptops in front of them and start answering viewers e-mail questions in real-time as they are received. Of course, the biggest question asked by far is whether Debby will become a hurricane.

Jack brings me my tea and joins me in watching the chaos. "Are we supposed to be doing something?" she questions and hands me two Lorne Doone shortbread cookies.

"Darned if I know."

"First off I missed the hurricane preparedness meeting they had here in the Pavilion. Then a nice couple, kind of hippie types, knocked on my door several weeks ago and said they were my neighborhood hurricane team leaders, or some such title." I nibble at the cookie. "I love these things, and gee I wish the Girl Scouts hadn't ruined the trefoils! Anyway, they quickly advised me I would have to take in the plant I have hanging by my front door, and anything else I may have placed outside that might become a projectile during a hurricane."

I pop the rest of the cookie in my mouth. "Do you think they would actually make me take in that big-ass pot I bought today?"

"I don't think even a hurricane could blow that thing away!" Jack laughs.

"So anyway, they said in the event that we would actually need to evacuate they will be responsible for directing me and the rest of the Glenhouse community here at the cove, out of here when it's time to go. They told me that my exit route is through the back-maintenance gate—wherever *that* is. They handed me a booklet from Publix enti-tled 'Your 2012 Hurricane Guide' and advised me to read it at my ear-liest convenience and put together my hurricane preparedness kit if I haven't already done so."

"Well… did you read it?" Jack asks. "And where's your kit?"

I am a little embarrassed. "I scanned the publication and I did buy a plastic tub to put supplies in."

"Where's the information?" she asks.

"Well," I say a little sheepish, "I think it might be somewhere in my bedroom."

Jack shakes her head, stands up and makes her way into my bed-room. "What would you do without me?"

"Maybe recycle it," I say under my breath. "If I haven't done so al-ready."

43

As we sit sipping our tea, Jack turns down the volume on the television, which subsequently intensifies the sound of the rain outside. She proceeds to tell me about the dream she was having before I woke her up.

"You know, usually I don't remember my dreams after a few minutes of being awake, but this one's still so vivid. I don't know how to explain it, Liz, but it seemed so damn real. When it began, I was at work in one of those windowless, huddle rooms P&G has, and I was so extraordinarily happy. Since usually those meeting areas are reserved for 'Gloom and Doom' announcements, that in and of itself should have been a clue I was dreaming!"

And we both give a chuckle.

"I'm eating a piece of cake. When I look down at what's left of it, I notice it's not a birthday cake but one with the remains of 'Congratulations' written on it and decorated with fondant flowers and white gumpaste bells. You know, the damnedest part was I felt sincerely concerned about all the calories I was consuming and the probability of gaining weight. Me, Liz, me who eats everything and anything was caring about my figure."

"Well, you do have a remarkable metabolism!" I say.

"Co-workers are handing me gifts, and I'm wondering how in the world I'm going to get them into my little car, and then my thoughts flash to how I'm going to pack them up for the big move."

"What big move?" I interject.

"Hell if I know," she says. "Anyway, once I get home and pull in the driveway, I open the trunk and start carrying bundles of boxes in. A man's voice calls from the kitchen, 'Give me a minute to stir my grits, and I'll be there in two shakes of a lambs tail!' and—"

"Who eats grits?" I grimace.

"Stop interrupting… now, here's the weird part, he comes out and exits the front door, and all I see is the backside of him in a pair of tight-fitting Levi's."

"Did you recognize him?" I ask, then quickly add, "Sorry!"

I get 'the look' before she continues.

"Not from that view or any of the subsequent rear shots to come," quips Jack.

"And you don't think dreaming about grits is the weird part?" I add, then quickly do the zipper across my lips gesture.

Jack exhales deeply then tries again. "So next we're filling moving boxes and all the stuff we're wrapping and packing are actual things I own. As I take each one in hand I reflect on where it's from or who gave it to me. I then have what…? Visions? That's it, I start having visions of that moment, or past events, happening within the dream. The thing is they were all actual real moments of time and came in quick flashes, pretty much scenes from most of my adult life chronologically one after the other. You know, like what individuals that have had near death experiences describe happening to them."

And with that a crack of ear-splitting lightning strikes somewhere out back, and the rear lanai eerily flickers and glows for a moment.

"Jeez, that was close!" I squeal.

"Too close!" adds Jack.

"Anyway, the mystery man, who by the way appears as handsome as one possibly can from the rear, calls my name and beckons me to follow him upstairs. He takes my hand in his and leads the way. We enter my bedroom and walk towards the bed. 'I think I have a pretty good idea of how we can say goodbye to this life,' he states, then pulls me down on the bed with him. And just as he's about to finally turn and look me in the face, you go and wake me up!"

Jack sips at her tea. "You got a shot of anything we can add to this stuff?"

"Wow!" I shiver. "That goodbye to life part's a bit creepy. Do you think he meant it literally, or just goodbye to how you're currently living?"

"Who knows, but I hope the latter," says Jack. "What about spiced rum?" She gets up and starts rummaging the wine bar.

"Oddly enough, I had a strange dream too," I say, and proceed to tell her mine, leaving out most of the intimate details. "Like your dream, it all seemed so real. I smelled, felt, tasted and experienced every detail. It was an actual living moment in time, yet it couldn't be… could it?"

Standing up I say, "I may have a couple of those airplane size bottles of liquor in my carry-on bag. Back in a sec."

"Well, I know one part that wasn't real in yours," Jack says. "There's no way in hell you can get from Cincinnati to Broadway in two hours and still fit in time for sex!"

Handing her two tiny bottles of Jack Daniels Old No. 7, we break down in giggles, as Mac gives us a disgruntled look and heads back to his bed.

We then settle down in silence listening to what for the moment has become distant thunder and a more peaceful rain. After about fifteen minutes, I stand up and tell Jack I'm going to try to go back to bed.

"You know, Jacqueline my dear, there are moments in life when you miss someone so damn much that you just want to pick them from your dreams and hug them for real once again."

I sigh and close my bedroom door quietly behind me.

44

I wake up to the smell of bacon and waffles.

"Guess you've stopped worrying about your weight?" I say as I enter the kitchen. "This wasn't necessary."

"I know." Jack smiles as she pours more waffle batter onto the waffle iron.

"I couldn't sleep, and the thought of cold pizza for breakfast didn't appeal to me, so I searched your cupboards. It's only Bisquick, but I doctored it up with a little brown sugar and a dash of cinnamon. I never found syrup, though, but you do have orange marmalade, which I'm warming up on the stove, and it'll work just fine. Oh… and why do you have so much bacon in your freezer?"

"I always forget that I have some, and when I'm at Publix and they have buy-one get-one, I can't resist," I say. "Didn't you notice all the Progresso Tomato Basil soups in the cupboard I purchased for the same reason?"

It's still raining as I stand in the kitchen slider looking out. "It's so rare to have an all-day rain down here, especially in summer. This looks like Ohio in November!"

"You set the table, and I'll dish it up," says Jack. "Hey, how's your toe?"

"Better," I say, "unless I physically move it."

Jack looks down at the now black and blue pinky. "Remind me to tape that up for you after breakfast."

I suddenly remember Mac needs to go out but Jack catches me looking at him.

"Been there done that," she says, "and yes I used the towel."

I can't resist hugging her and for a minute we just linger in each other's arms relishing the intimacy of the moment.

"Thanks," I say. "I needed that."

"We both did," she replies. "It's been one hell of a long night."

We chat during breakfast about her upcoming date, and she explains how Frank insinuated last night on the phone the possibility of seeing dolphins on a boat ride, along with something about enjoying dinner with a beautiful beach view and our toes in the sand.

"I'd take an umbrella," I say in jest.

We finish eating and I catch Jack slipping Mac the last piece of bacon before we clear the table.

"You know his vet has him on the green bean diet, and he isn't allowed people food," I scold.

To which, in her usual fashion, she replies, "It's not people food, it's pig." And then, in her best Charlton Heston impression screams out, "Soylent Green is people... it's people!"

She tapes my little toe to the one next to it and gives her doctor orders.

"Take two aspirin and call me in the morning. Frank is going to be here in a couple hours, and I need to get ready. Do you have a blow dryer I can borrow?"

She hops in the guest shower, and I use the time to get dressed. I have no intentions of going out in this weather, so I just throw on jeans and sweatshirt, as it feels a bit cool in here due to the lack of sunshine. Suddenly, the walk-in closet light goes out leaving me in total darkness. The house goes quiet, and I can tell the TV has gone off and the dishwasher stopped running.

"What the heck?"

It's normally dark in my little, hobbit hole even on the sunniest of days because of the many trees, but with the storm outside it's extremely gloomy. I walk out into the living room.

"Jack," I call out, "are you alright?"

At first there's no response and then the bathroom door slowly swings open and out she walks wrapped only in a bath sheet. "What now?" she says.

"I believe the power's gone out. There's one of those fuse box thingies in the front closet. Maybe we should look at it?"

We open the closet door, and it's pitch black in there.

"Where's your flashlight?" she asks.

"It went with all of Scott's tools and such, don't you remember? You had me put it all on the dining room table and I took a picture and then posted it on Facebook under the title: Handy Man's Special!"

"The big power tools I remember, but I emphatically told you to make a small toolbox with a hammer, couple of screw drivers, pliers, etc. and a flashlight and bring it with you for small projects. What happened to that?"

"I think I took it to Goodwill?" I say embarrassed. "Was it red or was that his tackle box?"

Jack pulls items out of the closet, like the sweeper and a stepstool, and finds the panel on the back-right wall. She starts feeling the breakers with her hand trying to decide if they're in the on position or thrown. In the meantime, I remember there's a box in this place somewhere that has vases, candles and mom's good candleholders' written on the lid.

"I think I know where some candles are," I say and take off on a search that's made nearly impossible in the murky light.

Jack comes out and joins in the futile hunt until we both give up and make our way to the lawn chairs to sit down in the dark. As best as I can tell, Jack looks at me and says in a defeated tone. "By now, if he hasn't been killed in the storm, if the roads are passable and, if he still even has any interest at all in taking me out, I'm guessing I have less than an hour to pull myself together. Yet… here I sit in a bath towel with wet hair in the dark!"

Hearing her sniffle, I try to sound as upbeat as I can.

"But you have the best naturally high cheekbones of anybody I know!"

45

Now, practically sobbing, Jack stands up. "If you'll excuse me, I'm going to go to my room now and see if I can feel-out something to wear."

"You work on the clothes," I say. "I have an idea for your hair."

I run off to the bedroom and, since I know where most of the items I need are kept, I find them with little effort. I return to the living room and call out to Jack.

"Need any help in there?"

"Only in figuring out if my tagless panties are on backwards!" she says with a laugh, and I know she's over the brief and uncharacteristic crying jag.

When she comes out I say, "That looks nice."

"Sure it does," she says. "What color is it?"

I gesture for her to take the seat in front of me that I've moved to the kitchen slider to get more ambient light and start by brushing out her damp hair.

"I feel like a little girl," she says. "I don't think another person has brushed my hair since my mother died. We used to take turns doing each other's when I would visit her in the home."

"That's sweet," I say.

"Perhaps," Jack laughs, "but have you ever seen what a seventy-five-year-old woman with dementia can do with a rat-tail comb on Hispanic hair?"

I chuckle. "I used to do Maggie's when she was a little girl. Before leaving the pool after swim meets, I would put her wet hair in a French braid. She used to look so cute that way. She would leave it in until the next morning and then take the braid out and brush out the subsequent waves and curls. That was how she would wear it until her next shower."

"So, you're telling me tomorrow morning you'll be having breakfast with Shirley Temple?" Jack wisecracks.

"Oh my God, I forgot to call the gate again!" I yell, dropping the hairbrush in a near panic. "Where's my phone?" I find it on the counter where I had it charging and call the front gate, "Hello, this is Elizabeth Blum in GL359 and I'm expecting a guest any minute now."

I recognize Jorge the ponytailed guards voice. "And what's your guests name Miss Blum?"

"Frank Landers." I reply.

"Spell that please!" he requests.

"L-A-N-D-E-R-S."

"And Frank?" he says.

"F-R-A-N-K." *How the hell else would you spell it?*

"And will he be staying with you?" he asks.

"Why?" I ask, wondering how that would be any of his business.

"Because it's currently the weekend, and he'll have to go to the office first thing on Monday morning to register for a parking pass if he is."

"No," I say. "He's just picking up my other guest and he and she are going out."

There's a pause. "Well Miss Blum, is your other guest registered?"

I put the finishing touches on Jack's hair as she takes advantage of the kitchen door light to check herself in a handheld mirror. I spray her entire head with a healthy dusting of TRESemmé.

She coughs and waves the air in front of her face with her hand. "What the hell was that for?"

"Protection," I say and then douse her with White Diamonds.

"Stop!" she yells. "I smell like an old woman in a beauty parlor. What made you do that?"

"It was the first bottle of cologne I grabbed in the dark from my vanity. Oh, I think he's here." I say as headlights illuminate the front hedge and shimmer through the unremitting rain.

"I need to run to the bathroom first," Jack squeals as she takes off into the darkness. "Stall him if you can since I'll have to leave the damn door open so I can see to pee!"

A few minutes later, there stands Frank at my front door, shaking out his umbrella and placing it on my porch. Mac comes trotting out of the darkness giving a few barks to announce his arrival. Frank's wearing one of his Hawaiian shirts with khakis, but it's somewhat tasteful—a solid color with an embossed palm leaf pattern. However, looking down, I notice he's wearing Crocs with socks. His unconventional footwear has the word Corona repeatedly printed on them.

"Won't you step in out of the rain?" I gesture.

He grabs my hand and starts pumping for water a big grin on his face. "Well golly gee ma'am it sure is nice to see you again. How y'all been gettin' along in your new place?"

I apologize for the lack of lighting and advise him that Jackie should be ready in just a moment.

He squints into the darkness. "The place sure looks nice."

I thank him and offer a lawn chair that's barely visible off in the distant gloom.

"Oh, no thanks ma'am, I'll just stand right where I am and drip on this here rug. I wouldn't want to make a mess."

Jack makes her way around the corner and slowly comes into view. As she approaches, Frank, and they find themselves face to face, there's an awkward moment as to what to do next. I pick up the vibe that I'm adding additional tension to the entire situation, so I excuse myself and aim into the blackness of my bedroom, calling back for Mac to join me.

"You two have fun!" I yell back.

To my surprise I believe I hear the smack of a faint kiss

"We'll see you later," Jack yells out. "Don't wait up!"

And then I hear the front door click shut.

Stormy
—Classics IV (1968)

46

For several hours I attempt to entertain myself in the dark. For a little while I play games like Angry Birds and Words with Friends on my phone until it suddenly dawns on me that, if I run the battery down, I have no electricity to recharge it.

Lunchtime comes and goes and I'm finding myself finally getting hungry, even after Jack's big breakfast. I'm concerned about opening the refrigerator for fear of how long the power might remain off. I open my pantry cupboard and search the shelves for items that won't require the stove or microwave.

Soup is out, I reflect, *it's got to be hot.*

I move around boxes of Minute Rice and Ghirardelli brownie mix and see a couple cans of Chicken of The Sea albacore tuna and decide, if I open the fridge door really fast I can grab the mayo out and make tuna salad. Well, minus a boiled egg, and I don't have celery, which is the usual way I like it. However, I know there's Wickles pickle relish in there somewhere, and maybe if I can find it fast enough, I can add that. I find a box of Ritz crackers and decide these will do, since I obviously can't use the toaster for bread.

I set everything on the counter, approach the fridge and plan my strategy. The Hellman's should be on the refrigerator door somewhere near the mustard and ketchup, but on which shelf is anyone's guess. Now the pickle relish could be on the door as well, however there's a chance it's on the second shelf down inside the fridge with the salad dressings and olives, or it might be on the bottom shelf by the sauer-kraut and beer brats I was planning on grilling for Jackie.

I fling the door open and the butter compartment is wide open and the dish, with a full stick of opened butter falls, butter side down, onto the floor. I ignore it as I quickly search the door for the mayonnaise.

"Eureka!" I exclaim and toss it on the counter. "Dammit MacArthur, quit licking the butter!"

The relish is not on the door, and I'm suddenly aware of all the cold air coming out of the fridge. It emphasizes the fact that the house is heating up without air-conditioning, and I'm now becoming warm in my jeans and sweatshirt. I scan the shelves and finally find the relish hidden behind the now sweating quart of almond milk on the top shelf.

"Why the hell is it there?" I slam the door, deliberately ignoring the fact that it is there because that's where I put it last.

I get a small mixing bowl and spoon out of the drawer, open the crackers, take the lids off the mayo and relish and pick up the tuna and walk over to the can opener—the *electric* can opener.

"Oh, good grief!"

I sigh and reverse the entire process by putting it all back. That is except the crackers. I walk to the cupboard, pull out the jar of Crunchy Jif and start spreading away.

Since our move to the Sunshine State, Mac has started requesting an afternoon potty break, and is now sitting at the front door giving me 'the Scotty eyes'. I ask if he would possibly give me a minute so that I may quickly change into shorts, tee, and a pair of deck shoes. I open the bottom drawer of the chest of drawers built into my closet and feel around blindly until I finally feel plastic. I take it into the kitchen where I can better see it.

It's one of the rain ponchos I held onto from when Scott and I went to Niagara Falls and rode the *Maid of the Mist*. I saved it partly be-cause it was still like new, but mostly because I'm sentimental and *Niagara* with Marilyn Monroe was one of our favorite film noir movies. I think about how Scott would have found this entire situation extremely funny as I don my poncho with the famous boat name emblazoned across the back. So now, with Mac on his lead, I aim out to face the storm.

We cross the parking lot, and Mac marks his tree. Standing below the arms of the great live oak, protected by the poncho and its hood, I take the moment to just breathe and enjoy some fresh air. It makes me realize I need to open up the house when we get back. Even though it's still raining, there is no longer thunder and lightning, so I decide to venture towards the Wilbanks clubhouse. I take the opportunity to glance into every condo we pass in an attempt to see if they might have electricity.

We actually come upon another dog walker and her large, black curly dog.

"Hahwahya?" she says with a Boston accent and introduces herself as Alise.

We both joke about how the dogs don't care whether there's a tropical storm or not, when you gotta go you gotta go. She shares that she and her husband are relatively new to Pelican Cove as well. Mac keeps pulling at the lead and looking back at me as he repeatedly shakes to remove the rainwater.

"Mine wants to head for dryer ground and get out of this rain," I say, "but yours seems to be relishing in it!"

"She's a Portuguese watta dog," she says, "and she thinks watta is the pissah!"

She then confirms that from her side of the cove, everything she passed was in complete dark. I advise it is the same on my side.

"Our objective was to make it to the Wilbanks, but I guess we'll just go back home and dry off."

As we turn to leave Mac eagerly leads the way. Alise says, "It was way wicked nice to have made youa acquaintance Maid of the Mist!"

47

Upon returning home, I open what doors and windows are protected from the precipitation by overhangs. The relief is short lived as, within the hour, I'm shutting them against the increased wind and rain. Additionally, the squall increases, coming down in torrents… hard and loud!

The sheets of rain are so intense, that I can barely see the trees right off the lanai doors. Walking to the front, Mac nervously following every step, I note the Pavilion lights are on and then watch as the parking lot lights blink to life. Lo and behold, next my condominium springs back to life, and the TV comes on, lights everywhere glow, and the dishwasher sputters back into operation.

"Thank you, Lord!" I say with a nod towards the ceiling.

The special report about Debby is still on the air, but all the key players have changed. There's now an attractive woman with the prettiest hair—and wearing pearls—alongside a horsey looking guy in a suit and tie. They both appear fresh and ready to go, compared to the fatigued middle of the night crew, and proceed to share the latest news on the weather.

The guy, whose banner identifies him as the Senior Meteorologist, advises viewers:

"Dry air, westerly wind shear, and an upwelling of cooler waters have prevented further intensification of the storm thus far. However, the NOAA Orion weather reconnaissance plane is reporting to us that they're currently monitoring sustained winds gusting up to 65 MPH. It appears the entire system has stalled in place and will continue feeding off of the moisture from the gulf, producing large amounts of rain for the Tampa Bay and surrounding Gulf Coast areas."

He ends his segment with a toothy grin as the camera swings to the anchorwoman who smiles attractively while adding, "All residents are encouraged to shelter in place and stay off the flooding roads. Police have advised us that only those with true medical emergencies, and first responders including medical professionals reporting to work, are permitted to drive. Coming up next: What to shop for when you're putting a hurricane preparedness kit together!"

The screen then goes to a 'No Malarkey call Mr. Sparky' commercial.

I walk around the house turning off the unnecessary lights and start thinking about Jack and Frank. I know that was a Tampa report, but all one has to do is look out the windows to know how bad it is. I open the front door and, gazing out, I am alarmed to see the usually dry and lifeless rock-lined creek bed, which runs thru the front yard, is now filled with rapidly rushing water.

As best I can see, it is dumping into the normally empty retention pond alongside Pelican Cove Road and filling it up to the top. It has prompted two fountains located in the center—fountains I have *never* seen operational—to spray water high up into the air. I stand mesmerized by the tableau before me until, once again, the winds change, and the rain now begins hitting me in the face.

Closing the door slowly on the tumultuous scene, I lean back against it clicking it shut, and look down at Mac.

"What in the hell are we doing here buddy? We should be in land-locked Ohio having a 3-Way at Skyline Chili right now."

I'm in desperate need of a tissue as my eyes well up with tears and my nose begins to run. My phone snaps me back to the moment playing "By the Seaside." I grab a paper towel off the kitchen counter and give a quick blow into it before answering.

"Hello, Liz Blum here?" *Dammit, why can't I stop answering like that?*

"Hi girlfriend it's, Jack. Everything okay there? You sound a little down."

"I'm fine." I say trying to sound perkier. "Just getting tired of all the rain!"

"You can't believe it out here," she says. "It's awful. At one point we were actually driving in water up over our tires… It's was nuts! Anyway, we're cutting our day short and heading back, but first we stopped at the Publix near you, down by Hooters off Stickney. I just wanted to check and see if you needed anything?"

"Why in the world are you at a grocery store?"

"Frank wouldn't let me come back to your place without buying a couple flashlights, a case of water, and something for dinner. That is if any thing's left in the store. It's a madhouse!"

"That's awfully nice of him," I say, "and shows that apparently my lack of preparation was a topic of conversation between you both."

"Only a small part, sweetie, only a small part! Anyway, is the power back on yet because that will make a big difference in what Frank's making us for dinner?"

"Yes, thank God, there's electric. But why is Frank making us dinner?"

"He offered so we could spend more time together while getting me out of the storm. He really is something else, Liz… I mean, *ma'am!*"

We both start to laugh. We chat a few more minutes, and before hanging up I say, "You might want to grab some butter while you're there. I kind of used my last stick while you were gone."

48

By the time Jack and Frank get to the condo it has cooled down considerably with the air now running again. They have dashed from the parking lot, across the bridge, and up the walkway as fast as possible. Still they are dripping wet and their shoes soaked by the time they enter the front door. I'm standing ready with Mac by my side and, this time, two towels in hand.

Jack gives me a look. "These aren't Mac's are they?"

"Only one of them!" I say.

I take the Publix bags they are each carrying and place them in the kitchen. They remove their shoes at the door, and Jack shows Frank to the bathroom and darts into the guest bedroom saying, "You try your best to towel off and give me a minute alone in here!"

She shuts the door behind her.

After first running to my clothes closet I go over to the guest bath where Frank is and tap on the door.

"It's Liz, Frank. I tend to buy some of my tee shirts in large sizes to sleep in. I'm afraid I can't offer dry bottoms, but I thought you might like a dry top?"

"Thanks ma'am, that's mighty kind of you," he says and opens the door—shirtless.

It's the first time I've seen this much of his bare body, and I'm surprised by how buff he actually is and by the amount of hair on his chest and how that ends in a 'happy trail' below his naval.

"Here you go!" I stammer and can feel the warmth of a blush on my cheeks as I turn away.

Back in the kitchen, I toss Mac a treat and then rummage through the grocery bags to see if anything is perishable and needs to be put away. I place the two flashlights, one yellow and one blue, and the package of C batteries on the kitchen counter by my phone for easy access.

"God forbid we need these again." I mutter.

The next bags have two bottles of San Pellegrino sparkling water, three bottles of Detox Water in mangaloe flavor, and a six-pack of Dasani sparkling berry. I wonder what these might be for but return to unpacking.

I place two packages of Caesar salad kits in the fridge along with a tube of Pillsbury French bread and a four-pack of unsalted butter.

I smile. *Good thing because who knew we were having bread?*

There's a bag with four bottles of wine and another with chocolate bakery brownies and a pint of Talenti coffee chocolate chip gelato.

I like how this guy thinks—bread, brownies, and gelato... screw the salad!

At the bottom of the bag there's a family-size Stouffer's Italiano lasagna. I take the liberty to turn the oven on and get a cookie sheet from the bottom drawer of the oven. I open the lasagna box and place the container on the sheet pan, get out my salad bowl and tongs, and then three bowls and three plates and set them on the counter. Afterward I head into the living room and sit in a lawn chair to await the oven's beep.

Jack comes out in dry clothes, her hair down, and takes the other lawn chair. Having taken the braid out she now sports a head full of damp ringlets.

"I thought Frank would be out here by now?" she whispers.

I tell her about giving him a spare tee so he could take off his drenched Hawaiian shirt and she credits me on being extremely thoughtful. Frank exits the bathroom and takes a stance directly in front of us and we both double over in laughter.

Frank maintains a straight face. "I want to thank you kindly ma'am for the use of the shirt."

When Jack can finally talk again she says, "Perhaps you weren't so thoughtful after all." Then covers her mouth with her hand trying to contain her snickering.

I apologize profusely to Frank, offering to search for another tee as the one he's wearing has a large blue anchor on the front decorated with red lipstick kisses and hearts. The arched line of type above it reads: "Hey There Sailor!"

The oven beeps and Frank excuses himself and insists on taking over from here. "After all, this was my idea ladies."

Jack and I half-heartedly watch the five o'clock news as at least they are talking about something besides the storm.

"So, you still haven't told me what you did today," I say. "I'm taking for granted toes in the sand was out?"

"We started the morning touring the Circus Museum of Art. It's a really beautiful place."

"I believe it's called The Ringling Museum," I say.

"Whatever, anyway he's a member and made a great tour guide of the place. We kept dry by hopping a ride on the covered tram, and it took us to the circus guy's house where he and his wife Melba lived. It's called something like the House of Juan. It so reminded me of your pictures of the villas in Tuscany, Liz. We toured it and then went into the protection of another building and saw a teeny tiny circus display. Everything was in miniature yet had such incredible details."

"First off their names are John and Mable Ringling," I say. "That much I know for sure! I haven't been there since the kids were very little. I don't remember anything but a museum building that housed circus memorabilia, like posters and ornate wagons, that we walked through which ended in a single ring live circus show. I mostly remember the clown's performance that involved audience participation."

"Anyway," Jack says, "he asks if I'm getting hungry yet, and you know me, I reply famished!"

"That little gal has a real healthy appetite!" Frank chimes in from the kitchen.

"That's because I'm a runner!" Jack says. "As I was saying, he asks about eating, and we dash for his car with our Ringling guide maps over our heads. Which, let me tell you, do little to no good against a tropical storm. He then drives us over to Saint Armands Circle. We cross over that large bridge on the way and I'm concerned his little Infinity is going to get blown right off into the ocean. Little did I know at the time that the winds were going to pick up even more on the way back?"

"Hey, how about we crack open a bottle of that wine?" she yells in the direction of the kitchen.

"Sure thing, Miss Jackie, I'll get right on that!" says Frank. "You want one too, Liz?"

"Yes please!" I call out, feeling a bit guilty that I'm just sitting here while a man I barely know is waiting on us hand and foot.

"So, he pulls up and lets me out at the Columbia. Have you been to the Columbia, Liz? It's unbelievable!"

I tell her how Scott and I ate at the one in Ybor City in Tampa many, many years ago when we were there on business.

"I'm not sure what we ate, other than I'm sure it was Cuban. However, I still remember our waiter making pitchers of sangria right at our table… and I do mean pitchers! I believe Tommy just may have been born nine months to the day after my last glass."

We all laugh at that, and I'm taken aback by the moment. Normally I do everything in my power not to mention my son's name, for it usually occasions a torrent of tears. But not today. It's not happiness I feel… more like comfort at being able to share a memory involving him.

Jack doesn't seem to notice. "Well, when Frank finally joins me, he looks like a drowned rat. He said he was lucky enough to find a parking spot on the street, but a waste management truck flew by and sprayed him with standing water from head to toe."

We break off for a second and thank Frank as hands each of us a glass of wine. Jack takes a generous sip from hers.

"Well, we didn't have sangria, my dear, but we did have a pitcher of their famous Mojito's. Oh my god! And those were made tableside as well. We both had black bean soup due to the insistence of our wonderful waiter who had the darkest most beautiful Latino eyes. Frank had a Cuban sandwich, and I had some kind of picadillo thing that was basically a beef stew type dish over rice. I loved it!"

From my vantage point, Frank seems to have scoped out my kitchen and made himself at home. He steps out of it just long enough to set the card table with dishes but does stop to ask where I might keep the napkins.

"Sorry," I say. "I'm alone most of the time so I just pull off a paper towel."

"Not a problem, ma'am," he says and returns to cooking.

"So like idiots," Jack says, "we try to walk around the circle and check out some of the boutiques and shops. We're walking under awnings as much as possible and ducking in and out of a couple of buildings along the way."

"I smell fresh bread," I interject while sniffing the air.

Jack assures me she's almost finished and that she got butter.

"We come to where we must cross the street and are making our way over in the crosswalk when all hell breaks loose. There's a downpour and the winds pick up. We both agree to bail, and Frank encourages me to wait under the cover of an ATM on the corner by a bagel shop, but we're both completely drenched so it doesn't matter and we just keep running!"

Frank starts going back and forth with food from the kitchen to the table. When my offer to help is yet again declined, I turn my attention back on Jack.

"Well we're soaking wet, and I ask him to turn off the car air as I'm freezing. We come to the bridge over to Sarasota, and this time I can't even see downtown due to the rain and winds. I'm actually a bit frightened, and I grab Franks upper left arm asking if we should turn back. He assures me we'll be fine as long as we take it slow. We get down to the corner of... what, the 41?"

I laugh. "I know Frank would have advised you it's called the trail!"

"Yes ma'am!" he yells from the kitchen.

"That's it. So there are police car lights flashing, and a policeman is actually out in the road waving us with a flashlight to go around. We look over, Liz, and honest to God, someone has run their car smack-dab into *Unconditional Surrender*, the huge statue of the sailor and nurse kissing from World War Two? And now both of them are laying on the side of the road in a rather compromising position!"

<h1 style="text-align:center">49</h1>

"Come and get it ladies," says Frank, "and please bring your wine glasses!"

As we make our way to the table, he actually pulls each of our folding chairs out, refills our glasses, and then his own. He goes back to the kitchen and returns with three plates carrying them on his arm like a waiter.

"Where in the world did you learn to do that?"

"I had to work my way through law school somehow," he states matter-of-factly.

Jack and I lock eyes and she hunches her shoulders as though to say, *Law school... who knew?*

I stick my fork into my salad. "Everything looks so—"

When the chandelier over the card table flickers twice and then goes out completely. The entire condo again falls quiet. However, this time it's later in the day and much darker, it might as well be midnight.

Frank stands up. "Stay put ladies, I saw where Miss Blum, uh I mean Liz, placed the flashlights on the counter." He comes back guided by their beams. "At least we can still see to eat."

"Hold on a minute," I say. "I did a little more searching and unpacking this afternoon." I rise, taking a flashlight from him, and head off around the corner. Returning in a matter of moments I have two Baccarat crystal candlesticks, with tapers and a box of matches, in hand. I give the flashlight to Jack and rearrange the table a bit to make room to place them.

"These were my mothers," I say while lighting them and then blow out the match. "I suggest we save the flashlights in case we need them later." And Frank and Jack simultaneously turn them off in agreement.

As I take my seat, Jack says, "Listen… what's that?"

We listen as the church carillon begins playing softly in the distance.

"It's the Methodist church on Vamo," I say. "It must only be six, but it sure seems a lot later."

"I think I know this song," says Jack. "It was in *Titanic*."

Frank grins. "Ma'am, that there would be 'The Navy Hymn' Some also know it as 'For Those in Peril on the Sea'!"

We sit embraced by candlelight, surrounded by darkness and listen as it plays poignantly over the din of the storm. I'm completely moved by the solemnness of the moment. Frank reaches out suggesting we all join hands and to my surprise he begins to pray.

"For food and all your gifts of love, we give thee thanks and praise. Look down, oh Lord, from above and bless us all our days. Amen."

And still holding hands, we all just sit in the silence experiencing the sanctity of the here and now as it continues to rain.

50

Still insisting on serving us his dessert of brownies and ice cream, Jack and I tell Frank to not bother putting any of it away, as the current situation calls for lots of chocolate. We also justify finishing off the gelato since it's going to melt by morning anyway. We ask Frank to get lost and find something else to do, as we offer to take care of clearing the table since he did the cooking.

He wanders away with one of the flashlights. "Well there are just so many things to do in the dark ladies that I don't know where to get started."

I wash as Jack holds the other flashlight up in the air over the kitchen sink. "My arm's getting tired," she says. "I would have just shoved them in the dishwasher and run it when the electric comes back on."

"Well, you must want to sleep with ants and palmetto bugs," I say, "because they can find a crumb of toast down here before it even hits the floor."

Trying to speak out of Frank's earshot I whisper, "You know that guy really is full of surprises, isn't he? First cooking, then law school, and finally leading us in a religious moment rivaling that of the Pope."

Jack agrees. "He has done nothing but take me by surprise since I met him, Liz."

"Did he finish law school?" I ask.

"Who knows? That's the first time I've even heard of it."

Frank has been peering out the back windows, as best he can in the dark, and joins us in the kitchen to suggest we close the inside sliders between the living room and lanai.

"The wind is howling through the back ones and some water is getting in."

"Sure thing," I say. "Let's batten down the hatches!"

"Have you taken Mac out recently?" Jack asks. "He's standing at the front door."

"Heavens no," I say, and Jack offers to do it while I assist Frank.

She places the lead on Mac, dons my Maid of the Mist poncho, grabs an umbrella and opens the door.

"Uh, Liz, Frank… I think you better come here!"

From the tone of her voice we come scampering immediately. Jack steps aside on the covered front porch to allow us both an unobstructed view. Where once there was this morning's rippling creek, there is now a raging river whose banks have crested to the edge of my front porch. It's difficult to see, but there are limbs and branches everywhere littering the yard and walkway.

"Good grief! What if the water enters my house?"

I look down in time to catch Mac as he relieves himself on the front porch. His expression says, *I have no intentions of going out in that!"* then he is dragging Jack back in through the open door.

"Without a weather radio, it's really difficult to tell what's going on," says Frank.

He reaches in his pocket and pulls out his car key. He slides on the crocs he left sitting by the door and makes a mad dash down the walk, jumping over a huge limb along the way.

"What's he doing?" Jack asks quizzically.

"He's either a deserter," I say, "or he's saving our lives." I take Mac back and remove his lead.

Jack remains at the door. "His headlights came on. You don't really think he's leaving, do you?"

"Not only do I doubt he's abandoning us now, but I have a feeling he's not going to be able to leave anytime soon! I'm guessing he's trying to find some weather information on the car radio."

The headlights have gone out, but there's still no sign of Frank. She closes the door as the wind changes direction and is again blowing rain into the house.

"I'm a little scared," I admit to Jack. "This is so different from an Ohio thunderstorm, or even a tornado warning, that is over in a matter of minutes. They used the term stalled on the news. Just how long can a tropical storm stall? Doesn't it run out of rainwater eventually?"

Jack just shakes her head at me and then gives me an answer I don't really want to hear, and I am embarrassed I hadn't thought of.

"There's a huge, entire ocean of water out there for it to feed on, my dear. I'm guessing it could churn in the gulf forever if it really wanted to."

By the time Frank comes back, one of the candles has totally burned down and the remaining wick emits an upward trail of soot. The second, aided by the opening of the front door, flickers and sputters as it joins the other. Jack and I are sitting at the card table with one of the flashlights, attempting to play Yahtzee.

"She's trying to get my mind off the storm," I say.

"We were ready to send out the Calvary," jests Jack, "but they all headed for higher ground. Did you find out anything?"

"I found out that Brandy was a fine girl and she'll make a good wife someday!" He smiles "And unlike TV, Miss Jackie, it takes a long time for anybody to even mention the news let alone the weather on the radio."

He then shares the good news that the storm is weakening and has started moving east, or inland, and is expected to cross the state and exit into the Atlantic. The bad news is all the Suncoast counties have declared a level 4 emergency and no one is allowed to drive on the roads.

"Seems the streets are flooded everywhere, and downed trees have brought down numerous power lines. Electric crews are attempting to return power as soon as possible, but in some areas, they say it could take days."

Frank sits down at the table. "Might it be possible ma'am for me to stay here for the night?"

"Of course, you can," I say. "I wouldn't let you go out in that mess no matter what!"

He thanks me kindly and Jack hands him the Yahtzee cup. "It's your roll, big boy… it's a brand-new game now!"

After Jack whips our butts by having three Yahtzees, I stand up. "I'm pooped and am heading to bed."

Mac follows me in and curls up in his bed. I come back out of the bedroom toting my trusty sleeping bag and a pillow.

"Here you go, Frank." I say. "It's not the most comfortable night's sleep, but it beats being out in the storm. Night guys!"

As I'm shutting my bedroom door, I hear Jack suggest opening another wine, and I don't hear Frank objecting. The day's events have been draining, and as I turn out the flashlight, I believe I hear Mac already snoring. I quickly drift off to sleep while thinking about how lucky I am to have these two friends in my life.

—

Later that night, Frank awakens, and it takes a minute to figure out where he is and why he's on the floor. He stands and stretches his lower back in an attempt to relieve the pain brought on by sleeping on Liz's thinly carpeted living room floor. Having no flashlight, he tries to maneuver through the dark towards the guest bathroom without tripping. He enters and decides he must leave the door ajar in hopes that what little ambient light there is might assist him with his aim. Wearing only boxers, having shed himself of the sailor tee, he proceeds to relieve himself.

Waking up in the guest room due to a full bladder, Jack feels around for the flashlight. She finds it, crawls off the air mattress and stumbles out into the hall towards the bathroom door. Upon nearing her destination, she flips on the flashlight and shines it straight into the bathroom. There stands Frank, the front of his boxers pulled down and penis in hand.

Startled, but unable to stop urinating mid-stream all he can think to say is, "Excuse me ma'am... Umm... I should be finishing up in just a minute, and the place will be yours."

Feeling extremely embarrassed herself, but unable to move an inch, Jack just stands there shining the light directly on his male member.

The Morning After
—Maureen McGovern (1972)
Songwriters: Al Kasha / Joel Hirschhorn

<h1 style="text-align:center">51</h1>

I wake up thrilled to find that when I try the switch to the lamp on my bedside table it actually comes on. "Hallelujah!" I exclaim to Mac, "we have power again."

He follows me to the bathroom where I begin my usual morning routine of running a brush through my hair and then cleaning my teeth. I grab my spa robe out of the walk-in and open the door of the bedroom whispering, "Ready to go out fellow? Let's try to not wake up Frank."

Mac pads along behind me close on my heels.

The living room is still dark, but the recessed lighting in the kitchen glows warmly. I glance outside, and I'm thrilled to see it has stopped raining. Grabbing Mac's lead from his cupboard we aim for the front door where I slip on a spare pair of flip-flops before we both make our way out to the yard allowing him to do his job.

The most difficult part of the process has been navigating over the limbs and debris covering the walkway and finding a spot of dry ground. Before going back in, I survey the Escape in the carport and realize I'm thankful for the cover of the parking spot's roof. Inside the house I remove Macs lead and, per usual, he trots off to go back to bed for a little more shut eye, with nary a look back in my direction.

Trying to move about as quietly as possible so as not to disturb Frank in the other room, I fill the Mr. Coffee with water, put in a fresh filter, and add eight heaping scoops of ground hazelnut coffee. I set the brew on bold, press the 'on' button and it immediately starts gurgling away.

"Shhhh!" I say to the coffee maker.

I get out three mugs from the cabinet and set them gently on the counter and then search the refrigerator for the French vanilla creamer, while worrying that the light may be shining too brightly into the living room.

Dawn is breaking, and I can see through the kitchen slider that, yes indeed, for the moment the rain has stopped, yet the sky remains overcast and gray. From this vantage point, I survey what I can of last night's high water in the creek, and it appears to have receded partially back into its banks. However, the pond is filled even more so than last night, and the fountains shoot even higher. I'm also able to determine that the damage to the trees and the foliage of my front yard is quite extensive.

I decide to tiptoe through the living room to the back lanai in an attempt to get a better look at the back yard and the probable damage there is to it. As I pass, quiet as a mouse, between the lawn chairs and the sleeping bag I notice that the bag is flat as a pancake and obviously Frank is not in it. I glance across the room towards the guest bath, thinking he may be in there, but am able to quickly ascertain that the door is open and it, too, is empty. I stop for a moment to ponder where he might be and then continue out to the lanai to check if he might be there.

Slowly, it dawns on me where he is after having spied the sailor tee tossed atop the sleeping bag.

I return to the kitchen and search the cupboards and fridge trying to discern what I can throw together for breakfast from the ingredients on hand. I open the egg carton find I still have eight even after Jack's waffles breakfast yesterday. I have a package of 'Simply Potatoes' hash browns and an onion. I get my trusty number eight cast iron skillet out and pour in some olive oil and set the stove burner on medium high after setting the oven to 350 degrees.

I dice some onion and throw it in the skillet working it with the spatula till they begin to become translucent. I empty the bag of cold shredded potatoes over that and they immediately begin to sizzle and pop loudly as I salt and pepper them generously.

No need to be quiet now. Frank is behind closed doors.

The kitchen is beginning to smell great as I break the eggs into a mixing bowl and beat them with a fork. I then add eight splashes of almond milk and a couple dashes of Tabasco and whisk some more. I recall during my earlier search seeing a can of Rotel tomatoes in the cupboard and return to grab them. I open them up and dump them in the egg mixture. While continuing to beat everything in the bowl, I slowly pour it over the items in the skillet. Moments later it starts to bubble, and I grab a bag of shredded cheddar from the deli drawer in the fridge and sprinkle some all over the top. I open the oven door and taking care to use a potholder to grasp the hot skillet handle I pop the entire thing on the center rack and set the timer for thirty minutes.

I look in the china cupboard trying to decide if I'm supposed to set the table for two and act surprised exclaiming when Frank pops out of the guest room. *Oh I saw the empty bag and took for granted you left...*

Or perhaps I should attempt to act like the hip with-it friend and set it for three to begin with and a nonchalantly greeting. *Why good morning Frank how did you sleep last night... And Jacqueline dear... would you care for something like a jumbo breakfast sausage to start your day?*

Jack surprises me by suddenly coming around the corner, beaming ear-to-ear. "Good morning, what in the heck smells so darn good?"

"I made one of my world-famous frittatas," I say. "You know, what I always make for a meal when there's nothing else in the house! It'll be ready in about ten more minutes."

Jack expounds on the joys of the clearing weather, as she peers out the window, and the miracle of electricity. She contemplates the probable current conditions of the roadways and comments on the large limbs down in the yard.

"Think this is the end of Debbie or is there more to come?"

By this point I think I'm going to burst. "Where the Hell is Frank?"

She turns from looking outside again.

"Why he left hours ago. He woke me up and said the rain had stopped and he thought he really should be going. He was concerned about his own place suffering damage. Why?"

Embarrassed at myself for thinking that perhaps my best friend and my realtor might have had a romantic encounter, and under my own roof no less, I try to act composed.

"Oh, no reason in particular, I just didn't want him to miss out on breakfast." I roll my eyes thinking of how lame an answer that was.

"Let me help," she says. taking the plates and forks to the dining room and returning to get a couple mugs full of coffee.

The buzzer sounds, and I take the frittata out and place it on a hot plate on the card table. "Do you want salsa on yours?" I ask carrying the jar in from the kitchen.

"Sure thing… the spicier the better! Oh, and speaking of spicy, wait till I tell you what happened between Frank and me last night!"

52

Since we're the closest of friends—and because Jack is always outspoken—she proceeds to tell me all the intimate details of last night. She starts with the accidental encounter in the bathroom and then the details of their ending up spending the night together.

"He was so embarrassed, Liz, I swear I could see him turn red even in the dark."

I can't help but chuckle visualizing her description of the toilet scene.

"So I apologize and go back to my room where I plop back down on the air mattress. Minutes later there's a faint knock at the door, and it's Frank apologizing for leaving the bathroom door open like that. A few ma'ams later, and before I know it, he's talked his way into the room and is now standing by the bed.

"Well, actually he's towering over me lying on the floor and you can guess where my eyes and my flashlight first focus. Frank and I joke about the situation and both start to laugh. In fact, I'm surprised you didn't hear us, as it was one of those contagious, I can't stop laughing sort of things."

"I was out like a light," I say with another chuckle while urging Jack to share more.

"Anyway, I reach up and take his hand and encourage him to kneel down on the air mattress…" Here she cracks up. "…which causes the release valve to make a farting noise from the escaping air due to his weight."

"Hold on a sec," I command. "I have to grab a tissue and possibly change my pants!" Returning, I hand one to Jack and she dabs at her eyes before continuing.

"I sit up and he then gently caresses my head in his hands and kisses me… I mean *really* kisses me, Liz, you know long and hard. Catching my breath, I lay back and invite him to come join me. He lies down beside me, and we embrace, my hands caressing his broad bare shoulders and strong upper arms then sliding down to feel the scapula and lumbar vertebrae."

"You felt his what?" I ask.

"His back," she says. "Sometimes my medical brain turns on. After another penetrating kiss we come up for air, and he asks me in that sweet sincere way of his, 'Do you really want to do this ma'am? I care deeply for you but would never want to do anything that might compromise our relationship.'"

"He paused, Liz, and looked so deeply into my eyes, well… I think he did because by now the flashlight has rolled off the mattress… and he says, 'Especially, Miss Jackie, at the risk of losing you.'"

"And sliding my hands under the elastic band of his boxers I grab onto his incredibly firm buns and tell him, I'm game if you are. You're one hell of a southern charmer!"

"And that my dear is as much of the sorted details as you're going to get out of me, well at least until after we have breakfast!"

While we are talking and finishing up eating, Maggie calls me, to see how I am.

"Sam the weatherman on Good Morning America has done nothing but carry on about Tropical Storm Debby for days now," she says. "And after trying to call you several times and getting no answer I started to get worried!"

I relay how we have literally been 'in the dark' a fair amount of the time due to the power loss and how Jacqueline's here visiting and that we're holding up fine.

"I'm just second guessing that it somehow affected the cell towers down here," I say, while looking outside. "It appears now that the sun is trying to peek out from behind the clearing clouds. I believe the worse is definitely over."

We talk for about fifteen minutes more, and when I glance across the table, I notice Jack smiling at me happily, as she is getting to witness first-hand my daughter and I interacting. The call wraps up with Maggie asking if it would be possible for her to pay a visit sometime around the holidays so she can see where I'm now living.

"I would be thrilled!" I say, ecstatic at the thought. "I wish you could come sooner. I can't wait to show you the place."

"And I can't wait to see you and to come to Sarasota again," she says. "I remember our vacations way back when..." Her voice trails off then.

"Way back when Tommy and Daddy were with us?" I say.

Yet again surprising myself at the ease with which I'm able to bring up their names.

"We are now, and always will be, a family, Maggie," I say. "And it's about time you and I move on while remembering that fact. I loved... no, *love* your brother and father as much as you."

We actually reminisce a few more moments about Siesta Key and other happy times from her childhood until time catches up with her.

"Well, I really have to go, Mom, but I wanted to make sure you were all right. I'll call with more details about coming once we get closer to the date."

"Thanks for checking on me, it really means a lot," I say. "You know I dearly love you!"

"Back at ya," she says and then... "Oh, and would you mind if I bring my boyfriend along?"

53

It's late morning when Frank calls Jack and tells her there's considerable damage to his neighborhood and that he's currently waiting on a tree service to come and get a large date palm off of his roof.

"There has also been damage to my screened lanai, but the pool looks fine, just dirty. I'm hoping to be able to swing by late afternoon and pick you two ladies up for dinner. Is it a date?"

"I can't answer for Liz," says Jack. "But I'll be ready and waiting."

"Last night was some kind of special." Frank adds in earnest.

There's quite a reflective pause before she replies. "For me too, Frank. Me too… see you soon!"

Jack comes into the kitchen to advise me of the plans. "He invited us both for dinner, but I say before that we try to hit a few furniture stores. What do you say?"

"I say fine to the shopping, but I would feel like a third wheel at dinner." I finish wiping out the cast iron skillet with oil on a paper towel before putting it away. "You know this darn thing has never been washed and it was my grandmothers?"

Jack scrunches up her nose. "NEVER?"

"Nope. Never!"

Jack returns to the conversation of Frank's dinner invitation to which I reply, "I would think that after last night's little tryst you two have a lot of things to figure out, or at the very least talk about."

"Who told you he was little?" says Jack with a chuckle. "Because he's anything but!"

Unwilling to rise to that comment (so to speak), I give it a second before I respond.

"This is important, Jack. The dynamics of your relationship will never be the same again. Once you've had sex with someone, well, there's no going back to just being friends."

"Wow, are you showing your age," she says. "Are you not yet familiar with the concept of *friends with benefits?*"

I roll my eyes. "Seriously Jacqueline, my question to you would be are you emotionally ready, and financially able, to handle a long-distance romance?"

Looking uncharacteristically serious Jack says, "This sounds so childish coming from a fifty-year-old woman, but I seriously don't know... I've never had one. Hell, I've barely had any long-lasting relationships beyond ours."

"And that, my dear, is why you two need to talk it out!" I say. "Now let me jump in the shower and let's go find me a dining room set!"

We spend the better part of the day negotiating our way around storm damage while shopping at Pamaro Shop, Baer's, Copenhagen Imports, La-Z-Boy, and more. By the end of this shopping spree, my head is spinning not only because of visual overload, but also from adding up the receipts from my purchases.

On the drive home I say, "I knew it was going to cost me to decorate the place, and I have budgeted for it accordingly. I just wasn't expecting to do it all in one lump sum. It feels like we spent a bundle today."

Jack snickers. "Well at least I'll have a place to sit, a table to eat at, and a real bed to sleep in on my next visit."

Jack gets a text that advises there has been a change to her plane schedule.

"Seems that due to the storm causing damage at the airport, my flight has been delayed till Tuesday. Can you handle me staying an extra night?"

"Out of everything that came about because of Debby, this is the only one I consider a blessing," I say. "And something tells me Frank will feel the same way too!"

That evening, Frank picks up Jack, and this time she's dressed to the nines. It's actually one of the few times I've seen her in heels. Jesting as they're leaving, I advise her not to break her neck. Frank attempts one last time to convince me to join them, and I bow out gracefully, agreeing to the next time for sure. Mac and I spend our evening trying to visualize what all our new furniture is going to look like in this place, while finishing off the leftover pizza and half a bottle of wine.

Around eleven o'clock, Jack calls my phone and advises me not to wait up for her.

"Frank wants to show me his place in Nokomis and, well… he offered me an invitation to spend the night." Now sounding like she's whispering she adds, "I'm hooked Liz. I'm crazy about him. What can I say?"

"Follow your heart my love," I say. "Follow your heart and you'll never go wrong."

54

Tuesday morning comes, and we say our teary-eyed goodbyes with a hug and a kiss in my parking lot. Earlier, Frank brought Jack by to pick up her suitcase, and has also offered to drive her back to the Punta Gorda Airport to catch her flight. Mac and I stand in the lot waving until the car turns the corner and out of sight.

"Well my friend," I say to Mac, "alone again... naturally." We begin walking, since I feel the desire to stay outside for a while.

Following the winding roads, we make our way towards the far harbor section of Pelican Cove. We follow Clower Creek Road and pause a moment to take in the view of the boats in the yacht basin and the gently waving American flag mounted on the dock. Three pelicans glide overhead and a couple of mullets jump into the air, creating ripples in the water.

We round a corner, and where the road crosses a small bridge, Mac stops to bark at a blue heron standing knee deep in the creek water below. I take out my phone and snap a picture before the bird flies up into a tree in an attempt to put a little distance between himself and the grumbling Scotty.

I text Jack the picture, writing:

Wish it had been this pretty while you were here!

She texts back right away.

True friendship can always weather the storm. Nice pic! XOXOXO

Mac and I continue walking, and I'm surprised that the road simply circles back at the boundary.

"Looks like we reached the end of the road, Mac."

It's very serene in this portion of the property, and there are no other individuals in sight. We walk towards a sign that points to a pool. Behind the hedges is a very small rectangular pool with nary a soul in it.

"It's definitely more peaceful back here, huh fella? Especially compared to our busy location in the heart of the cove with the pavilion auditorium, tennis courts and large pool."

As we wander past the end of the walkway to one condo, there appears to be two large ceramic sculptures of purple eggplants anchoring the walk. Mac sniffs at them both and then lifts his leg on the larger one on the left.

"Well, who knew you were such an art critic?" I say as he insists on pulling me further down the walkway of pavers towards the buildings.

Along the way are many smaller, terracotta statuettes—most are of nude women and many in poses that I couldn't even begin to try and replicate. We pause a moment in front of a particularly erotic one.

"Well, actually I may have tried that once in yoga."

I'm a bit wary as we meander between the buildings, with their mostly undraped windows, on a path that takes us to the very edge of the Clower Creek waters. I know we're allowed to explore anywhere we want on the grounds, but I can't get past feeling like I'm a trespasser of sorts. At this point the water is fairly wide and looking across I notice a park bench, sitting under a cluster of live oaks literally dripping with Spanish moss. It appears to offer a fine view of Little Sarasota Bay from its vantage point.

We continue on the trail parallel to the creek and behind all the condominiums we passed in front of earlier. Many have nice wooden decks off the back of them, beautifully decorated with outdoor furnishings and potted flowers. We make our way through a bamboo grove and pause a moment to watch a pair of large brown anoles mating on a bamboo stalk. It involves much gesturing and inflation of their dewlaps in the process.

"I think they got all hot and bothered from viewing all those naked sculptures," I say. "We best move on, Mac, before the neighborhood dubs us voyeurs."

Crossing the small bridge again we continue walking onto a dead-end section of the road, towards where I believe we'll find the welcoming bench in the pleasant setting by the water.

The land narrows to a point here with the creek on my right side, the entrance canal to the yacht harbor to the left, and Little Sarasota Bay straight ahead. The view is obstructed straight ahead by a clump of large oaks surrounded by some sparse, late blooming azaleas at the base. Even so, their fuchsia coloring makes for a fairyland setting to walk through. Rounding the plantings, I note that a tall, slender elderly man in a cowboy hat now occupies one end of the previously vacant bench.

Where in the world did he come from? I wonder. *He wasn't there a minute ago, and our route seems the only way of getting out here.*

He's wearing extremely dark glasses and staring straight ahead at the bay with his legs straight out in front of him and crossed at the ankles. Without so much as turning his head, he speaks.

"Well don't just stand there ya little filly. There's plenty of room on this here bench for two."

"Hello!" I say as we approach, Mac of course introduces himself by placing his paws up on the seat of the bench and whimpering for attention.

"Well, how-de-do! and who do we have here?"

The man is soft spoken and has a rather gentile manner. He gives a little chuckle as he pats Mac on the head and then pats the bench seat next to him several times.

"His name's Mac."

"Well isn't that just fine," he says. "I don't bite, come take a load off and sit a spell with me."

I take a seat and apologize for Mac's begging for attention.

"Oh, that don't bother me none, miss. Heck, I was kind of hankering for my two dogs back on the farm." And he does another round of chuckling. "Of course, they're working animals, and nowhere near as well-groomed as this dapper little fellow."

He reaches a hand towards me and with a firm, yet gentle handshake introduces himself.

"The names Erwin Williams, and what might yours be?"

"Liz," I say. "Liz Blum."

"So, what brings you here?" he asks smiling from behind those jet-black glasses.

"Please?" I find it necessary to mull my answer over for a minute, as I'm not sure if he means what brings me to this particular bench, or perhaps to Pelican Cove, to Florida, or even something more profound.

"Well," I say, "I was forced to retire early from my career of the last twelve years, and that prompted me to run away from home in search of paradise and hoping to catch hold of some crazy dream." I marvel at my response and how candid and comfortable I feel with this total stranger.

Another chuckle as he adjusts his Stetson to better shade his eyes. "So where in the Midwest do you hail from?"

"Cincinnati, Ohio," I say, surprised. "How did you know?"

"Well you see, Miss, I'm originally from Tippecanoe, Indiana, and you southern Ohioans have a particularly peculiar way of using the word 'please' when you really mean is 'what.'"

I consider that. "So you're a farmer back in Indiana?"

He reaches up and scratches his right temple and seems to reflect. "Well, I own a good deal of farmland in Marshall County, Miss. However, I'm fortunate enough to have some hired hands that work it for me. I'm retired now, but my actual career was as secretary."

"Oh, it's not often you meet a gentleman of your age… uhm, I mean stature, that's worked as a secretary. I'm always surprised how many men are going into nursing these days."

Mr. Williams hoots with laughter. "Please call me Erwin and may I call you Liz?"

"Of course, Erwin."

"Well Liz, I actually had a career with the government. I worked under the President as his Assistant Secretary of State in the early seventies. Let me tell you, those were some interesting times to be working in Washington. But that's all water over the gate now, so to speak."

He then seems to chuckle at some inside joke.

We watch the bay water as it sparkles and ripples in the midday sun. Mac has curled up on the ground and laid his head upon Erwin's shoe, a gesture signaling complete acceptance. I comment on how nice it is to be able to go outside after being housebound from the storm for so many days.

Still looking straight ahead at the view he answers with a conviction that surprises me.

"Every day we wake up is a blessing from God. And I consider each one of them the chance for a brand-new beginning!"

"That's a beautiful sentiment," I say. "How I wish I could adopt your point of view. Maybe then I could stop taking everything so seriously."

"It takes time to let go," he says. "But trust me, it will happen living here!"

I wonder again about what he actually means when without encouragement he adds, "Yes, siree, it can be mighty hard to leave your worries behind and just learn to breathe again."

Mac shifts in place and gives a yawn before settling back to sleep. We then remain sitting comfortably together on the bench as Erwin continues spinning yarns about Washington politics for the better part of an hour.

55

I finally stand up to stretch my legs, and Mac jumps up from his slumber to join me. My hair hits some of the Spanish moss hanging overhead and as I swipe at it.

"What the heck is this stuff anyway? I mean I know it's—"

"It's an epiphyte," he says as he struggles to his feet. "That means it draws all its nutrients and moisture from the air. It's actually a relative of the pineapple family. If you'll allow an old man the pleasure of walking with you part of the way home, I'd be obliged to tell you the plant's legend."

Thus, arm in arm we begin to walk as he continues to talk.

"Well Miss, if memory serves me right, the story goes something like this. A long bearded and villainous Spaniard by the name of Gorez Goz landed near these shores in search of ill-gotten gains and pirated booty. He carried a jagged scar across his left eye, a mouth full of rotting teeth from a lifetime of swilling south seas rum, and a disfigured right hand burned while retrieving gold bullion during a massive ship's fire during a night out marauding."

Erwin takes a handkerchief out of his pants pocket and wipes the perspiration from his brow. "Bit humid today, miss! But I digress, at the time an Indian tribe lived on this land, and even today tales are told of Pelican Cove being built on sacred land, most likely the burial grounds from a tribal settlement located at neighboring Spanish Point."

"I heard the cove is protected from hurricanes because of an Indian blessing on the land," I interject.

Erwin laughs aloud. "That's the romantic version of the story. But what the old-timers here will tell you is it's all because of our guard, Jorge. There hasn't been a hurricane yet that can figure out how to get past the front gate house!" He winks, and now we both are left laughing as I grip a little tighter on his upper arm and Erwin continues his tale.

"So, after anchoring their sloop the *Revenge* in the bay directly off the point, they tender over in a dinghy to the mainland and are greeted at the shoreline by the local natives. The elders always anticipate their yearly arrival and eagerly trade them pearls, abalone, pelts, fresh deer and fresh fruit for meager objects like beads, and colored string."

Mac pulls at the lead and proceeds to hike his leg on a clump of variegated Shell Gingers.

"However, during this particular landing, Gorez spies a beautiful, young Indian maid that he desires to take aboard ship for his own carnal pleasures." The old man stops to give me an investigatory look over the top of his dark glasses then continues. "Offering the chief an additional yard of braid, a bar of soap, and a bottle of Aguardiente, the young girl is quickly handed over to him."

"How horrible, today they would consider that part of the sex slave industry!" I say as Mac stops, yet again, to sniff the base of a Hong Kong orchid tree.

"That's so true miss," says Erwin. "So true."

"Well, it seems that the maiden is so terrified of this bearded beast, who is already manhandling her in front of the entire tribe, that she takes off running blindly. She loses him for the moment while climbing over the upper ridge of the midden outside the camp. However, in hot pursuit, the pirate quickly catches up as she crosses a glade and enters the dense forest surrounding what is now the cove."

"Tiring, arms and legs bleeding from the brambles, and unable to run one step further she begins climbing the tallest bald cypress tree she sees. She is quickly followed by the pirate trader as he pulls himself up branch by branch. He's furious and filled with rage he begins yelling in a strange language she doesn't understand, yet there's no misunderstanding his intentions from the tone: *Así, maldita pena cuando le ponga las manos sobre ti muchacha. Usted no va a estar tirando de esta mierda de toro otra vez!*

They both continue climbing, and as she reaches the top the thinning limbs weaken and bend. Knowing escape is futile she dives into the brackish water where the sacred creek meets the mighty ocean waters all the while praying to her gods to save her from this evil man: *Oh gwo lespri. nanm mwen Soti nan nonm sa a sa ki mal!*"

"Suddenly the sky darkens, and the ocean breeze kicks up. The top of the tree where the pirate clings begins swaying drastically. Looking down towards the water, the Indian maid is nowhere to be seen and he curses her aloud believing she must have perished in the fall. The wind becomes even stronger and it begins to storm furiously, causing the villain's long, grey whiskers to become entangled in the surrounding branches. Just then an enormous bolt of lightning strikes the tree, and Gorez Goz is lost as his lifeless body falls to the ground. However, as a warning to future intruders, his beard which torn from his face in the fall still lives on, forever growing on the limbs of our trees as the dangling Spanish moss."

"Wow, that's some story," I say wide-eyed. "So, how much of it is true?"

"All of it miss," he smirks. "Absolutely all of it!"

"Well, then how did it get to the Carolinas?" I giggle.

Walking After Midnight

—Patsy Cline (1957)

56

The months pass by slowly as I keep myself busy working on my place ahead of Maggie's visit. I've met a tall and extremely skinny man named Hans while on my walks. He always dons white painters' bibs and often approaches me, but completely avoids all eye contact and talks directly to Mac with a strong German accent.

"Hallo leetle dawgie. And how goes its with you twos?"

He drives a large van and the signage advertises faux painting techniques, interior painting, and ceiling popcorn removal among other things.

I have been living with the bare spots where the popcorn has fallen off long enough, so I decide to inquire of him about the cost to remove the rest and then painting my unit. He admits that his wife is the brains of the operation and an interior decorator as well. As best I can decipher, he advises me he'll have her stop by soon to give me a quote. Either that, or she's stooped over with a spoon on a boat?

One of my next-door neighbors is also having their kitchen remodeled by a local contractor whom I've also seen quite a lot of in and around the cove. They will gladly give me his name and phone number, but clutching the piece of paper with the contact information close to her chest the wife takes on a pleading look.

"He books up fast in here, especially when it becomes season, it seems like he's working for everybody now. So please, please, please… whatever you do, don't deter him from finishing our place before starting on yours!"

The contractor stops by one day after he has finished working on the neighbor's kitchen. He's stumpy and round in stature with a natural tonsure of grey hair. He's wearing a sweaty and well-worn Key West Sunset Ale T-shirt and when we go to shake hands, I notice he's missing the better part of his right thumb. He gives me an estimate for tearing out the fluorescent, illuminated dome ceiling in my kitchen and replacing it with drywall and canned lighting. My kitchen cabinets are plain white and in too good a shape to replace, so he suggests I just get new counter tops and maybe spiff up the cabinets with new knobs.

As well, I have contacted the Pelican Cove management office and inquired about getting the jungle in my backyard under control and installing a patio, like the ones all my neighbors have, so Mac and I can use the space. I also tell them about my stuck sliding glass door. Sharon, the woman I'm speaking with on the phone, advises me that the door is something I will have to take care of, but is kind enough to offer up the contact information of several places that do work in here.

As for the yard work, she informs me that I'll need to come to the office and fill out a work order detailing my request, which she will then forward to Mick, the manager of the grounds crew. He in turn will probably come and have a look for himself and then talk to me about what can and can't be done to improve the situation.

I'm excited to be taking the condo to the next level, but unaware, once the projects begin, of how big a disruption they are going to be to my life. The ceiling popcorn removal means covering or removing absolutely everything, including placing plastic drop cloths on all the walls and floors. During the week that this process takes place Mac and I stay huddled with my little TV in our bedroom, unless we're out walking or leave the cove entirely.

Hans, the painter and popcorn remover, has suggested we do my room last after all else is finished.

"Dees woulda bean mutch easier if da places she had bean emptied of all furnishings!"

A short time ago it practically was! I think.

Then several weeks later, my neighbor's handyman, Gene, begins tearing my kitchen out. I expected the ceiling portion of this project to be disruptive, but I had no idea the appliances would need to come out and the sink removed in order to replace the counters. And just as we're wrapping up that project, I have to reschedule Hans to come back and paint it all.

The wait is well worth it though as the Bimini Blue of the kitchen walls with the sand colored swirls of the granite counter and white cabinets—now sporting an array of brushed silver seashell handles—is exactly the "coastal living" look I was going for.

As for the backyard, Mick from the grounds crew has surveyed the area along with his master gardener, Sing, a diminutive and soft-spoken Vietnamese gentleman. They advise me that each unit is allotted a maximum thirty cement pavers of patio space, but because of the two huge trees just outside my lanai blocking the area, the configuration is only going to allow for twenty-four. Also, they are going to have to bring in a backhoe and a stump remover in order to make the area workable. After that portion is complete, Sing will meet with me personally to discuss the new plantings he has in mind. There is only one problem.

I can't understand a single word he says.

Finally, with my new furnishings all back in place and the current remodeling finished, I stand looking around in amazement, while pondering at how much my place has changed since the first time Jack and I saw it the day Frank tried to convince me not to buy. I start putting the last of the knickknacks back on the bookshelves, trying my best to replicate where Jack had placed them the first time.

I glance at my new coffee table and decide it needs a few of these items strategically placed on it. I was apprehensive at purchasing a round glass-top table at first, but Jack convinced me it would work well with the ell shaped sectional. Plus, I loved the nautical shell reliefs on the wrought iron legs and the extra shelf underneath for additional storage.

I set a basket full of shells on the bottom shelf and then take a book entitled *Cabinet of Natural Curiosities* from the bookcase and place it next to the basket at an angle. I peruse the shelves again for additional items then remember I have a beautiful hand-blown bowl somewhere in the other room, and I run to go find it. Returning to the table, I set it on the glass top and am pleased with how the aqua color looks with the couch, but the bowl looks pretty empty just sitting there.

I take off for the spare room again and dig through an open box—the one that contained the candles and holders on the night of the storm—and find the black silk drawstring bag I'm looking for. It contains sea glass that I have collected over the years from all my previous trips to Florida. It's kind of like taking coals to Newcastle, I think as I empty the contents into the bowl and they rattle loudly as glass hits glass.

Most of my magazine subscriptions have followed me south and have been forwarded along with the mail. I've been stacking them up on my bedside table because, until recently, it was one of the few tables in my house—also I tend to like to read them in bed at night before dozing.

So again, I dash off but this time to my bedroom and I come back with several magazines that I fan out on the table next to the bowl. I stand back and admire my decorating skills. *Cincinnati Magazine* somehow feels out of place here in Sarasota and I wonder that the subscription has not ended by now.

I determine the table is still missing something. If nothing else I have learned from my personal decorator, Jack, that one should decorate in threes for balance, not pairs. So, I shop my house again looking for that additional piece, and *voila* there it is. I grab the totem and place my naked, little tree man on the table. I shift things around slightly, then step back again and smile. That's when I realize my dining room and foyer want for natural light and that a new glass front door—in place of the current solid wood one—would do wonders for the place.

"Come here, Mac old boy… it looks like we're off to Lowe's!"

57

After sunset I slip on a pair of red jammie pants with black Scottie silhouettes on them and a matching plain red top with a single terrier on the chest pocket. Turning down the bedspread, I prop my pillows up against the headboard and climb into bed, grabbing the September issue of *Good Housekeeping* off the nightstand on the way. The rest of the house has gone to sleep, including Mac who's whimpering in his bed having puppy dreams and his stubby little legs are running a mile a minute.

Skipping mindlessly through the magazine one title jumps out at me: "Self Help Tips – Why it's never too late to start over!" Hoping to find some relevance to my current life situation I begin reading the article. The first woman identifies herself as being twenty-nine years old and not quite sure how to get back into the job routine after having her first baby. Skimming the paragraphs, it seems one of her biggest concerns isn't who will watch the baby, but the fact that she doesn't fit into any of her work clothes anymore.

"Oh, to be so young again."

The next woman is forty-something and has hit the invisible-to-most-men (yet extremely certifiable by all women) glass ceiling. Her concerns involve feeling that she is far from reaching her full potential at her current employer. She states she has gone as far as she can in her career without going back to school. Her major gripe being that there are various men working at the same company in similar positions making twice as much in salary. Ironically, she knows for a fact that they have nowhere near her own skill set or knowledge base of the industry. I turn the page searching for the end of her segment, curious if I happen to know her and if she works for P&G.

Startled by a gentle knock at the front door, I glance at the alarm clock. *Who would be knocking on my front door at this time of night?* Then another round of knocking occurs, much more rapid and louder than before. It's the knock of someone in trouble. It rouses Mac who takes off barking towards the door as I grab my robe and tie its belt around me while following, barefoot, close behind him.

The door has no peephole, so I ponder the wisdom of opening it wide to a possible stranger. While the dog continues barking his head off, I decide to make my way to the kitchen slider and see if I can possibly get a glimpse of who's banging at the front door. No matter how I strain, with the side of my face pressed against the cool glass, I can't see the area of porch directly in front of the door.

Another round of rapid pounding occurs, and I reach in the kitchen drawer where, thanks to Jack, I now keep a few tools and grab the hammer. Going back to the door I shush Mac.

"Who's there?" I call through the door but receive no answer. "Please identify yourself... Do you need help?... Do I know you?"

There's a hollow thud against the front door, not dissimilar to the sound of a dead weight like that of a collapsing body would sound like—or so I imagine. Mac has run out of barks and is now sniffing and snorting along the bottom edge of the door where it meets the threshold.

What the Hell?

I go back to the kitchen and again peer outside thinking perhaps I'll at least see their legs sticking out now, and maybe I'll recognize the shoes. Mac remains whimpering at the door and is now scratching at it, something he only does when he really needs to go out.

I don't know what to do. What if one of my elderly neighbors is in need. What if it's Marilyn with Tookie and she's had a heart attack or stroke after returning from synagogue? How would I feel finding them dead on my porch in the morning when I go out for the paper?

Still grasping the hammer, I take a deep breath and look down at short statured Mac.

"You go for the ankles. I'll go for the head!"

Turning the deadbolt and twisting the knob, ready to strike at the slightest wrong movement. The hinge squeals eerily as I open it—I actually make a mental note to get some WD-40 the next time I'm at Publix. *If there is a next time and I'm not murdered on my doorstep.*

Gazing outside there's absolutely nothing there. No neighbor, no varmint, no serial killer. Only darkness. However, Mac begins barking wildly again accompanied by guttural, angry growls and darts out the door off lead and into the darkness.

I'm panic-stricken. I run back to the kitchen drawer to grab a flashlight, and then realize I'm barefoot. I search for where I've kicked off my flip-flops and, finding them, run out the door with Mac's lead.

"Mac, Mac, here boy!"

I pause in the parking lot trying to determine which way he may have gone. Improbably I hear his bark off in the distance. Peering down Pelican Cove Road, through the tree bridges, I see him at the end under a streetlight barking. From my vantage point, he's positioned in what appears to be an aggressive stance.

Fool heartedly I take off in that direction just as he turns the corner towards the Wilbanks Clubhouse. I have no idea who or what he's chasing, of course, or what danger either of us might be getting ourselves into. I'm against guns, but I chastise myself for not at least bringing my hammer.

Reaching the corner of Pelican Cove at the tennis courts, I look north in the direction Mac's run, and I can just barely make out his small figure somewhere in the proximity of the Wilbanks Clubhouse shell path. I know I should call the guard house, but my cell phone is recharging on the kitchen counter.

I gather my breath and again take off jogging in that direction able to see well enough from the occasional streetlights to not require the flashlight.

"MacArthur, come here boy... MAC!"

In this quiet and refined community, I can't believe that the residents aren't running out of their condos in droves for fear that someone's being murdered in the streets.

I stop to catch my breath and lean against the trunk of the large African tulip tree near the entrance of the shell path to the rear of the clubhouse, chastising myself for how out of shape I have become. Panting I call for Mac again and hear his bark from somewhere in the rear of the property. I turn on the flashlight as only low decorative lanterns provide the trail lighting here.

Pausing on the back patio of the Wilbanks and looking towards the clubhouse pool, I'm struck at the sight of a huge orange full moon illuminating the rippling waters of the cove. Something about the fast moving cumulous clouds overhead causes me to swoon slightly. I lean on a handrail by the steps in an attempt to stabilize myself as the strong winds now blowing in from the bay causes the palms to sway adding to the whirling sensation. Yet, somehow, the scene is hauntingly beautiful, and I find myself wishing deeply that I could experience it sometime in a different scenario, rather than while chasing my dog, and all alone.

58

My head clears, and the moment has given me enough time to fully catch my breath. Mac's barking brings me back to the urgency of the situation. It appears to be coming from the woods to the left of the back lawn. Shining my flashlight, I locate the entrance to a trail, and again take off sprinting down the wild and ill-kept dirt path.

The winds have picked up considerably and leaves, needles and small twigs are falling all around me. The path appears to be narrowing the further down it I go, and the bushes and trees seem to be pushing in on me from both sides. Not able to hear Mac's barks over the noise of the rustling trees I start to panic.

"MAC! MAC! For God's sake Mac, come here right now!"

The generally well-groomed underbrush found in most of the cove has turned into a prickly thicket. Thorns and barbs are scraping at my legs and arms, and even through my nightclothes and robe I can feel their sting. Waving branches slap at my face, and I let out a scream as one hits me hard below my right eye. I wipe at the wound and using the flashlight I glare at the red blood on my fingertips.

I turn around, intending to return to the well-manicured back lawn of the Wilbanks clubhouse, but in the flashlight's now fading beam, I stand in total fear. Behind me, every sign of the path I just traveled has completely disappeared. A thick patch of shrubbery and dense underbrush now surrounds me on three sides. Most disturbing though is the fact that now, not two feet away and where I just walked, stands a large, gnarled oak tree. It's outstretched branches almost appearing to be extending towards me. And—*my God, have I lost my mind*—it feels like from somewhere within the trunk's woody tissue the damn thing is actually smiling at me.

"HELP ME! Can anybody hear me?"

I know that I'm somewhere behind a grouping of condos, but to my own recollection, I believe they're fairly far away and nary an interior light can be seen through the thick growth. Then suddenly I start remembering my conversations with the dog walkers and how they advised that "out of season" there's some seventy percent fewer residents living in here than in the winter months.

Filled with fear, and now running solely on anxiety, I continue moving in the only direction on the trail open to me, straight ahead, while still being pelted by the wind and brush. The dense vegetation continues to strangle the path, and I am now getting caught up in limbs and branches that almost seem to be pulling and tugging at me.

My clothes get snagged and my hair gets tangled. Something rubs at my breast and I feel another sensation against my inner thigh. The belt of my robe comes undone and it's as if something actually pulls at it, then it's gone. I'm left waving the flashlight around violently and fighting my way through the woods as fast as I can. I start questioning my sanity as at one point I would swear I hear the low, rhythmic beating of what—*are those native drums?*—coming towards me.

I trip over a large, lichen-covered log on the path and fall flat on my face. My flashlight tumbles and thumps into the bushes, and upon impact, the light beam flickers on and off twice before going completely out. Left in total darkness, and still in tears, I lay there for a second until I again feel something crawling up between my legs. I pull myself up, frantically swatting at my attacker while blindly still moving forward.

I keep one hand in front of my face to protect my eyes and the other outstretched pushing the limbs and branches aside. I now actually can *feel* it—something or someone is breathing down my neck. My senses, brought to an acute level by fear, pick up on the smell of something malodorous and putrid within each breath.

Suddenly I hear Mac again, the barking appears extremely distant now, but at least it's a direction to aim for.

"With God, all things are possible," I say, surprising myself. "With God, all things are possible!" It becomes my mantra as I fight to keep my panic at bay. I still call for Mac, still call for help, but I keep returning to it. With God, all things are possible. As I press forward, I can't help but feel I'm being watched from every direction… almost as if the trees had eyes!

I eventually come to one of the entrances to the boardwalk and grab the railing to steady myself from the relentless winds.

"Thank you, Lord!"

I turn around and stare into the darkness of the forest and primitive trail I just negotiated, fully expecting to see someone or something there to grab me. But now, with the aid of the moonlight out over the bay, it appears I'm actually alone and looking back at what appears to be a well-maintained mulch path.

I rush breathlessly towards the sound of my dog and am relieved to finally be familiar with my surroundings. I'm on the dock where Mac and I had our confrontation with the alligator. The full moon casts an abundance of light, and I'm able to easily spot Mac, safe and sound on the decking with his paws up on the lower railing looking out and barking madly at the water in the cove.

The wind blows my robe and hair about as I run to him. Taking him into my arms, he whimpers and starts licking my face. There's a mighty splash as something hits the water, and I look towards it in time to see the large circular ripples as they expand and lap across the footings of the dock.

<h1 style="text-align:center">59</h1>

My eyes fly open to the sight of Mac straddling my chest and intermittingly licking my face between whimpers. I bolt straight upright inadvertently knocking him aside and grab my chest. My heart is beating so hard it should burst. I jump out of bed while holding my clammy trembling fingertips to both my temples to check my heart rate.

"One thousand and one, one thousand and two, one thousand and three... Dammit!... Stop, stop, stop!"

Each of these motions were much too common for me, just a short time ago, when having a panic attack.

I pull down the red tee I slept in as it's practically twisted up to my neck. I'm sweaty, yet cold, as I race off for the medicine cabinet in search of my Librium. I knock a tube of Crest and a Secret deodorant stick into the sink while rummaging the shelves. I finally find the bottle I'm looking for, fight with the child-proof cap, and pop two black and green capsules into my mouth. I turn on the cold tap and, bending over, attempt to slurp enough water into my mouth, then stand up and swallow quick enough to get the pills down. It takes three attempts before they no longer feel stuck in my throat.

"What in the hell was that dream all about?" I cry out, as now I am talking incessantly to myself and walking in circles around the condo.

I've learned through the years I must do something—actually *anything*—to distract myself from thinking I'm having a heart attack, or worse yet, dying on the spot. I continue walking room to room straightening, opening and shutting drawers, looking in closets trying to pick out what I'll wear today… anything for distraction.

I dart for the bathroom as I need to use the toilet, but I fidget on the seat since it's terribly difficult to sit still. Washing my hands, I splash cold water haphazardly on my face in an attempt to calm down, leaving the mirror splattered and vanity top in puddles.

Looking in the mirror I attempt to talk myself down. "You're going to be fine. You're going to be fine. You're going to be just fine Liz… Like hell I am!"

And another wave of panic floods over me, and I'm off and running again. "No! No! No! Help me God!… PLEASE STOP THIS!"

I fly into the kitchen and attempt to get a drink of water but my hands are shaking so hard I can barely pick up the glass. I swing open the refrigerator door, swig orange juice straight from the container, then contemplate how the acidity will give me heartburn and I'm out of Nexium. Now I'm having a hot flash, so I stand at the kitchen slider where a ceiling air vent is pumping cold air directly down on my head. It's early morning, and I try to look outside and just take in the pleasant view.

"Just breathe Liz. In through your nostrils, hold… and out through the mouth slowly."

Mac sits at my feet looking up at me cocking his head as if to say: *"Are you alright, lady?"* During this process he has not left my side and has followed me on the entire route.

"I'm going to be okay, boy, don't worry. Mommy is just having one of her crazy spells."

Then finally it happens, the pill kicks in along with what I call the letdown reflex. My shoulders slump, my neck and back muscles re-lax, and my chest loosens and actually cracks. My arms, which were more animated than an Italian giving directions, now hang limply at my sides. I look back down at Mac.

"And now mommy is completely exhausted!"

Emotionally drained, I make my way to the couch, where I plop while plumping a fish print decorative pillow. I lie down and close my eyes thinking about what just transpired. I haven't had an anxiety attack that severe since the first time I took Jack to the airport. That one was prompted by the realization that I was left all alone in Sarasota to fend on my own. This one was triggered by a bad dream, actually a nightmare, where I get molested by trees of all things.

I'm just about to doze off when there's a startling knock on the door. My eyes fly open as Mac takes off barking.

This can't be happening again. I stand up, debating the wisdom of answering it after last night and exploring just how much I believe in phenomena like premonition.

I walk to the bedroom to get my robe as another round of loud rapping echoes through the place.

I have yet to have an unexpected visitor at my door, so my mind is running wild over whom this could be. Donning my robe, I reach for the belt and it's missing. I look on the closet floor below where it always hangs, but it's not there. I search the bedpost where I sometimes leave my robe before climbing in bed, but that too is of no avail.

Holding my robe shut with my left hand, I head towards the door, in time to hear additional rapping. I stop, take a deep breath, and contemplate that I must look a fright after the panic attack combined with bed head. I chastise myself for not running a brush through my hair while I was in the bedroom, but swing the door open wide anyway.

There stands a short, sturdy woman with choppy dishwater blonde hair that looks like she may cut it herself. She's wearing a sundress that reveals a lot of sun damaged skin, legs covered in bug bites, no bra, and little to no makeup. With what might be an east coast accent, she abruptly introduces herself as Bess and shakes my hand as assuredly as any man could.

"I'm with the Pelican Cove Social Club," she says "And I'm here to sign ya up!"

I apologize for my appearance, and am about to ask her what she wants, when she laughs and cracks her chewing gum.

"Don't ya worry none, Lizzy, you should see me when I'm not all dolled up."

She proceeds to just push by me and make her way in. Mac seems taken by her as he doesn't growl and allows her to pet his head.

"Hey, the place looks really nice!" she says kicking off her sandals and barefooting it around looking at the living room area. "Real nice Lizzy old girl!"

I'm curious how in the hell she knows my name, and then wonder why this stranger is comfortable enough to call me Lizzy. Till now, only my paternal grandmother endearingly called me that. And better yet, who's she calling old, she's no spring chicken? She's carrying some papers with her and she hands me one.

"You just pick which jobs you're willing to do and put a check mark by them. Have ya got a pen we can use? I left mine out in the car."

I feel obliged to offer my first visitor something to drink, plus I'm thinking a cup of coffee might help perk me up after the sedative.

"Any kind of beer ya got honey will be just fine!" she says then falls to the floor, on hands and knees, and begins barking like a dog at Mac. She grabs one of his toys and rolls around on the floor playing tug-o-war with him. I stare for a moment, from the backside, wondering if she recalls that she's wearing a rather short dress and then proceed to the kitchen.

Searching the fridge, I find one Heineken beer, all alone in the deli drawer, that I think was actually from Jacks first visit and then search for the opener.

Bess is now up and comes to the kitchen laughing. "That's a great little dog ya got there. Isn't that what Dorothy had in her basket?"

She sees me with the opener, grabs the bottle, twists off the cap and takes a long swig.

"Ah, that's good and cold. Thanks, honey." She tosses the cap, with a clink, into my kitchen sink where it goes down the disposal, I discretely set the pilsner glass that I had gotten out back in the cupboard.

I offer her a seat at the dining room table as she briefly discusses the social club and how it operates.

"Basically hon, its one party a month in season, and it's on the last Sunday at five thirty in the pavilion. Why you wouldn't even have to drive. Generally, it starts with a cocktail hour and open bar, hors d'oeuvres then dinner followed by dessert. It all wraps up with some sort of entertainment or dancing.

"Out of season there's a happy hour at six every other Thursday at the Wilbanks. It's BYOB and everyone brings a snack to share. Of course, I don't expect ya to hostess any of these events this year, but since you're so close perhaps we can use your kitchen!"

She instructs me to check off clean-up crew as I'm young enough to be able to heft the bags into the dumpster.

"Roz, poor thing, tore her rotator cuff cleaning up after the holiday party last year."

She also thinks I could handle being a food server as long as I don't overload the trays. She wraps up with, "We generally let the men run the bar, you know... just in case."

She gives me a wink and a snap of her gum, downs the last swig of beer, then jumps up gathering her papers and heads for the door.

"Mind if I keep this pen?" she asks clicking it several times. "Oh, and ya owe me fifteen dollars in back dues, sweetie!"

60

I lean back against the front door and start laughing till I cry.

Talk about mood swings. Just wait till I call Jack later and tell her about my first Cove visitor.

I put on a pot of coffee—half decaf, half regular—concerned about too much caffeine setting off my nerves again and aim for the shower.

I grab a clean white bath sheet and washcloth and start the shower running on hot. I disrobe and pull off the red tee and my scotty bottoms and throw them in the hamper. Steam is filling the bathroom and I reach in and turn the handle halfway towards cold and step in. I lean back wetting my hair and then grab the purple bottle of Aussie and lather up. While shampooing my hair I start thinking about the robe I just placed back in the closet—and the missing belt. Eyes closed to avoid suds and with water running over my scalp to rinse, I start visualizing clear as day. the belt being torn from my waist by a rather handsy tree limb.

My eyes pop open as I skip the conditioner and simply spread body wash all over and quickly rinse off with the hand-held showerhead, taking an extra moment to run the washcloth over my face. Stepping out, I wrap the bath sheet around me and scurry into the walk-in to get dressed. I stop at the vanity to brush my teeth and make a quick wet ponytail, then go back into the closet to retrieve my aqua Chuck Taylor All Stars and socks.

Out in the living room, I sit in the merry-go-round chair to put them on. Mac pads over always aware when I am putting on my shoes.

"Are you ready to eat something and go for a walk?"

He finishes up quickly and I place his gear on him and we aim outside for him to do his job. He wraps up his business and we take off following the exact route we took in the dream, only this time stopping to deposit his poop bag in a dumpster.

We get to the African tulip tree at the path head by the Wilbanks, and I touch it, reliving how I leaned against it and caught my breath while pursuing Mac. I bend down and pick up one of the vibrant orange flowers edged in red—*Hmmm, still no smell?*—and I toss it back on the ground.

We walk the path back to the patio, and in the morning sun, I take in the view of a glistening cove. Slender palms and a red blooming bougainvillea decorate the entrance gate to the pool. A young woman in a swimsuit rides up and parks her bike at the rack before entering the swim area. From another trail, coming in from the far right, there's an elderly couple carrying yellow swim noodles, their flip-flops crunching loudly along the shell path as they chat.

I look left towards the woods, "Okay boy, where's the trail you took?"

To my surprise Mac starts sniffing the ground and pulling me towards the trees. He pauses halfway to lift his leg and then leads me to a slight separation in the underbrush. Once entered it opens up to an actual dirt trail. As we walk down it in the daylight, I reflect on how it's quite wide and by no means confined like the one I dreamt about. At no point are there limbs or fallen logs blocking the way. The filtered light twinkling through the green leaves and creating dancing patterns on the bare ground is truly spellbinding.

We continue forward on the path when I see a coppery glint flickering in the light. I approach it, and, upon picking it up, note it's a Duracell battery, a C-cell. Remembering the flashlight in my dream, I look around the area, but come up empty-handed. I place the battery in my jeans pocket before continuing our walk. Rounding a bit of a curve in the trail, suddenly there it is...

My robe belt hanging from a weeping yaupon holly tree branch.

I walk up, touching it in amazement and wondering how in the world it actually got here. *It was just a dream, wasn't it?"*

I pull it off the limb and then just stand there looking around in all directions remembering the overwhelming feeling of being watched.

"The trees have eyes," I remember saying, and for some reason a shiver runs down my spine.

We come to the boardwalk entrance and amble out to the end of the covered dock. It's devoid of people, so I sit down in one of the deck chairs allowing Mac some slack on his lead to go chase crabs and sniff the cracks between the boards. I put my feet up on the railing and lean back trying to make sense of the entire scenario.

I had a bad dream, I tell myself. I possibly found the battery to my flashlight, and somehow, strangest of all, my robe belt was found hanging on a branch on a trail in the woods. I know for a fact that Mac and I spent the night at home in the safety and comfort of our own beds, *didn't we?*

There is a sudden whoosh of air and a wet snort snaps me back to the moment. I stand up in time to see a manatee breach the water's surface and then slowly submerge out of sight.

"Okay boy, it's time to go."

The first thing I do upon returning home is walk straight to the kitchen drawer and pull it open. There, next to the hammer and a Phillips screwdriver, is the flashlight. I pick it up, flip it on and it works. Curious, I unscrew the lens and dump out the batteries on the counter, they're Evereadys. Reaching in my pocket I pull out the one from the trail: it's a Duracell.

I have no clue what this means. I pull the length of material from my other pocket—but I know darn well this is my robe belt!

Doctor My Eyes

—Jackson Browne (1972)

<h1 style="text-align:center">61</h1>

A couple of weeks pass, and I've all but forgotten about the dream. I have made an appointment for a well visit to see a doctor down here because my one up north refuses to refill any more prescriptions without my actually coming into the office. I have practically used up my entire supply of Librium plus I know I should have someone available just in case I would really get sick.

I had called my Procter & Gamble retirement insurance in Cincinnati to inquire about getting a list of in-network doctors for my area. The customer service representative asked for my home address and after a few minutes came back on the line.

"Looks like you're near South Beneva. Is that right?"

"Yes, I live directly off of Vamo Road which turns into Beneva less than one block away."

"Well, there's a doctor Stu Robbins on South Beneva that's in-network, and it shows that he's accepting new patients." She sounds extremely pleased with herself. "Would you like the phone number?"

Several days later, leaving the cove for my appointment, I turn left onto Vamo and cross over the trail where the street name changes to Beneva. I go past the mall at Westfield Sarasota Square where I notice the address on a bank building is 8055. Looking at the Post-it note with the doctor's address, I'm seeing their street number of only 129.

I cross over Clark Road, I pass over Procter, noticing the addresses are getting smaller. I stop for the light at Wilkinson before driving on and crossing over Bee Ridge where a church on the corner is being torn down— the sign reads Coming Soon: Your Walmart Neighborhood Market.

The next intersection is Webber, with a funny little hot dog stand on the left-hand corner; this is followed by Bahia Vista where the light again stops me. At this point there's a flashing speed monitoring sign advising drivers to reduce their speed to 25 mph. There's also a wooden sign with an Amish horse and buggy carved on it that reads Welcome to Pinecraft.

I'm in awe as suddenly there are bonneted women and bearded men riding tricycles with handlebar baskets on them, as if they were driving cars. A sign pointing right: turn here for Der Dutchman, and to the left is Yoder's Restaurant and Amish Village. Having never driven this many miles down Beneva before, I'm taken completely by surprise at what I'm seeing. We have plenty of Amish communities in Ohio, but who knew they also dwelled in Sarasota, Florida.

The light finally changes, and I pass a wood-fired BBQ food truck parked next to a vegetable stand, manned by Amish children boasting last of the indiana sweet corn. But perhaps the shop that I find most humorous as I drive past is one named Pinecraft Golf Shop. The mental picture I conjure up of the Amish golfing— *What do they use, pony carts instead of golf carts?*—makes me laugh out loud.

I'm getting close. Thirty minutes into the drive I finally reach the 200 block of South Beneva. I make a mental note of a great looking garden center I pass on the right. I love plants and flowers, part of the reason I purchased where I did, and it's my hopes to add some color around my place in planters.

Still daydreaming about my plant purchases, I pass through a large intersection at Fruitville Road and become aware by the street sign that I'm now on North Beneva and the numbers are going back up.

I've gone too far. I turn around in a shopping center parking lot and aim back from whence I came. This time I see the doctor's office sign at the end of a drive leading into a woods across from the Eager Beaver Car Wash.

Pulling in it reminds me of the cove as no tree has been sacrificed in order to supply a parking place. In fact, even the rows are not in straight lines, but wind through the park like setting. I finally find an open parking spot, but it lies quite a distance from the main door. Looking around, as I get out of the car, I am totally amazed at how full the lot appears.

Can all these people actually be seeing the same doctor that I am? If so, I'll be here for days.

Once inside I realize it's actually a group practice containing numerous physicians. There are three receptionist windows, each with about eight doctor's names followed by credentials over them. I go to the one with Stu Robbins, D.O. over it and wait behind two others in line. This gives me time to contemplate the abbreviation D.O.

M.D. obviously means medical doctor. There's also a couple R.N.s (registered nurses) and N.P.s (nurse practioners). But what's a D.O.? I start mentally guessing, "Doctor of Ovaries, Deadly Optimist, Doctors Orders?" The insurance gal just called him a primary care physician on the phone.

"How can I help you?" Asks the extremely perky and cute Hispanic receptionist.

I give her my name and state I have an appointment with Doctor Robbins. Leaning in a little closer I whisper, "What does D.O. stand for?"

"Doctor of Osteopathic Medicine," she replies, then smiling hands me a clipboard with a pen on a chain attached to it containing no less than ten pages clipped to it.

"Fill out each page to the best of your ability. Skip the back of three and the front of eight. If you have a copy of your medical history from your previous caregiver place it in the back of the stack. Otherwise, fill in that portion on four with what you know and include your most recent doctor's contact information including phone number with area code. If you didn't bring all your actual medication bottles with you, at least list what you're taking including OTCs on page seven. And I'll need to make a copy of your driver's license and insurance card for our billing department, both of which I'll give back to you when you leave. Your copay today is going to be $45 Any questions?"

I know I must have a perplexed expression on my face. "Only one: what's osteopathic medicine?"

62

I take an empty seat between a nicely dressed elderly woman wearing wrap-around cataract sunglasses and surfer with spiked teal hair in floral board shorts and Adidas slides. Turning my phone off, as several signs request, I look up, and directly across the waiting room from me, I see the old woman from the antique store.

What did she call herself? It was Granny something...

Oh, she may not be wearing the cowboy attire now, and she's dressed in a colorful plaid blouse with blue jeans, but looking down I note she's still wearing her old Durango boots. As I look back up at her face there's no mistaking those stained tobacco teeth grinning back at me. Suddenly it dawns on me, Daisy, that's it! *"If you need anything else come see Granny Daisy."* Those were her parting words for me. She continues to smile and gives a slight nod of recognition my way then sticks her nose back in an issue of *Guns & Ammo*.

Slightly startled, I start filling out the forms. I am just flipping to page two, when a door opens and a young gal with braces steps out.

"Miss Blum," she says rhyming it with plum.

I stand up, gathering the clipboard, a book I brought in case I was left waiting, and my purse and giving the old woman a second glance as I pass her by.

"It's pronounced *bloom*," I say as I follow her down a hallway.

"That's nice, what's your height?"

"I believe it's around five foot ten, or maybe eleven inches."

"Step on the scale for me please."

256

I do as I am asked and the digital readout makes me flinch: 184 pounds. I haven't had a scale in my house for almost 10 months. And obviously it shows.

"Is your scale accurate?" I say. "I weighed myself at Publix once since being here and it wasn't that high!"

"Right this way, Miss Blum," she says (incorrectly). "We're going to examining room two."

"Why don't you just call me Liz. That will make it a lot easier for everyone." I apologize for not having the forms filled out yet and advise her that I was called back far sooner than anticipated.

"Don't worry, no one does!"

She then asks me to have a seat and takes my blood pressure and temperature. She takes a seat in front of a monitor and then inquires what meds I'm taking and what I'm seeing the doctor for. Then finishes up by quickly pecking away some more on the computer. While making a swift exit and with the door half-shut she calls back: "Doctor Robbins will be with you in just a minute Miss... um, well Miss."

And I'm left to myself in the examining room.

I'm curious if there's been some kind of mistake and they have placed me in the wrong room. The walls are covered in pictures of Labrador Retrievers, some are of old dogs and others just pups, and in chocolate, black, and yellow. There are also American Kennel Club awards and trophies, as well as ribbons and certificates of merit pinned everywhere.

I wonder if I'm at the vet and whether I should have brought Mac.

I actually get page three of the forms filled out when, and after a brief knock, Doctor Robbins comes bursting in wearing ceil blue scrubs. He's muscular, stocky, has a tuft of wiry chest hair sticking out of his V-neck and is a bit on the short side. He appears to be around my age and has an extremely pleasant smile and a mischievous twinkle in his eye. He reaches out a rather large hand and yet gently shakes mine stating.

"Hi, I'm Stu Robbins. What brings you here today?"

I explain again that I haven't had the chance yet to fill the forms.

That's okay," he says. "I'd by far rather hear your history and what's going on directly from you. Those forms are just so the practice can have them on file and cover its ass!"

I'm a bit taken aback as my past doctor was one for formality, even wearing a tie, and would never use such colorful language.

I start with my personal information advising I'm sixty years old, a widow and mother of two, well one now, for I lost my son. Also, recently I was forced to retire. I continue on with my known medical conditions such as arthritis, borderline high blood pressure, acid reflux, overactive bladder… "and my gut's a mess."

Then I tear up as I jump into my mental health issues, revealing I had experienced a complete nervous breakdown after being responsible for the death of my husband and child in a horrible car accident. I've had years of therapy, been diagnosed with anxiety attacks, panic disorder, and even went through a year and a half period battling agoraphobia, where I couldn't leave my house at times.

He hands me a box of tissues, and I blow my nose and take a deep breath.

"I'm on Librium, Wellbutrin, Lansoprazole, Pepcid Complete, Amlodipine, Benazepril, Lomotil, low-dose aspirin, a probiotic, and a multiple vitamin. There might be more, but I'm too upset to remember."

I blow again.

We sit and discuss what I've shared with him and his feelings about the diagnosis and current regimen of care. He takes my hands into his large and tender ones and looks me directly in the eyes.

"Want my honest opinion?"

I nod and my eyes well up.

"Miss Blum," he says, "you're carrying around a lot of anxiety and guilt. And, you're too damn young to have that much wrong with you and be on that many different medications!"

He announces that he's willing to fill my prescriptions since some of them you can't stop cold turkey. But he wants me to wean off some and go on what he calls a medical holiday from others. He advises that he'll have his medical assistant type it all up and give the dosage schedule to me, along with the new prescriptions that I can take to any Walgreens, or wherever, to have filled. I thank him, and we shake hands again as he tells me he'd like to see me in about two months to see how I'm doing.

I thank him and as he gets up ask, "What's with all the dogs, if you don't mind me asking."

"Not at all," he says, "those are my babies!" And with that he closes the door and is gone.

I'm still using up his box of tissues as I try to get myself together. I'm doing my best to fill out the forms, and I actually do finish them up when his nurse reenters the room. She hands me a stack of scripts and an envelope

"The doctor said to tell you not to open this until later when you're feeling better."

I chuckle, wondering what it contains. I look up at the nurse.

"I'm so sorry but I neglected to ask your name?"

"Tammy Faye," she says, and I can't help it—I begin to laugh.

She looks maybe a little hurt or perhaps just confused. "Honest to God it is!"

"I'm so sorry dear!" I say. "That's a lovely name." I reach for the box of tissues. "And just add these onto my bill."

I take the entire box with me.

63

Exiting the examination area through the waiting room, I can't help but look over to see if the Granny Daisy person is still sitting there. To my relief, she's gone. I settle my co-pay, and moments later begin the arduous drive back down Beneva, but this time when I reach Clark Road I turn west—at least I *think* it's west. I am trying to end up on Stickney Point.

Located at the corner of route 41 there's a Walgreens, and it's the closest one to my home that I'm aware of. I pull in and must circle the building to find a place to park, as it is very crowded. To even get in the door I must negotiate a man sitting at a table on one side wanting me to sign up for home delivery of the *Sarasota Herald-Tribune*.

"Already get it. Thanks!"

On the other side a guy dressed like a pirate—but for his red Skechers—who is hawking Captain Morgan Rum coupons in front of Walgreens Liquors.

Upon entering, I can barely see the pharmacy sign in the far back corner for all the crowded shelves stacked high to the ceiling. Making my way down an aisle lined with wine on my left and ice cream to my right, I find the end of the pharmacy drop-off line. To my amazement, the queue is about ten deep.

As I stand there, I soon realize I'm one of the few individuals that appears to speak English. Truth be told I might be the only American in line, as the rest appear to be foreigners—I'm guessing Siesta Key vacationers. Boisterous conversations are going on between apparent family members, accompanied by much gesticulation and reprimanding of small children.

Most of the men are dark and tanned and wearing Hawaiian-style shirts, short shorts with a protrusive bulge, and leather sandals. They stand arms crossed over their beer bellies in defiant stances when not speaking. The posture displays gold Rolex watches on hairy arms that match religious cross necklaces tangled on furry chests.

Seemingly unconcerned about cancer or age spots, the equally tawny woman are more Rubenesque than their American counterparts in stature, but in all the right places. They appear to favor beach cover-ups that barely cover their butts or short dresses one or two sizes too small. Cleavage is spilling out everywhere, and when the woman in front of me turns around and smiles, it's difficult to know exactly where to look so prominent are her nipples.

All of them are balancing on strapless mules or sandals with heels and are somehow able to execute every motherly move while wearing them. They also don an abundance of gold jewelry and there's not a one that hasn't spent big bucks on a mani-pedi and foil hair highlights.

I glance down at my left unpainted hand and chastise myself for not at least having clipped my hang nails. The line moves slowly, and now I can hear some of the conversation going on with the pharmacy tech. Some are explaining that their child has a fever or perhaps a sore throat. Others share concerns over sunburn or having sinus problems with headaches. Time and time again I hear: "I wishes to speak to the pharmacista please" or similar variations of broken English.

Then I come to the realization of why this is happening, and why it's taking so long. From my past travels I know that, in many countries, a visit to the pharmacy is similar to our trips to the doctor. Individuals share their symptoms with the pharmacist and they in turn prescribe what remedy they feel would be best for it. A totally different concept from our American way of self-diagnosing and purchasing a medication right off the shelf that we deem appropriate to cure our ills—well, it's either that or we run to the Urgent Care or ER.

I mentally drift for a moment recalling a time in Rome and having a headache that I just couldn't shake while I was out shopping. I saw a Pharmacia's green cross on a corner and popped in to grab a bottle of aspirin. Upon telling what I recall as being the most attractive model-like salesgirl that I wanted some aspirin, she scurried off with a concerned look to get the pharmacist. A stern looking woman in a white lab coat approached me and began spewing out Italian faster than I could comprehend.

Struggling I said, "*Sono Americano. Parlo poco Italiano* [I'm American. I speak little Italian]." Then I whipped out my translation book from my purse. "*Aspirina per favore. Voglio aspirina* [Aspirin please. I want Aspirin]!"

The pharmacist started talking a mile a minute again as I tried to look up one or two of the words I was hearing that sounded vaguely familiar. Fortunately, a kind expatriate American man standing next to me made an offer to assist and told me that the pharmacist wanted to know my symptoms and how long I'd been experiencing them. After going back and forth between me telling the man, and he telling the pharmacist, she finally shook her head, appearing disgruntled, and handed me a small pouch of aspirin powder.

"Grazie!" I said (to both) and received the usual "Prego!" from the gentleman and left the shop laughing, barely able to wait until I could share this story with Scott when I caught back up with him in the Piazza Navona.

Focusing back to the moment, I'm finally next at the counter. When I am called forward the girl asks for my prescriptions. I hand them to her, and she pecks at the computer then says she can't find me in the system and wants to know if I'm new to Walgreens. I tell her that I've used them for many years back in Cincinnati, but this is my first time in Sarasota.

"That's probably the problem," she says. "What's your Ohio phone number?"

I give it to her.

She taps away at the computer again, but this time for five minutes or more, then proudly looks up from the screen.

"There now, I've linked your two addresses and phone numbers so you shouldn't have any more problems when you're traveling between your two homes."

And she runs off with the scripts.

"I can see one problem," I say. "Somebody else lives in one of the houses now!"

There are only four chairs in the waiting area, and every one of them is filled, some even with two individuals as fathers have now taken to holding a child on their lap. I decide to kill time by walking around the store. The first thing that tells me I'm not in Cincinnati anymore are the beach products. Because of the proximity to Siesta Key, there are beach chairs, balls, towels, shoes and more. There's a major selection of sunglasses and suntan lotions. The next aisle rivals any seaside gift shop as it's lined with decorative shells, shot glasses, water globes of shakable beach scenes, and starfish salt and pepper shakers. There are T-shirts, sweatshirts, hats, mats, and jackets all embellished with Siesta Key, Florida!

But the most humorous aspect to me is for an ostensibly health-related store to have so many refrigerated coolers full of beer, and more wine bottles and displays than a master sommelier could identify. On top of that, there's a full liquor store attached.

I kill some more time in the Hallmark card aisle and actually pick out one to send Jack. It simply reads, "I often find myself saying a little prayer of thanks for knowing you!" and has two women walking hand-in-hand along a beach on the front.

Then in the "As Seen On TV" section of the store, I'm actually considering the Miss Belt, for an instant hourglass shape after my weigh-in at the doctor. It's at this point I finally hear: "Prescription ready for Blum!" (like plum) over the loudspeaker.

I make my way back to the pharmacy where I'm forced to start over again waiting in a line of people. While waiting, I decide this should be handled like Starbucks; there should be a completely separate window for pick-up with my name misspelled on my cup. I also contemplate, yet again, on how no one in Cincinnati seemed to mispronounce my last name.

<h1 style="text-align:center">64</h1>

When I get home, I put the teakettle on, select a Tazo Zen green teabag out of the canister, and place it in my favorite hand-thrown mug. In the bedroom, I change out of the clothes I wore to the doctor and slip on something more comfortable, deciding it's definitely time for shorts and flip-flops.

The kettle is whistling as I return to the kitchen. Carefully pouring hot water over the tea bag, I then place a saucer upside down over it, and set the oven timer for five minutes.

I retrieve the envelope from Doctor Robbins in my purse and open up the lanai sliders and breathe in the fresh air, before taking my seat in a wobbly lawn chair, reflecting that I should pick up wicker chairs or something better. Mac does what I call working the sliders, as he walks up and down the track between the doors and the screen sniffing and snorting. The highlight of this game is when he discovers a chameleon or anole running across the screen he then gets to grumble and "Scotty snap" at it causing his teeth to click.

I tear the sealed envelope open and unfold the typewritten letter:

Miss Blum,

Hopefully by now you're feeling better and can be open-minded enough to consider my recommendations to help make your life a bit better. I know we only met once, but trust me on this, I can help you! The following is a bucket list of sorts, and I'd like for you to see how many items you can accomplish before returning for your follow-up appointment with me in a few weeks. Enclosed is my card with my personal cell phone number written on the back. Please don't hesitate to call should you find yourself in a panic and in need of my assistance.

Sincerely,

Stu Robbins

Stu Robbins, D.O. – Intercoastal Medical Group

The timer goes off on the stove, and I go remove the saucer, twist the tea bag out around a spoon, and then use it to stir in a squirt of honey.

He's taking a lot for granted, I think, for I haven't decided if I'm going back to him at all!

Returning to my seat, I read over the list he's included.

- Volunteer to do something, anything that helps others for no personal gain.
- Exercise – perhaps yoga?
- Take a class, any class for fun or education. Just be sure to learn something new!
- Socialize – Either entertain guests yourself or attend someone else's party.
- Eat healthy daily, but don't diet.
- Okay, cheat and have chocolate & wine… but make sure it's good chocolate & wine!
- Take a walk in the woods or garden or go to the beach. Mainly just get outside.
- Get a dog. They're a great reason to walk in the woods! If you don't like dogs (Heaven forbid) then get something else to take care of.
- Forgive yourself… fate, destiny, life, whatever you care to call it is out of your hands! Every day look in the mirror and tell yourself, "I love you, and you are perfect just the way you are!" Keep doing it until you believe it!

I sit dumbfounded by the list, wondering if my issues are that stereo-typical, or was this guy really able to read me like a book in a single office visit. I have seen shrinks and counselors for years, and they've never suggested anything other than medications and rehashing—over and over again—life's past tragedies until I'm reduced to a puddle of tears and emotionally exhausted.

I jump up searching for a pen and quickly place a checkmark by one of his suggestions.

• Get a dog. They're a great reason to walk in the woods!

"Well, I already have that one licked, Mac old boy. Now if I can just get past the anxiety of wandering aimlessly out in a forest."

Then suddenly remembering the night of the bad dream, and prac-tically being sexually assaulted by trees out in the woods. I look at Mac. "Maybe we'll try a busy public park with paved sidewalks and in the daylight!"

Taking the list, I pin it to the front of my refrigerator using a heart shaped magnet that reads:

Love thy neighbor,
but don't get caught!

65

It's mid-October and fall is in the air (well, as much as it can be in Florida where the temperatures still regularly top out in the mid-eighties). I'm surprised when, overnight, a roadside pumpkin patch has popped up at the corner of 41 and Stickney Point. It has piles of pumpkins, stalks of fodder, and bales of hay. There are scarecrows staked everywhere, and a sign boasts of face painting this weekend. Truth be told, if it weren't for the coconut palms and saw palmettos surrounding the scene, you might think you were in Ohio.

Maggie calls to say she'll be flying into Tampa on JetBlue Wednesday, November 21st and leaving Sunday the 25th. I tell her how excited I am that she's coming for Thanksgiving. "I wish you could stay longer," I say. "I'm going to cook a turkey and everything!"

"You do remember the year you caught the oven on fire and Dad threw the entire roaster, turkey and all, out in the snow?"

"You're right," I say. "Maybe I'll just order from Publix! And I can't wait to meet your boyfriend."

Then there's a moment of complete silence on the other end. Then: "Well, I've got his ticket here in my hand. Now we'll just have to see if he comes?"

Not knowing what to say to that, I let it ride.

"Aunt Jack is going to join us for dinner," I say. "She has a new, uh" –I almost say lover, but don't– "acquaintance. They met down here of all things, and she'll be visiting him. I've invited them both to eat with us on Thursday."

"Great!" she says. "I get to see Aunt Jacks and a bit of Sarasota in one fell swoop! Bye mom, I'll see you when you pick me up!"

I tell her goodbye and disconnect, but I am in a daze. I stand there, phone in hand for a moment until Mac gives a low bark.

Having to pick Maggie up hadn't even occurred to me. I can't get the vision of that damn Sunshine Bridge out of my head, and my palms start to sweat. For God's sake, it's more than a month away and there's alternate routes.

I grab Mac's red harness and lead. "Want to go for a walk?"

Of course, he does. Placing them on him he "Scotty talks" back to me while wagging his tail.

"You're right," I say, "I'll take 75 all the way to Tampa and then cut over on that pirate road they have up there again."

As usual, Mac leads me towards the grove across the street where his favorite tree stands, surrounded by other large oaks and white pines. To my surprise there's a gathering of men and woman deep in conversation right where Mac generally chooses to do his job. They are, each of them looking up at something. Unabashed, Mac drags me to the center of the group and poops.

Embarrassed I say, "Hello everyone," and bend over with a pet waste bag to pick it up.

The group snickers for a moment at our antics, and I sense we've helped relieve some sort of tension I detect in the air. Their faces return to dour as soon as the conversation picks up again.

"Poor Neville," says one woman. "Ever since Natalie died, he hasn't been right."

"Oh, don't I know it," says another returning her gaze to something overhead. "Her fooling around with Niles drove him crazy, but her death has just about done him in!"

I try looking up, but I see nothing but treetops and an occasional glimpse of the sky.

"I don't think he's eaten in days," adds an older gentleman.

"How long has he been up there this time? the man beside him says. "And any ideas on how we can talk him down?"

There is a shaking of heads and a consensus of no, and one elderly woman, balancing on a cane, dabs at her eyes with a handkerchief. "I don't know what I would do if I didn't see him at the pool every day!"

Meanwhile a tiny, little man in a scooter, complete with a bright orange safety flag flying from a six-foot fiberglass pole on the back of it, takes off and starts circling the trees frantically.

Still gawking, I am doing my best to encourage Mac to move to allow me to change positions so I might get a better look. However, he is so enthralled with their antics that he just keeps tilting his head and wagging his tail.

"Shouldn't we call someone?" I suggest. "911, the fire department or the police?"

Several individuals standing near glare at me quizzically, including one rather large woman in an Eva Gabor wig. "What good would they do?"

"Well, I mean—"

"No, she's right," says the woman with the cane. "We probably should call Sarasota County Animal Services to help us. I'll do it when I get home from bridge club."

I turn to the man on the scooter who has now pulled up and stopped right next to me.

"Animal Services?"

"Well my dear," he says, "pray tell, whom would *you* call to succor a depressed peacock?"

I Believe I Can Fly

—R. Kelly (1996)

66

Tugging on Mac's lead, we move on down the road, with me contemplating the peacock 'group therapy' encounter I just witnessed. I decide to aim towards the harbor. We pass the office, and straight ahead, between the condos and a carport, is a footpath leading towards the water. We follow the shell path until it ends at the top of a small set of steps leading down to the dock.

A sign reads:

No dogs allowed on the docks
unless providing ballast for their master's boat.

We also ask that they avoid the barques!

"Well Buddy, that means you," I say. "Maybe someday we can get a boat..."

Standing there daydreaming, I take in the various types of boats while Mac sniffs a rail post that's apparently been visited by many a canine sailor. From this vantage, there are a few cruisers and large sailboats that could easily take their occupants to the Bahamas. There are smaller boats, too, many of them the center console fishing types, and even a pontoon party barge or two.

Directly in front of me, tied to the dock, bobs a romantic looking sloop with beautiful lines, varnished wood and a unique paint job. For me, the boat conjures up images of a Harlequin paperback hero with his broad, bare chest and flowing flaxen hair reaching out to me. *"Come here wench and we'll sail away to the Caribbean, where I'll have you in ways you've only dreamt of!"*

The name carved across her stern is *Summer Wind.*

"Let's go Mac," I say with a smirk, "nobody calls me a wench!"

We make our way back to the road and, turning right, walk down Pelican Point Drive. I've lived here for ten months now and I still have no clue what each of the streets is named. The road weaves and turns and, rounding a corner with yet another bougainvillea in full bloom, I come upon the artsy, gray haired woman who's always in a rush. She doesn't disappoint as she's currently running around her own front lawn gathering up leaves and palm fronds.

Mac sits in place, and I find myself drawn to the scene unfolding before me. She has set up a four-cornered tent of sorts, covered on three sides in what looks like plain burlap or muslin cloth. The front remains open, showing an interior with what appears to be boughs and lemons covering the walls and ceiling. She lays the fronds, carefully crisscrossing them across the top of the structure, and then continues scattering the leaves and other yard waste atop that.

She rolls out a polychromatic woven mat and spreads it on the floor of her hut, then runs into the front door of her condo and immediately exits again with her arms full of colorful, decorative pillows. She spreads them around the interior and then stands back to admire her work. That's when she spies me trying to sneak away unnoticed, but my dog has decided to bark eagerly at her antics.

"Hello there, you two!" she cries, racing towards us. She bends down taking Mac's head in her hands. "How are you?"

He grumbles at her brash move and I feel obliged to answer on his behalf.

"We're fine."

"Okay," she says. "I know this is short notice, but would you be my guest for Sukkot tonight? I just finished building my sukkah, isn't it a beauty?"

I'm not sure how to answer. "It looks very nice," I say somewhat tentatively. "Are you camping out in the yard tonight?"

She laughs. "I didn't think you were Jewish! Let's back up... I'm Sarah and we've said 'hello' in passing but never really met. And who might you be?"

"Liz, Liz Blum," I say. "And this guy here is Mac."

She wrinkles up her nose. "And, with a name like Bloom, you're not Jewish? Oy vey!" And she raises her hands towards God.

She explains that it's a Hebrew holiday and tonight is the first day of Chol HaMoed. She's having some neighbors over where they will feast, drink wine, say prayers and tell tales known as lessons in the sukkah. She explains that it is customary to invite a guest, and would I please be hers.

Remembering the doctor's orders to try new things, I surprise myself. "Yes, I would love to. What can I bring? I make a great chipped beef cheeseball."

Sarah abashedly grins as she explains that not only is she vegetarian, but her kitchen is also kosher. She also tries to explain that there's some sort of problem with just even having meat and cheese on the same table, much less purposefully mixing them together and forming it into a ball. Then, to my surprise, she gives me a tight hug.

"Just yourself, Liz Bloom, just bring yourself!"

67

When I arrive, Sarah is wearing a long-sleeved steel blue blouse with a gray colored gauze skirt and silver flats. Her head is covered in a hand painted, multi-colored silk scarf, making her body covered from head to toe even though the night is extremely warm. Her boyfriend, Tobias, makes his appearance in the sukkah wearing some kind of shawl with tassels over a long white cotton robe and, upon his head, a tie-dyed woven kippah yarmulke. They both look so beautiful together, yet so foreign to me.

I'm the only woman in the group wearing slacks and a sleeveless top. I also went out of my way to wash and curl my hair. Every other woman has hers covered, at least partially, in some manner or other. One elderly lady is even wearing an obvious wig. I note Sarah sensing my uneasiness and then sneaking off to her condo. Upon her hasty return she wraps a beautiful shawl around my shoulders, whispering in my ear, "Hopefully this will make you a little more comfortable."

It's a beautifully quilted masterpiece of batik squares in a combination of ocean colors and pieced together in various hues of earth tones. When I tell her how beautiful it is, she tells me she just completed it yesterday and believes it will be her entry in this year's Pelican Cove Art Show in the fabric category. Worried I'll soil it in some way—since I'm notorious for spilling red wine—I start to remove it.

But she stops me. "Art only becomes more beautiful if it's loved and used." She goes on to explain there's an amazing three-day show here each spring and I won't believe the talented artists that live right here in the community.

As the evening readings continue, I find I'm feeling just fine after my first encounter with matzo and charoset plus a couple glasses of Terrenal, a red kosher wine. Offering up yet another glass, Sarah advises she'll pour as the carafe of wine must remain *mevushal.* I laugh to myself wondering what that might mean and what was to become of the bottle of Barefoot Bubbly Pink Moscato I brought her for a hostess gift.

When the time comes for me to bid my goodbyes to Sarah and the other neighbors I've met tonight, she kisses me on the cheeks, European style, and whispers in my ear.

"I want to have Tobias drive you home since the sun has set and it's getting late."

"Oh, that's not necessary," I say. "It's so lovely out, I want to walk. I'll stick to the roads with their streetlights. I promise!"

"Fine," she says. "Then I'm walking you as far as the corner."

Walking down Pelican Point Drive towards the four-way stop, I thank her again for including me in her celebration. I enjoyed myself very much. As we're passing under the branches of the tree canopy I'm suddenly startled by a loud and sudden "Kyow!" from overhead.

"Heads up through here," says Sarah. "There are two nests of green heron up in those trees, and you're liable to get pooped on."

She then points down at the pavement that is splattered white with droppings.

"Once in the Piazza Navona in Rome," I say, "I was pooped on by a pigeon at the Fountain of the Four Rivers. The crowd around me broke into a great applause. Perplexed, I found a tissue and wiped at my shoulder as best as I could and continued on my way. Only later, when re-telling the story at dinner with Italian friends, did I find out that it's considered *estremamente buona fortuna un segno di ricchezza principale proveniente dal cielo*! Extremely good luck and a sign of major wealth coming my way from heaven."

"Well I don't know if heron poop brings a person good luck or not." Sarah smiles. "But I do know a story about the trees they're nesting in."

"Do tell." I nudge.

"Well let's see... these particular trees are called trees of gold or technically speaking *Cassia fistula* or some such thing. During the hot season, they are in full bloom with beautiful yellow blossoms. Once spent, the branches release their hold on the blooms, and they pirouette to the ground like dancing fairies."

"It seems that in the heart of Brittany there's an ancient village named Tréhorenteuc in the beautiful Brocéliande forest, which is considered to be the home of Morgana, queen of the fairies. If one explores the dense woods at just the right time of year, on exactly the right day and at the precise hour of dusk, one might be guided by a glowing blue fairy to an alluring lake known as *Miroir aux Fées*, the Mirror of the Fairies."

We walk slowly as Sarah speaks. "The lake is surrounded by trees in various stages of growth and decay. Yet, one tree stands out because of its obvious age and since it is coated in gold. Despite centuries of trauma, it stands proudly in the forest shining for all to see. What's more, it stands in the Valley of No Return. Its message being that once you become gold and shine, there is no turning back to what you were."

She hesitates next to a lamppost that illuminates her slender outline and casts an elongated shadow across the road. "It's an old French story of survival and revival. Those that have been fortunate enough to be led there say they are forever changed and always for the better. It's also said that Merlin's tomb lies beneath the magical tree."

"Wow! Such a colorful story."

Reaching the corner of Pelican Cove Road, we pause again as I hand her back the beautiful shawl. We part, promising to stay in touch and I begin walking towards home, glancing back in time to see her silhouette twirl and her skirt billow as she passes under the last streetlight She calls out then.

"I think we're going to become fast friends, Liz Bloom!" Then she disappears into the night.

68

As I make my way home, I glance over at the long-closed Pelican Cove office, and I'm surprised to see a young girl sitting all alone on the front steps, holding some sort of large book or tablet. She appears to be maybe ten or eleven years of age and wearing what looks like a lacey white nightgown. As I approach her, it becomes apparent she's either writing or drawing busily on the sketch pad pages.

"Hello Sweetie, what are you doing out here at this time of night and all by yourself?" I ask. "Is everything all right?"

She answers without looking up from whatever she's doing. "I'm fine."

Not sure what I should do. I feel uncomfortable simply leaving her here all alone. "Do you live here Honey?"

She remains focused on the task at hand. "Yes ma'am."

"Are your parents nearby? Won't your mommy be worried about you?"

"They're just down yonder a piece," she says, pointing south in the direction of Vamo Road. It's the first time where she has actually looked up, allowing me to see her angelic face surrounded by a head of long dark curls.

"Can I walk you home?" I ask.

"That won't be needed none, ma'am."

I stand wondering what to do and reach in my pocket for my cell phone to check the time. It's quarter to eleven, and there's no way I'm going to just leave her here alone in the dark while I walk home.

Since I have my phone out, I decide to call the guardhouse and ask if the night roaming guard—who meanders around the property in a golf cart—could possibly come and assist with the situation. If nothing else, perhaps one of the guards will know who she is and take her home.

The gate house guard picks up. "Hello, this is Kenny. How can I help you?"

I identify myself and explain the situation. He requests her name and says he can then look her up in the computer system and contact her parents to have them come pick her up.

"Hold on," I say, turning to the girl. "What's your name, honey?"

Still frantically doodling, or whatever, she says, "My new family calls me Figgie now. The nice people in here all refer to me as Miss Sherrill. I don't talk to the bad ones! But Mommy and Daddy named me Mary, although my sister used to call me Beth."

"So, your name is Mary Sherrill?" I ask, trying to make heads or tails of what the heck she just said.

I repeat the name to the guard, and I can hear him pecking away at the keyboard of his computer.

"I'm sorry, Miss Blum, but I have no one in the system registered under the last name Sherrill. I even did a cross search under the name Mary and all of the known Marys in the system are much older, long-time residents here, with very different last names."

I'm asking him how we should handle this, and he says that he's going to send the night guard my direction right away and asks if I'll kindly stay with the little girl till he arrives. As I'm assuring him I wouldn't think of leaving her alone, she jumps to her feet, darts across the road and scurries off down the path towards the Wilbanks.

"Mary! MARY!" I yell out but she continues running.

I take off after her while advising the guard of what's transpiring. He says he'll need to hang up so he can contact the night roamer in his golf cart and have him assist me. Thanking him, I end the call, stick the phone back in my pocket and, taking a deep breath, attempt to catch up to her.

She takes the path around the back of the clubhouse, and I do my best to follow her but trip over several of the large, sausage-shaped fruit laying on the ground from a kigelia tree growing beside the building. Picking myself up, I rub my knees then round the corner and pause again on the back patio.

Looking out towards the pool and the cove with the moon glistening on the water, I'm suddenly all too aware of how similar the current situation feels to the dream I had of chasing after Mac. Perhaps supported by the lingering effects of too much wine, I actually question whether this is real or if I am going to wake up in the morning only to realize it's just another dream? I look down at my scraped knee with its trickle of blood and, sensing the pain, decide that if this is a dream it's awfully damn real!

I just catch her figure and a glimpse of white as she heads down a mulch pathway behind the row of treehouse condos lining the bay. I sprint to the trailhead and pause, filled with fear, remembering the horrible feeling of being molested by the trees as the path closed in on me. I tell myself that it's not the same trail. But it's still dark and scary and this time I don't have a flashlight. However, some of the condominium buildings are occupied, and their interior lights are casting random spots of light out into the woods and onto the much-trodden path.

Thinking I can't leave this child out here alone—and praying that the guard catches up with us soon—I take off down the trail.

"Mary! MARY, please wait up!"

I continue yelling as an older man's voice yells down from one of the condo balconies.

"You kids be quiet down there, here me? It's way too late to be playing in the woods." Then, as he retreats inside, "Damn renters!"

I finally start to catch up to her as she approaches a small set of steps leading down to the dead end of Bayhouse Court. She glances back, and sees me, and it appears she's actually laughing.

"This isn't a game of tag!" I yell after her and pause at the top of the steps to catch my breath. Now looking out at the road illuminated by streetlights I can see Mary hugging a huge laurel oak that is practically growing right in the middle of the road.

She smiles up at me and beckons with her hand and disappears to the far side of the tree.

"Mary!" I call breathlessly, "this isn't hide-and-go-seek either!"

Attentive to my surroundings, I approach the tree cautiously, well expecting to find her standing on the other side with a little girl's coy smile on her face ready to yell, *"Now you're it!"* I know she hasn't gone any further or I would have seen her running down the well-lit roadway.

Rounding the tree, I'm perplexed to find no one there. I circle the entire oak, and she's nowhere to be found. I call out her name while searching between the cars in a nearby carport. Suddenly two small head lights come racing down the road heading directly towards me.

"Miss Blum… I say, miss is that you?"

"Yes, it's me."

After he pulls up beside me, I proceed to tell the guard in the golf cart my story. He advises that I take a seat in the cart as he gets out his flashlight.

"I'm going to take a look around, and I think it best if you stay right here. This place can be a little tricky to navigate in the dark."

Some fifteen minutes later he comes back with having found neither hide nor hair of a little girl. He offers to drive me back to my unit, and on the way, I share my concern over leaving her out there alone.

"I wouldn't worry too terrible much, miss. We get folks from all parts of the country. Heck, all parts of the world staying in here, and some of them have some peculiar ways of doing things if you know what I mean. I'm guessing she's with a family of renters or visitors and by now has found her way back home."

Pulling up in front of my unit I thank him and get out of the cart. He waves goodbye and does a U-turn before heading back down Pelican Cove Road. Crossing the troll bridge to my walkway, I can hear Mac give several barks, and I pick up the pace, rushing to get in the front door.

"I'm sorry I'm so late, good boy. How long have you been waiting at the door with your legs crossed?"

69

Rising early from a restless night's sleep, I swing my legs over the edge of the bed and stretch. Mac climbs out of his bed and stretches as well, straightening out his back legs while pushing his belly into the carpet. Then he tilts his head quizzically several times while staring my way.

"I know it's early, but I can't stop thinking about that little girl!" I bend down and pat his head on my way to the bathroom.

I grab my robe off the hook. "Want to go out?"

Since we're on the early side of our usual schedule this morning we run into our neighbor, Marilyn, taking tiny Tookie out to do his business. As usual Tookie gets excited to see Mac coming his way and twists his lead in and out of Marilyn's walker and between her legs.

"Don't move, Marilyn!" I yell out while hurrying to get there and unwrap her before she trips and falls.

"You are so good to me, honey."

"It's no trouble at all."

"So kind," she says, then: "Say, if you're going to Publix today, can you get me a quart of whole milk? None of that watery two percent stuff. Oh, and I do so like those little chocolate brownie bite things you got me the last time!"

I ask her if she knows of a Sherrill family living in the cove that may have a little girl of about ten named Mary.

"No Honey, there's the Sherbacks and the Shermans and that one woman on the board of directors, her name might be Cheryl, but she's way too old to have children. Oh, did I tell you I'm going to be a great bobeshi again?"

I detail the events of last night to her, starting with Sarah's sukkah to running through the woods after the young girl. When I finish my tale, she simply looks at me sort of perplexed.

"Well I'll be, I never knew her name was Mary. You must be very careful, honey, when dealing with the dybbuk. You don't want to have spirits talking directly to you like that!"

"Dybbuk?" I figured this was probably a Jewish thing.

"Spirits, like I said."

"What do you mean by spirits?"

"Well let's see… Have you ever looked out your lanai windows, sweetie, towards our shared backyards, and seen a woman with long, flowing white hair wearing all white clothes tending to the azalea garden? She pulls weeds, picks up limbs, and rakes up the longleaf pine needles and cones that fall in that area. It's usually just after dawn or right before dusk. I can't reckon that I've ever once seen her during midday."

"I have seen her!" I exclaim. "I jokingly refer to her as the ghost gardener."

"Well it isn't a joke, hon. She goes about working old mister Eckstein's garden—he's the original owner of unit GL355—and the person that put in the original azalea beds."

"You're telling me that I've witnessed an honest to God ghost, gardening in my backyard?"

"Well, I prefer to think of the ones like her as friendly spirits or maybe even guardian angels that have attached themselves to individuals. You know, to help or care for them here during their time on earth. However, in her case, Mr. Eckstein has been dead about three years now and that condo you see her enter when she's finished raking… well, it sits totally empty now. They say it's held up in probate due to a nasty family squabble amongst his children. Feh!"

I am trying to digest everything she just shared. "So, you've also seen the little girl Mary, and you're telling me she's not real?"

"Well, there's lots of spirits in here, honey, and I can't say if the little girl that haunts the Pelican Pavilion is your Mary or not. Does she like to doodle and draw things?"

"Oh my God, yes!" I gasp. "She had some sort of tablet and pencil and was busy drawing the entire time we talked."

"Well then, sweetie, I guess I have seen your Mary from time to time backstage in the storage area during several of the Rinky Dinks' line dancing performances.

70

Marilyn proceeds to explain to me that Pelican Cove is actually built on an ancient Indian burial ground. "As well, this exact spot appears to have been the tribe's spiritual center adjacent to the sacred waters of the bay. It's all documented, sweetie, that the tribal village itself was located at the current site of Spanish Point. Have you been there, Hon? It's just down the road. You can see the Indians' garbage dump and some old bones, pots and whatnot."

"No, I haven't been there yet," I say. "But I pass by it all the time and know where it is. From the road it looks like an old schoolhouse and from the sign I thought it was just a Sarasota County library."

Attempting to bend over to pick up her dog she grunts. "It's said that when the foundations of these very condos were under construction the builders found all sorts of bowls, totems, and even skeletal remains."

Marilyn straightens back up, Tookie tucked under her right arm and boob. "Some pieces went to the Spanish Point Museum and many others actually went to the Smithsonian. I dare guess a few things went home with the workers." She laughs at that.

I laugh along with her but in my case it's because all I can see of poor little Tookie is his pink nose sticking out from beneath her abundant breast.

Her story immediately brings to mind my totem purchase from the shop by Spanish Point, and I begin telling her about it.

"Oy Gevalt!" she says, clearly alarmed. "You mustn't fool with idolatry my dear. Why, in the Torah it's the first of God's ten commandments."

"It's not an idol, or at least not to me. It's a decorative piece, a carving if you will. It's of a man, but, well, he looks like a tree, or maybe it's a tree that looks like a man." I attempt to describe the figure further and then regret that I even went there. "He's extremely virile looking with a rather large... well, a large uh—"

"Nose?" she says, "like those Easter Island guys?"

"No," I say. "No, he has an extremely big" –I lower my voice– "well, erection."

She doesn't hear me correctly.

"Direction? What direction is he pointing in, Sweetie? That might mean something!"

"No, not *direction*," I say, "erection. He has an extremely big erection. A huge penis!"

"Do you worship it?" she asks squinting disapprovingly at me.

"My goodness no!" I advise. "It's just a decorative piece sitting on my coffee table."

"So, you've given a false idol a prominent place in the heart of your home?" she says. "You must rid yourself of that graven image. Why it's like an open invitation for all the wandering spirits to come stay at your house!"

"Well," I say, "I don't know about—"

"Here's what I want you to do. Return it to where it came from. This isn't as easy as having a sales receipt, honey. You need to try to find out where it was originally found and then take it back to that place. You need to sincerely believe and give the totem back to those that created and worshipped it. Tell them you're sorry to have disturbed it."

I try to take in the entirety of what Marilyn has said, and the rational side of me is debating how much to believe of everything she has shared with me today. "I really haven't disturbed it very much," I find myself saying to her. "All I really did was polish it up with a little Lemon Pledge."

Spooky

—Classics IV (1967)

71

I've come to love Publix No Sugar Added Yogurt for breakfast, especially the peach. I like to sprinkle Mona's Honey Almond Granola on top. After feeding Mac and taking him out, yet again, I jump in the shower then get dressed. Today's goal is to follow up on several volunteer opportunities I've heard about.

"I'm in dire need of getting out among the living, Mac." I grab my Radley London Scottie purse and head out the door. "But it's going to be a little harder on you being here all alone. I left the TV on *Animal Planet* so you won't feel so abandoned. Back soon!"

Heading out on Pelican Cove Road I suddenly feel obligated to deviate away from the exit gate and drive the opposite direction down Bayhouse Point Drive. I take the next right onto Bayhouse Court, the street where I last saw Mary, and proceed till coming to the tree in the middle of the road. Nailed directly onto this side of the tree is a sign reading, Narrow Road – Proceed with Caution!

Leaving the Escape idling and the air on, I slowly get out of the car and tentatively approach the huge laurel oak before me. I consider how, during the entire running around of last night, I hadn't even noticed the sign on the tree—or the fact that it's actually not a single tree but two.

About halfway up, and smack dab in the crook where the oak tree branches out in all directions, there is the crown of a totally different species of tree sticking out. From the light green foliage and shape of the glossy leaves, I recognize it as a *Ficus benjamina* or weeping fig tree. I consider how I had a small bonsai one in a shallow red and green glazed pot on my coffee table back in Ohio. Three miniature Chinese fishing mudmen figurines were positioned in the soil at the base of it.

Rounding the oak to the far side, I stop dead in my tracks and just stare. Since moving here, I've become acquainted with the term epiphyte—basically a plant that grows harmlessly upon another—but I've never seen anything like what I'm witnessing now. The head of the fig tree is not as prevalent as it was from the other side. Its trunk runs the length of the parent tree and is attached tightly to its bark. The smooth textures of the rhytidome along with its light coloration convey the appearance of youthfulness when compared to the dark and rigid outer bark of the larger oak. However, there is no other way to describe the sturdy little tree other than voluptuous.

The fig's trunk, near the top, takes on the appearance of slender female shoulders. The torso is vivacious and curves lasciviously around the oak's trunk. Two limbs embrace the older tree warmly as if in a romantic hug. What appears almost as a well-endowed buttock at eye level curves sensually from the full hips of a young female of childbearing age. But the most expressive portion of the tree's growth is the way two distinct roots branch off from either side of the main trunk and wrap themselves around the oak in a manner reminiscent of a woman coupling in the cowgirl position.

From what one would take to be hands and feet, run long tendrils of roots like fingers and toes, some even attaching to the ground and apparently growing down deeply into the sandy earth.

By far though, the most startling of all sights is that protruding from the massive oak—in the region directly between the fig tree's "legs" if you will—is an enormous gall or growth of sorts that for all the world resembles a male phallus with testicles. I'm surprised that I'm actually feeling embarrassed regarding the scene before me. I stand in place feeling like a voyeur looking into someone's bedroom window.

I'm startled back to reality by two squirrels chasing each other around on the tree limbs overhead. The pursuer only pauses to look down for a moment; it makes a chattering noise while looking straight at me, before scampering off after the target of his desire. I return to the car and sit and stare at the trees and try to make sense of it all. I replay in my mind the encounter with Mary, my discussion with Marilyn, and now this.

Turning the car around I start heading out of the Cove toward my appointments. I reason that I've not been made *fearful* by these unusual goings on, so much as confused and somewhat uncomfortable.

Pulling through the gate and left onto Vamo Road towards the Trail, I find myself singing to myself.

"If there's something strange in your neighborhood, who ya gonna call? Ghostbusters!"

72

After returning home, I put my trusty teakettle on and take a seat on the back lanai to call Jack.

"So," she says, "what's new in the Cove?"

And by golly I tell her! It takes well over an hour and two cups of tea since I start with the party at Sarah's, continue with chasing after Mary, and then today's conversation with my neighbor Marilyn.

"Don't think me crazy, Jack, but I swear everything started happening the minute I purchased that totem figure from that Daisy woman in Osprey."

I finish up by telling her how I was compelled to drive back over and view the spot where I last saw Mary with my own two eyes.

"Honestly Jack, wait till you see it. For all intents and purposes, I was looking at a couple of trees that appeared to be stuffing the turkey! Oh, that reminds me. I'm planning for around one o'clock for my Thanksgiving dinner with Maggie and her boyfriend, so plan your arrival accordingly."

Jack tends to laugh it all off—as she does most things in life—but does suggest that I might consider throwing the damn tree-man away or at least buying him a loin cloth. I end the call by telling her about applying for a couple volunteer jobs today.

"One was doing nails for elderly women in a retirement home, and the other was reading books to preschoolers with ADHD. I passed on them both, but it was good experience since I haven't interviewed in what twenty some years?"

When the call winds down, we end it as we always do.

"Love you."

"Love you more!"

I finish out the week with no additional monkey business. I had contemplated attending church again months ago but hadn't acted on it. Now that it's the Sunday before Thanksgiving, I determine it's a good way to start off the holidays. I always enjoyed the services, music, and messages prevalent at this time of year. I determine my decision is partly brought about because of my doctor's suggestions to become involved, and I sincerely miss the feeling of fellowship. But I also am aware that I am quite moved by the devotion many in the Cove—such as Sarah—have to their faith and how they have no reservations about displaying it.

Yes, I've concluded that religion is definitely something that's been missing in my life. I haven't stepped foot in a church since Scott's funeral at College Hill Presbyterian in Cincinnati followed, almost two weeks to the day, by my son Tommy's. It's odd, I think, how those times where faith and some kind of belief in a higher power were most warranted were the times I've tended to turn away and apostatize myself.

I'm well aware that, for me, that fire was built of guilt and fueled by anger. For months after the accident I would walk around angrily ranting to the heavens. If you truly are a merciful and loving God, I would argue, how could you tear my life apart and take my husband, my love, my soul mate and leave me so all alone. And, what kind of Lord allows a little boy, my beloved son, to suffer like that and eventually die. Hell, he was only ten years old and had an entire life ahead of him.

I have lived out each day ever since believing my own hands brought about all this pain. The script in my head doesn't change: For God's sake, why in the hell did I have to be driving that rainy night? Why? Why is this my cross to bear?

So, deciding to try Siesta Key Chapel over on the island, I drive over the Stickney Point Bridge and then north on Siesta Key. The chapel sits a good distance off Ocean Boulevard, after driving through the village, and is situated in the middle of a wood.

One could easily miss it if they weren't sure what they were looking for. Pulling in I'm again amazed at the lack of a designated parking lot. Cars are parked every which way on the grass, around and under the multitude of live oak trees whose branches seem to be embracing the house of worship.

Approaching the structure, I'm reminded of the thatch roof chapel in the movie *Hawaii* with Julie Andrews (though more refined, of course). One navigates a rather steep and long ramp up to the second level of the building, then steps onto a large deck that wraps around the entire exterior. I follow several parishioners to the left and find the entrance flanked by two greeters, who both shake my hand and bid me a warm welcoming.

"Thank you for joining us today!"

The first thing I notice upon entering the sanctuary is how simplistic it is. There is no resemblance, whatsoever, to the magnificent cathedrals I've visited around the world. No golden figures, crosses or candelabras. There are no stained glass windows depicting biblical scenes, no majestic pulpits or clergy seats that resemble thrones, and no massive organ with enormous ceiling-to-floor pipes.

No, the room is absolutely beautiful because of its lack of embellishments.

The walls—where there are walls—have been crafted out of beautiful lumber, possibly yellow pine, and large wooden beams and trusses support the ceiling. Three sides of the space feature numerous sets of double glass sliders that offer a wide-open view of the rampantly green surrounding forest.

As well, the altar is constructed of wood and upon it rests a conch shell and what appear to be hand-woven offering baskets. It contains a very simple wood podium with a single candle atop a large carved wooden holder. Behind it all, centered on the only unbroken wall, hangs a simple driftwood cross, and above it all is an open window showing an unobscured view of Heaven.

There are no wooden pews, but actual upholstered chairs—many with arms. I find a row and enter it as an usher hands me a program and bids me a good morning.

Then there's music and singing coming from behind me. I glance back to see a choir loft and small organ complete with orchestral accompaniment performing "We Gather Together to Ask the Lord's Blessing."

The minister enters through the same door I came in and proceeds down the aisle. To my pleasant surprise, she's a woman. She has long, wavy black hair and is wearing a lengthy white robe. Her stole is covered with items such as wheat shocks, pumpkins, and gourds. Beside her, walks a young, shorthaired blonde woman, carrying a basket full of can goods. She approaches the altar and then turns to face the congregation smiling warmly

"Good morning!" Her voice is jubilant.

The audience echoes her greeting back as one.

"This is the day that the Lord has made," she says. "Let us rejoice and be glad in it!"

And again, the rear balcony erupts in a joyful noise to the Lord our God.

73

It's Tuesday, November 20th, two days before Thanksgiving, and like a crazy nut, I'm headed to the new Trader Joe's in Sarasota. The place has been packed since its grand opening in September. I was a grocery shopper and avid procurer of their Two Buck Chuck back in Cincinnati. However, it took driving across town on the Ronald Reagan, from Colerain to Kenwood, for well over a half hour each way to do it.

Now, it's less than ten minutes away.

Pulling off Tamiami Trail onto Robinhood Street, just past Chili's Grill, I can easily assess from my vantage point that there are no further parking spaces in the store's actual lot. Cars are backed up, waiting for an open spot, and I'm left sitting dead still on the side street. To my surprise, as we start to inch along, the back-up lights of a gun-metal grey Jaguar come on, and I stop where I am, allowing them to wiggle their way out of the spot while I zip in.

Getting out of my vehicle and looking at the sea of cars, I question the wisdom of choosing to come here this close to the holiday and wonder how in the hell I'm ever going to get out again. Adding to the lack of parking, a white tent has been set up in front of the store with a display of gourds, pumpkins, fall arrangements, and fresh cut flowers. I'm drawn to a wicker basket overflowing with miniature pumpkins.

Suddenly, experiencing some otherworldly communications from Martha Stewart, I decide on using them for place card holders on my Thanksgiving table. Since I haven't hosted a dinner party in years, and

Maggie's coming for her first visit and bringing a guest, I want everything to be extra special.

Let's see...

I start by picking the best-looking Jack Be Little pumpkins I can find. One for Jackie and one for Frank. This one looks like Maggie, and I need one for her boyfriend. *What's his name? Oh, she mentioned it... Bob... no, Bill?* I've also invited Marilyn, so I'll need another one. And, last but not least a pumpkin for me. I also grab a fall bouquet before entering the store with a shopping cart.

It's a madhouse!

I weave my way through the sea of bodies and buggies to the produce section. I select sweet potatoes, little red potatoes, and brussels sprouts. I pick out several large Vidalia onions and a package of celery hearts. In the bakery section, they have pre-made bread cubes for stuffing, and I select two bags of the old fashioned sage seasoned ones.

In the next aisle of open freezer chests, a young woman is giving out samples of Trader Joe's frozen pumpkin pies. Shivering from the cold, I elbow my way to her table and, after devouring one bite, I make my way to the case behind her and grab two boxes, knowing I can't begin to make pumpkin pie that good.

Moving on to the cheese wall, I select a caramelized onion cheddar along with a 1000-day Gouda. I then search for kalamata olives and some pita bite crackers before hitting the wine aisle and stocking up on several bottles each of both reds and whites. With the assistance of a rather bohemian store clerk, I also grab a bottle of kosher Terrenal Tempranillo for Marilyn.

The checkout lines are some ten people deep, and customers are having a grand old time ringing the bells announcing the need for additional cashiers. Problem is it's quite obvious every single register is occupied and operating as fast as humanly possible.

Due to the landscaping and cement curbs in the parking lot, it's impossible for me to take my cart directly to my car. And even if I could, I doubt I could negotiate it across the street through the busy traffic. So,

I'm forced to leave it in the lot between two parked cars and lug my groceries, two bags at a time, over to my vehicle. It takes three trips, and I'm extremely grateful that the paper bags have handles, making them a bit easier to carry. What I'm not thankful for is the angry looks I get from drivers thinking a spot is opening up each time I leave the car to go back for more.

My next stop on my way home is Publix in the Landings to get the bird. I purposely waited to the last moment to buy one because I would never be able to fit it in the incredibly small freezer of the old Frigidaire that came with the place. I sit and review my grocery list before getting out of the car. I decide to add a disposable, aluminum roasting pan to it, since I suddenly—and quite vividly—recall setting my mother's speckled enamelware roaster on the dining room table and posting it to Facebook before the move.

What was I thinking?

I wasn't.

Once inside I'm forced to return to the parking lot in search of an abandoned cart. A Publix employee is pushing a long train of them in my direction and gladly rids himself of one. This store is total chaos as well. People are running around every which way, and all wear the same dour expression one that cries, *I'm on a mission and don't even think of getting in my way!*

I negotiate my way straight for the meat department while still considering what size turkey I should get. I recall being advised by my Cincinnati butcher—Greg at Langen Meats in Cheviot—to plan on a half-pound per person and then double or triple that according to my plans for the leftovers. Surprisingly, the meat section is far less crowded, and as I wheel my cart up to the large open chest freezer—Thanksgiving Turkeys Fresh and Frozen .49/lb—I quickly understand why I'm all by myself.

The freezer case is completely empty.

I stand dumbfounded just staring deeply into the empty chest as if, by some holiday miracle, the perfect bird is going to materialize. I feel the onset of panic and start chastising myself for setting myself up for failure by even offering to host the holiday dinner. Suddenly there's a butcher pushing a cart stacked sky high with hams standing beside me. He reaches in front of me.

"Excuse me ma'am." He takes down the turkey sign. "Is there something I can help you with today?" he asks politely as he starts placing hams in the empty freezer.

"Yes, there is," I say, trying to keep my tone light. "Would you have any more turkeys in the back?"

"No ma'am. We sold the last of them probably about two hours ago. Can I interest you in one of these nice, honey-glazed Smithfield hams?"

"Hams are for Easter, you turkey!"

I blurt it out and then feel bad as the poor man's face becomes sullen. I apologize profusely while digging through my purse for a Librium. I experience all the telltale signs of an anxiety attack coming on. Chest muscles tighten, senses become hypersensitive, and my hands are becoming sweaty as I drop my little cloisonné box, causing pills to spill everywhere onto the tiled floor.

"Shit!" And then. "Sorry. Again."

"Let me help you, ma'am." Perplexed, the butcher starts scurrying after a pill that's rolling towards the seafood section.

"Just grab the green and black ones for God's sake!" I yell. "You're chasing after a Centrum Silver!"

I take a deep breath and attempt to blow off any debris that might be on the Librium I've picked up before dry swallowing the pill whole. The butcher hands me the vitamin, and I thank him repeatedly while, at the same time, apologizing one more time for my bizarre behavior.

He looks genuinely concerned on my behalf and offers me his apron to dry my now tear-filled eyes.

"Stay right here," he says, "and let me take a look in some of the backroom refrigerator cases."

He disappears behind the counter and I attempt to get my act together while waiting for the medicine to kick in. Moments later, he comes hurrying back all smiles with several plastic wrapped meat packages in his arms.

He is excited. "I know it's not a whole turkey, ma'am, but I'm confident you can make it work." He places them one at a time in my cart. "This is a small turkey breast. It's only two and a half pounds, but it's all white meat and boneless. This package has three good size legs in it. Why they're almost eight pounds total. Now see this meaty top portion on them?"

I nod. "Yes."

"Well, that's basically the thigh. It's dark meat, but very flavorful and juicy. And this last package has five turkey wings in it. You'd be surprised how much meat you can pick off of those bones, or lots of folks just enjoy gnawing on them whole. Then again, you might consider using them for making your stock."

I stand there, now sedated and confused. "What do I use to put it all back together… is Elmer's Glue edible?"

He suggests roasting the breast and legs first and then adding the wings a couple hours or so later so they don't dry out.

I thank him for his patience and again beg his pardon for my being a bit snappy.

"Oh, don't you never mind, ma'am. It's just the beginning of the holidays. Just wait till the December snowbirds arrive and Christmas hits if you want to see crazy!"

I finish up the rest of my shopping then jockey for position in the checkout lanes that, here too, are all several customers deep. When I finally reach the cashier, I'm amazed at his friendly demeanor and the up-beat attitude of the young woman bagging. They share playful banter about the holiday, and both wish me a happy Thanksgiving.

I suddenly realize stressing out isn't going to make the meal or the entire season turn out any better and resolve right then and there that, from here on out, my motto will be *go with the flow!* But I also realize that this aphorism can soon be reconsidered when it comes to making my New Year's resolution.

The bagger insists on helping me to my car and even assists in loading the bags in the back of my Escape and wishes me a Happy Holiday.

I pull out of the lot and navigate down 41. Driving south and only about two miles from home I pass a small shop sitting back from the road called Geier's Meat Market & Sausage Kitchen. There, out by the side of the road, handwritten on their sandwich board sign it reads:

Fresh Amish Turkey's
We Still Have Plenty to Go Around!

I can't do anything but break into laughter. *Now you tell me.*

74

Arriving back in the Cove, I park in the carport and juggle as many paper grocery bags as I can in my arms while aiming towards the condo. I'm well aware this is going to take multiple trips to complete. I negotiate my way through the hedge, over the little troll bridge, and down the path as best I can, since the fall floral arrangement is sticking out of the middle bag right in front of my face.

"Mom… uh, Liz is that you?"

The voice is coming from the direction of my front porch, and I recognize it as Maggie's.

"My goodness, sweetheart, you're a day early!" I am navigating my way down the small pavers. "And how in the world did you get here from Tampa? I have my map and medications all planned out for tomorrow!"

She's seated at the wrought iron café table on the front patio, and immediately, from between the yellow pom-pom mums and the orange gerbera daisies, I can see she's pregnant. And, it appears she's brought three suitcases and a couple carry-on bags.

"Staying long?" I say then before she can respond. "Correct me if I'm wrong, but you appear to be carrying some extra baggage?"

I fumble with the keys and end up passing them to her.

"Can you please unlock the door before I drop these bags?"

She pulls herself up out of the seat with a slight groan and toddles over, grabbing the keys and the bouquet I am peering around, and proceeds to let us both in. She's greeted enthusiastically by Mac who immediately recognizes her. He still gives her a good once over from the ankles down, with Scottie snorts and sniffs, before letting loose with several loud and tail wagging barks of acceptance.

"Hello Mac," she says in a slight singsong. "I'd bend over and pet you fella, but I might not get back up!"

I set the bags on the kitchen counter and turn to hug her. We embrace and she starts to weep a bit.

"Oh, Mommy…" (A moniker I pretty much thought I would never hear again.)

Soon the floodgates open and she is clinging on to me for dear life. To my surprise, I relish in the warm embrace, but don't break down in tears myself.

"Seems like we have quite a bit to talk about?" I say, trying to lighten the mood while giving her a *mother's* once-over from head to toe.

I realize she looks just like me when I was pregnant with her, carrying it all in front like a basketball.

"Why don't you have a seat while I finish unloading the car? Stuff tends to melt or go bad quickly down here, even at this time of the year."

"I'm not crippled, Mom, just baby bump impaired. I need to bring in my luggage. Where should I put it?"

"Well, you'll soon learn that you can stand in the middle of the living room and pretty much take in the interior of my entire condo. But there is a guest room and bath to the left. You should have no problem finding it!"

It's not long before we've brought in our respective loads.

"How about some hot tea?"

"If you have decaf," she says, "that would be great. But first, I need to visit that bathroom and pee!"

We settle in on the sectional.

"Pregnant women really do glow," I say. "You look absolutely beautiful, sweetheart!"

"Well I don't feel beautiful," she says. "Especially when I stand sideways and naked in front of a full-length mirror."

I'm anxious to know the who, why, and when of her situation but decide to get there gradually.

"Now tell me, how did you get to Sarasota? Why, I was already getting anxious today just thinking about driving to Tampa to get you tomorrow."

"Well, since Bob wasn't coming, the airlines actually refunded me for both our tickets and—"

"That's it, *Bob*!" Then. Sorry, go on," I say, patting her hand.

She rolls her eyes. "Actually, it was only after I told them he died, and that I was left all alone and pregnant." Her cheeks flush at the admission.

"My obstetrician advised that he felt it best that I not fly since I have had a little cramping and spotting, so I bought a bus ticket."

"You rode a bus all the way from New York City to Sarasota?" I ask, wide eyed.

"I sure did!" Maggie says, sounding rather proud.

"My God, how long did that take?"

"One day, thirteen hours, twenty-four minutes, and approximately seventeen bathroom breaks." She laughs still dabbing at her eyes with a tissue. "I lost count somewhere around Jacksonville."

"And Bob..." I say.

"Long story short, he and I haven't been together for a while now. I'm sorry I couldn't tell you all this the last time we talked, but it was much too fresh a wound. At least now it's had some time to form a scab, even if every now and then I unexpectedly knock it off and it has to re-heal."

"Seems that fatherhood doesn't maintain a place in his acting and Hollywood bound career goals, and at the time we hadn't completely figured out what we were going to do about the baby. Oddly enough, I can semi understand him as it's always been my lifelong dream to achieve stardom too."

"Oh Maggie..."

"But the part that hurt the most is that apparently neither does marriage or a long-term relationship of any kind. By the time he decided to share all this with me, I felt the baby move for the first time, and I knew immediately in my heart what my decision was going to be. Unfortunately, it only made the situation all too real for him, and he was out the door by the next morning."

"I'm so sorry, Maggie," I say. "You've had so many bumps in your young life along the way… and, well, you didn't really need another one."

"Well, if I have to face yet another bump, at least it's a baby one!" she says with a wry smile.

"So how far along are you? Have you been well, and do you know what you're having?"

"Well, I'm told it's been a fairly easy pregnancy so far," she says. "I actually haven't experienced morning sickness since the first few weeks, and even then, it was mild. My doctor estimates I'm at five months and that the due date is around the middle of March."

"Hold on a minute," I say, and run off to the kitchen to grab a box of Pecan Sandie's then quickly return.

"Okay, continue." I take out two cookies and hand the opened box to Mag.

"Still hooked on cookies, I see."

I give a slight shrug.

"Well, anyway, I had foolishly signed us both up to take birthing classes before her father got cold feet."

"*Her!*" I shout. "Oh my, goodness a girl."

"Yes, the ultrasound showed it's a girl and that everything looked as it should. They did mention she's a bit big for her age and perhaps later they may need to adjust the due date. But as my doctor said, babies don't carry calendars, and they come when they're darn good and ready!"

I'm compelled to reach over and hug her again.

"I'm so excited that you're here," I say. "But I can't lie, I'm a little taken aback by the prospect of being a grandmother. Hand me another cookie."

She does.

"So, what are your plans now that what's-his-name has left you. I'm guessing stage work and your own career have been put on hold due to your condition?"

"Well, yes," she says. "Unless Rosemary's Baby the Musical is being produced for Broadway."

Maggie has to hold her tummy as we both laugh, and the mood definitely lightens a bit.

"I've been in these clothes for two days, and my immediate plans would be to take a shower and a nap."

"Of course, sweetie. There are towels on the bookcase shelves in the bedroom, and under the vanity, is just about everything you might require—body wash, shampoo, a blow dryer. Just let me know if you need something else."

I run Mac outside and then decide a nap doesn't sound half bad. After the angst of shopping, the anxious moment with the butcher, Maggie's early arrival, and now trying to process the prospect of becoming a grandmother, I too could use a quick escape from reality.

I scan my living room bookcase for something to read, while thinking I need to get a Sarasota County library card sometime soon. I grab *Fear Nothing*, an older novel by Dean Koontz, and go to my room. Lying sideways across my comforter, I soon hear Mac settle into his bed, and before I can finish the second chapter, I'm fast asleep.

75

I shoot straight up in my bed, sated with fear—a scenario that has repeated itself much too often recently. Unable to discern whether dreaming or real I pinch myself. It smarts—then I recall how, even in my past dreams, I experienced pain.

I distinctly recall hearing muffled cries.

"Help! Hello? Mom…"

I remain in bed, sitting Indian style, as I hear Mac grumbling and scurrying out of the room to investigate for himself.

"Mom! Can you hear me? I could use some help here!"

And suddenly, through the fog of slumber, I remember Maggie is here and realize something is terribly wrong.

"I'm coming Sweetheart!" I yell. "Where are you?"

"In the bedroom, on the floor!"

Entering the guest room, I see her, lying on her back in the middle of the partially deflated air mattress, rolling side to side in an attempt to get out of it. Wearing gold colored sweats, she resembles a street vendor hot dog, topped with deli mustard and nestled in a royal blue steamed bun.

"Oh honey, are you stuck?" A foolish question.

"Not only am I stuck, but if you don't get me out of here soon this will become a waterbed. Those two cups of tea we had have kicked in!"

I can't believe that I never considered that I was sending a pregnant woman to lie on the floor. I flip the switch on the air mattress motor, and it begins humming and sluggishly puffing up.

"Oh Maggie, I'm so sorry. I never gave the bed a second thought when you said you were coming. Heck your Aunt Jack even called it comfortable, so I figured you'd be okay for a couple days."

I then quickly regret that I can't get the mental picture of Jackie and Frank and what may have actually occurred on said mattress out of my head.

The bed slowly becomes firm, and with my help, she rolls to the side and I pull her to her feet. "For the rest of your stay you're sleeping in my bed!" I insist. "You'll be much more comfortable there."

"I don't want to put you out," she says, or cause problems."

"Nonsense, it's just for a few days, I'll be fine!"

The next day is spent in pre-Thanksgiving preparation. I start in on the cooking prep work of dicing onions and celery for the dressing while setting the bread cubes out in a colander to dry further. Mom always swore that stale, day-old bread made for a better stuffing. I also load the dishwasher with grandma's china that I intend to use and then set about ironing my one good tablecloth that fits the new table.

In the meantime, Maggie has volunteered to Swiffer the place, giving it the once over. I catch her doing a little additional straightening up as well and I make her promise not to overdo by trying to move heavy furniture. She vows to sit and put her feet up each and every chance she gets.

Always true to her word, she sits on the couch as she removes each item from the coffee table to dust them off.

"You have any window cleaner for this glass top?" She calls out.

"Sure thing, let me bring it to you."

Setting the Windex and a roll of paper towels on the table for her, I begin to head back to the kitchen where I am now attempting to brine the dismembered turkey pieces.

I decide to use the Pioneer Woman's brine recipe that I saw her make last week on the Food Network. I've gathered up all the spices, sugar, salt and apple cider and placed them by the large pot on the stove that contains two gallons of water about to come to a boil. I focus on attempting to peel the rind off a large orange without leaving too much pith.

"What *is* this thing?" Mags asks picking up the naked, male tree statue. "I don't recall ever seeing it around the old house."

"You wouldn't have," I say. "Our conservative neighbors would have reported us to the sheriff's office for harboring pornography. You know how right wing Cincinnati is."

The joke goes over her young head. "Aunt Jack named him Peter, for obvious reasons. He's a prehistoric Indian totem of some sort."

"My first guess is fertility," says Mags. "Obviously I won't be needing his services!"

"Well it's obvious you know what you're looking at!" And we both giggle.

I wander into the living room and proceed to tell her all about the odd little antique store where I purchased the totem, complete with details of the elderly wild west granny who sold it to me.

"That's some kind of tale mother, you sure you haven't been reading too much Stephen King?"

"Sometimes I wonder," I say. "So many strange things seem to have happened since I brought that thing home." I then proceed to tell Maggie of the dreams, real or proposed, and about the night I met Mary. I wrap it up by explaining the stories that Marilyn told me.

"You sincerely believe this figure had something to do with all of that?"

"I know it sounds a bit silly." I smile. "But yeah I do… I really, really do!"

"Aren't you even the least bit spooked over all this spirits and ghost talk by your neighbor?"

"Well, that's the strange thing," I say. "There's actually something sort of comforting about it. I especially like Marilyn's explanation regarding guardian angels being here on earth watching over all of us."

I can't resist placing my right hand on Maggie's belly and kissing the top of her head.

"I'm just so glad that you're here" I say. "I better get back to my mess in the kitchen, or we won't have dinner tomorrow!"

It's finally Thanksgiving morning, and I rise early to finish the dressing, prepare the sweet potato casserole, and put the little red potatoes on to boil. I wash and clean the brussels sprouts, and with a paring knife, make little x's at the end of each and every stem to help them soften up faster. I drain the turkey pieces from the brine they sat in overnight in the fridge. After patting them dry, I give each piece a quick massage with real butter then grind black pepper over them but omit additional salt since the brine was quite salty to begin with.

Out of my bedroom and rounding the corner into the kitchen comes Maggie. "It already smells really good in here. What can I do to help?"

"Grab a cup of coffee and an apron," I say, "and I'll set you up!"

Suddenly I remember that she's avoiding caffeine. "Or how about I make you a cup of that decaf tea? I'm afraid I didn't make a big breakfast in anticipation of today's dinner. Can I interest you in a pack of blueberry Belvitas?" I ask, holding up an opened package. "They're what I'm having. Or, I believe I have some Thomas's blueberry bagels in the freezer?"

"Umh… guess you've forgotten; I don't like blueberries. Do you happen to have any white toast, creamy peanut butter and Welch's grape jelly… oh, and maybe a dill pickle?"

For the Beauty of the Earth
—Mormon Tabernacle Choir, Craig Jessop & Orchestra (2003)
by John Rutter

76

Everything is either cooking or under control in the kitchen. I finish setting the table and put the final details on my little pumpkins by writing each guest's name on them in script with a metallic gold Sharpie. Maggie sits on a bar stool at the counter, putting together the centerpiece for the middle of the table.

"I wish you'd have gotten a few more flowers," she says. "It looks a little skimpy. Is this big thing your only vase?"

"I have others, but they're packed away in boxes somewhere." I look at the vase and see that she's right. "Why don't we stretch our legs and take Mac for a walk. I know where we can pick up some free filler along the way."

"Sure, I really want to see more of this place!"

I go to the kitchen to retrieve a pair of heavy-duty scissors and the dog's lead.

I say, "Somebody want to go for a walk?" …and from out of nowhere Mac is soon by my side, tail a-wagging.

Walking south from the parking lot on Pelican Cove Road, we soon pass two floral opportunities planted together where the road forks with Treehouse Circle. A huge Hong Kong orchid tree is in full bloom with beautiful, purple flowers. I easily snip off several of the lower hanging blossoms, and we both agree that the color will be a welcoming addition to the mostly orange and yellow fall bouquet.

We stand admiring the large bed of red roses that surrounds the base of the tree and soon agree, even though pretty, they somehow seem more summer than fall. I suggest that down the road and around the corner is a large stoplight croton we should check out.

"The leaves are in shades of gold, red, and green and much slenderer than most other varieties. That should allow you to use them as filler and round out your floral design."

Mag smiles. "Always good to have someone who's studied this stuff."

"Once upon a time, before you kids were born, I studied ornamental horticulture and botany at Miami University. Oh, that seems a million moons ago," I say. "But it has come in handy, especially since living here."

"I can imagine," continues Maggie. "This place looks like the set of *Land of the Lost*... Well either that or a real-life Krohn Conservatory."

"You're not far off." I smile to think about it. "Back in Ohio most of these tree-size specimens are simply mere house plants."

We continue around the block chatting and laughing as we take in the 80-degree weather and fresh air this Thanksgiving day has to offer. We pause for a moment while Mag catches her breath.

"By the way," she says. "I meant to tell you, I had the most interesting dream last night. Surprisingly, the memory of it is still extremely vivid. It was quite detailed and resembled what you told me about yours and how every aspect of it was so lifelike."

I stop where I am and encourage Mac to sit. "What was it about?" I feel a bit anxious and perhaps it shows.

"There was nothing particularly scary about it," she says, picking up on my unease. "In fact, there wasn't even a spook or a ghost in it. I'd say it was more of a dream come true of sorts."

"I was performing on stage playing the part of Sister Mary Robert in *Sister Act*. I remember explicitly how good it felt to be doing what I love, acting and singing before a full house. I recall longingly searching the audience for a familiar face, and upon seeing the two empty seats that I had reserved, feeling extremely disappointed. You know Mom, I swear, I sincerely felt acutely hurt... like I said, everything was so real."

I nod acknowledging my understanding and for a moment I recall how vivid my own recent dreams have been and how in reality one usually forgets every detail before their feet hit the bedroom floor.

"Anyway," she says, "then it's intermission and I feel the need to break away from the rest of the cast and get some fresh air. I go out the stage door and it's a beautiful night. The air is warm, and I make my way down a palm-lined walkway towards a large body of water. The moonlight dances across the waves as a gentle breeze causes the Catholic nun's habit I'm wearing to billow. I just stand there and take in a huge cleansing breath of ocean air."

"Then I hear the slam of a door behind me and my name repeated several times. 'Maggie… are you out here Maggie?' I assume I've lost track of time and the stage director is concerned I'll miss my next curtain cue."

"Turning around, I'm pleasantly surprised to see Bob coming down the walk with our three-year-old daughter in his arms. I run towards them in time to hear him saying, 'Don't be afraid Mary, it's only mommy in a costume.' I hug them both tightly and tell them how glad I am they finally showed up. Bob sets our daughter down, and we all hold hands as we walk back towards what I can only describe as the biggest purple monstrosity of a building I have ever seen."

Mac is now pulling at the lead to move on and wants to take a side trail through the woods that will pass the Glenhouse pool. I allow him his head.

"Well, you're right," I say, "it's not a nightmare by any means, but it's definitely interesting! It seems logical for you to dream about your chosen profession, but the part about Bob and the baby kind of surprises me."

"Surprises *you*!" exclaims Mags. "It flabbergasted me! He's in California right now, chasing his own dream, and it's a fairly slim chance that I'll ever see him again unless it's on television."

"I'm most taken aback by the baby's name of Mary," I add. "It's a bit unnerving considering my recent experience with the young girl by that name, real or otherwise, here in the Cove. Is that actually the name you've picked for your baby?"

"I believe it was sublimely placed in my head, Mom, by you sharing your story with me. Actually, my current front-runner is Lillian."

"Well I might give that a second thought, dear." I laugh. "With your last name, the kids in school will be teasing her about being a Lilly bloom."

Walking into the condo it smells like the holidays. I peek in the oven at the turkey pieces and they're golden brown. I decide to cover it and the sweet potatoes with foil and turn the oven down low. I throw the sprouts in boiling water and drain the red potatoes to mash. I decide to leave the skins on thus making them look rather rustic.

"If anyone complains, I'll advise them it's the exact way the pilgrims made them," I jest aloud.

I also set the pumpkin pies on the counter with the intention of baking them while we're eating.

Maggie has gone to change for dinner, and I take this last half hour before our guests are due to arrive to do the same. I don't recall wearing a dress since I got here, and decide on a loose-fitting Alexander McQueen crepe number that I actually bought down at Fifi's fine resale apparel in Venice. I chose it, even though it's a bit smart for the occasion, as it has lots of breathing room, and I intend to eat absolutely everything.

77

There's a light-hearted knock at the front door.

"Mag," I call out, "are you able to get that? I'm still putting my face on."

"I'm already on my way!" she shouts in my direction.

Opening the door, there stands Jack and Frank who's holding a couple bottles of wine.

"Aunt Jackie!" exclaims Mag and she motions for both of them to come in.

Jack does a scan of Maggie's figure and smiles.

"You either have a lot to tell me, or you swallowed the Thanksgiving turkey whole."

After a long hug and a slightly tearful moment with Jack scolding, "It's been way too long since I've seen you baby girl!" she then introduces Frank.

I come out of the bedroom moments later and give them both a kiss on the cheek while grabbing the wine from Frank.

"What say we open these and get this party started?" Leaning into Jack, I whisper, "I wish I'd have heard what noun you used to introduce him as I struggled with that question earlier."

Jack follows me into the kitchen. "Gigolo!" she says and then offers to help.

I give her a questioning look and shoo her off.

"I knew you'd be surprised when you saw Maggie's condition." I am going to start a roux for the gravy. "Why don't you just go to the living room and catch up. I've already heard most of the long and the short of it all."

"Okay," she smirks. "But which was *he*... the long or the short?"

I give her my best disapproving glance before we both break into giggles.

"That's fine," she says. "I know when I'm not wanted." She then takes the wine bottles back from where I placed them on the kitchen counter. "But let me pop the cork on these babies and start pouring first."

While she's reaching up to open the cabinet over the sink where I keep the wine glasses, I suddenly see it.

"Oh my God, Jacqueline Hernandez! Is that what I think it is on your finger?"

She is beaming ear to ear. "Isn't it the biggest damn rock you've ever seen? I'm tempted to run to the jeweler at the mall and see if it's real." She holds her hand out to show me. "I swear it looks like it was plucked off of some southern woman's Georgian, crystal chandelier!"

"It's gorgeous!" I say as we hug tight. "I'm so happy for you, Jackie. I just knew there was something special about that guy. When did he give it to you?"

"Just Tuesday night. Heck, I haven't even gotten used to feeling it on my finger yet."

"And you didn't call to tell me?" I question further.

"Well it's a bit difficult when there's no cell service where we were."

"Where did he ask you?" I continue.

"Oh Liz, you're not going to believe this story!"

"Well, since the sun sets so early this time of year, he suggested we leave mid-afternoon and maybe grab a drink at some tiki bar and walk the beach in Venice before having dinner."

"Oh, how nice the seashore at Venice Beach," I smile. "That's a very romantic place to propose."

Jack rolls her eyes and says, "That's not it!"

"So, we're in his little sports car with the top down, just driving along talking, when he pulls this James Bond like move and sharply turns into the Venice Municipal Airport. He continues driving at top speed straight down the runway directly towards a plane whose propeller is spinning. He circles the plane and skids to a stop on the door side of the plane, and I can then see it's some sort of an amphibious aircraft."

"He hops out, opens the trunk to the car and takes out a small carry-on bag before coming to open my door and help me out. So, I'm completely wide-eyed and I ask him, 'What's up?'"

"'Oh, I just thought I'd take you to one of my favorite places for dinner, Miss Jackie, if you would be so kind as to join me,' he answers with that toothy coy smile and a twinkle in his eye."

Suddenly I realize I haven't been stirring my roux and the butter and flour mixture has scorched to the pan. "Darn!" I admonish and place the mess in the sink and turn on the water. "So much for having gravy... now go on, I'm all ears!"

"Well, let's see... he then helps me to board the plane where the waiting pilot greets us, 'Good evening Miss. Looks like we've got great weather for flying all the way to your destination!' So of course, I ask, 'Where is my destination?' And he replies, 'I'm afraid that's confidential information ma'am.'"

"Oh my gosh, I gasp, How romantic. You got engaged on a plane while flying over Sarasota County."

And again, Jack makes a face. "For God's sake, Liz, that's not it either! Let me finish."

I gesture zipping of my lips as she takes a deep breath while feigning exasperation and continues.

"So, after takeoff Frank gets up and goes back to a small galley area where he has champagne stowed. He pops the cork, which ricochets off the cabin ceiling, and then hands me a flute that's engraved with, 'Love isn't something you find. Love is something that finds you!'"

She poses, "Isn't that just the best thing you ever heard?"

Now afraid to talk, I just nod enthusiastically.

"So, we toast to the inscription, share a long wine laced kiss and continue flying south to who knows where."

Suddenly, Frank pops into the kitchen asking, "Whatever happened to that wine ladies?"

Jack then hands him both the bottles. "There's a corkscrew in her bar back in the other room. You pour and we'll follow."

I get out the cheese and olive plate I put together earlier and grab the basket of crackers as we go to the living room, where I clear a spot for the appetizers on the coffee table.

I congratulate Frank and quickly we catch Maggie up on where we are with the story.

"Before you go any further," I state to Jack then turn to face my daughter. "Maggie is there anything I can get you to drink since you're not doing wine?" She advises she's just fine with her ice water as we settle in all ears.

"We fly over the Everglades National Park, and it's absolutely beautiful from the air. There are a lot more open areas of water than I expected. In fact, we saw a couple airboats and a colorful group of kayakers. Oh, and lots and lots of birds. Frank, what were those pink ones called that weren't flamingos?"

"Those would be roseatte spoonbills, ma'am."

She stops to take a sip of wine and I hand her a cracker with cheese.

Maggie says, "Sorry, but this would be a good spot for an intermission," and heads off for the bathroom.

I can't help but notice that Frank is beaming as he looks at Jack and, as their eyes make contact, I swear I can see the proverbial sparks fly. Mag hurries back to her spot on the couch as Jack picks up where she left off.

"We come to the Upper Keys and continue flying directly above Highway 1, the overseas route from mainland Florida to Key West. Frank says there are about eight hundred islands that make up the keys. Can you believe that? Eight hundred."

And now we all start talking amongst ourselves, contemplating how there can be that many islands, how most must be extremely small and who in the world counted them?

"Anyway, Frank is so knowledgeable. He points out Key Largo and that we're approaching Lower Matecumbe Key, followed by Craig Key and then the city of Marathon. Then we fly parallel to the Seven Mile Bridge. It's so long Liz, but I think you could do it, as it's practically flat on the water."

"How do you know so much about the Keys?" I ask Frank.

"Y'all need to remember I was born and raised here. My daddy use to love to dive and fish, and well, I reckon there ain't nowheres finer for doin' both them there things than in the Keys, ma'am!" And then there it is, his signature grin.

Jack gives me a side glance that says loud and clearly, *Let me finish my story!*

"So, then we pass over Key West, and it's already crowded, and the pre-Thanksgiving weekend party is in full swing. We circle around a fort, and Frank advises it's the Dry Tortugas National Park. And then we descend towards a small island and the plane actually lands on the water before floating up to the dock."

"The pilot announces, 'Welcome to Little Palm Island, miss. Give me a moment to tie up, and I'll help you off the plane.'"

By now both Mags and I are on the edge of our seats in disbelief waiting for the remainder of the story.

"We were greeted at the dock by our host and escorted to a private bungalow on the water. It was unbelievable, Liz, decorated so smart and with every amenity. I took pictures with my phone that I'll show you later!"

"Well then, Frank hands me a small carry-on suitcase and suggests we get changed. I open it and all that's inside is a rather skimpy two-piece swimsuit and a few toiletries, like a toothbrush and sunscreen. I give a smart aleck remark of some sort regarding the lax dress code here, and he just laughs as he pulls off his shirt and drops his pants right there, revealing he's already wearing his swim trunks underneath. 'Welcome to the real Florida Miss Jackie!' he says and then, well… we'll skip what happened next."

"Are you actually blushing?" I say.

"Only because there are children present," as she pats Maggie lovingly on the belly.

78

Jack is about to finish up her story when, out of habit, I look over at the grandfather clock to check the time. I still can't get used to it not working since the move, and I very much miss hearing the Big Ben chime.

I turn to Frank, who always wears a watch. "What time is it please?"

"One twenty, ma'am."

And suddenly I feel the need to check on Marilyn.

"If you can hold your thoughts, Jackie, for just a moment more, I'm going to run next door and see what's holding up my neighbor from joining us."

I knock, knowing full well to allow ample time for her to hobble to the door with her walker. I can hear Tookie barking on the other side. The door opens part way, and I can see she has the security chain on.

"Hello, hello… who in the world is it?"

"Why it's me, Marilyn, it's Liz. I was expecting you at one o'clock for Thanksgiving dinner."

I hear fumbling and then the clink of the chain as she slowly swings the door open.

"*Oy chorbn*, I was just searching everywhere for your phone number. I know you gave it to me at least three times now, but I'll be darned if I can remember what I've done with it."

She's wearing a floral nightgown with a pink fleece bathrobe over it. On her head is what appears to be a shower cap of sorts and she looks a bit pale and fragile.

"Are you all right?" I ask, and she gestures for me to lean closer towards the door and then whispers through the screen.

"I got the dysentery, honey... real bad." She frowns and shakes her head. "Got it last night right after eating a spicy shakshuka, and a leftover meat-stuffed Kibbeh... Oh, and I found a couple potato latkes that I had with horseradish sour cream. You don't think the sour cream did it, do you, honey? Heck, it was only a few days after the expiration and, let's face it, it's already sour to begin with!"

I'm not sure what in the world some of the things even are that this woman's been eating, but I suggest maybe a large Thanksgiving dinner wouldn't be the best thing for her today.

"I'll bring you over a plate later that you can keep in the refrigerator until you're feeling better."

We smile at each other. "You're just way too good to me, sweetie pie... way too good."

And I take my leave after assuring her she will be sorely missed.

Back home I give the short synopsis of my visit. "My next-door neighbor isn't feeling well, and she apologizes for not getting to meet all of you."

Jack refills my wine glass. "Drink up. You're a glass behind the rest of us! Oh yeah, and something smelled like it was burning so I turned the oven off. By the way I couldn't keep from taking a peek... what in God's name did you do to that poor bird?"

My phone begins playing "By the Seaside" from the charger on the counter, and I walk over and answer it.

"Hello, Liz speaking."

"Oh my, oh my, honey. This is Marilyn, sweetie. I was just wondering if you made a pumpkin pie or not?"

"Well as it happens, I'm just about to put them in the oven."

Well, hon, if it's not asking too much, I'll take two pieces with extra whipped cream. Do you make your own?"

Jack then shouts, "Everybody just shut-up and sit down for five more minutes so I can finish this damn story!"

I reassure Marilyn there's plenty of pie, but the topping will just be Cool Whip, and hang up.

Jack takes a deep breath before proceeding.

"So, as I said, this place is unbelievable. Our private concierge magically appears from nowhere and sets up our personal dining table for two at water's edge with fine china and crystal. He lights a romantic bonfire on the beach and then opens and serves another bottle of bubbly before quietly advising Frank, 'Just let me know when you want dinner served, sir.' And then disappears from the open-air room."

Jack lays hold of her wine and after a slightly noisy sip continues. "Frank suggests we explore the private beach and watch the sunset. And as the sun explodes in a tremendous orange ball and the clouds glow pink Frank takes my hand, drops to one knee and says, 'Miss Jackie, I sure do love you. As I already shared with you, love isn't something you find, love is something that finds you! And, ma'am, I'm so very thankful that you found me.' Then from somewhere in his Speedo he pulls out this ring," she explains while holding her finger out. "And he says, 'Will you marry me?'"

By now I'm shedding a tear and sniffling while Maggie's hormones have her blubbering uncontrollably.

Frank stands. "Why don't I see what I can do in the kitchen? And I was wearing surfer trunks with a pocket!"

And with that he leaves the three of us to gather on the sectional and hug.

"Oh Jack, That southern boy's the whole package. I'm so happy for you," I say.

"Aunt Jackie that's possibly the most romantic thing I've ever heard. It could be on Broadway!"

Unanticipated, there comes clanging and banging from the kitchen. "Shucky darn!"

"Hold on." I say. "And I'll come help you."

"Oh, there ain't no problem, ma'am, that I can't take care of… dinner will be ready in about five minutes."

I turn to Jack. "And we already knew he knows his way around a kitchen. Hang on to this one!"

Frank makes several trips between the kitchen and dining table and then announces, "Y'all come and get it while it's hot!"

We girls excuse ourselves for a moment and head off in separate directions to fix our faces and pull ourselves together. Returning to the table, I advise everyone to find their names on the pumpkins and take a seat. Briefly, I glance at Marilyn's place beside me that remains' empty and feel a pang of sadness.

Frank senses my discomfort. "You know ma'am, my momma, God bless her soul, used to purposely set an empty place at all of our holiday tables in remembrance of all the loved ones that couldn't be with us that year. It was her way of dealin' with the inevitable way the holidays have of remindin' us of those who have passed. My daddy would attempt to lighten the mood by telling us young'uns that 'should any hungry stranger in need of nurturing come a knockin' at our door today we will graciously invite them in to break bread with us.'"

Maggie and I both make eye contact, and I know in my heart of hearts we're both thinking of the exact same two people, Scott and Tommy.

I suggest we revive an old family Thanksgiving custom and all join hands. "Now would be a good time for each of us to state what we're thankful for this Thanksgiving."

I start off by saying, "I'm so thankful for each and every one of you in my life I sincerely don't think I could have survived this adventure without you. And praise be to God for blessing me with the addition of a new family member who'll be joining us soon." And, I give Maggie's hand a little squeeze.

The others in turn share their sentiments and we end on a communal, Amen.

Jack looks at the platter that Frank has placed in the middle of the table. He has creatively arranged the turkey breast in the center, two legs on one side and one on the other and then five wings fanned out around it. Then she looks up at me.

"So now my dear please do tell, what the hell happened to this pitiful turkey!"

79

The next day is Black Friday, and Maggie and I both agree that neither of us are stepping foot near the mall or any other shopping venue for that matter. All morning the news has replayed two extremely graphic scenes of violence that occurred in the wee hours of the morning.

In one incident in Los Angeles a woman, with two children, pepper sprayed fellow shoppers waiting in line for an Xbox 360. Twenty people were treated for minor injuries in the resulting battle for a Christmas present. At another location in Long Island shoppers burst through the doors of a retailer at five am, trampling to death a thirty-four-year-old seasonal employee and injuring a pregnant woman.

I turn the TV off while voicing my disgust for the human race sometimes. "Only in America would people trample each other for sales, just one day after giving thanks for everything they already have."

Mags and I sit at the table, picking at an Entenmann's cheese-filled coffee cake, discussing our non-violent options for the day and decide a leisurely walk through beautiful Marie Selby Gardens suits our needs.

Maggie asks if we might see a beach as well and I suggest lunch on St. Armands Circle, followed by a stroll on Lido Beach. We both head towards opposite bathrooms to get ready and determine we should be able to make ourselves presentable and be out the door in about forty-five minutes.

Driving down the Trail, I point out things she might remember, like the Hooters at Stickney we went to when she was small.

"You were so disgusted, and even though there were other families, you voiced your concerns over our bringing your little brother into that kind of a place. On the flipside I recall your brother ogling the sea of bouncing boobies and beaming. Of course, so was your father!" That brings a laugh and it feels good to be comfortably talking about both of them.

Traffic is heavy and moves slowly. I point out the new Trader Joe's and P.F. Chang's, as well as how they are raising funds to turn the old Sarasota High School into a modern art museum.

"Oh, see that Publix near 301? It's new, and I just went there a few weeks ago. The first level is a parking garage and the actual store is upstairs. They have a sort of escalator thing for carrying your cart up and down between floors. It's a great design for urban grocery stores."

"I never did understand why Kroger's never built a prototype store smack dab in downtown Cincy. Especially since they have their corporate headquarters there. It would have given P&G a place to test market products or try out new shelf sets and end cap designs. Marketing would have loved it."

Mags smirks. "You really can't let go of work, can you?"

We pull into Selby, and it appears this was a good idea, as we easily find a primo parking place. By the time I pay for two admissions, I can become a member and use my membership at various reciprocal gardens here and across the country. Plus, I intend on visiting here in the future and even take some information on the upcoming 'Lights in Bloom' for the Christmas season.

We meander through the rather warm greenhouse with its amazing array of orchids in full bloom. There are more varieties in every shape, size and color than one could ever imagine. Maggie asks for help pulling her sweater off.

"I can't seem to regulate between being hot and cold anymore."

"I was exactly the same way when I was pregnant with you," I say. "I remember one time when it was snowing outside, and I had the bedroom window wide open trying to get some fresh air. Your poor father nearly froze to death. Come the next morning, I cranked the heat up to eighty and he walked around the house with shorts on."

After another connecting bout of laughter, we step outside into a wonderful display of bonsai. "I always wanted to learn to do these," I say.

"How hard can it be to stick a small tree into a clay pot?" she says.

We walk further down the paths as I try sharing what little I know, about the idiosyncrasies of bonsai gardening.

"Did you know some of those little trees have been tended to for well over a hundred years? They take a lot of care with pruning and shaping the tops and trimming of the roots to maintain them and inhibit growth. I think there's something almost mystical or fairylike about them."

We stop at a little cottage restaurant where we purchase a large, unsweetened peach iced tea to share. We take a seat on a cement bench for a moment, watching multi-colored koi swimming to the edge of a decorative pond to beg for food. I dig for a quarter and a gumball type machine dispenses fish feed into the palm of my hand. We sit, feeding them one pellet at a time, and marvel at their jumping skills and long whiskers.

We continue meandering through the gardens enjoying the sunny day and the light ocean breeze coming off Little Sarasota Bay. We come upon a huge banyan tree whose support roots are numerous, creating the appearance of being its own forest in miniature.

I marvel at the sight of it. "It's almost like an enormous bonsai isn't it?"

Mag reads aloud from a sign posted in front of the magnificent tree.

A banyan is a fig that starts its life as an epiphyte (a plant growing on another plant) when its seeds germinate in the cracks and crevices of a host tree. When those seeds grow, they send roots down towards the ground, and may envelop part or the entire host tree, giving banyans the menacing moniker of 'strangler fig'.

Older banyan trees are characterized by their aerial prop roots that grow into numerous thick woody trunks which, with age, can become indistinguishable from the main trunk. In a banyan that envelops a support tree totally, the roots eventually apply enough pressure to ultimately kill the tree. Over time such an enveloped dead tree rots away so that the banyan becomes a 'columnar tree' with a hollow central core. In rain forests and jungles such hollows are particularly desirable shelters to many animals.

A chill creeps down my spine as the tale brings to mind the immense oak tree in the Cove that Mary ran to that night. Originally, I was haunted by the thought that somehow the old, lecherous male tree was, what… holding poor, young Mary captive in the form of a delicate young fig tree for his own demented sexual pleasure? But after hearing Maggie's narration I find myself reconsidering.

Is the little fig actually strangling the life out of the old oak instead?

I just stand there, impassive, lost in my thoughts for several minutes.

Mags has waddled on, and as I catch up, we approach yet another unusual looking tree. Around its base are folding tables manned by several women. Each table contains bright colored strips of satin ribbon displayed on them. There are also several containers holding black Sharpie markers. Hanging off the limbs of the trees are mesh baskets made of wire, reminiscent of garden ones that hold flowers, or the ones that hold fruit, like bananas, that people hang in their kitchen.

One of the volunteers manning a table motions for us to come closer and take a look and we oblige her. She informs us that, throughout the holidays, they are hoping to fill the baskets, thus cover the bottom limbs of the tree, in a rainbow of ribbons and best wishes for the Earth. She holds up a poster that shows the meaning behind each color ribbon and what it represents to the universe.

"Yellow is a symbol of support for all the world's people," she explains. "Green, concern for the world foliage including trees, fruits and vegetables. In other words, prayers that the world can continue producing enough food to feed the masses. Blue denotes concerns for the oceans, lakes and fresh water, red represents health and well-being and so on and so on.

"We're asking that you choose the color ribbon that represents something in the world you most care about and, using a marker, write your blessing, prayer or wishes for the planet on it. When you're ready, you can tie the ribbon onto one of the many baskets hanging from the Buddha tree. It's our hope that by New Year's Day the tree will be filled with heartfelt sentiments for 2013."

I quickly grab a blue one since I now have a renewed concern for the oceans, and sea life in general, since moving here. I quickly write, *Protect the manatees and all God's sea creatures!* on mine. Maggie seems perplexed as to what to pick and is still reading the board explaining the color choices. She smiles and grabs a white one and begins to write.

"What does white stand for?" I ask.

"Purity, protecting the world's children and pro-life," she states, as I put my arm around her waist. We go tie our ribbons to the tree.

Sitting cross-legged and barefoot on a Jaipur rug behind the tree is an East Indian woman with luxuriously long, ebony hair. With motioning hands on slender arms decorated with henna tattoos, she signals for all to come closer while bidding, "Namaste." We join a small group that has gathered in a semicircle around her as she begins telling the story of the Buddha Tree.

"The Bodhi or Buddha tree is one of the earliest Buddhist symbols and objects of reverence. According to the Buddhist scriptures, people asked the Buddha whom should they pay respect to when he was absent, and he replied that they should pay respect to a Bodhi tree. 'Look at the shape of the leaves; they represent my heart that will always be with you.' Since then Bodhi trees have been planted in Buddhist temple gardens all around the world. They remind us of the forest origins of the Buddhist tradition and of the dependence of our lives and achievements on nature and to be kind to all living beings."

The woman does several mudras—or hand gestures—then places her hands in a praying gesture on her chest.

"This particular tree at Marie Selby has had an interesting spiritual life all its own. In 2001 Hurricane Gabrielle uprooted this very tree and dropped it into Little Sarasota Bay right over there."

She nods towards the open waters visible from where we're all standing.

"Horticultural scientists, botanists, and the garden staff all deemed the tree a total loss from root exposure and subjection to saltwater. However, much like the ribbons you hung on the tree today, employees and volunteers alike had faith that the tree could possibly be saved. So, they directed a major effort that involved bringing in a fifty-ton crane on a large barge. The tree was lifted from the bay waters and gently returned to its upright position on the Selby Garden grounds. Leaves yellowed, many shriveled and thousands more littered the ground below it. However, with a little extra care, additional feedings and a bit of pruning, over time it not only survived, it thrived. And, as you can clearly see, it continues to flourish to this day."

The crowd applauds and begins to disperse. Maggie and I choose to walk over to a group of park benches lining the bay and sit a spell, reflecting on all the stories this magical oasis has shared with us today and gazing out at the glistening, teal water.

80

After finishing our tour of the gardens, and with Maggie expressing her need to eat something, we drive over the Ringling Bridge to St. Armands Circle on Lido Key. Entering the circle from Ringling Boulevard, it's apparent that parking is nowhere as easy to come by as it was at Marie Selby. We slowly drive the circle twice looking for a place to park, but to no avail. The traffic is horrendous, since it appears even here, all the Black Friday shoppers are out in full force. Numerous out of state vehicles have no idea how to handle the large roundabout comprised of eight one-way side roads that fan out from the ring of boutiques and restaurants. Cars either suddenly cut in front of us, after finally spying the side road they want to turn on—or stop dead in front of us contemplating their next move.

I pull up in front of the Crab & Fin.

"Maggie, you jump out and get our name on the list. Sitting outside where we can people watch would be nice, but tell them we'll take first available. If I never come back take a cab home!"

She laughs while pulling herself out of the Escape as an impatient red Maserati convertible lays heavily on its horn behind me. The driver then observes her visible condition and mouths, *Scusi.* Complete with Italian hand gestures and accompanying facial expression. *Mi dispiace!*

I decide to try the back streets and turn down Fillmore Drive where there's a public parking lot. Its filled with bumper-to-bumper traffic—drivers who will possibly be searching for a spot until well after sunset. I weave my way down Monroe, over to Washington, and turn left at the Tommy Bahama, ending up back onto the far end of Ringling Boulevard. There's a car pulling out, and I swiftly parallel park in the vacated spot.

Damn I'm good at that!

I beam in the rear-view mirror and then dig in my purse for some lipstick and a hairbrush.

After walking over half the circle on foot to get back to the restaurant, Maggie is nowhere to be seen. I survey both the line of people waiting at the host stand and the street side tables, all filled with prattling diners. I go in and find her seated in a lone chair just inside the door.

"The kind man outside thought it best if I have a seat in the air-conditioning until a table becomes available. He said I look like I've been out in the sun too long. Do I look red to you?"

"Well, maybe a little," I say. "We really should have put more sunscreen on you, and probably a hat, before walking around that garden!"

"They should be calling our name in just a minute," she says, and sure enough, moments later, the name Blum—like plum—is announced outside and then again inside through the opened door.

"Here!" I say. "And it's Blum, like bloom not Blum like plum."

The host smirks, checks his seating chart, claps his hands twice and announces, "Michelle, please show Miss Plum and her guest to their table!"

Maggie has Charley's chowder and I the shrimp bisque. We share an entrée of fish tacos and then split a piece of key lime pie.

"Nothing against yesterday's Thanksgiving dinner," She says, "But now I feel like I'm really eating in Florida."

We finish our late lunch and, despite our previous protests, shop a bit of the circle on the way back to the car. We both agree that we've gotten too much sun for one day, and Mag suggests she's now ready for a nap anyway.

"Maybe we can go to the beach later for sunset?" I say. "Either way, we'll make sure to get there before you leave!"

Turning right on 41 and driving towards home, we pass the vacant site where *Unconditional Surrender*—the larger than life statue of the World War Two sailor and nurse kissing—use to stand. I'm compelled to share Jack's tale of the car wreck, which then leads to the highlights of surviving a tropical storm. Then I digress for a moment.

"You know, I just read the other day in the *Sarasota Herald-Tribune* that the statue is almost finished being repaired and should hopefully be reinstalled before Christmas."

About three miles before reaching Pelican Cove, we pass a small shopping plaza on the right consisting of tiny white cement block cottages each with pine-green colored roof shingles and matching shutters. The complex, built as a semi-circle, appears to have been an old motel left over from the days before I-75 and when the Tamiami Trail was the only major highway on the Gulf Coast.

The storefronts contain a real-estate office, an insurance agency, and such. However, one end unit, nearest the road, stands out. The sign proclaims **Readings by Vivian** and on the door in bright red it says OPEN.

"Can we stop?" yells Mags excitedly, and intuitively I quickly turn the wheel, and we fly into the lot.

"What is it dear?" I ask. "Are you feeling carsick?"

"No, no… please don't think I'm crazy, Mom, but before I got pregnant, Bob and I were out with friends in Chelsea one night. We walked past this storefront psychic, and we all joked about getting a reading. Looking in through the glass pane of the front door I could see through partially opened curtains, in a mid-century modern floral pattern of drab olive and gray, hanging in the interior doorway, a woman seated in a bleak back room kitchen. She's sitting on a metal step stool and slurping soup, or something, with a mixing spoon from right out of the pot.

"Her dark eyes were staring straight at me, and she was beckoning us with a hand wave to come in, and strangely enough, I felt compelled to open her cracked glass door and go in. I wasn't comfortable with the situation, and I clung tightly to Bob's arm. As we all went inside the empty storefront, she came through the curtains, pulling them shut dramatically behind her, and then, with an overly dramatic twirl, stood facing and greeting us all.

'Hallo… Seet my children, please seet.'

"With olive skin and long dark hair she looked like a gypsy and spoke to us with possibly a Hungarian accent. Bob whispered in my ear saying we needed to get out of there! But then we each sat in a semi-circle of folding chairs in the middle of this otherwise dimly lit and empty room.

"She whipped off her multi-colored, knit gypsy shawl and while dramatically throwing it aside said, 'So, whom vill goes first I vonder?' Rubbing her chin hairs with a crooked finger, she looked us each directly in the eye before stopping in front of me. 'Crosses my palm vit de silver!' she said, so I opened my clutch, took out my change purse and picked out all the silver coins I had on me and placed them in her hand.

"She continued to stare directly in my eyes without even blinking. Confused as to what to do, I dumped the remainder of the coin purse into her hand, which of course was only copper pennies and a Canadian nickel. She continued to stare. So, I took out my wallet and tried a one, then a five, and finally a twenty. She stuck the money in a pocket of her frayed Bohemian skirt and then said, 'Geeve me your handsa!'

"I reached out and she grabbed them both firmly and then inspected them diligently, front and back, for what felt like fifteen minutes. Every now and then she snorted or groaned and even once gave a slight cackle.

"Then she started her reading. 'I sees from your right handsa's hearts line your hearts, she breaksa easily. No?'

"I nodded and she continued.

'Youva experienced emotionals trauma anda losses. Too, too manys for a younga womans lika yourselves!' She ran her malformed finger along another part of my hand. 'Youra head line, she says you be the very creative persons. Arteest, dancer or actoressa maybes? Howevers, all dees criss-a-crosses through the line tellsa me yousa been faced with momentous decisions. No?'

"She seemed to pause for a response, but before I could even answer, she said, 'Youra life line, she shows youa be maybes too cautious when it comesa to relationships, loving, sexa?' And she smirked and then winked. 'I also sees a sudden changes in lifestyles in youra past. Per chances you moved, maybes twicea?'

"I acknowledged my moving to New York to pursue my acting career. Then advised her that I lost my brother and father in a terrible car accident.

"Showing no emotions whatsoever, she let go of my right hand and focused only on my left. 'This handsa holds the futures. Youra fate line she's a strong… yes good and deep. Youra future it be strongly controlled by the fates, however. You a must yields to the support offered by the family and friendsa. New life shea springs from your loins in one, ora maybe twoa years.'

"And that was it, she moved on to reading the rest of the group. It eventually dawned on me that apparently I'd paid for a group reading!"

We both just sit there in the car quietly for a moment. I'm sure with me looking completely dazed. "Wow," I say, "that's some story. So, what brings us here now?"

Maggie reaches over and takes my hand. "The details of that reading have haunted me since that day, and it scares me a bit how accurate that woman was!" Whether she realizes it or not, she is patting her belly. "I've often wondered if another psychic would see things the same way. But mostly, now that I'm pregnant, I'm curious if they can read and share any details about the baby. You know, is it alright, healthy, will it grow up to be happy?" She chuckles, "Am I carrying the first woman president?"

I reflect on my response since this is all new ground for me.

"I've never been to a place like this before, and I'm a bit leery. However, if you're asking me to escort you inside, I say, let's go on in and see what this Vivian has to say!"

Witchy Woman

—Eagles (1972)

Songwriters: Don Henley / Bernie Leadon

81

We enter Readings by Vivian, and it's nothing like I pictured Maggie's apprehensive New York experience. The small room is painted bright white, and with the large, exposed windows, it's actually quite light and cheery. Royal blue fish netting has been draped above the windows as swag curtains, and each contains metallic silver stars of varying sizes randomly attached to them.

Along the walls are sunny–yellow decorative shelves containing an array of self-help and wellness books. Intermixed among them are other materials artistically placed, items like incense, candles, and crystals. Seated at a shabby chic desk that has been painted pink is a bejeweled, heavy-set young woman with a flamboyant updo of aqua-blue hair.

"Welcome," she says, "please come in! Have a look around. If I can be of any help just let me know."

The woman then goes back to some sort of journal she's writing in, which causes the numerous bangle bracelets she's wearing to jingle pleasantly.

I follow behind Maggie as she approaches the woman.

"Actually," she says, "I was wondering if you were available to do a reading."

"Oh, sure thing, hon," says the woman and points with a quartz ringed finger, bracelets tinkling, to one of the two wing back chairs facing the desk. "Have a seat, and I'll be right with you."

Maggie sits and I follow suit, taking the other chair. The seats are beautifully upholstered in a luminescent fabric of astral designs.

"I'm Vivian," says the woman.

"Maggie."

"And what kind of reading were you looking for, Maggie? I do astrology, clairvoyance, crystal ball gazing and channeling." She takes a breath, clearly part of a well-practiced script. "Palmistry, runes, numerology and tarot Readings. I'm just learning lithomancy, but I'm game to try it if you are. And, I absolutely refuse to do clairsentience anymore as it's way too emotionally draining on me. Heck, the last one I did, my client and I must have cried for two hours!"

"Right," says Maggie, sensing that Vivian is not done.

"I don't do groups. It's all individual, so it will be a separate fee for the two of you. Also, if desired, I have a small room in the back for private readings. So, what will it be ladies?"

She smiles like the Cheshire cat showing extremely straight, white teeth through painted hot-pink, botoxed lips.

"A simple palm reading," replies Mag.

Vivian turns her gaze to me.

"I'm just here for moral support," I say.

"Right," she says. "Okay, Maggie was it? Have you had your palms read before?"

Maggie states, "Yes." to both and gives her a short synopsis of the New York experience.

"Well palms don't change regarding the past, and I would be unable to tell you anything you don't already know. What say we focus on the future?" There is a twinkle in her eyes and another dazzling smile.

She leans back in her chair, rubbing her hands together. "Unfortunately, I insist we settle on the financial part of the reading first."

"Let me get this," I say and grab for my purse. Dumping the contents of my change purse on the desk, I start to mutter. "I really thought I had a lot more silver on me."

Vivian gives a quizzical look as I then search my wallet and pull out three singles.

"I don't carry much cash on me either," I say apologetically. "I'm afraid I usually use plastic."

To which the psychic's smile broadens. "I take Visa, MasterCard and American Express!"

After that things are settled quickly. Then she turns her attention to Maggie.

She gently takes her left hand. "You're right-handed correct?"

"Yes."

"Good, then your left hand holds all the details of your future that are visible to me at this time. It's important for you to remember that what I see is not necessarily how things will be, but more of how things are headed right now. Your final story hasn't been defined yet and is subject to chance. However, I must warn you, left unchanged, your destiny will be strongly guided by a pre-determined fate, and if I see a negative outcome from your reading, I won't be held responsible for the consequences."

The room suddenly takes on a sullen attitude as Vivian switches off the Muzak retail music, and I begin to fidget nervously in my chair. Then, after adjusting the interior lighting with the aid of a dimmer switch on her desk, the psychic looks eanestly at the palm of Maggie's hand as she begins.

"You continue to long for acceptance and approval. This seems to be about a job or profession rather than personal relationships. You've been advised you're not good enough, and you'll spend your life trying to prove them wrong. Will you succeed?... That's unclear."

I look over and see Maggie smile as the reading continues.

"You have many loose ends you continue trying to wrap up. Someone... a man, yes, a tall man whose name begins with D or B has hurt you recently. He has hurt you deeply however, this person will be in your life forever, and you would do best to remember that fact and try to make amends. You are with child... a girl, yes, I'm seeing lots and lots of pink around your aura!"

I again look over at my daughter and think the 'with child' part was fairly obvious when we came through the door—and to that end she had a fifty–fifty chance with the girl thing.

"You're filled with consternation about your baby's well-being, aren't you?"

Maggie nods and tears begin to fall.

"Not to worry, my love, she will make it through the troubles ahead for her. Your fears are well founded, but all will be well in the end!"

I dig through my purse for my Puffs-to-Go and can't find one. Vivian quickly picks up on it, reaches under the desk and hands a tissue to Maggie, who dabs at her eyes with her free right hand.

"You've carried your burdens and personal belongings a long way and hope to stay where you are for a while. No… forgive me, I see you *must* stay, as your past has closed the astral door with a slam, firmly shut behind you, signaling a completely new beginning for you now. Your concerns, beyond the baby, seem to be around an unstable relationship that is only recently being rebuilt. It involves your birth mother or another matriarch figure assisting you, but there are many more souls guiding you on the astral plane. As well, you worry financially about what the future holds for you."

Vivian pauses, closes her eyes and breathes in deeply. When her eyes open, she looks straight at me.

"You're her mother?"

"Yes"

"My dear, your daughter needs you now more than the time she had chicken pox and was hospitalized or in the midst of your family's personal tragedy. She won't be leaving Sarasota any time soon, but it's unclear how long she'll stay with you. I see a wonderful future for her as a possible outcome, but I also see possible catastrophe filled with much sadness and personal loss. Remember, fate is the cards the dealer hands you, but how you play them is of your own free will."

Vivian now reaches out from across the desk and takes my hands in hers. "Make future decisions placed before you both *very* carefully, for there is a proverbial fork in the road ahead. You are surrounded by spirits, some good… some extremely evil. One such wraith was actually invited into your home by one of you. Others have roamed the land for a very, very long time."

I feel a bit dazed, but Maggie is smiling ear to ear as she thanks Vivian for the reassurance of her unborn daughter's well-being. We leave the shop, but not until the palm reader convinces Maggie to purchase a Mama Mio Candle for yet another $26 dollars.

"It has a mix of mandarin, neroli, and ylang ylang essential oils," she claims. "It's all natural, and the delightful aroma reduces the stress of pregnancy. Personally hon, I like to keep one in my bathroom!"

Back in the car, I take a cleansing breath. "Well, that was informative, and different… actually very, very different. So, when were you going to tell me you're not returning home?"

Maggie looks at me credulously.

"Most people would have surmised that when I showed up at their front door hauling absolutely everything I own for a weekend visit!"

By the time we are pulling into the Cove I have regained my footing somewhat.

"I need time to think and digest all this stuff. Like evil spirits and you staying with me." I glance over at my daughter. "I can't even begin to discuss it now, but later, when we do, there's going to need to be ground rules… lots and lots of ground rules."

"Well, that sounds inviting," says Mag under her breath with a roll of her eyes.

I pick up on a heavy sigh. "How do you know they aren't mostly for me?" I say. "The ground rules that is." I manufacture a slight chuckle.

She quirks an eyebrow at me and I can feel some of the tension fall away.

"And for the time being," I say, "you better get used to that grump at the front gate who just leered at us when we drove in. His name is Jorge!"

82

The next day I announce, over salt bagels with salmon cream cheese, that my number one priority is to buy a bed… yet again!

"If we're going to share this tiny place, I'm going to require my own space," I say. "And that, my dear, means I want my bedroom back! I hope that's what's on your list to Santa because it's what she's giving you this year."

"Sounds good to me."

"The process should go much quicker this time," I say, "as I've already seen what every store in Sarasota has to offer."

I run to put my face on and change tops. Meanwhile, still in her pj's, Mag grabs her iPad and starts surfing the web. By the time I come back out she has news.

"Macy's has a Macybed queen mattress set with a grand plush super pillowtop, and it comes complete with the bedframe. It's regularly $1,079 on sale for $639, but today there's an extra ten percent off on all online orders, making it $575 including free shipping. It can be delivered to the door and set-up in just three days." She smiles beaming, "That doesn't even figure in your gas savings from our not driving all over town. Where's your Macy's card?"

Amazing.

Now back in Ohio, Jack calls with exciting news.

"Before my leaving Nokomis to go back north, Frank told me he's decided to come to Cincinnati for Christmas this year. It will give him the chance to see where I live and also to meet my brother and his tribe."

"Oh goodness," I snicker. "Have you warned him about how fertile your brother is?"

"I just told him it's a little crazy at Christmas at their house since I have quite a few nieces and nephews. I kind of left out the fact that there's seven of them plus his wife."

"I'm actually thinking about going the whole nine yards while he's here and having a few friends and coworkers over for a small party. You remember Little Debbie from Procter, right? She's the one who left to start her own catering business last year. She's agreed to help me out with the appeteasers. If you were here, I'd sign you up to help as well. Any chance of you coming north?"

"Ha! Not *this* year," I say, and with that I brief her regarding the goings on of the last week with regards to my Maggie.

"I have to be honest," says Jack, "I was so excited when you two reunited, you'll never know. But full-time and under the same roof and with a soon-to-be-born baby, well... it just seems like you might be pushing it. Too much too fast, after so many years of having a relationship built on loss, pain and distance."

"Trust me," I say. "Don't think I haven't questioned the wisdom of this decision. But what was I to do? Turn my only daughter out on the streets along with my first grandchild? Mag swears it's only temporary, and somehow, I believe her. I think that helping her to get back on her feet just might help me to get back on mine. It's about damn time we both had a relationship based on love and healing!"

"Well, even though I think your choices might be questionable and a bit crazy at times," says Jack, "there's one thing I'm quite certain of. You've come a long way this last year, and it's good to have spent Thanksgiving with put-in-near the old you!"

"Put-in-near?"

"Blame Frank." She laughs. "Pretty soon ma'am this Cuban gal will be sayin' y'all!"

That evening after dinner, I suggest we take Mac for a walk and try to catch the sunset. "There's nothing like a little fresh air and a sunset to end the day. It helps keep things in perspective."

Maggie finishes putting the last of the plates in the dishwasher, places her hands on her hips, and arches her back to stretch. She stretches and moans in a manner that causes her inner porn star to accidentally come out.

I laugh out loud. "I'm guessing it's noises like those that got you in your current condition!"

Mag smirks. "I think you two better go ahead without me. Look at my swollen ankles. I need to put my feet up!"

On our way to the boardwalk, Mac and I stop for a moment to say good evening to Marilyn and perform our usual untangling of Tookie from her walker.

"You know, sweetie, you gave me so many of those 'Thanks for the Giving' leftovers that I just finished eating up the last of them tonight. They were delicious! Say, do you cook like that for your Christmas celebration too?" She has a playful glint in her eyes.

I assure her that if I do, I'll be sure to save some for her or, better yet, invite her over to dinner again. She says that sounds just fine and turns and aims back towards her condo.

"Remember, hon, I don't eat ham, the cloven hooves thing and your brussels sprouts gave me gas something terrible!"

We enter the boardwalk behind the Wilbanks and slowly walk while gazing out at the cove water and the jumping mullets amidst the rookery. Fluttering in slowly on the surrounding red and black mangroves are brown pelicans, cormorants, egrets, and a great blue heron all nesting down for the night. Suddenly an American kestrel circles the sky overhead in search of some prey.

Reaching the end of the walk, at the point where a fishing pier with benches is constructed, we take in the view of Little Sarasota Bay. A petite, middle-aged woman with a short curly 'do is seated on a bench.

She's wearing sunglasses, and lying at her feet is a black Labrador retriever. The dog lifts its head from the warm wood of the boardwalk and Mac gives two sharp yaps in reply.

"Well, hello there!" the woman says pleasantly. "I thought I felt somebody walking along the boards. Who do we have here?"

I find it odd that she continues to look forward and directly at the setting sun instead of in our direction. Maybe Mac does too because he gives another bark.

"My name is Liz, Liz Blum, and this talkative little fellow is my Scottie, Mac. He's extremely opinionated. Mind if we watch this beautiful sunset with you?"

"Why heavens, no! By all means come sit down." She pats the seat next to her.

"I'm Barb Lancer and my gal here is Susie," she offers up while reaching down to pat her dog's head. "She's not working right now if you'd like to pet her."

Unsure what she means, I also give Susie a pat, and tell her what a good girl she is as she smiles up at me with those big black Lab eyes.

"She's kind of small for her breed," I suggest.

"Oh, is she?"

We sit quietly watching the sunset, taking in the beauty of the moment.

"Oh look," I say after a few moments, "the white pelicans are gathering out on that sandbar over there!"

Still staring straight ahead she says, "I'm blind dear, but I would love it if you would see them for me."

Of course, she is blind. I feel like an idiot.

"See them for you..."

"Well, if you would be so kind as to describe in detail what you see, I can then watch with you through my mind's eye. You know, I can visualize it."

"Oh, I see." I cringe over my choice of words. "Uhm, I understand."

"I wasn't always blind, my dear. My sight slowly faded, and I didn't completely lose it until I was a sixteen-year-old girl. My mental concepts of shapes and colors may not be correct anymore, but they're mine and as real to me as any that you might see. Okay, now tell me what we're looking at!" She then takes hold of my right arm and settles back.

I'm not quite sure how to begin. "Well, pelicans are rather funny looking birds, they're big, very big and nothing like a regular bird like a cardinal. They look kind of prehistoric, like those big dinosaur birds."

"Pterodactyls!" she jumps in.

"Yes exactly!" I exclaim. "They have huge bills, long ones for scooping up fish, that when filled with their catch hang and sway like my grandmother's neck use to do when she was eating."

I look over just in time to observe Barb pulling at the sagging skin of her neck as she laughs aloud. "I believe it's referred to as 'turkey neck' my dear."

I continue hoping I haven't offended. "Their heads kind of look like little, old bald men when they look at you. These are white instead of the usual brown ones which actually look kind of grey to me," I add. "I've been told they only return to the Cove during the winter months."

Barb surprises me again. "I read that too!"

And I contemplate how to continue as the sun now approaches the rooflines of the high-rise condominiums on the Turtle Beach end of Siesta Key.

"The sun is a huge, perfectly round ball setting in the sky tonight. It's bright orange, that's it… it's the color and shape of an orange, only it's on fire. The peel of the blazing orange is a brilliant white, almost blinding." And then I pause, suddenly embarrassed, yet again, by my poor choice of words.

"Oh, please continue!" pleads the woman. "It sounds amazing!"

"All the trees and buildings on the distant island are turning black and becoming silhouettes. The rays of the sun are now hitting the bottoms of the clouds and turning them into gold. Let's see, the color of jewelry like wedding rings, like pirate coins, or the goose's golden egg. The tops of the clouds are purple, blue, and grey. They remind me of Elizabeth Taylor's eyes, periwinkles or morning glories and battle-ships."

Pausing to deeply inhale through my nose, I savor the pleasure to the senses of the evening's ocean air. After a moment I continue.

"Overall the sky reminds me of wisps of smoke coiling slowly from a once blazing, but now smoldering hot, campfire."

I look over and conclude that I must be doing okay as even in the fading light I can see the woman is beaming.

"The sun has disappeared completely below the horizon, and all the vivid golden hues are fading and becoming lighter in color. Now they appear as the light-yellow curls of a toddler's hair, a golden retriever's silken coat or an old sepia tone photograph of a farmer's fallow field.

I pause to take another breath and Barb simply sighs. "Oh my, oh my!"

"The color is all but gone now," I tell her. "And the clouds appear dark, grey and hanging heavily in the sky. Strangely, I've noticed this is the time when most people get up and leave. I've watched groups at the beach, that have been waiting for hours to see God hand paint the sky with color, pack up everything and head for their cars, or go inside their artificially lit condo's. All when the finale is yet to come!"

And right on cue, the purples and pinks start to come, kissing the bottom of each cloud and then streaming out their last bursts of color across the entire sky.

"It's magical... Oh!" I gasp, realizing I was lost in the moment. "I forgot to describe it in detail for you."

"Not only did you do a wonderful job, my dear," she says, while maintaining a tight embrace on my arm. "But I do believe that was possibly the most beautiful sunset I have ever seen!"

83

By now it's past twilight, and feeling genuinely concerned, I ask Barb, "May Mac and I escort you and Susie home? I'll worry about you walking as it's actually quite dark out here now."

I reach in my pocket and pull out a small Eddie Bauer flashlight. "I always carry this torch with me for walking around the Cove in the evenings."

Barb laughs, amused, as she stands up. "Liz, through these eyes the world looks just the same each and every day and at any hour of the day for me. It can't get any darker, my dear. Besides, you'll be putting Susie here out of a job as she's my eyes as well as my best buddy. That's what she does."

She brings out a guide dog harness that's been leaning unseen at the end of the bench and Susie allows her to easily slip it on her. Shining the flashlight on the fluorescent yellow sign attached to it I read Working Guide Dog – Please Ignore! And the moment the harness is in place, I can observe a total change in the dog's demeanor, as she is now all business.

"May I pet *your* dog?" Barb asks, "I've never seen a Scottie before." She continues bending over and chuckles. "Where the heck *is* he?"

"Scotties don't have legs." I jest. "Here, let me bring him up to your level."

I lift Mac up and she rubs her hands all over him from head to tail. Her delight is obvious.

"I never knew they were so short. And his hair feels so different from Susie's."

We part ways both agreeing we hope to see many more sunsets together.

Before we go in, Mac drags me to his tree for one final piddle. Then we cross the parking lot and aim for the front door. Inside we find Maggie curled up on the couch watching an old rerun of *The Golden Girls.*

"Thought I better see what life for us is going to be like from now on," she jokes.

I roll my eyes this time. "As long as I'm not Sophia."

"Not to worry," she laughs aloud. "You've got the part of Rose completely covered!"

"Gee thanks, *Blanche!*"

"Oh, I almost forgot," says Mag as she leverages herself up and goes to retrieve a message from the counter near where I keep my cell phone charging.

"I hope you don't mind, but your phone rang three different times, all coming from the same number and the caller ID was Dr. Stuart Robbins (Cell). I started to think it might be important, so I answered it. He wants you to call his office first thing in the morning, let the receptionist know who you are, and she'll put your call right through to his private line."

She hands me the message and I read it for myself, feeling a little dumbfounded.

"Is everything all right Mom? You look upset."

"Do I? No, I'm not upset, dear, I'm just a bit surprised that my physician would be calling at this time of night and slightly concerned that he wants me to call his office first thing in the morning."

I read the note one more time as if my eyes might see something written there this time that I didn't see before.

"I've only been to his office twice," I say. "Once shortly after I moved here and I was looking for a primary care physician, and the second time when I tried volunteering at the nursing home and had to have a Tdap vaccine. Did I tell you about my attempt at painting the nails of old ladies with Parkinson's disease? It's trickier than one might think."

"Maybe it's just a follow-up call to check on your health, or some test or lab results that finally came in," says Mag, in an attempt to comfort me.

"They haven't done labs since the blood work at my first visit," I say. "And what doctor these days calls just to see how you're doing?"

I start overthinking the entire thing while making busy work as I grab the Windex and a paper towel and just start wiping down everything.

"I must be dying!" I say it out loud. "And I'm never going to see the baby!" I blurt out in Maggie's direction. "I need the bathroom! QUICK, look in my purse and find your mother's pills!"

"Will do, *Dorothy!*"

<h1 style="text-align:center">84</h1>

The next morning, I anxiously wait for the doctor's office to open at eight am. I actually call twice prior to the office opening and each time get the recording, *If you are having an actual emergency please hang up and call 911. Otherwise, please call back during normal office hours!* The third time is a charm as the call is answered by the receptionist.

"This is Elizabeth Blum, B-L-U-M. I'm returning Doctor Robbins call from last night."

"Sure, thing Miss Blum. Please hold one minute, he's been expecting you."

I nervously walk into my bedroom and sit on the edge of the bed. *He's been expecting me?* I'm left waiting on hold while still second-guessing the nature of the call. About five minutes later he comes on the phone, friendly and bright.

"Why hello there."

"Hi Doctor Robbins, this is Elizabeth Blum returning your call."

"Oh, I appreciate that, and please call me Stu."

"Okay, uhm Stu," I stammer. "What's your reason for calling me… am I dying?"

He chuckles as he apparently thinks I'm kidding. "Heavens no, Liz, may I call you Liz?"

Which is followed by an extremely long and awkward pause by me, as I can't recall having ever been asked before by any of my doctors in Cincinnati if they could address me in such a personal manner. Hell, even my shrink called me by my proper name, Elizabeth, once we got past the Mrs. Blum phase.

"Sure… Stu, Liz will be fine." Now I question his intentions even more.

"Well, I have this sort of doctor thing," he starts in. "Actually, it's a kind of formal dinner and dance at the Ritz-Carlton downtown. Frankly… um, it's a holiday party thrown by the practice every year for the entire staff and their significant others. And… well, I just wondered, well Liz… would you be my date?"

Again, it's followed by complete and utter silence as I'm taken aback—firstly that my doctor is asking me out on a date, and secondly when I realize it's been well over forty years since anyone has actually done that.

Even over the phone line he senses the awkwardness. "I promise to practice proper physician–patient privileges the entire evening. And I won't check your pulse unless you want me to!" And then laughs at himself.

He continues by sharing the date and time and waits for my response. Finally, able to speak, I surprise myself with my answer.

"Sure Doctor, I mean Stu, I would love to go."

After hanging up, I quickly call Jack, dying to share the conversation.

She answers briskly. "Hello Liz? I'm in the car driving into work and expecting another call so make it fast."

"Oh my God!" I yell, "Wait till you here this."

I quickly recount the conversation in brief and then chastise myself for saying, *I'd love to go.*

"I think I sounded desperate! Why didn't I just say something like that might be nice, let me check my calendar?"

Jack clears her throat. "You're way overthinking it again, my dear. I'll call you later and we'll discuss this further, but whatever you do, don't have a panic attack and change your mind. It's about time you were seen out in public with a man. I can't continue being your date forever, you know. Plus, now that I'm with Frank, I believe that's called a ménage à trois. Bye, Love you the most!"

Coming out of the bedroom and glancing towards the lanai, I see that the glass slider and screen door have been pried open. Mike, head of the grounds crew, has advised me that my yard and patio projects have been pushed back till after season. It seems there are so many urgent work orders and requests being placed by the snowbirds that his employees have had to prioritize their tasks. It's starting to become clear to me that full-time residents just may be on the bottom rung of this communal hierarchy.

Yet somehow, and through the overgrown underbrush and my huge trees, I can see Maggie outback with Mac.

"How in the world did she get that damn door open?" I question. "I swear I've tried no less than twenty times to do it myself."

The dog is hiking his leg on the trunk of a good-sized magnolia and Mag appears to be talking with someone as she gesticulates, just like her mother, while conversing.

My daughter steps aside to say something to the dog, and my jaw drops in disbelief. I can't believe my own eyes.

There she is, the ghost woman!

Wearing a flowing white robe, skin as pale as new-fallen snow and long, white hair gently blowing in the breeze coming off the bay. She reaches out touching Maggie's belly, and I actually gasp wondering what kind of curse she might be placing upon my unborn granddaughter.

From my viewpoint it actually appears as if Mag is laughing. She turns around and starts walking in my direction. This, while the spirit retreats and seemingly floats amongst the shadows of the garden she so diligently tends. Then the specter simply fades through the open slider into the darkness of a supposedly uninhabited condo.

My heart is pounding wildly as Maggie and Mac make their way back into the lanai.

"What in the world do you think you're doing?" I plead. "Are you nuts?"

Maggie stands dumbfounded for a moment. "I really didn't think you'd mind my taking the dog out as he needed to go. And as for the door that you say is broken, it's actually just stuck. I think a little WD-40 might make it good as new again."

I sit down on one of the new wicker chairs now on the lanai and beg Mag to do the same. She lets Mac off lead, and as he scampers away, I begin telling her the tale that Marilyn shared with me about the dybbuks (or ghosts) haunting the Cove.

"Mom you already told me this," says Maggie with a roll of the eyes.

I then reiterate the warning that Vivian the palm reader gave us. "I don't want to scare you honey, but this place was built on an ancient burial ground, and I've actually seen yet another apparition in here named Mary. She's but a child that apparently wanders the grounds. By the way, when that spirit touched you, well... placed her hand directly on your belly what did she say to you?"

Maggie shakes her head with a slightly sarcastic grin.

"Mother... she said she remembers being pregnant, albeit many, many moons ago, and that she just loved each and every minute of it. She also said it was good to see younger people, like yourself, moving in here again and she also hopes I'll stick around long enough to come pay a visit with the baby once it arrives. And by the way, your ghost's name is Lynnea, but she prefers Lynn. She's lived here twenty years come January."

I sit there dumbfounded and taking it all in for several moments.

"Did that dear, sweet woman really call me young?"

85

It's now less than three weeks till Christmas, and the population of the Cove has more than doubled as the snowbirds continue their migration south in full force. Almost daily now, the news reports five car pileups involving an RV along their flight path of I-75. In fact, two different neighbors have returned to their condos which have stood empty all year. The couple to my left, Maynard and Evie, couldn't be nicer.

They're an interesting mix of cultures. He's a slightly stern speaking German cardiologist with a guttural accent. She's a vivacious Haitian woman, also with a medical office background, which is how they met. He's as pale as she is dark, his hair's thinning while hers is a head of thick and lustrous black curls. He's tall and thin while she's demure and curvy; he runs and swims while she reads and attends Pelican Cove University classes. It is a case of *opposites attract.*

They have invited me over for a little impromptu happy hour of wine and cheese twice now and I'm really feeling the need to reciprocate soon. While there, Evie doesn't hesitate to share numerous photo albums, showing off pictures of their children and grandchildren. She has every right to be proud as it seems when you mix a Central European with an island girl the genetic results are super models.

Above me, as they say, a couple of really 'strange birds' have perched. Beverly is from New York City and her boyfriend Vinny is from Hoboken, New Jersey. Maggie has started referring to them as the train wrecks! They are two extremely short, vociferous individuals who appear stuck in a psychedelic time warp. They have a penchant for wearing tie-dyed or hand-painted tee shirts and bejeweled ball caps. Each of them has to be hovering around eighty years old, yet they both sport colorful sets of tattoos and body piercings.

It's a bit hard talking face-to-face with Bev as she never wears a bra and the girls are now hanging somewhere around her waistline. And with Vinny it's even harder as the lech truly believes he is still God's gift to women. The entire time you're forced to speak with him you can feel him undressing you with his eyes. He smokes menthol Tiparillo cigars, and his smoker's breath is bad enough in a regular conversation, but when he leans in to whisper such lines as, "Hey there pretty little neighbor girl, how about some sugar for an old man?" it's absolutely repulsive.

Maggie broaches the subject of what we're doing for Christmas.

"Well," I say, "I guess the usual except I won't be going to New York City or you won't be coming to Cincinnati. I thought we'd go to Christmas Eve service and then out for a quiet dinner. How's that sound to you?"

"That would be fine," she says. "But I was talking more about decorations and a tree. It's a little 'Bah Humbug' around here. In case you haven't noticed the train wrecks upstairs have a virtual automated light show set up on their deck. Why, they've even wrapped the stair banister from up there in multi-colored twinkle lights that have proceeded into the bushes and are encroaching on your front porch."

"I did notice that the other night when Mac and I went out," I say. "Your point?"

"My point is even the Cove has wrapped all the lamp post along the roads in white twinkle lights. And I've even seen a few condos with porches decked in Chanukah blue and white, or at least they have a lit menorah in their front window. But this place... hell, it looks like the Grinch herself lives here!"

"Maggie you know darn well I haven't put a tree up since... well, since that last Christmas. We'll burn a few candles and watch *It's A*

Wonderful Life together. Maybe we could bake cookies? You'll see, it will be fine."

"Do you even still own decorations and ornaments?"

"Unbelievably, I moved absolutely everything that we have ever owned to this tiny little place. I didn't have the heart to go through it to condense it, and I couldn't fathom throwing anything away. Check out the office closet sometime, the majority of those boxes in there are crammed full of holiday trimmings."

After that she lets the subject drop, but over the next week I notice a simple strand of white lights has been placed around my front door. Later, an artificial pine wreath with pinecones, holly berries, and a red ribbon has mysteriously joined it. And lastly, I come home one afternoon to find a small Christmas tree, decorated with miniature ornaments and icicle garland, sitting on the credenza in my living room.

"It's beginning to look a lot like Christmas!" I announce smugly and then give Mag and the baby a big hug.

It's Friday, and tomorrow night, is my date with Doctor Stu (as I've started referring to him). Rummaging through the closet, I try on anything and everything, but nothing seems right. Maggie walks into the closet to ask if I want some tea.

"You have a spare maternity frock I can borrow for tomorrow night?" I ask. "God, I have nothing appropriate to wear to this thing!"

"Go slap on your lipstick and let's run up to the Sarasota Square Mall," suggests Mags. "We can get a cup of tea there, then do a little shopping."

We start at Macy's where my loving daughter announces everything that I pick out looks matronly. We next check out J.C. Penny's, avoiding Sears, and then hit the mall shops. I actually find a dress I like at New York and Company but decide to keep looking, as it would require new shoes and accessories to go with it.

Maggie keeps hounding me to try something younger and more *with it.*

"Unless you really think he wants to go out with his mother?"

She smirks.

Becoming tired and discouraged she marches me into rue21, and before I know it, I'm purchasing a bright red sequined party dress that I insist is cut two sizes too small for me.

"Admit it, Mom, you have great legs, for a woman your age, and there's nothing wrong with showing them off. Now let's go over to Victoria's Secret and get you some decent underwear to hold that top up."

On the way out of the mall we stop at the Bobbi Brown make up counter in Macy's, and Maggie makes me an appointment for a professional makeover at two o'clock tomorrow.

"What's that for?" I ask. "Oh, just a little trick I learned in New York when you have a casting call and can't afford to buy new make-up!"

The next day I shower and shave, and then my personal stylist takes over.

"Take a seat in that crazy swan chair of yours," she says and then proceeds to put my hair in curlers and then paint my finger and toenails in Jordana – Red of Hearts nail polish. When my hair feels dry, she asks, "Where's your stash of bobby pins?"

"I don't have many, but look in the drawer of my bathroom vanity."

She returns with an elastic ponytail holder and a handful of pins and proceeds to create a mile high 'coiffure' that she sprays heavily with hairspray. I try telling her about Jack's first date with Frank, and my doing her hair in the dark, but I'm so gasping for air from the over-spray fumes that I can only get half of the story out.

"Damn!" Maggie yells, looking first at the non-working grandfather clock, and then running into the kitchen to see the stove's timer.

"Quick!" she yells. "Put on a button-up blouse so we don't have to pull anything over your head. We have just twenty minutes to get you to the mall."

I do as I'm told as we dash out the front door.

"What about Mac?" I question. "He hasn't been out."

"He can hold it," She answers. "He just may have to cross his legs for a little while!"

Nearly two hours later we're back home where I stand questioning my judgment in the bathroom mirror.

"I look like Liza Minnelli," I exclaim.

"You look great," says Maggie, as she takes the dress off the hanger. "Change your underwear to the new red satin and lace numbers we got you and put the dress on. Call me when you're ready for the back to be zipped up."

In the bedroom, I reflect that I finally have the opportunity to wear my black lace Manolo Blahnik heels. That alone pleases me more than it should.

When I step out of the bedroom looking for assistance, Maggie's eyes light up.

"You look *hot!*"

"I'm not sure hot is a good look for a sixty-year-old soon-to-be-grandmother to have on her first date with her doctor whom she hardly even knows."

Now, concerned and nervous, I feel the need to FaceTime Jackie for moral support.

"Oh my goodness… did somebody run off and join the circus?" asks Jack, with nary a 'hello.'

"Very funny," I reply. "I'm calling for a boost of confidence and you're joking around."

"All right, all right… put the phone on speaker and have your daughter hold it out so I can get the whole effect. Perhaps you were just a little too close to the camera lens for me to really appreciate it. You know, like how your pores look like huge craters in those magnifying mirrors?"

Maggie does as told, and Jack requests for a scan from head to toe so she can get the total effect.

"Liz, turn around a few times!" Then. "Hand the phone back to your mother Maggie. We've got some work to do!"

"Liz, take the damn phone off speaker and listen up girlfriend."

I follow her orders as she starts right in.

"I want you to do exactly as I tell you, and don't argue with me. Wash that clown makeup off with soap and water and put your face on the same way you always do except for two things. Wear some mascara, even though you hate it, and use a little blush on those apples, but for God's sake don't overdo it or you'll look like somebody's grandma."

"I am somebody's grandma."

"Yes and for heaven's sake whatever you do please, please don't mention that on the first date!"

"I want you to brush your hair out and wear it like you always do. Then take that quarter of a yard of material off and give it to your daughter. She'll look super-cute in it after she drops the baby weight. What have you got on under it?"

I proceed to tell her.

"Now that sounds hot. I say go with it just in case… well, you know?" And she gives a kind of naughty snicker.

"Jacqueline Hernandez, I'm an absolute nervous wreck about carrying on a decent conversation with this man, and possibly having to dance with him," I say. "There's no way in hell he's ever going to get a glimpse at my underwear."

"That's what they all say!" She laughs, in a way that only she can. "Now, put on the pretty little beige number that you wore for Thanksgiving. It was overkill for a family dinner, but it'll be just perfect for this event. Keep the shoes you have on and accessorize simply. Less is more. Got it?"

"Got it!" I reply.

"Do as I say sweetie, and he'll be eating out of your hand. Let's face it, this guy has seen you crying and not looking your best in his doctor's office. He also knows you come with a tragic history and a bit of baggage. Yet, there's still something he sees in you or he wouldn't have asked you out."

"Maybe he was just desperate," I wisecrack.

"Stop that. You're a wonderful person and he sees that. Just be yourself and have a good time," says Jack, preparing to end the call. "Remember what you told me about going out with Frank, if nothing else comes of this at least you've made a new friend!"

The Way You Look Tonight

—Jerome Kern (1936)

86

From the moment he knocks on the door and hands me a corsage, he's nothing but sweet, considerate, and surprisingly funny.

"From the way the florist fiddled around making this thing, I'm guessing they aren't very popular anymore," he chuckles. "But I couldn't show up empty-handed, and giving you a bottle of wine might have been misconstrued as attempting to ply you with liquor. Although, as your doctor, I could have advised that red is good for your heart!"

"It's lovely," I tell him, and then proceed to pin it to the evening bag I'm carrying. "There, that's just the touch this plain, old black clutch needed to dress it up!"

"Speaking of dressing up," he says, "you're looking exceptionally lovely this evening, Liz."

And suddenly I can feel my face blushing at the unexpected compliment.

I'm immediately struck by the fact that I'm not accustomed to having a man open a car door for me, let alone chauffer me to my destination. Generally, I feel the need to always be in control of the situation in order to curb my anxieties. I'm taken aback that, somehow, I'm content allowing someone else take the wheel, so to speak. Perfectly timed to coincide with the end of yet another beautiful Sarasota sunset, he pulls his Long Beach metallic blue BMW Coupe under the portico of the Ritz-Carlton, in front of a splashing fountain. We valet park, and taking my arm, he escorts me into the lobby.

The interior lobby is breathtaking with polished marble floors, golden drapes, and shimmering crystal chandeliers reflecting in enormous gold-leaf mirrors. Taking center stage is a huge, magnificently executed gingerbread house. Reading the placard beside it we realize we are looking at an exact replica of John and Mable Ringling's Ca' d'Zan mansion, albeit six feet long, four feet wide and three feet tall.

"It's amazing what you can whip up with a little flour and sugar," quips Stu.

"Six hundred and fifty pounds of sugar, 350 pounds of assorted candy, 300 pounds of royal icing, and 250 pounds of fondant doesn't sound little to me!"

An elegant hand-painted sign positioned on a gilded easel advises, Suncoast Medical Group Holiday Affair – Grand Ballroom, and an arrow points the way.

The room is replete with distinctive iron and crystal chandeliers with matching wall sconces, while richly colored Irish woven carpets cover the floors and beautiful Italian fabrics adorn the walls. The tables are set with Waterford dinnerware—in the Lismore Lace gold pattern—paired with brocade linens and banquet chairs upholstered in a rich gold fabric. The stemware on the tables is a luxurious cobalt blue color, and simple seasonal centerpieces, arranged in Lennox Lady Anne crystal bowls, complete the scene. It's magical!

At the center of each table is a small piece of signage containing the names of each individual practice. Stu spies Beneva Family and steers me towards it. After brief introductions to various doctors and staff members, he suggests getting us a drink and excuses himself as he heads to the bar.

Returning, he appears to have a short clear beverage garnished with lime for himself; he hands me a glass of red wine.

"I take you for a wine drinker," he states assuredly.

A look must pass across on my face.

"Was I wrong?" he asks

"No, no… not at all. I'm just amazed how you could know that about me. I don't remember that being a question among all that 'new patient' info I had to fill out?"

He chuckles. "Actually, Liz, it wasn't really that hard, especially since there were two bottles of red wine on your bar, and I spotted another one in the kitchen."

A quartet begins playing holiday tunes, as servers start placing salads of baby arugula and port wine poached pear with Roquefort in front of each guest.

"Excuse me," I say to the young man as he places mine in front of me. "Is this salad already dressed?"

"Yes, ma'am, with a citrus vinaigrette and spiced walnuts. Would you prefer a plain one?"

"Might I get it on the side?" I request.

"Of course." And he picks up the salad plate and takes off quickly towards the kitchen.

I'm amazed at how comfortable the conversation around the table is and also how easy I find it to talk with Stu. He shares with me that he was married once.

"It was way back in med school, and we were just kids. We were more in lust than in love. Once I started my internship at Mount Sinai on Long Island, she packed up and moved back to Baltimore near Johns Hopkins where we met. Seems she couldn't put up with a doctor's hours."

I surprise myself by opening up and share how Scott and I met and about how fortunate we were to have traveled the world on the company's purse strings. He admits he has an affinity for Italy, much like myself, and we find out we have many shared experiences in Rome, Naples, and Venice to name a few.

The server removes the empty salad bowls and replaces them with a generous filet of poached swordfish with a side of baked polenta cakes and grilled asparagus covered with a tapenade cream.

"Excuse me," I whisper motioning with my index finger for the server to come closer. "I hate to be a bother but…"

"Would madam prefer the cream sauce on the side?" he interjects.

"Why yes, that would be lovely."

And again, he scurries off towards the kitchen doors dinner plate in hand.

After dinner an attractive, middle-aged black woman with spikey, white hair, wearing a silver sparkling gown, takes the dance floor.

"Good evening everyone, my name is Lady Jazz. I'll be joining the party." And she extends a hand towards the musicians, which encourages the crowd's applause.

"Like I said, I'll be accompanying these gentlemen with a few time-honored standards and your holiday favorites. Please, won't you join me on the dance floor?"

She breaks into a smooth "I'm Dreaming of a White Christmas," and as she strolls over to join the band on stage, couples leave their tables and begin filling the dance floor.

"Would you care to dance?" Asks Stu.

And after some contemplation I say, "Sure, thank you. However, I feel the need to warn you it's been a long time, so watch your toes."

"I'm definitely no Fred Astaire, and it's you who better be watching your toes my dear as I'm no featherweight." And we both take to the floor laughing.

The singer next belts out a fabulous version of "Fly Me to the Moon" after which we both leave the floor a bit winded and return to our seats. Waiting at our places are beautiful presentations of mango cream tarts with crème fraîche ice cream and lemon raspberry coulis. Seeing our server attentively standing by should his services be required, I motion for him to please come my way yet again. Attempting to second-guess me he picks up another dessert plate and a petite sauce pitcher and heads my way.

"Might I trade out madam's current dessert for this one with the sauce on the side?" he smiles proudly.

"Oh no, this is perfect just the way it is. I just wondered if you could package it to go?"

87

We spend the remainder of the evening alternating between dancing and sitting at the table swapping stories. Every now and again we acknowledge the others at our table and even catch on that, if we laugh when they laugh, they seem to believe we're actually following along with their conversations.

At one point, Stu asks me what brought me to Sarasota. I try my best to answer with my usual tales of family vacations and love of the beach. But surprisingly, Stu sees through me.

"But why here where there's still so many reminders of your husband and son? I understand needing to start over and leaving the past behind. But what made you pick here of all places?"

I think about it for a few minutes before answering. "I honestly don't really know. If I tell you I felt like someone or something was pulling me here, would you think me crazy?"

He gently takes my hand and looks into my eyes. "Liz, I think you're anything but crazy. A little quirky maybe, but you're not crazy. Now answer me this. If I tell you I think I've been waiting for you to get here, would you think me nuts?"

The evening eventually comes to an end and the ever-watchful server scurries over with a container advising. "I left the ice cream out for fear of melting!"

We bid our goodbyes to the few people remaining at the table before getting up to leave.

"Do you have a curfew?" asks Stu with a wry smile. "Or would you care to join me for a night cap under the stars?"

We make our way back to the lobby to what Stu advises is a newly opened restaurant named Jack Dusty.

"Good evening, two for a late supper?" asks the hostess.

"Yes, two, but we're just here for a drink. Is there something available outside?"

"Of course, Sir, Madame if you'll follow me."

She leads us out to an expansive terrace with waterfront views of the marina, and we're seated in Georgica rattan lounge chairs and the sumptuous environment is complete with comfortable decorative pillows and the ambiance of burning candles. Across the walkway from us is a two-sided gas fireplace framed with glass that adds just the right touch to the setting.

We take in the scene, framed by lighted palms, which includes the harbor and the Hyatt Regency across the way. We can also see various high-rise condominiums some of which have decorated their balconies with Christmas lights. In a few condos a tree can be seen glistening within.

The night is a bit chilly for Florida, and I suddenly become aware that I haven't thought to bring a shawl or a jacket. Observing me with my arms folded across my chest for warmth Stu stands up, removes his suit coat and places it on my shoulders. I can still feel the warmth from his own body heat and smell a hint of his spicy, woodsy cologne. I was first taken aback when we danced as I believe it to be the scent of Vétiver—the only fragrance Scott would ever wear.

"Thank you," I say, "But now you'll be cold."

"I'm fine," he responds. "My Latin blood runs on the hot side."

We both laugh aloud, but I can't help second-guessing that his statement may have had sexual overtones, and I'm suddenly well aware of my new underwear and how the waistband may have rolled. When the waiter approaches for our drink orders, I ask for a glass of red wine. The fellow begins spewing off a wine list that's a mile long and I attempt to interrupt him when he finally takes a breath.

"Honestly, just your house Cab Sav will be fine thank you!"

"And for you, sir?"

"I'll have a snifter of Rémy Martin."

We continue chatting in the same comfortable rhythm we had at the party. Most of it is friendly banter about favorite beaches, places to eat or comparisons of Baltimore versus Cincinnati. I inquire as to whether he actually has Latin blood and he advises me that his mother's family had escaped to Argentina during the war where she fell in love and married. Then at one point, he asks, "What synagogue do you go to? I worship at Temple Sinai on Lockwood Ridge."

"I've sort of been church hopping in hopes of finding a new place of worship. I think I may have found it at a chapel on Siesta Key. However, I also like spending one-on-one time with God on the beach. Sometimes a Sunday morning beach walk can do more for my soul than any sermon. And you have to admit, the ocean makes for one beautiful sanctuary."

Stu looks quizzical. "You mean you aren't Jewish? I mean your name… well, Blum. Well… I just took for granted. I'm sorry."

"Sorry?" I ask. "For what? For asking if I am Jewish? Or for my not being?"

And for the first time the entire evening there's an awkward long silence from him.

After a few sips of wine and an unrelated remark about the clear skies and stars out tonight, I finally have to ask, "Did you not notice me singing along with all the Christmas songs at the party? Or how, when we first came out here, I pointed out the Christmas lights on the buildings? Or, here's a big clue, what about the white lights strung around my front door and you had to notice our little Christmas tree in my living room?"

He chuckles and, after finishing off his brandy and setting the empty snifter firmly back on the table, states. "Guess I was hoping it might be a Chanukah bush!"

88

The drive home is cordial but nowhere near as upbeat and buoyant as the trip was going downtown. Glancing out the passenger side window I catch my own downhearted reflection as holiday luminosity goes speeding by. Believing I'm talking to myself I internally mutter, "Why does my doctor have to be Jewish?" To my surprise a reserved reply comes from Stu. "Well, actually it comes from my mother."

He insists on walking me to the door—and talk about awkward, we both stand there like two kids at our first sixth grade school dance. Neither are comfortable with direct eye contact, and the scene ends with a peck on my cheek, followed by a thank you for accompanying him this evening. He leaves me fumbling with my keys with no mention of a future phone call or further contact.

Mac runs to greet me at the door, and I bend to pat his head. "You're not used to me being out this late, are you boy? Did you wait up?"

The house is filled with the sounds of carols, and turning the corner into the kitchen, there stands Maggie. She has on a holiday apron that depicts a German dirndl laced up so tight that her *Fräulein's* appear to be popping out above her pregnant belly. Her face and hands are dusted with flour, and my kitchen counter and sink are an absolute mess.

I muster out a forced, upbeat, "Something smells good!"

"The last batch of Christmas cookies are in the oven now and all your holiday baking will be done!"

"Thank you dear, but I didn't even know I would be doing holiday baking this year."

"I read that list you left on your dresser from the doctor advising you to bake something and give it away. So I thought what better time than the holidays to do it? Remember when we were little how you would make us deliver your cookies to the neighbors?"

I am now totally flabbergasted. "You read my personal letter?"

Maggie's face turns from "Holly Jolly Christmas" to "You're a Mean One, Mr. Grinch," and she starts to tear up.

"I was just looking for some socks because my feet were cold. It was just lying there open and well, I was just trying to help."

Engendered by her condition, there comes a flood of tears, and I'm compelled to stand in the kitchen hugging her.

"Oh hey. No. It's okay. Everything's all right!"

The timer buzzes on the oven, and with a complete mood swing, she lets go of me.

"My cookies have to come out before they burn!"

I look down at my dress, and it's covered in tears and flour.

"And to think I made it all the way through dinner and an abundance of red wine without spilling anything on myself," I say. "Let me go change, and I'll help you clean this place up."

Passing through the living room on my way to my bedroom, I spy the coffee table has been cleared off and Maggie has started a Christmas jigsaw puzzle of the Coca-Cola Santa.

"Well I see you've done some additional rummaging through the storage boxes!" I call back in Maggie's direction.

"Yes! I had all but forgotten about this naughty apron of yours!"

Continuing towards the bedroom door, I stop dead in my tracks. Spinning around I see where she has stacked the coffee table magazines in the merry-go-round chair. Sitting directly atop is the tree man, penis erect, and I do a double take—I swear he's actually sneering at me. I know Maggie had to have touched the totem in order to move it.

I should have rid myself of you back when Marilyn cautioned me to, I think. *You better behave yourself!*

I wave a stern finger.

After the kitchen is put in order, and Mag is back looking for the straight-sided pieces of the puzzle border, I decide to give Jack a call.

"What the hell. Do you know how late it is?" she mumbles. "This better be good!"

She continues, voice cracking, sounding more like Brenda Vaccaro than Jacqueline. Looking towards the grandfather clock, I again realize I still haven't gotten it to work.

"Oh, my God Jack, what time is it?"

"You called me to find out what time it is?" she chastises. "Surely the clocks on your oven, microwave, computer still work?"

"I am so sorry," I say in my most sincere of tones. "I wasn't thinking when I called you. I just wanted to download regarding tonight's experience."

"I figured as much, but I expected to hear the details over my morning coffee," she says. "So, since I'm up now, let's hear it!"

I proceed to share the evening's experience including all its splendor and positive moments.

"Unfortunately, at the end it took an ugly turn."

"You didn't tell him you're going to be a grandmother, did you?"

"I believe I mentioned that before we even parked the car!" I joke.

"No, it seems the good doctor mistook me for Jewish. My name, the nose, my idiosyncrasies', Pelican Cove… who could blame him?"

"That's a deal breaker for him?" Jack asks.

"Apparently," I advise. "He lost me totally when he started telling me that he has 613 mitzvot to live by to my mere list of ten!"

"What's a mitzvot?" questions Jack.

"I'm guessing it's like a commandment?" I reply. "Either that or it's a Jewish reference to David Letterman's top ten list."

I go on proclaiming all the bright spots of the evening and how compatible we seemed to be.

"I couldn't believe how comfortable I was and how easily we were able to talk to each other. Religion is an important factor in my life too.

And it would be nice to share the same belief system with someone. However, I was simply at the beginning of the *let's become friends* phase, and apparently he is looking for a life partner."

"Well, Mrs. Robbins *does* have a certain ring to it."

"Sure," I say. "I'm guessing his first wife thought so as well!"

We end the call promising to talk over the holidays.

"Give my love to Maggie!" she says.

"Yes, and mine to Frank."

89

Maggie is startled awake by the warm sensation between her legs and under her bottom. She feels her panties and realizes they are wet. Swinging her legs over the side of the mattress, she does her best to roll the bulk of her pregnant belly out of bed. Feet on the floor, she switches on the bedside light and is relieved to see it's either urine or water and not blood. She slips off her nightgown and stands there naked and confused.

"Mom?"

Fearing she's perhaps ruined her new mattress she strips the bed and carries the wet sheets and sleepwear towards the bathtub.

"Mom! Can you hear me… Mom?"

And then it hits her, excruciating pain and cramping of the abdominal muscles. Doubled over she drops the bedclothes and sits on the toilet lid as she lets out a scream. Clutching her belly, she whimpers through the tears

"Mother, where are you? Dear Lord, please help me God!"

After another wave of pain, Maggie realizes she's in labor. Cramping shoots from her abdomen to her lower back. This is followed almost immediately by the sensation to push.

"Good God! Mom, I need you *now!*"

She slides to a squatting position using the toilet to keep her balance. The urge to bear down is even more intense as the duration between labor pains gets closer.

She lets out a scream of pain. Panic has her.

"Help!"

Unable to see past her stomach she feels between her legs and realizes she is touching the wet and slippery top of her baby's head. Oddly, her thoughts turn to wondering if the child will have dark hair like her father. Bearing down she uses every muscle to push, while continuing to cry out for Liz. She feels nauseated and dizzy as she gives one last push, and out slides the baby covered with a mixture of blood and vernix onto the sheets she's dropped on the bathroom floor.

Crying from a mixture of pain, joy, and relief, she wipes at her eyes with the back of her hands as she lowers her bottom onto the coldness of the tile floor while still attached to the newborn by the umbilical cord. Motherly instincts kick in as she realizes that the baby is not moving or crying. Becoming panic-stricken, she starts wiping frantically at the cheesy like covering on the baby, especially her face and head. Maggie then abruptly stops what she's doing and lets out the most earth-shattering scream yet.

Nooooo!

She stares in disbelief at her daughter's face, which appears to be a combination of cork like material and tree bark. The top of the head is covered with algae, lichens, and moss—resembling the complex environment of a forest floor. The baby's ears are formed from basidiomycete mushrooms, like ghost fungus, and her nose an apparent bracket fungus. The child's mouth is but a mere fissure in the bark, thus explaining the lack of sound.

The newborn stirs, and its limbs begin to shudder. Her would-be hands open revealing appendages covered with tiny buds that begin unfurling displaying spring green colored miniature leaves. The seedling then branches out and, reaching towards the bathroom light, appears to take in its first breath via the stomata on the surface of its compound leaves.

Wishing to put distance between herself and the plant, Maggie pushes herself backwards, scooting across the floor towards the bathroom door. Unfortunately, due to the cord that attaches mother and child like a diligent root system, she does nothing more than drag the life form along with her.

Labor pains and contractions—mere aftershocks now—seem to be further triggered from physically pulling the creature along by the cord. Wishing to separate herself from the monstrosity, Maggie spies her curling iron on the vanity above, still plugged into the wall socket. It takes several attempts at reaching to retrieve it, but eventually she has it in her grasp and turns it on extra-hot. She squeezes open the spring clamp and snaps it down on the umbilical cord. The smell of burning wood, like a slightly damp morning campfire, is unmistakable as she burns herself free of the baby.

Moments later Maggie expels the placenta and the accompanying blood and bodily fluids flood the floor.

90

I wake up and squint through my left eye at the alarm clock on the nightstand. It's a quarter to six. The dog.

"What the hell's wrong with you, Mac?"

He is grumbling loudly and sniffing at the bottom of the door.

"Fine… I'll take you out to pee!" I say, dragging my body out of the bed. Being up later than I have been in years, and consuming more alcohol and carbs than usual, had apparently placed me in something of a food coma.

Still half asleep and functioning in a mental fog I pull on my white spa robe and search for something to put on my feet. Suddenly there's an ear-shattering scream followed by aggressive barking from Mac, the likes of which I've never heard. I dart through the door and sprint across the living area heading towards the guest bath where I see light beaming out from underneath the closed door.

Mac is close on my heels, still producing low guttural growls, as I swing the door wide open. On the bathroom floor is a pile of sheets and atop them is what appears to be Maggie's nightgown. The toilet seat is up and inside the bowl the water appears red in color, the color of blood! Various cosmetics are knocked over on the vanity top and my daughter's plugged in curling iron appears to have been knocked into the running water of the bathroom sink.

"Mom!" Maggie's voice from the bedroom.

I race in to find Maggie naked on the bed and in the throes of an apparent nightmare. She says something I can't make out.

"Maggie, Maggie, wake up. Mother's here, wake up!"

Tossing and turning frantically while seemingly trying to push her pillow away she opens her eyes and wildly screams.

"No, no, no getaway get away…"

Eyes still wide with fear as tears stream down her face, Maggie slowly stops fighting the unseen evil and sits up in bed. I take off my robe and wrap her in it as she clutches me.

"Oh God, Mom, I just had the worse dream of my life!"

She frantically feels her belly and is relieved, at least for the moment, to find she's still pregnant. When she realizes she's naked and the bed stripped a fresh wave of horror washes over her.

"Oh no… Mom, what's going on?"

"I'm not exactly sure what took place," I say, trying to remain calm for her sake. "But the bedclothes and your nightgown are on the bathroom floor."

I see a bit of blood on the mattress cover. "I think you're spotting, Mags? Do you remember getting up and using the toilet last night?"

"I… what? No. The dream…"

"That's what it was. It was just a dream. Why don't you put on something comfy and stretch out on the living room couch, okay? I'll quickly gather stuff up in the bathroom and come out and sit with you and you can tell me all about it."

Five minutes later there is a load of laundry going, Mac has done his business outside, and I am sitting with Maggie listening to her memory of the dream that had so upset her. It upsets me too, but I manage to keep that to myself.

"Other than upset and shaken how are you feeling? I mean, are you cramping or uncomfortable?"

"I feel fine," she responds. "However, I'd feel a lot better if the baby would kick or move."

"I can take you to Sarasota Memorial if—"

"No that's okay. Let's give it a moment," she says. "I really could use a calming cup of decaf chai tea right now."

"If it's a matter of money," I say (for I know Maggie doesn't have health insurance), "I can cover it. I don't want that to be an issue."

"I have no intentions of us becoming a financial burden to you," she says. "But I guess I will need to find a doctor near you at some point soon."

Going into the kitchen, I put the tea kettle on and take the moment to call Stuart's private number even though fearing the moment might be a bit awkward. It rings twice before he picks up.

"Hello?"

"Stu? This is Liz. I apologize for calling at such an early hour. I'm sorry if I got you up."

"Actually, I was up and about to go out for my morning run. You sound a bit upset, Liz, is everything all right?"

I share the details of Maggie's condition with him, and he insists that I bring her in at eight when the office opens. He says he'll examine her, to make sure her vitals check out, and then ask his associate, Doctor Taylor, a female OBGYN, to do a quick consult.

"She owes me a favor anyway," he chuckles.

"Thank you so much, Stu. That means a lot to me," I say. "I guess I owe you a favor now too."

"Not at all." He states and then after some hesitation. "Just give me the chance to apologize for the way I acted last night by having dinner with me this Saturday and we'll call it even-steven!"

These Dreams

— Heart (1985)

Songwriters: Bernie Taupin / Martin Page

91

I'm relieved when Stu advises me that all Maggie's vitals are exactly in line for a pregnant woman entering her seventh month. I'm further comforted by the fact that Doctor Taylor says the baby is just fine and that Maggie may have simply been over doing it the last few days, moving around boxes of Christmas decorations and baking holiday treats to all hours of the morning. She's been prescribed a few days of bed rest and ordered to keep her feet up.

She's also agreed to accept her as a new patient and deliver the baby. Maggie is relieved that the doctor has also advised her that, if we work out a payment plan in advance, she will accept an uninsured cash discount for her services, but that we will still have to work out the hospital billing with them directly.

Back home and snuggled up on the couch with Mac and *Miracle On 34th Street* playing on TV, Maggie easily dozes off. I make my way to the bedroom where I remove a pair of Sperry Topsiders from their shoebox and place them on the closet floor. I then go to the kitchen to retrieve a large set of mint-green Tupperware salad tongs. Returning to the living room, I set the box atop Santa's puzzle face on the coffee table and turn to face the little demon.

Even now, defiantly situated on top of the stack of magazines in the chair stands the totem… still erect, still grinning, still staring with a malevolent glint in his eyes. The only physical difference is the appearance of a carmine colored substance, possibly dried blood, on the figure's hands and genitals. I take the tongs and, before squeezing them around his tree trunk body, I look towards the heavens. *Please, dear God, protect me!*

I grasp the totem, place it in the box, and quickly fit the lid on top. Carrying it to the kitchen, I find a roll of packing tape and proceed to wrap the tape around the box several times, in both directions. I then carry the box back to my bedroom closet and return it to the exact shoe nook from which it had been taken.

You stay put until I decide what to do with you. Marilyn warned me that I needed to return you back from whence you came, and according to the old, cowgirl shop owner, you came from Spanish Point.

I switch off the closet light and shut the door tightly behind me.

With Maggie napping and the totem safely stored, I figure that now might be a good time to pass out the Christmas cookies as the holiday is a mere four days away. Since I wasn't planning on giving out cookies, I haven't purchased any containers in which to place them. I suddenly remember seeing a packet of lunch bags down in the cabinet where I keep napkins and paper plates.

Counting out a dozen bags, I look through the junk drawer for scissors and a hole punch. Going to the spare room, I rummage through the holiday boxes until I find a roll of red, green, and white curling ribbon. Returning to the kitchen, I fill each bag with an assortment of cookies and fold over the bag top. Punching two holes horizontally about three inches apart in the flap, I begin threading the ribbons in one hole and out the other. I tie them in a bow and then scrape the scissors along each of the strands causing them to curl festively.

Standing back, I admire my work but decide I need to take a red Sharpie and write *Merry Christmas from the Blums'* on the sacks. After writing the first one, it dons on me that perhaps *Happy Holidays* would be a better sentiment, considering my neighbors' varying religions. By now Maggie's awakened from her catnap, and she gives her approval of my handiwork as she shuffles to the fridge for ice water.

I pick up two of the bags. "I'm starting out with the next-door neighbors, then going to the condo just past theirs where Marilyn lives. When I get back, I'll do the latent hippies upstairs, although they'll probably be disappointed they're not laced with pot, and the remainder I'll likely drive through the Cove to deliver later."

Knocking on my neighbor's door Maynard answers with his German accent. "Vell, hallo there, Lizzie. How is you, and von't you comes in?"

I thank him and enter the condo where he offers me a seat at the dining room table.

"Evie she be oust mit da shoppings. She'll be saddened that she misses you!"

I offer up my small parcel and bid him a Happy Holidays. "It's not much, but hopefully you'll enjoy the cookies my daughter Maggie has made."

In front of him lies a block of wood and various carving tools, mallets, and chisels. Shavings of wood litter the tabletop and several curls have found their way to the ceramic tile floor.

"What are you working on?" I ask. "It looks lovely."

"Since me hands are no longer those of a young man, and I be unable to perform de surgery, I have to find somethings to keep them busy. De vood carving seems to fill de bills." And he gives a jolly chuckle.

He proceeds to hand me the handwritten story of the scene he's carving of Saint Nicholas and Krampus, a horned monster with a whip.

There seems to be little doubt as to his true identity for, in no other form is the full regalia of the Horned God of the Witches so well preserved visually. Krampus travels around Central Europe preceding a child's visit from Saint Nick. His sole purpose is to scare the misbehaved children so badly that they soon become good ones. On his misshapen back he carries a woven pine bough basket in which to throw the misbehavers and carry them away to his cave and later to be eaten.

I quickly realize that my jaw must be down on the table as the story seems a bit gruesome, and in extreme contrast to our North Pole visions of a jolly Santa Claus and his hard-working elves.

"That's quite a tale."

"Ja, but it kept me in line as a youngster!" And again, he gives a raucous chuckle.

I ask him to give my best to Evie and excuse myself.

"I need to keep making my deliveries, or the cookies will be stale by the time people get them. I know our neighbor Marilyn is a talker so that won't be a quick visit either."

And this time I initiate the laughter, but quickly become aware, I'm completely alone.

Maynard sets down his tool and mallet on the table and stands up. "Vats dis you say?"

I repeat my statement and my observation and it clearly strikes a chord with him.

"Has you seen Marilyn yourself?"

"Why yes, of course I have. All summer and fall I spent my time helping her and Tookie become untangled from his lead around her walker and bringing her occasional meals and treats. Many an early morning we walk and talk our way around this small block of the Cove."

He stands there obviously dumbfounded and thinking hard of what to say next.

"What is it?" I ask. "Has something happened to her that I'm not aware of?"

He suggests I sit down again and looking me directly in the eyes says in a very enunciated manner, "Marilyn vas a dear und vonderful neighbor to us. Sadly Liz, she died of a heart attack on board a plane to Israel."

I am shocked. "When? How? I just talked to her a few days ago."

Obviously feeling almost as confused as I, Maynard takes the seat across from me.

"Abouts three years ago my dear. Ja, abouts three years."

92

Stunned, I make my way back home and Maggie's intuitive instincts pick up on something right away.

"What's the matter with you?"

"I don't know what to say. Apparently, I've been feeding a ghost! You've seen my neighbor Marilyn and her tiny little dog, haven't you?"

Maggie thinks for a moment. "Is that the tall blonde elementary teacher with Nellie, the cute white dog that wears ruffled dresses? The athletic woman with the cute grey haircut that jogs, bikes, and walks a shih tzu called Quincy? Or the skinny, diminutive woman that drives the silver convertible, waves like a prom queen, and walks that prissy footed little Chihuahua. Either she or the Chihuahua is Ginger and the other is Maryanne—I can't remember which is which but I always think of Gilligan's Island.

I shake my head. "How in the heck do you know all those people?"

"Well, whenever I take Mac out, it seems he and the baby bump just brings them out of the woodwork. You really are surrounded by a lot of nice people, Mom. Except *those* two," she says pointing up. "What the heck is all the stomping noise about up there all the time? I swear for two little people they must be wearing some extremely heavy diving boots or something. So now tell me, what's this you say about nourishing a phantom?"

I steady myself against the kitchen counter.

"While I was at our neighbor Maynard's house giving him his Christmas cookies, I mentioned I was going to Marilyn's place next to

387

deliver hers. He got this surprised look on his face and then confided that she had died three years ago on a plane to Israel. I told him about how I've been keeping an eye on her and taking her meals for months now. Hell, I've even picked up doodies after her damn little dog! He just acted as surprised as I and tried to console me."

"Hold on, wasn't it this Marilyn who advised you that your backyard neighbor Lynn was a ghost?"

I nod distractedly. "Sure," I say, "what are you getting at?"

"Well, just maybe, she was confused over which of them was the dead one."

Picking back up the bag of Christmas cookies I had dropped on the counter with the other ones I head for the door.

"Where are you going now?"

"Well there's only one way to settle this thing," I state. "I need to visit Marilyn."

Once in front of her condo, I open her screen door and knock. After a few minutes I rap harder and louder. Finally, I pound thunderously while calling out her name.

"Marilyn... Marilyn, it's Liz. Are you in there?"

Even after hearing Maynard's story, I have visions of her laying helpless on the floor somewhere. I step over to her kitchen slider and attempt to peek between the vertical blinds, but they are pulled tightly shut.

Weren't these wide open the last time I was here?

It suddenly dawns on me that I could have just called her since I have her phone number on my phone. I scurry back down the road and over the bridge and, bursting through the front door, head to the charger on the counter.

"Damn!" My iPhone is not there, and I suddenly realize the last place I remember seeing it was in my purse.

Maggie jumps to her feet when she hears the door slam against the entry hall wall.

"What's up now? You act like you've seen a ghost."

"Not yet I haven't. She won't answer the door!" I call back while entering my bedroom and rummaging through my purse. Unable to locate the phone I dump my bag out on the bed.

Et Voilà!

Swiping through the contacts, I come to Marilyn's name and hit call. The phone rings and rings before going to voicemail.

"Hello... Oh yes, this is the Spitznogle residence. We can't get to the phone right now. Please leave us a message after the recording machine thing beeps.... <Say goodbye Marilyn...> Goodbye!... I think I did it Morty... should I just hang up now? <oy vey>" BEEEEEP

Trying not to laugh.

"Marilyn this is Liz. I'm a bit worried about you since I knocked and knocked at your door and you didn't answer. Please give me a call back... Oh, and I have Christmas or uh I mean *holiday* cookies I wanted to give you!"

When I end the call Maggie is standing in the doorway.

"Let me get this straight. You just left a voicemail for a dead woman, letting her know we baked something for her?"

I drop the phone back in my purse and start collecting up the rest of the debris from my bed.

"Yes, sweetie, but we haven't confirmed that she's actually dead yet and it is the holidays!"

93

Maggie returns to her place on the couch and sits Indian style. "Mom, are you honestly going to tell me that you find Pelican Cove and all these strange goings-on normal? Heck, I've only been here a few weeks, and it's made my top ten list of America's strangest places."

"Oh sweetheart, try to remember you're in Florida. There's always an odd story on the news taking place in this state. Why remember the other day on *Good Morning Suncoast* when that anchorman, Don what's-his-name, advised that an eighty-year-old North Port woman was outside feeding her birds and was startled when she looked inside her house and saw a shirtless man standing in her kitchen window trying on her brassiere?"

Maggie rolls her eyes as I continue.

"Or what about that Walmart store in Tampa where the dad was waiting in line to renew his hunting license for the black bear hunt while his wife gave birth in his pickup? I can't believe they have three other kids who were watching! You can't make this stuff up, honey!"

"I'm talking more about all the supernatural things, Mom. The ones that you, Jack, and heck all of us have experienced in this place. That disappearing Mary girl, getting felt up by trees, the bad dreams, and obviously the grinning little man with the huge pecker! Heck, the Florida crazies are a whole different story that pale in comparison!"

Upset, I reach for Marilyn's cookies and begin feeding my angst.

"You realize, don't you, that now I either have to skip one of my neighbors, or you have to bake more cookies? Damn, these are really good!"

"I say we buy bakery cookies from Publix and repackage them," says Mag, without even looking away from the television. "Heck, if you add a little frosting and sprinkles to them, nobody will be the wiser."

I grab another cookie out of the bag and make my way to the back slider on the lanai. I struggle again trying to pull it open.

"I have no idea how you ever opened this thing."

I hear a moan come from the couch, and soon she's standing beside me.

"Move it, old girl, and let a younger woman give it a try."

She grabs the handle and tugs making a low *umph!* Then she tries it again. She pauses, looks at the handle and then flips the lock. Giving me a look, very similar to Mac's evil eye, she simply slides the door open.

"How in the world did you ever get that thing to slide so easily?" I ask.

"You never did get any WD-40 like I told you to, so I used extra virgin olive oil with a little aged balsamic, we might be able sell the stuff!"

"I need a little fresh air." I make my way down what semblance of a path there is through the growth. "I say we make dinner easy and order Hungry Howie's pizza when I get back."

"Can we get a veggie with extra green peppers and onions on Cajun crust?"

"Y'know, pregnancy and heartburn go hand in hand—or they did for me anyway." Then I smile. "Not to mention the fact that indigestion can cause bad dreams."

Once outside I look over the backyard and again reflect on how lovely this could be if they ever build my patio. It would be a great setting to dine alfresco or perhaps sit and sip a glass of red wine.

Maybe I can even have a grill?

I decide to mosey my way down the trail towards the back of Marilyn's condominium in hopes to get a little look-see inside.

Making my way through the pines, I quickly notice that the rear of our units are full of pinecones and think in terms of quick and free seasonal wreath or decoration. *I need to remember this for next year.*

The path weaves through a small dense forest of areca palms until opening up behind Maynard and Evie's patio. I'm in awe as the setting is replete with table and chairs, a gas grill, and a chaise lounge. The scene is only made more splendiferous by the pots of brightly colored annuals in full bloom placed strategically here and there.

My God. How can these people live next to my unkempt garden and untrimmed trees covered in Spanish moss? Dear Lord, they even have decorative candles… and what are those, actual garden steppingstones?"

Moving further through the rear of their yard, I come to a large oak hung with various planters of blooming orchids. The array of sizes, shapes and colors are bewitching.

Approaching the edge of Marilyn's area, the scene suddenly matches more the look of my yard, only it includes a vacant patio, null and void of furnishings. I view the sets of glass sliders that run the length of this portion of the house only to find that, here too, the vertical blinds have been pulled shut. I figure *what the heck* and try knocking and calling her name out yet again.

I suddenly become aware of music. The sound is coming from somewhere in the direction of the upstairs condo, one unit further down. The male voice singing sounds despondent or melancholy in tone, yet hauntingly beautiful and familiar.

"When I was a young man and never been kissed
I got to thinking it over what I had missed.
I got me a girl, I kissed her and then
Oh lord, I kissed her again.
Oh, Ohhh, kisses sweeter than wine,
Oh, Ohhh, kisses sweeter than wine."

I'm compelled to follow the tune in hopes that perhaps this person may be able to shed some light on what may have happened to our mutual neighbor Marilyn.

Blocked from view by an entanglement of Carolina allspice trunks and their offshoots that have grown to be some nine feet high is a steep set of rear steps.

"I asked her to marry and be my sweet wife,
And we would be so happy the rest of our lives.
I begged and I pleaded like a natural man,
And then, oh lord, she gave me her hand.
Oh, Ohhh, kisses sweeter than wine,
Oh, Ohhh, kisses sweeter than wine."

Looking up there must be some eighteen open runners to the top step. At the summit is a screened in porch, or lanai, with a single screen door for entrance. I pause at the base of the stairs for a moment, taking in the scent coming off the sweet-smelling shrubs. There's something reminiscent of the smell of my grandmother's dresser drawers from childhood about them.

"I worked mighty hard and so did my wife,
Workin' hand in hand to make a good life.
With corn in the field and wheat in the bins,
I was, oh lord, the father of twins.
Oh, Ohhh, kisses sweeter than wine,
Oh, Ohhh, kisses sweeter than wine."

I begin climbing the steps and then pause again, about a quarter of the way up, to listen as the melody continues.

"Our children they numbered just about four,
They all had sweethearts knockin' at the door.
They all got married and they didn't hesitate;

I was, oh lord, the grandfather of eight.
Oh, Ohhh, kisses sweeter than wine,
Oh, Ohhh, kisses sweeter than wine."

From this vantage point, all I can see is the very top of a thinning head of gray hair that appears to be nodding in time with the music. Not wanting to interrupt I stand my place waiting for the song's completion.

"Now that we're old, and ready to go,
We get to thinkin' what happened a long time ago.
We had a lot of kids, trouble and pain,
But, oh lord, we'd do it again.
Because she had, kisses sweeter than wine,
Oh, Ohhh, kisses sweeter than wine."

There's the hallow thump sound and accompanying string vibrations that are made from an acoustic guitar being set down too roughly on a hard surface. It's followed by the sound of a canned beverage being popped open and seconds later a long drawn out 'Ahhhhhhhh!' followed by a belch.

"Hello? Is somebody up there?" I ask even though the answer is obvious.

"Who the hell are you?" The voice is rather gruff and sounds nothing like the harmonious one that was singing just moments ago. I now hear the flipping sound of a lighter and can see smoke billowing up above the gray head.

"I'm a neighbor from a few doors down, and I just wondered if I could have a word with you?"

Sniffing at the air again I note it smells much more herb like, not tobacco, up here.

"Well if it's about the damn music, tough shit. It's before ten p.m., and I can play anything I want." And that's followed by a raucous coughing fit. "And lady, if it's the smokin', then screw you because as per the frickin' Pelican Cove *Rules We Live By,* I can smoke like a chimney in my own damn place!"

Startled by the crude response, I take several more steps up in an attempt to make eye contact. There, seated in a hanging papasan chair next to a pyramid of empty beer cans, sits an extremely thin and wrinkled, older man with long gray hair and smoking a marijuana cigarette.

"Oh, excuse me!" I gasp as the most startling thing about the scene before me is he's totally naked. "I'll just be going!"

I continue and as I'm about to turn and go he uncrosses his legs, leans forward placing his hands on his knees and with feet flat on the floor it leaves absolutely nothing to the imagination.

"Hey, what's the hurry baby? Care for a beer?"

I turning my back to him and preparing to descend the steps. "I'll need to take a rain check."

As I continue down, he calls after me "What's your name?"

"Liz, Liz Blum," I say and then, out of habit. "What's yours?"

Hearing the chain on the chair squeak, and then the sound of bare feet slapping on tile, I take for granted he's now standing at the screen door and looking down at me.

"Tiger!" he says, emphasizing the T, and then gives an exaggerated growl. "You can just call me Mr. T."

I stop, still keeping my back to him. "Is that your real name?"

"Hell no!" He laughs. "That's just what Pete dubbed me when I was playing with the Weavers. It kind of stuck with me for life."

"Well... Mr. Tiger, uhm sir, I was just wondering if you knew our neighbor Marilyn? She has a little dog named Tookie."

He hems and haws for a moment. "There's one hell of a lot of you old ladies with dogs around here, Liz. In fact, if I'm not mistaken, I believe you have that yappy little black one? You'll need to be a little more specific than that."

I describe both her and her tea-cup poodle in great detail, including the housecoats and walker. All the while contemplating in the back of my mind how this long in the tooth and naked hippie just called me an old lady.

"Never seen her out back… ever," he says. "But I've definitely seen her walking down Pelican Cove Road numerous times before. It's usually around dusk, but shit, I'm never up before noon."

"So, you have seen her?" I ask excitedly since I take that as a confirmation that Marilyn is real.

"Sure thing, Babe, but I have to tell you, it's been a long, long time!"

94

Walking back through the pleasant-smelling shrubbery, I hear him call down to me.

"Come on up anytime you're cutting through back here, Liz. But next time bring a six-pack and I'll roll us a fat boy! Ya hear?"

Always the girl scout I reply, "Sure thing. Thank you very much!"

Back home, I open the slider and Mac comes running and barking to see who's breaking in.

"It's okay, boy," I say. "It's just Mommy. And by the way… you're officially now known as the yappy one!"

"Feel better after some fresh air?" asks Mags, still in the same spot on the couch.

"If you like the smell of cannabis mixed with grandma's potpourri, then yes."

I share the Tiger experience, and after us both cracking up, we decide this goes more in the weird Florida category than the 'Supernatural' one.

"Was he honestly stark raving naked?" asks Maggie still laughing.

"I saw more of that neighbor than I've seen of any other neighbor or care to see again!"

"Was it actually more?" She jokes pursing her mouth in a self-satisfied smirk.

"Well, yes it was… but do realize, my dear, your mother is only working from memory!"

My phone begins playing "By the Seaside," and I dash to get it.

"Hello, this is Liz." Then, because I hadn't taken the time to check the caller ID. "Marilyn is that you?"

"No, it's me, Liz, Stu. I guess you are expecting a call, I hope I'm not a disappoint."

"Oh… Stu, why not at all," I stammer, not quite prepared to speak to him. I find myself straightening my clothes and checking out my reflection in the microwave oven door.

"I just wanted to make sure we were still on for tomorrow night."

"Tomorrow night?" I say all the while thinking, *You're not FaceTiming with him. Stop fiddling with yourself.* "Why, what's tomorrow night, Stu?"

I hear him take a breath as he seems to be gathering his words.

"I thought we had a date for Saturday night. We made it at the time your daughter came into the office for me to check her out when she was… well, when she was having some spotting. I had asked for the opportunity to make it up to you for my bad behavior on our last, well technically I guess our first date."

"Oh, Stu, I'm so sorry but I totally forgot about it. What with everything going on with Maggie at that time I'm afraid it totally slipped my mind. I can't believe that I didn't put it on a Post-it note or add it to my calendar. Heck, I have to write everything down anymore."

"Actually, knowing a little bit about how you are, that's why I called to check. Hopefully you're still willing and able to give me another chance?"

Just then my phone starts vibrating indicating another call is coming in. This time I look, and the screen name reads Marilyn – Cove Neighbor. It also asks if I want to accept or ignore the call.

"Oh Stu, I hate to do this to you, but I have another call that I have to take. I'll phone you back later!" And I hit the accept button with the tip of my finger.

"Hello Marilyn! Is that you?"

"Why yes, sweetie it's me," she says then chortles, "I'm so sorry to have worried you, but how nice to know that somebody cares. I was out of my Mogen David Blackberry wine and low on Manischewitz

Matzos, and I like to keep both on hand for Chanukah. Plus, my little Tookie was out of dog treats. Say speaking of treats, what kind of cookies did you bake, honey? They are homemade, aren't they?"

"You're home right now, correct?"

"Why of course I am. How the heck else would I have gotten your message?"

"Don't go anywhere!" I say, "I'll be at your front door in a matter of minutes!"

I snatch up Marilyn's bag, attempting to replace the missing cookies by throwing in a handful of Holiday Kisses wrapped in red, green and silver foil and retying the now limp ribbon into a bow.

"I'm running over to Marilyn's place to give her the cookies." I call out from the kitchen in Maggie's direction.

"Be sure to check her pulse!"

Sarcastic.

I knock, and Marilyn almost immediately answers the door. Standing there on the other side of her screen door she seems pretty much normal.

"Hello again," I say and then begin to consider how never, ever, in the past months has she under any circumstances answered the door that quickly.

"Howdy doo to you too," she says cheerily.

Every other time she takes a good five minutes, and while Tookie is barking at the inside of the door, she is calling out things like *Hold your horses, I'm coming* and *Give an old lady some time*—all to the sound of her walker dragging across the parquet floor.

"My goodness," she continues with a sparkle in her eye. "Would that little bag be for me?"

"Yes, it is," I say. "They are holiday cookies that my daughter Maggie made."

She fiddles with the latch on the door, giving a couple 'oys,' before getting it open. She reaches out for the bag, and as she does, I take her arm and pinch it.

"Ouch!" she screams. "What the hell was that for?"

"I'm sorry," I blurt out. "It's an old family custom. A way of wishing friends and loved ones a Merry Christmas… MERRY CHRISTMAS!" I exclaim loudly.

"Goodness, honey, your family must be all black and blue this time of year." She laughs under her breath and sotto voce adds, "And you gentiles think our customs are strange?"

"Mind if I come in?" I ask. "I can put these cookies away for you."

"Oh, now don't you never mind," she advises as she slips her way out the screen door and onto the porch. "I doubt they'll last that long around me," she teases. "Let's have a seat on my front porch bench, shall we?"

We both take a seat on her green painted park style bench. "Where's Tookie?"

"Oh, he's plum tuckered out from our little excursion. I'm guessing he's in my room taking a nap. He was as good as gold sitting in the basket of the motorized shopping cart at Wynn Dixie. I wish you'd have seen him."

Remembering Mags comment made in jest as I was going out the door, I take Marilyn's hand in mine. As we continue with idle small talk, I slowly start sliding my hand out of hers and up her left arm. I try my best to position two fingers atop the pulse point of her wrist. Struggling to feel any sign of a beating heart Marilyn suddenly breaks free and grabs the cookies sitting on my lap.

She unties the bow, opens the bag and sticks her nose in and takes a big whiff.

"Oh… they do smell good enough to nosh on right now." She reaches in and comes up with a hand full of chocolate Kisses. Perplexed she says, "I thought you said your daughter made these. Is she from Hershey, Pennsylvania?"

95

Walking back home, I check my mailbox situated out on Pelican Cove Road, and as I enter the house, I hand my daughter a letter, noticing it's postmarked from Los Angeles, California. The remainder of the mail consists of bills and the January 2013, issue of *Reader's Digest.* The front cover boasts "Be Young and Fit for Life."

It might be a little late for that, I think as I place the stack on the pass-through counter to the kitchen.

Maggie, heads for her bedroom, rips the envelope's flap open along the way, but not before glancing back at me. "So tell me, what happened with your neighbor. Is she a ghost?"

"Well, the jury's still out on that one," I snigger. "But I can tell you, that even though I wasn't able to detect a pulse, I was able to inflict severe pain."

Maggie shakes her head and continues into her room.

"I'm starting to think I just might know who may be the crazy one here in the Cove?" She starts pulling her door closed then pauses. "I'll be in my room if you need me after your neighbor reports you to the police!"

I decide a cup of tea is in order and it will afford me the opportune time to call Stu back. Opening the cupboard, I peruse my selection of teabags and quickly choose Constant Comment. The smell of its sweet spices and orange rind has always reminded me of two special things, Christmastime and my dear departed mother.

Settling into my favorite phone calling spot in the wicker chair on the lanai, I bring up recent calls on the screen and tap Stu's to recall. He answers almost immediately.

"Hello?"

"Hi Stu, I'm so sorry for having to hang up on you earlier. Please forgive me."

"I believe it was I who was calling to ask forgiveness."

"Well, I hope you realize you got it," I say. "Now what's this about tomorrow night?"

We chit and chat for over forty-five minutes, and I'm touched by his suggestion that we take Maggie with us to dinner, and then take a ride on the Sarasota Trolley Tour of Holiday Lights. I say I'll check with Mag, but with Christmas just a couple days away it should be a lot of fun.

"Oddly, I think I'm missing *Holiday In Lights* a Christmas drive-thru display back home." I add.

Tentatively he says he'll pick us up at six o'clock tomorrow night as the trolley pulls out at exactly eight-thirty.

Ending the call, I carry my tea mug into the kitchen and place it in the sink. I hear Maggie's bedroom door swing open and the sound of Mac scampering to meet her.

"How do you feel about joining Stu and I for dinner tomorrow night and then going to see Christmas lights?" I say. "It would be an opportunity for you to get to know him better, and I always love viewing other people's luminescent spectacles."

Maggie comes around the corner to the kitchen. She stands there with tear streaked cheeks, the letter in hand.

"Bob?" I question.

She cocks her head to one side. "Yes, who else?"

I reach out and she comes over and throws her arms around me.

"He wanted to know how I am doing in Florida. He has a small part in an upcoming television series, but he's hoping it will turn into something bigger once they see his work. He said it should air at nine o'clock on either Tuesday, February 12th or 19th on ABC, and I should look for him. He says he's the one in the handcuffs."

"Well that's good news, sweetie. He's getting work. And his contacting you is positive, isn't it?"

She starts to weep, loosens her grip and, looking at me face-to-face.

"Two goddamn pages about himself and what he's doing in California. At no point, not even once, did he ask about the baby!"

Love of My Life

—Freddie Mercury, Queen (1975)

96

I've been successful in convincing my dear daughter that Christmas lights will cheer her up, so she's agreed to go but with a bit of apprehension.

"Eight thirty seems awfully late for this thing to start," she says. "I'm usually in bed by then."

"Oh, I imagine it only lasts an hour or at the most two." I tell her. "Heavenly days, both of us should be able to stay up till ten-thirty on a Saturday night."

That night, I quickly feed Mac and run him out to take care of his business and then change the TV station to *Animal Planet* for him.

"You watch 'My Cat from Hell' and be a good boy while were gone," I say while waving my index finger in his direction. "And no big parties!"

It's already six fifteen, and it appears that Stu is running late. Trying to expedite things a bit, I suggest we go wait under the carport, as that will save several minutes of negotiating the walking paths and crossing the troll bridge. Maggie grabs a shawl as I pick up my purse, and we head out the door, as Mac stands dutifully, tail wagging, at the kitchen slider watching us depart.

While we stand waiting, Mag tells me that the blonde woman with the white Bichon Frise now coming our way is the elementary school teacher she told me about.

"Hello there!" the woman shouts as she approaches arms waving. "I'm Eileen Birch, and this little cutie patootie would be my Nellie belly." She bends over picking up her dog and placing it in my face. "I've just been dying to meet you. I met your adorable daughter… is it Myrtle?"

"Close," she replies, "It's Maggie."

"Oh, hi Margie… and this must be your mother? Oh my God, you two could be sisters!" she beams.

I introduce myself and she insists we stop by her place this Monday night, Christmas Eve, as she's having a small holiday soiree.

"Nothing fancy. I have no family down here and neither does anyone else," she announces loquaciously. "So years and years ago, you know I'm a founder in here, right? I started having an open house for the holidays. It'll be a great chance for you to meet some of the other neighbors, well except for Ann since we're not speaking, and a few of my teacher friends from Venice Elementary. Oh, and a couple tennis pros I play with at the club. Tell me you'll come? Please, please, please!" She is almost pleading, with a bit of a pout and working her big blue eyes.

"Well, that will be nice," I say. "The only definite plan we have is going to Christmas Eve service. How about you, Maggie?"

And before she can open her mouth the woman practically squeals.

"Great! Maybe we could all go together?" she states eagerly. "I go to Midnight Mass at Saint Thomas More Catholic Church in Gulf Gate."

I smile. "We're planning on going to the seven o'clock service at Siesta Key Chapel. But how about we stop by your party beforehand, since it's on our way?"

"Great!" she shouts again. "That's a tad on the early side, but I'll put you down for a hot hors d'oeuvre." And she scurries off rambling away to her dog about how, if she's a good girl, she'll let her open a present on Christmas Eve… maybe two!

As she disappears down the road, I get out my phone and see that by now it's after six-thirty. "How strange that we haven't heard from Stu," I say. "You want to go back in and sit down for a while?"

"No, I'll be fine but I'm going to waddle over to the pavilion and pee. I'll be right back!"

Of course, the moment she disappears through the pool gate to the clubhouse, Stu's metallic blue, little, sports car takes the turn onto my portion of Pelican Cove Road. Although the speed limit inside the compound is an enforced fifteen miles an hour, he zooms up beside me doing at least triple that.

The passenger window is down.

"I'm so sorry Liz for being late. I had a medical emergency and was needed at the hospital. Please forgive me for not calling, but I left my phone in my office and didn't realize it until I reached in my coat pocket and it wasn't there."

I lean in, and place both hands on the car's open window.

"Stu, please, please listen to me… if this relationship has any chance in hell of ever going anywhere both of us have got to quit apologizing for everything!"

Maggie, all smiles, comes bounding down the walk towards the car.

"What's up?" I ask.

"Oh my gosh!" she beams. "There's several old ladies in the kitchen inside there bickering at each other about Jell-O. Seems there's some kind of holiday dinner party tomorrow night and one lady is extremely upset that all they have is red and green Jell-O shots. She's scolding that someone was supposed to make Berry Blue for Chanukah."

Stu gets out and comes around to open the door for us. I suggest I sit in the back, after he leans the passenger seat forward, since in Maggie's current condition we may not be able to pull her back out. Moments later we're off and running, and to my surprise, Holiday tunes are playing on the car radio.

"I must say, it seems your taste in music may be evolving?" I joke.

Looking up at the rearview mirror for any signs of reaction in his eyes. "I just thought it might get us all in the mood for the evening's festivities," he says, making eye contact.

Winking coyly I repartee, "Kind of like how Marvin Gaye gets one in the mood for—"

"Oh my God!" squeals Maggie. "I already feel like a third wheel, but this is getting gross."

We pull into Madfish Grill at Cattleman and Bee Ridge Road.

"The trolley leaves from the Regions Bank parking lot right over there," Stu says, as he helps pull me out of the back seat. "I thought we could easily just walk over to catch it after we eat." He checks what looks like a Rolex watch and announces that it's now five minutes till seven. And Maggie notes there seems to be quite a line of people out the door of the restaurant.

Stu suggests we wait at the back of the line while he makes his way to the front to check on our reservation. Along the way he is greeted by sneers and taunts that say anything but 'Happy Holidays'.

The hostess finishes up with the couple in front of him and then belts out, "Next!"

She looks up and recognition spreads across her face.

"Oh, Doctor Robbins, how are you? I thought I saw your name on the reservation list for later tonight. Ah, here it is Robbins. Party of three for eight-thirty. How can I help you?"

Confused, Stu attempts to explain. "My secretary was supposed to make reservations for six-thirty, and yes, that would mean we are now late, but according to you we're actually early."

She pats his hand. "Let me see what I can do, Doctor Robbins. My mother still swears you saved her life! You know with all the snowbirds without reservations, and it being a holiday weekend, this place is a total zoo tonight."

And off she runs deep within the restaurant.

Stu looks back in our direction and gives a palms-up gesture with a shake of his head in other words, *Who knows what's up?* The hostess returns about five minutes later, and it seems there are only two seats at the bar available, and one of us would have to stand. However, if we would like to take them and have a complimentary drink, she will work us in as soon as possible.

Making his way back through the hangry mob, Stu joins us and proceeds to fill us in on the situation.

"It's already after seven. And even though the tour begins at eight-thirty the tickets advise to check-in at least fifteen minutes prior to departure." He takes a deep breath. "So what do you say, is it a dinner of alcohol and beer nuts or perhaps a late bite after it's over?"

Maggie pats her belly. "I'm on the wagon, Doc, but right over there I see a MacDonald's. How about a compromise and we get the mother-to-be a Big Mac, fries, and a large chocolate shake and you two can grab something later… and on your own?"

97

Since we're on a roll, literally, Stu parks closer to the bank and we can see several 1920s-style red and green trolleys in position and what looks like families already boarding them. Everyone is in queue and appears to be reporting to one of the costumed individuals positioned outside the door to each vehicle. I tuck my purse under the car seat, and Maggie grabs her shawl. We get out of the car and make our way to the first trolley line.

After waiting our turn to get up to the jolly elf, complete with curled toes, who is working ours, we are greeted with, "Happy Holidays! Have you got your tickets?" She scans the list of names on her clipboard, as the bells on her hat constantly tinkle, then announces, "Robbins, party of three?"

"That would be us," we answer almost simultaneously as Maggie starts swaying to Burl Ives *Holly Jolly Christmas,* which is blaring from the vehicle's open windows.

"I'm so sorry folks, but this trolley is now full." And she hands us back the tickets. "If you'll move on to the next available one, I'm sure you can get on it!"

We dutifully walk to the next line of people, and this time there's an older man in a Santa hat, but he's donning his own home-grown, white beard. Stu hands him the tickets and he states, much like the elf did, "Robbins, and there will be three of you tonight?"

"Yes," Stu says.

Santa takes our tickets. "Please watch your step boarding." The latter directed mostly to Maggie, as he helps her up the rather high first tread.

"Have fun tonight everyone… Ho, ho, ho!"

Glancing out the front window, I note that the trolleys ahead of us are already pulling out. We wait, however; parents are blocking the aisle as they secure places by the windows for their offspring. Others are handing out treats and beverages before storing their coolers overhead. A prodigious woman in a graphic Christmas sweater, replete with flashing lights, is passing out song books as she bumps bellies with Maggie and chuckles, "Oopsy-daisy!".

I whisper to Stu, "I'm not sure we're properly prepared for this. Why, I don't even have a bottled water."

Stuck about midway down the aisle, I suddenly become aware of someone tugging at my skirt hem.

"I said your high heels a diggin' inta my damn boot."

I twist sideways attempting to look back and gasp "Excuse me, I—"

and grab Stu's upper arm in a death grip, for I'm looking straight into the face of the old cowgirl from the shop in Osprey.

Now conscious of the pungent scent of tobacco smoke intertwined with peppermint, I begin feeling both nauseous and claustrophobic and sense the onset of an impending panic attack. I'm compelled to continue apologizing as I begin to feel sicker by the minute.

"I'm so, so sorry!" I shout out as Stu turns to give me a concerned look and then glances down at his now rumpled sleeve.

"I do declare dat old granny be seein' more of you den my own kin folk in dis here town. How's your new leetle pecker friend been a treatin' ya, sugar? Any problems with'm?"

Stu gives me a questioning look as he misconstrues the comment as pertaining to him.

By the time everything settles down, and the gal with the carol books has taken up a full double bench for herself, it becomes apparent that there's not enough seating left for all of us. In fact, there's only room for approximately one and a half of us.

Santa boards at this point.

"We can't take off till you take a seat folks. Please make your choices quickly as we wouldn't want to miss anything!"

All eyes then turn on us, and one little girl cries out, "Mommy, why does that lady look like she's going to throw-up?"

We quickly explain our situation to Santa where on he returns to the front and takes a radio hand piece from the driver.

"Breaker, breaker North Pole this is Papa Claus on Trolley Three come in please. Over." We move back up to the front, but not before my making eye contact once again with the old woman and her tar-stained grin.

We all listen, through the static, along with Santa for a response.

"Hello, Papa Clause, this is Rudolph; how can I help you? Over."

The guy spells out our circumstances to the home base and awaits their reply. In the meantime, he has asked us to please step off of the vehicle as we are creating a fire hazard, which I do with great relief. I realize my pill case is in my purse and struggle with telling my doctor how I currently feel or asking him for his car keys and just running off like hell towards it.

Several moments later, after we have observed a lot of head nodding by Santa, he steps off the trolley into the parking lot and advises,

"I apologize profusely, but it appears we have somehow overbooked for tonight. Another trolley is on its way from the depot and should be here soon." He then points towards the other end of the lot where there's a small group of about twenty gathered and states, "If you'll just go wait with the others, we should have you on your way in no time." He gives a final, "Ho!" steps on the bus and off it zooms blaring *I Want A Hippopotamus For Christmas*.

98

As the parting trolley pulls out onto Cattleman Road Stu realizes that Santa still has our tickets in hand.

"Well hopefully your name's on this trolley person's list." I offer a comforting pat on the arm that's actually an attempt to unrumple his dress shirt sleeve. "You really didn't know what you were getting into when this evening started, did you?" I manage to hold back nervous laughter.

"I have a feeling, Liz, that I didn't know what I was getting into the moment I met you!"

While Stu offers to wait with the group, I ask him for his car keys, and Maggie and I quickly slip into the Burlington Coat Factory, situated before us, to hunt down the little girl's room. After my anxiety filled experience on the trolley, I feel the need to pop a pill and freshen up, or I may have to bail right here and now.

As we walk away the first thing Stu notices is that this group does not seem to be made up of happy little families like all the others. In fact, there's not a child to be found. Also, all the guys appear to be with a buddy or the gals with a girlfriend. He soon makes eye contact with a woman clutching a clipboard and she comes charging straight for him. The larger than life woman is coiffed with a mound of white hair that would make Marge Simpson jealous. She's wearing flashing dingle-ball earrings that are swinging wildly as she struts up to a point well within the boundaries of his personal space.

"Hey there, cutie pie, you flying solo tonight?" she asks, while obviously checking him out from head to toe. "Nice little Christmas package you have there!"

She smirks, and then gives a flirtatious smile and an exaggerated wink of the right eye showing off extremely long false eyelashes. Stu is not sure what to make of this woman. She is taller than he is with the shoulders of a linebacker and is dressed in skin tight red sequins and sprouting a set of skinny bird legs ending in strappy stiletto heels.

"Oh yes, hi," says Stu. "We had tickets for the Holiday Light tour, but couldn't fit on the trolley. Santa kept our tickets, but said we could join your group. Are we on your list?"

"Oh… you're on my list big boy. Now tell me, did Santa happen to say if you've been naughty… or nice?" She grabs Stu's crotch with her holiday manicured left hand while thrusting two of the pointiest and hardest set of boobs that he's ever felt into his chest area.

Just then Maggie and I walk up.

"Everything all right, are we on the list?"

The woman lets go of Stu and, while glancing over her shoulder and strutting away like Marilyn Monroe in *Niagara.* "Oh, he's on *my* Christmas list, honey, so you better keep an eye on him during the entire tour!"

Mag looks around at the others and starts giggling. "Oh my God, you two, this is a gay group."

"Are you sure?" I ask. "I mean they all seem quite happy and what not, but how do you know?"

"Mother," She says, rolling her eyes. "For God's sake I lived in New York City and work in theatre… what don't I know?"

Stu suggests we leave the tour as he discreetly turns around and adjusts himself, but since my Librium has kicked in, I exuberantly insist we join in the fun and go see some lights.

We board the trolley last, and the big, busty woman introduces herself as Eartha Quake and advises that her counterpart is Miss Beneva Fruitville. She then turns to the other riders who have settled in and claps her hands loudly.

"Attention… I said, attention everybody! It seems we have several 'Straights' joining our Holly, Jolly, Christmas Trolley tonight." She pats Maggie's belly for emphasis. "Especially this one!"

And the entire trolley breaks into uproarious laughter.

"Okay, let's keep the evening gay, but not so queer that we embarrass them," she says and then actually asks us to introduce ourselves.

We do.

"Hi Stu, Liz, and Maggie!" comes a raucous response from the others on board as we make our way down the aisle to the open back seat that spans the entire rear of the vehicle.

A male rider grabs my skirt hem and asks, "Wherever did you get that Sweetie? I have a blouse that would match perfectly!"

The overhead bright lights suddenly go out and the entire interior comes alive in Christmas colored twinkle lights, including a mirror ball hanging in the middle of the ceiling as the trolley pulls away.

"Many of you know our driver Ziggy from last year's party," announces Eartha. "He will be taking us to some of the best sights to see in all of Sarasota. Well, except for getting to see me perform!"

And with the flip of a switch, Mariah Carey's "All I Want for Christmas is You!" starts playing loudly through the trolley's speakers as Eartha lip syncs and begins to quake, shimmy, and strut her stuff down the center aisle, and the other riders take turns stuffing dollar bills into her garters.

We make our way through entire neighborhoods that have lined their streets with flashing arches of lights. Amongst the decorated homes in another subdivision there's a large two-story that the owners have gone to great lengths to turn into a genuine gingerbread house, including a costume clad real-life gingerbread family out front waving 'hello' to every passer-by.

Along the way wine and Champagne bottles start popping, and beer cans snap open with a 'fssst!' sound. The interior starts to smell like a mix of bowling alley with a hint of pot. Tupperware and Christmas tins circulate through the trolley, and when we are offered a container of brownies the guy handing them to us leans in.

"I really don't think Maggie should be tripping out if you know what I mean!"

Continuing on, we're taken to an exact replica of the National Lampoon Christmas Vacation home complete with a large full moon atop the gable of the roof and the silhouette of Santa's sleigh flying by. The show of lights and music continue until we pull into the driveway of the Grace Baptist Church, somewhere in the countryside and miles out on Bee Ridge Road.

"Okay folks," Eartha announces, "This is about the halfway point of the evening and your only chance to tinkle. The outside light show repeats on the half-hour. Inside you'll find musical performances in the sanctuary and complimentary homemade cookies and hot chocolate in the lobby. And trust me, those Baptist ladies can bake! We'll only be here for a half hour so be back on the bus by ten-thirty or we'll leave without you!"

And with that, everyone jumps up and, once off the bus, goes running straight towards the light display like brightly sequined moths to an incandescent bulb.

We get off the bus to the final chords of "the Hallelujah Chorus" and stand there in amazement with our mouths hanging open. The orchestration ends to thunderous applause in every direction from the audience. Mag asks me to help get her shawl around her shoulders when suddenly every light goes out and we're standing in pitch darkness.

"Don't move!" warns Stu. Before the blackout we all had the opportunity to notice the electrical wires running every which way on the ground. Suddenly out of the gloaming the outside speakers come to life and begin playing "I Heard the Bells on Christmas Day" and one by one the light display comes back to life in varying shades of celestial blue.

I heard the bells on Christmas day
Their old familiar carols play
And mild and sweet their songs repeat
Of peace on earth good will to men

Every inch of this prodigious church and all its out buildings are covered in lights. They begin to fade from blue to green and then touches of red start showing up and quickly blend into purple. There are mechanized, spinning Christmas trees actually moving towards us on small tracks similar to those of a train. There are snowflakes and stars that start showing up, first here and then there, and joyfully twinkling everywhere. And then, in the middle of it all, a huge flagpole covered with conical lights comes to life transforming into the biggest and brightest tree of all.

And the bells are ringing (Peace on Earth)
Like a choir they're singing (Peace on Earth)
In my heart I hear them
Peace on earth, good will to men

I lean my head on Stu's shoulder, and Maggie takes my hand as we stand, mesmerized and deeply touched by the scene unfolding before us, which is only intensified by this incredibly stirring rendition of the song.

Then rang the bells more loud and deep
God is not dead, nor doth He sleep (Peace on Earth, peace on Earth)
The wrong shall fail, the right prevail
With peace on earth, good will to men

Mag asks if I have a tissue as she starts to sob, and I advise that I left my purse back in Stu's car.

"It's my damn hormones, [sniff] and well… the holiday season," she whimpers.

Overhearing us, Stu reaches in his back pocket and pulls out a white, folded handkerchief which he hands to her.

"Don't worry it's clean," he says. "I only use it to wipe my sunglasses." Now the entire scene turns from shimmering gold to blazing white.

Then ringing singing on its way
The world revolved from night to day
A voice, a chime, a chant sublime
Of peace on earth, good will to men
And the bells they're ringing (Peace on Earth)

Like a choir they're singing (Peace on Earth)
And with our hearts we'll hear them
Peace on earth, good will to men

We gather ourselves and make our way into the narthex and Maggie lets out a yawn.

"I can't believe it's going on ten thirty and we're only halfway through this thing."

"I know sweetie. Are you doing all right?"

"I'm fine, just getting tired and I need a lady's room."

"Well I'm getting hungry!" I say and aim straight towards the church ladies. Most wearing long skirts and sporting hair buns—more importantly though, they are handing out cookies and cocoa left and right.

Back on the trolley the tour continues with one splendiferous display after another through additional Sarasota neighborhoods. Maggie has leaned her head onto me and is actually snoring through most of it. The waking point is when we pull over in front of the Klein residence where Ziggy, the driver, takes over. He sounds a little like the Swedish chef from the Muppet Show.

"This will be our last stop for the evening, ladies and gentlemen. My dear friend Mrs. Klein and her little dog Dixie have been waiting all night for our arrival. She insists you get off the bus and come see her display that she's been working on all year!"

Dutifully we all pile off the trolley again, but this time it's to Dolly Parton singing "Hard Candy Christmas." Waiting at the gate of the picket fence that surrounds her modest house stands Mrs. Klein, all smiles. In her arms she holds little Dixie who strikes me as the second runner up to the annual World's Ugliest Dog contest.

"I don't see her as the winner," I jest. "But she's a strong contender!"

As Mrs. Klein is explaining to us how she scours the thrift stores and Goodwill's from Venice to Bradenton, starting in January each year, to find all her holiday treasures, a burly man wearing a tan colored uniform with the name 'Bud' stitched on the right pocket, and toting an actual classic metal thermos lunch box, walks up. With nary a word he opens the gate, kisses Mrs. Klein on the cheek, and continues down the walk and into the house, screen door slamming behind him.

Ziggy, all smiles, enthusiastically announces, "Oh, how lucky we all are! That was Mr. Klein everyone, arriving home from his job. He works second shift to help Mrs. Klein fund this glorious vision laid out before you!" And he does a sweeping hand gesture towards the property reminiscent of Carol Merrill on *Let's Make a Deal.*

Ziggy then leads us on a tour of the place, and for all the taste and sophistication that every other display showed us earlier, this one is the exact opposite. Every conceivable lighted figure, from plastic snowmen to the Grinch and his dog Max fill the front lawn. From our vantage point it appears that the porch is piled high with various forms of stuffed animal ever made. Many of them seem to be held in place on the wrought iron porch railings by green garbage bag ties and it's obvious that the once fuzzy characters have weathered their share of storms.

The picture windows of the home are dressed like 1900s department store displays, replete with animated Victorian style caroling figures. Each is dressed in holiday velvets—now covered in dust—and holding candles or song books as their little motors grind, arms jerkily move, and mouths clap open and shut. Watching their struggling movements, they appear to be the offspring of Frankenstein.

As we move on towards the carport Mrs. Klein excuses herself.

"I have to go in and get Bud's Hungry-Man dinners out of the oven. I do declare that man can eat two of their Salisbury steaks. Please stay as long as you like, Merry Christmas and thanks for coming!" And up the walk she goes still towing the dog.

As we pause at the scene before us, trying to take it all in, the screen door again slams shut.

We are now viewing what appears to be Santa Claus, after returning home late on Christmas night after a hard day's work, and the irony of the similarity to Bud is not lost on the crowd. Santa sits, stocking feet up, in a recliner and he's watching *The Tonight Show with Johnny Carson* on an old, black and white TV with rabbit ears. He's removed his familiar red coat, and it hangs on a coat tree along with his cap. Of course, in his fist is a cold can of Pabst Blue Ribbon beer.

Mrs. Claus is in the kitchen preparing a traditional Christmas feast complete with a huge turkey defrosting in the sink. Her mechanized arm is in continuous motion stirring one of the pots atop a 1950s Tappan gas range. Every detail, including the canisters on her counter, sport a holiday motif.

Apparently earlier in the day, Mrs. Claus set the dining room table with the familiar Spode Christmas Tree pattern, only in Melmac, and in the corner of the room stands a full-size Christmas tree mimicking the same dish motif. Ziggy bids us to please follow him, but to be very careful on the walkway to the backyard as the pavers are a bit wobbly.

The scene takes on a somber tone as the side yard is dimly lit and the backyard music transitions to "Silent Night." Here the only decorations are a life size nativity scene with a flood-lit flagpole behind it and the American flag and MIA flag flapping in the mild evenings breeze. A realtor style sign stuck in the ground beside the manger holding the baby Jesus reads Keep Christ in Christmas!

As we gather ourselves to leave and aim towards the trolley, Ziggy points out a large, plastic piggy bank at the end of the driveway.

"Please feel free to leave any gratuities you feel are appropriate for Mrs. Klein in the pig. Her FPL bill is ginormous!"

By the time we get back into Stu's car it is twelve-thirty in the morning. "What an experience." I say and sigh.

"I'm pooped," says Maggie.

Stu too looks a little rough around the edges. "Well one thing's for sure. That's a heck of a lot of entertainment for fifteen bucks!"

<h1 style="text-align:center">100</h1>

We all agree to call it a night and aim back towards the Cove. Driving in on Pelican Cove Road Stu's headlights catch a red fox, darting out of the darkness of one side of the jungle and disappearing into the other. Once in the Pavilion parking lot, Maggie quickly jumps out of the vehicle and heads towards the condo calling back over her shoulder as she fishes keys from her purse.

"You know where I need to go!"

Stu gets out pulls me from the back seat. In the distance, I can hear Maggie fumbling with her key and Mac giving a couple *Who's there?* barks. Then the front door clicks shut.

"May I walk you to the door?" asks Stu in a seemingly solicitous manner.

"I can find my way," I say, "and you really should be going. It's late, and I know you're tired, plus you have to drive home yet. By the way, where *is* home?"

He proceeds to tell me how he lives in Southside and asks if I'm familiar with the SMH area and Morton's Gourmet Market.

"I've been there once or twice since moving here," I say. "I was looking for a Jungle Jim replacement but found the place rather pricey."

"I could be wrong," he says. "But I really don't think they sell children's play sets there. And by the way, where would you put one?"

I laugh at that. "No not a jungle gym. Jungle Jim's… it's a megamarket near Cincinnati, sort of a huge grocery, deli, bakery, wine and liquor, cigar, fish monger, foreign food, garden center and kitchen accessories store. With the Campbell's Soup Kids swinging from the ceiling and animated singing animals throughout. Oh, and an award-winning port-o-let. Honestly, Stu, it's hard to explain what the heck it is, but I sure do miss it. If you ever find yourself in Cincinnati, well, you have to check it out for—"

He leans in with a surprise kiss. Our lips slowly part creating a soft smacking sound, and I can feel the warmth of his lips lingering afterwards on mine.

"I'm sorry if that was too forward," he says. "But I have really been wanting to kiss you for quite a while now."

We stand looking into each other's eyes for a moment. "Not at all. In fact, it was very nice." And to my surprise, this time, it's me who initiates a second kiss.

Stu offers a soft smile. "What are you doing New Year's Eve? If you don't have plans already, I would love for us to go out."

"Well, I did have plans to watch *New Year's Rockin' Eve* with Ryan Seacrest and Pitbull with probably a fifty/fifty chance of still being awake when the ball comes down. But since you've tempted me with a better offer, I think I just might take you up on it."

"Great!" he says as he jumps in the car and starts the engine. "I'll pick you up around five, and wear something that's appropriate for being on the water."

He pulls out, giving a friendly single honk as he drives off. Checking my neighbor's windows for any signs that he's awakened them, I proceed over the troll bridge and down the walk.

Hang on, I think, *Isn't five o'clock kind of early for New Year's Eve?*

Mac's at the door and, since it's so late, I just let him trot out off-lead and he runs to the front yard to relieve himself. Once Inside, I see Maggie's already had time to get into her pajamas and is now in the kitchen getting a glass of milk.

"That took quite a while just to say goodnight." She grins from ear to ear. "I thought you were tired?"

I walk to the kitchen cupboard, get out a small juice glass, pop the wine stopper out of an open bottle of Cab Sav on the counter, and pour. We clink glasses.

"Salute," I say and toss back the wine.

"What's gotten into you?"

"Your mother's been, as you young people say, *sucking face.*"

"Trust me, young people *don't* say that, Mom. But that doesn't matter... dish!"

As Time Goes By

—Jimmy Durante (1964)

Writer —Herman Hupfeld (1931)

101

It's finally Christmas Eve day, and I must say, I'm suddenly feeling in the spirit of things. After putting *Sounds of the Seasons* on Comcast, we enjoy a continental breakfast of cinnamon rolls—albeit only Pillsbury Pop'n Fresh—toasted almond coffee, and a large grapefruit, picked fresh from one of the trees in the backyard. Maggie made everything before my even getting up. She even fed Mac and took him out.

I get up from the table and kiss her forehead.

"Thanks, Sweetie," I say, clearing my place. "That was terrific."

I then go lock myself in my bedroom to wrap the last of my Christmas gifts. I know I told my daughter that her new bed would be her only gift this year, but I have picked up some little cosmetic things for Santa to place under the tree, and also some newborn outfits for the baby. I hold up an adorable Baby Aspen hooded elephant bath towel and washcloth set, that I spotted at Target just yesterday, and I can't help but coo over it anew. The big pink bow over the elephant's ear is simply adorable, and for a moment I find myself remembering how fun it was to shop for my own two babies.

I decide to take a shower and do my hair early. We are going to church later and beforehand that party at... *What the heck was her name?* The elementary school teacher. I remember her dog's name is Nellie. *Or is it Ellie?*

Actually, now that I think about it, I don't recall the names of most of the people Mac and I run into on our daily walks, but I can usually remember their dogs. I will say, "Hi Sassy!" or ask, "How's Buddy doing today?" but their owners merit little more than "Nice day." Or "How are you?"

Sarah, with her artsy flamboyance, is one of the few I remember by name—most of the others, not so much. I'm reminded that a couple weeks ago I bought a Chanukah card at Hallmark for her and Tobias, and I need to walk it over there later and drop it in their mailbox. *Would it be right to take them some Christmas cookies?*

Returning to the main part of the condo, I find that Maggie has cleared and reset the dining table with holiday placemats that I haven't seen in years, and she is now in the kitchen starting the dishwasher.

"You're just full of energy."

"I just feel so darn good for some reason."

I look at my daughter with her tall stature, flowing auburn hair, and pronounced pregnant belly and begin to beam. "You are possibly the most beautiful woman that I've ever seen!"

"You are too kind."

"Care to run to Publix with me?" I ask. "I've decided to make my hot artichoke and parmesan cheese dip for tonight, and I don't have any mayonnaise and I need a baguette."

"Thanks, but I think I'll pass," she says. "I think I'll use this time to clean up and jump in the shower just like you did. Say, do you have any nail clippers that I can borrow?" She glances down at her fingers. "I swear my nails grow so darn fast that I could trim them every other day now!"

"Sure thing, look in my vanity drawer," I say. "Y'know, I remember saying the same thing many moons ago to the obstetrician that delivered you, Dr. Boiman. He advised me it was due to the higher levels of estrogen in my body, plus the prenatal vitamins or some such hormonal thing. I'll look for another pair while I'm out."

Later that afternoon I'm in the kitchen taking my dip out of the oven when Maggie rounds the corner sniffing the air. "Boy, doesn't that smell good!"

She's dressed cute as a button in a red, green and white floral prairie skirt and ruffled peasant top that she has pulled slightly off the shoulders. Her hair is pulled back in a curly, off-center ponytail held together by a single red, sateen ribbon.

She stops dead in her tracks and, after giving me the once over states. "Is that honestly what you're wearing tonight?" And then just frowns.

"Why?" I answer, while looking down and pulling on the sleeves of the black polyester scrunch neck that I paired with a simple black slack. "I thought it was fine."

"And what are those things on your feet?" she asks. "You look like you're going to a funeral, not a holiday party."

"Well, I was actually dressing more for church and not so much for the party." I recognize how defensive I sound. "Actually Mag, I was mainly just trying to smell good and look clean!"

She leads me by the hand into the bedroom where she begins tossing several choices from my walk-in onto my bed.

"This will be the first impression many of your neighbors will have of you. Heaven forbid if there happens to be any eligible men in attendance—they'll likely mistake you for the hired help and ask you for a drink refill."

Once she's satisfied with my appearance, she excuses herself and aims towards her side of the condo simply shaking her head, leaving me looking in the full-length mirror on the back of the bedroom door. The peacock blue dress that I have only worn once before never looked so good. Maggie has loosely tied a purple and fuchsia silk scarf around the waist at a slight angle and affixed it with an Anne Klein silver and blue crystal dragonfly pin that was my mothers. She insists I leave the neckline plain and the only other jewelry I'm wearing are my diamond stud earrings.

Not bad, Maggie. Not bad at all.

102

I cover the warm dip with aluminum foil and place it and the sliced baguette into an old Longaberger picnic basket that I've been using to carry things to parties for years now. I've included a bottle of 19 Crimes red blend wine for me and a Sanpellegrino with gas for Maggie.

"Ready to go, Hon?" I ask.

"Ready as I'll ever be!"

Walking down Pelican Cove Road past the tennis courts and both of us comment on just how beautiful a December afternoon it really is.

"Hard to believe that this is Christmas Eve." I smile. "The weather sure doesn't hint of it."

I share with Maggie the details of that final holiday week I spent in our old family house in Cincinnati before the big move. I end the tale with my moment of melancholy memories about Christmases past and my toast goodbye to the neighborhood from my front porch in the falling snow.

As we continue sauntering towards the corner, Maggie shares her favorite New York City yuletide memory of a remarkable evening planned entirely as a surprise by Bob.

"After having dinner at Casellula, our favorite little cheese & wine café near the theatre district, we strolled over to Central Park where he had reserved a carriage ride for us. It was freezing cold and snowing heavily that year. We snuggled in under a blanket the driver provided, and Bob held me so tight, concerned that I was on the verge of hypothermia. I told him that perhaps if he would kiss me it might possibly help to warm me up. And by golly, that's exactly what he did… about every five minutes during the entire ride. You know, I think that's the actual moment that I knew I was falling in love with him. Either then or when I saw how he handled that Pig's Ass Sandwich they're famous for at the restaurant!"

We cross the street arm in arm, laughing, and make our way down a path through a courtyard garden replete with candlelit lanterns. They hang from various oak limbs spread out like an octopus and dripping with Spanish moss. We navigate the open steps to the landing one flight up and find two different front doorways.

"I believe this one is her place on the left."

Beside her door the hostess has placed a small round table decorated with a live seasonal floral arrangement and several lit votive candles. The smell of holly berry and pine permeates the air. There's a hand-written sign that reads 'Help Yourselves To A Shot of Holiday Cheer!' as she has left shooters of peppermint schnapps waiting. Pop music, not necessarily holiday, can be heard even through the closed door and windows.

"Well, here goes nothing," I say throwing back a shot. "Per doctor's orders, it's time to experience my second Cove party!"

Taking a deep breath after rapping on the front door, I open it to reveal a very large party in full swing in a rather small space.

Somehow our hostess spies us from across the room and starts maneuvering her way through the raucous crowd.

I lean in to Mag. "I feel so bad I can't remember her name."

"It's Eileen, Mother. She's an elementary teacher, and she's lived here since 1979, making her one of the longest Pelican Cove residents."

I shake my head. "Honestly… I don't know how you know these things."

"I'm so glad you came!" Eileen blurts out and then hugs and kisses us both on each cheek in an over-the-top theatrical fashion. She yells over the clatter.

"Everyone this is Lizzy Blum," she says, pronouncing it like plum, "and her daughter Margo. They bought Susanne's old place." She turns to me with a concerned look. "My God, that place must have been a mess. She was such a tight wad, and after she died, they let that granddaughter of hers live there and keep that smelly horse of hers in the place."

I'm taken aback by her straightforwardness. "She had a *horse?* Well, that might explain the smells the first time we saw the condo."

"Heavens no!" She howls, and then finishes off what looks like a martini in one huge gulp. "It was a bullmastiff, but I swear you could ride it." She cackles and elbows me in the side. "And, I think that donut bumper just may have, if you know what I mean Lizzy."

The foyer where we're standing is adorned with framed vintage circus posters commingled with what look like black and white publicity photos.

"These are interesting," I say, uncomfortable with the conversation thus far while trying to make additional chit-chat.

"Oh, those old things," she says then yells out, "Tommy... Tommy honey, I need a fresh drink. Those are just faded memories from my circus days, sweetie... Thomas! Where the Hell are you?"

Then a nice-looking older gentleman with an agreeable smile says, "Hello." And he is exchanging Eileen's empty glass for a new one. This one appears to be rimmed with red sugar crystals and has a small candy cane in the glass, which the woman uses as a stir stick then runs her tongue over it sensually before tossing it aside in a decorative bowl on a foyer table and continuing on.

She points at a picture of an extremely dark and handsome young man sporting a handlebar mustache. He is wearing a tailcoat and vest, tall boots, and a top hat and is holding a whip.

"That's the Ringling Brothers Ringmaster and the reason I ended up here in Sarasota, gals. Well, *after* I made him my second husband."

She then sips at her drink. "Good job, Tommy," she calls out to the room, "but next time skip the sugar rim, I'm dieting!" Then, turning back to me...

"You might say, as a young girl, I actually ran off and joined the circus." And then she laughs at herself while slapping me on the back.

As if on cue, her little Bichon Frise prances up to her, and Eileen—on bended knee—slaps her chest twice and yells, "Jump!"

The dog leaps from floor to knee then into her arms and she balances its front paws in the palm of her hand.

"Up Nelly, up!"

As the dog kicks its back legs up and balances itself on the flat of her hand, she continues to move her arm about to assist the animal in keeping aloft. The other guests standing around us break into thunderous applause, and Eileen beams ear-to-ear as she flips the dog over in midair, and then assists it in jumping down to the floor. The dog trots off, but not before both she and her owner take a bow.

"I apologize, what can I get you two to drink?" she asks— as we've been left standing there this entire time with my basket still in hand.

"Oh, I have a bottle of wine here and my daughter is sticking to sparkling water."

"Oh, how sweet, you didn't need to do that," she says.

She grabs the bottle of wine out of the basket, and off she scurries as she places it under her Christmas tree, completely decorated in only gold, and then continues to mingle amongst the other guests.

About an hour and a half into the party, I suggest we say our good-byes so that we can get to church on time. On the walk back home, we talk about the interesting assemblage of Pelican Cove guests in attendance. I ask Mag if she met the cute little couple who were also with the circus.

"She was the band director and he played the licorice stick. They have played in every major city around the world, but they find it quite humorous to share how they tied-the-knot one night when the circus train broke down in Intercourse, Pennsylvania."

"Well I can top that," Maggie says. "The Asian man in the red embroidered kimono who was walking around with the little tasseled cap on. Well, now he's a famous fine artist, but when younger and studying in Peking, now Beijing, he was required to paint the sides of buildings

with larger-than-life portraits of the communist leader Mao Zedong...
can you imagine that?"

I see that Marilyn's lights appear on even through her pulled blinds
and propose we stop by so I can check on her.

"I'll need to bring her some leftovers from tomorrow's dinner."

We are crossing a small bridge to her unit, not dissimilar to the path
leading to mine. Suddenly the place goes black, and I suggest that she
must have just gone to bed.

"I hate to disturb her," I say. "Plus it takes her so long to get to the
door and we're running late."

Maggie grabs my hand and we turn back, mid-bridge.

"I must say, you take darn good care of her considering she's an ethereal being!"

103

Crossing the Stickney Point Bridge to Siesta Key and turning right onto Midnight Pass we find ourselves in a visually stunning winter wonderland. Each and every condominium community has attempted to outdo the other with their Christmas light displays.

Nestled under candy cane–striped Cuban belly and slender Carpentaria palms are illuminated figures of every kind. From traditional Santa's and snowmen to glistening sea creatures like octopuses, dolphins, and whales—the displays stretch all the way from the drawbridge to the village.

"Well, if that doesn't put you into the holiday spirit, I don't know what will," I say, taking in the scenery.

Maggie grins and says, "Besides the fact that I'm sweating... I believe most of these people staggering around in shorts and flip-flops are going to be sleeping off their 'Holiday spirits' most of the day tomorrow and totally miss Christmas morning."

At the corner of Ocean Boulevard and Canal, under the garland draped gazebo, is Saint Nick himself. A conglomeration of individuals, ranging from families dressed in church clothes to bandeau and Speedo-clad beach goers are lined up to make their last-minute requests of the big guy. On the opposite corner in front of the Hub Baja Grill is a young group of carolers, who make us both chuckle when we see them wearing winter hats and scarves with bikinis and board shorts. I roll down my window and we catch a stanza of "Deck the Halls" as we pass by.

Mag says, "Remember the Christmas before… well, y'know, before our last one all together?"

"Any part of it in particular?"

"We had gone to Aunt Margaret's for her annual Christmas Eve party. I used to love how she made what she referred to as 'Sleepy-Time Punch' for the kids. As I recall, it had lime sherbet scoops and maraschino cherries floating in it? She said it would guarantee that we would sack out the minute our heads hit the pillow so Christmas morning would arrive sooner."

"Oh yeah, that's right. I had forgotten all about that head-game she played on you and your cousins. You know, it actually worked, and it tasted pretty darn good at the same time. Well, once the adults slipped a bit of 'The Captain' into their glasses!"

"I wouldn't know?" Questions Maggie. "I've tried to make it a couple times, but it never tastes quite like Auntie Mags."

She remains quiet for a moment and I can tell there is something.

"I noticed that you received a Christmas card from her a couple days ago." she says. "She used to send me one too, but I haven't heard from her in years. What happened?"

"I can't say for sure, sweetie, but I think she just misses your dad her twin brother very, very much. And maybe… just maybe, we're too much of a reminder of him for her to handle. What say we make that our New Year's resolution to work on together in bringing Aunt Margaret back into the fold before the next holidays?"

"That sounds good, Mom."

"Heck," I say, "if someone would have told me I'd actually be enjoying Christmas again I wouldn't have believed them, but thanks in part to you showing up at my front door here I am, celebrating the season big time!"

We reach Siesta Key Chapel and it's apparent the lot is full and that this is going to be one packed church service. We continue down Gleason Avenue and turn left onto Lotus, circling behind the church. Every space in the other lots and along the street are taken. We come to Higel, where I turn right and then immediately turn right again onto Ralph.

We find a spot at the Out of Door Academy marked Teacher of the Month Parking Only, and I quickly pull in.

"I'm sure the school is closed for the holidays and hopefully they gave this *special* teacher the night off! You think Eileen was ever teacher of the month?"

We jump out of the car and make our way back the two blocks to the church.

Upon entering the narthex, a greeter hands us a program advising we'll need to share because he's running out. He then asks us to wait a moment as the service has already started. Moments later the pastor finishes with…

"…such a special night for all of us to gather together to celebrate the birth of Jesus the Messiah."

And with that, the musicians start playing their instruments, and the choir begins to sing "Oh Holy Night" as the congregation rises to their feet and join in.

An usher wearing a suit jacket and tie—but with red and green plaid, Bermuda shorts—then gestures to us.

"This way ladies!" He scurries us down the center aisle to what appear to be the only two vacant seats left in the entire sanctuary. They are located in the very front row and smack dab in front of the pulpit. We join the others in song, and after its completion, the congregation takes their seats.

The Pastor, who introduces herself as Kathie, remains standing, opens the bible to the page marked by a purple trinity ribbon and begins to read aloud.

"Therefore, the Lord himself will give you a sign: The virgin will conceive and give birth to a son, and will call him Immanuel."

With that, an angel swoops down the center aisle, her left wing brushing Maggie's right shoulder as she starts reciting.

"Do not be afraid, Mary; you have found favor with God. You will conceive and give birth to a son, and you are to call him Jesus. He will be great and will be called, uhm… called… *<the Son of the Most High>* Oh yeah, his son most high. The Lord God will give him the throne of his father, David, and he will reign over Jacob's descendants forever; and his kingdom will never end."

The child beams.

She is followed by a continuing procession of Sunday school shepherds herding adorable pre-school toddler sheep, and majestic kings, all interlaced with additional scripture readings.

A teenage Mary and Joseph, toting a chubby and squirming baby Jesus, enter the scene and lay the baby in a wooden cradle. The congregation and cast commence singing "Away in a Manager" as the Christ Child begins to wail loudly. Instinctively, a young woman wearing a red cashmere sweater and pearls jumps up from her pew and pokes a Binkie into Jesus's mouth.

The audience laughs, and the reverend embraces the frivolity of the moment.

"Oh, what Mary would have probably given to have the kings bring one of those things to the manger!"

After the laughter subsides she continues.

"As is the tradition of our church, we have reached the candlelight portion of the service. When the ushers come up the aisle, will the person on the end please hold out your candle to be lit, and then light the person next to you in the pew, and so on and so on."

Now, as the room begins to take on the warm glow of candlelight, the chandelier's hanging from the ceiling slowly dim. Pastor Kathie makes her way from the podium down to the floor where she pauses in front of Maggie and me.

"I hate to tell you two, but you drew the short straw tonight." She smiles showing off a dimple. "On my cue, I need you to lead the congregation down the center aisle, exiting the rear door to the left onto the exterior deck, and then make your way slowly around the perimeter of the entire church while leading us all in song."

"Are you up to it?" She grins again with a flutter of the eyes while acknowledging Maggie's condition.

Both of us nod.

"Yes." "Yes."

"Only one question," says Maggie. "How slow should we go?"

"Well don't do the bridesmaid walk, but don't rush it either. We have about seven carols to get through before calling it an evening."

The organ and musicians introduce the first movement of "Hark the Herald Angels Sing." And just before the choir begins belting out the first verse, the pastor nods her head in our direction. We rise to the occasion and commence to lead the entire congregation down the aisle and into the heart of Christmas.

104

Turning right off the Trail onto Vamo Road, I advise Maggie I'm making a breakfast casserole for tomorrow morning.

"I couldn't decide if I wanted sausage or bacon in it, so I bought some of each. And your choice would be?"

Mags scrunches up her face as if struggling to decide. "How about both!"

"I like the way you think!"

A moment later we are pulling up to the Pelican Cove gate. An older guy with a Wilford Brimley style mustache, whom I've never seen before, is manning the guard house. He scrutinizes us and our parking sticker for a ridiculously long time, then slides open the side door on the building, and I roll down my car window in response.

"Merry Christmas ladies!" he says with a smile and slowly reaches for the button that opens the gate.

"Merry Christmas to you!" we yell back as I proceed maneuvering down the drive.

"That really surprises me," I say.

"What?"

"First, you know it's never quick getting in this place," I say. "And basically, that guard was comfortable bidding us a Merry Christmas when the odds are about seventy-thirty in here of us being Jewish."

Mag shakes her head. "Honestly Mother, you slay me... How many Jewish people do you know that drive around in a car decorated with a big red nose on the grill and antlers on the roof top?"

"I forget that you found those decorations too!"

We're rounding the blind curve by the dog park when suddenly, from a driveway on the right, darts a small child all in white. They look directly at me and then continue running off down the shell path and disappear into the night.

It had startled me to the point where I'd stomped hard on the brakes.

"Oh my God," I say. "That's Mary! What the heck is up with that kid? Don't her parents ever keep an eye on her?"

Then I remember my pregnant daughter.

I reach out and touch her belly at the point where the seatbelt has been pulled tight across it. "Are you all right?"

"I'm fine," she says. "No harm done. So, is that the strange little girl you told me about that you chased through the woods?"

"Yes," I say. "Yes, it is. And did you happen to notice how oddly that child was dressed?"

Maggie unbuckles the seatbelt to adjust it and make it looser. Then she Turns to look directly at me and answers in perfect deadpan.

"I saw a hell of a lot more than that, mother dear. Didn't you notice how your headlights shined right through her?"

We continue on in total silence, and once back home, I sit at the dining table, utterly shaken, while Maggie runs off to pee.

"I'm just baffled by this place," I yell in the direction of the closed bathroom door. "There's a strange little girl who runs around and talks to me but who is apparently a ghost. Then, there's the gray-haired gardener who looks like a ghost lady but isn't, yet she hasn't uttered a word to me since I moved here. As well, I have Marilyn that walks her little dog, and whom I feed frequently, yet my neighbor, Maynard, advises me she died several years ago… good grief!"

Mag walks back out into the room and shrugs. "I'm not sure your darn realtor gave you a full disclosure statement with regards to this place?"

"Maybe I'll just confront him about that the next time I see him. After all, Frank is your Aunt Jack's fiancé."

105

I'm awakened—as per usual—by Mac's grumblings at pretty near six o'clock on the dot. Slipping on flip-flops, we shuffle our way outside and across the street where he squats while I try to hide, in my bathrobe, behind a bush as two joggers pass by.

"Hi Liz!" Calls out one of the women, sounding a bit winded. "It was nice meeting you last night."

The other one waves and, with a New York accent, comments at twice the volume.

"Judy here was just telling me all about youse guys. We hafta get together ovah some wine and discuss how fercockt dis crazy place is."

Then off they both trot going left onto Treehouse Circle, while I linger behind the bush wondering who the heck they are and what the last one even said.

Back inside, I try my hardest to move about quietly and not wake my sleeping daughter, as I get the breakfast casserole out of the fridge and into the oven. *What the hell is fur cocked?* I wonder. I start a pot of decaf so Maggie can have a cup, then walk into the living room to turn on the Christmas tree. I stand, arms crossed, and admire the lights and ornaments and can't help but give a little smile as I reflect, yet again, on how glad I am that this holiday has found its way back into my life.

Looking down at the small array of presents arranged beneath, my eye catches one I haven't noticed before. I figure Maggie snuck another gift under here even though I told her enough already.

I reach down to pick it up. It's a medium size, rectangular box, wrapped in plain brown Kraft paper and simply tied with jute twine. Knotted into the bow is a single sprig of dahoon holly sporting several red berries.

There's a live gift tag made from a white mangrove leaf attached, and when I flip it over it simply reads, 'To Liz.'

What the heck? I wonder who it's from because, at that moment, I am sure it's not from Maggie after all. *But if it's not from her, how did it get here?*

The Mr. Coffee starts beeping in the kitchen bringing me back to the moment, and I place the package back and return to the kitchen.

I pour myself a cup of hot coffee, lace it with sweet cream, grab my phone from the charger, make my way back to the lanai. I take a seat in my comfy chair and placing my feet up on the new stool I picked up at Beall's Outlet when buying a few additional baby's things. I sit, sipping slowly at my drink, watching the backyard come to life.

Daybreak rises over the adjoining condo building, and bright, ubiquitous beams of sun filter through the foliage and dance across the yard. A varying array of bird calls can be heard outside, and I rise to open the back sliders, allowing the outside to make its way in.

The tick, tick, tick of a pair of cardinals. Loud screeching calls of a party of blue jays. The humorous squawking's of a flock of Quaker parrots passing overhead.

I know after our many years of friendship that Jack is a creature of habit and will assuredly be up by this hour. However, my only hesitation about calling is I don't know exactly what she's doing right now, and I don't want to bother or wakeup her brother's entire household. I wait until the time on my phone reads seven-thirty on the dot and then make my call. This is the longest we've gone in ages without talking, and I'm about to bust with curiosity over how things are going with her and Frank in Ohio.

"Hello?" Jack is whispering for some reason. "Is that you Liz?"

"Yes, Merry Christmas!"

"Shhh!" she murmurs. "Give me a minute to put something on."

I hear faint noises of movement and maybe a drawer and then I hear a chain unlatching and the closing of a door. "Okay," continues Jack, "I'm out in the hall."

"Why are you out in a hall?" I ask. "Aren't you at your brother's place in the guest suite?"

She proceeds to tell me about how her stay with the family has been going so far and all the holiday happenings they've attended.

"So, you see with Frank being single and not used to all the commotion, he finally advised me yesterday morning that he'd be glad to pay for a hotel room for the remainder of our stay."

"Makes sense to me," I say. "I've been to their house!"

"And… well, we really hadn't been alone for quite a while and… so, you know… one thing led to another. Actually, it led to two things and it lasted until about one in the morning. And—"

And, that's more than I need to hear.

I tell her about what Maggie and I have been up to and how much I am enjoying the holidays for the first time in many, many years.

"When was the last time you saw lights strung on my house or heard me sing "Silver Bells" along with grocery-store background music?

"Wow!" she says "Next you'll be telling me that you put up a tree"

"No, but you're close. Maggie did it!"

Jack goes on to tell me about how damn cold it is in Cincinnati and the warmest thing Frank brought was a windbreaker and a Lido Beach chambray sweatshirt. "We actually went to Walmart to get him the warmest, cheapest winter coat we could find."

"You can imagine what little selection there is left the week before Christmas. The only thing left that even fit him was an Onyx Hunting and Flotation Jacket in sort of a dirty brown and moldy green camouflage fabric. It's ugly as hell, but he says" –and she clears her throat and attempts her best Frank imitation– "It sure enough does keep a body plenty warm, ma'am."

Her impression—which is getting better every time I talk to her—and the thought of Frank in that jacket makes me laugh hard enough that I need to put down my coffee.

It's Beginning to Look a Lot Like Christmas

—Perry Como & the Fontane Sisters (1951)

106

I'm still on the phone when Maggie steps out on the lanai. She gives a little wave of her fingers and mouths *Good morning.*

She then patters off towards the kitchen where I hear the clank of a coffee mug being placed on the counter. I ask Jack to hold for a minute.

"Hey Sweetie, please take the casserole out of the oven and place it on the stove. Thank you!"

"Will do," she calls back.

The conversation takes on a more serious tone as Jack advises me that this trip has proven to be beneficial in several aspects.

"First of all, staying with my brother, his wife, and their seven off-spring caused Frank to share that he really doesn't want children. Of course, I just smiled, thinking, *well, thank goodness for that since at fifty my periods have become unpredictable and hopefully will soon be ending.*"

"He *does* know how old you are, right? I only ask because you honestly don't look it."

"Well, thanks, but it's never really come up in conversation. He's never asked so he's clearly not too concerned one way or another."

"Nor should he."

"Right, anyway the second piece of news is that we've also decided to put my house on the market and are meeting with a realtor next week. Frank says he would move to Ohio if I really wanted him to, but the poor Florida Cracker has been shivering the entire time he's been here... and that's spending most of our time in the house with the heat set at seventy-eight and a fire in the fireplace!"

"Isn't that a bit premature?" I ask. "I mean, where are you going to live while you work?"

"Well that's sort of the number three thing." She clears her throat. "I put in my resignation at P&G, and we've decided—speaking of age—what in the heck are we waiting for. We're going to move all my things to Frank's house in Nokomis, and I'm thinking spring is a fine time for a wedding."

"Oh Jackie!" I burst out. "I couldn't be happier for you, and selfishly I love the idea of us being so close together again."

"Me too, but I think I hear Frank rattling around in there, so I'm going to let you go."

"Of course, Jack. You two have a great Christmas. I love you!"

"Love you more!"

Once I end the call I just sit where I am looking out at the beautiful day that's waking up in my backyard.

Thank you, Lord. What a great Christmas gift.

Maggie calls out, "Can I dig into this thing yet? I'm starving."

"I'm on my way right now… find a spatula and wait till you hear the good news."

When I tell her, Maggie is almost as excited for Jack as I am. We both must be hungry because we tear into the casserole. But I'm still chewing my last bite when she practically jumps from her chair.

"Good grief, Mom. How much longer before we open presents?" Suddenly before me is the same young tyke I knew so many years ago.

"I thought I made myself perfectly clear," I say. "All Santa got you was a big girl bed this year."

"Oh, I'm quite aware, and my back and the baby thank you—or rather *Santa* very, very much. However, I have noticed he left several additional packages under the tree, and there's even a couple addressed to Baby Blum."

I advise her to select one from under the tree with her name on it and take a seat on the couch while I get us refills on our beverages. I return and set the mugs on the coffee table as she has already begun ripping the paper off.

"Why Santa you shouldn't have." Maggie smirks. "Stretch mark cream, maxi pads and lidocaine spray all packed up in a sitz bath."

I pick up my mug and lift it in a salute. "I was a mother too you know, and trust me on this one, you're going to thank me for all of them later."

Maggie's a little less anxious to get at the other practical presents until she opens the ones for the baby.

"Oh Mom, how cute!" She coos while holding the outfits up, smiling and admiring each of them. "They're so tiny they look like doll clothes. And this little pair of Converse sneaker booties are just killer!"

<h1 style="text-align:center">107</h1>

"Nature calls yet again." And after Mag gets herself up from the couch, she says, "It's your turn. Grab one and wait till I get back to open it."

Upon her return she jokes about the stack of gifts piled on the table. "Looks like somebody was a good girl this year."

I take a sip of my coffee. "I saw no reason to keep getting up and down, so I just grabbed them all."

I'm practically brought to tears after opening one from Maggie. It contains two T-shirts, one an adult size and the other infant. The large one states, Somebody stole my heart! and the small one says, I'm that somebody. Each contains a little sequined bling in various heart shapes.

I then pick-up a package that was professionally gift wrapped by the looks of the crisp folds, minimal tape, and perfect bow. It arrived via a UPS box about a week ago, and the return address on the shipping box advised it was from my old buddy Jack. Opening it, and digging through the glitter strewn tissue paper, I find it's filled with numerous smaller packages. There are name tags that read to Liz as well as Maggie and even one made out to Fetus.

"That is so Aunt Jacks."

The remaining gift is the rectangular package wrapped in brown paper and tied with a simple cord that I spied earlier. A mangrove leaf name tag with my name on it.

"Is this from you?"

"Not me," she says.

I attempt to untie the bow, pricking my finger on an extremely sharp holly leaf spine. Blood droplets splatter on the brown paper

"Here!" says Maggie, handing me her napkin to hold on it.

I remove the twig of holly leaves with red berries and instinctively smell it. The aroma is earthy and fresh like a conifer forest laden with morning dew.

"That showed up at your front door yesterday," Maggie says, "while you were in the shower getting ready for the party and church. I thought I told you about it."

I shake my head, examining my throbbing finger.

"Well, I was watching Live! with Kelly and Michael and heard a knock on your door. By the time I rolled off the couch and waddled to the front door there was no one there, except that package sitting on your welcome mat."

"How strange. I can't imagine who it could be from."

"Probably a neighbor," she says. "I mean there's no postage on it. It was just dropped off. Maybe it's something that the Cove does for the residents?"

I carefully proceed to unwrap the paper. I sit with an exposed shoebox atop the paper on my lap and quizzically read the imprinted label on the side.

Sperry Topsiders – Red – Size 8M

I look over into my daughter's wide eyes. "I believe this is *my* box."

Then I just sit there, still holding the napkin on my finger since it won't stop bleeding, staring at the parcel.

"Well, for God's sake open it!" shouts Maggie. "The suspense is killing me!"

Knowing damn well what I had stored in this very box—stored and *hidden away*—I hesitantly remove the lid to find the shoebox is filled with what appears to be Spanish moss and dried live oak leaves. Cautiously, I begin moving the debris around with the index finger on my left hand, not wanting to get dirt into the wound on my right one.

"This has to be a joke of some sort," I say as I nervously pick through the contents of the box.

I discover what looks to be a stick or twig poking out and, grasping it between my thumb and forefinger, proceed to pull it loose from the packing materials. Even though I had anticipated what I would find. I gasp aloud when the figure is exposed, and I find myself holding the erect penis of the wicked little totem man.

Abruptly letting go of his manhood, he tumbles back into the box and, now laying atop the rubble, he appears to be grinning devilishly up at me—I swear again that he's winking.

Startled by my actions Maggie grabs her belly in a protective manner. "I thought you got rid of that damn thing! How in the hell did it get under the Christmas tree?"

Placing the lid back on the box and slamming it down on the table, I get up.

"After that night when you had that horrible dream and we had to get you into the doctor… Well, I decided enough was enough and placed the little bastard in that shoebox. I even taped it shut with packing tape and hid it back in my closet. I remember thinking at the time that it was only a temporary fix and, as Marilyn had warned me, I'd needed to get it out of my house as soon as possible and for good."

I pick up the box and walk towards my bedroom with the intentions of checking out my closet, where the box use to be, when I suddenly stop dead.

"That's it! Marilyn is the only person, other than you and Jack, that I have even talked to about this hideous thing." I continue while shaking the box in Maggie's direction, "But how in the hell did she get in here to take it, and better yet, why in the world would she wrap it up and give it back to me?"

108

An hour slips by and Maggie glances up from a *Sarasota* magazine as I angrily stomp out to the kitchen to retrieve the packing tape dispenser from the junk drawer, and then tromp, vexed, back into the bedroom. The sticky high-pitched rip of the tape as I pull it from the dispenser echoes through the entire condo

"So what are you up to now?" she calls from the couch.

"Oh, not much," **–reeep–** "Just securing tribal boy's box lid again." **–reeep–** "then I'm getting myself dressed" **–reeep–** "and marching over to Marilyn's with some damn leftover breakfast casserole and a shitload of questions!"

There's a moment of silence, followed by lots of water splashing, before Mag hears the cry, "Bring your mother her pills!"

I make my way over to Marilyn's, toting a harvest gold Tupperware Servalier container and a taped-up shoebox. I knock but get no response. My knock turns into a thunderous pounding as I also commence loudly calling out her name.

"Marilyn… MARILYN! I'm pretty darn sure you're in there somewhere. I found out Hanukkah ended on the sixteenth, yet you kept taking food from me all the way through Christmas!"

I suddenly realize I've drawn the attention of several people in tennis whites making their way to the courts.

"Hi there!" I say offering a nervous wave in their direction. "Enjoy your movie and Chinese food later!" I add, rolling my eyes over what I just said.

I stand there trying to remember the last time I actually saw Marilyn and Tookie and what we even talked about. Now concerned that, if she's alive perhaps she's fallen, or even worse died in her sleep, I decide to walk down to the office and ask them if they know anything about her condition, or perhaps what I should do to help.

Making my way up the steps to the structure and onto the porch I can see there's some kind of notice on the office door printed on celadon green copy paper.

The Pelican Cove Office will be Closed
Monday, December 24th and Tuesday December 25th for the Holidays. We will re-open on Wednesday. In case of an actual emergency please contact the guard at the front gate. Thank you!

I'd taken it for granted there was someone running this place at all times. Never assume.

Just as I'm stepping down into the parking lot, a golf cart comes whizzing up driven by a plump little Hispanic guy.

"Hallo Miss. How might I helps you?"

I explain my concern about my neighbor and that I was hoping the office could assist. He suggests I come back tomorrow at nine o'clock and attempts to console me that she's probably just fine.

"Maybes she goes to the church for Navidad?" he suggests.

"I seriously doubt it," I answer. "She's Jewish."

He looks a little at a loss as to what to say to that.

"Have you had breakfast?" I ask.

"Sí, but I can always eat." He pats his paunch and grins in a manner that curls the tips of his handlebar moustache.

I hand him the container with the casserole in it. "It's probably cold by now, but if you use the microwave in the Wilbanks it will probably taste better."

"Gracias, gracias." He seems genuinely touched by the gesture as he gets back in his cart. "Are you the Jewish too, miss?"

I smile. "No, no I'm not."

"Well then," he says, "Feliz Navidad, Señorita!"

"Merry Christmas to you too, Señor," I say and offer a wave as he drives off.

I then think to yell, "I'm going to want my Tupperware back!

109

Feeling a bit anxious over all this, I discern I want to escape the house, so I ask Maggie if she is up to a little beach time. I'm filled with the desire to place some distance between us, the totem, Marilyn, and the Cove.

"I'll place the honey-baked ham under foil in the oven on low," I say. "It should be just fine while we're gone."

"Sure, what the heck?" She places her '*Bump*' magazine back on the table. "But I won't be getting in the water for fear someone might mistake me for a whale," she says. "Well, that and the fact that I can't get into my swimsuit anymore."

I suspect it shouldn't be crowded at all with it being Christmas day, comparing it to Sunday mornings and how empty the shores can be until church lets out.

"I'm going to go get ready," I say. "You be sure to put on plenty of sunscreen Missy. We'll stop at Starbucks on the way and grab a green tea frappuccino."

"Sounds good," she says. "As long as they come in decaf?"

I better get low test too, I think, *or I'll find myself feeling anxious.*

We decide to head south and take the scenic route to Casey Key. Turning right off the Trail onto Blackburn Point, we pass the Fish House restaurant before crossing the swing bridge over the Intracoastal Waterway. Making a sharp left onto the extremely curvy and very narrow Casey Key Road we begin the mere five-mile drive that can take anywhere up to twenty minutes or more to navigate.

I let out a heavy sigh. "I can't get Dick out of my mind!"

"Who the heck is Dick?" says Mag. "Or should I have said *whose* dick?"

I give her a disgusted smirk. "I'm talking about that damn totem guy with the enormous… thing. I had to call him something?"

She takes a sip of her Frappuccino and nods. "First name, Dick; Last name, Johnson."

Giggles!

The road continues to curve its way along the length of the extremely narrow key offering views on one side of the Intracoastal Waterway and the Gulf of Mexico on the other and, at times both. Along the way, you can view some of the most expensive homes in all of Sarasota County. However, there remain several original sprawling ranches, and my personal favorite, a few gingerbread cottages that hold their own sort of old Florida charm.

"Stephen King has a place somewhere on this little spit of land," I say.

"Yeah, I read that in a review somewhere back when *Duma Key* came out. I hear he has a new neighbor in Rosie O'Donnell. You know, with her bigger than life personality, Stephen just may have some new fodder to write about."

"Oh my God," I laugh. "I read about that too in the *Tribune*. Imagine having her and those five kids as your neighbors. You know, now that you mention it, I wonder if he's ever been to Pelican Cove? That, my dear, would provide him with some unbelievable writing material!"

We reach the Nokomis Public Beach where the parking lot is packed.

"What the heck?"

"I guess other people had the same idea," Maggie says.

Continuing on, we come to a small dirt lot on the left side of the road across from a beach pavilion. I pull in and negotiate a spot next to a two-door, fusion red Tesla Roadster positioned between two palm trees and facing back out towards the road.

"At least we won't be blocked in if this lot fills up like the other one."

"Sure," says Maggie, "I just hope we can tell which red car is ours when we come back?"

I grab the beach chairs and hand her my drink. "That's easy. Mine's the one that's not yet paid for!"

We cross the road, and as I ascend some rather steep steps, Maggie makes her way up a zig zag handicap incline. I wait at the top until she makes it up. She is breathy by the time she reaches me.

"Where the hell's the beach?"

"It should be just on the other side of this building," I say. "And look, there are restrooms right here."

We make our way down a boardwalk directly behind the structure that ends at the beach head. We pause, taking in the cloudless, baby-blue sky that melds into the turquoise of the ocean waves. I remove my flip-flops so I can feel the sand between my toes and bend over to pick them up.

"You want yours off too," I say. "I'll be glad to help you so you don't have to bend."

She looks down. "Did I wear them? I can't see a thing. Mostly I'm afraid if I take them off we'll never get them back on again… I'll be just fine."

Glancing up and down the beach, I'm amazed at how many people are actually here. However, instead of individuals staking out their personal space on blankets aligned in comfort zones across the sand, people are gathered in large groups and appear to be doing more socializing than swimming.

We stake out our own spot, and Maggie suggests we stroll a little prior to her settling into a chair with her book and a drink.

"Once I'm down I may never get back up again."

"Okay, just let me grab a Publix bag from my beach duffel to collect shells and garbage in."

We decide to aim south towards the north jetty and the further we walk the more we realize this is no ordinary day at the beach.

We come across groups of thirtysomethings who have set up portable folding tables covered in plastic holiday tablecloths and filled with platters of food. The centerpiece of the entire scene is a completely decorated artificial Christmas tree, and it's not the only one we see as we peruse the other parties we pass along the way.

"I can't imagine hauling all my Christmas decorations to the beach!" I laugh.

Bending over I pick up several shells at water's edge.

"Know what they call this one?" I ask

"Not a clue, but it's beautifully translucent. What is it?"

"It's called a Roman Coin due to its shape. Perhaps you've noticed I have a mason jar halfway filled with them on my dresser."

"I figure, once it's full I can take it to the Pelican Cove office, and it should pay for at least a month's HOA fees."

"Ha. You wish."

We pass kids building sand snowmen and actually see a family pulling plastic sleds across the shore. People are literally making snow angels in the loose sand on the beach, while others are running around with lit sparklers.

Occasionally individuals call out a Merry Christmas in our direction. Or they extend a welcoming invitations for us to join them and attempt to wave us over.

I show Maggie another shell. "This one's called a lions paw for obvious reasons. They always remind me of when I went to Beijing and saw the guardian lions."

"Oh, I've seen those all over Mott Street in Chinatown," She says. "The lions, not the shells... I've actually seen the Chinese rub their heads, kind of like they do to Buddha's belly."

"Well, the lions are usually depicted in pairs," I say. "They consist of a male leaning his paw upon an embroidered ball representing supremacy over the world, and a female restraining a playful cub that is on its back, representing the nurturing aspect of women."

We come upon a group that appear to be either Mexican or Cuban. They are grilling something that smells like fajitas and playing "Mi Burrito Sabanero" by Juanes on a boom box as the little ones whack away at two colorful, Christmas present shaped piñatas.

I am surprised when Maggie begins singing along.

"How do you know that song?"

"Oh, Bob and I had a couple of Hispanic friends from the theatre who were from Spanish Harlem. They were notorious for their holiday parties… and flamboyant lifestyle!"

I joke that her New York City experience is a lot like living in the Cove and actually Sarasota itself. Both are a microcosm of the world.

"I have never lived anywhere in America that has had such a European flair and feel as this place," I say. "I actually love hearing all the different languages being spoken and my only catching every tenth word… It's great fun!"

We're so overcome by the smells, sights and sounds that, before we know it, we're standing at the North Jetty Beach Park. Looking back from whence we came we can barely make out the tiny specks that may or may not be our chairs. Maggie puts her hands on her hips and stretches her back.

"I need to get out of this heat and sit for a minute," she says. "Plus I think I see a bathroom over by those picnic shelters."

As she takes off, I spy a concession stand and buy a couple of Zephyrhills bottled waters with the credit card I had the foresight to stick in my cover-up pocket along with my ID. However, I can't believe we left our Frappuccino's back with the chairs, and I'm sure they're warm and melted by now. *That's ten bucks down the drain.*

Maggie staggers out of the Ladies room holding wet towels on her forehead.

"You don't look so good," I say.

She shrugs. "I don't feel so good." And she finds a bench in the shade under a shelter on which to sit.

I see the road exiting the parking lot and deduce that it must be the same one we parked on, and that walking on pavement would be quicker than walking on loose, drifting sand.

"You sit here under cover and drink this water while I go get the car and then come back to get you."

"It's a deal," says Maggie still wiping her brow. "And don't forget our chairs and beach bags. I'm spent and ready to go home!"

110

I clean up following dinner and, after wiping down the glass stove top and starting the dishwasher, turn off the lights.

"The kitchen is officially closed for the holidays!"

I enter the living room to find my daughter has found a burning yule log on YouTube TV and it's accompanied by instrumental Christmas music.

"How nice is this?" I ask while walking over to the bar. I peruse the wine selection inside and select the bottle of 2011 Mascota Vineyards Unanime that came with the gift basket from my old co-workers when I first moved here.

"I can't believe that it will soon be one year that I've been living here," I say. "I guess it's about time that I opened this. Care for a glass to toast the holiday?" I ask. "I personally don't think it will hurt either of you."

Maggie contemplates but only for a moment. "Sure, why not. But only half a glass please. Maybe it will help me sleep."

"Haven't you been sleeping well? I thought you loved your new mattress?"

"I do. I just can't get comfortable anymore no matter which of my three flat sides I lay on. Plus, I still keep having some really strange dreams."

"Well, todays long walk and tonight's big meal should go a long way towards knocking you out," I say. "You know this has been a very nice day. Heck, overall it's actually been a truly wonderful Christmas." I lift a glass in Maggie's direction. "Thank you, thank you very much!"

Maggie blushes. "But you did everything mom."

"Oh, I think we both did our part to bring the spirit of the season back into our splintered lives." I smile. "Plus, you know what they say my dear, a baby changes everything!"

A Baby Changes Everything
—Faith Hill (2008)
Songwriters: Craig Michael Wiseman / James Timothy Nichols /
Kimberly Kerryann Wiseman

111

Before pouring myself another glass of wine, I ask Maggie if she would care to join me. But she places her hand over her glass.

"I'm finished for the night and not just with the wine. I'm struggling to keep my eyes open now." She gets up and aims off towards her bedroom as Mac patters off in the opposite direction towards his own bed.

"Goodnight you two," I say aloud to the empty room. "See you in the morning."

I finish my pour, curl back up where I was on the end of the couch, and sip at my glass as I stare mindlessly at the simulated fireplace on the screen. The music has stopped playing, and now the only sound is an occasional snap or crackle from the flames, or the intermittent shifting of the logs causing the embers to rekindle and burst back to life. It's absolutely mesmerizing as I stare at it and reminisce about my current living situation compared to the actual home fires of long ago in Ohio.

Suddenly, I'm startled awake by the chiming of the grandfather clock striking twelve.

What the heck? It hasn't worked for almost a year.

From my vantage point, I can see that the lyre pendulum is actually swinging back and forth and the reflection of the tree lights are dancing on the circular brass bob.

I'm slumped sideways with my head on the couch arm and as I sit up, I'm horrified to see a red wine stain on my new couch's cushion and the wine glass lying on the floor.

"Damn it!"

I must have dosed off and dropped my glass. Jumping up I run towards the kitchen to grab the can of Love My Carpet I keep on hand just in case Mac has an accident. That's when I notice that the front door of my condo is standing wide open and dried oak leaves have blown into the foyer. *What the hell?*

"Mac?" I call out. "Mac… come here, boy."

But there's no reply. I run to my bedroom and flip on the light. His bed is empty and Marvin the Moose—his favorite Kong toy that he's had since puppyhood and always sleeps with—is not there either.

"Mac! Where the heck are you?"

Recalling the open door, I'm filled with dread at the thought that he's gotten out and is running amok through the Cove. God only knows how long he's been out there.

I think, and then try to remember what time it was when Maggie and he went to bed.

"Maggie!" I shout and run to her bedroom door slowly opening it. The bedside light is on and she is nowhere in the room. Her top-sheet and duvet are tossed to the side, and the fitted sheet is halfway pulled off the mattress in the direction of the door. Almost as if someone had been clinging onto it. Also, one of the pillows lying on the floor has droplets of what looks like sticky tree sap on it.

Looking around I note there are more oak leaves scattered about and Spanish moss hanging from the shade on the lamp by the bed. But, strangest of all, the room has a musty, damp, woodsy odor about it. Not dissimilar to the fall aroma of decaying leaves combined with the scent given off by a handful of moist soil.

I glance into the bathroom. Empty

"Maggie, Mac where in the world are you two?"

I become nauseated, return to the bath, lift the lid on the toilet and puke.

I lurch to the sink and, gathering some water in the palm of my hand, I slurp it up, swish it around my mouth and spit it out. I gaze into the mirror. My eyes are desperate.

Dear God, what's going on here? Please Lord, please help me! —but also— *God... I really need a haircut.* Which causes inopportune laughter.

Returning to the front door I slide my flip-flops on and grab my phone from the counter. I contemplate calling 911, or at least the guard house, but hesitate. What if Mac had to go out and Maggie simply took him outside?

Sure, that's it, she saw me on the couch and simply didn't want to disturb me.

Then the terrifying feeling of dread rushes back over me as I realize that thought wouldn't explain the mess in Maggie's room, Mac's missing toy, or the front door standing wide open after I know damn well that I locked it.

112

I scurry down the path, crossing the troll bridge and exit the carport, making my way into the open parking lot of the Pavilion.

"Maggie, Mac... are you out here somewhere?" I say quietly not wanting to arouse all that are surely sleeping. "Please, answer me!"

I pause, in awe, after looking down Pelican Cove Road to the East and observing an enormous, and amazingly luminescent moon with a bright star to the lower left of it.

It is an amazing sight and were this the celestial spectacle some two thousand years ago, I can see why the Magi followed it.

Upon closer observation I believe the star shows a small red spot. *Jupiter maybe.*

Seeing neither hide nor hair of either of them, I decide to follow the Christmas star and continue down the street allowing it to light the way. The scene is actually sort of magical, as the twinkle lights wrapped around every lamp post have turned the place into a wooded fairyland that appears full of fireflies.

I come upon one of the lanes running off to the right on Pelican Cove Road and see what appears to be the silhouette of a dog walker down at its end, strolling in and out of the shadows impishly. It's way too dark to pick out if it's them, but I softly announce their names in that direction.

"Mag, Mac... Maggie, is that you?"

There's a slight *yip,* but I can't discern if it belongs to my dog. Then before I can even blink, they disappear completely into the dark, dense foliage at the end of the road.

"This is really stupid!" And I take off in their direction, doing a slow jog in an attempt to catch up. Reaching the point where I saw the figures last, the pavement abruptly comes to an end. I am left with a choice of three paths.

I find the flashlight app on my phone and turn it on in hopes of better viewing my options. To the left is a rather rough dirt trail that seems to go under an upper condo's back steps and then off into complete darkness. Straight ahead is an actual poured walkway, but it's extremely narrow and looks more to be a drainage channel for storm run-off. Worse yet, it's in total blackness as well.

Standing there, I can see into the back sliders of a bottom floor unit that's eerily illuminated by the glow of a large screen TV. I recognize the show as *Jimmy Kimmel Live!*

Also, peering out from this condo's lanai and staring straight at me, is a life-sized carved pelican statue with a sinister grin and the tail of a fish hanging out of its bill.

To the right, and in the direction I *think* they may have actually walked, is a meandering mulch path covered with long-leaf pine needles and larger than life pinecones. It proceeds behind a long line of unlit condos. However, at least here and there are actual light posts positioned through the woods partially brightening the way, albeit lacking the addition of twinkle lights.

Still using my phone, I cautiously make my way down the path until it emerges into a large open lawn area that's densely wooded around the perimeters. Looking up, I'm somehow comforted by the reappearance of the moon and its companion shining down on me and illuminating the grass.

Through the closely compacted foliage, I see a mysterious, bluish glimmer off in the distance. it is dancing off the undersides of the various tree leaves and the partially visible portions of the condo buildings.

As I start to approach it, I can make out what looks like smoke or fog rising from the glow.

"What the heck?"

I cautiously continue down the trail in its direction, rounding the exterior of an unlit wooden structure that sits secluded by fishtail palms and huge banana tree leaves. I find myself standing at a fence gate, looking inside at a swimming pool. I know, then, where I am—the Glenhouse pool.

I have never approached it from this side and especially not in the dark of night, nor at this late time of day. Truth be told, I've actually only swum in it once. The coolness of the winter night air, mixed with the eighty-degree heated pool temperature, has created a misty haze rising up from the water reminiscent of the hot mineral springs in Yellowstone.

There's no sign of either a walker or their dog, much less Maggie and Mac. I'm compelled to cautiously unlatch the gate and enter the pool deck. Stepping inside I can barely see through the low-lying fog to the other side, but I soon become aware, nonetheless, that I'm not alone.

I make out the vague form of someone sitting at the far edge of the pool. From this distance all I can see are a set of legs from knees down and diminutive feet making ripples across the surface by gently paddling them in the water.

Not wishing to startle whoever is there, I speak as I begin making my way around the pool edge in their direction.

"Hello. I don't mean to interrupt your late night swim, but have you seen a young pregnant woman with a little, black, Scotty dog come through here?"

I continue walking finding it rather odd that I receive no response. Rounding the final corner, where the ladder for the deep end is located, I stop dead in my tracks.

"It's you. What in the world are you doing out here all alone at this hour? Not even an adult should be out swimming in this steamy fog unsupervised!"

The mysterious young girl, Mary, turns her head slowly in my direction and it becomes quite apparent that she's crying. I note that she's still wearing the strange, old-fashioned white dress she always wears, and on the edge of the pool lies her sketch pad and what appears to be charcoals.

"Are you all right?" I ask and squat down beside her so as to be closer to eye level.

"We saw you run across the road last night," I say. "And now you're here at this time of night. Enough is enough. There's no argument this time young lady. I'm taking you straight home and talking to your parents!"

I try to grab her arm, but my hand goes right through it. *What in the world?* Then, trying to embrace her tear streaked face, my hands simply meet together with a simple clap in the center of her sorrowful expression.

I'm so startled, I lose my balance and end up flat on my butt, staring into the teary eyes of what I now realize is an actual ghost.

"Mary," I whisper to her, "are you... dead?"

She blinks her eyes in a bewildered way causing a flood of additional tears.

"I don't think so," she says in the manner of a puzzled child, even innocently hunching her shoulders a bit for emphasis.

As I get myself up off the pavement, and she mimics my movements. She picks up her sketch pad and is soon standing in front of me looking up. Without even glancing down, she flips open the book to the first page and holds it up, showing me what she apparently has been drawing.

"He says he's tired of me," she says softly. "He wants the baby."

She rips out the page and begins to weep uncontrollably.

I take the picture from her, and at first, I am completely amazed at the details of the piece.

"Did you draw this, Mary?"

"Yes!" she says proudly and even shows signs of possibly starting to smile.

Upon closer inspection, the drawing seems to be of a majestic—and quite manly—southern live oak holding someone, a woman, captive as she struggles to free herself from the grip of his sweeping limbs. Limbs that plunge towards the ground before lifting skyward.

The tree's devilish eyes send a chill down my spine as I immediately recognize them as belonging to the totem. One of the smaller limbs shooting awkwardly up from the crown is hoisting a baby skyward, as if gloating over its newly claimed prize. Alarmingly, from the newborn's stomach, an umbilical cord is still attached.

Following the tether that supplied the life-providing food and oxygen to the unborn infant, it twists and turns from branch to branch until it reaches the mother. It is now quite apparent to me that the woman is screaming, for her newborn child has been ripped from her womb.

I shift my gaze back to Mary who is still looking up teary-eyed at me, and before I have a chance to ask about the woman in the drawing, she answers.

"It's Maggie!" she cries.

113

Heart pounding wildly, I jump up mid-panic attack while grabbing my chest in an attempt to calm myself. My feet come down hard on a pile of fur...

"God, sorry Mac!"

He looks up at me as if to say, *What was that for?*

I can see a red wine stain on my new couch's cushion and my wine glass lying on the floor.

"What the hell?" I gasp. *I just did this.*

My mind fast forwards to my last recollection before waking. Ghostly Mary's horrid picture of Maggie with her baby wrenched demonically from her body as she screamed in horror and torturous pain.

The holiday fireplace scene is no longer on the television and has been replaced by an infomercial hosted by Larry King. He is touting a product called Omega XL and how it miraculously reduces joint inflammation.

Feeling quite anxious and a bit sick to my stomach, I run towards the pantry to grab something to clean up the spill. I pause on the way to take in the grandfather clock that sits idly in place—pendulum frozen, and both hands hanging lifelessly in the six-thirty position, just as they have since moving here.

In the kitchen I flinch seeing the digital stove clock flicker from 11:59 to 12:00 midnight and I brace myself for clock chimes to play and signal yet another dream. *They do not come.*

472

I grab the carpet cleaner and several damp paper towels, as I nervously rush back to the living room to attend to the stain. But then panic hits me again, and I drop everything haphazardly on the floor and run off to my bathroom vanity. With shaking hands, I pull open the drawer and grab the bottle of Librium and toss two green and black pills in my mouth, while spilling the remainder on the counter. Turning on the faucet, I bend over and slurp up enough water to get them down.

I look in the mirror and recall the observation made, mid-nightmare, that I needed a haircut. Attempting to smile I give a half-hearted chuckle stating. "My God… I really do!"

As my thoughts start to calm I am struck again as though by a rogue wave. *Maggie!*

Darting off towards her room to check, I turn on the hall light so I can see in without disturbing her. I slowly open the door and look. I can see she's in bed, lying on her back, and easily make out the outline of the ever-growing baby bump that houses my soon-to-be-born granddaughter.

"Thank you!" I say, glancing heavenwards.

I quietly pull the bedroom door shut and return to the living room, where I attempt to distract myself by scrubbing at the Cabernet spatter. I carry the empty wine glass and soiled towels back to the kitchen and pause at the kitchen sliders to gaze outside. I slide them open in an attempt at taking a deep cleansing breath of fresh air, while waiting for the pills calming effect to completely kick in, and the debilitating tightness in my chest to release. I would welcome the exhaustion that always follows.

Suddenly, out of the corner of my right eye some movement out in the darkness catches my attention. Glancing in the direction of the other bridge to my property, I'm just in time to see Mary darting across in the soft moonlight, wearing her all-too-familiar dress. She looks over her left shoulder, directly at me, and I swear she's mouthing the words, "Run Liz, run… run!"

114

I have no recollection of when the medication took effect, nor when I actually laid my head down on my pillow, but I awake to Mac yipping and begging to be taken out. I'm fully dressed, except for my shoes, and as I make my way to the walk-in to find them, I catch a glimpse of myself in the vanity mirror.

You're a hot mess, I tell myself as I run a quick brush through my hair and adjust my brassiere.

I slide on a pair of Vionic, Beach Flip Flops. "Come on boy," I say and grab his lead as we head out the door.

When we return, I put on some coffee, and when it's ready, I pour a cup and make my way out to the lanai and my usual chair.

Sipping away at my hazelnut cream, I keep replaying the scenario of last evening's nightmare over and over in my head. The sights, sounds, and smells of these damn dreams are so darn real every time that it's difficult to discern fact from fiction. Yet I'm totally convinced of two things: Mary is real (well... a real ghost, whatever that means) and that friggin', scary totem has got to go.

I reflect how ever since that cursed thing came into my life it's been nothing but trouble. Staring blankly outside, a male and female cardinal flit from branch to branch tick, tick, ticking to each other and cocking their heads at me.

Then breaking my gaze, I remember that day vividly at the peppermint scented, collectibles store and the old, weathered, smoking cowgirl that I bought the darn thing from.

Granny Daisy. That was her name. *Daisy.*

Her name seems to summon her voice, and with her voice comes her words: *Oh, I reckons y'all been travelin' a bit more than dat on dis current journey y'all are on.*

Then for some reason a fleeting image of the young woman I'd seen leaving her shop comes to mind: *Thanks again for everything… It literally changed my life!"*

Changed my life? I wonder if possibly *my* life hadn't changed since I bought it from her. I further ponder if a bit of it wasn't for the better?

Unexpectedly, all the positive events since the totem's purchase come flooding to mind in rapid progression. The first day of ownership and how Jorge, the guard, miraculously ushered me through his interrogation gate around all others. Finding my daughter sitting on my front porch and her sharing the blessing of a forthcoming granddaughter. In turn, how Maggie restored a feeling of family back into my life, and reintroduced traditions like Thanksgiving and Christmas. Then there's Jack, falling in love with Frank and, thank God, their decision to settle down here in Florida and be near me.

I've made new friends here in the Cove as well, and I personally know more of my neighbors now than I ever did in Ohio. I've attended parties and events out in public, and I've found a new doctor, and more importantly a friend, in Stu. I linger for a moment thinking of Stu and how we're to go out next week for New Year's Eve. I wonder about where our relationship might be going and, for the first time, realize I don't feel guilty, or like I'm cheating on my husband Scott for having such thoughts. In fact, somehow, I think he's actually saying, *It's about damn time, Elizabeth, that you got on with your life.*

It pains my heart but makes me smile at the same time.

First things first, however. The Cove office reopens from the holiday vacation at nine o'clock this morning, and I'm going to be the first one there. Somebody has got to check on Marilyn! So, off I trod to put my face on and dress.

115

I'm sitting on a park bench on the righthand side of the Pelican Cove Office front porch, as a green Jeep Wrangler pulls into a spot to the left of the building. This is quickly followed by a White Chevy Silverado that parks on the right. The truck's rear cargo door is covered in bumper stickers all regarding horses and riding. But one in particular stands out.

Cowgirl Attitude, it Ain't for City Girls!

Two women independently exit their vehicles and make their way up on the porch where I'm seated. The one taking out her key and opening the front door, I recognize as Sharon who mans the front counter in the office and has assisted me several times regarding my questions about living in Pelican Cove and the plethora of rules and regulations involved.

The other, wearing a white bullhide cowgirl hat with an up-turned brim, I recognize as Bonnie Long the general manager. We've never met in person, but I recognize her from the picture included, every month, in the "Bonnie's Corner" commentary of the *Pelican Cove News*. The in-house publication has been a great asset for finding out what's going on, both socially and bureaucratically in this place.

I introduce myself to her as Sharon holds the door open for us to enter.

"Hi Bonnie, my name is Liz Blum in GL-359." She shakes hands rather firmly for a woman. "I was hoping to speak with you for a moment about some concerns I have regarding one of my neighbors, Marilyn Spitznogle."

She gets a peculiar look on her face, "I recall seeing your name on your paperwork when you first moved in here. Give me a moment to run upstairs to my office first and put out one of last night's fires. Sharon will you please show Miss Blum" –pronouncing it like plum– "up in about five minutes?"

Once I'm upstairs, she offers me a seat across from her desk, in front of a large picture window showing off an enormous *Kigelia Africana* or "sausage tree." Its fruits dangle from long stems and are reminiscent of Genoa or Mortadella hanging in an Italian deli window.

"So, tell me," asks Bonnie, "what did you want to know about Mrs. Spitznogle?"

"I actually have a genuine concern about Marilyn living all alone, and I worry about Tookie becoming intertwined with her walker. It's a real trip hazard you know! I'm also worried she's not eating regularly..." going on to explain how I take her leftovers or pick up groceries items for her whenever possible.

The woman shifts uncomfortably in her desk chair and now sports an even more disconcerted guise on her face.

"I've been calling her phone," I say, "as well as knocking and knocking at her door, for the last few days and she hasn't answered. Heck, I even went around back and attempted to peek in her windows. I'm terrified that she's fallen in the shower and broken a hip. Or worse..." –I clear my throat– "well, that's she's dead on the floor in front of the kitchen sink and beginning to smell!"

Bonnie seems at a loss for words as she stares at me with questioning eyes and a wide-open mouth. Finally she manages to collect herself.

"Are you saying you've actually met and talked to this woman?"

Now it's my turn at being confused.

"Of course, I have. She's my neighbor. Why, I even drove her to Temple once."

Standing up, Bonnie approaches a file cabinet on the other side of the room and pulls the drawer open. Arriving at the divider labeled S, she thumbs through the files until she comes to what she's looking for and pulls it out. Returning to her desk, she sets the folder down, and I can easily read the header on the tab—Mortimer (Morty) & Marilyn Spitznogle—and hand-stamped in red at a slant across the cover another word.

DECEASED

She opens the folder and pulls out the death records for both the Spitznogles.

"I usually consider resident files strictly confidential and wouldn't think of sharing the personal details of our condo owners' files with anyone but the owner. However, with these documents being of public record, I see no inherent problems from sharing them with you."

I gaze down and can't believe what I'm seeing... *the couple's death certificates.* According to the documents, Marilyn's been deceased since January 17, 2009.

"My other neighbor, Maynard, was right..." I whisper. "She's been gone almost three years."

I look up at Bonnie. Astonished.

"Who in the hell have I been feeding for months on end now?"

The Sound of Silence

—Simon & Garfunkel (1964)

<h1 style="text-align:center">116</h1>

It takes quite a bit of convincing, but finally Bonnie agrees to take me to see Marilyn's condo.

"I couldn't live with the thought of an elderly woman, even if it's not really Marilyn, lying dead on the couch two doors over from me, with the *Price Is Right* on, and no one doing anything about it!"

"I'm sure no one is in the condo or it would have been reported to the office by now," she explains. She waves me out of her office and down the steps. As I ponder, "I liked Bob so much better than Drew, didn't you?" Pausing, she gives me a quizzical look, then turns and tells Sharon that she'll be right back as she continues ushering me out the front door.

"It's mandatory for all units to have a condo checker to examine the interior monthly when the unit is vacant," she says as we speed off in a white, canopied golf cart.

"They look for things like water damage, pest infestation, and assuring the air conditioner is operating correctly to prevent mold. I should have checked to see who's on file for that unit before we left," she says as we speed down Pelican Cove Road. "Undoubtedly, the caretaker would have stopped by the office to advise of a dead body watching television."

She glances over at me. "You don't think you've inadvertently been caring for the condo checker, do you? Or maybe it's a vagrant that's taken up residence in there." But that doesn't sound right, and she knows it. She takes a sharp left onto my section of the road almost tipping the cart.

"I just saw a report on the news about a couple in North Port coming home after an extended vacation and finding a married couple living in their home with their four children," she says. "Besides the fact that they had trashed the place, they were now insisting they had a legal right to stay there until they could relocate and were threatening to sue the owners. Now is that crazy, or what?"

She skids to a stop in a vacant guest spot next to Marilyn's empty carport. We hop out and she unclips a ring of keys from her belt loop. I follow her across the small wooden bridge and we march up to the front door. I'm guessing that it's out of politeness that she knocks three hard raps on the door, before inserting the key in the lock and opening it.

Straining to glimpse around Bonnie's head, I can see the interior is completely dark. "I want you to stay here," she says, "while I hunt for a light switch and check things out inside."

As I stand there holding the screen door open, I catch the whiff of something foul that vaguely reminds me of the odor that greeted us the first time I looked at my own place.

Lights come on and I can see from my vantage point that the place is sparsely furnished and has an abandoned and uninhabited appearance. Moments later Bonnie calls out for me.

"Miss Blum [like plum], come here please… I'm in the kitchen."

I enter with trepidation, my head swiveling every which way, taking in the grime, cobwebs and the overall feeling of emptiness in the place. I pause to wipe a finger across the arm of a lone side chair and observe that it's covered with dust.

Moving further into the interior I access the kitchen and there stands Bonnie frowning and pointing at the counter and recessed sink.

"*What the hell?*"

The countertop and double sink are filled with various Rubbermaid and Cool Whip bowls and include Ziploc baggies that are piled everywhere, still filled with various food contents.

"These appear to be mostly mine!" I say. "I recognize them."

I take in the scene before feeling completely perplexed. The smell in the condo is obviously originating from the rotting contents still visible through the transparent containers.

"I don't get it?" I say, shaking my head in confusion. "She not only would call to thank me for the meals and tell me how much she enjoyed them, but she would also place special requests. Heck, I would even pick up the chocolate iced brownies and cinnamon-pecan schnecken she liked from Publix bakery!"

Bonnie walks over and swinging open the turned off refrigerator's door states, "And, that might explain this."

As she steps aside displaying numerous Publix tan grocery bags lined up on the shelves each appearing to also be filled with decaying packages of food. There, amongst it all, I spy the bottle of kosher wine from Trader Joe's that I bought her for the holidays.

I grab it from the shelf. "I'm taking this back… something tells me I'm going to need it!"

117

"Would you like all your storage containers back too?"

Asks Bonnie as we cross back over the bridge and pause by the golf cart. I barely hear a word as my mind is racing wildly, attempting to comprehend the fact that Marilyn isn't real.

"Hell, I even picked up her phantom pooch's poop," I mumble.

"The property was held up in probate for a time," says Bonnie, while taking a look back at the condo. "Marilyn and her husband Morty were large supporters of the Serious Fun Children's Network. As a matter of fact, Marilyn was on a flight to the opening of the most recent Paul Newman Hole in the Wall Gang camp in Israel when she died. I believe they were to receive some sort of award, or honor, for all of their charity work over the years."

"She died on the plane?" I ask, coming out of my daze.

"Yes, sadly, on her way there. Y'know Paul Newman, himself, came to Pelican Cove to meet with them. That caused quite a ruckus, let me tell you!"

"Anyway, yes, probate," she says picking up the dropped thread of her conversation. "So it seems Marilyn left three quarters of her estate to Mr. Newman's cause and a quarter of it to her estranged daughter in New York City. Apparently, part of the hold-up in the court settlement was because her daughter contested the will, feeling she should receive one hundred percent of the family fortune. The other part was that the woman refused to set foot in the state of Florida. Whatever the reason,

I've been advised by several of the residents that she hadn't even visited her parents' home in Pelican Cove... ever!"

"That's so sad," I say. "So what happened?"

"Well, it seems the courts decided on a fifty–fifty split, and part of that meant the daughter got the condo and all its contents. One day, about two years ago, a man pulls up with a moving van, and the movers load up all the valuables, antiques, and their extensive Jewish fine art collection and quickly drive away. I received one phone call three days later from the daughter asking where to send the monthly HOA fees, and we haven't spoken since."

"Why didn't they just sell it?"

Bonnie shrugs. "Who knows? There's some pretty strange things that go on in here. Maybe I'll get a few answers when I call the daughter and tell her about this situation. Say, speaking of strange, you never answered me... do you want your food containers back? I can have Amie on our custodial staff clean them up and give them back to you."

At first, I'm too taken aback by the supernatural situation—and the thought that I've been befriending a ghost—to consider wanting any of my dishes back. I say my goodbyes and thank Bonnie for not laughing at me and letting us into Marilyn's place.

Still dazed I finally react, "How about just the vintage, pastel-colored Tupperware? Some of those pieces were my mother's... Oh, and she can toss all the Cool Whip and butter bowls!"

118

For the remainder of the morning, I keep replaying in my mind every encounter that I've ever had with Marilyn. Maggie attempts to console me, but I can tell she's finding the entire situation to be somewhat comical. In particular, she wants to know how one can actually drive a so called specter to synagogue for Shabbat service and have nobody take notice.

"First of all, we were late, and we sort of snuck in after it had already started and took seats in the back. It was a Saturday morning service that Marilyn had specifically chosen because it's not well attended. And prior to it ending, she had excused herself, advising me she needed to use the little girl's room.

"When she never came back, I exited with the others, and the two women beside me insisted I stay for a little something to nosh to better get acquainted. I asked where the lady's room might be found, and they directed me down the hall, to the left, before the catering hall and kitchen.

"Marilyn was nowhere to be found inside. I even checked the stalls and a broom closet. Becoming concerned, I made my way back to the main doors, and upon glancing outside I saw Marilyn standing by my Escape.

"As I approached her, she seemed upset and was wringing water out of her shawl. I asked what was the matter and if everything was alright. And she said she'd dropped her prayer shawl in the commode 'like a klutz.'

"When I suggested that she just pop it in the washer and dryer when we get home, she looked at me like I was nuts or rather 'Meshugah' I think was what she called me. It was made of mulberry silk from the Holy Land and had been an anniversary gift from her Morty."

Maggie and I also discuss my encounters with Mary and eventually get around to the totem and the series of visions everyone that touches him has been experiencing. I reiterate my belief, that even though some positive things have occurred since penis boy entered my life, I think it's about time I returned him, just like non-existent Marilyn had advised.

"You and the baby are the greatest blessing of them all," I say and we embrace in a long hug, ending with a kiss. I guess it's the culmination of everything that's happened, but my emotions get the best of me and I begin to cry uncontrollably.

"Mom… are you alright?" She asks. "I won't let the boogeyman get you!"

"I'm fine, just fine," I sob while searching for a tissue. "I believe they call these happy tears."

119

The next morning is Thursday, December twenty-seventh, and I'm enjoying seven grain, Italian toast with almond butter and honey when Maggie joins me.

"You think the stores are open today?" I ask.

"Of course, they are. I believe many of them are now open on Christmas day… why do you ask?"

"I'm thinking now would be a good time to take the tree-man figure back home to the cowgirl. Want to come along?" I try to sound light and casual, but I really do want her to come along, and I'm sure it comes through in my voice. I look at her with my best puppy-dog eyes.

"I'm sorry, but I'm having a bit of a problem and I think I ought to stick around here for a while."

"What's wrong?" I ask, alarmed. "Is it the baby?"

"The baby is fine," says Mag. "I'm just not myself."

"What's the matter? Are you nauseous? Achy? Do you have vertigo?"

She rolls her eyes. "No mother… none of those things. I'll be fine. It's—"

"Spotting? Cramping? Oh my God… are you having contractions already?"

"For goodness sake, Mom, I'm constipated! I haven't had a good BM for days. I've eaten everything the book says, apples, bananas, figs, and strawberries. Hell, I even ate sweet corn, but nothing works. I'm pretty sure soon I'm going to explode! There, are you happy now that you know?"

Then off she waddles to the kitchen for a glass of water. "Oh, and enough water to float a boat, but all I do now is pee even more than before."

"Oh sweetie, been there, done that, and again believe it or not it was with you. What say I pick up a mild laxative at CVS while I'm out and you give that a try?"

"You really think that would be alright?"

"You turned out pretty good, didn't you? But as a first-time mommy I suggest you call your doctor while I'm gone and get her okay first. Call me and let me know what she says."

I retrieve the shoebox—now aggressively secured with packing tape—from my closet and set it on the dining table. I then scour my purse, looking in my wallet, then the top drawer of my bed-side table for a Librium to place in my pill case, and finally I scour the shelf in my walk-in where I keep my checks, bank statements, and receipts.

When I come back into the living room Maggie is sitting on the couch, her phone in hand, playing elevator music through the speaker.

"I'm on hold with the OB-GYN office. What do you need?"

"I can't find my receipt for Dick... Do you think she'll take it back without one?"

"Honestly mother, what does it matter? If it were me, I would throw it out the window as I was driving by at sixty miles per hour!"

I continue out the door as the music on the phone abruptly stops and a female voice breaks in.

"Intercoastal Medical Group, Maria speaking."

"Yes, Hello. This is Maggie Blum calling..."

After passing Spanish Point, I pull into the gravel parking lot of the strange little shop, my tires grumbling until I come to a stop. I read the sign promising Fine Antiques & Rare Collectibles and think about how much better I would feel if someone were with me for moral support.

I wish Jack were here—*she's so damn good at retail manager confrontations.*

I make my way towards the shop door, negotiating the front porch steps. The electronic chimes sound and, just as before, it takes my eyes a moment to adjust to the ambient lighting in the store.

I'm immediately greeted by the smell of peppermint and pipe tobacco, and as soon as I can see clearly, there she stands, the weathered old cowgirl herself staring straight at me.

"Well I'll be dagnabbit, child is dat you?" she asks. Then. "What in tarnation took y'all so dang long to git here?"

120

Not totally understanding her comment or its meaning, I start right in with what I have awkwardly rehearsed in my head.

"Do you take returns? I don't know your policy, but I have something I'd like to return. It's a…" –and I fumble for a moment as to what to call it– "a tree man… a fertility guy with a huge… uh package. I think your receipt said something like prehistoric native totem. Anyway, I've misplaced it and can't find it."

She gives me a puzzled look. "Is ya sayin' dat y'all lost da dab blame totem?"

"Heavens no, no. I know exactly where he is!" And I slap the taped-up shoebox on the glass countertop with a thud. "I've misplaced the receipt, and I wish to return him. Is that possible?"

She pulls a large pocket knife out of her Wrangler jeans pocket. It's been personalized with the name 'Daisy' carved across the wooden handle. Switching open the sheepsfoot blade, she quickly slices through the packing tape and releases the lid. Flipping it open, she digs through the dried oak leaves and moss with her gnarly, yet well bejeweled with silver and turquoise, fingers until she finds the figure.

Lifting it out of the box she holds it up to her face and gives it a good once over with her eyes, almost as if she's nearsighted.

"My, my," she says, while slowly shaking her head side to side. "I ain't seen dis leetle dickens fer quite da time." She is literally holding him by the balls. "Has ya cum back home ta Granny Daisy, leetle man?"

"Well anyway, I remember what I paid for it," I say, trying to get the conversation back on track. "But if you have some kind of policy regarding returned merchandise without receipts, or that you only take items back at the current sale price, I completely understand. To tell you the truth, all I really want to do is get rid of it."

"Y'all wanna gits rid of it, huh?" She cackles, and then breaks into the smokers cough I remember all too well from the first visit.

"Well maybe I should have worded that differently," I stammer nervously. "See, my friend Jackie helped me to decorate when she visited from Ohio. And, well, after living with uhm… the little man for a while I just feel like it honestly clashes with the couch. Well, actually my entire décor."

I take a breath as I try to figure out what inspired me to babble on like I just did.

"Anyway ma'am, if your policy is for an even exchange, I'm sure I could be quite happy with one of these lovely stones in your case." I am stammering while acting as if I'm perusing the array of pieces in her rock collection under the glass.

She squints one crepey eye, and looking directly at me through the open one asks, "How goes it wit yer sexy lives, sweetie?"

Then she laughs so hard she has another coughing fit. This time she pulls a red and white paisley kerchief from her back pocket and loudly blows her nose in it before dabbing at her eyes.

"Sorry bouts dat." She smiles "Dang oak spores." and continues staring straight at me apparently awaiting my response.

Uncomfortable with the question I simply reply, "I'm not sure why you ask, but I consider that subject personal, and not appropriate to discuss with a store clerk."

Straightaway her demeanor changes and the look on her face can't be described as anything other than a scowl. She pops a peppermint ball into her mouth, grinding it veraciously between her tobacco stained teeth before stating.

"Is dat whats y'all tinks dat ole Granny be… jest da sales gal?" She leans forward over the counter spewing her tainted, hot breath in my face.

I step back after literally inhaling the tobacco & peppermint breath and swear I can taste it in my mouth. The thought turns my stomach and I begin to feel sick. "I'm going to puke."

I apparently say aloud, but not realizing it. The old woman grabs a peppermint ball and begins tearing the wrapper off of it as she makes her way to the front side of the counter.

She grabs my cheeks with her left hand in a manner that makes my mouth pucker open like a guppy and pops the ball in it before letting go.

"Dare ya goes, sugar," she says. "Dat works eferytime fer old Granny. Whatcha bally well think I keeps dem on hand fer?"

Let's Have Another Cup Of Coffee

—Irving Berlin (1932)
sung by J. Harold Murray and Katherine Carrington

121

"Y'all best come set a spell in da keetchen wit me," she says, taking my arm and dragging me towards a back room in the store. "Ya be turnin' green as da maters come fall."

She snickers as she pulls aside a chintz calico drape and leads me to a Formica dinette set in teal, reminiscent of fifties diner furniture.

"Y'all jest set right cheer while ol' Granny pours us a mug a da jamoka."

She grabs two mismatched mugs from a cabinet above a heavily stained farmhouse sink and slaps them with a clank on the table. She then retrieves a chipped enamelware percolator from the burner of an antique gas stove and commences to pour. The dark liquid almost appears thick, like beef bouillon, and adheres somewhat to the sides of the cup.

"Does ya takes da cream or sugars? Me self, I likes mine ta be jest as black as da backwaters in Okaloosa County."

First, I consider how hard even really good coffee can sometimes be on my empty stomach and then question what kind of havoc this sludge may cause on it. Feeling the need to be polite, I answer with a tinge of fear.

"Do you have a touch of cream? Possibly French vanilla or hazelnut?"

She shoots daggers at me with her eyes as she crosses the scuffed black and white checkered floor and opens the rusting door to an ancient Kelvinator. The heels of her boots clomp loudly as she marches back and slams a half gallon jug of skim milk on the table.

"Hopes dat werks fer ya? My doc said I has ta reduce da fats and da fried foods!"

My first thought is that the woman is so thin a level one hurricane would blow her into the next county. But I now remember the day I saw her sitting in the waiting room of the medical office where Stu practices.

Does he attend to this crazy cowgirl too? I make a mental note to ask him.

Picking up my crazed mug with a chip on the handle I notice the imprint on the front:

Never Squat with Your Spurs On!

God help me.

I take a sip. To my amazement it has an earthy and wonderful flavor.

"Your coffee is delicious," I say, surprised. "What brand is it?"

She gives me a bit of a devious grin.

"Dat dare be da chaga yer a tastin. Y'all likes mushyrooms? Day be dang good fer what ails ya! My elder sister geets it from da birch trees in da south of da Carolinas lowcountry den sends dem to me. Dat be where she practicin the Gullah wudu, sorta like ol' Granny be doin heres in Sarasotie. Drink up, sugar," she insists with a wink. "It'll settle yer gut down."

"I really didn't mean to be a bother," I say, trying to explain my visit. "But ever since that totem came into my house, I've had some really strange dreams."

The old woman squints her eye, again, and appears to be intensely listening.

"Actually, my daughter and my friend have had some issues with it as well!"

Her eyes grow big.

"Ya don' mean they be a usin' it also?" She leans forward waiting for my answer.

"I'm not quite sure I would call it using the little guy," I say. "It's more like just picking him up or moving him to dust. Add in the situation with my dead neighbor Marilyn haunting me and the spectral figure of a little girl running amuck, and basically all I want to do is rid myself of him."

She leans back, picks up her mug and takes a hard sip of the steaming beverage before lighting up a Marlboro.

"Dat dare leetle man was meant fer ya and only fer ya, and nobodies else shoulda bean foolin' wit it. Y'all came to ol' Granny yearnin' fer da affections, an dats what ol' Granny gave ya. As fer da perished neighbor problems, well dat ain't got nothin' ta do wit me!"

In the middle of the table is an antique tin cake cover. It's mint green and decorated with hand-painted pink roses. In the center of the lid is a white ceramic knob. The handle shows the accumulation of built up grime from years and years of fingers removing the lid and leaving behind their dirt and oils. And as I look on, Daisy lifts the lid yet one more time revealing what appears to be a pie of sorts.

"I jest made dis apple boggy-top dis mornin'. How 'bouts I slice a beeg piece for y'all and ol' Granny?"

She gets back up, takes a couple small, harvest gold, Melmac plates out of a cupboard, pulls open a drawer and grabs a couple mismatched forks, and returns to the table. Taking her pocketknife back out, she slices the pie and uses the blade to dish it up.

"Goes ahead, sugar, deeg in," she says, taking another puff on her Marlboro. "You ain't et better dan dis I can promise ya dat. Why, dis here pie won ol' Granny first place in da nineteen and thirty-six Winston-Salem Apple Festival. Wanna see da ribbon?"

Just then the kitchen screen door slams behind me.

"Hi, Granny. How are you today? Oh! I'm sorry, I didn't know you had company."

The voice sounds vaguely familiar, and as I turn around to see who's arrived, I'm taken aback, for it is Bonnie Long, the manager of Pelican Cove.

"Why Miss Blum—pronouncing it like plum—what a surprise seeing you here at my grandmother's shop. Don't tell me she's sucked you into her world of sorcery?"

The old woman gives Bonnie the evil eye.

"She already be a payin' customer Miz Smart Ass Pants. But I was jest gettin' rounds to explainin' how dis here place works to her."

Suddenly the front door chimes and Granny Daisy jumps up.

"Da payin'customers dey always comes first!" And with that she dashes out of the kitchen, pulling the curtain shut behind her.

"I'll put your groceries in the fridge!" calls out Bonnie from behind her. Then she shakes her head and takes a seat at the table. "I swear, that woman at ninety-seven years has more energy than I do."

Bonnie reaches over, taking Granny's piece of pie and begins digging in.

"Go ahead, try it. Did she tell you that it's award winning?" This last comment makes her laugh at herself. I take a bite, and just like the coffee, I'm amazed at how great it tastes.

"What did she call this thing?" I ask. "It was some kind of funny name."

Bonnie nods.

"Boggy-top? She probably referred to it as a boggy-top. Basically, Miss Blum, it's a cowboy version of an apple pie without crust. Her daddy was a cookie on a chuck wagon, and it's his own recipe."

122

Bonnie gets back up, finds another cracked mug, and pours herself a cup of the mushroom jamoka. Then tops off mine.

"Thank you," I say. "It really is surprisingly good."

She takes her seat again. "So what brings you here?"

I tell her about the day I first stopped in and met her grandmother, and how she kind of steered me towards Digger Doug's shelf way back here by the kitchen.

"I spotted this kind of totem thing, and I don't know why, but the piece just kind of spoke to me, you know artistically. But there was something more to it… like I was compelled to purchase it. I almost felt like if I didn't get the darn thing something bad might happen. Does that sound crazy?"

Bonnie sets her mug down after taking another sip and smiles.

"Not if you're under the spell of a granny witch," she says matter-of-factly, and then seems to wait for my response.

"Are you saying your grandmother is a witch?" I am feeling a bit uncomfortable with my surroundings again.

"Well, if it makes you feel better, she's what they refer to as a white witch. I however, prefer to think of her more as a folk healer. Per the local Florida crackers, she's quite the herbalist, and they come from far and wide to get this medicinal coffee you've been raving about. Oh, she'll be the first to tell you it's healing powers are in the mushrooms and the mind, but most assuredly they wouldn't work half as well if she didn't add her own special touch of magic to them."

"I'm not sure about the hocus pocus part of this stuff I'm drinking, but I do know I'm no longer nauseated, and neither am I jittery. Heck, sometimes after two plain cups of Folgers I'm anxious and bouncing off the walls."

I go back to telling Bonnie the abbreviated version of what I'm doing here by explaining all the strange incidents that occurred to anyone touching the totem.

"I can't begin to tell you how lifelike and vivid those dreams were," I say before wrapping up my tale.

I then go on to describe the most recent incident and my unwrapping the damn thing after it mysteriously showed up under my Christmas tree. I get up and set my empty mug in the old sink.

"Anyway, I came here today to return it. Heck, I'll even just give it back to your grandmother if she'll take it. I'm just absolutely certain about one thing... It isn't coming back home with me!"

123

We leave the kitchen and slowly make our way through the various rooms of the store, heading towards the sales counter and exit. I pause in front of the life-size cigar-store Indian—*where on my first visit I had jokingly snapped a selfie and sent it to Jack advising, 'If I show up missing look for the body here.'*

I turn to Bonnie.

"Did you ever get ahold of Marilyn's daughter?"

"Why yes. Yes, I did. Actually, she gave me a call at home last night on my cell. I must say this is a strange one Miss Blum because—"

"It's Blum like B-l-o-o-m, but what say you call me Liz, and I'll call you Bonnie?"

She reaches out a hand and as we shake on it.

"It's a deal, Liz." And instantly I sense a rapport building with this woman.

"Anyway, it seems Marilyn's daughter, Miriam, tried calling the condo checker, and her phone is no longer in service. She says she tried several times and then remembered she had the address where she sends her quarterly payments to the woman. Apparently, she lived in unit #17 at the Beneva Place apartments.

"When she finally got a return phone call from the manager, the man advised her that his tenant no longer lived there. In fact, she hadn't lived there for over a year. Miriam was frantic and wondered who'd been caring for her mother's place, and I advised her obviously nobody. She's wasn't a happy camper when I described the smell and the mess you and I found in the place. We ended the call with her asking if I could assist with getting it listed with a realtor and out of her hands as soon as possible."

I'm not quite sure why, but I feel a bit sad at the thought of Marilyn's place on the market. Somehow, as silly as it seems, I still can't totally convince myself that she's not real. In my heart, I'm sure that, later, when I take Mac out to his favorite tree, I will surely need to walk over and untangle Tookie's lead from around Marilyn's left leg and in-between her green tennis-ball walker coasters.

Bonnie picks up on my change in demeanor.

"Is everything alright, Liz?"

"Fine. I'm fine."

Bonnie looks around and changes the subject back to her granny and the shop.

"Y'know, some of this stuff she's been collecting her entire life. Yard and estate sales, flea markets and the likes. The rest she takes on consignment from the locals or as payment for her healings, like your purchase from Digger Doug."

"Well, this Doug fella is more than welcome to have the darn thing back," I say. "I just hope he knows better than to try and dust the damn thing off!"

Bonnie smiles. "My grandmother really does do a lot of good for the people around here. I would venture to say one-hundred percent of the tourists and snowbirds and possibly some eighty percent of the residents are oblivious to the poverty surrounding them in the Sarasota area."

"Granny is always questioning how Sarasota County, an area known for luxury homes, waterfront restaurants, and other symbols of affluence can also boast that nearly one in four Sarasota children are unsure about the source of their next meal.

"Why, up in Rubonia and Newtown, or out in the muck as they call it in places like Myakka and Arcadia, she's been midwife to their mothers and delivered many of those kids herself. She then cares for and doctors the young and old alike with her potions and recipes. Most times she operates on the barter system, but in some cases, it actually ends up costing her."

"That's commendable," I say. "But wouldn't you say that what she did with the totem was cast a spell on it and then surreptitiously send it home with me?"

Bonnie begins to laugh and places a hand on my shoulder.

"More than likely, what she may have actually done my dear, is make Digger a few bucks to live on while she cast her rough-hewn charm on you!"

124

As we enter the front room, Granny Daisy is managing a transaction with a woman. She's bent over the counter, pointing her gnarled and bejeweled index finger in the customer's face.

"Y'all just leaves it ta me ta remedy da sitchy Asian darlin'. He's sorry arse won't be a visitin' dat floozy Flora Shay's horror house evers again, I'll tell ya dat much. Why I has half da mind ta makes his willy shrivel up and den falls off in his frickin' hand next time he be a jerkin' on it!"

Granny suddenly notices that we've entered the room and straightens herself up.

"Sorry bouts dat last part ladies… I tend ta gets carried aways with da fornicators."

She hands the woman a Ziploc bag that's filled with what looks like oregano or possibly marijuana.

"Ya be a sprinklin' dis heres potion on his evenin' vittles. It won't be matterin' iffin it be gettin' on yours as ya ain't gots any a dose nasty man parts to worries about.

Granny Daisy then reaches under the counter and brings up a small amber colored vial capped off with a black rubber dropper.

"Now dis here's be awful strong sugar and ya daren't gets any of it ons ya. Y'all jest be puttin' two drops, nots a drop more, on da bastard's peller before he hits da hay." She gives a coy smile revealing her tobacco-stained teeth and lowers her voice. "Ol' Granny promises ya dat after da nighty mare visions get planted in his brain dat he won't

503

be thinkin' 'bouts puttin' his pecker anywhere other than where it be-longs!"

The woman has faint tears streaking down her face as she thanks Granny and picks up a picnic-style basket from off the floor and places it on the counter. Opening the hinged wooden lid, she reveals quite a few oranges mixed with key limes.

"I should be able to bring y'all another dozen or so next week."

She then removes a paper egg crate and hands it over to Granny who flips open the top.

"Oh my, my, my… dem be soma da beegest brown eggs dese old eyes has laid sights on of lates. I be a guessin' dat ya gave dem dare hens of yours dat corny meals feed mixture I ground up fer ya. And damn, ifin it don't work every darn time. Looks like ol' Grannies a gonna have her-selves an omi let for breakin' da fast in da mornin'!

125

The woman places the items Granny gave her into her basket, gives a nod of recognition in our direction, and exits the shop door, causing the bells to chime.

"Guessin' y'all be wantin' ta settles up wit me now regardin' ol' lubber boy?" Daisy asks, staring straight at me before popping another striped peppermint ball in her mouth.

"Well ma'am, like I was saying… well, honestly I just want to give it back to you… or I guess to that Digger fella."

She turns around, takes the shoebox I brought the figure in off the shelf on the wall behind her, and sets it on the counter. Reaching into the leaves and rubbish, she pulls the figure back out and sets it down in front of herself.

Viewing it in profile, and obviously leaning in and giving close inspection to the erection, the old woman tips back on her boot heels.

"I ain't nevers ridden da cowboy dat had a one-eyed snake beeg as dit one. Whatabouts y'all?" she asks, looking to both of us for a response.

I'm sure I'm blushing seven shades of red when, to my surprise, Bonnie chimes in.

"Remember that gaucho from Ocala I almost married? Antônio. I'll be damned if that Brazilian wasn't hung like that old Texas longhorn bull you used to have!"

Grandmother and daughter laugh raucously as I stand there a bit taken aback by their slightly crude discussion. Bonnie then slaps me on the back.

"What about you, Liz? You ever been the recipient of too much of a good thing?"

Baffled at what to say I surprise myself.

"It's been so long since I've had… I mean, been with someone that it's hard to remember. Heck, to be totally honest I've actually only been with Scott, he was my husband, so I don't have a lot to compare it to."

Granny Daisy's face turns serious.

"I sensed dat bouts ya da minute y'all stepped inta my shop. Dat ya be lackin' the lovin' in yer life. Why dats be da reasonin' I sended da old totem here home witya. And dat, my dears, is how dis heres place werks. Y'all come's ta me wit da problems, and I sends ya homes wit da cures. Give me dat left wrist of yours."

And as I hold it out, she places a hand-crafted bracelet made from yak bone and inlaid with coral and turquoise and three distinct metals: copper, nickel, and brass.

"Ya always wears it on da left, honey," she says with a wink of her wrinkled eye. "Never evers on da right."

She reaches under the counter again and brings up her old cigar box.

"I can'ts do nuthin ta stop ya iffin ya don't want my help." And she begins counting out singles, one, twos, tree, fer… Iffin yours happy, den ol' Granny be happy. Twelves, turteen, fourteens… Whatta I cares iffin ya dies an ol' maid!" And she gives a cackle as she continues counting.

"Twenty an da three, twenty an da four, twenty an da five. Here ya go, sugar. I'm put-in-nears sure dats whatcha paid fer it!"

I hold my hand out to take the money and then pause.

"What happens with Digger? Didn't you say you sell the items for him?"

I'm not exactly sure how she manages to do it, but Granny Daisy's face takes on an even more serious demeanor.

"Oh dunt ya be frettin' over dat none, honey. Dat Digger's a good man, an dat minute I be a tellin' him ya brought it backs he'll be a given ol' Granny at least a ten-spot and a batch a da froggy legs and few gator steaks ta pays me back."

As she turns her back to us to place the figure back on the shelf, I quickly lift the cigar box lid and drop all the bills inside. Before we say our goodbyes.

Heading out to our cars Bonnie reaches out and puts her hand on my shoulder.

"You know that was really very nice of you to allow my grandmother to hang onto her money. She's really not a wealthy person… well, unless you're counting friends."

"No problem. I'm just glad to be rid of the damn thing and it's so called magical spell. Plus, I think I made out pretty well."

I smile, holding out my wrist and showing off the bracelet.

"I believe your granny called it a Tibetan healing bracelet. Whatever it is, it's beautiful, and I definitely got the better end of the deal!"

Bonnie rolls her eyes. "We'll just see about that…" she says under her breath.

I stop staring at my wrist.

"What did you say?"

"You know, I like you, Liz Blum. What do you say we stop at the Hoosier Bar just down the road for a cold one? Did I tell you I'm originally from Indiana?"

Day Drinking

—Little Big Town (2014)

126

The first thing I do upon getting home is call Jack.

"Howdy doody, cutie patootie. How's my best BBFF..." Then I break into giggles and a hic-cup. "I guess that would make you my best, best friend forever and ever?"

I giggle some more but this time follow it up with a brief snort. "Excuse me."

"Liz dear, are you okay? You sound a little... well, snockered."

"Oh, you're so silly," I say with another longer, nasally snort. "I just had three... or was it four?... beers after breakfast with the granny witch's granddaughter. I really like her Jack, really I do, but don't worry, she can never take your place... plus she's a cowgirl. What in the hell would we have in common?"

And that hits me so darn funny I snicker aloud and slap my leg.

"I'm not sure you should be driving."

"No worries there, I'm already home, sweetie. Bonnie, the cowgirl, rounded me up and brought me straight home in her pick-him-up truck."

And now, I just laugh bawdily straight into the phone.

"Isn't that the funniest thing Jack, *pick-him-up*? She says it works like a charm when she goes to the rodeo out in Arcadia. Did I tell you she's a cowgirl and a barrel racer?"

I then proceed to tell her about trying to return the well-endowed totem—to a white witch no less—and the entire goings-on while I was at her shop. I transition to how I found out from Bonnie, the cowgirl, who actually manages Pelican Cove, that my neighbor, Marilyn, was really dead and that you wouldn't have been able to meet her at Thanksgiving, even if you'd wanted to. I finish with the tale of the evening I dreamt I encountered Mary, the ghost, at the Glenhouse pool and her warning about the tree wanting to take the baby.

"Honestly, Liz, how much did you drink, and is all that crap for real?"

We go on chit chatting about it until I finally yawn directly in her ear. "I think I need a nap now."

"You go sleep it off," she says, "but if you'll permit me to change the subject, I wanted you to know the latest news. Frank canceled his return plane ticket, and we are busy loading up a U-Haul, right now with most of the things I plan on keeping. He's going to drive it down and store everything at his house until we decide what to do with it. My house is listed, but I decided I didn't really need to be here to sell it so guess what…?

"What, honey bunny?"

There is a pause on the other end of the line.

"I gave my two weeks' notice at Procter. I'm guessing that just about the time you sober back up I should be living in Florida. Bye!"

I go to put my phone back in my purse and glimpse a Ziploc sandwich bag that Granny Daisy had also handed me before I left the store. It looks a lot like the one she gave the woman with the womanizing husband. However, these greens are fresh and the package cool to the touch.

I give a little rap on Maggie's door before entering her room.

"Come in!"

When I enter, I find her, maternity top pulled up, standing in front of the full-length mirror checking out her baby bump.

"Is this dark brown line from my naval to my nether regions normal?"

"I sure hope so," I chuckle trying to hold in a belch, "because I had the same thing when I was carrying you."

She lets the front of her top drop and appears a bit dispirited. "So what's up with the big brown nipples?"

I give her a motherly hug and then hand her the small baggie of greens.

"What the heck is this, a small salad to go?"

I tell her the details of my visit to the strange little shop to return the totem man.

"…and just before leaving the old woman handed me this bag and told me to give it to 'my baby-making daughter'." *Snort.* "She said it was dandelion roots and that you should boil several of them daily and drink it like a tea. She claims it helps with the birthing pains."

Mags exams the bag. "I'm not quite sure I'm comfortable brewing some weeds from a total stranger and then drinking them. Heck, my doctor even warned me not to drink any homemade eggnog during the holidays!"

"You know what?" I add. "The strangest thing is I don't recall mentioning you in any conversation I had with that woman. And even if I did, I'm fairly sure I never mentioned you were pregnant… Oh well, mommy has to go… I think I'm going to be sick."

Later that night I call Jack back and apologize for our earlier conversation.

"I really shouldn't drink before noon."

"The trick, my dear, is to *continue* drinking."

We recount the fact that she's actually moving and it's going to be soon.

"I can't wait till we can be together again. I miss us." I then go on to tell her how nervous I am about my New Year's Eve date with Stu, which is coming up in a matter of days.

"First, he said we'd be on the water and to dress accordingly. That actually confuses me a bit as practically everything here is on the water so what difference does that make? Secondly, it's on a Monday this year. To me, that always seems like an odd night to stay up till midnight and party."

Jack laughs.

"Per usual, my dear, you're over thinking it. Wear what you would normally to any restaurant for dinner with a man, but make sure it has a touch of holiday sparkle. And as far as it being Monday night, what the hell does it matter? You don't work anymore. I sincerely can't wait to be in your shoes. Say, speaking of shoes, did you keep those black, silk, Ann Taylor trousers we bought one time at Saks during our lunch break? Wear those with black heels and something with a little cleavage at the top and you'll be set to go!"

127

I walk out of my bedroom emulating my best model's twirl in front of Maggie, who is planted cross-legged in her usual spot on the couch, performing a massage on her belly with both hands.

"Well how do I look? Come on, be honest."

Mags chooses her words carefully. "Mother, we've been here and done that too many times now. It doesn't matter what I think, you'll still dress like a plain Jane conservative."

I start to return to my room, now questioning if I look alright, when she pipes up.

"Do you have something more dangly and sparkly in earrings to choose from? Those tiny studs aren't doing it, but the rest of the outfit's okay."

I come back out a moment later.

"Now those are better," she says, appreciating the smoky, teardrop Swarovski crystal earrings that I'm wearing.

"I've only worn these once, and that was years ago." I am rummaging in my evening bag for my lipstick. "Strangely enough, I've always avoided wearing them not because they remind me of your father, but because they bring back memories of the one time I could have left him."

Maggie sits up a little straighter. "Daddy did something to hurt you? I'm guessing you two may have had a fight at some point, but God knows we kids never saw it."

I twist the tube on my lipstick and up pops Lancôme "Ooh La La pink" and hold up the mirror on the flap of the clutch.

"Some things are private, Mag, and I intend to keep them that way. Let's just say, when it comes to selecting men, we may have more things in common than you think."

Maggie gets herself up off the couch and lets out a moan as she grabs her back.

"Are you okay?"

"I just keep getting these pains in my lower back, especially when I stand up. I think I may have over done it by walking your dog all around the Cove this afternoon. I just felt a little antsy and needed to get out of the house."

Just then there's a knock at the door, and Mac takes off on his stubby legs, wobbling and grumbling towards the entry. I answer and there stands Stu. He is wearing cotton capri shorts and a Saint James nautical striped tee with a pair of navy Bass boaters on his feet. Atop his head sits a yacht cap not unlike the one the Skipper wore on *Gilligan's Island*. In his right hand he holds out a dozen lavender long-stem roses in my direction.

"These are for you!" he says and grins when I invite him in.

"You sure look nice tonight," he says as I close the door behind him

"Thank you! And you sure look... well, seafaring," I say. "Very J. Crew."

He gives me a quizzical look.

"This is pretty typical attire for boating on the water. I must say, personally, I've never seen a first mate dressed in high heels and a cashmere sweater before. But trust me, you do look lovely!"

"You mean we're *actually* going boating... on a real boat? I thought we were just going somewhere to eat on the water."

He smiles. "We are having dinner on the water; we just have to set sail first. The *On Call II* is my yacht."

"Oh, I..." I give a nervous laugh. "Can I just have five more minutes before we go? Why don't you chat with Maggie for a minute?"

And off I run closing the bedroom door behind me.

A moment later, I return to the room.

"...well humor me," Stu is saying to Maggie, "if you're still uncomfortable in the morning please get in to see her as soon as possible."

"Will do," she says, turning and giving my look a once-over.

"What's going on," I say, "is there a problem?"

Mags shakes her head. "Only with what you've now chosen to wear!

<h1 style="text-align:center">128</h1>

Yet again I'm impressed by Stu's manners. It's all the little things, but little things that make a big difference when you haven't had a man to do them for you in such a long time.

Like helping me slide my sweater on, opening the car door, pulling out a chair. Sure, they are all things one can easily do for oneself, but inside I realize I miss the little nuances that separate the sexes. Smiling to myself, I suddenly understand that, even though I'm sixty years old, I much more enjoy perceiving myself as a woman and not just as a grandmother who's retired.

"I said is this music okay?" repeats Stu as we make our way north on the Trail.

"I'm sorry," I reply coming out of my self-absorption. "What did you say?"

"I asked if you like the Rat Pack or if you'd prefer some other music?"

It's "Fly Me to the Moon" that is crooning from the speakers.

"No, no… this is perfect. I adore Dean, Sammy, and Frank. As a matter of fact this is one of my favorites!"

"Mine too," he says, as he reaches over, taking my hand. "*Mine too…*"

Pulling into Marina Jack Restaurants and Dockage, Stu drives straight up the roadway to the valet parking stand and rolls his window down.

"Good evening, Doctor Robbins," the smiling redheaded attendant states. "Are you here for the New Year's party upstairs or the yacht?"

"We'll be ringing in the New Year on the water, Andy," Stu says. "Can you take us to the dock and then find a place for the car?"

"Sure thing, Doc!" the boy answers as he sprints around the car and opens my door. We all get into a sleek, six-passenger, limo golf cart, and Andy whisks us off in the direction of Stu's boat. Along the way, I spy Stu slipping the driver a couple twenty-dollar bills.

I'm flabbergasted by the yacht... it's huge. The captain greets us with a tip of the hat as we board.

"Good evening Doctor Robbins. Welcome to the *On Call II*, ma'am. I've charted tonight's course as directed, sir. Please let me know of any changes to your itinerary." And off he aims towards the flybridge.

Stu leads me into a beautifully appointed salon, and as he approaches the bar on the starboard side, he proceeds to tell me a bit about the vessel.

"She's an eighty-five-footer with five cabins and custom built for island hopping and worldwide travel."

"She's absolutely beautiful," I say, as Stu hands me a glass of Cab Sav. He takes a sip of what I assume is brandy from a snifter.

"How long have you had her?" I question. And his reply catches me by surprise.

"I got her shortly after Salomon Rosenfeld's shivah. A gift from his now departed wife who joined him in Olam HaBa shortly thereafter.

"*Where* did they go? Isn't that off the Mediterranean Coast."

"I'm fairly sure, Liz, that you probably refer to it as Heaven."

He smiles then and initiates a toast.

"To this life, L'chaim! Here tonight, with you."

Our glasses clink, and I smile.

<h1 style="text-align:center">129</h1>

The dockmaster assists the captain and two crew members to cast off, and we're soon underway. We slowly pull away from the dock, turning west and exiting the marina, as the captain gives two short blasts of the horn.

"Is that how you signal the dock that we're leaving?" I ask, while taking in the many even larger boats we're passing moored in their berths.

"No, it's not. That's the captain's way of signaling other boaters in the channel of his intentions to pass them on our starboard side."

Stu points to the opposing L-shaped sofas, adorned with numerous decorative pillows, that line both sides of the room beneath the large windows. "What say we have a seat?"

I choose the one portside that has a long teak coffee table with matching stools to set my wine glass on.

Before joining me on the couch, Stu flips a switch and the artwork on the fore salon wall rises revealing a large, built-in LED television screen. It blinks to life, showing a live feed from the forward bow, allowing us to view where we are going. With another switch, the room is completely filled with the surround sound of light jazz music.

He then flips a third switch and smiles. "What's wine without a little cheese?"

And from the galley, located behind the wall with the screen, comes a young woman in braids, donning a black chef's coat and a bistro apron.

"Good evening Doctor Robbins, ma'am."

She sets a cheese filled marble cutting board and breadbasket on the table. "This is an English Blue Stilton Half Moon, this one a Cave Aged Cheddar Truckle from Italy, and finally we have a French chèvre or goat cheese with herbs de Provence and Le Grand Miel honey. In the basket you'll find an assortment of water crackers and a warm baguette that I just pulled from the oven. I'll be right back with the fruit plate."

As we navigate Sarasota Bay, Stu points out that the piece of land we're looking at across the lagoon is Bird Key.

"See that house with the red barrel tile roof, that's where Brian Johnson, lead vocalist of AC/DC lives. And there, on the corner with the waterfall spilling into the infinity pool, is tennis great Martina Navratilova's place."

Passing the southern end of the island, Stu chuckles. "See that sort of crazy colored, old-style ranch home with the yard flamingo's over there? That's tabloid talk-show host Jerry Springer's house. That fella has made millions off of a stripper pole, bar room type brawls, and countless infidelities. Not to mention that, in my opinion, some of the most questionable guests to be part of the human gene pool to ever appear on television."

I grin and take a sip of wine. "Bet you didn't know *this* about him..."

"What?"

"Jerry was once the toast of Cincinnati, anchoring the number one rated evening newscast and winning the position of mayor of the city from his constituents. The latter even after admitting that he solicited the services of a prostitute at a Newport, Kentucky, brothel and actually paid for it with a signed personal check."

Stu spits his brandy across the room, quickly apologizing as he grabs a cocktail napkin off the table, wipes his chin, and attempts to blot off the couch.

"I'm so sorry," he exclaims. "But that's the funniest thing I've ever heard. Why he could be a guest on his own show!"

We travel on through Big Pass with South Lido Key to the starboard and North Siesta Key to port. Entering the Gulf of Mexico, we continue west straight into the sun until we reach the channel and then turn and navigate due south at full throttle.

130

Maggie has been pacing the condo for the last hour, waiting for the doctor to call back. Being New Year's Eve, it came as no surprise that, when she called around seven, she got the answering service. She now questions her decision to tell the woman it wasn't an emergency and that she would wait for a call-back from Doctor Taylor.

Hell, I never asked if the call back would even be tonight!

Feeling anxious, but also because she's still in her PJs from the night before, Mag carries her phone into the bathroom, reaches for the bathtub faucet and turns it on warm. She sets the phone on the vanity, but within reach of the tub in case it rings. She unties and steps out of the plaid pants bottoms and pulls off the matching floral V-neck top.

Looking down at her bump. *Where are my feet?*

Feeling another round of back pain starting, she sits facing backwards on the toilet seat and leans forward placing her forehead on the cold tank.

This actually feels better.

And once the ache has passed, she steps into the tub and starts the shower. The warm water flowing over her body begins to work its magic, by calming her and feeling great pounding against her lower back.

Soaping and lathering takes twice as long as it used to, and she can only pray that anything below the naval somehow saw some soap and water. Taking care not to slip, she steps out of the tub onto the mat and attempts to towel off when suddenly she's overtaken by another round of pain. However, this time it's accompanied by an equally strong abdominal cramp.

"Damn it…" she screams. "I can't do this alone. I need you, Bob!"

So Far Away

—Carole King (1974)

131

Stu refills my wine glass as I indulge in another round of appetizers. The cheese selections are fabulous, but I can't stop eating the cantaloupe and honeydew melon balls wrapped in a paper-thin Italian Prosciutto di Parma. The presentation includes seedless watermelon cubes, kiwi slices and large holiday grapes.

"This really is a lovely way to ring in the New Year," I say, feeling comfortable enough to curl my legs up on the couch. "Now explain to me again how this yacht was heaven sent."

Stu explains that, when he first started his practice in Sarasota, Mister and Mrs. Rosenfeld were among his initial patients.

"I was in my early thirties, and I would have sworn they were eighty or ninety if not for their medical records. However, in retrospect, they would have been around our current age right now."

"At that time, they lived alone in a magnificent Mediterranean revival home in Laurel Park, on a street made of brick pavers lined with large laurel oaks dripping with Spanish moss."

"Isn't that downtown?

"Why yes, yes, it is," he says. "It's part of the historic district. Anyway, they had only one son, and he had been shot down during the Korean War, and Gerta, Mrs. Rosenfeld, wore a locket with his picture in it till the day she died. Seems even though she went on with her life, she never completely got over the loss of her precious Bernie. Neither did Sal who'd always intended to pass along the family business and wealth to his son.

"Well, I guess you could say they adopted me. I was recently divorced, and just starting out in Sarasota, when they took it upon themselves to introduce me to their friends and neighbors who would soon become my patients. In fact, we had a standing engagement for me to join them most Saturdays in the late afternoon for Shabbat and Havdalah. I would only say my goodbyes with a kiss on their cheeks after three stars would appear in the sky, and we had ushered in the new week."

Stu appears to be reflecting on his narrative and the silence feels a bit uncomfortable.

"So you were like a son to them," I say. "As much as a doctor."

"Well, I guess kind of doctor first, pseudo son second. At the end primary caregiver would better describe our relationship. Although I must say, I dearly loved them both with all my heart."

"So, I'm guessing you inherited their estate and that included the boat."

"Not really, no. The majority of their monies and property were willed to various art organizations in Sarasota, all of which they were already large supporters of."

"The one exception in the legal documents was directed to me. I was to receive Sal's yacht, clear and free, and the fee for the boat slip at the marina was to be paid yearly out of a trust account that had been set up in my name. The only caveat was I had to sign an agreement to take quarterly vacations on the yacht and promise not to work so hard or the agreement would be deemed null and void."

We clink our glasses again.

"That's a great story. I wish I had court ordered vacations!" I chuckle. "They must have really cared about you."

Stu smiles. "I believe they cared even more than my actual parents."

And he leans in and gives me a quick kiss on the cheek before standing up.

"I think it's time for me to check on our dinner, if you'll excuse me."

Dinner? I'm already full.

132

Maggie struggles to get a pair of pink polka-dot maternity panties on. Slipping one arm at a time into her white Turkish terry robe, she knots the belt loosely around where her waist used to be and then runs a brush through her still damp hair.

Suddenly she feels cold and actually starts shivering.

A minute ago, I was having a hot flash…

Making her way out to the thermostat in the dining room, she checks the digital gauge which reads 77 degrees.

I wonder if I'm actually getting sick and that's why I'm achy?

Abruptly she feels a popping sensation immediately followed by a sudden, large gush of very warm fluid that soaks through her panties, down her inner thighs and puddles on the floor.

"Damn it!"

She attempts to reach the kitchen and a towel…

"Mac stay back!"

But, with each and every subsequent move a little more fluid leaks out. Then comes another round of pains.

She slides her panties off and, grabbing the roll of paper towels, does her best to clean herself. The white towels highlight the fact that the fluid is tinged pink with blood.

My God my water broke. I'm in labor… and I'm all alone!

Then another, even stronger contraction hits.

Should there be blood?

133

Stu returns to the salon.

"Inside or out?"

"Inside or outside of what?" I ask.

"Would you like to have dinner inside, where it's warm and less windy at the dinette off the galley, or outside at the table on the mezzanine?"

He waits patiently as I ponder my decision.

"If you have a jacket I can borrow, in case I'm cold, I believe I'd like to sit outside. But first might I use the little girl's room?"

"Sure thing," he answers, "I'll run below and grab you a boating jacket while you use the head. It's fore through the galley and to port."

"Where's that now?

He laughs. "Go forward around the TV screen, through the kitchen, and it's on the left."

"Great, I'll meet you back here."

When I return, Stu leads me to the mezzanine where several candlelit hurricane lanterns grace the table and cast an inviting glow on the scene. Two square white Mikasa place settings have already been set and paired with Yamazaki Gone Fishin' flatware. White napkins with a red and blue anchor pattern are folded to look like sailboats and sit in the middle of each dinner plate.

Stu pulls out my chair and gestures. "Madam."

As I take my seat, he pushes it in. Yet another one of those gentlemanly behaviors I so miss. I think to myself before saying,

"Thank you."

A moment after Stu is seated, the chef appears on deck and offers us both a menu. She walks to a small wet bar, retrieves both a bottle of red, and a bottle of white in a silver chiller, and places them on the table. After popping the corks, she says, "I'll be back to take your orders in a few minutes." And discreetly disappears.

"A menu? Why this selection could have that poor girl cooking all night!"

Stu grins. "That poor girl's name is Francesca. She's in the Culinary Arts Program at the Suncoast Technical College. I wouldn't feel too sorry for her as she actually gets college credit for the time she works around town. And on top of that, I pay her an extremely fair stipend every quarter that she works for me."

"Well, that's very kind of you," I say. "But that still doesn't mean she won't be cooking all night."

To which Stu fills our wine glasses and again initiates a toast.

"And, here's to a happy and healthy New Year. The best is yet to come!"

Clink!

134

For the first time—well not counting a bad bout with stage fright—Maggie believes she knows how her mother feels during a panic attack. Head spinning, heart racing, she dons her robe and grabs the phone and hits redial on the last number called.

You have reached Beneva Family Practice after hour line. If this is an actual emergency, please hang up and call 911. If you would like us to contact the doctor on call, or if this is an obstetrics related call please stay on the line and someone will be with you as soon as possible!

Then a strange operatic version of "Stairway to Heaven" kicks in mid-stanza.

Maggie waits and then a Hispanic sounding woman comes on the line.

"Hallos. Please holds."

And Mag is back on hold as someone—*not* Robert Plant—is singing about pipers and reason and forests that echo with laughter.

"Hallo's, how can I helps you?"

"Uh yes, hi, I called an hour ago and left a call back request for Doctor Taylor."

"Doctor Taylor she no in. Office closed now. She'll be back tomorrow."

"I *know* that!" Maggie's voice comes out as a growl as yet another contraction begins to build. "I believe I'm in labor, and I asked for her to call me back. Ow!"

"You says this emergency?"

Maggie can feel panic building.

"Yes, I says this emergency… Get my damn doctor on the phone!"

"Well… no reasons to shouts at poor Rosarita, miss. I'll try getting the doctor now. Holds on please!"

And now it's humming heads and stairways and whispering winds and a guitar solo, and Maggie wants to scream. At her feet, Mac has picked up on her anxiety and is now circling and whimpering.

"Hallo, you still theres, miss?"

"Yes, yes Rosarita… I'm definitely still here."

"Goods! Doctor Taylors, I have Maggie the Blum on the line. She's in the labor of pains… Go ahead Miss Blum."

"Hello, Doctor Taylor this is Maggie Blum. It seems my water broke, and I'm pretty sure I'm in labor!"

"Okay Maggie, is somebody there with you?"

"No… I'm all alone," she says, sure that the doctor can immediately detect the fear in her voice.

"The first thing I want you to do is calm down and concentrate on your breathing. Let's try to slow it down a bit. I want you to hear what I'm about to say and believe it… Everything is going to be just fine. Come on Maggie, repeat after me, everything is going to be fine."

"EVERY DAMN THING'S FINE!"

"Okay, now I want you to take a deep, organizing breath. That's it. Now as soon as the contraction begins let out a big sigh. Try to focus your attention on an object Maggie, something nice to look at."

Maggie looks around and then positions herself in front of the Christmas tree with its twinkling lights and glistening bulbs.

"Have you found something?" asks Doctor Taylor.

"Yes," she says as the longer she stares the more her peripheral vision disappears, and soon all she's conscious of is an ornament with the Virgin Mary holding a newborn baby Jesus painted on it.

"I want you to slowly inhale through your mouth and exhale through your nose. Can you do that for me?"

"Yes, yes I'm doing it."

"Try slowing it down some more, sweetie... you're doing great! Now, with each exhale I want you to focus on relaxing a different part of your body. Let's start with your head and work our way down. I want you to think, Maggie, as you focus on your breathing, my head is warm, heavy and relaxed... again, my head is warm, heavy and relaxed... again..."

135

For the first course, both of us have chosen lobster bisque. Chef Francesca has convinced us that it's one of her signature dishes, and the lobster was caught fresh that morning. When she brings it to the table, it is presented in individual, white crocks and topped with a lightly browned puff pastry. The bisque also comes with a small pitcher of Manzanilla that she recommends drizzling on top.

My second course is a beautiful piece of cedar plank salmon with a glaze that hints at lemon and garlic. Accompanying the fish is a brown rice pilaf ramekin and petite white asparagus spears. Stu has chosen a medium rare prime rib with horseradish sauce paired with a sea salt–sprayed baked potato with sour cream and plenty of butter.

"No vegetable, Stu?"

He winks. "Don't tell my patients."

Francesca sets a silver basket of warm orange blossom muffins between us. "I apologize, I forgot the honey," she says and scurries back towards the galley.

Next I'm served a roasted beet salad with candied Marcona almonds and a tangerine and sherry dressing.

"It sounded healthy and light," I say, but I question my decision when I taste the sweet syrupy dressing and the almonds that taste better than peanut brittle. Stu has a curried crab salad with watermelon served on a bed of Arugula.

"Do you eat like this often?" I ask. "I know, if I did, I'd be as big as a house. Why I can barely breathe!"

"Not hardly. Remember, I'm a bachelor, and believe you me, I eat like one. Usually after leaving the office, I pull into Yoder's Market and buy one of their prepared meals. I can just pop it in the oven while I take a shower, after getting home and taking out the dog."

"That's right, you have a dog. I remember all the photos in your exam room. What kind was it?"

Actually, I have three, and they are Labrador retrievers. They make quite the handful."

I suggest my terrorist Mac could give them a run for their money!

The music that has played through dinner, even on the outside deck, starts playing Rosemary Clooney's 'Hey There'.

"You know she's a Cincinnati girl, don't you?" I say. "Well actually, across the river in Maysville, Kentucky, but Cincy likes to claim the Clooney's as their own."

"Oh really? And I guess next you'll be telling me you dated George?"

"Not quite." I smile. "But as the saying goes… I wouldn't kick him out of bed for eating crackers!"

Stu stands up and extends a hand. "May I have this dance?"

After pulling my chair out he escorts me forward to the bow of the ship where we begin to dance under the stars.

"You look lovely tonight, Liz."

His whispers in my ear cause chills to run down my spine. As he holds me closer, and I smell his familiar cologne, I start recalling how well we fit together when we danced at the holiday party.

The warmth of his hand in mine, the firm but gentle pressure of his hand at the base of my back, the rough but manly stubble on his cheek when it brushes against mine. It's been so long since I've felt some of the feelings raging inside me that I find myself looking up at the stars in a form of prayer.

Please God, don't let this evening ever end.

Hey There

—Rosemary Clooney (1954)

136

"Good job, Maggie. You sound much more in control now. I know you're alone, but we need to get you to the hospital. Is there a neighbor, friend, or relative close by who can help you? Where's your mom?"

"A date," she says. "With Doctor Robbins somewhere. I've tried calling, but each time it's just a dropped call. It doesn't even go into her voice mail."

"Is there no one else you can call?"

"I can go check with one of my neighbors and see if they can help me," she says and suddenly envisions knocking on Marilyn's door and asking for a ride from their ghostly neighbor. This makes her laugh out loud.

"Is everything alright?"

"I wouldn't go that far but something just struck me as funny."

"Well that's an improvement. Now go see if a neighbor can help you, and I'll wait on the line."

Mag goes out front and is taken aback by the number of vehicles and headlights she can see moving about in the Pelican Pavilion parking lot. As she passes by the troll bridge and the opening in the hedge, she views men in suits and ties escorting women in long dresses into the building across the way. There's a small search light at the clubhouse entrance, circulating and shining its bright, beam skyward.

Must be the New Year's Eve Dance starting, Maggie thinks, recalling the posters she saw on several of the bulletin boards, during her walks with Mac these past few weeks.

Continuing on the path to the next-door neighbors, Maynard and Evie's, Mag commences knocking and knocking. She can tell that there are lights on inside, but no one answers. Walking to the bottom of the steps that lead up to the place above her mother's where the two train wrecks, Bev and Vinnie, live she looks up. It appears they're having a party too. She can definitely see through the kitchen slider that people are moving about inside. They also have their front door wide-open and old-time rock and roll music is playing and it sounds like vinyl. Helium filled mylar balloons are tied to their balcony and candles burn on various steps leading up to the unit.

Grabbing the banister with both hands Mag starts the climb up the steep stairs while trying to avoid catching her robe on fire from the candles. About halfway up, and as a gust of wind blows through the open steps, she becomes blatantly aware that she's not wearing underwear.

"Oh my God!" she gasps and stops to make sure that her robe is shut properly.

About three steps from the top, Maggie experiences another contraction. Sitting down on the step in an attempt not to topple, she repeats the breathing exercise that Doctor Taylor taught her. She moans then begins to choke on the overpowering scent of patchouli incense burning in a lotus leaf holder on the step beside her.

Just then she looks up straight into Vinnie's face. He's bent over and looking down at her as he blows out a huge puff of smoke that smells like cannabis. He is practically dissolving into laughter.

"Are you having an orgasm doll?"

"Vinnie, it's me, Maggie, from downstairs... actually, I'm having a baby!"

"Oh groovy, are you here for the party? Bring the little tyke and come on up."

"Truth be told, I was hoping that you, or preferably Bev, could help me get to the hospital. How's Bev doing? Has she been smoking or drinking?"

"Oh Bevie, hasn't toked in years, she just enjoys getting a second-hand buzz. There's something about it not mixing well with all her heart pills."

He slurs something about how she still likes an occasional beer, then appears to be trying to look down her robe.

"She does love her bubbly though, but again because of her meds she was trying to hold off till midnight so she doesn't pass out. I'll be right back after I ask her if she thinks she can take you. She's a little afraid of driving after dark since her last accident and what with the one remaining cataract."

As he straightens up and enters the doorway.

"You just stay put babe and I'll be right back," he calls back over his shoulder.

And then she hears him yell from somewhere inside.

"Hey Bevie, my love, you know that preggers that lives below us? Well, she needs ya to take her to the hospital tonight along with her kid. You ain't been eating any of them brownies have ya?"

137

Now, we are standing at the bow in a stance reminiscent of Kate and Leo's scene in *Titanic*—well maybe if they had been on a senior cruise. Stu puts his arms around me.

"Cold?"

"A little chilly perhaps, but by no means cold. I think I've had enough food and wine to fuel me and keep me warm. Plus, your arms aren't doing a bad job either. Hey, what are all those lights over there? Is that a runway I see in the middle of it all?"

"It is. That's the Naval Air Station in Key West."

"What! We're in Key West?" All humor has evaporated from my voice. "I thought we were just floating around in circles somewhere off Sarasota till midnight. What the heck are you up to? Is this a kidnapping?"

Confused, Stu steps back. "First, if my intents were to abscond with you I believe the proper term would be shanghaied, since I used a boat. Second, I didn't realize you had a limitation on how far from home you could travel. Hell, you're the one that likes to talk about how you've been to Europe, Asia, and who knows where else all the time."

"Time! Oh my God... What time is it?"

Stu looks at the Rolex Submariner on his wrist.

"It's only eleven o'clock, unless you're on Keys time and then it's always five o'clock somewhere." Then he slightly chuckles.

"It's not funny, Stu. I'm guessing that if we turned this showboat around right now, we wouldn't be back in port until six in the morning.

I have a pregnant daughter at home whom I advised I'd probably be home by one at the latest. Come morning, she'll probably call the police thinking I'm dead!"

"First off," says Stu, "I didn't realize I should have gotten your daughter's approval for this date before shoving off. And then, if I may be totally honest, I was really hoping that we would celebrate the New Year on Duvall Street and remain in the keys for the night. I truly anticipated having brunch with you as we slowly made our way back north to Sarasota."

"You honestly thought I would spend the night with you on what I consider only our second date?" I stammer angrily. "What kind of woman do you think I am?"

Stu moves closer and embraces me in his burly arms, covered in dark hair, and tipping me back slightly, plants the most intense and deep kiss I have experienced in many years—no, actually, in my entire life!

Pulling away slightly, to catch my breath, I look deep into steely blue eyes that appear to be sparkling from the ambient lights on the shoreline.

"I'll be right back," I state softly. "I need to go call Mags and tell her I'm running a little late. Remember where we were!"

138

Mags comes back inside and picks up her phone.

"Doctor Taylor are you still there?"

"Yes, Maggie I'm here. Any luck finding someone to drive you?"

"None whatsoever. At least no one that I'd get in a car with. By the way, I've suddenly noticed I can breathe a little easier. You know, I can take a deeper breath now."

"That's completely normal, Maggie. It just means the baby has dropped and is settling into your pelvis, taking the pressure off your diaphragm. Now, here's what I want you to do. Let's hang up and you call for a taxi. In the meantime, I'll head for Sarasota Memorial, and I'll be waiting there for you when you arrive. By the way, it would probably be best for you to enter through the ER."

"What? Are you saying this is an emergency?"

"No. No, I'm not saying that at all, sweetie. It's just that they are better equipped to expedite maternity cases, plus the admitting desk in the lobby will be closed at this hour. Remember what I told you Maggie… everything's going to be just fine! See you and your baby girl soon."

Mags starts to head for her room to get dressed and then realizes the new pressure on her bladder means she needs to pee, badly. While sitting on the pot, she recalls that she needs to phone for the taxi first.

Her mother, she knows, keeps an address book on her dresser, and that it has all kinds of business cards in it.

I bet she has the number for a cab company. Better yet, I wonder if they have Uber here like in New York.

Entering her mother's room, she flips on the light, finding the book right where she last saw it. Flipping through it hastily, a business card falls out landing face down on the glass top of the dresser. There is a note handwritten on the back:

> *Frank's number if you need him*
> *but remember he's mine.*
> *He's a lot closer to you than I am.*

There's a squiggly sort of heart shape and it's signed, 'Jack'.

Turning it over, Mags sees the name Frank Landers with Sunshine Real Estate. It also includes his office phone number and his cell. Scurrying back to her phone, she lurches and pulls out a dining room chair to sit on, as she experiences another intense labor pain.

It's going to be fine, she thinks. Slowly breathing in through her nose and out through her mouth… Then another labor pain hits.

"God, help me!"

She punches in Franks cell number and waits for the ring. It rings several times before Frank picks it up.

"Happy New Year, don't forget to eat your black-eyed peas!"

"Hello, Frank? This is Maggie Blum, Liz's daughter. We met at Thanksgiving when you came to our house with my Aunt Jackie."

"Well hello, Miss Maggie. Yes, of course, I remember you. How y'all doin'?"

Maggie proceeds to download the events of the evening, possibly including too many intimate details for such a proper southern bachelor man to handle.

"I can literally be at your mom's place in less than ten minutes. I'm right here in Nokomis, and I'd be honored to help."

"Thank you so much," Maggie practically weeps into the phone. "I don't know what I would do without you."

"Well, there is one little thing that y'all can do for me, miss."

"What?" she asks while wiping her nose and watery eyes on her robe sleeve.

"Please call the Pelican Cove gate and tell them I'm coming. That dang guard is apt to not let me in without showing him my real-estate license and succumbing to a strip search. Especially when I show up in a U-Haul!"

139

Stu joins me back inside the salon. "Did you speak with your daughter?"

"No, I couldn't get ahold of her. It seems I have no bars out here at sea." I sigh, while putting my phone back in my purse and trying to suppress the angst I feel building in my chest.

"I really need to switch from Cincinnati Bell now that I'm down here."

"I'm sorry but I never bring mine on board,," says Stu. "I can have the captain call ship-to-shore if you give me the number. However, at this point, by the time it goes through, we'll be docked at the key, and I'm sure your phone will pick up a signal there."

The captain docks the boat at the Galleon Marina located on the Key West Bight. Stu advises me we're a mere stone's throw away from Old Town and its famous Duvall Street.

We make our way off the dock and cut through the Sunset Tiki Bar at the marina resort. He says something, but it is extremely loud and crowded and I can't make it out.

"What's that?"

He leans in a little closer. "I asked if you'd ever been here before?"

"No, I haven't." I am practically yelling as we exit onto the boardwalk, and he grins a bit cynically.

"Well, you better brace yourself because this is where the weirdos and party people go professional."

We make our way through the crowd on Front Street and turn left and begin walking down Duvall. We continue passing funky boutiques, various art galleries and numerous bars. Some forty-three of them according to the map a corner vendor hands me. Written at the top it reads, *"Every single bar must be visited to complete the infamous Duval Crawl. Is your liver up to the challenge?"*

A seventy-something woman in spike heels, gold metallic short-shorts, and a mile-high bouffant knocks into me.

"Hey toots," she mumbles, "watch where you're goin'! Whatta y'all been drinkin' or somethin'?"

She then takes a long swig from the brown paper bag she's carrying.

A young couple, arm in arm, are aiming straight for us. Both are dressed as pirates complete with eye patches and a live scarlet macaw perched on the guy's right shoulder. They split apart, allowing us to pass between them, and as we do the bird cocks his head.

"Nice tits, lady. Awk! Let's kiss and make up."

"This is insane," I shout, while searching my purse for my pill case as we make our way through the horde.

"There's so many people. It reminds me of New Orleans and Mardi Gras."

"Well, there's not much difference. Mix too much booze with too many people, in too small a space, plus throw in a holiday and you get one crazy party. So, what's your choice?" he asks. "Do you want to ring in the New Year seeing a bosomy pirate wench lowered from the mast of a schooner at midnight? It's very near here in the Historic Seaport."

"Perhaps, view the big conch shell that's lowered from atop Sloppy Joe's Bar each year? Trust me, that one's a crowded and boisterous affair that draws all the regulars and locals."

"You sound like your speaking from experience," I say with a nervous titter.

"Or finally, and quite possibly the most famous tradition of them all—well, at least per CNN that is—is the lowering of Sushi in the final moments of the old year. She's a local drag queen, and quite the celebrity, dropped sensuously from a balcony on the Bourbon Street Pub, while riding in a huge, red, high-heeled shoe. Needless to say, that's a gay affair in oh so many ways. Your preference?"

"Wow, one just sounds better than the next," I say, hoping Stu didn't notice the rolling of my eyes. "I don't want to come off as a party-pooper, but do you think we could try to find a quieter place first where I might try calling my Maggie again? And, I think my ability to handle this crowd just may call for another Cab Sav and a nerve pill!"

140

Frank pulls in under the hospital portico, swings open the driver's door, gets out and scurries around to the passenger side to help Maggie out of the cab of the moving van.

"Just take your time, I'll help y'all. Just hold on to the grab handle and slowly swing yourself down. I won't drop ya Miss... Promise!"

Mags does as instructed and swings her body out of the U-Haul truck and into Frank's arms.

"That a girl," he says as he sets her firmly on the ground.

"As I said before, Miss Maggie. I'm so sorry that my car wouldn't start. I think it sat way too long without being driven while I was in Ohio with Miss, I mean your *Aunt* Jackie. I'll have to get it jumped in the morning, but thank goodness I hadn't yet turned in this truck I used to help move her down here!"

Frank keeps hold of her left hand with his as he keeps his right arm around her waist while assisting her towards the building. Approaching the ER, the doors swiftly slide open and they step into the blinding lightness.

An older, female aide or possible volunteer runs up to them, and addressing Maggie directly.

"I think I know why you're here mommy-to-be. I want you to wait right there at the door while I grab a wheelchair. Can you do that for me?"

And off she goes prattling something about we may have our first baby of the New Year.

"Sure," says Mag, quickly followed by another agonizing, "Ow!" that causes her to squeeze the heck out of Frank's hand. "But make it quick!"

As soon as Maggie is settled into the wheelchair, the aide zips off down the hall, but before rounding the corner she calls back.

"I think it's best if Daddy registers our mommy back at the reception desk while I get her up to the third floor, since she appears to be in a little bit of distress."

They're both gone from view before Frank can even finish to mutter his clarifications.

"We're not married and I'm not the..."

Time of the Season

—The Zombies (1968)

141

Trying to get off of Duvall, Stu steers me south down Caroline Street where at the corner of Whitehead we approach Kelly's Caribbean Bar and Grill. The well-weathered white sign with red lettering hanging out front advises that the building is:

Birthplace of

PAN AMERICAN

WORLD AIRWAYS

Climbing the five brick steps that lead up to the hostess station, I practically trip over a black cat darting across them.

"Whoa!"

Stu grabs me under my left arm just in time to keep me from falling.

"Did it have six toes?" he laughs.

"I wouldn't know it was moving so fast, why?"

"Because you then could blame Mr. Hemmingway for any bad luck it brings your way."

We wait our turn in line, and then Stu steps up to the young woman at the door.

"Hello there Erica, I don't suppose you remember me?"

"Of course, I remember you, Doctor Robbins. Are you here for the New Year's Burlesque Show out in the garden? I don't recall seeing your name on the VIP list."

"I'm not quite sure what the evening will bring," he says. "But I was wondering if my friend here might borrow your office phone for a minute to call home. Seems she has no service down here in the Conch Republic, and her daughter is expecting."

"Sure thing, Doc," she says. "Hey Jenny, can you show Doctor Robbins and his lady friend to Kelly's office. They need to borrow the phone."

Entering the office, I head straight for the phone on the desk and dial Maggie's number. While it rings, I start noticing personal pictures and framed, signed posters that include a beautiful woman who looks familiar to me but whom I just can't place.

The call finally goes into voice mail.

"Hello Maggie darling, it's Mom. You must already be in bed. Hope this doesn't wake you up. Well, it appears I won't be getting home until sometime tomorrow which is New Year's Day. Oh, that reminds me, if you still want to have Reubens you need to get the pumpernickel out of the freezer to thaw. Anyway Stu, you know Doctor Robbins, surprised me with a boat ride to the Keys… Oh my God… I just realized whose office I'm in. I'm calling from a restaurant because my phone doesn't work down here. I'm sure you're doing fine, and I'll see you soon!"

I end with a double kiss smacking sound before hanging up.

I turn to Stu who's perusing the signatures on a movie poster on the wall by the door.

"Kelly's Caribbean Bar and Grill… as in Kelly McGillis?"

"The one and only," he says. "Check out this photo of her in *Top Gun*."

"Oh, like you don't remember Harrison Ford watching her taking a sponge bath naked in a cow barn in *Witness*." I laugh. "I do love that movie."

Suddenly, we can hear the countdown coming from the courtyard.

"Five, four, three, two, one… Happy New Year!"

Horns blow, party poppers crackle, and revelers whoop and cheer. Stu takes me into his arms giving me an extremely slow lip kiss while ever so gently introducing just a bit of tongue.

"Happy New Year, Liz."

"Happy New Year to you too," I say while slowly opening my eyes and gazing straight into his.

His eyes are smiling.

"Well, what do you want to do now? This place never closes you know. Just name it."

I take his hand in mine and look earnestly into those starry blue eyes again.

"What say we go back to your beautiful yacht? I was having a pretty great time alone with you there!"

142

Frank realizes he's still holding on to Maggie's purse when he hears a phone ringing faintly in it. He also has a jacket draped over his arm; Maggie ripped off on the way in, saying she was hot. He notes there's a bottled water in each of its two pockets weighing it down.

"Sir… sir, I need you over here please!"

He walks over to a counter of four admitting desks. A young woman behind the only desk open on New Year's Eve yawns loudly then looks at him apologetically.

"Oh, excuse me."

"A long night," he says.

"Please take a seat." She gestures and then takes a big gulp of coffee, placing the cup down on a first-year nursing textbook.

"Bear with me," she says. "This darn computer is running slower than a two-legged dog on tranquilizers." And at that she gives a slaphappy laugh at herself.

Frank just smiles.

"Okay, we're up and running!" she says, sounding like the coffee may have finally kicked in. "Now tell me, is your wife pre-registered?"

"Here's the thing," he says blushing for some reason. "She's not my wife. She's the daughter of a friend who called me in a bit of a panic."

"Oh, I see. Well, let's start with her name?"

"Maggie," he says. "Yes ma'am, it's Maggie."

"And her last name?"

Frank gets a bewildered look.

"Hmmm. Well, I know her mama's last name is Blum. But I don't rightly know if they share the same surname, that is to say—"

"Well, let's take a look-see. Let me just run a quick name search." She types in BLOOM and clicks search. "I have nothing in the system but an eighty-seven-year-old woman visiting from Poughkeepsie with… Oh wait, she passed. I'm sorry, sir, but I have no one else under Bloom."

"Now, how did you spell that, ma'am? I know they spell it B-L-U-M but pronounce it like bloom. I know because I was her realtor."

"Her realtor…"

"The mother's."

"Right well…" She types and moments later has her answer.

"Bingo! It's actually under Margaret Maria Blum," she says—pronouncing the last name like plum. "Why I see she's a patient of Doctor Taylor, and she just passed through here about a half hour ago. Looks like she's all registered and ready to go, sir. Now, all I need to get from you is her insurance card so I can make a copy of it, and for you to promise to pay by filling out your info on this Responsible Party - Guarantor Form."

143

Back on board, Stu asks if I would like that glass of wine now.

"I can't distribute whatever medication you were referencing for fear of losing my license. However, I can prescribe a nice glass of Hall. It's a dark garnet Cabernet Sauvignon from Napa Valley and one of my favorite vineyards."

"Well, if it's doctor's orders, I'm all in. However, only if you'll join me."

I toss aside two decorative pillows and take a seat on the couch.

"You of all people should know I always carry my own pharmacy with me… just in case!"

Stu walks over to the bar and, after preparing two sizable pours, flips yet another switch, and the entire salon dims to the amber glow of mood lighting.

"Too dark for you?"

"No not at all," I say. "Don't you know that every lady looks her best in soft lighting?"

Smiling, he hands me my wine glass. "Oh, do they?"

And now I straight out laugh while curling my legs under me on the couch.

"Of course, we do… it hides all the wrinkles."

We clink glasses.

Similar to our conversation at the holiday party, we talk easily and without hesitation. Both of us sharing intimate details, good and bad, about the choices we've made in life. Stu tells some hilarious tales of 'dates gone bad' after his divorce. While I describe what I call the *isolation years.*

Stu leans back into the couch. "I was desperately dating and constantly searching for the next Mrs. Robbins. I felt like there was a giant void in my life that needed to be filled. It wasn't until I moved to Sarasota that I realized there's more to life than identifying oneself as a married man, somebody's husband."

His tone now reminds me more of when I first met him at his office. "I finally stopped looking for love in all the wrong places and started living my life's purpose... doctoring in earnest and making people's lives better, while in turn improving my own. Meeting the Rosenfeld's and their reintroducing me to my roots and religion during Shabbat played an intricate role in my healing."

"I did the exact opposite," I say, and again I surprise myself at the ease with which I can talk about my family and my emotional issues with him.

"After my husband died, I swore off not only men, but all human contact. My son dying shortly thereafter only reaffirmed my belief that the world was a terrible place. Then, when my daughter got old enough and left home, leaving me with literally no reason to get up in the morning, I grew depressed and struggled with panic attacks. I also then trapped myself in my own sort of hell with agoraphobia.

"Truth be told, if anyone had told me that someday I'd be floating around out in the ocean with a man I barely know, and partying in the New Year down in the Florida Keys, I would have said they were nuts!"

Stu holds out his wine glass again. "I like someone who is a little crazy but coming from a good place. I think your invisible scars are sexy because it means you lived life hard and survived to tell the world all about it."

Clink.

And this time, it's I who leans in to kiss him.

144

The woman pushing the wheelchair has brought Maggie to the birthing room. She is grinning ear-to-ear.

"You just stay put, honey, until your assigned maternity nurse, Barbara, comes in. You're in really good hands. She's an old-timer here, but a real sweetie and has assisted in hundreds of births. I hear say there's been some ten plus baby girls named after her on the spot! And get this, her maternity patient's grown daughters are now delivering here."

My, Oh my.

Maggie looks around at the softly lit room decorated in tans and teals. There's a large recliner in the corner and a pullout couch located under the large picture window. There's a baby bassinette to the right of the bed and a workstation with a computer monitor to the left. The bed appears rather hospital standard.

In the corner, rests a large blue birthing ball. Next to that on the wall are squatting bars and just past them, recessed into the wall, is a hydrotherapy tub.

An older, petite woman, in scrubs covered with whimsical, colorful owls, scurries into the room. She has a pretty, made-up face, but with a little boy's short haircut.

"I'm hoping you're Margaret Blum," (pronouncing it like plum) she says.

"That's me."

"Well, I'm Barb, your nurse, and I'll be staying with you till the bitter end whether you want me or not."

She reaches in the closet and takes out two hospital gowns. One's baby blue with sharks on it and the other coral pink with bunnies.

"Which one?" she asks holding them up in front of Mag. "Some people are superstitious. I can find you a plain one in that horrible hospital teal if you prefer?"

"The pink I guess."

Barbara helps her change from street clothes.

"You can call me Maggie and my last name is *Blum,* like what the flowers do."

Here we go again!

Barb helps her into bed and elevates her head so she's sitting up. "Is that comfortable, or do you want it down a little?"

"It's perfect. It hurts either way." Then she sighs. "But is there a chance that I can get back up and pee?"

"Now is a very good time while I'm here to help."

She gets Maggie back on her feet.

"While you're in there, can you leave a sample in the clear cup with the lid on it? I'm going to leave a form here on the tray for you to fill out. I'll pick it up when I come back with some ice chips and a blanket."

Mag returns to the bed and picks up the clipboard and #2 pencil before working her belly under the sheet and reviewing the paperwork.

We are committed to help you achieve the birth experience you and your family desire.

Patient Name:

Due Date:

Labor Companion:

Healthcare Provider:

During Labor I Prefer...

( ) Dimmed Lighting

( ) Music played (I will provide)

( ) To bring items in from home like blankets, aromatherapy scents, massage oil.

( ) The room as quiet as possible

( ) To wear my own clothing

( ) To walk during early labor and try multiple positions during labor

( ) I understand that if I get an epidural I will be confined to bed

( ) I would like to stay hydrated with clear liquids whenever possible during labor

( ) A saline lock if the placement of an IV is needed for hydration during labor.

( ) To be intermittently monitored in early labor so I can walk and move freely.

( ) To walk while being monitored by telemetry.

For Pain Relief...

Nonmedical Options:

( ) I'd like to use relaxation techniques such as:

( ) Various labor positions

( ) Visualization Massage

( ) Birthing Ball Breathing Techniques Tub/Shower

( ) Hot/cold packs

Medical Options:

( ) Analgesics (Narcotics) Epidural

Maggie breezes through her name and due date of February 17th. However, she's stumped on Labor Companions.

It was supposed to be Mom. How in the world can I ask my Aunt Jack's fiancé to stay here with me?"

Barbara has advised that her companion will be in soon, as she has him gowning and scrubbing up down the hall.

The thought of him seeing her naked and giving birth seems repulsive.

I wonder if he can just hold my hand and lend support and then leave near the end?

As for the list, it appears to be something she should have considered and filled out way before this point. After reviewing all the choices, she simply writes her own direction in the blank space at the bottom.

I'll take all the drugs, Broadway music, and adult drinks you can give me!

145

As the fireworks over Key West begin to fade, so do I. Embarrassingly, I yawn right in Stu's face while he's sharing tales from his childhood with me.

"Oh Goodness, I am *so* sorry."

He looks at his watch. "No need for apologies. Who knew it was going on three o'clock in the morning?"

"Obviously I didn't bring a little overnight bag with me. Heck, I only brought this small purse, or I might at least have had a toothbrush."

"Not to worry," says Stu. "Your stateroom should be stocked with pretty much anything you might need, including a brand-new *complimentary* toothbrush."

We both laugh, but I'm compelled to ask.

"Do you bring young ladies out to sea very often?"

"Not really," he smiles. "But it never hurts to be prepared."

He takes my arm in his and shows me to one of the three staterooms via a beautiful curved teak and stainless-steel staircase that leads us below deck. The room is forward on the ship, and when he opens the door, I'm amazed by the accommodations.

Centered into a built-in console with drawers and shelves is a queen size bed. The furniture is teak with silver fixtures and wraps totally around three walls of the room. The spread and decorative pillows are a nautical theme in coral and navy colors. Two hand-blown glass sconces, the emerald blue color of the ocean, cast a fan of light upward to bounce off the soffit running the length of the wall above the bed.

Inside the decorative molding are small, canned lights that beam down onto the bed pillows. Small, live floral arrangements atop the console adorn either side of the bed. As well, each side contains a small bank of buttons and switches that, I imagine, control the lights and God knows what else.

There's a large, private head with a seamless, glass shower done in opalescent glass tiles and a vanity with blue marble countertops. Stu turns back to the room and points out several steps along the wall that lead up to an overhead hatch.

"If you get a hankering to see the moon, that leads to the foredeck."

"I hope you'll be comfortable in here," he adds. "Again, If you look inside the drawers and chifforobe you should find just about everything you need. If not, I'll be in the room straight aft... Uhm, in the back of the boat."

He gives me a peck on the lips, not quite the kisses I've been getting and turns to leave.

"Thank you, Stu, for such a memorable and lovely day. I'm sure I'll be just fine in here."

I say, left standing there all by myself...

And as the door clicks shut, I feel a little... abandoned at sea.

In the Wee Small Hours of the Morning
—Carly Simon (1990), composed by David Mann (1955),
lyrics by Bob Hilliard

146

Doctor Taylor gives a polite three, little knocks and then enters the room looking concerned. "How are we doing in here since I last came in?"

"I'm eager to end this," says Maggie. "The contractions seem to be not as frequent to me, but the pains are ten times worse!"

"Well, even though I've asked Barbara to help you change positions several times now, and to do a little walking, the fetal heart monitor shows the baby is in distress. My biggest worry is that she's not getting enough oxygen. Add in that your labor has slowed way down and your cervix is only dilated to about six centimeters, I think we need to discuss doing a C-section, and very soon. First though, I'd like to do another quick internal exam to see if she's still in the occiput posterior position or if she finally flipped."

"Is there something else we could do besides surgery?" asks Mag, obviously feeling anxious and concerned just as another intense contraction begins.

"Dammit, I want my mother," she yells.

"*Screw you Bob... Ow!*"

Frank grabs the cool washcloth and wipes her brow with his right hand, while he watches the fingers of his left one turn bright red from her fierce grip.

"Well, I could order a shot of Pitocin to see if we can get your labor back to what it was. I could also use forceps to physically turn the baby, but I think we're way past that option. As I said, I'm truly concerned about her heart rate, and I think we need to prepare for an emergency Cesarean."

Mags begins to cry. "But you told me this wasn't an emergency and that everything would be all right." And as she becomes more anxious, she starts to hyperventilate and obviously panic.

"Maggie, remember to breathe in through your nose to the count of four, hold for four, and out through your mouth in four."

Grabbing Frank by the shoulders she quickly tutors him in what she calls the hypnobirth breathing technique and subsequent use of concentrating on a focal point.

"Frank, find something for her to focus on while you calmly get her to breathe slower," she says and then pats Maggie's arm. "I'm going to go get everything ready in the OR while Barbara preps you. I'll see you in a few minutes."

Doctor Taylor then darts out the door, while Frank stands there holding up a blue bedpan about two feet in front of Maggie's face pleading, "Just breathe while a lookin' at this thing Miss Maggie. One, two, three..."

147

I strip down to my bra and panties after finding a white terry spa robe in the closet to put on. Entering the bathroom, I'm amazed to find such a complete array of products available including a packaged hair and toothbrush, both of which I can't wait to use. I then take a navy washcloth from atop the stack of white ones on the shelf and wipe my face with lukewarm water, never soap. I quickly use the commode, re-belt the robe and head towards bed.

As I'm removing the decorative pillows and comforter from the bed, I notice my bare wrist, and suddenly remember that while Stu and I were talking the night away I slipped off the Tibetan Healing Bracelet Granny Daisy gave me. That and my wedding ring—which I still wear—and placed them both on the coffee table.

Dang! better run up there and get both before I forget them.

I quietly make my way back up the stairs, and even in the unlit salon I easily find my jewelry by the lights of the marina coming through the picture windows, aided by the brightness of the near full moon. I slip into the kitchen and, fumbling around, I find a glass to get water from the front of the refrigerator.

My mouth is incredibly dry from red wine. I gulp the cold drink down and return for a refill.

Good grief I'll need to get up and pee again in two hours.

Placing the glass in the sink, I tiptoe my way back to the top of the stairs, pause one more moment to admire the waxing moon shimmering on the water, then make my way slowly down the curved stairwell.

Halfway down the open stairway, I peer down the aft corridor through the half-opened door of a dimly lit stateroom. Sitting up in bed, bare-chested, and positioned under a single recessed spotlight, sits Stu who appears to be reading a book with the aid of a pair of cheaters.

I'm compelled to walk towards the room and ask if everything's okay, since it's so late and he's still not sleeping. I rap on the door softly with just two knuckles.

"Stu, it's Liz. I couldn't help noticing your light is on. Are you all right?"

"Yes. Yes, please, come in," he says. "Did I wake you up?"

"Heavens no. I thought perhaps it was I who disturbed you with my creeping around upstairs."

I proceed to tell him what I was up to, extending my arm to display the bracelet and ring as if for proof.

"Is that Stephen King you're reading? He's one of my favorite contemporary writers. Which one is it?"

"It's called *Duma Key,* and so far, so good. The interesting part is it takes place in Sarasota, well actually, I believe Duma is a possible pseudonym for Casey Key. You may want to read it when I'm finished, who knows maybe it mentions Pelican Cove?"

"Oh wow… Maggie is reading that."

And then… a long and uncomfortable silence takes place that I finally feel compelled to break.

"Well, I'll just be going back to my room now." I smile and step backwards while pulling the door closed.

"Hey, Liz?"

"Yes."

"Please don't pull my door completely shut. It's a quirk of mine, but I can't sleep in a room with the door shut."

"Oh, I'm sorry…" I push the door back open.

Stu removes his glasses and our eyes lock.

"And I would also prefer not to sleep alone."

Setting the book aside on the night table, he proceeds to turn the sheet back on the other side of the bed.

148

Nurse Barbara wheels a cart into the room and asks Frank to step out into the hall. Moments later a dark-haired Asian man in scrubs arrives. The nurse puts the head of the bed down and helps Maggie to roll over on her left side.

"Like I explained before, this is Doctor Wú, and he's here to administer your epidural."

"Try to relax and just keep breathing normally," instructs the anesthesiologist. "This will only numb you from below the boobs on down. You'll be wide-awake and aware of everything going on."

"Don't you worry," the nurse chimes in, "Doctor Taylor's the best, she'll talk you through the whole procedure once we're in there."

Barbara calls for Frank to come back into the room before turning to Maggie.

"Do you want your birthing coach to be with you in the OR?"

"Me?"

Mags contemplates a concerned looking Frank's expression.

"I would love it, but the better question is whether or not he wants to be there. After all, it's a lot more than what he signed up for when I called him for a ride."

Frank ambles up to the bed and, taking Maggie's hand in his, musters a smile.

"I'd be right pleased, ma'am. However, I feel I should warn y'all that I faint at the slightest sight of blood!"

The nurse whisks him out of the room to go prep.

"I promise that you'll see far less blood because of the screen between Maggie and the doctor than if she had delivered vaginally."

As they continue towards the operating theater, Frank contemplates on the term *vaginally*. He's pretty sure it's the first time he's even heard that word used aloud by proper lady folk, and he wonders what other firsts might lay ahead for him on this unexpected evening.

149

Hesitantly, I enter his room while fumbling to undo the belt on the robe. Trying to remain calm, yet attempting to look sexy, I let the robe fall open, revealing I'm only wearing my undergarments. I'm suddenly self-conscious of the fact that my hot new red underwear, he was possibly to see, is in the hamper and that my current bra and panties don't match.

What the hell were you thinking, Liz! Of course most of my New Year's evenings to date haven't involved stripping on a yacht.

Not seeming to notice, Stu smiles. "You're really quite a beautiful woman, Liz."

And I can tell that he's waiting for me to climb into the bed next to him.

"I think I should go to the… Oh darn, what did you call the bathroom?"

"Head," he says. "Or bathroom."

"Well, I'm going to use both of them real quick if you don't mind?"

I scurry into the room off of his, practically slamming the door behind me.

"Sorry!"

Looking in the vanity mirror I take a deep breath and say to myself. "What the heck am I doing? Look at me, I'm out of shape and old. For goodness gracious I'm a grandmother-to-be!"

A grandmother-to-be in the Florida Keys with her G.P.... or D.O.? Hell, some kind of doctor... For God's sake, for all you know he's a mass murderer who's going to leave your dissected body in the Dry Tortugas.

I then pull the top elastic down on my panties.

Worse yet, you've still got stretch marks!

I put the lid down and take a seat on the commode. It's been so long since I've had sex, I wonder if I've forgotten how to do it. I imagine it's like riding a bicycle. I'm sure the basics are the same, but then I wonder, aren't I the one who is supposed to bring a condom now?

He probably has one.

But I wonder what it feels like. Is it rubbery? Scott never used one and I was on birth control pills when we were younger. Maybe Stu won't use one. It's not like I can get pregnant. But what if he has AIDS or some horrible STD like Gonorrhea.

He's a doctor for God's sake surely, he practices safe sex.

Suddenly, I am swamped with anxiety.

Lord, I need a Librium!

I spastically dart back out of the bathroom, exiting through the bedroom door, and about halfway down the hall I yell.

"I'll be right back... I think... Well, maybe!"

Behind me Stu is nonplussed, and I don't blame him.

"Okay?" he says. "Just let me know."

150

Frank comes out of the scrub room and makes a wrong turn, ending up in the Maternity Waiting Room.

"Hmm," he thinks, "Maggie's room must have been the other way?"

A stalky, little woman is seated behind a walker. Beside her is a young girl in some sort of nightgown, and she is staring straight down at the wood laminate flooring. The woman smiles and gestures in his direction for him to come over.

"Hi honey, you don't rightly know me, but I'm one of Liz's friends and neighbors."

"Oh, you live in Pelican Cove?"

A look that Frank can't quite read passes over her face.

"Well, I guess you might say that, but actually I suppose, it's more like I reside there. Anyway, I just stopped by to see how her daughter was doing. Is everything all right with the baby?" She digs a tissue out from her bosom and blows her nose.

Frank questions how much to share, but decides what harm can it do to advise a friend who's been good enough to show up at the hospital?

"She's about to have a C-section. Seems the baby's in distress of some sort, and the doctor feels it's for the best. I'm sure everything will be just fine. I really must be going."

Frank turns to leave.

"Well l'chayim," she says. "Give my blessing to the mother for me."

"Will do, ma'am."

At this point the little girl beside her looks up, bleary eyed.

"He wants the baby!" she mutters to Frank, sending a chill down his spine as he walks away.

Once back with Maggie, Frank discloses the conversation he just had with an elderly, Jewish woman, omitting the ominous statement from the girl.

Her speech beginning to slightly slur. "Well, there's so many old women in the Cove I'd be hard pressed to determine which one it might be. If they know my mother, I'm sure I'll be hearing about it. Aah, I think the drugs are kicking in... I can feel I'm having a contraction, but it barely hurts."

"Well now, that's just fine ma'am." Frank blushes.

"Before they wheel me out of here please try calling my mother again for me. Will you please? My phone is in my purse in the locker, and her number should be in the recent calls."

Frank retrieves the phone and hits redial next to a number assigned to Mom/Liz. The phone rings and then is marked as a dropped call similar to the prior ones.

"Wherever she is," says Frank, "it's off the grid."

He's about to put it away when he notices something at the bottom of the screen.

"Now hold up," he says. "It looks like you have a voice mail. I suppose that—"

"That's got to be her. Please check it for me!"

Frank puts it on speaker and hits the play button.

Hello Maggie darling, it's Mom. You must already be in bed. Hope this doesn't wake you up. Well, it appears I won't be getting home until sometime tomorrow which is New Year's Day. Oh, that reminds me, if you still want to have Reubens you need to get the pumpernickel out of the freezer to thaw. Anyway Stu, you know Doctor Robbins, surprised me with a boat ride to the Keys... Oh my God... I just realized whose office I'm in. I'm calling from a restaurant because my phone doesn't work down here. I'm sure you're doing fine, and I'll see you soon!

There are kissing noises and then the message ends. Frank gives her a smile as he saves it and returns the phone to her purse.

"Well, that explains a lot!" says Mag. "I hope she doesn't have her heart set on Reubens!"

Follow You Follow Me

—Genesis (1978)

151

I grab my purse, dump its contents on the bed, and rummage for the small cloisonné pillbox I always carry with me. Spilling its contents into the palm of my hand, I pick out two of the all-too-familiar half black, half green pills and pop them in my mouth. I try dry swallowing them, but they stick in my throat. Panicking further and convinced I can't breath, I now dart for the bathroom sink and, tilting my head sideways, begin slurping from the running faucet...

The *hot* water faucet.

Damn!

I swallow anyway, melting the gel coating and further sticking the Librium's to my throat.

Dear God, now it's melted to my larynx! I'm going to suffocate... I just know I'm going to asphyxiate myself and die on this damn boat!

I then run around the room flapping my arms and checking my pulse repeatedly.

"Damn, damn, damn... I have no heartbeat!" I exclaim as I place my fingers to my temples and actually take a breath, after finally convincing myself that my heart is, in fact, beating. Then new panic. "It's so damn fast!"

Lord help me.

Spying a container of Cherry Passion Tic Tac's, in the small pile on the bed, I struggle to flip it open with my shaky, sweaty palms and pop several into my mouth, hoping I'll make enough saliva to get the pills the rest of the way down.

Stop over-thinking you idiot!

Wait, did I just say that out loud? Just swallow... Just breath...

The hallway is spinning as I run down it and taking two steps at a time make my way up the stairs. Heart pounding wildly, I pause, teary-eyed, peering up at the moon pleading.

Please help me God!

I continue into the kitchen where I fling open cabinet doors until I finally find a baggie containing what's left of the baguette from dinner. I rip off a crusty piece and begin to chew it frantically and then swallow. The bread is so damn dry that now it, too, feels as if it's stuck in my throat along with the pill.

Panicking further, I grab the glass I placed in the sink and run to the fridge to fill it with water. Gulping it down I feel the bread and pill ease down my esophagus on their way to my stomach. Almost Instantly I feel my shoulders un-tighten and my anxiety ease.

I can breathe!

Teary eyed, I look down at the front of me where, in my anxiety I spilled about half the glass of water down the front of me, and now I have a soaking wet brassiere. I have also left a small puddle on the floor that I clean up with paper towels. I replace the glass in the sink, put the bread back in the bag, and brush the crumbs off of the counter. Taking a deep breath, I feel my chest crack as I start to aim back downstairs. Pausing again at the top of the steps, I look directly up at the man on the moon.

I know, I know, I'm a nutcase!

Back in my room, I take a look in the bathroom mirror and then take a hand towel to the left side of my hair that got drenched when I was first slurping from the sink. Next, I take my bra off, give it a ringing out then hang it from the showerhead to drip dry. Now wearing only panties I slip the robe back on and approach the bed. I refill my purse with the scattered contents, place it back on the console and take another deep, cleansing breath.

"I think I'm okay now." I say it out loud.

But I feel the lurking apprehension I always carry for a while after a full-fledged panic-attack. I'm exhausted from the experience. Also, according to the clock, it's about five in the morning.

I make one last attempt at brushing my hair and actually pinch my cheeks in lieu of having any blush with me. Straightening the robe, I make my way down the corridor towards the dim light of Stu's stateroom.

"You must be wondering what in the world happened to me?" I say softly as I slowly swing open his door flirtatiously and try my best to seductively saunter in. And there he lies, mouth wide open, eyes closed tight and obviously fast asleep!

152

"I can't see you, Doctor Taylor!" Maggie's voice sounds anxious. "Are you there?"

"I'm right here, sweetie. I'm inserting a catheter. Can you feel this?"

"No, I didn't feel anything."

"Good. That's real good. Barbara is washing your belly down with an antiseptic solution right now."

The nurse peeks over the screen between us revealing her capped head and masked face and gives us a little wave with her blue, latex-gloved hand.

Mag glances over at Frank and offers a tired smile.

"You look pretty professional yourself."

He's sporting a full set of scrubs and even a cap. Truth be told he looks a little pale as he gives her hand a squeeze.

"Thank you, ma'am."

"I don't know how to ever repay you."

"Now don't you go worrying yourself any about that, Miss Maggie. Why, we're almost family now!"

Doctor Taylor peers over the screen.

"Do you want a mirror? I don't recommend watching the surgical part of the procedure, but you may want to see your baby being born. It's your call."

"Yes, I would love to," says Mag. "Frank, I think you'll probably want to turn away."

"You got that right, ma'am," he says, sounding slightly queasy.

"Well, here we go… First I'm going to be making a small horizontal incision in your lower abdomen. It will be right above your pubic hair line, and I promise, with the neat suturing that I do, it will be fairly unnoticeable."

"So there goes my bikini?"

"No, you should be fine, unless you wear an itsy-bitsy teeny weenie one!"

"Now this might feel somewhat like your skin is unzipping, you know, a little bit of pulling, but it shouldn't hurt. Are you doing okay?"

"So far, so good," says Mags. "I actually didn't feel a thing."

"Well, let me know at your first sign of discomfort."

"Now, I'm about to make the second, and somewhat trickier incision into your uterus. I just want to be very careful while cutting to stay clear of the baby. I've decided to do a vertical cut down the middle of your uterus because your baby is nestled low and backwards. Still all right?"

"Yes!"

"Frank, what about you?"

"I'm trying not to listen," he whispers.

"Okay, I'm getting rid of the amniotic fluid now and then I'm going to be bringing your baby into the world. You may feel a little tugging, but again that's normal."

Maggie hears suctioning noises and the sound of instruments clanking on perhaps a metal tray and then utter and complete silence for two or three seconds.

"Barbara, please take the mirror away."

A subtle ripple of confusion passes through the room. Frank gives her hand a squeeze. Doctor Taylor's voice is low and muffled through her mask.

"What in the world…"

Either Barbara, the nurse, or another member of the operating room staff, gasps.

"Oh my."

"What's wrong," says Maggie now on high alert. "What's happening?"

"Everything's going to be all right, sweetie. I just need you to stay calm until we're finished here. Barbara, will you take the baby away please?"

153

Standing at the end of the bed and staring at Stu, I think about going back to my own room and getting some sleep.

Maybe it's the wine. Maybe it's my prescribed medication that's kicked in. Maybe it's just plain loneliness and I am starved for affection and the human touch. My gut feeling is it's a combo of all these things.

I allow the robe to fall to the floor and slide into bed with him.

Hoping to hide my flawed body in ambient light, I fumble with the panel of switches and buttons next to me in the nightstand. First, I have the television rise up from a console at the end of the bed. Then I have the mechanized shutters on the stateroom's windows opening and closing. Next the bath lights go on and off before causing the entire bank of spots to come on overhead and a ceiling fan to twirl.

I mutter a curse under my breath, and pressing a large red button, eureka everything goes dark. Lying there I realize it's a little too dark, as now I can't see a damn thing. Wearing only panties, I feel my way out of the bed and towards where I believe the head should be. Unfortunately, I stub the same little toe that I broke back when Jackie and I were weathering the storm together and she had to perform triage.

Reaching the bathroom's doorframe, I make my way in. Finding the light switch I shut the door, hobble over to the toilet and take a seat while holding my foot and rocking my body in place waiting for the pain to subside.

Once the throbbing stops, and the sick-to-my-stomach feeling has passed, I leave with just the shower stall light on, pulling the bath door partially shut so I can find my way back to the bed. In the meantime, Stu has rolled onto his side with his back to me, undoubtedly partially awakened by my shenanigans.

I get back into the bed and lay my head on the pillow.

Now what?

I'm compelled to slowly scoot closer to Stu, in what appears to be a king size bed, and the process seems to take forever.

Where the hell is he?

Reaching out with my left hand in an attempt to judge distance I touch his back.

It's hairy.

I'd seen his bushy chest earlier when I first came to his room… but a hairy back? Scott wasn't very hairy, and he would shave what little hair he did have because he was an avid cyclist. *Today they call it manscaping or some such thing?*

Pushing my arm under his, in an attempt to sort of spoon up against him, my hand falls directly on a male body part I haven't felt in a very long time.

I feel obliged to pull away, but my curiosity won't let me as I actually begin to physically examine his penis.

It's larger than I remember—I mull over as I lightly squeeze it—*but it's much more flaccid than I recall them being.* Stu stirs slightly and emits a slight moan. I move my hand down and now realize I'm feeling his furry testicles that are being pushed out from between his closed legs.

My God he reminds me of a palomino I saw once on my uncle's farm.

When Stu's eyes flutter open and his hand finds mine, he rolls part way over in an attempt to see me, his voice is sleepy and earnest and sweet.

"Can I help you find something?"

154

Maggie struggles to pull herself upright in an attempt to see over the operating screen and in turn Frank tries to hold her down. He's well aware from the serious look on Doctor Taylor's face that something is not quite right.

"Please Doctor, what's going on with my baby? What's wrong with her?" Maggie's newly founded motherly instincts have kicked in. "Damn it... Somebody talk to me!"

"I need you to lie still, Maggie. I've removed the placenta and I'm trying to stitch up your uterus. After that, I'll need to do your abdominal stitches. It generally takes me about half an hour give or take a few minutes. I don't want to cause you undo worry, but the OR staff has taken your daughter to the neonatal intensive care nursery."

"Why? Is she sick?"

"She was born encased in a skin that resembles a yellow shiny film. We technically refer to them as collodion babies."

"What are you saying?" Pleads Mags, "My baby is yellow? Is she going to die?"

"No, no. I didn't say that. But it can be very serious. They are currently making her comfortable and running some tests for me. After they get the results, your baby will no doubt require the care of specialists like a geneticist and a dermatologist. They'll be better able to advise you of the depth of her condition.

"But when can I see her? I want to see her."

"Let's let them get her cleaned up, fully examined, and into a humid-ified, neutral temperature incubator first. For her skin's sake it's impor-tant that she be in a controlled environment as soon as possible. More than likely her doctors will order emollients to keep the skin moist and topical steroids to reduce secondary inflammation."

Maggie's head spins from the overload of information that she can't quite grasp. She turns to Frank and begins to cry. Not quite sure how to react, he digs under the gown and then gives her his handkerchief.

"It's a clean one, ma'am. I promise!"

"Thank you," she says then dissolves into uncontrollable sobs.

155

I wake up disoriented and rub my eyes. The scant light coming through the plantation shutters adequately illuminates the cabin and my brain begins to connect the dots.

I'm on a yacht, in the Keys, with my doctor.

Then I see my purple cotton panties lying on the floor and it all comes flooding back to me.

My doctor with whom I've just had sex.

I slowly roll over, contemplating what I might say to someone I just slept with other than 'Was it good for you?' To my surprise his spot in the bed is empty.

Was it so bad that he snuck away in the night? has he jumped overboard? I get up, retrieve my underwear en route, and move on to use the bathroom.

Climbing the stairs, while tying shut the bathrobe, I'm greeted by the aroma of prepared bacon. Looking out the windows, it's quite apparent the boat is moving. Crossing the salon, I enter the galley and there stands Stu at the stove, wearing only a pair of boxers, frying bacon, and flipping an egg.

"Good morning sleepy head," he says. "Ready for some breakfast, well... brunch or probably late lunch?"

He sets the spatula down, walks towards me, takes me in his arms, gives me a long kiss and a bear hug that ends with his hands caressing my butt cheeks through the robe.

"I haven't brushed."

"That makes us even."

He takes my face in his athletic hands. "I think I could get used to this. You and I fit well together."

He gives a gentle peck on my nose and then goes back to tending the eggs he left sizzling in the bacon grease.

Awkwardly, the only thing I can think to say.

"What time is it anyway?"

"It's a couple minutes before one, my dear." He opens the oven door revealing toast he has started under the broiler. "I had the captain shove off first thing this morning. In fact, we're about halfway home by now."

He suggests I take a seat at the galley, dining table as he serves me a flute of orange juice. "Let me dish this spread up, and I'll join you. Hey, do you eat fresh grapefruit?"

Taking a sip, I realize it's not orange juice at all.

"Wow this is delicious. What is it?"

"It's a pineapple coconut mimosa. Do you like it?"

"I love it, but I'm prone to question your motives of plying me with alcohol this early in the day."

"Ah but remember, it's actually the afternoon by now. Plus, as they say in the Keys, it's five o'clock somewhere!"

At first I'm a bit taken aback at eating breakfast with someone's hairy chest in plain view, but somewhere in the midst of dipping my toast into the perfect yolks of the eggs, and several sips of my drink, I settle into things. We are, after all, on a boat in the Gulf of Mexico. And Stu's boxers aren't entirely dissimilar to swim trunks, especially since they're blue with little red crab motifs on them. Plus, who am I to talk—I'm sitting here in only a robe and panties.

The light conversation about the sights and sounds of last night's experience on the Key takes a sudden turn when Stu takes my hand.

"I see you still have this interesting bracelet on." Admiring some of the intricacies to be found in the pattern he then adds, "I can't help but also notice though, that the rock you were wearing seems to be missing from your finger."

I'm caught off guard and a bit surprised that he even noticed. Hell, many times Scott wouldn't notice a new dress or hair change until I pointed them out to him.

"This may sound silly," I say, "but when it became apparent to me last night that I may be sleeping with you, I felt compelled to take my wedding rings off and put them in my purse. I know my husband isn't actually here, but it felt too much like I was being unfaithful, you know, cheating and right in front of him."

Then several tears run gently down my cheeks. "Damn, I wish I wouldn't cry!"

Stu continues holding my hand and looks me straight in the eyes.

"First off, Liz, I never want you to feel you have to do anything you're uncomfortable with when you're with me." He dabs at my eyes with his napkin. "Secondly, I don't ever want to make you cry."

"What about happy tears?" I say. "I really enjoy happy tears!"

Your Cheatin' Heart

—Hank Williams (1952)

156

When she is finished, and the screen has come down, Doctor Taylor speaks matter-of-factly with Maggie, letting her know that the C-section went smoothly and there ought to be no complications on that score.

"That being said, you're going to need to stay a few days recovering from the surgery," says Doctor Taylor, "And I know you're going to want to stay close by the baby, so I'll finagle a few days extra with the insurance company due to complications."

"I know there are a lot of other things for me to worry about, and you may not remember, but I have no medical insurance. I mean my mother was going to help pick up the cost for the delivery, but now with the C-section and—"

"Don't stress yourself with that now," says Doctor Taylor. "I will stop by the cashiers office personally and talk with a financial advisor. They will meet with you personally once you've been assigned a room."

Mag has calmed down a bit from the IV sedative the doctor ordered, along with a round of antibiotics to prevent infection and oxytocin to help contract her uterus and control bleeding.

"I can't go to my room without seeing my baby," she says through heavy eye lids and a feeling of total mental and physical exhaustion. "Please Doctor, I need to see her!"

"How about I see if I can arrange for a compromise?" says Doctor Taylor. "You're in no shape to walk into the NICU, and we can't very well wheel the bed in. What say we pass by the window of the nursery and see if the nurse can roll the incubator over so you can see her? That way the staff can continue evaluating her while you get some rest."

Barbara secures Maggie in place in the bed and raises both the siderails with a clank. She checks the tube on the IV bag and makes sure the port is secure on the back of her patient's hand.

"I'm going to need to empty your bag from the catheter when I get you into the room," the nurse advises. "I'll check with the Doctor but I'd guess she'll just have me remove it."

Mag asks that her head be raised a bit.

"Frank, I know this has been an unexpected ordeal for you, but do you mind staying with me for a few more minutes?"

"Not at all, miss, not at all."

Doctor Taylor has gone ahead to arrange the reunion between mother and child. Barbara is reviewing a checklist of what to expect after surgery with Maggie, as a young male attendant navigates the bed down the hall. They pass the regular nursery window first and lined up in bassinettes is a row of newborns, each wearing either a little pink or blue hand-knitted cap.

"The volunteers knit those caps to keep the newborns heads warm" says Barbara. "Aren't they precious?"

"Oh please can we pause for a moment?" asks Mag, trying to sit up a bit higher in order to see through the glass.

She reads the cards, posted at the foot of each bassinette, containing the surnames of all the little ones: Baby Boy Nash... Baby Girl Motz... Baby Girl Gryder... Baby Girl Kleiman... and Baby Boy Lowe.

Maggie suddenly feels sad thinking about how happy their parents must be. The thought of intact families makes her even more grief-stricken, as she contemplates raising her daughter all alone without the father. She simply sighs, "Oh Bob."

Doctor Taylor sticks her head out of a glass door about fifteen more yards down the hall.

"Hurry on down here. They have her set up so you can see her through this door, but our time is limited."

Closing the door behind her the doctor waits in the hall for the bed to arrive. She stops the procession just prior to the NICU door and, choosing her words carefully, begins to inform Maggie.

"Now the membrane she was born with has already begun to desquamate..."

A look of confusion has come over the already sedated mother's face.

"Sorry, that just means the baby's skin is flaking and peeling. That's why we have to keep her in a highly humid, but sterile environment. I know she doesn't currently have the skin of the pink and brown little newborns you were looking at. Just keep in mind the team of professionals currently being assigned to her case will do everything possible to make sure she has as normal a life as she can."

The bed moves parallel to the door, and Barbara adjusts Maggie's pillow to prop her up. Peering in excitedly, Mag sees two nurses, a woman in pink and blue butterfly scrubs and a man in shades of navy camouflage, moving a large object their way. It's like a white chest of drawers with a closed plastic box situated atop. There's what looks like a modern desk lamp attached to it and IV bags hang on hooks to the side. A small monitor on the side coming towards them blinks regularly and appears to be registering perhaps heart rate or respiration.

The two staff members turn the incubator sideways positioning it centrally in the glass window of the door. Maggie peers in, blinks twice as if clearing morning eye floaters away and looks again.

She emits a shrill scream that echoes down the maternity corridor and faints dead away. The NICU nurses quickly wheel the cart away as Barbara grabs the smelling salts taped to the head of the transporter bed, breaks it open and places them under Maggie's nose.

"Oh dear!" cries Doctor Taylor. "The poor thing. I feared it might be too much for her. Barbara, please just get her to her room stat, she's had a bad shock.

Frank, who had involuntarily produced an audible gasp and then quickly turned three shades of gray, softly begins to pray.

"Our Father who art in Heaven, hallowed be thy name..."

157

Still seated at the table, sipping our third mimosas and chatting away, the conversation between Stu and I has taken on an air of frivolity. We swap tales about where and how we grew up, first loves, first broken hearts, the time I stuffed my bra with tissues, and other embarrassingly funny stories from our respective childhoods.

"Remind me to tell you about where I stuffed a tube sock once and how it fell out on the dance floor at my cousins Bat mitzvah." Chuckles Stu.

Chef Francesca apologizes as she enters the kitchen via a hidden stairwell located starboard aft that leads up from the crew's quarters.

"I'm sorry to interrupt, Doctor Robbins, but I was wondering if you would still like me to prepare a lunch for the two of you?"

Stu glances at me with a questioning look.

"Heavens no, Francesca," I say. "We just ate. But thank you!"

"Very good. Well then if you'll allow me, I'll clear the finished dishes from the table for you and straighten up the kitchen a little bit. Also, why don't I leave a light crudités and cold-cut platter on the salon bar in case you get hungry later on?"

"That would be fine," says Stu, standing up and pulling my chair out.

"Oh, and I made some of that cognac mustard you like so much, Doctor Robbins. I'll be sure to set that out too."

Stu suggests we finish our drinks in the sky lounge and give Francesca some room to maneuver.

"I always feel bad about the mess I leave for that girl," he whispers, "but I just love to cook a big breakfast whenever I'm out on the boat. I think it's the fresh sea air that gives me an apetite."

We re-enter the salon, where forward and to port, we climb yet another spiral staircase that leads up to an enclosed room with sweeping views off the bow of the ship.

The captain is seated in a centerline helm chair.

"Good day, sir, ma'am! Any changes to our charted course, Doctor Robbins?"

"No, Captain, straight ahead for Marina Jack in Sarasota. The lady is a bit anxious to get home."

Stu motions aft of the helm where there is a small wet bar to port with a double sofa and another L-shaped sofa to starboard.

"Have a seat, won't you?"

We continue chatting, but it's back to a more serious tone again as at one point Stu comes out and lets me know the question foremost on his mind.

"Do you ever think about getting married again?"

I contemplate the question, but even more so, what's behind it before replying.

"It would take the right person, in the right place at the right time. I'm afraid that I've been single for such a long time now that I would probably be pretty annoying to live with. You know, set in my ways and used to things being done just as I like them."

Taking the empty flute from me and aiming towards the bar he asks, "Another?"

"Oh my no," I say. "I don't believe I've ever had three cocktails before lunch in my entire life!"

Then laughing to myself, I suddenly recall my recent beer binge at the Hoosier Bar with Bonnie.

"I hope you don't mind, but I believe I'm going to make my way below. If I can find my stateroom again, I would love to take a hot shower and then put the rest of my dirty clothes back on."

And, for whatever reason, that hits me as so funny that I give a resounding laugh, but also let out a loud, champagne-and-fried-egg-tainted, belch.

"Oh my goodness. Please excuse me!"

Blushing, I give Stu's cheek a quick peck and depart down the stairs.

158

Mag wakes up quite some time after her fainting and has to orient herself to her whereabouts. Looking around the hospital room, she sees Frank napping in a recliner over in the corner.

A young nurse raps on the door before entering the room, and upon seeing Maggie awake, brightens.

"Oh good, you're finally up. I need to check your incision and a few other things, and I was afraid I would have to wake you. I came in earlier and you were sleeping so soundly that I decided to come back later."

"What happened to Barbara?" whispers Mag to the nurse in an attempt not to wake Frank.

She takes the cue and whispers back. "She's strictly O.B. and her shift ended. I imagine she's gone home. However, since you'll be with us for several days, I'm sure she'll stop back in to check on you. She usually likes to keep an eye on her patients."

"Is there any news about my baby?" asks Maggie and her eyes begin to well up with tears as she begins to physically shake.

"Let me go grab a warm blanket to put on you. I'll also check your charts and actually run down to the NICU myself if I need to. Don't you worry, honey, the doctors on her team are all really, really top notch!"

She darts out the door, returns in a matter of minutes with the wonderfully warm blanket and a cup of hot tea and then scurries back out again.

"I'll be back, and I'll also see if I can't get your doctor to prescribe something to help you relax."

Frank stirs in the chair and then his eyes flutter open and he smiles in Maggie's direction.

"How y'all doin?" he asks sincerely, while wiping off a little drool with the back of his hand.

"Obviously, I've been better. What about you?"

"Puttin' near good as new since I rested my eyes," he says. "But first I need to scope out the men's room." And he gets up and heads for the door.

"Uhm Frank," says Mag, "There's a bathroom right over there. Just shut the door, and I promise not to listen."

When he emerges again, he washes at the sink and also splashes water on his face and looks more alert.

"Do you know where they've put my purse and phone?" she asks.

"I believe they put everything in a large plastic bag and brought it up here with us from maternity and the operating room ma'am. Let me check out this here locker."

He looks in and sure enough there are her clothes, shoes, and purse.

"I really want to try to get ahold of my mother again. It's mid-day and she has to be home by now. I would think she would be calling me concerned over where in the world I may have gone off to."

Then suddenly it hits her.

"Oh my God, Frank… if she doesn't answer from home, I have yet another big favor to ask of you. Would you please run to my mom's house and let Mac out? He hasn't done his business since sometime late last night!"

159

I finish brushing my teeth, walk over to the glassed in shower, and turn the faucet on hot. Taking off the robe, then slipping off my panties, I test the water temperature with my hand, adjust it, and then step in. Tipping back and letting the water cascade over my hair and run down my back, I literally groan in ecstasy over how good it feels.

"What a night!"

I turn around, adjust the shower head setting to rain and close my eyes. I allow the gentle spray to wash over my face and down my chest.

"God this feels good!" I exclaim.

I'm taken by surprise when I hear, "I'll bet it does. Would you like some help with washing your back, Liz?"

Stu strips out of his boxers, opens the glass door, and is in the shower with me before I can even begin to reply.

"Can you hand me the body wash please?"

"You're being a bit bold," I say, still squinting from the water dripping in my eyes.

"What?" He shrugs. "Do you have something to hide?"

"Well, if I did, I guess you've already seen it."

He squirts a sizable amount of Philosophy 3-in-1 bodywash in his palm and then hands me the bottle. Standing behind me he has me tilt my head back and begins lathering my hair.

"That smells fantastic," I say then look at the label.

Falling in Love, shampoo, bath, and shower gel. Created to fill your bath or shower with a sensual scent that is absolutely irresistibly sexy.

"Wow! Is this stuff legal?" I jest.

He rinses my hair with a secondary, handheld showerhead, then grabs the loofah and suds up my shoulders and back.

"God, that's great. I'll give you an hour to quit," I laugh.

He requests the soap again and, after squirting another generous amount into both hands, the bottle slips to the floor.

Still standing behind me, he reaches under my arms and places a soapy hand on each breast and, after teasing my nipples ever so lightly, proceeds to lather up the front of me while kissing the nape of my neck. I can now detect that he has become aroused as I feel his penis head sliding against the crack of my bottom.

Stu's right-hand shampoos my pubic hair as his left one goes back to massaging my breasts. He begins nibbling on my left earlobe as his middle finger slips even lower and, with the aid of the slightly lubricating soap, he begins to gently massage my clitoris.

"Oh Stu," I moan, while attempting to reach behind me and feel his erection.

Feeling as if I may explode, I'm finally able to turn and face him and offer him a long and intensely passionate kiss.

"I'm a bit leery to try this standing up against a glass wall. And, I can't fathom getting back up off the wet tile floor once I'm down there. What say we dry off and head for my bed?"

Now, with the *On Call II* docked back at Marina Jack, the captain has notified the dockmaster, who in turn has sent Andy with the limo golf cart to pick us up. The first thing I do is start digging in my purse for my phone, and once find it I hit redial on Maggie's number.

Mag answers the call immediately.

"Mom, Mom is that you?"

"Yes dear, it's me." I can hear the concern in her voice. "What's wrong, honey?"

"Oh Mom!" is all Maggie gets out before bursting into tears. "She's… she's sick mom."

"Who's sick, honey? Calm down, it's not good for either you or the baby to be so upset."

That comment sets off an even louder and clamorous deluge of tears and wailing.

"Sweetheart, you're scaring me. What's going on?"

"Her skin."

Are the only words I understand out of a tear and sniffle filled rambling followed by loud nose-blowing.

"Maggie, answer me! Where are you sweetie, home?"

There's more uncontrollable bawling before I catch, "The hospital… she's in intensive care."

I finally begin to understand.

"Mag, don't tell me you had the baby while I was gone."

A definitive, "Yes!" blurts out of her before another voice comes on the phone.

"Liz, it's Frank."

"Frank… my word, what are you doing there?"

"Long story short, I gave Miss Maggie here a ride to Sarasota Memorial. She went into labor last night, and well, obviously she had the baby."

"Is everything all right?" I ask. "She mentioned intensive care."

There's a period of quiet before his cautious answer.

"We don't know the entire details yet, ma'am, but a doctor is supposed to come in anytime now to talk to your daughter."

His words remain guarded as he's standing next to Maggie's bed.

"The baby is alive, and they did say she's good size for being premature." He stalls a bit struggling for what to say next. "She just has a bit of a skin issue and, well… that's why she's with all those specialists now."

After telling Frank that we'd be right there I hang up and fill Stu in on what few details I know. Having overheard the conversation, the driver takes us pronto straight to the car. We jump in, and Stu squeals through the red light at Marina Plaza and onto Bayfront Drive, heading south towards the hospital. As he navigates the sharp bend right before Marie Selby, he pats my leg and reassures me Maggie and the baby will be just fine.

"They're in good hands at Sarasota Memorial." He consoles. "Plus congratulations Babe! You know, you're pretty darn good looking for a grandmother."

Baby Mine

—Bette Midler, *Beaches* (1988)

—Disney animated feature *Dumbo* (1941)

161

Stu hangs a sharp right onto Osprey and continues flying through the residential neighborhood of Southside—that is until flashing lights and a siren from a police motorcycle bring us to a screeching halt at the cross street of Floyd.

"Oh dang," I mutter.

"Don't worry, Liz. I know how to take care of this."

"I'm not worried about you, Mario Andretti, I'm concerned about getting to Maggie and the baby.

As the officer removes his helmet and makes his way up to the open driver's window, hands on hips.

"Do you have any idea how fast you were going in a 25 MPH zone?" He smirks while peeling off his right glove and glancing over at me in the passenger seat. "Driver's license and registration please."

Stu digs his wallet out of his back pocket and removing his ID he hands it to the officer. He then excuses himself for reaching in front of me and proceeds to get the registration and insurance card out of the glove box, handing them over as well.

"I'm sorry officer, but I'm a doctor and there's an emergency…"

"Hold that thought, sir."

The officer walks back to his radio on his bike. It's difficult to understand a single word from the garbled conversation he's having with someone on the other end.

Several minutes later he returns to the car.

"So Doctor Robbins, what's this about an emergency?"

Stu explains where we are headed, and for all intents and purposes he really doesn't lie, but he does stretch the truth a little bit regarding the situation's medical necessity.

And we're soon back on our way

As we pull into the hospital's parking garage off Waldemere, I finally exhale.

"That was some smooth talking, Doctor, if ever I've heard any."

Looking at me with those baby blues, he shrugs.

"What? It was all the absolute truth about the patient and her baby. I just may have forgotten to advise him that I'm not the attending physician."

We wait for what feels like days for the garage elevator. We stand for what feels like hours at the information desk to get Maggie's floor and room number. It then takes forever for the volunteer to make out our adhesive nametag guest passes.

I'm bitching and bemoaning the situation as we head towards the elevator bank.

"It's okay, Liz, we're doing really well. We've made great time. It's only been thirty-five minutes since we got off the boat!"

<h1 style="text-align:center">162</h1>

Without so much as a knock, I abruptly fling the hospital room door open, and it hits with a bang against the interior wall.

"Oops, sorry."

All eyes turn to look at me. Mag is in the bed and surrounded by two doctors, a nurse, Frank, and a janitor with a mop and wringer-bucket. Stu remains in the doorway as the group parts like the Red Sea to allow me through.

"Mom, thank God!" exclaims Maggie with her arms out.

As we embrace.

"What the heck's going on?"

Mag begins to cry and the nurse speaks up, gently.

"Now you don't want to get yourself all worked up again to the point where you vomit. Plus, it pulls on your stitches."

"Can someone tell me what's wrong?" I urge, and the older of the two doctors introduces himself.

"I'm Doctor Joshua Blair, and you must be the Grandmother." he states while offering an in earnest handshake. "I'm a dermatologist. Your daughter's obstetrician, Katherine Taylor, brought me onboard to outline a care plan and course of treatment for the baby."

And with that, he smiles warmly.

"How do you do?"

He continues by introducing the much younger and extremely nice-looking gentleman beside him—Doctor Geoffrey Martin. He reaches out to shake my hand as well, and all I can think of is that he looks a lot like Doctor McDreamy on Grey's Anatomy.

Doctor Martin advises, "I'm a geneticist and have been brought in to confirm the primary diagnosis and help determine the best prognosis for this case. We want to approach her treatment with options that will promise the best results for a normal future."

Dazed momentarily I sit on the edge of Maggie's bed to get my balance. I suggest that Frank and Stu go find the cafeteria and get a coffee.

Taking a moment to gather my thoughts.

"So what exactly do you believe is wrong with the baby? And I could use some layman's terms please."

I take Maggie's hand in mine and squeeze it, partly out of support and love and partly because I'm scared to death over what we're about to hear.

Fortunately, the weeping has ceased leaving only their streaks upon her cheeks and through an occasional sniffle says, "Yes, please tell us, doctor, what's wrong with my little girl?"

"I'm afraid," says Doctor Blair, "that your daughter was born with a genetic defect that first presented itself with the collodion membrane she was encased in."

"I'm sorry to interrupt you already, doctor," I say, "but I don't quite understand. *What* was she encased in?"

"It's a tight shiny membrane that resembles Saran plastic wrap completely covering a newborn's body." He takes a deep breath followed by a productive pause before continuing.

"To be honest it's an extremely rare condition. In what few cases I'm familiar with the membrane usually dries up, cracks and then peels off slowly over the course of say several weeks to a month. However, in your granddaughter's case the process seems to be accelerated."

He again pauses to make eye contact with Maggie.

"Even though we have kept her in a humidified incubator and applied a thick layer of emollients to keep the skin moist and topical steroids to reduce inflammation, she is already cracking and peeling."

"Is that a good or a bad thing?" asks Maggie sounding concerned, but still in control of her emotions.

"To be totally honest, Miss Blum," –pronouncing it like plum– "we don't know what it means. At times, what happens is that after the membrane completely sheds the infant does not display any other skin involvement. It's a phenomenon we call a self-healing collodion baby."

"But, in the majority of cases, and I feel I must be honest here, that's a little over 90%, I'm afraid the infant will display one of several ichthyosis skin types such as CIE, lamellar, harlequin or even Netherton syndrome. The results of her genetic tests, even if they identify a specific mutation, will not tell us how mild or severe a condition we'll be dealing with. Basically, only time will tell."

I am utterly overwhelmed. "So much for layman's terms, I guess."

Maggie returns to tears, and I grab the box of tissues off the bedside table, pull several out, and hand them to her while reserving one for myself.

"I'm sorry, doctor, but please help me try to understand this thing. What are these icky whatever skin problems you mentioned?"

"Honestly, it would be terribly confusing and an ill use of my time to describe each of them in detail to you, states the doctor matter-of-factly. Once we have a distinct diagnosis, then we can focus on what it is and where we go from there. In the meantime, I want to get back to treating the baby."

"Can I see her?" I ask, jumping up. "She's my first grandchild."

The doctor gets a concerned look as he thinks about my request.

"I guess it would be all right, but only for a few minutes. And, you'll need to scrub and gown up first before going into the NICU."

163

Doctor Blair escorts me to the neonatal intensive care unit via the same elevator I used to come upstairs. Getting off on the floor marked Labor & Delivery, we follow an arrow that points to Nursery & Waiting Room.

"I want you to be prepared for what you're going to see," advises the doctor, as we continue walking down the hall. "I know every grandmother's dream is to mollycoddle a little pink bundle of joy, and in time, I'm fairly hopeful that will happen. But right now, we're dealing with an extremely ill baby that may have a serious deformity to cope with for life."

"I've seen a lot of things, Doctor Blair, in my sixty years on this earth, and trust me, not all of them have been pretty." I exhale, "Trust me!"

As clear as if it happened yesterday, I can see my son Tommy's frail and broken body lying comatose in the hospital bed. His head partially shaved and bandaged, an intubation tube coming out of his mouth and his left leg being held up in traction. I then fight hard not to see the lasting impression I carry with me of Scott's terrible burns on his chest and face.

"I'll be okay, doctor," I repeat tentatively, then totally regret my decision to not pop a preventative pill while I was up in Maggie's patient room.

Focus on the baby...

Passing through the waiting room, with Doctor Blair still doing his best to prep me, I stop dead in my tracks and gasp.

"Are you all right?" questions the doctor. "We haven't even seen the child yet."

There, sitting in two of the vinyl upholstered chairs, are my dead neighbor Marilyn and the neighborhood wraith Mary. Marilyn motions for me to come over while Mary raises her head just enough to display her shockingly sad, sunken eyed and acutely pale face.

"I'm sorry, Doctor Blair, I just thought of something I forgot to do."

Seeing a door marked Public Ladies Room I step back. "Will you please excuse me for a minute? I think I better pop in here before we enter the nursery."

Appearing a bit baffled, the doctor advises me on where to find the scrub room and that he'll just meet me there after I'm finished. He nods, then departs with a concerned expression before taking one more glance back. As I open the bathroom door, I can see Marilyn get up, out of the corner of my eye, with the aid of her walker and its green tennis balls. She starts to shuffle my way with Mary in tow.

I holding the door for them.

"What in the world are you two doing here?" I check under the stalls to make sure we're alone. "I'm damn well sure that doctor saw you!"

"Now honey, don't be foilishtik. That fellow couldn't see us. Well, not like you can. He may have seen a shadow against the wall or, upon second glance, caught sight of a glimpse of movement. But he isn't receptive enough to experience us the way you and a few others do. No, metukà, he isn't nowhere as sensitive to us as you."

"Seems kind of young doesn't he?" She smirks while taking a moment, adjusting what I presume is her girdle.

"Sweetie, these old bones need to sit down on something." Marilyn swings open a stall door and awkwardly maneuvers herself and the walker inside before lowering herself down on the toilet seat. "I've become such an old klutz." She snickers and then gets her usual tissue out of her bosom and blows her nose.

"Your daughter's baby is in big trouble," she says. "Why it's all the talk in the woods of Pelican Cove... He wants the baby, sugar! Go ahead, Mary, tell her. Come on girl don't be shemevdik. Go on now, speak up!"

Mary looks up for the first time since entering the bathroom. "I told you that night by the pool, Miss Blum, when I showed you the picture I drew of the live oak with the devilish eyes." She is weeping softly as she speaks. "Remember it Miss? The one where he's hoisting Maggie's baby skyward with his gnarled branches and gloating over his newly claimed prize? He's tired of me," she says. "He wants the baby."

"I'm pretty sure that was a dream," I say, looking at both of them. *I'm having a conversation with two phantoms in a Sarasota Memorial ladies' room.*

Just then the main door to the restroom begins to swing open.

"This is custodial," I say. "We have an old Jewish woman causing a bit of a mess in here, so you'll need to find another one to use."

The person on the other side is a bit thrown off.

"Do you know where I..."

I lean my back against the door and hold it closed with all my weight.

Mary goes back to staring at her bare feet again.

"My reality and yours are two different worlds. I have to communicate with you on whatever level you'll listen to me."

"Most people think we're nothing but a lot of bobbemyseh," says Marilyn, with a determined look. "But with your aid and my keinehora to ward him off, we're going to help save that baby!"

I shake my head.

"What in the heck did you just say? You know I only went to temple with you once and didn't understand half of what the Rabbi said." I look around the bathroom and realize something. "By the way, where's your dog Tookie?"

The old woman grins.

"I left him with that circus woman, Eileen, down the street from both of us. He just loves playing with her little Bichon Frise, and between you and me, she's none the wiser that he's even there."

164

I grab the door handle and shake the index finger of my free hand at them.

"I can't deal with the two of you right now. I have a doctor waiting on me and a newborn granddaughter I'm anxious to see. I appreciate your concern… I think… but I need you both to butt out and let the professionals handle this."

I swing the door open and make my way across the waiting room and down the hall.

Compelled to look back over my shoulder, I observe Marilyn shuffling with her walker and Mary following behind her still staring straight at the ground. Unnervingly, I witness both figures pass *through* two nurses reviewing a patient chart. The specters continue coming towards me as I turn to confront them once again.

"Okay girls, where in the hell do you think you're going?" I shout—or do I think it? No one seems to look askance at me.

Marilyn's eyes twinkle. "Why to save the baby, of course. We haven't been sitting here all night for nothing!"

Putting my hands on my hips I begin to chastise both of them as an older couple in street clothes pass by and turn to stare at me as they cautiously continue on.

Left alone again, I contain myself and lower my voice to a whisper.

"I need you both to go home, or wherever you stay when you're not out haunting. I'll take care of things here, and if I need you, I'll give you a call. I do have your number, you know, Marilyn."

"Oh honey, that number won't do you no good," she says. "That dang Pelican Cove woman had my place cleared out, and one of those cleaning rascals took my cell phone from right off the counter while I was yelling at her."

She gets an anxious look.

"Well, all right, I really do need to take Tookie out, so I guess we'll be going and leave you to be for now. I've already taken a peek at the little bubala earlier, and trust me, sweetie, you're going to need our help."

She pats my hand, and its warmth surprises me. With that they both take off towards the elevators and the last words I hear are Marilyn scolding Mary.

"Keep up girl, stop your dawdling. We're going to miss the last #5 bus to Sarasota Square Mall, and you remember what happened the last time we tried hitchhiking!"

165

Helping to tie the back of the procedure mask over my nose and mouth before entering the NICU, Doctor Blair again warns me of what I'm about to see.

"As we discussed, her epidermis is already desquamating." Sensing my continued confusion by the look in my eyes, he explains again, "That is, it's cracking and beginning to scale and come off in pieces.

"Right now, she is extremely sensitive to temperature changes due to her hard, cracked skin, which doesn't prevent heat loss. That's why we are keeping her in a temperature-controlled incubator. By using the glove holes on the sides, we're going in to care for her, not taking her out to be with us.

"Ready?" he asks.

"I think so."

We proceed into the nursery, and I'm immediately struck by just how many babies seem to be in here, and the enormous amount of staff running around caring for them. Several parents are actually sitting in rockers and holding some of the tiniest little beings I've ever seen in their arms. Surprisingly, the room I was expecting to be filled with immense sadness radiates with a feeling of pure love and kindheartedness.

Progressing across the sizable room the doctor continues to explain to me the situation.

"Her breathing is also being restricted by the tight skin, which impedes the chest wall from expanding and drawing in enough air. This can lead to hypoventilation and respiratory failure. To prevent that from happening, we have her on a CPAP, so expect to see small tubes inserted in her nose. She also has a central line so we can administer meds. Patients are often dehydrated, as their plated skin is not well suited to retaining water. Thus, we are also administering fluids intravenously."

On the back wall we approach a bank of sliding doors leading into several small private patient rooms. The lights inside the one we enter are dim, yet I can see a male nurse inside tending to all the dials and gadgets associated with the elaborate looking bassinette.

"We can only stay a few minutes as, unfortunately, you pose one of the greatest risks of all to her at this time. Infection. You won't be able to touch her, but you can see her, and I will have the nurse dial up the lights a bit once we're inside."

We enter the room, and the nurse makes eye contact with me over our masks and says softly, "Hello."

Even though it can't be seen, I smile proudly from behind my mask.

"I'm the grandmother," I whisper,

The doctor moves over to where the nurse is standing, and they have some sort of conversation that causes the nurse to nod in agreement, prior to the doctor coming back to my side. The nurse dials a switch, and the incubator begins to glow dimly from within. Doctor Blair puts an arm around my waist and taking my right arm leads me up to its side.

I may have gasped, I don't know. What I do know is that I suddenly feel like all of the air has been knocked out of me, and I'm having difficulty getting a breath. My first instinct is a desire to rip the mask off of my face and take off in a desperate search for an open window.

Then my stomach clenches, and I feel as though I want to throw-up. Feeling wobbly, as my legs are literally shaking, I'm grateful that the kind doctor has strengthened his grip around me. Finally, I am able to catch my breath.

"Oh my..."

The baby is completely undressed and lying on her back. Her eyes are closed but her mouth is doing a suckling motion. She appears to be trying to move her arm and perhaps get her fingers to her mouth.

"The poor thing can hardly move," I say.

Doctor Blair nods.

"It's because of the rigid skin."

The baby is completely covered in a cracking layer of tissue that's drying out and turning various shades of tans and brown before curling up on the edges and peeling off.

"It looks for all the world like the bark on the pine trees in the Cove," I murmur. Then it hits me like a truck.

She resembles the tree man! That damn totem I bought from Granny Daisy... well, minus the penis.

The baby's eyes flutter open, and suddenly my grandmotherly instincts kick in as I realize I'm looking directly into Maggie's big brown eyes. I can't help but cry.

Damn, where did I stick that tissue?

The nurse says, "I'm afraid it's time for you to go."

The slider sweeps open, and I step out.

What in the hell did that crazy Daisy woman do to her?

Wild Horses

—The Rolling Stones (1971)

166

Re-entering Maggie's room, I'm just in time to hear the nurse advise, "That pill should help you get some much-needed rest. The doctor is worried you'll be too weak to tend to the baby if you don't take care of yourself."

Maggie makes eye contact and smiles at me in a manner that lets me know exactly what she's thinking—namely, that there may not be a baby for her to care for—and now that I've seen for myself I'm thinking the same thing.

The nurse says, "I'll just let you two visit while I do my rounds. I'll be bringing you some dinner in a little bit." She then scoots out the door and shuts it softly from behind.

"Well? Tell me!" says Maggie, her voice desperate. "How's she doing?"

Pulling the bedside chair up closer to the bed, I grasp my dear daughter's hand in mine and take a deep breath.

"She's sick sweetheart, but trust me, they are taking very good care of her. She has her own room, equipped with her own private nurse."

"She's getting medicine, and they are slathering her in lotion to keep her skin moist. Uhm, let's see... oh, and she has a little tube down her nose so she gets some extra oxygen. I think that's about it?"

Maggie's eyes are getting heavy from the drugs, and as she gives a yawn, she squeezes my hand. A tear rolling down her cheek.

"I know you, Mother. What aren't you telling me?"

I stall, and as I do her eyes struggle to stay open.

"Is she going to live?" she mutters groggily.

My response before she's sound asleep is something of an evasion.

"She's very, very ill, sweetie. Our little girl is in big trouble."

I stand up and kiss her forehead goodbye, while pulling up her blanket and tucking her in. I stand there looking for a moment at the sweet face of my own little girl, and when I start to cry again, I grab a tissue off the side table and give a good, long blow.

Keep it together, Liz. You've got work to do!

I find Stu and Frank sitting in the hospital lobby. Frank's eyes are closed, and Stu is thumbing through a beat-up December issue of *Ladies Home Journal* with Ina Garten on the cover.

"Learning anything from the Barefoot Contessa?" I ask.

"Who?"

"Never mind," I say. "How long has poor Frank been out?"

"Quite a while. He's been up all night."

I shake his shoulder gently till his eyes pop open.

"Oh, I'm sorry, ma'am. I must have dozed off for a minute."

"Not a problem, Frank," I say. "I think you need to go home and get a little shut eye. I don't know how in the world I can ever thank you for everything you've done. You're a special kind of guy." Then I give him a huge hug. "I'm so glad you came into our lives."

Frank, Stu and I exit the hospital together.

"We're parked in the hospital garage," I say. "Where are you parked?"

He points to the large orange U-Haul truck parked across the way. "That would be mine, ma'am."

I break into much-needed nervous laughter to relieve the tension.

"Wait until Jackie hears about all of this."

We part ways, and as we walk to the garage elevator, I start telling Stu about the actual condition of the baby.

"I just couldn't bring myself to tell Mag what the poor little thing looked like."

The doors open, we step in, and Stu pushes floor three. He takes me by the shoulders and turns me to face him.

"Don't be so hard on yourself, Liz. You didn't actually lie to your daughter. You were just protecting her. From what I know, that's what a mother is supposed to do."

The doors part and we continue towards the car, arm in arm.

"I've been in these same clothes for two days now," I say. "I must reek. I really need to get home, shower and change."

"I thought we already showered earlier," Stu says with a grin, trying to lighten the mood.

"That *particular* shower left me feeling a wee bit dirty!" I state sarcastically.

167

Stu insists on walking me to my front door even though I've pleaded it isn't necessary. Mac is barking incessantly, while darting from behind the door to the kitchen sliders in an attempt to get a glance of me.

"I'd invite you in, but like I said, I really want to strip down, take a shower and take some time to think."

Stu embraces me tightly and whispers in my ear. "I can help you with the first two."

"Another time, Stu. I promise."

We kiss goodbye. Actually twice, as I instigate the second round, and as he walks away I call to him.

"Thanks again for a memorable evening. Happy New Year!"

He disappears over the bridge and through the hedge and I hear his car drive away.

From the above balcony, I hear the familiar Jersey accent of my neighbor Vinnie.

"Hey Liz ol' girly girl, how's it goin'? Noticed you were gone last night… Did ya get any?" He expels his sleazy old man laugh before breaking into a smoker's cough, undoubtedly coming from the faint pot odor I routinely smell.

I fumble with the key.

"Oh, by the way, hon," he says, "I think your daughter's out somewhere havin' a baby!"

I give a little mutter of disgust. "Thanks Vinnie for letting me know."

Upon opening the door, I'm attacked by a whimpering Mac as I step on a soggy entry rug.

"I can't recall the last time you had an accident, boy, but I can't get mad at anyone who tried to hold it as long as you must have."

I take him out, quickly feed him and contemplate taking a preventative Librium.

I'm not going to need this, I think while placing it back in the bottle. *That weathered old witch doesn't know who she's dealing with.*

I can feel my face getting hot. Then I start laughing as I can hear best friend Jack advising, *Stand back everybody... Liz is having an 'I need a manager!' moment.*

Looking around the house for a weapon, I pick up one of my mother's candlesticks

No, wait, I couldn't bear bending this. I place it back on the table.

I run to the kitchen where, on the counter by the stove, sits a Gunter Wilhelm knife block. I grab the honing steel and place it in my purse.

I start to leave the room, but quickly return and open the spice cabinet taking out the cylindrical box of Morton salt. Mac is looking at me.

"I don't know what good your salt can do," I say to the little girl with the umbrella. "But in all the really good horror movies they always seem to use it."

"Mac, behave. I'll be right back!"

I dash out the door and take off in my red Escape, driving way over the posted Cove speed limits. My mind is racing.

I don't know what the hell that wretched, wrinkled, cowgirl and that darn totem had to do with all this, but I'm damn sure going to see they make it right!

The nasty old guard, Jorge, leans his ponytailed head out of the guardhouse calling after me.

"Hey lady, slow it down. I'm going to have to write you up with the office!"

My tires squeal as I swing out of the Pelican Cove entrance onto Vamo Road. Glancing into my rearview mirror, I stick my arm out and flip him the bird.

168

I fly off the Trail and into the gravel lot, almost taking down the dilapidated picket fence separating the parking spaces from the building. Dashing through the arched trellis, my shoes crunch loudly on the shell path leading to the orange sherbet and teal colored cottage. I mount the steep steps and march across the porch, attempting to see inside through the front windows that are still cluttered with sale items.

The open sign that has hung on the front door on every previous visit is noticeably absent. It's been replaced by a taped down goldenrod post-it-note:

Closed for the

Holidays!

Damn!

I make my way around the building, peeking in all the side windows.

Rounding the corner, I come to the back entrance and climb the few steps attempting to see in through the jalousie window in the kitchen door. It's covered with such a film that I'm guessing it's from the ageing cowgirl's tobacco tar, and I can barely see in.

I start frantically pounding on the door, and when there's no response I start yelling.

"Come on, old lady… I know you're in there!"

I continue the process several times before finally hearing noises from the inside that sound like someone fiddling with the lock.

"Holds on to y'all's horsies!" I can hear her holler. "Ol' Granny's tryin' her bestest to unlatch dis dang ting."

And with that the door swings open with a bang and slaps against the metal pipe banister.

There I stand with the honing steel in hand and raised in a threatening manner above my head. The old woman looks at me calmly, as her hoary, loose hair swirls wildly around her head.

"Y'all didn't stop by jest ta sharpen my kitchen knives, dit cha?" she says, and flashes a grin that shows off her brown stained teeth.

"You better damn well tell me, old woman, what you and that wooden penis man did to my newborn granddaughter. She's a tree!" I scream. "She's a frickin' loblolly pine, and her skin is made out of bark!"

Granny Daisy gives me a scornful look as she slowly reaches into the pocket of her pink, chenille robe. As the grizzled woman begins to pull something out of it with her arthritic hand, I start to panic and pull out the salt and throw a handful directly in her face.

"Take that you, you… white witch!" I shout. And then wait for her to either melt, or at least back away in complete and utter terror.

"What in da hell is y'all doin' now?" she asks as she brushes the crystals off her nose and clothes.

"Making you obey my every command," I stammer. "I want you to get that little man out here pronto. And, dammit, I want you and him to cure that baby… NOW!" I scream as I toss another hand full of salt at her, but drop the cylindrical container causing it to bounce off the back stoop.

"Honey, I ain't got no idears what in tarnation ya be talkin' bouts. Buts iffin' y'all will come insides and set with old Granny fer a spell, I'll see what I can do fer ya. Oh, but first y'all better throws a pinch a dat dare salt over da left shoulder and put dat dang sharpenin' stick down before y'all hurt somebody."

The old woman enters the duskiness of the kitchen, flips on the light over the dinette table, and makes her way to the stove where she picks up the percolator and then takes it to the sink to fill with cold water.

"I'll jest makes us a cup of da jamoka dat y'all was so fond of on yer last visit." She turns and takes a quick glance of me standing confused and hesitatingly in the doorway then returns to what she's doing.

"Come on, sugar, come belly up to da table. Don't be feared none. If I was gonna harm y'all, I would have already done did it wit da peestal Ima packin' in my robe pockeet."

I enter the kitchen and, without even turning around again, the old woman says, "Can't helps but notice dat y'all be a wearin's da bracelet Granny gave ya. I also can't help but notice dat it works."

And she practically cackles with unrestrained laughter before breaking into her smoker's cough.

"What are you saying?" I demand as I tear the bracelet off my arm and slap it on the table. "Is this what effected the baby?" I ask while pointing at it. "Did you place some kind of spell on that thing that deformed my granddaughter? Oh my God!" I scream again. "And to think I carried it into the hospital on my own arm!"

"What in da hell are ya ranting bouts now?" she asks then turning to me. "Y'all be a glowin' honey, jest as rosy as da schoolgirls' blush." She ponders for a moment. "What's dat dey say dees days... y'all got your groove back? Dat's it!"

And she cackles and coughs again. She takes her pipe out of the ashtray on the table and placing the stump between her tar stained teeth.

"Listen up, Liz... Da only spell old Granny put on y'all was ta git some lovin' back in yer life."

She strikes a kitchen match and sits down at the table directly across from me, picks up the bracelet, and while fingering it looks me directly in the eyes.

"How was it, sweetie?"

Then she lights her pipe.

169

Feeling my anger draining, I set the honing steel on the table before taking a deep breath. "I'm not here to discuss my sex life with a person I hardly know. However, I will tell you I am quite fond of one Doctor Robbins with whom I spent New Year's Eve."

It then dawns on me that I've taken the bracelet off and Daisy had just insinuated it was responsible for my relationship with Stu.

"I won't lose him because I took that thing off, will I?"

She smiles at me reassuringly. "Heavens no, child. Da power in da bracelet was to give y'all da urges and erase da fears of tryin' ta feel da lovin again. Dat, and a beet of help wit de virginial dryness. It had nuttin' ta do with pickin da feller. Hell, fer all I knows ya coulda picked da mailman."

I take a sigh of relief and literally feel my chest crack and relax.

"I really do like this thing," I murmur as I place the yak bone with its jewel and metal inlays back on my wrist.

Granny pours us each a mug of coffee and, to my surprise, goes to the fridge and gets out an International Delight French Vanilla creamer and sets it in front of me.

"What? Y'all don't think dat I knew ya was comin by?" She then reaches for the bottle. "Let me try dat dare fancy-pants stuff."

I begin telling her everything I can remember from the very beginning. My first visit to her shop, the lifelike dreams that seemed to coincide with bringing home the totem and then touching it. I continue with Mary the poltergeist and how she became intermingled with the dreams. I include the tales of the groping trees in the woods and how Mary actually became intertwined with a huge, and extremely manly live oak, while she seems to be trapped in the form of a diminutive fig tree.

I share that, several times, I've received the warning that he, which is to say the oak, "wants the baby!" And finally, I go into great detail regarding my deceased neighbor Marilyn and what a voracious appetite she has for a dead person.

"Heck," I say, "there's even a phantom dog named Tookie whose poop I have picked up,"

Granny Daisy soaks it all in and not till the very end does she speak.

"Goodness to da gracious, child, y'all gots more of da turd eye den me!" She then sips at the mug. "I'm gonna have ta get dat granddaughter a mine Bonnie ta git more a dis flavorsome creamer."

I am confused. "What's a turd eye?"

She wrinkles her nose up and begins to count.

"Furst, seconds, turd, fours. We all's only gots two eyeballs a showin', but we all's got a turd. It's called da chakra... da spirit eye and, honey, urin's seems most powerful!"

She lifts the lid off the cake holder still in the center of the table.

"Care for a Huckdummy? Jest made em dis mornin'"

I have still not eaten any lunch and it's now past dinner time.

"Don't mind if I do." I'm pleasantly surprised, much like last time, at how delicious it is. "My god, but you can cook."

"Oh shucks, why it don't take nuthin' ta throws together a beescuit wit some dried up huckleberries."

She continues to mull over everything I shared with her. "Well, ta be honest dat totems been in and outta dis here shop more times than I cares ta count. Originally it was some kind of da fertility idol from dem Spanish Point natives. Howevers, in your case I knew yer eggs was all shriveled and dried up, so I jest used it to git yer motor runnin'. Y'all know, Lizzie... horny!"

I nearly spit my coffee across the table at the nonchalant way the old woman uses the term.

She slaps the table. "Sure enuffs, y'all be a glowin'!"

She takes a bite of one of the rolls. "Dem are pretty dang good ain't dey? Now dis here's Mary and da tree is a whole nutter can of da worms and none of it has ta do wit old Granny. Y'all wants s'more coffee?"

She gets up and grabs the pot. "Sounds ta me like she's a being held against her wills by dis tree demon."

"Demon?"

"Why yes, child. Da spirits of the wicked have walked dis ert since da beginins of da times. Day enters into da weak folks dat are alive and kill dem from da insides out. Pocessin' dere souls for dere own use. Your Mary, poor ting, is deader dan da doornail, and heaven only knows what vile tings dat creature makes her do for him.

"But how can she be held captive as a tree, by a tree, and also appear as an apparition running around the Cove, heck the city, in the form of a girl?"

"Oh da world be full of da shapeshifters, honey. Y'all can't imagines da number of times ya probably thoughts ya was pettin' a cat whiles actually 'twas a divine intervention or da black of da magics a visitin' wit ya."

"Well, what about Marilyn and Tookie?" I ask.

She breaks out into her cackle of a laugh yet again.

"Your dang neighbor's simply a ghost wit a leetle doggie dat she deeply loves. What more can I tell ya, sweetie?"

170

Granny Daisy clears the table and places the dirty dishes in the coffee-stained farmhouse sink. She runs the hot water over them and adds a squirt of Dawn dish soap and sniffs the air.

"I jest love dis heres apple smells." She grabs a dish rag, and keeping her back to me, she starts to wash them while she shares her additional thoughts on everything.

"Now, honey child, I don't want to cause ya ta shakes in yer boots, but ta me dis sounds like yer dealins wit a Green Man. Why deres been tales about dem bein' amongst us since da early times. No doubts ta me dat dose Spanish Point injuns dat lived right chere in Osprey believed dat da trees were an important part of da fertile ritual." She turns to face me, shaking a dripping, soap-water spatula. "Hell, dat dere totem of Digger's proves dat much now don't it?"

"Did y'all know deres a deerect link between da tale of a virgin mother givin' birth ta save da world durin' da bleak spell on ert, and da tales of da Green Man fertilizin' old mutter nature ta bring about new life, dus savin' da world as well. Both tales sprout outta da stygian blackness of da mid-winter night. And it all lines up wit what y'all calls da Christ mass."

"I know that certain aspects of the holidays are based on pagan traditions," I say. "You're obviously referring to the winter solstice."

Granny places the last dish in the wooden drying rack, grabs a tattered tea-towel and dries her hands, turning to me. "Ain't dat what I jest said?"

She returns to the table taking her seat and asks me to describe every additional detail I can muster about Mary and the Green Man.

I repeat my story of the night that the trees grabbed at my robe and actually felt and groped at my breasts and crotch region. I retell the horrifying dream where Maggie gave birth to a tree baby on the bathroom floor. I share the night Mary showed me her drawing of the tree ripping the baby from Maggie's womb and claiming it as his own.

"Tells me effery ding abouts where he actually stands. Y'all mentioned earliers dat ya found 'im and circled 'im. Tells me bouts dat!"

Granny suggests I close my eyes as I begin.

"Well, the morning after chasing Mary through the woods, I drove over to the tree located in the exact spot on Bayhouse Court where I lost her. Actually, I thought she had vanished into thin air. I slowly got out of my car and tentatively approached the huge laurel oak. I remember how during the entire running around of that night that I hadn't even noticed the sign reading 'Narrow Road – Proceed with Caution!' nailed on the tree, or the fact that it's actually not a single tree but two.

"Halfway up and smack dab in the crook where the oak tree branches out in all directions there is the crown of a totally different species of tree sticking out. From the light green foliage and shape of the glossy leaves I am second-guessing it as being a weeping fig tree."

"Rounding the oak to its far side, the one facing the woods, I remember I stopped dead and just stared. I've become well acquainted since moving here with the term epiphyte, basically a plant that grows harmlessly upon another, but I had never seen anything like what I saw then."

"Goes on, honey. Do tell, do tell," coaxes Daisy. "Whatcha all see?"

"I can't see the head of the fig tree like I did from the other side. But, the body of its trunk runs the length of the big tree and is attached tightly to its bark. The smooth textures of its bark and light coloration make it appear quite youthful when compared to the dark and rigid outer bark of the old oak.

"This may sound silly, but I remember thinking that somehow the little tree looked voluptuous."

"How old does ya tink da tree would be iffin it were still a person?" asks Granny Daisy.

"Still a person?" I question with a quizzical look.

"Jest git on wit da describing', sugar, and we'll git back ta dat."

"Well, from what I can recall of it, the tree's trunk near the top looked like slender female shoulders. The torso was vivacious and seemed to curve sensually around the oak's trunk. I remember that two limbs embraced the older tree as if in a romantic hug."

"Well Liz, I has seen plenty of da huggin' trees in da wild," states Daisy. "I tink dats kinda natural like."

"Well, how many times have you seen what appeared to be a well-rounded rear-end and, curving sensually from either side of it, two distinct roots branching off the main trunk and wrapping themselves around the oak tree, similar to a woman having sex in the cowgirl position?

"Now dat is da bit of da differents I must say," Granny chuckles.

"Well, you haven't heard it all yet. From what would be hands and feet, were this a 'real person' as you say, run long tendrils of roots like fingers and toes, some even attaching to the ground and growing down into the sandy soil. But the thing that startled me most was that growing from the massive oak, and in the region directly between the fig tree's so called legs, was an enormous gall or growth of sorts that for all the world resembled… resembled…"

"Spit it outs, honey!" urges Granny Daisy.

"Well, an enormous man's penis, complete with testicles… Sounds pretty crazy, huh?"

"Well, da good news, honey… wells sorta, is da Green Man ain't gots da hold of dat babins of yers. I'm not quite sure's ta what his intentions be, but I gots a few idears. No, da problems be wit dat ghost of urin, what y'all calls her? Mary?"

"Yes," I respond, "She goes by several names, but Mary is what she responds to with me."

Y'all de scribes her as da pre-puberties and being dressed in da all white showin' she's still of da pure soul."

"I'm sorry I don't quite know what you mean."

Granny Daisy wrinkles her brow and practically bellows at me.

"Da child ain't been tetched by that dang demon fornicator. But, my oh my, heavens help da poor gal dat he gets his retched hands on. Her after da lifes will be nuttin buts a livin' hell!"

If You're Going Through Hell

—Rodney Atkins (2006)

171

Granny excuses herself, but before leaving the room she advises, "Y'all jest stays put. Dis might takes me sum times!"

She dashes off through the chintz-draped doorway that separates the kitchen from the store, leaving me sitting alone at the table. After about fifteen minutes or so, I contemplate hunting for her and seeing what she's up to. I get up and peek through the drape, but all I see through the dim lighting is the cast shadows of the objects in the closed store.

"Daisy!" I call out. "Is everything all right?" I await her response, but there's no reply.

Upon returning to my seat, I dig through my purse before getting out my cell phone to check the time. It's only seven fifteen, but with all that's happened it feels like it should be well after midnight.

This has been one long and emotional day. What with yachting to the Keys, becoming a grandmother, meeting with the baby's doctors.

...and God knows, thanks to Stu, I didn't get a lot of sleep last night.

Now, of course, I'm dealing with my neighborhood witch, and I'm exhausted!"

The old woman breaks my train of thought as she finally returns to the kitchen carrying a long silver pole. She has it in both hands, and the damned thing it is longer than she is tall by more than a foot.

She huffs and puffs and while laying it across the table.

"I be so sorry, child, but I had ta fetch dis from da attics, and dat damn iguana a mine was pissed as hell cuz I forgot to take em a bees-cut."

The pole is actually in a loose-twisted square bar pattern, from about halfway up, and ends in a sharp arrowhead point. Midway is a large amber glass ball that the pole passes directly through. The glass is cracked and looks like a piece of antique Blenko crackle glass and contains a pontil mark distinguishing it as handblown.

The bottom portion of the silver pole is smooth and has a blackened patina. Three legs are attached with separate hinges that make it sort of appear like a camera tripod. However, attached at the bottom tip of the main shaft is a length of 8-gauge electrical wire that's been coiled up into a bundle. Lifting the piece up out of curiosity, to ask what it is, I'm first taken aback by its weight.

"No wonder you were out of breath," I say.

"Dat dare tings made of da solid silvers, includin' dat groundin' warer.

I continue to study it. "I still have no idea what this thing is, and I definitely don't see how in the world it could ever help me with the baby. Is it a medieval weapon of some kind?"

Granny Daisy grins and shakes her head. "Dat be one way a lookin' at it, honey. It's da 1800s lightnin' rod, dadburnit, and iffin y'all does as I tells ya, we jest might save dat babins!"

She takes my hands in hers.

"Duz ya gits da weatherin' news on da telly visions?"

"Yes," I say. "I think it's channel 520 on Xfinity."

Granny scrunches her face up appearing confused.

"Whatever, honey. Now here's what yer a gonna do…"

172

I enter Pelican Cove with the back-hatch window open on my little Escape, and the lightning rod's pointy end sticking out. Jorge, the guard, immediately sees me and waves me over to his lane at the gate, keeping the arm down so I can't enter until he grants his consent. I roll down my window and listen to a five-minute dressing-down regarding the clearly posted fifteen miles per hour speed limit of all roads on the property.

I'm advised to re-read my 'Rules We Live By' manual which is available at the office if I've misplaced the copy I was given and signed off on when I moved in.

"Rules are rules!" he commands. "Refer to page seven, article two, paragraph three, Miss Blum (like plum). This time I will not write you up, but next time I'll be forced to advise management, and it will go on your permanent record."

Good grief, that damn thing followed me from kindergarten in Ohio all the way to Florida!

For a moment I start to consider explaining to him everything going on in my life, and even stretch the truth a bit by telling him I was rushing off to save the life of my newborn granddaughter. But I quickly come to my senses.

Screw him!

I simply smile. "Thanks for reminding me Jorge. Happy New Year."

As the gate goes up, I make a mental note to have a little talk with Bonnie about this nutcase and then begin to laugh.

Better yet, I'll sic her grandmother on him!

Back home I apologize to Mac, again, about leaving him for so long and offer up a Milk-Bone dog biscuit as a gesture of sincerity. I enter my bedroom walk-in and totally strip down. I toss the dirty clothes in the hamper, grab a teal bath sheet and wash cloth, and aim for the shower. I stand there for what feels like an hour simply letting the hot water run over my head and down my body… and then again, I start to cry my heart out.

Getting out, after wrapping my dripping hair in another towel, I slip on my white spa robe and aim straight for my iPhone, charging out on the pass-thru countertop.

"Please pick up, please pick up!" I repeat as Jack's phone continues to ring.

"Hello. This is Jacqueline Hernandez, now you say something." BEEP!

"Hi Jack, its Liz. If ever I needed a friend, it's right now. I know you're busy wrapping everything up so you can get down here. Honestly, this weekend can't come soon enough, and I can't wait to see you. Oh, by the way, it's a girl. I'm a grandma, and long story short, Frank practically delivered her. I know I've said it before, but that guy of yours is some kind of special! I'll try calling you tomorrow. Bye."

Suddenly the weight of the day hits me like a ton of bricks. After placing the phone back in its charger, it feels like it takes every ounce of strength I have left to make it into my bedroom, where I pull back the covers and fall into bed. I'm asleep, it seems, before my head hits the pillow.

173

Entering the hospital lobby, I practically bowl over Doctor Martin, the geneticist brought in on the baby's case.

"Excuse me," I say while bending over to pick up my dropped car keys.

"Aren't you Maggie Blum's mother?" he asks.

"Why yes, yes I am."

"I was just upstairs running a few additional tests on the baby, and I also had a talk with Maggie." He pauses, appearing to choose his words, and then stammers, "I'm afraid I left her pretty upset, so it's probably a good thing that you're here for her now… I mean both of them."

He excuses himself and runs out the front door, heading towards the hospital garage. Concerned over his comments, I hurry upstairs to Mag via the elevator, while contemplating what news he may have shared that would add to this already upsetting situation.

I enter my daughter's room to find her sitting up in bed with an untouched dinner tray in front of her. Tears are flowing as she grabs for a tissue and blows her nose.

"Oh Mom!" is all she says as I come to her side and attempt to comfort her.

Pushing the tray table aside I take a seat on the side of the bed, grasp her hands in mine.

"I know the baby's terribly sick, but she's going to get better. Doctor Blair even said some infants come through this with little or no side effects."

I try to take on an even more sanguine tone. "I have high hopes, that with a little divine intervention, everything is going to turn out to be just fine. Trust me on this... your mother's going to do everything she can to make things right. Now tell me, what did that other doctor, Doctor Martin, have to say?"

Maggie wipes her eyes and takes a deep breath.

"It was all so technical and confusing. Something about the results of a progeny test and phenotypes and genotypes. And then he described the need to do grafting, rooting, taking cuttings and performing some additional tissue cultures.

She blows her nose again before continuing. "Oh, and that he would need to collect her apomictic seeds to assist with classification and determining her genus and species. Why he might as well have been speaking a foreign language. He also said our best bet is to probably bring in a horticulturist!"

Before I have the chance to respond there's a two-knuckle rap on the door and a jolly young nurse, who's all smiles, wheels in a bassinette.

"Time to try breastfeeding." She laughs. "We can't expect this wee sprig to thrive if we don't nurture it."

I stand up expressing surprise that they would bring the baby out of isolation, especially after what Doctor Blair shared with me about the danger of exposure to infection.

The nurse walks over and undoes the tie on the back of Maggie's robe and then pulls down the shoulders of it exposing her breasts. She pulls a Kimwipe from the container on the nightstand and proceeds to clean her breasts and nipples.

"Can't be too careful," she chuckles. "Now it's your choice which side to do first, but I recommend you give equal time to both of them." And then she tee-hee's a bit more.

"This may not be the best time for this, nurse," I state firmly. "My daughter is extremely upset, and I know from experience that nursing and trying to remain relaxed during it can be a bit of a challenge. Can't it wait?"

The nurse returns to the bassinette and leaning over picks up a small bundle swaddled in pink.

"Come on sprout, it's about time your mommy got to meet you."

"I'm anxious to see her," beams Mag, while wiping away the last of the tears with the back of her hand.

"Try to remember everything the doctors and I have been telling you," I say. "She has a severe skin condition and is probably covered in lotion."

"Oh, we stopped slathering her in that stuff a while back, dear," the nurse says with that now familiar chuckle. "In fact, I think they stopped giving her medications altogether except fertilizer... well, that and water. Lots and lots of water."

And with that, she hands the baby over to her mother who lets out an earth shattering scream the minute she lays eyes on it.

The nurse breaks into hysterical laughter and grabbing the baby from Maggie she tosses her in my direction cackling.

"Let's toss another log on the fire! Whatta ya say grandma?"

I barely catch the bundle before it reaches the floor. Holding it close I pull back the blanket that has fallen across her face and find myself gasping for words.

"What have you people done to her. My God she's a... a... tree!" I falter.

"I think technically she's timber," says the nurse. "But look at that cute twig sprouting out where her nose should be."

Looking down again, I watch as the infant opens its eyes, and momentarily, I can see Maggie in them again. The bark covered thing grimaces as if in discomfort and then opening its knot of a mouth it proceeds to projectile vomit a sap type substance straight into my face. Dazed momentarily, I'm then taken aback by the permeating smell of warm Vermont maple syrup.

174

Disconcerted, my eyes flutter open, and I sit up in bed to the sound of my phone's "By the Seaside" ringtone going off in the other room. It takes me a moment to adjust as I find myself in total darkness. Glancing at the illuminated alarm clock, I see it's quarter to one. It takes my mind a moment to comprehend that it's twelve forty-five in the afternoon.

Throwing back the sheet, I switch on the nightstand lamp, just as the phone stops ringing. I sit on the edge of the bed and recount the gory details of the nightmare I just had. Taking a sniff of the air, I can almost swear Mrs. Butterworth must have made a pass through my bedroom at some point. The whole thing causes a chill to creep up my spine and sets my hairs on end.

I make a quick pit stop in the bathroom, mostly brought on by nerves, before going to retrieve my phone. Checking the recent calls list, I see I've missed four, including the most recent one, from Jack and one from Maggie. There have also been two voice mails left from my dear friend and one from Mag.

I listen to my daughter's message first as I'm concerned it may be additional news about the baby, and I'm also feeling tremendously guilty that I slept so long without getting back for visiting hours.

"Hello Mom, it's me. Believe it or not, they got me up and walking. They let me go to the nursery to see the baby. Oh Mom, it's so sad.

"I just had to see her for myself. The doctor says she's peeling so rapidly that he's never seen anything like it. He says we won't know what we're dealing

with until she sheds the collodion membrane totally. Anyway, I can't believe they handed me a beer and had me pump my breasts while I was down there. Something about wanting her to get the colostrum to build up her natural immunities or such. Anyway, the nurse has wheeled me back to my room, and I'm completely pooped and tipsy. I just wanted to tell you I'll talk to you later. Love you. Bye."

Relieved that Mags sounds as good as she does, I walk into the kitchen and put the tea kettle on before listening to Jack's messages.

"Oh my God! She had the baby already. How are they doing? What are the stats, and who does she look like? Can't wait to get my hands on her. Oh... what's with the 'if I ever needed a friend it's now' part? What aren't you telling me? Call me!"

Message two is less about the baby and more about how she's getting concerned.

"This is my fourth call, and you haven't picked up. It's well past midnight, and I'm about ready to jump in my car and start aiming south! Call me, I'll be up... Well, at least till Jimmy Kimmel is over."

175

I take my tea mug and phone to the living room, switch on the cable, and search for the Weather Channel just as directed by Granny Daisy. There's a Chevrolet Camaro commercial currently airing as I dial Jack's number.

She picks up practically mid-ring. "What in the world's going on down there? Well, besides that you're a grandmother!"

I take a deep breath. "I'm not sure where to start."

"The beginning is always good."

"Well, this time I think I need to start just about halfway in and then back up with the juicy details. But, before we begin, I am a bit surprised that you don't already know everything that's going on. I would have thought Frank would have filled you in by now? God bless him!"

"Funny you should mention him. I've tried calling him several times, but it just goes straight into voice mail. You said something in your message about him practically delivering the baby. Do tell, I'm all ears?"

I start to explain that I was out with Stu for New Year's Eve when Maggie chose to go into labor.

"To be fair," she says, "I don't think that's something you get to pick."

"Probably not, but hear me out," I say. "Mag wasn't able to drive herself, and there was no one else in the Cove to take her. The poor thing was in pain and panic stricken, but miraculously came across Frank's contact information and called him."

"Oh, hang on! You're going to have to hold for a minute," I say. "Jim Cantore is on, and I have to watch the weather!"

"Liz, It's one fifteen in the afternoon. I'm at P&G preparing for my exit interview in forty-five minutes. I think the weather can wait."

"Shush!"

He begins talking about a cold front on the west coast that will gather up moisture off the Pacific and bring snow to the Rockies, but that it won't help to alleviate the drought conditions in California and Nevada.

"In the Midwest we have Des Moines, Iowa currently under a tornado watch. This occurrence ties into the same cold front pushing across the country and, when the cold air meets the warmer air, we tend to see these scenarios start to set up."

"For God's sake, Liz, are you still there?"

"Yes… Be quiet, damn it!"

"Now adding to the weather picture, we have an Alberta Clipper dipping down through the Great Lakes Region and sweeping through the Ohio River Valley. I believe at first we're just going to see lake effect snow in places like northern Ohio and up-state New York, but later in the week we could be looking at some accumulation for the East Coast."

"I'm hanging up," she says, more than a little put out. "Call me back when you're done planning what to wear or whatever the heck you're doing!"

"Hold on, they just scanned down towards Georgia and Florida, and I need to focus."

"Focus on what? Isn't the weather down there pretty much the same every day, give or take a hurricane or two?"

"We have an interesting scenario setting up down south. Now it all depends on how far that northern clipper and its cold front dips down, but I do believe

that the Panhandle and places like Pensacola and Tallahassee may see some ice and maybe even a snowflake or two by the weekend."

"Did I hear snow? Are you worried about the cold?" asks Jack. "You do have a furnace, don't you?"

"Shh!" I spat at the phone.

"See this late season low pressure area down in the Gulf of Mexico? Well, it's collecting a lot of moisture from the still relatively warm waters down there. The National Weather Service has it listed as an unnamed storm, but as it continues to develop it will be the first storm of the season for 2013 and named Andrea. Spaghetti models are all over the place on this one currently, but most agree it's headed somewhere towards Cuba and possibly Florida. I'm going to go out on a limb here and predict we'll be seeing some severe storm activity along the Gulf Coast of Florida by the weekend. Now it's time for your local weather on the 8s."

"Okay, I apologize, I can talk now."

"What in the hell is going on with you, Liz?"

"Oh Jack, I'm sorry. The baby is sick… very, very sick, and I have to do everything in my power to save it."

"Well of course you do, honey, but what in the world is wrong with the baby? And what in the hell does that have to do with the weather?"

"The poor little thing was born wrapped in some sort of film. The doctor referred to her as a colostomy baby or some such thing and—"

"I'm sorry, Liz, I'm no doctor, but I was a field nurse, and I can promise you colostomy is not the word you're looking for."

"Either way," I say. "Her skin is all cracked and peeling off. I swear Jack, it resembles tree bark. You know the pine trees in the Cove with the deep fissures in their trunks that curl and peel off? She looks just like one."

"Oh my…"

"She's in the ICU nursery and under the care of various specialists. Oh Jack, I tear up every time I think of what she's going through. They have her on all sorts of tubes and oxygen and are slathering her constantly in various salves and lotions.

"But I have a plan. Well actually, I was told what to do by that granny witch cowgirl I bought the totem from. It looks like the best opportunity to execute it will be this weekend, and I could really use some help. Think you can get here a day earlier and arrive on Friday?"

"Sure thing, but it's going to cost you big time!"

"It always does," I say. "What is it this time... a bottle of Dom Pérignon?"

"No, I'm serious. This time it's really going to cost you. Do you have any idea of the fee Delta's going to charge me to change my flight with this short of notice?"

I continue filling Jack in with regards to the baby's condition.

"That's just terrible, poor thing," says Jack. "And I can't begin to imagine what Maggie's going through. Has she contacted the father? What's his name, Rob, Bob, Slob..."

"You know, I have no idea. It really hadn't dawned on me, but I suppose he has some right to know what's going on."

I then proceed to tell her about the letter Mag received from him and how I know she mailed one back to him.

"I also heard her on the phone one night, and well, I'm taking for granted it was with him. Let's just say, if that was a disagreement they were having, it sounded rather hot and heavy if you know what I mean. Say, speaking of hot and heavy," I say. "Wait till I tell you about how I brought in the New Year. You're never going to believe it in your wildest dreams what your prudish friend did!"

You've Got A Friend

—Carole King & James Taylor (1971)

176

Friday, January 4th arrives quicker than I anticipated. I'm sure the running to and from the hospital, and the amount of time I've spent supporting Maggie while meeting with additional specialists has played a key role in that fact. As well, I've also been keeping a keen eye on the Weather Channel.

As I'm cleaning up the kitchen after a quick breakfast, while placing the Coffeemate Peppermint Mocha creamer back in the fridge, my phone rings, and I don't recognize the number.

"Hello, Liz Blum speaking."

"Howdy-do ma'am, it's Frank Landers. Did I catch y'all at a bad time?"

"Heavens no, Frank. I'm just glad to hear your voice. The last time I talked to Jackie, she said she couldn't get ahold of you."

"Oh about that, ma'am, seems my phone battery died that night at the hospital and the minute I got home I crashed before charging it. Slept a full six hours before wakin' up, and then had to wait a spell for it to recharge. She's given me all manner of grief over that one."

I laughing out loud. "I'm sorry to laugh, Frank, but I'm guessing you got to see a side of Jack she genuinely only shares with her really close friends. Now how might I help you?"

He goes on to explain that he's currently at the real-estate office and a last-minute showing has come up.

"It's the third time this couple has looked at this listing, so I think this is finally it. Hopefully they're ready to make an offer. Unfortunately, it's at almost the exact same time as Miss Jackie's plane arrives at SRQ. I hate to impose ma'am, but is there any chance you could pick her up for me? I'd be all kinds of grateful."

"Frank, I owe you so much for all you did for Maggie and the baby, that I couldn't begin to ever repay you. And secondly, you know the two of us will chat like crazy on the drive home, as we have a lot of catching up to do. So, no problem, consider it done!"

That entire trip up 41 on the way to the airport, whenever I'm stopped at a red light, I glance towards the sky. It's unbelievably bright blue and filled with Toy Story clouds.

Where the heck are the severe storms that weather guy, Jim whomever was promising?

I park in the short-term lot and enter the Delta building. Making my way up the escalator, I check the arrival board and smile: the Cincinnati flight is flashing, 'At the gate.' I approach the waiting area and, after glancing in the large aquarium displayed by Mote Marine, take a seat in front of the closed doors to the terminal. Each time they slide open, and a handful of people exit, I look up with the hope of seeing my friend.

About ten minutes later, Jack waltzes through the opening looking like a million bucks. I can tell she has a fresh cut and color—*maybe even some new foil highlights?* She's wearing a black Eileen Fisher scoop neck paired with a Vince Camuto pencil skirt. It's all tied together with a black and white paisley print silk scarf that's dramatically billowing behind her as she struts her stuff in a pair of Jimmy Choo black and white calf hair pumps, while pulling a zebra striped carry-on behind her.

Approaching her through the other passengers her expression actually drops from elation to disgust right before my eyes.

"What in the hell are you doing here?" she asks, hands on hips.

"Wow, that's a fine 'how do you do' for your bestie."

She begins to smile and as we kiss and hug.

"If I would have known you were picking me up, I would have simply worn jeans and a sweatshirt. I'd have been a lot more comfortable the last two hours and wouldn't have had to worry about seatbelt wrinkles."

"Well, for what it's worth, you look fabulous."

"Thanks, I was hoping to impress my fiancé and maybe get as much action as you did on New Year's."

She snickers as I smack her in the upper arm.

"We've been apart since after Christmas," she says, "and I was getting kind of fond of waking up to a little somethin' somethin', if you know what I mean?"

We both laugh aloud as we step arm in arm onto the down escalator.

"So, what's the plan?" asks Jack as I aim south, back down the Trail.

"Well, like I told you, the dermatologist is treating the baby with various ointments, and they still have her on IV fluids and in the temperature-controlled incubator. It's really difficult seeing her that way as my grandmotherly instincts are to pick her up and comfort her."

Jack touches my arm. "I'm well aware of *those* plans for the baby, Liz. What I'm not clear on is why you wanted me here as soon as possible to help save the baby's life, and what the heck it has to do with Jim Cantore?"

"That's it, Cantore!" I say. "I've been racking my brain all the way to the airport trying to remember his last name."

Making the bend at Ringling Boulevard, I look out towards Little Sarasota Bay and the Ringling Bridge, smiling when I see storm clouds moving east and rolling in off the gulf. The mass of cumulus clouds projecting their growing thunderheads portends what I'm praying is one hell of a storm.

"Remember how I said I went to visit that old woman at her shop again?"

"Sure," says Jack. "But you never exactly shared the plan she gave you for helping the baby."

"Well, promise me you'll be open minded," I say. "Because this is going to sound a little crazy!"

I go on to explain the details of the scheme to her, and when finished, she simply stares at me before speaking.

"I think maybe you've been living in that fairyland you call Pelican Cove with those spirits of yours for a little too long. I've tried to be open-minded with all the tales about dead neighbors and vanishing little girls. Hell, I even tried to empathize with you regarding that damn totem, the dreams, and the groping tree limbs. But honestly, Liz, I don't see how killing a perfectly good tree is going to make any difference with regard to the baby's condition."

Making the turn to the right at Route 301, in front of the Ford dealers' huge American flag, I become teary eyed.

"You've trusted me all through our friendship, even when I've asked you to do some pretty silly things for me. Why, remember the time I asked you to hit on Scott at that Halloween party we were all at because I was sure he was cheating on me again, and I wanted to see if he'd take the bait?"

"Oh, I remember, *trust* me. He laughed so hard at my come-hither flirting's, especially since I was dressed as a chicken, that I felt bad about myself for at least two weeks." She laughs stating, "I really fail to see how that relates."

"Well, I'm not sure either," I say, "but it does prove you'll do anything I ask of you." I wipe my eyes. "And it lightened the mood, don't you think?"

I pull into Sarasota Memorial. "Is it okay if we visit with Mag for a minute before we massacre the big, Green Man?"

"I'd love to give my girl a hug and wish her well. But explain again, why the hell are we after the Jolly Green Giant?"

178

As we exit the hospital, the outside world has turned to shades of gray. It's not raining, but the sky is simply one large cumulonimbus cloud.

"I thought this was the sunshine state?" says Jack. "Do we have time for you to drive me down to Frank's in Nokomis before we go on a killing spree? I'm not quite clear what my role in this venture is, but I'll bet I'd prefer casual clothes and comfortable shoes over what I'm currently wearing."

I stick my head out the car window, looking up at the sky like a storm chaser. Pulling stray strands of hair out of my mouth.

"I guess that would be okay, but you can't dawdle as it will be getting dark soon. The particular woodsy part of Pelican Cove where we're going can be pretty dark."

"Do I have time to kiss Frank if he's home, or should I just wave at him?" Jack Laughs, then slides her heels off. "Oh my God… that's better!"

About thirty minutes later, we're entering the Cove as the first few drops of rain hit the windshield.

"I was so hoping to get this thing set up *before* the storm hit," I share. "Do you have an umbrella?"

"For God's sake, Liz, look at me… where would I be hiding an umbrella? All I grabbed was this tiny wristlet I brought for the plane with my ID and maybe twenty bucks in it."

"That's all right," I say, "I hung on to those *Maid of the Mist* ponchos."

I ask Jack to feed and take Mac out while I run to my bedroom then aim for the lanai area to get the lightening rod.

"Is he still eating green beans?" she calls from the kitchen.

"Yes, a whole can to half a cup of dry kibble," I yell back before disappearing into the laundry cupboard. "And be sure to rinse them!"

I clank and clang loudly as I attempt to get the long pole out of the small utility area without hitting the ceiling light fixture or banging it into the side of the dryer. It's taller than the room's door opening, so I have to exit at an angle and hold the rod under my arm, sticking it out ahead of me like a knight holding his jousting lance.

I navigate my way through the lanai without a hitch until I step up into the living room and a bright flash of light fills the room, followed by an ear-shattering crack of thunder, which startles me from behind. I swing around without thinking and knock one of my new Italian glass table lamps to the floor with the metal rod. When it hits, the bulb shatters everywhere.

"Shit! That's brand new!"

I set the pole on the floor, pick up the lamp, relish that it's not damaged, and return it to the table, before going back to the laundry room where I keep the Dyson.

All I need is for Mac to cut his paw and we have to run to the emergency vet yet tonight.

I drag the Dyson out and vacuum away.

Jack returns advising in a cooing tone that's directed at the dog.

"He was such a good boy, and he did both his jobs even though that was a heck of a crack of lightning, and it's sprinkling harder out."

She then looks over at me. "I thought you were in a hurry, why in the world did you pick now to start cleaning?"

Once I'm sure all the glass is up, I turn off the sweeper and leave it where it is and still plugged into the wall.

"Come over here and help me carry this thing," I say. "You have the sharp end so just be careful I don't poke your eye out!"

"Where are we going with it?" asks Jack.

"First to the car, then to the tree," I say. "But we also need to go across to the pavilion auditorium. I know they keep a large extension ladder over there in the storage closet behind the stage. Oh, and grab that flashlight on the counter."

179

It's only been a matter of minutes since her mother and Aunt Jack have left the hospital when in walks the baby's doctor. His face is solemn, and his eyes tell of news better not delivered. Mags immediately succumbs to a feeling of dread, and Liz's description over the years of what anxiety feels like, prior to pure panic, comes to mind.

The doctor takes her hand in his and forces a smile.

"The good news is your baby's epidermis, or top layer of skin, is sloughing and the tissue underneath appears pink and normal. The process is allowing her care-team to actually get the meds and emollients in contact with the underlying dermis."

Still attempting to comfort the young mother he takes a seat on the side of the hospital bed and continues.

"The bad news is she is still on oxygen and a ventilator and not able to breathe on her own. She's exhibiting symptoms of 'failure to thrive', having dropped almost two pounds since birth, and she refuses to accept the bottle. Currently her only nourishment or fluids is through an IV drip."

He pauses allowing Maggie the chance to probe.

"What will happen to her if she can't breathe and eat?"

He is hesitant with his reply. "I'm afraid, my dear, she won't make it."

He gives Mags the time to process and cry, then hands her the box of tissues.

"I think we may have missed one important factor in caring for your daughter." He pulls together a smile. "Are you familiar with the term kangaroo care?"

180

Pulling onto Bayhouse Court with both the lightning rod and ladder sticking out the back of my car, I note that the road is practically deserted. Oh, there's a few cars under the carports, most bundled up in car covers, but only a handful of the condos are lit from within. I surmise that it seems even darker because what Christmas lights are still up have been left dangling, as unlit reminders of a holiday that's passed.

"The world is always so dark and bleak after the first of the year," I say as we continue toward the end of the road.

The towering live oak comes into view and looms ominously, silhouetted by nature's light show in the sky behind it. As my headlights illuminate the front side of the old and gnarled tree, its lower boughs sway in the storm like the arms of an angry old man suffering from Huntington's chorea.

"Don't I know it," sighs Jack. "That's why I always left a strand of colored lights up year-round on my back patio. Besides that, I would just have to rehang them for Carnival in April."

And that breaks the tension in the air as we both smile, recalling several wild parties at her place involving Diplomatico rum and Cuban cigars.

"You know Frank is going to have a lot to get used to, especially now that we're moving in together," she says. "He actually told me that he hasn't put a tree up since leaving home for college. He saw no good reason for decorating the place for one person. Isn't that kind of sad?"

"It is."

"Wait till he sees what's in half of those boxes he trucked down here!"

I pull into a guest parking place and turn the car and its lights off. Stepping out of the vehicle only accentuates the darkness and, except for the wind gusts, intermittent rain, lightning and occasional thunder, it's extremely quiet and void of people.

"I guess the group of snowbirds that showed up right before the holidays have already cleared out."

"This place never ceases to amaze," says Jack. "And they probably paid first class airfare from Europe!"

Switching on the flashlight, I direct Jack to help me get the ladder out and over to the tree. We set the foot of the ladder down, and I ask Jack to hold the base, while I pull on the rope threaded through a pulley to begin extending the fly section to its full length.

"Pull the bottom back away from the tree some," I say. "It needs to be at more of an angle."

It takes every ounce of strength to pull on the rope, and about halfway up the ladder strikes a limb, just as the skies start to rumble loudly again.

"We're going to have to move the ladder over to the right some," I say. "Can you maneuver it while I hold onto the rope? If I let go, the top section is going to come sliding back down."

"Sure… no problemo," mutters Jack sarcastically.

A steady breeze carrying light rain begins, sending a rare chill through the air, reminiscent of Ohio in November. Just then a lightning bolt strikes nearby with a thunderous clap, startling me to the point that I let go of the rope and the top portion of the ladder slams to the ground, causing Jack to let out an involuntary scream of surprise, mixed with colorful expletives. As she suddenly lets go of the entire extension ladder, it falls sideways, banging into the driver's side of my car and clamoring to the ground with the distinctive clinkety-clank sound of heavy aluminum.

"Well *that* went well," says Jack, trying to regain her composure. "What now?"

"First we wait to see how many neighbors come running out, thinking there must have been a major car wreck in the parking lot."

After several minutes there is nary a response.

"Good, they probably just thought it was more thunder."

"Well dang," say Jack, "I was dying to hear how you were going to explain to them what you were doing outside their condos, at night, during a storm, with this big ass ladder and a lightning rod."

"Trust me," I say. "If I were to advise some of these nutty, professor types in here that I'm reenacting a Benjamin Franklin experiment, they would beg to join in!"

Rainbow

—Kacey Musgraves (2018)
Songwriters: Shane L McAnally, Kacey Lee Musgraves
and Natalie Hemby

181

Jack walks over and after hoisting up the bottom end of the ladder. "This time you do as I say."

She orders me to pick up my end and follow. She rounds the huge tree trunk and, upon reaching the back side, shines the flashlight directly on the obvious phallus, protruding out at about eye level.

"Well, well, you weren't kidding, were you? This big boy makes your little penis man look like a real weenie!"

She sets her end of the ladder on the ground and we both walk it up, hand over hand, until the top is leaning against the trunk of the tree. She explains that this time she's pulling the rope while I steady the base. Suddenly the drizzle turns into a torrential downpour, and its arrival is announced by a sky full of lightning and booming cracks of thunder.

Shining the flashlight up and down the rungs, illuminating the clamorous raindrops before pulling up the top section, Jack yells out in order to be heard.

"I think we need to pull the bottom angle out a little more or we may get hung up on his male member and end up performing a bris. That reminds me, did I tell you that Frank's not circumcised? Let me tell you, is that strange looking!"

I stand there in my now soaking wet clothes with my bangs dripping water in my eyes.

"Honestly Jacqueline, that's a mental picture I won't be able to shake the next time I see him."

Dried leaves are falling like snow, and an occasional acorn can be felt pelting my skin as the wind strips them from the old oak. The tempest has picked up, and between the sound of the storm and the rustling tree limbs, we have to now literally scream at each other in order to communicate.

"I forgot to bring the ponchos!"

"Yes, he thinks he looks quite macho!" says Jack. "Now get your mind back on the task at hand!"

She yanks hard on the rope, and it clanks its way up to its full extension until the two hooks clamp in place holding the top part of the ladder up.

"Now we need the rod!" exclaims Jack.

"Yes," I say, "we should definitely pray to God!"

We return to the car to retrieve the lightning rod, and I'm dismayed that I left the back window open with the rod sticking out and now not only is the hatch interior soaked, it's also full of blowing, wet leaves. We make our way back to the tree, and I cupping my hands so I can talk directly into Jack's ear.

"I'm the one that has to do this according to Granny Daisy. I may need your help getting the dang thing up the ladder, but I want you to seek shelter once I'm up there. There's no sense in both of us risking our lives."

I check the ladder one more time for steadiness before mounting the bottom rung and making my way a quarter of the way up. Looking back over my shoulder I yell down to Jack to hand it up.

Jack holds the pole up in my direction, and I grab it with my right hand. I realize not only is the dang thing heavier when hefting it alone with one arm, but now it's slippery when wet.

"Get in my car and wait for me!" I call to my friend who looks like a drowned rat. "The keys are in it so you may want to turn the heat on?"

I continue to clamber up the ladder, the lightning rod clinking and clanking with every step, against each rung that's directly below me.

Silhouettes of the gnarled and menacing tree limbs blowing in the wind come to life as the cumulonimbus clouds repetitiously flash white, followed by resounding thunder that's so strong that the vibrations can be felt through the ladder.

Hanging on for dear life with eyes closed I pray silently.

With God, all things are possible... with God, –Crack!– all things are possible.

The rain, leaves, and bracts continue to pelt me in the face.

Feeling my way up the ladder, I finally grasp the top rung with my left hand and, squinting, look up only to realize it falls about three feet short of reaching the top of the tree's canopy. By now the pole in my right hand feels like its weight has doubled due to my exhaustion. I fear letting go and watching it topple all the way back down to the ground.

While reaching up and grabbing a limb for support, I suddenly think of Maggie all alone and crying in the hospital bed, while that poor baby, with her cracked and peeling skin, struggles to survive in that bassinette contraption in the NICU.

I can't begin to imagine the amount of pain that little thing is in. I begin to cry aloud.

Dammit, Liz, keep it together. Your family needs you!

Wiping at my eyes with the back of my hand, I continue on with the balancing act of standing on the top step of the ladder, while hanging on for dear life to the rather flimsy limbs up here at the top of the tree, and also not losing the lightening rod.

Crack! There's the fiercest lightning strike yet from somewhere directly behind me, that causes my hair to actually stand on end, and startles me to the point that the rod slips from my hand. It clanks about two steps down against the ladder and the trunk and pauses just long enough for me to grab the loop of wire attached to it. The piece continues to fall, but only about halfway to the bottom, and I cling tight to the wire that feels as if it's now cutting deeply into my hand.

Supporting myself by hooking a limb with the crook of my arm, I begin pulling up the rod, hand over hand, with the aid of the wire. I become cognizant that the wetness and difficulty of holding on is not simply brought on because of the deluge, but actually the bleeding from the lacerations to my hand where the wire has cut into my flesh.

I raise my eyes upward, as I continue pulling.

Please God... help me!

As the lightning rod finally comes into reach. I balance it on the top rung of the ladder while I position myself in a more secure stance amongst the swaying branches.

Crack!

Once I feel fairly secure, I attempt to pull the sleeves on my Prada ribbed-knit cardigan down over my hands much like mittens. As the skies continue their light show overhead and the rain is relentless, I find myself questioning my wardrobe choices per usual.

The damn thing is dry clean only and how in the world will they ever get the blood out?

182

"Kangaroo care," says Doctor Martin, "is when you lay your diapered baby between your bare breasts. It's also called skin-to-skin care because your baby's bare skin is touching your bare skin. The NICU nurse will put a blanket on your baby's back to help keep her warm."

"You mean I'll finally get to hold her?" says Maggie. "What about all the fear of germs and infection and the need to remain in an incubator to live?"

The doctor is nodding.

"At this point," he says, "I think it would be more detrimental to the child's health to keep her in isolation and not bonding with her mother. It's proven kangaroo care can help a baby maintain a regular heart rate and assist in breathing."

Mag sits up, wipes her eyes one last time with a tissue. "That sounds great!"

"I believe this will be good for you as well. It should help you produce more breast milk, which in turn should allow you to breastfeed, and hopefully add some pounds to the baby. Another benefit to you is it should alleviate some of your stress and help you feel closer to her."

He gives a gentle pat to her hand.

"I'll go get the ball rolling on transferring the baby to your room. It helps that it's a private one, but we will still have to take precautions and also limit the visitations. But the first thing we need to do is have environmental services do a thorough cleaning of your room. Stay positive for me!"

183

I wipe at my face in an attempt to clear away the rain lashing down. Similar to surfacing through pool water, I flip my bedraggled hair back and momentarily the water ceases running straight in my eyes. Looking up and through the tree canopy there's still plenty of flashes and lightning streaks traversing the night sky. I maneuver cautiously up through the opening to the treetop, holding tight to the ever-thinning limbs, with the rod still in tow.

Rumble!

Terrifyingly, I find my head protruding above the rustling leaves and swaying twigs. I have a front row seat to the Lord's most heavenly light show. Even though the rain still continues to pelt down on me, the fast-moving clouds overhead open up for a moment revealing a full wolf moon and allowing it to illuminate the entire scene of the sleeping Cove stretching before me.

I take advantage of the moonlight to open the tripod legs and jam the end of the lightening rod into the pocket of a visible tree crotch. The apparatus holds, but only for a brief moment, before the strong winds blow it back into my arms. Looking about for a preferable group of branches in which to place the rod, it abruptly dawns on me. Who said it can't be upside down?

I painstakingly maneuver the rod amidst the swaying branches, while endeavoring to maintain my balance atop the careening oak and its captive ficus tree. The clouds have covered the moon again, and I'm enveloped in darkness. Yet, I can still make out where I made my first attempt to secure the lightning rod. Mustering all the strength and anger I have left inside me, I raise it up above my head and thrust the pointed end directly into the fork of the limbs.

Clap!

Exhaling deeply, I let go. Hesitantly, I wait…

…and, thank god, It stays put.

Holding onto the attached wire, while letting it out slowly, I maneuver myself downward until I feel my foot touch the top of the ladder. I then cautiously step down onto the top rung with both feet and expel a long sigh of relief.

Almost done!

Carefully I continue making my way down the wet and slippery steps holding tight to the cable in my left hand, feeling the tension and anxiety lessen, as I can now detect the ground below is only a few steps way.

KABOOM!

Abruptly, all I can see is the brightest of white lights. It blinds me. I'm experiencing the dreamlike sensation of flying through the air unsupported like a bird… no, I'm vertical, more like an ascending angel.

Suddenly, across a long expanse of white sand, I visualize Scott coming towards me on the beach, with two ice-cold beers dripping with condensation in one hand, and our son, Tommy, grinning ear-to-ear as he kicks at the sand, in tow with the other. I smell the familiar scent of Coppertone suntan lotion and then the smell of Tommy's hair when freshly washed. It's Johnson & Johnson. I smile.

…Then everything goes black.

184

Moments before the lightning strike, Jack feels the hairs on her arms stand on end and a physical tingling sensation throughout her body, yet mostly in her extremities. A blinding flash fills the night, and she's unable to focus clearly for several minutes as she tries blinking and rubbing them.

There's a loud BOOM! followed by a cracking sound and several loud thumps that vibrate the vehicle. Her first instinct is to cry out.

"Liz!"

She finds the interior light switch in the car. Once on, it helps her eyes to adjust and soon her peripheral vision returns, and the white dot in her center field of vision fades.

"Liz!" she screams again, as she flings opens the car door and jumps out.

Shining the flashlight in the direction of the tree, she stops in place and for a moment simply gasps.

The large oak is completely split in two.

Half has fallen across the road and is resting against the side of the condo on the other side of the street. The other has fallen on a neighboring carport and has collapsed the structure's roof onto at least one blue car that she can see. From the looks of the bark littered ground every bit of the trunk's exterior has been completely blown off.

A light flickers on in one of the condo windows, and through the unabating rain, Jackie can just barely make out the silhouette of a small figure peering out.

Knowing that Liz and the ladder were positioned on the far side of the tree, by shining the light back and forth, she does her best to try and figure out how to climb over to the other side.

"Elizabeth Blum… answer me dammit!"

From her vantage point, it seems the only clear shot she has is to go straight through the middle where the tree has split to the ground. Approaching the base of the tree, she focuses the flashlight on the inner portion of the oak and is amazed to see that it's completely rotted out and hollow inside.

Stepping inside so as to pass through, Jack shines the light out the other side and the beam glistens off the silver of the aluminum ladder.

"Liz. Can you hear me?"

"Where in the Hell are you?" Jackie sighs.

Glancing back into the tree at the half that hit the condo she's startled and freezes in place. Imbedded into the deteriorated and rotting interior are partially decomposed skeletal remains. Eerily, the eye sockets of the intact skull seem to be staring straight at her. Her first thought is irrational.

"Liz… is that you?"

But her medical background and common sense take over and tell her she's looking at the remains of a young—perhaps teenage—girl that's been dead for a very long time.

"What the hell's next?"

She steps out of the tree trunk and onto the ground on the other side. Swinging the light frantically about, illuminating the ground, bushes, and scattered limbs and leaves from the exploded tree, Jack quickly spies one of Liz's shoes and—about seven yards away—Liz herself. She is face down on the wet ground.

Quickly transitioning into combat triage mode, Jackie flips her friend over and checks for a pulse.

"Thank God you're alive."

Competently she begins pulling up Liz's clothes, checking her head to toe for broken bones, open wounds and burns from the lightning strike. She first finds what look like first degree burns to her left palm and, far worse, third degree ones on her wrist where Liz was wearing the Tibetan bracelet that the old Granny woman gave her. Where once was Yak bone, jewels, and precious metals, now resided the blistered skin outlining the exact shapes and patterns of the piece of jewelry completely encircling her friend's wrist.

Continuing her examination, Jack finds a pinpoint exit burn wound on the bottom of Liz's left foot, the one that's missing a shoe, and after removing the right sneaker is relieved to find it's unhurt.

Cradling Liz's head in her lap and trying her best to shield her friend's face from the rain with her jacket, she pats her cheeks and encourages her to come to. This, while trying to push back her knowledge and fears of possible heart, neurological, or brain damage from electrocution.

"Come on, Liz. Wake up. Please wake up. Open your eyes for me girlfriend. You can do it. I know you can!"

The rain starts to let up and the rumblings and lightning flashes are moving away from the bay water and off to the east. Jackie looks to the sky and pleads.

"Okay Lord, I know you and I don't always see eye-to-eye, but this lovely lady truly believes in you. After seeing the amazing way you have helped her to heal this past year, and then brought her daughter back into her life well… I'm probably a bit of a believer too. However, please, please, please do me this one thing. Please God, let my dear, old friend wake up and be alright…"

Jack then continues softly in prayer

"Padre nuestro que estás en los cielos

Santificado sea tu Nombre

Venga tu reino

Hágase tu voluntad

En la tierra como en el cielo

Danos hoy el pan de este día

y perdona nuestras deudas

como nosotros perdonamos nuestros deudores

y no nos dejes caer en al tentación

sino que líbranos del malo.

Amen."

Jack realizes the water running down her cheeks are her own tears and no longer raindrops. She can taste their saltiness as they run across her lips. She wipes at her eyes with the back of a muddy hand and to her great surprise she hears the faint voice of her dear friend as Liz clears her throat.

"Who the hell are you calling old?"

185

There's an almost inaudible tapping on the hospital room door, and Maggie's heart leaps, anticipating the baby's arrival

"Come in!"

The door slowly swings open, and a middle-aged Latino man, dressed all in black except for his white clerical collar, enters. He smiles as he approaches the bed and introduces himself as Father García.

His demeaner quickly changes, however. His appearance turns quite serious and he starts speaking in somber tones.

"I'm the Christian clergy on duty at the hospital today. In my heart of hearts, I'm hoping that you don't construe what I'm about to share with you as a HIPAA privacy violation."

Maggie's confusion over the statement clearly shows on her face. "Alright…"

"I was taking lunch in the cafeteria, as I usually do, and at the end of my table were two NICU staff discussing a patient's dire condition. Being a man of the cloth, and not a physician, I honestly only understood about every fifth word. But what did come through loud and clear was that the baby they were speaking about was very, very sick."

Mags holds up the flat of her right hand signaling 'pause' as she reaches for more tissues and proceeds to blow her nose and wipe her eyes.

Father García moves from the foot of the bed and positions himself right next to Maggie.

"When it became clear during their conversation that the mother was still in the hospital, I was compelled to ask your name and room number. Both quickly offered them up as they felt a pastoral visit might offer you some comfort."

The priest now takes her hand with a look of compassion in his eyes.

"Are you familiar with the Sacrament of Anointing the Sick?" He takes a deep breath. "It's a final rite administered to the sick and dying."

He pauses in an attempt to read Maggie's reaction which now appears staid and serious minded.

"What do you do?" she asks.

"Basically, I'll lay my hands on the head of the baby. I'll then proceed to anoint, with the blessed Oil of the Sick, plus her forehead and hands. That accompanied by prayer."

"Through this holy anointing may the Lord in his love and mercy help you with the grace of the Holy Spirit. May the Lord who frees you from sin save you and raise you up'. These are the sacraments that prepare us for our heavenly homeland."

Mags thinks about the priest's words before looking him directly in the eyes.

"Thank you, Father, for coming to see me and for sharing the hospital staff's sincere concerns. It truly touches my heart."

It's now her turn to take a cleansing breath.

"I'm not quite ready to throw in the towel yet, Father. I have great faith in God and a mother's intuition to keep trying and moving my baby's care forward. What I will ask of you, if you're able, is to baptize her while you're here today."

I Can See Clearly Now

—Johnny Nash (1972)

186

Jacqueline is attending to me where I fell and begins by shining the flashlight directly into each of my eyes, checking to see that they dilate.

"Good…" she says. "Now don't move your neck, but slowly try moving your arms and legs for me."

I do as I'm told.

"Anything feel broken?" she asks.

"No, just stiff."

"Mind if I poke and prod a bit at your ribs and belly?'

"Not unless you start your wisecracks about my lack of boobs and need to start a diet."

As Jack continues the examination, we both hear the snapping sounds of someone or something approaching and stepping on the scattered broken-off twigs and tree branches.

"Hello!" Jack calls out. She turns back to me.

"I saw someone in the window of that condo. God, I hope no one was hurt. As it is, we could have a lot to answer for, Liz."

I hadn't thought of that.

"…or better yet, maybe it's one of your night guard guys coming to help us. Hello, is somebody out there? We're over here!'"

"I'm cold," I mutter.

Jack rubs her hands together and places them on mine.

"It's probably mild shock," she says. "We need to get you to the hospital."

Some more rustling occurs out of the darkness, and Jackie shines the light straight through the split in the tree, where the beam strikes the hazy form of a figure dressed all in white on the other side.

"Hey… over here. We have an injured person and could use some help!"

There's no reply.

"Do you know, has someone called 911?"

Still silence.

"Do you have a phone and can you at least call the guard house and report there's been an incident?"

The individual moves forward and appears to step *into* the trunk of the splintered oak. I say nothing though I have my suspicions who it is. I see fear creep onto Jack's face. The figure stoops as though examining something. Jack's grip on my hand tightens.

"Jack, what is it?" I ask.

"I was so worried about your condition that I may have forgotten to share a minor detail with you," Jackie whispers into my ear.

"What's that?"

"Well, there's a dead person, no… a body, well… actually what appears to be a young girl's skeletal remains inside that blown-to-bits tree."

I struggle to sit up, while still leaning into her, so as to get a view of what she is pointing the light on. The figure straightens up and takes a step towards us out of the tree.

Jack gasps as now it's quite apparent that the bright beam is shining straight through the ghostly figure and illuminating the trunk's interior.

"It's Mary," I say and lean back.

187

I let out a slow ragged breath. "So you can actually see her," I say,

"Hell yes, I can see her! At first, I took for granted she was one of your crazy neighbors coming to help, but now… I mean—"

"Her name is Mary Sherrill," I say. "She's the little girl that I told you about who's been running wild around the Cove with a drawing pad… Well, her spirit has anyway!"

Mary pauses before us, and it's now quite apparent she's about six inches off the ground. We also notice she's crying, but with a huge smile and a child's innocent twinkle in her eye. It soon becomes obvious to me that they are tears of joy.

"Mary…" I say.

"Yes'm," she says, her voice reedy and ethereal. "Oh, thank you, thank you, thank you. I'm finally free from that horrible creature."

The young spirit brings her arms forward from behind her back and I gasp. Before me she is holding the totem man, erect penis and all.

"Ma'am, she said it's up to you to finally take care of everything and you know what you have to do."

"Who said that?" I ask. "Who is she?"

"Why your guardian angel… Marilyn. She said, when the time was right, I should give it to you."

Guardian angel? I wouldn't have thought so, and how the heck had Marilyn gotten that thing back from Granny Daisy?

Suddenly, Mary appears panicked. "Where's my mother?"

"Honey, do you know what year it is?"

The child looks confused. "Year? I don't know what you... I mean to say, well... I believe it's 1881, but is there something special about that? What..."

It's possible she is going to run off, start crying, or both.

"It's okay, Mary. Shhh. Don't you worry. Now where did you— I mean *do* you live, honey?"

"Well, our home is back north in Brooklyn, but we're wintering in Hill Cottage at a place called Webb's Winter Resort on Spanish Point. Can you take me there?"

I think back to my last conversation with Granny Daisy. "That's exactly what we are going to do, sweetheart!"

I turn my attention to Jackie who has been frozen, dumbstruck by all this.

"Jack... Jack! Please go look in the back of the car for a Cincinnati Reds stadium blanket and bring it to me."

"I... What? Oh are you still feeling cold? We should have gotten you somewhere warm by now!"

"No dear," I whisper in an attempt to not include Mary, since it appears she has no understanding that she's actually dead. "You're going to use it to collect up that poor child's bones from inside that damn tree."

188

After positioning the naked baby between Maggie's breasts, a folded cloth diaper under its bottom, the nurse adjusts, then tapes, the portable ventilator in place.

He then gently covers the baby's exposed backside with a hospital receiving blanket. He positions the side table within Maggie's easy reach and stocks it with ice water, tissues, and the call button.

"Are you comfortable?" he asks.

"Can my head be raised a little more?"

"Of course." And the nurse adjusts the bed. "How's that?"

"Better," she says.

He gives her a smile. "Alright, now how about I get something for the mother?"

He leaves the room and quickly returns, popping the top on a Michelob Light beer. He pours it into a tumbler with a flexible straw and adds it to the table.

"Is that for me?"

"Sure is," he says. "Doctor's orders, in fact. And there's two more where that one came from when you want them."

"Does he want me drunk?"

"Drunk? No, though it wouldn't hurt if we could get you to relax a bit. More to the point, it helps with the let-down reflex and your ability to produce more milk!"

He heads for the door stating, "I'll just dial down these overhead fluorescent's a tad while you two try to moderate your breathing and relax. Press the call button if you need me."

189

Jack gathers up the blanket and ties it shut much as a hobo would. She cradles it, with most of the bones, back to Liz's Escape. As she picked up the larger pieces several connected smaller pieces, such as fingers and toes, just disintegrated. Items such as the skull, sternum with rib cage, pelvic girdle and a femur were still pretty much intact.

Upon opening the car's back gate, she spies a Publix reusable shopping bag and decides that placing the blanket in a carrier with handles would help to keep all the pieces together.

It's not until she secures it in the cargo area that she notices the bag is decorated with graphics of fruits and berries and the tagline: Publix - Always Fresh & Ready for the Picking!

"Well, probably not this time," she mutters and slams the hatch shut. She returns to find me hobbling out of the oak tree, embracing the totem.

"I told you to wait for me!" she says

"I'm okay. It's just hard to walk with the hole in my foot."

Jack supports me as we slowly make our way to the car.

"I'm still not sure exactly what we're up to, but is it important for us to have all the pieces of that poor girl with us?"

"Why, what did you leave?"

"Basically, a handful of dust."

"I don't think that'll matter."

She places me in the passenger seat and once inside cranks up the heat.

"Sarasota Memorial?" she asks. "Or what's that other one, Doctors Hospital?"

"Neither," I say. "First you're going to my house and letting Mac out. Then back in my laundry room I keep a small spade for gardening, grab it. After that we're visiting Spanish Point... Oh, and get me a Cab Sav in a to-go cup with a lid."

"I don't think Spanish Point is open at this hour."

"Since when in the hell has a little issue like that stopped us?"

"And, I'm not sure this is the time for wine."

"Fine, check the fridge. You can probably find yourself a cold beer!"

As we pull away, the car's headlights briefly illuminate the interior of the fallen tree. I glimpse Mary within, looking down at the location where her remains once lay.

190

The beer, the warmth, and weight of the baby on her chest, along with the rhythmic beat of the ventilator have all lulled Maggie into a half-wake, half-sleep world. The nurse, having now turned off the overhead lights, and pulling the blinds from the storm, adds to her feeling of well-being.

Before she realizes it, she's humming "Too-Ra-Loo-Ra-Loo-Ral" to the baby and then softly singing...

"Over in Killarney, many years ago
My mother sang a song to me, in tones so sweet and low..."

Upon suddenly hearing someone gently blowing their nose, Maggie slowly opens her eyes, and finds a short squat elderly woman, supporting herself with a walker, standing beside her and staring.

"Oh honey, I hope I didn't wake you. Oh vez mear, sometimes I can be such a nudnik."

"What?" stammers Mag. "Do I know you?"

"Well, I sure as heck feel like we do," she chuckles, while placing her used tissue inside her brassiere. "I'm your mother's neighbor, Marilyn Spitznogle. Howdy do."

Maggie squints to see better in the semi-darkness of the room. "But, aren't you dead?"

"Oh, your mother, the shiksa. She's like mishpocha to me, like I'm her bubba. However, she has some meshuggina ideas about things in Pelican Cove."

Not understanding a thing the women has said, Maggie's thoughts turn to concern for the baby.

"The nurse said we are under quarantine and only hospital staff are permitted in the room. You need to go before you expose my daughter to any germs or infections. She's extremely vulnerable with her skin condition."

She reaches for the call button, but Marilyn takes it in hand before she can reach it.

"What are you doing?" says Mag, "Nurse!"

"Honey, now don't go all hok a chainik on me here. Think about it… If I'm a ghost what possible germs can I be carrying?"

She smiles, and the apples of her cheeks turn rosy, as she announces,

"Today is the first Shabbat after your daughter's birth and I'm here to perform the b'rit bat for her."

"Perform what?" Maggie asks. "I really need you to go!"

"Why the ceremony to welcome your baby girl and to present her with her Jewish name. Of course, we can't have a kiddush, but it's the thought that counts!"

"Jewish name? I'm basically an agnostic," says Maggie, now totally confused.

"No one need know you don't eat meat, sweetie… now let me see this beautiful child of God."

Bridge over Troubled Water

—Simon & Garfunkel (1970)
Songwriter: Paul Simon

191

Before the Visitors' Center at Historic Spanish Point, there's a sign and then an entrance driveway. Our first obstacle is a guardhouse with a steel barrier arm gate lowered across the drive and secured with a chain padlocked to a cemented pole on the left side.

"At least there's no guard on duty, apparently, since it's all dark," points out Jackie. "Any suggestions on what we do now?"

"Yes. Hop out and get one of those maps in that card rack beside the ticket window."

She does as told and, upon returning, hands it off to me. I place the totem on the dash, flip on the overhead reading light, and unfold the map.

"Dammit!" I grumble, as I dig through my purse for a pair of readers.

The map of the grounds is broken down to four color-coded sections with a key in the lower right-hand corner.

Prehistoric: Yellow

Webb Pioneer: Orange

Bertha Palmer Period: Blue

Plants & Gardens: Green

There are also numbered dots 1–25 that correspond to a legend below the key.

"What in the hell are we looking for?" Jack asks, as she scoots over beside me to get a better look-see.

"Well, first we need to find Yellow-22."

"There it is," she says. "Out on that peninsula piece of land sticking into Little Sarasota Bay. What's there?"

"That's the prehistoric shell midden where, more than likely, Old Grannie's friend, Digger Doug, found the totem. She had said I needed to return it to where it belonged."

"What the heck is a shell midden?"

She reads the description aloud which explains that it was an area where the early tribes would deposit shells, fish, and animal bones and other accumulations of waste from their daily lives.

Jack scrunches up her face.

"It's a damn garbage dump… like Rumpke back in Ohio. Yuck! How do you know she meant for you to bring it here? Maybe, she just wanted you to stop by the Visitors' Center and give it to the person at the front desk!"

I give her the stink eye over the top of my glasses. "We then need to make our way back to Orange-8 and 9, Mary's Chapel and Pioneer Cemetery, with Mary's remains."

"You're not telling me that this chapel is named for the same Mary who floated out of a tree, and whose earthly remains I stuck in a Publix bag in the back of your car, are you?"

"Believe what you will, my dear, but I hardly think it's a coincidence!"

192

My voice takes on a somber tone as I grasp my best friend's hands in mine and explain exactly what I need for her to do.

When finished I ask, "Do you know how much I love you?"

"Ditto!" she says with a kiss on my cheek, as she exits the car and heads towards the back. She opens the hatch and grabs the shovel in one hand, the Publix bag in the other. Slamming the rear shut, she makes her way to the passenger side, where I roll down my window and hand her the totem.

"I hope this is the last time I see you, Big Boy!" I murmur.

"Give me the map," she says holding out her hand.

I pass it to her. "Good luck!"

Regretting my inability to walk, I watch as she ducks under the bar blocking the roadway and disappears into total darkness.

Left alone, sitting in the shadowy moments of the wee small hours, I think back over the last few years of my life. Leaving my job, giving away many of my possessions, moving a thousand miles, settling into the Cove, meeting Stu and experiencing the feeling of love again...

and the sex, Liz, let's not forget about that.

Then there is my reconnecting with my daughter and the blessing of a grandchild. Teary eyes begin to water as I begin thinking again of that poor helpless baby and her struggle to live.

Suddenly, out of the darkness, heading straight towards me, are two bright lights bouncing along that resemble the glaring eyes of a great gray owl. The image settles on the far side of the gate, and after a moment, the figure of Jacqueline Hernandez walks out of the light.

She walks up and opens my door.

"Did somebody here call an Uber?"

Giving a slight snivel I wipe the tears from my eyes on my sleeve.

"May I see some form of ID please?" I jest.

She assists me in limping to a tram decorated with Spanish Point emblems and also a sign reading, 'Complimentary Guest Shuttle to Parking Lot'. We climb into the engine car, and Jack makes a big U-turn and aims back into the park

"Where did you wrangle this thing?"

"A little ways down this drive there's a parking lot with a gazebo in it. Believe it or not, this baby was parked right there with the keys still in it. The biggest problem was getting it in gear. I'm glad I've driven a jeep before!"

Using the flashlight on my phone, I take the map and advise her to veer to the right.

"We should pass a large, ancient burial mound."

We come to a crossroads where there's a picnic ground.

"Continue on straight and Acorn Cottage should be on our left. Then the next thing we should see is a place called the White Cottage. It says that it was in this area where John & Eliza Webb first settled with their family and named their new home Spanish Point."

"Well, if nothing else," says Jackie, "we're getting our local history lesson for the night!"

"Okay, slow down. Somewhere along this wall and atop that ridge is the midden. We're looking for a set of steps."

She slows the vehicle and proceeds at a crawl as abruptly, amidst the rocks and foliage, a set of wooden steps come into view and she comes to a stop. The essence of night blooming jasmine carries pleasantly on the air.

"I'm not sure what that is, but it sure as hell smells damn good for a garbage dump."

Jack waits at the top of the steps with the totem and spade in hand, as I slowly make my way up, one tread board at a time, since they are slippery from the earlier rains. At the top, I pause to catch my breath and survey the surroundings.

It appears this ridge, a long running mound, built along the water's edge of Little Sarasota Bay and now topped by a walking path, is in fact the shell midden. Straight ahead, the full moon dances on the water and the silhouettes of large houses located on Casey Key can just be made out in the distance.

To the right the path abruptly ends amidst a forest of trees. Walking to the left, we come upon a large sunken garden, and built over to the far side is a white pergola covered in small white flowers on climbing vines. Beyond that point, the trail continues into complete darkness.

"Well we found out where the great smell is coming from," says Jack as she points at the trellis topped columns in the distance. "Frank and I need to get some of that for the yard."

193

A different nurse introduces herself and proceeds to take the baby and place her back in the enclosed bassinette. After attending to the infant, she then assists Mag with tying the back of her gown and adjusting her bed and tray table. She grabs Maggie's chart from the end of the bed.

"Did you have any success in getting the baby to latch on when the earlier nurse was helping you?"

"No, but if my boobs get any bigger, they're going to burst," She says—then, a bit embarrassed. "And they're leaking."

"Great!" says nurse. "That means your milk has come in. I'll go get you a breast pump and show you how to use it. We can save the milk and try to bottle feed her with it. Do you want another beer?"

"No thanks. Those last two left me in a daze. However, it's been months since I had a real Coke with caffeine. Any chance that you have one somewhere?"

"Sure thing," she says. "I'll be right back."

Mags tries to get comfortable but realizes she needs to use the toilet. She rolls out of bed and shuffles to the bathroom. Upon her return she stops to check on the baby.

"I'm so, so sorry little one. If any of this was brought on by anything your mother did... well, I apologize. I promise you, with all my heart, that I will never give up on you and will take care of and give you the very best life I possibly can."

The young mother picks up her phone and stares at it for several minutes.

What do I expect him to say or do when I tell him?

She goes to contacts and flips through the list of names until she sees Bob's number. Hesitantly, she hits the call button and immediately it begins to ring on the other end. After listening to the fifth ring, she hits 'end call' and sets the phone back on the table before it goes to voice-mail.

She positions herself back in bed, adjusts the pillow, and soon drifts off in a restless sleep.

194

"Well, this looks like as good a place as any," I say. "Grab the shovel and help me dig a hole in that geranium bed over there."

We plant the totem as deep as we can and then fill the hole with dirt and tamp it down.

"Good riddance you little prick!" I smirk.

"Think they'll notice there's a section of flowers missing?" says Jack.

I think about that for a moment. "Take a few plants from each of the other beds for filler. No one will ever be the wiser."

After we're back on the tram, I grab the map and my phone light again.

"Okay, now we're off to the Pioneer section, so orange; numbers 8 and 9, the chapel and cemetery." I glance down at the Publix bag full of bones nestled between my feet.

"Mary, Hold on, you're next!"

"So, where *is* Mary by the way?" says Jack

"Between my legs," I reply.

"No, I mean the apparition we left standing by the remains of the old oak tree back in the Cove?"

"Good question. Somehow, I can feel her right here, now, encouraging us to continue on."

Jackie starts the engine. "So which way co-pilot?"

"We need to go back the way we came."

She gives me a hard look. "You honestly expect me to back this baby up all the way to the parking lot? Look at this skinny road we're on.

Plus, it's surrounded by jungle on both sides with no room to pull a U-turn."

"All right, up ahead there's another road off to the right that appears to loop around and bring us back to that crossroads we went through by the picnic grounds. There's only one little issue… we have to cross a body of water called Webb's Cove via Cock's Footbridge."

"A footbridge!" She struggles with the gears again, and slowly we begin to chug forward. "How in the hell am I supposed to drive this big ass thing across a footbridge."

"Let's hope it's a misnomer," I say—then, under my breath, "as we should be coming up on it any moment now."

"You know, I really can't believe we haven't been discovered yet, or at least awakened people," I say. "Why this train alone makes enough noise to wake the dead with the way it clinks and clangs."

Jack pauses and looks directly at me.

"Did you honestly just say 'wake the dead' when we are riding around a foreboding forest in the middle of the night, looking for a graveyard, with the remains of a deceased person rolled up and stuck in a Publix bag?"

195

"The map states that the original footbridge was constructed in the 1890s but was recently replaced with a boardwalk," I say, and sure enough, when we reach it, it's the same width as the path.

Thank God!

Still taking it cautiously across the creaking boards over the brackish bay waters, I'm relieved to note that the tide is out. The full moon has exposed the bottom and it is covered with oyster beds forming rock-like reefs.

"You're a Floridian now," states Jack "is it true what they say about oysters and sex?"

"Why would my living in Florida have anything to do with my knowledge of oyster sex?"

"Come on," laughs Jack "don't tell me you're not familiar with the belief that they're an aphrodisiac?"

"Not only am I unawares," I blush "But I wouldn't put one of those slimy things in my mouth on a dare. Would you?"

"Not only would I," She chuckles suggestively "but now that we live here I think I'm going to start including them in most of Franks meals!"

Her own wit causes Jack to slam on the brakes as we both double over from laughter.

You slay me...

The roadway comes to a dead-end, with signage pointing left to the Frank & Lizzie Webb Guptill House on the shores of Little Sarasota

Bay. To the right is Duchene Lawn and Classic Portal of Bertha Palmer as well as the exit.

We turn right, and after exiting the dense foliage, we find ourselves back at the crossroads with the burial mound and picnic grounds.

"Now what?" asks Jack.

"Straight ahead and take the second left, Lovers Lane."

"Lovers Lane? In this haunted forest of no return!"

We round a bend and the tram's headlights shine through an old wrought iron fence. They also illuminate, within the cemetery grounds, an unkept, haphazard array of careening headstones and above-ground vaults of various sizes. Jack comes to rest with the car lights illuminating a charming, little, white chapel.

"It's adorable," I stammer.

There are several wooden steps leading up to double doors that are swung wide open. The wood paneled interior gives off a warm orange glow similar to the illumination of candlelight.

Jack turns off the vehicle lights and now the stained-glass windows down both sides of the church, and one at the front chancel area, can be seen backlit by the full wolf moon.

"It's perfect!" says Jack. "I can't wait to show Frank."

"Perfect for what?"

"My wedding silly. It's just the right size and feel."

"In a graveyard?"

"I believe we'll take our vows inside!" she says with a smirk.

Stepping out of the tram, Jack takes the spade, and I grab the Publix bag. We approach, I hobble, towards the chapel, pausing to read the small plaque out front.

Mary's Chapel is named for Mary Sherrill, a young woman that disappeared and was presumed dead while staying at the Webb's Winter Resort circa 1881. In 1986 this reconstruction was completed and contains the six original stained-glass windows and bell salvaged from the deteriorated original building.

Climbing the steps, we enter, and to my surprise, sitting in the back pew against the far right wall are Marilyn and Mary.

Needing to get off my sore foot, I join them. Jack, instinctively knowing what she needs to do, excuses herself and retreats out of the church and towards the cemetery.

"I don't know what I expected," I say. "But, I'm not sure I anticipated seeing both of you here."

Mary appears solemn and fixated on her hands clasped in prayer. Marilyn turns to me.

"Poor little thing came to me all confused and completely lost. She shared with me what happened. After talking to Daisy last week, when she gave me that little fellow who has the schmeckle with the orl intact, I put two-and-two together. I then brought her here so that I can function as her spirit guide to the other side."

"By the other side, do you mean Heaven?"

"There's no telling where the soul is destined to go when we pass, sweetie. But I'm guessing that for this shayna punim, who has suffered so long, only something good can be awaiting her."

I believe

—Robson & Jerome (2009)
Songwriters: Bobby Rivkin Bobby Z

196

After several more minutes of awkward conversation, with me contemplating what does one really say to a ghost, Mary turns to Marilyn.

"I think I'm ready now Ma'am."

They both stand, and I step out into the center aisle allowing them to pass. To my surprise they aim the other way, towards the sanctuary altar. Marilyn looks back at me and mouths, "The Kaddish Prayer." Both facing the alter I hear them pray.

Marilyn begins: "Exalted and hallowed be His great Name."

Mary follows: *"Amen."*

"Throughout the world which He has created according to His Will. May He establish His kingship, bring forth His redemption and hasten the coming of His Messiah."

"Amen."

"In your lifetime and in your days and in the lifetime of the entire House of Israel, speedily and soon, and say, Amen."

Mary responds: *"Amen. May His great Name be blessed forever and to all eternity, blessed."*

"May His great Name be blessed forever and to all eternity. Blessed and praised, glorified, exalted and extolled, honored, adored and lauded be the Name of the Holy One, blessed be He."

"Amen."

"Beyond all the blessings, hymns, praises and consolations that are uttered in the world; and say, Amen.

"Amen."

May there be abundant peace from heaven, and a good life for us and for all Israel; and say, Amen.

"Amen."

He who makes peace in His heavens, may He make peace for us and for all Israel; and say, Amen.

"Amen."

Marilyn, takes the young girl's face in her hands. "I will recite a kaddish for eleven months from today so that you will know you're not forgotten."

Both spirits turn around and slowly move down the aisle, towards the front door, reciting Psalm 23 in unison.

"The Lord is my Shepherd; I shall not want. He has me lie down in green pastures, He leads me beside the still waters. He revives my soul..."

I precede them outside, and in the graveyard, find Jackie finishing digging a good size hole. She wipes her brow.

"Even though this is nothing but sand, I'm working up a sweat, and I could sure go for that beer now that you offered me earlier!"

"Well, I'm afraid that needs to wait, as now I'm expecting the deceased and her ghost buddy to be exiting the building."

They arrive graveside, Mary afloat and Marilyn holding her arm lovingly. They make eye contact and bid final goodbyes. Mary then turns to me with a benevolent expression upon her face.

"I can never thank you enough for saving me, Miss Blum (like plum)."

"You're welcome my Dear... and, it's pronounced bloom."

Jackie unties the blanket and gently places the remains in the hole.

"Do you see the light, Mary?" asks Marilyn

"Not yet."

I pick up a handful of the sandy dirt from the pile and toss it atop the remains. All I can think to say is, "Ashes to ashes and dust to dust."

Jack picks up the spade and begins filling in the remainder of the hole.

Mary begins to beam with a child's innocent smile, so radiant with unadulterated happiness.

"Mommy, Mommy is that you?"

"Go child, run to her," Marilyn pleads. "That's it, go now baby!"

Before our eyes, Mary's image slowly dissolves into the night air until she's totally gone. Marilyn gets out her well used tissue from her bra and blows her nose and mutters,

"Hamakom y'nachem etchem b'toch sh'ar availai tziyon ee yerushalayim."

"These things always make me verklempt," she says, as I realize I can see right through her. Jack finishes tamping down the ground with the back of the spade as I watch the figure of Marilyn fade away as well.

197

Pulling into the ER at Sarasota Memorial, the first rays of the morning sun are throwing light on the front of the hospital in glorious shades of rose gold.

The concierge opens my car door and, glancing over at Jack, asks if he can park the vehicle for us.

"No thank you," I say. "We're good. Jackie, You go find a place in the garage, and I'll go register. I'm guessing I'll still be waiting my turn by the time you get back."

When she does return, I'm sitting in the waiting room near a woman throwing up in a barf bag. Another woman several seats down is applying her face make-up with the aid of a mirrored compact. There is a homeless man sleeping in a hospital wheelchair who the uniformed worker from the guard desk is trying to rouse.

"Come on buddy, I need you outta here before the hospital opens. I only let you in last night because of that nasty storm."

"I'm over here," I call to Jackie as I see her enter through the glass sliding doors.

She walks over and looks around, raising an eyebrow at the collected humanity. Then, something passes between us. A wordless moment of shared recognition between two people who have just been through something remarkable together. Both knowing there is no way of ever explaining fully to another living soul what the Hell happened last night.

Jack takes the seat next to me and for quite a while, we simply hug.

"Please do me a favor and go upstairs and check on Maggie and the baby for me. Just tell her that her klutzy mother burned herself and that I'll be up once they've cared for me down here. Whatever else you say or do, don't tell her the real story. That can wait until we're all better and back home again in Pelican Cove."

"Whatever you do," chuckles Jackie, "be sure to invite Frank and I to that show and we'll bring the wine!"

An orderly comes into the waiting area with a wheelchair, "Elizabeth Blum?" (pronounced like bloom).

"I'm right here. And, you pronounced my last name right!"

"How else would you say it?" he questions. "I'm going to take you into triage now, would your companion care to join you?"

"Her companion has two other patients to visit while I'm here," says Jack. "Liz, you call me if they decide to release or move you to a room."

She gives me a quick peck on the head before aiming off to find the elevators.

198

Jack gets off on the fifth floor, locates Maggie's room, and finds a hand-printed sign on the closed door indicating STAFF ONLY. Undeterred, she retraces her steps back to the elevator and makes her way to the central nurses' station.

"Hi," she says, to the nurse on duty, "I'm here to visit Margaret Blum in room 517."

The harried nurse searches through a stack of clipboards for a moment before pulling one out.

"Are you family?"

Jackie smiles. "Why yes, yes I am. I'm her aunt."

"I'm sorry, but there's a notation here from the doctor that the only family member who has visitation privileges is her mother."

"Well, currently her mother is downstairs," says Jackie. "She's—"

"Well, if she wants to see her daughter, she'll need to come *upstairs*," says the nurse, grabbing a ringing phone line while fumbling with more paperwork.

Jack walks over to the elevator, presses the down button and returns to the lobby. Spying the door to the ladies' room she decides to take advantage of the facility before returning to Liz. After finishing up and washing her hands she begins to beam ear-to-ear in the wash station mirror.

Worth a try...

Fifteen minutes later a middle-aged woman exits the washroom. She appears a bit conspicuous; her dark hair is tied back with a paisley print, boho scarf, and she's wearing dark sunglasses and ruby red lips. Her black skinny jeans are rolled up several turns at the bottom creating the look of capris, and she has a dark windbreaker style jacket tied around her shoulders.

She commands attention with her shoulders-back posture and cat-walk approach to the elevators. The doors open, and after several others exit, she steps in and the doors go closed.

Back on five, Jackie takes a deep breath and steps out. The nurse's station is vacant and for a moment she keeps thinking to herself, just keep walking, just keep walking…

Suddenly, a young nurse in a kitten covered scrub top pops out from behind a row of file cabinets and smiles. Jack freezes and feels compelled to speak.

"Happy New Year!"

"Same to you," replies the nurse. "Can I help you?"

"Yes, my name is Liz Blum. My daughter's a patient here, and I've come to visit," says Jackie. She is trying her best to disguise her voice but sounding more like a Latino, Morgan Freeman, than her friend Liz.

"Her name and room number?"

"Margaret Blum, B-L-U-M, in room 517."

Looking into the breakroom behind the file cabinets, her heart skips a beat as she spies the original nurse she spoke to, just sitting down at a table and unwrapping a McDonalds breakfast sandwich.

Jackie tries to scooch to the left and out of her line of sight. "So how's the baby doing?"

The nurse lifts the clipboard containing Maggie's file and scans it.

"Well, guess what? They have moved the baby out of NICU, and she's in with your daughter right now. You should be able to see for yourself."

"That's great news. Oh, I'm excited. Thank you so much," she says and scurries down the hall towards the room before any more questions can be asked. Entering the room, she finds Maggie sitting upright in bed watching the first hour of *Good Morning America* on TV with the sound on low.

"I'm sorry, but this is a private room without visitors," She announces. "I'm going to need you to please leave."

Jack steps forward allowing the room door to swing shut behind her. She removes her dark sunglasses and loosens the scarf from her hair.

"Even if it's your Aunt Jack?"

199

Jackie makes her way over to the bed, arms outstretched, and embraces Maggie in her usual bear hug fashion

"That one's from your mother too." Pulling away she adds, "My, oh my, have the girls gotten bigger? Your mom's going be jealous of those things when she sees them."

They both giggle like schoolgirls.

"That's apparently what happens when you start nursing." Mag looks down at her chest and smiles. Then… "Oh shit, and apparently you leak every time you think about the baby. Hey, you mentioned Mom. Where the heck is she?"

"Downstairs." Jack breaks eye contact while stammering for a moment about what to say. "See, we were starting to make breakfast, and you know your mother, she's a tad bit accident prone. She was taking a hot rack of bacon out of the oven and spilled grease on her hand which caused her to drop the entire pan on her bare foot." Relays Jack with eyes rolling. "She screamed and ran to the bathroom shower to run cold water on it, but I came running, took one look and insisted we head to the ER pronto."

"I thought Mom said something about giving up bacon." Responds Mag quizzically. "Something about Stu saying she needs to watch the saturated fats and nitrates."

"Well she was probably making it for me." Spouts Jackie while impressed with her own quick thinking. "Long story short, she's down there now and asked me to go check on you. Oh… and the baby. Hey, speaking of the baby, can I take a look-see?"

"Of course, she's right over there in the bassinette. Surely, Mom has shared all the problems the poor little thing has had, and what she's been going through since birth."

"Oh Maggie, my dear, none of that is important now. No matter what the future holds, you know your mother and I will both be here to support you and… and, what the hell did you name her?"

"Now promise me you won't laugh?"

"Of course not," says Jack as she crosses her heart. "and hope to die."

"It's Daisy. Daisy Esther Blum." Maggie is beaming when she says it.

"That's absolutely adorable. Did you know Daisy in Spanish is Margarita, one of my faves? Now, let me see that little flower."

Jackie approaches the container with the baby inside and gives out a slight gasp, "Oh my." followed by a booming, "Oh, you dear little bambino!"

Maggie jumps out of the bed and joins her as Aunt Jack puts her arm around her assumed niece.

"Your mother painted such a horrible and bleak picture of the baby's condition and what she looked like that I was concerned with how I might react the first time I saw her. I see a few flaky rough patches here and there that look like dermatitis to me, but look at that face, she's an absolute angel!"

"It's amazing, Aunt Jack, but after they let me hold and feed Daisy, her condition kept improving. The outside layer of skin started sloughing, and as I held her to my bare chest, I was able to easily peel various pieces off. Underneath was the purest white skin I had ever seen."

Maggie, her young face mantling with emotion, reaches into the baby's bed and adjusts the swaddling blanket.

"If we stay in Florida, I'm afraid she'll never be able to go outside without my slathering her head-to-toe in SPF 50 sunscreen."

About thirty minutes later I burst through the door with a heavily bandaged left hand, a white sock on my foot, and one crutch jammed into my armpit.

"Somebody get me a chair!" I bark.

"Mom! Are you okay?"

"Now, now. Don't you worry about your old mother," I say between gasps to catch my breath, after dragging myself upstairs and down the long hall to her room. "It's not as bad as it looks. I just stumbled over that damn ottoman in the living room on my way to answer the door and let your Aunt Jack in."

Maggie looks at Jackie, then back to me.

"Were you carrying a hot tray of bacon at the time?"

"Was I what, now?" I shoot a glance to Jack—no help there—and when I turn back to Mag she has crossed her arms and has an interrogative look on her face.

"All right you two, what gives?"

"First things first," I say. "I need to see that baby."

After viewing the baby's amazing transformation for myself, we all sit down. I search for a Librium but change my mind, and Jack and I proceed to tell Maggie the entire story from beginning to end.

While I describe my confrontation with Granny Daisy while wielding a honing steel, plus my flinging Morton's salt all around at her kitchen door, we all can't keep from laughing. In contrast, when Jackie and I describe the torrential storm and the difficulty of placing the lightening rod in the big oak tree, you could have heard a pin drop.

In pops a nurse, and she immediately questions what we're all doing in the room.

"I'm the patient's mother and this is her Aunt," I reply.

"Well, I just reviewed the patient's chart before going on shift and it appears *you* can stay and *she* needs to go," he says, pointing at Jack. "I'll give you all five minutes to wrap it up!"

Jack quickly explains the story of my climbing to the top of the tree and consequently getting struck by lightning and knocked off the ladder. She tries to soften her description on my injuries and her short-lived fear that I might be dead when she found me.

"Oh mother!" Mag says, and we embrace and break into tears.

Jack continues with the tale of finding Mary's remains, then I jump in, explaining her actual apparition and request for us to take her home to Spanish Point. I also include our returning the little totem man to his rightful place in the ancient midden amongst the people that worshipped him.

"So now my dear," I say, "it's your choice as to what you want to believe about what we did last night and its effect on things. But I, for one, have become a believer in the fact that there's some unexplainable events that can happen in this world. Just look at that little miracle you gave birth to right over there."

"And, I truly suspect that Pelican Cove is one of the hearts of said magic," adds Jack with a grin.

"Now, your mother has had a rough few days, and I'm about to fall on my face. So, before they have to admit me for complete exhaustion, I need you, my dearest friend Jackie, to take me home and tuck me in bed."

We stand to leave, and I struggle to get my bandaged hand through my jacket sleeve. Jack hands me my crutch, and once I am properly balanced, I turn to Maggie.

"Now, how in the world did you come up with Daisy as a name?"

"Funny thing," she says. "This elderly woman from registration came in and asked if I had chosen a name yet. She stated it was customary to fill out the birth certificate before leaving the hospital. I told her I was struggling between several choices, and after hearing her repeat them with my last name I really didn't like any of them. That's when she suggested Daisy and how sweet it would be with Blum. Long story short, I liked it a lot. She tossed me a wrapped peppermint ball and said, 'consider it done!'"

My jaw drops as I consider the possibility that Granny Daisy was here and, to top it off, named my granddaughter after herself.

"Did she look like an old cowgirl that had been ridden hard and put away wet?" I ask.

Mag gets a confused look. "She was an older, blue hair in a floral smock. That's about all I remember. Why?"

"Never mind," I mutter as I lean in to kiss her goodbye.

"Oh, and by the way, your deceased neighbor Marilyn came in yesterday and had some sort of a Jewish service for the baby and said that she was presenting her with her Jewish name. She chose Esther stating it is one of her favorite characters from the bible. Don't worry, a priest came and baptized her Christian too. I guess she has all her bases covered."

I shake my head. All I can do is grin. "I'm really going to miss Marilyn and her little dog. She was one of the most lovable neighbors I've ever had!"

On the way home all Jack and I can talk about is the miraculous recovery of the baby. She does me a favor and takes Mac out, then comes into my bedroom and sets a mug of Sleepy Time tea on my nightstand and gives me a peck on the forehead.

"I'll give you a call tomorrow to check on you."

As she goes to exit and unlatches the front door, the grandfather clock in the entry begins to strike twelve noon.

"Well, I'm glad to see you finally got that clock working!" she yells out as she closes the front door behind her.

200

Negotiating the Stickney Point drawbridge, waiting for the traffic light to change at Midnight Pass, jockeying for a parking spot and the long hike across Siesta Beach to the shoreline never changes. Butts, guts, tits, crystal quartz sand and lots of kids digging holes for adults to avoid lest they end up with a sprained ankle.

"Which beach attendant shall we ogle today," asks Jackie, "red, blue, green, or yellow lifeguard station?"

"Hey you, you're a married woman now," I laugh.

"I'm still allowed to look, and I say green, just check out those red trunks on the bare-chested blonde one with the surfboard."

We find a vacant spot near water's edge and spread out our oversized beach blanket. Jack anchors her two corners with her water shoes and Costa beach bag, and I cover the other two with my Igloo cooler and flip flops.

I check my phone. "About another hour till showtime."

Jack smiles. "The sunsets here never get old. Just look at those shelf clouds rolling in." She pops the cork on a bottle of Nineteen Crimes, Red Blend. "Have you ever seen the phone app I have for these wines?" she asks as she digs through her bag. "It's creepy as hell I tell you!"

She holds her phone up to the bottle's label and the likeness of John Boyle O'Reilly magically comes to life and begins telling his tale of extradition to Australia for his numerous crimes.

713

"That's amazing!" I exclaim. "Having worked with package design at Procter & Gamble, I'm extremely impressed. Why, labels could easily advise consumers of the advantages and directions on using their products."

"Oh my God, after all this time you really can't ever quit working, can you?" laughs Jack. "I honestly haven't missed one damn minute of the corporate world since I left!"

Both women pick up their plastic tiki glasses of wine and 'clink!' as Jack toasts to now living their lives in paradise, and I give a big thanks to William and James for making it possible.

"Thank goodness for P&G stock splits!"

I sit my glass atop the cooler and begin nervously rubbing my left wrist. The evening takes on a more somber tone as I feel the permanent, risen scar that's an exact replica of the Tibetan bracelet I was wearing from Granny Daisy at the time of the lightning strike.

"So much has changed over the almost two years since this adventure started. I was sad, lonely, anxiety ridden and much too dependent on medications. I remember the trepidation of selling my home and buying the condo in Pelican Cove. Leaving my job, my Cincinnati doctors and you. Who would ever think things would work out this well?"

We tap glasses again.

"How are Maggie and Bob doing?" asks Jackie sincerely with a look of concern.

"They are taking it very slowly," I reply. "Now that he accepted the artistic director position at the Venice Theatre, and has an apartment on the island, it's obviously easier for him to have a relationship with Daisy."

"What about the relationship between him and Mag?" Jack questions further.

"I'm not sure how I was supposed to take it, but I interpreted it as a compliment when she said, 'You know Mom, you're living proof that you don't always have to have a man at your side to be a success. You've done pretty damn well for yourself.' But I know she's talked about taking her relationship with Bob slowly because of how much he hurt her."

"Smart girl. That sounds like an approach her aunt would take!" she says as she refills our glasses.

"Oh, does it?" I chuckle. "I never saw anyone jump on a relationship as fast as you and Frank did."

We watch the sun dip below the horizon and set the sky aglow. I continue with my thoughts.

"Anyway," I say, "You're not the one with two extra people living in your teeny-tiny condo. I'm not sure how much longer I can take it."

"Have you met said Bob in person yet?" asks Jackie.

"Yes, and strangely enough I like him. I'm sure you'll have the opportunity to judge for yourself on the Fourth of July when you and Frank come over to grill-out burgers."

"So true my dear, I'll try to bite my lip and behave. Oh, by the way, I've decided to bring my mother Mildred's macaroni salad."

Jack stares up at the last remnants of the sunset's scattering before nightfall.

"I imagine it can complicate the romance side of dating Stu?" she says.

"Honestly, between his home and the boat, we make do just fine."

I glance to the side of our blanket, looking for the flashlight I always carry to the beach for getting us back to the car in the dark. Flipping on the light, there they are, two green tennis balls attached to the front legs of a walker. Slowly looking up, there stands Marilyn blowing her nose into a tissue and sticking it in her brassiere.

"The sea air always opens my head up. You two gals ready to give this old yenta a ride back home? I need to take Tookie out!"

A Million Dreams

—Pink (2017)
The Greatest Showman
Songwriters: Benj Pasek and Justin Paul